THE
COMPLETE
ECHO
POWER
TRILOGY

OTHER BOOKS BY ANNA DURAND

THE COMPLETE ECHO POWER TRILOGY

Echo Power Trilogy, Books 1-3

ANNA DURAND

JACOBSVILLE BOOKS JB MARIETTA, OHIO

THE COMPLETE ECHO POWER TRILOGY

ISBN: 978-1-958144-47-3 (paperback)
ISBN: 978-1-958144-48-0 (ebook)
ISBN: 978-1-958144-49-7 (audiobook)

Jacobsville Books
www.JacobsvilleBooks.com

Publisher's Cataloging-in-Publication Data
provided by Five Rainbows Cataloging Services

Names: Durand, Anna.
Title: The complete echo power trilogy / Anna Durand.
Description: Marietta, OH : Jacobsville Books, 2024. | Series: Echo power trilogy, bk. 4.
Identifiers: ISBN 978-1-958144-47-3 (paperback) | ISBN 978-1-958144-48-0 (ebook) | ISBN 978-1-958144-49-7 (audiobook)
Subjects: LCSH: Magic--Fiction. | Survival--Fiction. | End of the world--Fiction. | Man-woman relationships--Fiction. | Romance fiction. | Paranormal romance stories. | BISAC: FICTION / Romance / Paranormal / General. | FICTION / Romance / Fantasy. | FICTION / Romance / Suspense. | GSAFD: Love stories. | Occult fiction. | Romantic suspense fiction.
Classification: LCC PS3604.U724 E241 2024 (print) | LCC PS3604.U724 (ebook) | DDC 813/.6--dc23.

ECHO POWER

Echo Power Trilogy, Book One

CHAPTER ONE

Allison

I CAREEN ACROSS THE GRASS, STUMBLING OVER A HOLE IN THE GROUND, and stagger sideways while my boots bump into things I refuse to look at, things that might be human bodies. I can't stop. Not now. Maybe never. Anyone on the ground is beyond saving, anyway. Overlapping screams pierce the air behind me, but I cannot look back. Green sparks ignite in the unnatural twilight, sizzling and snapping, nipping at my skin. My foot slips in the mud, and my ankle twists sideways, but I keep running. *Don't look down, don't look down. I can't help them.* No one can.

Ahead of me, a hulking figure seizes a smaller one around the neck and jerk its hand. The crack of bones snapping resonates in the air.

The smaller figure crumples to the ground.

Bile surges into my throat. All I can do is gulp it down and keep moving even while my muscles burn.

The ground falls away. I sail through the green-sparked air to smack down hip first. Clawing for a handhold, I lose the remnants of my balance and tumble down a hillside, spinning and spinning as I hurtle sideways down the slope toward where I'd sat to eat my lunch earlier today. The slope that's now drenched in blood. The warm liquid clings to my skin and infiltrates my mouth, its taste tangy and salty with a hint of sweetness that makes me gag. I slam into a barrier. Though I've stopped moving, my head keeps whirling, trapped in an illusion that the world is spinning. I choke back my gorge, but it tastes of blood. *Oh God, no.* I heave myself up onto my hands and knees. There beside me lies the object that halted my fall.

The headless remains of a human being.

I can't focus on anything else, my gaze riveted to the gruesome sight. Pain still throbs inside me from my tumble down the hill. But I just slump here, immobile, my heart pounding so hard my chest hurts while the pressure of nausea thrusts up into my throat. I slant sideways and retch, over and over, until my abdominal muscles ache and my throat burns. When at last the heaving subsides, I struggle to catch my breath.

Out of the corner of my eye, I glimpse the dead man.

So many lifeless bodies litter the area, but I'd managed to avoid looking directly at them until now. This one... Christ, it's impossible to avoid seeing that.

I must keep moving. The beast chasing me will catch up any second.

With an effort that screams agony through my muscles, I hoist myself up and run.

***

THE APOCALYPSE BEGAN AT TWO O'CLOCK ON A SUNNY WEDNESDAY AFternoon, but no one in this city noticed anything unusual at first. We kept going about our business, even when the sky turned a darker, more intense shade of blue like nothing seen on earth before today. I was in the public library shelving books near the front windows when I realized something had changed, something more than the color of the sky. I felt the change deep inside me, and I heard it too. A silence deeper than the void of outer space enveloped the world while an irresistible impulse seized me, luring me outside.

I pushed through the doors and shambled across the portico, past the tall pillars, and out onto the street.

People poured out of vehicles and other buildings, all of us mindlessly drawn down North Main Street toward the viaduct. We crossed the bridge to gather on the grassy hill just past the trail that skirted the river, as if waiting for something to rise up from the water below and land in front of us. We glanced at each other in confusion. Why had we come to this place? Why was the sky a deeper blue than ever before? We didn't speak to each other, but somehow, I knew we were all thinking the same thing.

What on earth is happening?

High above us, the eerie sound of music started up, softly at first, then escalating into the strains of a string symphony like none ever heard in this world. The music surrounded and infiltrated me, the melody beautiful and terrible and mesmerizing, its purpose and meaning beyond comprehension. It vibrated through my soul, wringing tears from my eyes. All around me, people sobbed and dropped to their knees, their gazes glued to the cobalt sky, as hypnotized by the music as I was. I fell to my knees too, helpless to understand what was unfolding around me. Deep inside, though, I sensed the horror hidden beneath the beauty.

If only I had understood a few seconds earlier...

No, nothing would have changed. A power beyond imagining had unleashed itself on the world.

The music froze on a single, discordant note that stretched on and on, making my ears ache and pulsating through my flesh. Then the music stopped—and an unearthly roar erupted, impregnating every molecule of air with its cacophony. I slapped my hands over my ears, but the roar penetrated into me so deeply that I couldn't breathe. And then...

The sky split open.

A rupture in the fabric of the world distended across half the horizon, from high above down to ground level, while a shredding noise grated on my eardrums and reverberated off buildings throughout the city. The hole in the sky disgorged a river of writhing shapes that spilled onto the earth, spreading outward as the amorphous shadows became creatures with arms and legs and heads. They growled and screeched like demons sent up from hell itself.

And then they came for us.

The demons grabbed human beings and tore them to shreds. Screams of agony and terror echoed around me, mingling with the wet sounds of flesh ripping and the cracking of bones. I stood frozen, unable to even blink, witnessing events in mute horror as the creatures ripped men, women, and children asunder. My heart pounded so hard and fast that it robbed me of breath.

A creature raised the severed head of a human being, hoisting it high, and roared in triumph.

Run. Do it now, before those things come for you.

I bolted back down the hill, clinging to the only coherent thought in my mind. *This can't be happening.* But it was. While I fled toward the bridge, fireballs shot out of the rip in the sky and slammed into the earth. The green sparks had snuffed out, and the only light emanated from the meteorites crashing down on the city. But they weren't objects from outer space. They came from another world, from the place on the other side of the rupture in the heavens.

Buildings exploded. Trees burst into flames. Pavement melted. I scrambled up the hill and onto the bridge, heading for...I didn't know where. Anyplace but here.

At the center of the bridge, hunkered a huge beast.

I halted so quickly I almost tripped over my own feet, and a frigid chill iced through me from my skin down to my soul. Behind me, demons rampaged. Ahead of me, this creature blocked my only escape route. He must've stood over six feet tall, a mountain of muscles and wild black hair with a scruffy beard that hid most of his features except for the scar that slashed across his cheek. Every flash of the fireballs lit him up. His long, battered leather coat fluttered around his thighs. It was black, just like his shirt and his worn leather pants that stretched tight over his thighs. I glimpsed hints of tattoos revealed by his partially unbuttoned shirt.

The beast stood there, legs spread, as if he had no intention of allowing me to pass. His gaze landed on me, and his lips peeled back from his teeth, though not in a smile. He sneered at me, fisting his hands at his sides. Jabbing a finger toward me, he growled, "You."

That beast wanted to kill me. I sensed it, though I had no idea what I had done to enrage him. He must have come through the rupture, which made him an alien monster like the others. What could I do? Behind me lay carnage and death. Ahead of me, maybe I could still find a place to hide or a way to escape.

I whirled around, and before he had time to react, I ran back the way I'd come as fast as my battered body could go.

And the beast barreled after me.

~

THAT'S HOW I WIND UP PELTING ACROSS THE VIADUCT YET AGAIN, DODG-ing other creatures and getting stung by molten fragments of the fireballs that hurtle past overhead. Every explosive impact makes the earth shudder beneath my feet. I need to escape, that's all I know. The hoarse bellows of the beast pursuing me reverberate off the shattered carcasses of the buildings that once formed a city. Now it's a wasteland. Where can I hide? How can I get away from that monster? More creatures, just as terrifying, maraud through the city. I *can't* get away.

But I must try.

My legs tremble, and my ears ring. Any second, I'll pass out. I know this. I have no choice but to stop and rest, though I realize the beast will catch up to me if I do. There must be someplace I can hide, for just a few minutes, long enough to regain my strength and catch my breath. I race past a building I would probably recognize if it weren't reduced to rubble, but up ahead, I see a structure that seems mostly intact. It's a pharmacy. I'd never visited the place, but I drove past it every day on my way to work.

I risk glancing over my shoulder.

The beast is nowhere in sight.

Maybe I've caught a sliver of luck. Veering onto the cracked sidewalk, I leap through a broken window into the pharmacy building. Shelves lie broken and scattered while their contents have sprayed across the blood-spattered floor. I leap over the biggest pile of rubble and drop to my knees, breathing so hard that black spots speckle my vision. I take a long, slow breath. Then another. And another. The ringing in my ears has subsided, and those black spots no longer obscure my sight.

In the gloomy space, I notice a refrigerated case nearby, one that would've held beverages, though its glass front has been smashed. Crawl-ing over the debris, I feel around inside the darkened refrigerator until my fingers close around a plastic bottle. Of what, I don't care. I need to drink something, anything.

When I pull out the bottle, I realize it's water. *Thank heaven.* I unscrew the cap and guzzle the still-cold liquid.

I allow myself a few minutes to finish my drink and rest. Then I know I need to get moving again. As I make my way over the rubble and out the window, I move cautiously so I can scan the vicinity. Just as I step out onto the sidewalk, a solitary fact at last sinks into my brain.

Though it's afternoon, the world is cloaked in twilight. Sure, I'd noticed the semi-darkness before. But the fact the sun had been vanquished didn't hit me until right now. No stars glitter above me, either. Fireballs keep hurtling out of the tear in the sky, seeming to emerge from a black, disk-shaped hole at the center of the rupture. A rim of silvery fire surrounds the disk.

Behind me, footfalls crunch on rubble.

I spin around and yelp as I slam into a manlike creature, stumbling backward.

The beast who had pursued me seizes my upper arms and drags me into his body. His impossibly broad shoulders encompass me. He hoists me off my feet. My boots dangle several inches above the ground. My face is so close to his that I feel his scruffy beard rasping over my chin.

"Everything that's happening"—He snarls his words while spittle peppers my face with every syllable he utters—"it's all your fault."

This brute speaks with a British accent. That's weird, considering where we are, but I have bigger issues to worry about now. It feels like a rock has gotten stuck in my throat, and swallowing hard does nothing to alleviate the constriction. Though I don't want to do it, I force myself to meet his unearthly gaze and not cringe at the brilliance of his golden brown irises. "What are you talking about?"

"This happened because of you."

"No."

He spins me around, my feet touching down on the cracked pavement, and cuffs my wrists behind my back with his much bigger, rougher hands. I try to kick him, but he lashes one leg around both of mine. "Stop fighting. It won't help."

His fingers wriggle as he ties something around my wrists. Rope? Not sure, and it hardly matters. I've been captured by a monster who blames me for the apocalypse unfolding around us.

"Kick me again," he snarls into my ear, "and I'll bind your feet too. Understand?"

I nod.

He shoves me forward while keeping hold of my bindings. "You're coming with me."

"Where?"

"Somewhere else."

"Who are you?"

"If you must have a name, call me Dax." He yanks on my bindings, making me trip over a lump of shattered pavement. "No more talking, Allison, or I'll gag you too."

He knows my name. *He knows.*

I shut up and let the beast haul me down the streets of what used to be a thriving city. It's metamorphosed into a wasteland populated by monsters and whatever survivors remain. The world has died. Whatever is replacing it seems like nowhere any human would want to live.

This used to be Fort Worth, Texas. What will it become now?

Chapter Two

Dax

I GIVE THE GIRL A SHOVE EVERY SO OFTEN TO ENSURE SHE KEEPS MOV-
ing, despite the nasty looks she flashes me over her shoulder. Allison
Dahl is the reason for all of this. I know it, and she must know it too,
though she refuses to admit the truth. This world has been laid waste because of her. And I've been trapped in hell for the same reason. The time has
come to extract the truth from her by whatever means necessary.

Screams and unearthly roars echo through the ruins of this metropolis. I
have no idea where in the mundane world I've wound up, but the city's name
hardly matters now. It no longer exists, not in any form its residents would recognize. I haven't recognized myself for five years. Allison thinks I'm a monster,
I'm sure, and she is correct. I have become one of the things mundane humans
fear will crawl out from under their beds to devour them.

The only creature I want to devour is Allison Dahl. But she wouldn't like
the way I'd fuck her. No, she seems like one of those women who would never
allow a man to defile her in filthy ways. I haven't been with a normal woman
in far too long, which is the only reason Allison's body intrigues me. Even
through the dirt and blood spattered over her from head to toe, I can tell she
has a body any man would want to sink his cock into for hours.

I don't have time for that.

Allison stumbles over a chunk of pavement that's been blasted out of
the ground and nearly falls flat on her face. She catches herself just in time,
despite her bound hands. Her dark hair falls around her face, but I can still
see the deep blue of her eyes as she glares up at me.

No, I will not help her. She destroyed the world.

We need a place to hide, a location where I can interrogate her and
find out the truth behind what has happened today, and even earlier, when

events were set in motion. A safe place? No such thing exists anymore. Fireballs rain down every few minutes, slamming into any remaining structures and igniting whatever they touch, while silver tongues of lightning punch into the ground. Every strike, of lightning or fire, makes the ground tremble beneath our feet.

I don't know this city. But Allison does.

"Where can we hide?" I ask, stabbing a finger into her back, between her shoulder blades.

"How should I know? Everything's destroyed."

"Think of something, or I will break your fingers one by one until you give me the information I need."

"Do you seriously think threats help? I can't focus with all this…" She chokes back a sob. "There's no word for how horrible this is."

"Of course there is. It's an apocalypse. Judgment Day, if you prefer that term."

"Whose judgment?"

Someone screams from high above us, and a dark shape flies off the top of a half-destroyed building. The body smacks down a few feet to our left, hitting with a wet crunch of bones and flesh.

Allison jumps and yelps, then turns her head away, squeezing her eyes shut.

I swallow hard, refusing to glance at the human being who just hit the ground, and shove my prisoner onward. "Keep moving. And think of a place where we can hide. You have two minutes to come up with something, or I will remove your smallest finger with a very dull blade."

She sniffles but keeps trudging forward, sidestepping other bodies and climbing over heaps of rubble. We've just mounted a large pile when she freezes.

"Keep going," I snarl.

"Wait. I think I see a hiding place."

She uses her shoulder to point toward something ahead of us.

From our vantage on the mountain of debris, we have a good view of this section of the city. I have no idea where in the old world I've landed since nothing here resembles anything I remember, and I certainly have no idea how this new world being thrust upon us has changed the topography. But Allison seems to recognize a structure. I squint in the direction that she indicated.

"I don't see anything," I growl. "You're delaying."

"No, I am not. It's an underground place."

"What sort of place?"

She turns toward me, her pale face colored by the glow of a fireball streaking across the sky. "There are tunnels under the city. I guess we'd be relatively safe there, at least for a while."

"If it's underground, how can you see it from here?"

"Can't. But I do see the remnants of the stockyards, and the tunnel is under that, under what was East Exchange Avenue. Don't know what it is now."

I gaze down at the remnants of buildings ahead of us. "What city is this?"

"Used to be Fort Worth, Texas. Why do you care what city this is? You're a monster from another dimension or something."

"Or something, yes." I don't care if she calls me a monster. That belief serves my purposes. I'd never visited America until I was thrown into this city. "Take us to the tunnel."

"I've had enough of you pushing me around. If you want me to take you to a good hiding place, better start being at least marginally polite to me."

"Polite?" I slant toward her, bringing my face to within millimeters of hers. "This is only the beginning of the apocalypse. Etiquette is a bygone concept, you stupid chit. Haven't you noticed the world is being torn apart around us?" I grab her bound hands roughly and force her to bend all the fingers on her right hand except for one, the smallest digit. Then I bring out my knife, holding its long blade to her hand. "Your choice. Do what I say, or lose a finger. Afraid I can't bandage it with clean gauze or disinfect it with alcohol. You will develop an infection and die slowly while in great agony."

"You're evil. Do you know that?"

I chuckle like the beast she thinks I am. "Of course I'm evil. But so are you."

"Me? I—"

A roar erupts behind me, reverberating off the remnants of the buildings. I glance back, searching the darkness but not seeing the source of the animalistic sound.

I seize Allison's arm and start dragging her toward the location she'd indicated a moment ago. "Something is coming. You'd better take us to that underground hideaway now, or we might both wind up as puddles of blood and pulverized bone."

"Please untie my hands. I can't move very fast this way."

She does have a point, though I dislike admitting it. With at least one creature approaching us from behind, we need to find sanctuary, fast. I remove my leather belt from her wrists and stuff it into my pocket. "If you try to run, you lose two fingers."

Though she puckers her lips, and I'm certain she wants to curse at me, she doesn't do it.

I grasp her arm again and urge her to move.

Allison struggles to keep up with my pace as we scramble down the other side of the rubble mound, but she doesn't complain or fight against my hold on her arm. Whatever creature had roared before issues the same noise twice more, sounding closer every time. Soon, we reach a street that has less damage than in the other parts of this city that I've seen. The human carnage seems not to have reached this area yet, since I haven't noticed any bodies, alive or dead. None of the buildings look sturdy enough to qualify as a safe hideaway, so I let Allison lead me toward the place she had called the stockyards.

We pass by structures I can't identify, and I don't ask her what they are because it doesn't matter. She stumbles twice as we navigate more rubble. My hand on her arm is the only reason she doesn't fall, and I keep hold of her strictly because I need her alive to answer my questions, not because I give a toss about her well-being. At last, we come to a place where the ground slopes downward, leading us into a gloomy space beneath the city.

Allison stops near the entrance to the tunnel. "It's dark in there. Don't suppose you have a flashlight or something."

"You think I had time to grab a torch before the Echo thrust me into this world?"

"The Echo? What are you talking about?"

As if she doesn't know. She must. Once I have her in a reasonably secure location, I mean to interrogate her and get the answers I know she must have.

I drag Allison back over the rubble mound we had just scaled and head for a large structure on the other side of what's left of the street she called East Exchange Avenue. The building seems like a shopping mall. Allison trips and crashes to her knees, hissing in a breath when her kneecap strikes a sharp piece of broken asphalt. Her entire face wrenches with pain. I start to reach for her, to help her, but stop. I shouldn't care if she's injured. I don't care. Let the cow get herself up off the ground.

She clambers to her feet, favoring her knee, and glowers at me. "Thanks so much for the assistance."

"Better get used to helping yourself."

I clamp a hand around her upper arm once more and haul her toward the building. One half of it has collapsed, but the other side seems to have minimal damage as far as I can see. One pillar of the portico that leads to the mall's entrance has been shattered, leaving the roof tipped at a precarious angle. We hurry toward the glass doors. Some of the panes have cracked, and the frames have been warped, but I manage to yank one door open.

The lights are still on in here. They flicker but provide just enough illumination to show me the way. I have a feeling the power won't stay on for much longer, not with the impacts of fireballs and lightning shivering through the ground. The sounds grow closer every second.

"We can stay here," Allison says. "Can't we?"

"No. The storm is getting closer, and I doubt this building will survive it."

"Storm? I thought this was an apocalypse."

"It's the same thing."

We pass a restaurant, but the kitchen seems to be on fire, and the flames consume more and more of the dining area. As we hurry through the building in the flickering light, I spot what looks like a shop. I tow Allison along as I search for a torch—a flashlight, she said—or something else I can use to light our way. Finally, I discover an electric lantern.

"That needs batteries," Allison says.

"Obviously," I growl. "Do not speak again unless I ask a question. You are my prisoner. I could kill you—"

"Thought your favorite threat was to cut off my fingers with a dull knife."

"Shut up."

Allison lifts her chin. "Screw you."

The arrogant girl has no idea how much I need to take her up on that unintentional offer. I ignore her comment and hunt among the toppled racks and shelves in the store until I locate what I need—a package of twelve alkaline batteries, double-A size. To insert them into the lantern, though, I'll need to let go of her arm. Unacceptable. If I release her, she will run.

"Open this," I say, handing her the package of batteries.

Despite the fact I'm gripping her arm, she can still use both hands to open the package. And she does that, though she glowers at me first. She keeps flashing me disgusted glances while she struggles to tear open the plastic and cardboard packaging. Once she's completed her task, she thrusts the batteries at me.

I hold out the lantern. "Put them in here."

She puckers her lips, but then snatches the lantern from me and inserts the batteries. She shoves the lantern at me again. "Here. I hope you get electrocuted using the stupid thing."

Every time the chit defies me or insults me, the beast within awakens, and the heat of lust rushes through me. I despise her, but I wouldn't mind shagging her.

I lean in until the whiskers of my beard graze her cheek. "Do not speak to me that way unless you want me to ravage your body for my own pleasure, strictly to silence you."

"If you try that, I'll find a way to slit your throat."

"No, you won't. You're a weakling, not a warrior."

I've never forced myself on a woman, but I can't think of a better threat to intimidate her.

Before she can say anything else, I clamp my hand tighter around her arm and drag her through the store toward the entrance. Allison digs her heels in, pulling with all her strength to stop me. She accomplishes nothing more than to make me growl again. But I stop at the store entrance just long enough to shoot her a dark look.

"We should stay here," she says. "It's a safe place, and we can probably find food in one of the restaurants."

"This is not a safe place. The apocalypse began over the river, but it's coming this way like a plague of insects swarming across the earth. Unlike locusts, this plague will rip you apart in seconds."

"I haven't seen a single living thing since we got to the stockyards district."

Thunder explodes above us as a bolt of lightning punches through the roof right over our heads, plunging deep into the earth beneath the building. Debris and dust choke the air, but through the haze, I see a massive chunk of the ceiling teetering on the verge of tumbling down to crush us. Just as I push Allison, compelling her to run, the ceiling slab crashes down mere feet away from us. We both fall down amid the debris, tripping on the chunks of concrete that once formed the foundation. The lightning tore it apart. Hard, sharp edges slice into our skin, but we have bigger problems right now.

In the corridor outside the store's entrance, figures move around amid the shadows.

Allison is coughing. In the shaft of muted light that shines down through the hole in the ceiling, I can tell she's bleeding from multiple cuts. I'm bleeding too, but I don't care.

Because the real beasts are about to find us.

CHAPTER THREE

Allison

My skin stings all over from the knife-sharp cuts that form a patchwork on my exposed flesh. Maybe I don't have as many cuts as I think, since the blood coating my skin makes it hard to see exactly how much damage has been done. What just happened is impossible. Lightning shouldn't do that. When a bolt hits a building, it can fry electrical stuff and damage the roof, but it can't drill a massive hole through the entire building and the foundation.

My ears ring, thanks to the deafening force of the explosion, but at least I don't think I have any broken bones. I push up until I'm on my knees, surrounded by debris. Dax is kneeling beside me, but he seems focused on something ahead of us, in the direction of the corridor outside the store. Shadows writhe out there, with only the grayish twilight to pierce the darkness. Dark shapes, that's all I can see.

As the ringing in my ears fades away, I start to hear other sounds. Growling. Grunting. Snarling reminiscent of a rabid dog.

"What is that?" I ask.

Dax swivels his head to glare at me. "Monsters, obviously."

"How is that obvious? All I see is shadows moving around out there."

"Those aren't shadows. They're creatures." He seizes my arm and stands, forcing me to scramble to my feet too. "You think I'm a beast, but those things out there make me seem like a sweet little puppy."

Worse beasts than him? I don't want to meet those things.

But I don't have a choice. We can't get out of here unless we go through the corridor.

He reaches inside his leather coat and pulls out a large knife, the one he'd threatened me with earlier. The sharp edge has an elegant curve to it, but the barbs on the opposite edge look like they could shred flesh. He snatches the battery-powered lantern off the shattered floor and seizes my arm again, dragging me toward the store's entrance and the corridor beyond. The corridor full of terrible beasts, according to Dax. Maybe he's just trying to scare me. He seems to enjoy doing that.

The jerk thinks I caused the apocalypse. He's insane and dangerous, but I guess that's what I need in a protector. I have no idea how to defend myself against the creatures that have invaded the city, but Dax at least has a weapon. Maybe he's got more hidden inside his coat. As long as he believes I know what the hell is going on and why, he will keep me alive. Right? My brain isn't running on all thrusters, but I'm pretty sure the beast of a man hauling me away is my only shot at survival.

For now.

I'm a librarian, not a woman warrior. What do I know about combat? Zilch, that's what. I hate feeling helpless.

Just as we step out into the corridor, Dax freezes. He swerves his head left and right, eyes narrowed.

A gang of freakish creatures has gathered in the corridor. I count at least six of them. Each looks different, but every single one of them scares the shit out of me. One has long fangs that protrude from its mouth, extending down its chin. Another has reddish-brown hair all over its body and eyes that flicker with red fire. And those are the nicest ones in the bunch. Every creature growls or snarls or gnashes its teeth, sometimes all three at once.

So this is what hell looks like.

Dax keeps hold of my arm, but pushes me behind his body. He waves his huge knife around like he's showing the monsters what he's got. They don't seem impressed.

"Back away," he growls, though his voice isn't as scary as the animalistic noises coming from the gang of creatures. "Let us pass, or I will be forced to destroy you."

Saliva drips from Fang Boy's mouth. "Give us the woman, and we will let you pass."

The creepy monster speaks? Yeah, this is definitely hell. That hole in the sky must've pulled demons out of the bowels of purgatory and dropped them off here just for fun.

Red Eyes chuckles, trickling a shiver down my spine. "Yes, give her to us."

"No," Dax declares, his voice so commanding and dangerous that another, harder shiver rakes through me. "She belongs to me. Leave now or die."

He brandishes his knife. It glistens in the backlit glow from the hole in the ceiling of the store behind us.

Fang Boy charges us.

Dax shoves me backward and rushes at Fang Boy. He slashes his knife across the monster's throat. Blood pours from the wound, and the creature crumples to his knees, gasping and gurgling.

Red Eyes makes his move next, roaring as he throws himself at Dax.

My sort-of protector dispatches that creature too. He stabs his knife into Red Eyes' gut and yanks it upward, gutting the beast.

I wince and look away. I've seen enough blood and gore today, but I doubt this will be the last.

The other monsters gallop away.

Dax turns toward me with the knife still in his grip. Blood coats his entire hand as well as the blade, and crimson liquid drips onto the floor. He stalks up to me, halting inches away, and wipes his knife off on his shirt. Then he tucks it inside his jacket.

I can't help cringing a little. He just murdered those two creatures without any remorse, without even trying to chase them away. Maybe he had no choice, but I've never witnessed such ferocity.

Breathing hard, he speaks through his clenched teeth. "Let's get back to that tunnel. We can't be above ground when the Echo reaches this section of the city."

He mentioned the Echo before, but he hasn't explained.

I don't get the chance to ask. He plucks up the lantern, then seizes my arm and tows me out of the building. I stumble over debris as we rush across the street, heading for the stockyards tunnel. A new pile of rubble blocks most of the entrance, but Dax tows me through the narrow opening without slowing down. My arm is starting to ache from how tightly he's gripping me. Not that I think he cares about that. Of course he doesn't. He might not be as hideous as those monsters in the mall, but he is a beast just like them.

Terrifying. Merciless. Alien.

A chill ripples through me. I'm the prisoner of a beast from…who knows where. Why hadn't I ever bought a stun gun or at least a can of pepper spray?

Dax halts and switches on the lantern. He sets it down on the cracked terracotta tiles of the floor. "You will stay here while I secure the tunnel at both ends."

He pulls his leather belt out of his pocket.

The creep wants to bind my hands again. Screw that. No more letting him drag me around.

I race for the tunnel's opening, scrambling through the narrow gap in the debris pile.

Large, powerful hands clamp onto my ankles and pull me back into the tunnel. Dax hoists me to my feet and lashes his arms around me, squeezing me to his body. "That was a stupid mistake. You can't outrun me. You can't overpower me. Give up."

"Never."

"Your sudden desire to be feisty will only make your situation worse." He snatches his belt off the floor. "You leave me no choice. Remember, this was your doing, not mine."

He spins me around until my backside is pinned to his front. His thick, musclebound arm restrains me, and I can't get any leverage that I might use to free myself. He's too damn strong. Too damn big. Too damn evil.

Before I realize what he's doing, Dax has bound my wrists with the leather belt. He shoves me against the concrete wall, then kneels in front of me. The jerk uses my own shoelaces to bind my feet. I'd worn my favorite boots today, leather ones with strong, thick laces. If I'd known what would happen today, I would have worn my Velcro tennies instead.

Dax takes a big step backward. "You have no choice now."

He stomps over to the debris that's blocking this end of the tunnel and starts shifting large chunks until he's sealed the entrance.

"What are you doing?" I demand.

He ignores my question and stalks down the tunnel in the other direction, disappearing from my view. Even the sound of his boots clomping fades away. Silence pervades the space, and the smell of blood fills my nostrils. My blood? Most of it probably is. But my boots had crunched on things I couldn't think about when I fled from the epicenter of the apocalypse. Who knows what I've got glued to my body.

I slide down the wall until my butt meets the terracotta floor.

Footfalls clap closer and closer, louder and louder. Dax emerges from the shadows, stopping just inside the circle of light from the lantern.

"You blocked us in, didn't you?" I say. "We're trapped."

"For our protection."

"How are we going to breathe with no ventilation? The air in here won't last forever."

"It will last long enough. I can reopen either entrance as soon as the worst of the Echo has passed through this area."

Time for the cretin to explain a few things. "Why do you keep talking about 'the Echo'? What does it mean?"

"You know as well as I do."

I want to cross my arms, but I can't do that with my wrists bound. So I scowl up at him instead. "Stop telling me I know what's going on. I don't. And I certainly did not cause it."

"That's bollocks." He walks toward me, then crouches close enough that our knees almost touch. "You are responsible for everything that's happening."

"No, I am not. I don't even know what 'the Echo' means."

He studies me for a moment, his expression giving away nothing. "The Echo is the power driving the apocalypse, the power that will merge both worlds."

"There's only one world."

"Wrong. There is this world, the one normal humans live in. Then there is the Echo, the world populated by desecrations of the human form."

"You said the Echo is the power behind what's happening, but now you're calling it a different world." I lean forward. "It can't be both."

"Of course it can. The Echo is the power generating the change, and it is the world that I and the monsters rampaging through this city came from."

I shake my head as I struggle to decide if I should believe him, if I should trust him to tell me the truth about even one thing. "Why do you keep saying I caused what's happening?"

"Because you did."

"No, I did not."

He mutters something that must be a curse, based on his tone. "Enough of this. Tell me about the magics. Tell me the truth or I will torture it out of you."

"Okay, here's the truth." I lean even closer, his breaths reflecting off my face. "I have no fucking idea what you're talking about."

"That's too bad—for you." He brings out his knife, holding its tip to the underside of my chin. "Last chance."

"I can't tell you about 'magics' that I know nothing about."

He presses the knife's tip into my flesh just enough to make his point, but not enough to break the skin. "Tell me about your relationship with Sefton Stainthorpe."

Cold floods through me, raising goosebumps on my arms. "Dr. Stainthorpe? I don't have a relationship with him. I barely know the man."

"Of course you know him. He created the Echo for you, with your help."

"What? You're insane."

Dax draws the knife across my skin, but again without piercing it. "You admit to knowing him. If you won't explain how the two of you did this, then tell me what happened in the days leading up to the merging of the worlds."

I glue my back to the wall, lift my chin, and spit my words at him. "Go to hell."

"We're living in hell already." He touches the knife's wickedly serrated edge to the underside of my ear. "Tell me what I want to I know, or I'll start slicing."

Nothing I can tell him will help because I have no idea how or why the apocalypse came to be. But I might as well share the events that happened before the Echo crashed into my world. Maybe that will satisfy him, though I doubt it.

"I have to start a few weeks ago," I say. "When Dr. Stainthorpe first visited the library."

Chapter Four

Allison
Three Weeks Ago

I'VE GOT THE EVENING SHIFT ON THIS TUESDAY, MANNING THE CHECK-out counter at the public library as I do five days a week, sometimes on Saturdays and sometimes in the evenings, working whatever hours I'm asked to take. While I prepare books for shelving, applying an adhesive plastic covering to paperbacks, I keep glancing at the clock.

Seven forty-two.

My shift ends at nine, closing time. Groaning and rubbing my aching neck, I return to my task. With a ruler, I smooth the bubbles out of the plastic sheath on a Nora Roberts novel. If only real life provided happy endings for everyone, the way these novels always do. Instead it doles out pain far too often and leaves me to slave away at a minimum wage job that doesn't require the master's degree I'd worked so hard to earn. I don't have anyone to go home to either. No parents. No real friends, just work buddies. No loved ones at all, only a long string of bad dates and failed relationships.

I won't tell Dax about that. My past and my private thoughts are none of his damn business. Instead, I get back to my story.

A man pushes through the main doors, stepping off the portico and into the open area in front of the check-out counter. As he walks toward me, I can't help noticing several things about him. He's attractive, with dirty-blond hair cut short and bright blue eyes. The guy has a trim build too, and I can see muscles stretching his suit jacket, though he doesn't seem like he works out obsessively. His suit looks a bit rumpled, just like his hair. He sports a shadow beard too, but based on his unkempt clothes, I suspect he simply hadn't bothered to shave, rather than his stubble being a fashion statement.

I paste on my polite smile as the man shuffles up to the counter, which comes up to waist height. Now I can see his blue eyes are bloodshot and dark circles rim his lower eyelids.

"Good morning," I say. "How may I help you?"

"I am in need of information about alchemy."

He sounds British. I've met quite a few Australians who emigrated to North Texas, but this guy is my first Brit.

"Alchemy?" I say. "Let me check our catalog, but I doubt we have much on that topic. Most people check out novels or kids' books."

The man observes while I type keywords into the search screen on the computer. Just like I thought, we don't have anything about alchemy.

"Sorry," I tell him. "We don't have those kinds of books in our collection, but I could probably get some on interlibrary loan. Or you could try the research databases we have access to. I can show you how to use them."

"That would be brilliant. Thank you, Miss…"

"Allison Dahl."

He offers me his hand to shake. "I am Dr. Sefton Stainthorpe."

"Nice to meet you, Dr. Stainthorpe."

"And you as well, Miss Dahl."

"You can call me Allison."

He tugs at the collar of his shirt and clears his throat. "I prefer formality, if that's acceptable to you."

"Sure. Whatever you want."

I get to work collecting all his info to sign him up with a library card, so I can request books for him via interlibrary loan.

Dax interrupts my story. "Sefton lived in Texas?"

"He gave me a local address, but it could've been fake. The library didn't run background checks on patrons. May I continue?"

"Yes."

Dr. Stainthorpe leaves with my promise to hunt down some books on alchemy. What an odd subject to study. Creating gold from lesser metals? It sounds like nonsense to me. No one can transform one thing into a completely different thing. Can they?

Maybe I don't get the whole alchemy thing, but I always do my job and go the extra mile for my patrons. Two days later, I phone Dr. Stainthorpe to let him know I've found several books for him as well as a ton of articles he can download on his home computer using the library's gateway. He asks me to print them out instead since he "can't understand the internet." Whatever. Printing out weird articles is part of my job.

A week after I'd first met Dr. Stainthorpe, he returns to the library to pick up the stuff I've gathered for him. I'm pushing a cart around while I reshelve books when Dr. Stainthorpe finds me in the stacks.

"How are you this eve, Miss Dahl?" he asks.

I suppress a chuckle. This eve? Nobody talks that way. "Is there any chance I can convince you to call me Allison?"

Shoulders hunched, he averts his gaze. "It seems inappropriate. We aren't well acquainted."

"We can change that." I pat his arm. "Let's be friends, hey?"

I swear his cheeks turn faintly pink, and he still won't look me in the eye. "Perhaps we could be friends. You've gone to a great deal of trouble to find those books for me. Might I take you to dinner?"

"Um…" Not sure if that's ethical or a good idea. But then, I don't have a great track record with men. Dr. Stainthorpe seems nice enough, but I've only met him twice and spoken to him on the phone once. Something about him makes me uneasy, though I can't put my finger on what it is. "Maybe another time. I'm always wiped out after an evening shift."

Yeah, I'm trying to let him down politely.

He looks disappointed and follows me back to the check-out counter in silence. While I scan the barcodes on the books I'd ordered for him, he keeps watching me. When I set the stack on his side of the desk, along with the papers I'd printed out, he scratches the back of his neck and almost winces.

"Do you have any books on quantum physics?" he asks. "I'm particularly interested in string theory and quantum entanglement."

"Uh, let me check." I perform a quick search of our catalog. "Sure. We've got some books on that. If you want in-depth stuff, I can hunt for more ILL books. That means interlibrary loan."

"May I see the books you do have?"

I guide him into the stacks and straight to the science section, then skim the call numbers on the spines until I locate the right ones. I hand them to Dr. Stainthorpe. "Any of these work for you?"

He flips through each of the books, then nods. "Yes, these will do. Though I would appreciate it if you could find more for me."

"Sure. ILL is the best way to get stuff on unusual subjects."

We say goodbye at the desk, and Dr. Stainthorpe leaves.

He returns several times over the next two weeks, always on days when I'm working. We don't chat much, and he doesn't ask me out again. I know nothing about him except his name and that he's British. One day my curiosity gets the better of me, and I search his name on the internet, coming up with only one result—his faculty listing on the Oxford University website, which contains little information about him. He's an associate professor with research interests in physics and the history of science. That's all I learn.

No matter how often I see Dr. Stainthorpe, I can't shake the unease his presence always triggers in me.

Three days before the apocalypse, Dr. Stainthorpe waltzes into the library looking like a different man. The rumpled scientist has put on a crisply pressed navy suit with a white handkerchief in the breast pocket. He has not only combed his hair, but has also brushed it back in a style that accentuates his beautiful face. Wow, he's a hottie. But I still can't muster any interest in him beyond our professional relationship.

He stops at the counter, holding one arm behind his back. Chin raised, he gazes at me with a slight smile on his lips.

"Good morning, Dr. Stainthorpe," I say. "How may I help you today? I hope those books and articles I got you were useful for your research."

"Yes, they have been enormously helpful."

"Glad to hear it."

He whisks his arm out from behind his back, revealing a bouquet of pink roses he holds in his hand. "These are for you, Allison. As thanks for all your hard work."

I accept the bouquet and sniff the flowers, enjoying their sweet scent. "That was very thoughtful, Dr. Stainthorpe."

"Would you call me Sefton?"

"Sure, but I thought you preferred formality."

"I have changed my mind."

"Okay." I set the bouquet on the desk. "Thank you for the roses, Sefton."

"You are the most beautiful woman in the world, Allison."

A shiver lifts the hairs at my nape. I'm not excited by his compliment, though. I feel weird about the whole conversation. The guy who couldn't look me in the eye a week ago is now flirting with me.

Sefton glances around as if he's watching for someone or something. Seeming satisfied with what he saw or didn't see, he zeroes his gaze in on mine. "Have you ever wanted to change the world?"

"Not really. I mean, everybody wishes the world were different, better, but too much is out of our hands."

"What if we could control the world's destiny?"

"That would be fabulous. If I could rule the world, I'd make sure everybody was happy."

He leans forward, arms braced on the desk, and bores his gaze into mine with such intensity that another shiver ripples through me. "I'm not talking about pie-in-the-sky dreams about improving the world. I mean real, tangible change. You and I, we could remake the world together."

"Not sure what you mean."

He lowers his voice to a whisper. "This is no joke, Allison. I want to give you the world, literally. You and I can change everything. I do not speak metaphorically, but in the most literal, concrete sense."

As I stare into his eyes, I realize he's serious. This man believes he can remake the world. "What exactly are you talking about?"

"You will see soon. Then you will understand I've done all of it for you, Allison."

The sound of a cell phone chiming, announcing a new text, emanates from his side of the desk. He pulls out the phone and checks it. His brows furrow, then his eyes light up. His entire expression becomes...excited.

"Please forgive me," he says as he backs away. "The moment is almost upon us. I will come to you when the event is nigh."

Before I can speak, he rushes out of the library.

Alchemy. Quantum entanglement. What do those two things have in common? Nothing that I can see. But clearly, Sefton believes those subjects hold the answers he needs to complete his insane quest to "remake" the world.

The day before the apocalypse, Sefton tracks me down deep in the bowels of the library where I've been shelf reading to make sure all the books are in their correct places. Sefton still dresses like a businessman as he had the last time I saw him. But his eyes are wild, and he seems incapable of standing still, instead bouncing on the balls of his feet.

"Sefton?" I say. "Are you okay?"

"The time is nigh," he announces, his tone and his expression full of excitement. "You must come with me, Allison. I can protect you, but only if we stay together."

"Protect me from what?"

"You will see." He grabs my hand and tugs. "Please. Hurry."

I yank my hand away. "You're scaring me, and I'm not going anywhere with you."

He throws his arms around me, dragging my body into his, and mashes his mouth to mine. I clamp my teeth shut to stop him from pushing his tongue inside and struggle against his hold. He keeps his lips glued to mine as a strange, almost electrical sensation zings into me through our joined mouths. The room spins around me, then settles down, leaving me dazed.

Sefton releases my lips but maintains his hold on my body. "I love you, Allison. And you love me too, I know it."

"No, I don't." I wriggle out of his arms. "I'm sorry, but I just don't feel that way. Please get out of here before I call the police."

He bows his head, knifing his fingers through his hair. "No, no, it wasn't meant to be this way."

"Leave, Sefton. Right now."

"Yes, yes, all right. I will go. You need more time to see, and tomorrow, all will become clear."

He hurries out of the library. I know he exits the building because I trail after him to make sure.

The next morning, I go to work as usual. After reshelving books for an hour, I return to the check-out counter to find someone has left me a note concealed inside an ivory envelope that feels like it's made from high-end paper. My name is scrawled on it in an elegant, sweeping hand.

I cautiously open the envelope and unfold the note.

"Stay in the library until I come for you," the note says. "To change the world, we must first dismantle it."

I stare at the note, at Sefton's elegant signature, and swallow against a tightness in my throat. Then I toss the paper into the trash can.

23

CHAPTER FIVE

Dax

HOW CAN YOU CLAIM TO BARELY KNOW SEFTON STAINTHORPE when you had a relationship with him?" I grip the belt that binds her wrists and pull her closer. "Stop lying to me. You were deeply involved with Sefton, which means you conspired with him to bring about the merging of worlds."

"I never conspired about anything. And I never really knew Sefton. I thought he was a nice guy—strange, but nice—until I found out he'd been hiding his true self until the day he couldn't hide it any longer." She curls her lip and hisses, "He's a whackjob, just like you."

Does she honestly know nothing? I refuse to believe that because Sefton spoke of her with deep emotion, as if she meant far more to him than a casual acquaintance. And I know she aided him.

"Perhaps he is insane," I say, "but you must have cared for Sefton. Stop lying and tell me how to find him."

"No idea." She yanks her wrists, tearing the belt out of my fingers, and slumps against the wall. "Go on and kill me or rip my fingers off or whatever you want to do. I don't care. The world has become a nightmare, and we'll both die sooner or later when monsters rip us apart."

"You can't escape me that way." I grasp her chin, forcing her to look at me. "Not yet, at least. I will keep you alive until you tell me where Sefton is."

"For the umpteenth time, I don't know. Are you deaf *and* stupid?"

A boom shivers through the tunnel. Bits of the ceiling tumble to the floor.

The woman who won't tell me the truth snaps her spine straight and peers up at the ceiling, eyes wide. "The ceiling might collapse any second."

"It will hold."

"How do you know? Are you an expert on tunnel construction?" When I don't respond, she huffs. "No, I didn't think so."

Naturally, she's being sarcastic. That makes me want to shag her even more. My cock doesn't care about the apocalypse raging above our heads.

If I want answers from her, I need to take a different approach. "You mentioned Sefton's note urged you to wait in the library until he came for you."

"Yes."

"But you didn't do that."

"I was hypnotized, like everyone else. Duh."

"Hypnotized?" I tilt my head to the side as I study her expression and body language, but I can't find any clues that suggest she's lying. "You weren't mesmerized when I found you. No one was. You were all screaming and running from the beasts."

"Yeah. But before that, the music put us in some kind of trance. We couldn't stop ourselves from going outside and congregating on and around the viaduct."

"That was the bridge across the river."

"Yes." She shuts her eyes, her lips trembling. "The music was almost worse than the monsters that came when the song ended."

"I didn't hear music," I tell her. "It must've happened before I arrived. But I have no doubts it wasn't a normal melody, but something borne of the Echo. That's why I need to find Sefton."

She opens her mouth as if she means to speak, but instead shuts it. Allison scrutinizes me for a long moment, her gaze traveling over me in what seems like an appraisal, though I have no idea what she's attempting to figure out by analyzing me from head to toe. "You know Sefton, don't you? That's why you keep calling him by his first name instead of saying Dr. Stainthorpe like everyone else does. He only asked me to call him Sefton a few days ago."

"Who or what I know is not your concern."

"It damn well is my concern. You're holding me hostage and threatening to dismember me."

"Only your fingers." I squeeze words out through my clenched teeth in a deliberate attempt to cow her. I know she fears me, but she has enough backbone to defy me in spite of that. My only option is to terrify her. "If you keep testing me, I might change my mind. You have many more appendages I can hack to bits."

"Go on and do it. I don't care anymore. The world is ending, and if I have to get hacked up by a beast, it might as well be you."

"The world is not ending. It is transforming."

She stops blinking, her gaze nailed to mine. "What do you mean it's transforming?"

"You'll see. Right now, I need to know where—"

"Gah!" she shouts so loudly that it reverberates through the tunnel. "For the last time, I have no fucking idea where Sefton Stainthorpe is."

Strangely, I believe her. "All right. That means we must wait until the first wave has passed through this part of the city, then we can check the library. Maybe Sefton is waiting there for you."

"Great. A field trip into hell."

I move to the opposite side of the tunnel, directly across from Allison, and sit down on the terracotta floor. All we can do now is wait. The strikes of lightning and fireballs have been lessening in frequency, but even after the skyborne chaos ends, we will need to contend with the monsters that have been dumped here. And we're running out of air in this tunnel, which means we can't wait much longer.

"Are you going to drag me through the city again?" Allison asks.

She can't walk with her feet shackled. But I can't trust her not to try to run away. I'll need to bind her to me somehow, maybe by strapping one of her wrists to one of mine. I have a little time to consider the options. Only when the first wave has passed will I attempt to reopen the tunnel.

Assuming we have enough air to last that long.

Once we venture outside again, we will have other problems. "Is there a shop in this city that sells weapons?"

"Like I'd tell you even if I knew. You probably want to torture me."

All I can do is growl. This woman seems determined to harass me until I snap and do something we will both regret. I'll wind up ravaging her, though not with torture devices.

"Where are you from?" she asks.

"Silence, woman."

"I told you everything I know about Sefton. Time for a little reciprocation, if you want me to cooperate."

Do I believe she will ever cooperate? Of course not. She's trying to wheedle information out of me. So I pretend I didn't hear her question and shut my eyes, listening to the sounds of chaos outside as they dwindle gradually. I swear I can feel Allison glaring at me, her gaze piercing me like a hot, sharp needle thrust into my eye.

She clears her throat. "I don't understand—"

"Silence. There will be no discussion. Do as I say or suffer the consequences."

The infernal woman huffs. "If you want my help, better start giving me some explanations. Otherwise, you can sit there sulking until the next millennium because I will not go anywhere with you."

"You are a fool if you think you'll have a choice. I can force you to do anything I want because I am stronger and larger than you."

"Go ahead and try it, creep. See how far you get."

I can't help it. My lids fly open, and my gaze gravitates to her. The look of sheer defiance on her face makes me want to...do things to her that I should never do. Sex should be the last thing on my mind in the middle of an apocalypse, but maybe this is exactly the time I should indulge my lust. One last shag before we all die.

To claim the woman Sefton coveted… No, jealousy is not the reason I'm behaving this way. It can't be.

Springing to my feet, I stalk up to her and shove my arms under hers. Then I hoist Allison off her feet and pin her to the wall with my body. I'm sure she can feel my cock hardening against her belly. Instead of cringing or struggling to get away from me, she stares into my eyes, not blinking, while her lips turn a deeper shade of pink and her pupils dilate.

Oh yes, she wants me. The woman despises and fears me, but a primal instinct drives this need we both feel. I despise her too, but I haven't been with a woman in so long…

I crush my mouth to hers.

Neither of us moves for a moment, both frozen by the shock of what I've done. Kissing her? It's insanity. I must stop this, despite everything inside me urging me to do the opposite. Not sure I can control myself, not today, not with her. *Back away right now, before you go too far.*

Allison moans low in her throat—and thrusts her tongue between my lips.

I try to pull away, but my body refuses to obey me. Every swipe of her tongue amplifies my hunger until I can no longer hold back. I ravage her with brutal lashes and nips, our teeth clashing and her moans growing more fervent. The scent of her lust makes me drunk, stripping away the vestiges of my control, though I cling to the tatters for as long as possible. Ravenous grunting noises emerge from her as she devours me as wildly as I'm consuming her, our kiss imbued with desperation and fear and something far darker too. With her arms trapped between our torsos, she wriggles against me like she wants to get free and wrap her entire body around mine. Never have I experienced lust like this. It erodes my willpower and propels me to rub my hard length into her belly. I should stop. To do this here and now…

Have I really become the sort of bastard who does a thing like this?

I tear my mouth away from hers, breathing so hard I feel almost light-headed, and set her down on her feet. A matter of inches separates our bodies, and her cheeks have turned pink. Her lips are slightly swollen too, while her gaze has gone glossy and unfocused.

I plant my palms on the wall, bracketing her shoulders, and lean in. "When I fuck you, it will be even more brutal than the way I just kissed you."

"That's never going to happen," she says, though her breathless tone proves less than convincing.

Despite her statement, I know it will happen. Neither of us can fight the overpowering need our kiss inflamed. That's why I must get away from her. Once she takes me to Sefton, I won't need Allison anymore. Can I make myself walk away, leaving her alone in this vicious new world? I'll think about that later.

Perhaps I am starting to believe her story.

No, never.

Her breasts rise and fall with every breath, and her lips are parted as if she wants me to kiss her again.

I slant in more until my lips graze hers. Then I growl, "Remember this the next time you consider harassing me."

"Remember what?"

Ignoring her question, I kneel to untie her bootlaces and unshackle her feet. Then I surge to my full height and liberate one of her hands so I can secure that end of the leather belt to my wrist. This will leave her with one hand free, but she won't get the chance to escape me. If Allison makes the slightest move to do that, I will stop her.

I grab the lantern and drag her down the tunnel to the entrance we had come through earlier. With one boot, I kick at the debris I'd used to seal us in. The chunks of concrete and rock fall away, revealing the twilight outside. I pause and tilt my head to the side to listen. Though I hear distant screams and feral noises, I don't detect any signs of fireballs or lightning.

"Move," I growl as I climb out through the opening, towing her after me.

She clambers over the debris, and I lead her away from the tunnel and onto the street. East Exchange Avenue, she had called it. Not that the name matters anymore.

"Which way to the library?" I demand.

"Um…" She squints and bites her lip. "Not sure."

"No games. Take me there now."

She plants one hand on her hip. "I didn't memorize a map of the city. Give me a minute to think. Everything looks different now."

"You have one minute."

"Until what?"

I tug her into me and lower my head to hers. "Until I walk away and leave you to fend for yourself. Without me, you'll be dead in five minutes."

She spits in my face. "I don't need you. And if you ever try to kiss me again, I'll grab your dick and twist so hard you'll scream like a baby."

"Our kiss was consensual. And you'll beg me to take your body."

"I didn't ask you to kiss me."

"Your desire was unmistakable." I tap her lips with one finger. "And you thrust your tongue into my mouth."

"That was—Ugh, I hate you."

I'm certain she does, but I'm equally as certain that she wants me inside her as much as I need to sink my cock into her soft, willing body. She is beautiful, passionate, fiery, and clever. Of course I hunger for her body. But that's all it will ever be—sex to satiate our mutual needs and numb the fear and pain.

She starts walking, and I let her lead me away. Whether she knows where she's going… I'll find out soon enough.

CHAPTER SIX

Allison

I'M TETHERED TO A MONSTER, AND I LET HIM KISS ME. EVEN WORSE, I kissed him back—with tongue. What on earth is wrong with me? I blame the apocalypse and the terror I've experienced ever since chaos descended on the city. How can a girl think clearly when the world is literally falling apart around her? I see no other explanation for my behavior back in the tunnel. Well, maybe I've suddenly developed a taste for crude, mean, obnoxious assholes who treat me like dirt.

No, I don't like that kind of man. So I guess I like grizzled, grimy, unkempt assholes instead. *Ugh.* Worst of all, I liked that kiss. Whatever that says about my mental state, I don't have time to think about it.

We scrabble over mounds of debris, tripping over dead bodies as we rush headlong back toward the epicenter of the destruction. But it doesn't seem as chaotic and terrifying as it had at first, and I'm not sure that's a good thing. I should still be horrified, but maybe I've just gotten numb from the shock.

I still glimpse demonic creatures now and then, but they seem less interested in us than in the corpses that litter the streets. No, I cannot think about that right now. Even if they're feasting on the lifeless remains of human beings, there's nothing I can do about it. No one can help the dead.

Survival. That's my only goal.

Others must have survived, right? Somewhere. Somehow. They would've run just like I did.

My legs burn and ache from trudging who knows how far today, and I feel like I can't catch my breath. Sweat pours down my temples. It must be two or three miles from the stockyards to the library, and I've already walked at least that far today. I haven't eaten since lunch either, when I had yogurt and a banana. How many hours have elapsed since then? Feels like forever.

"Stop," I tell Dax, tugging on our bindings. "I can't walk anymore."

He doesn't stop. He doesn't even slow down or glance at me. His jaw is firmly set while his gaze has narrowed, focused on the path ahead of us. This used to be a street, but I can't recognize enough of it to remember the name.

With all the strength I have left, I yank him hard enough that he stumbles.

Dax glares at me. "What do you think you're doing?"

"Trying to get your attention, obviously." I mop sweat from my forehead with the only part of my shirt's hem that's not soiled with things I refuse to identify. "We have to stop and rest. I'm hungry, exhausted, and probably dehydrated. You've already dragged me miles across the city, and now you're doing it again. I'm not a robot."

He stares at me without expression, though I swear I see a muscle in his jaw ticking.

My knees buckle. I hit the ground hard, slumping my entire body, though my left hand remains bound to his wrist. My arm hangs from his, and it's the only thing that keeps me from collapsing on the ground.

With a growl, Dax squats in front of me. He removes the leather belt that shackles us to each other and shoves it into the pocket of his coat. Then he picks me up and throws me over his shoulders in a fireman's hold. I'd already felt slightly nauseous and dizzy, but with my head upside down, I feel like the world is gyrating around me.

Dax sets off down the street again.

This makes no sense. The man who threatened to cut off my fingers is carrying me because I'm too weak to walk anymore. He terrifies me. I hate him, and he hates me. Yet we kissed, and now he's carrying me, which implies he cares about my welfare.

Minutes tick by, though I have no way to gauge how many. Hazily, I notice when we cross the Paddock Viaduct that spans the West Fork of the Trinity River, though I shut my eyes while we traverse the bridge because I know it must be littered with bodies. I can't take seeing more carnage. After a span of minutes that I can't count, he gently sets me down on what used to be a sidewalk, though the remnants around me only hint at the original purpose. I'm too exhausted to move, and I slip into a restless sleep.

Strong hands shake me. "Wake up, Allison. I found food and water."

I recognize that gruff voice. It's Dax.

"Huh?" I'm gradually rousing, but my head feels like it's full of cotton balls instead of brain cells.

"I have food." He slaps my cheek, though not hard. "Wake up and eat."

I push myself into a more upright position and realize I'm leaning against the brick wall of what used to be a building.

Dax hands me a plastic bag. "Your meal."

I notice he's holding an identical bag in his other hand. I take the one he offered me and pull out the contents—a sub sandwich, a bag of chips, and a bottle of water. He has a backpack slung over his shoulder. It's pooched out like he's filled it with stuff.

"What's that?" I ask, nodding toward the backpack.

"Enough water and food to keep us going for a while." He sits down near me, though not too close, and pulls out his own food. "There was a sandwich shop in a building over there"—He waves toward a semi-ruined structure across the street—"and I took all the food I could find."

"Where did the backpack come from?"

He turns his head to the side, almost as if he's ashamed to tell me. "The person it belonged to no longer needed it."

"Oh."

My throat goes thick when I consider the ramifications of his state-ment. The original owner of the backpack has no use for it now, but that bag might save our lives.

I dig into my food, wolfing down my sub sandwich faster than I prob-ably should, but I can't help it. Ham and cheese with tomatoes, onions, and fresh spinach never tasted so good in my life. I devour the jalapeno cheddar potato chips too, despite the fact I hate spicy stuff. Can't be choosy when the world is transforming. Into what, I have no clue. Dax doesn't want to tell me.

He studies me while I eat, his eyes flicking this way and that like he's searching for something in my expression. "Why aren't you worried about your family?"

"What?" I say with my mouth crammed full of food. A sliver of lettuce tumbles from my lips, and mayo dribbles down my chin. I swipe it away with the back of my hand.

His mouth twitches, almost like he wants to smile, but the expression fades quickly. "You haven't once expressed concern for your family or your mates."

"Neither have you."

He squints at me, which he seems to think will intimidate me. *Sorry, pal, no dice.* I've been through literal hell today, and I've grown a much thicker skin.

But I decide to be honest. "I don't have a family anymore. My parents died in a plane crash when I was eighteen, and I was an only child. As for friends, those were people I worked with and never saw outside of the library."

"Why don't you have real mates?"

"None of your business." No, I don't want to share my painful past with him. I've given him enough info for now.

After we're done eating, we just sit here for a while. Maybe he's not as indestructible as he seems, because I get the impression he needed rest and sustenance as much as I did.

Finally, I have to ask. "How is the world transforming? All you said before was that I'll see."

"I'm not entirely certain what it is becoming. Only Sefton can answer that question."

He rises, hooking the backpack over his shoulder, and grabs my hand to urge me to stand too. Then we head out again. Despite the destruction, I start to recognize some of the buildings. At last, I spot a street sign that affirms my belief we're going in the right direction. We're on Throckmorton Street, which means we need to get on the next block over to find the Central Branch of the Fort Worth Public Library. We scramble around the remnants of a parking garage and at last reach Taylor Street. Now we stand just behind the library, directly across from the Tarrant County Plaza building.

I spread my arms. "We're here."

"Is this the front entrance?" Dax asks. "If so, we can't get into the building. The facade has collapsed and blocked our way in."

"The main entrance is around the other side."

He follows me down Taylor Street until we reach West Third, then we walk side by side down that street, stopping in front of the portico that shields the main entrance. The four pillars in front have been shattered, and large chunks of them lie scattered around the area. For a moment, I gape at the damage while my brain struggles to come to terms with what I'm seeing. What I keep seeing. Everywhere I look. This can't be real, but it is.

Dax shoves me from behind. "Get moving."

We wend our way through the remains of the columns and step through the shattered glass doors, careful not to get cut. The interior is dark. That means we not only have no lights, but no ventilation either. It's beyond stuffy in here, and I start to sweat just from hopping over freestanding shelving units that have toppled over, spewing books across the floor. When we reach the check-out counter, which is miraculously intact, I stop and face Dax.

Naturally, he glowers at me.

"Well, we're here," I say, waving at our surroundings. "Don't see anything alive in this place except for you and me."

He digs the lantern out of his backpack and switches it on.

I pray there are no bodies in here. My gut twists when I think about that, and I will not go any further into the building to find out. There's no point. The dead can't be saved. I hate that circumstances have forced me to harden myself to the death and destruction around us. Later, I'll feel everything. Won't I?

"Where would Sefton find you whenever he visited the library?" Dax asks.

I shrug. "Wherever I was. Sometimes I'd be at the check-out counter, but other times I might be in the stacks or in a storage room."

"We will check everywhere, then."

"Everywhere? In case it escaped your attention, being a thickheaded lout, this is an enormous building."

He slants toward me. "Better start searching."

The only way I'm getting out of this building is if I find evidence that Sefton was here and left, or if I find a way to disable Dax for long enough that I can escape from him. Option two seems improbable. The bastard is a hulking mass of muscles. So I go for option one and lean over the waist-high check-out counter to rummage through any papers I can find.

"Nothing here," I say.

Dax grasps my ass in both hands, then pushes me up and over the counter. While I crash onto a chair and tumble off it, he watches me with a smug expression. "Look harder."

I scramble to my feet and do what he commanded. What choice do I have? Unless I find a weapon here or suddenly develop superpowers, I'm stuck with the grizzled jerk. He watches me while I root through the papers strewn across the floor, shoving a computer monitor out of the way and avoiding the staples that litter the carpet.

Then I see it. An envelope.

Crawling under the desk, I grab the ivory-colored envelope. It feels and looks like the same fancy paper on which Sefton had written his note that urged me to stay in the library until he came for me. I recognize the elegant handwriting too. "For Allison," it says. Dax will want to see this, I know, but I need to find out what Sefton said before I tell my captor. I kneel under the desk, sitting back on my heels and slouching forward. Then I peel the flap open and pull out the folded sheet of ivory paper tucked inside the envelope.

A shiver tingles over my skin, from my scalp down to my toes.

Whump.

A pair of large, booted feet land in front of me. Dax bends over to seize my arm and drag me out from under the counter. He hoists me off the floor with my feet dangling in the air and our faces aligned. The barely contained fury on his face makes me shiver again.

"You found a note from Sefton," he snarls. "Didn't you? And now you're trying to hide it from me to protect your lover."

"I am not involved with Sefton Stainthorpe. But you're never going to believe me, are you?"

He lets go of me.

My tailbone smacks into the counter's edge. I wince and hiss, but he doesn't pay any attention because my suffering means nothing to him. So what if he scrounged up food and water for me? He wants me alive until he finds Sefton, that's all.

I'm leaning against the counter now with Sefton's note clenched in my hand while the throbbing pain in my tailbone gradually fades.

Dax snatches the note from me. He reads the handwritten text, and his brows knit together. "What does this mean?"

"That Sefton is loony tunes."

"No, it has meaning." He thrusts the note at me. "And you know what it is."

"The only part I understood was 'Dear Allison, sorry I missed you.' The rest is insane."

He throws an arm around me, mashing my body to his, and reads the now-crumpled note. "Through the alchemy of worlds, the alchemy of souls, the Echo shall reveal the true nature of all."

"Crazy talk, like I said."

"No, I don't think so." Dax pins his gaze to mine. "You left out the bit where he vows to find you again."

My best option right now is to say nothing. He won't believe anything I say unless I tell him what he wants to hear, but that would be lying. It's not my fault Sefton became obsessed with me when he tipped over the edge, tumbling headfirst into madness. The alchemy of worlds? What does that mean?

Dax told me the world isn't ending. It's transforming.

The beast clutching me to his body sweeps me up in his arms and climbs over the counter, thumping down on the other side. Then he sets me on my feet and grabs my arm, towing me out of the library.

All those books about alchemy and quantum entanglement... Sefton must have wanted them as part of whatever he did to transform the world. But what is it becoming?

Chapter Seven

Dax

WHAT DOES THE NOTE MEAN? I ASSUME THE ALCHEMY OF WORLDS HAS already begun, but the alchemy of souls is yet to come. I don't know exactly what Sefton meant by those terms. Still, I'm certain it doesn't herald the beginning of utopia. No, a deranged mind like his would dream up something much worse than what we've seen so far. Sefton always was a master planner.

But I could never have envisioned what he would become—or what he would do. Am I as deranged as he is?

Allison and I exit the library, and I start walking down the pockmarked street for several yards before I realize she is not following me. The bloody-minded woman isn't trying to escape, though. When I turn to look for her, she's sitting on the edge of the pavement in front of the library with her feet on the roadway, holding the wrinkled note. She stares at it with a blank expression.

With a heavy sigh, I stalk back to her. "What are you doing? We need to keep moving."

She holds up the note. "Do you know what this means? Because I don't have a clue."

"Only Sefton knows what it means. That's why we need to find him."

"Told you I don't know where he is." She crumples the note and tosses it away. A breeze latches onto the ball of paper, whisking it across the street. "Might as well start chopping off my fingers."

Why must she keep repeating the threat I'd made earlier? Maybe I should follow through on it, but I don't have time for that right now. I am not delaying because I feel bad for issuing that threat. Her feelings mean nothing to me. Her safety only matters because I need her to take me to Sefton.

I don't care what happens to Allison Dahl. No, I don't.

What I should do is walk away now. Leave her there looking miserable and alone. But I don't do that. For reasons I can't comprehend, I sit down beside her and pull a water bottle out of my backpack, then hand it to her.

Surprise flashes on her face, but only for a second. She accepts the bottle and unscrews the lid, taking a long drink of water. "Thank you."

"Don't thank me. I'm only keeping you fed and hydrated because—"

"Yeah, yeah. I know you hate me. But you're obsessed with the asinine idea that I know how to find Sefton Stainthorpe." She holds the water bottle between her palms, turning it side to side while she studies me. "Why do you hate me? I've never done a damn thing to you."

Not sure I know how to answer that question. From the moment I first saw her, I had been determined to capture and interrogate her, to wrench the truth out of her by whatever means necessary. But do I despise her? Or am I afraid of what she might do to me? She can't hurt me physically. Perhaps I'm afraid of what I might do to *her*. This lust she inflames in me… I don't know what it means or if I can control it.

Since I refuse to answer her question, I change the subject. "Where else might Sefton go in this city?"

"Not a clue."

"That's bollocks. You know him. He left you a note, which must mean he expects you to find him. Sefton needs your help. You are the catalyst, after all."

"I'm the what? If you're implying I conspired with him to start the apocalypse, you're even more wacko than I thought."

She thinks I'm insane, but it's Sefton who deserves that label.

What time of day is it? Hard to tell while the sky still roils with dark energies that all but blot out the heavens. A false twilight had overtaken the city earlier, but sooner or later the real thing will descend on us. True night may prove much deadlier. The city has no electricity which means no lights—except for the battery-powered lantern I nicked from that store. I have no idea how long its batteries will last.

Allison snaps her fingers in front of my face. "Hello? Are you awake?"

I swat her hand away. "I was not asleep."

"Good. Then you can tell me what the hell you meant when you said I'm the catalyst."

Telling her seems like a bad idea. Then again, she might be more cooperative if she understands what precisely is going on since she claims to have no knowledge of what's happened.

"Do you honestly know nothing about the Echo?" I ask.

She groans and rolls her eyes at me. "For the umpteenth time, I do not know anything about any of this. "

I pull out another water bottle and swig half its contents, only in part to delay answering her question. "I told you before that the Echo is the driving force behind the apocalypse and that it will transform both worlds. The Echo is a magical construct. It requires dark energies of such power and scale that no one can comprehend its vastness."

"Ditch the hyperbole and explain."

"It's not hyperbole. Magics of that scale require both a catalyst and an anchor. Otherwise, the construct would crumble."

She swivels toward me and smacks her water bottle down on the pavement. "I am not a catalyst. Whatever Sefton might've done, it's not my fault."

"In his warped mind, he believes he loves you. The magnitude of his obsession fuels the Echo, but he needed you to set the machine in motion."

Her eyes narrow, and her lips flatten. "I had nothing to do with any of that. If Sefton is obsessed with me, that's his problem. I never agreed to become his catalyst."

I believe her, though I can't imagine why. Might Sefton have used Allison as his catalyst without her knowledge? I'm hardly an expert on magical constructs or dark energies, though I learned enough during my time in the Echo to comprehend what my brother has done. But Sefton is a scientist who has spent years learning about and experimenting with things most people think are utter rubbish.

"Perhaps you didn't willingly or knowingly help Sefton," I say. "But he used you to trigger the process. You are the catalyst, and I am the anchor."

"Does that mean you're holding the Echo together?"

"I'm not sure. That's why I need Sefton. Only he understands the intricacies of what he's done."

"Can he stop the worlds from transforming and merging?"

"That's a question for the man who created the Echo."

Allison glances up at the sky, at the dark, seething maelstrom that marks the opening into the Echo. "If you stop threatening to dismember me, I'll go with you."

"You're going with me either way."

"Try saying 'thank you.' It wouldn't actually kill you to be a little bit nice."

I can't help growling softly. "We are not friends. You are still my prisoner, and I still do not trust you."

"Ditto." She offers me her hand. "No dismemberment, and I won't run away without just cause. Do we have a deal?"

She gave herself a way out by including "without just cause" in her statement. But she will regret it if she tries to escape. The situation is too dire for me to be even "a little bit nice" to her.

I shake her hand. "Yes, we have a deal. Now, tell me where else Sefton might have gone."

"I don't know."

"Think, Allison. There must be another place that has meaning for him, something related to you."

She closes her eyes as if she's racking her brain for an answer. Her entire face becomes slightly pinched.

Roars and screeching sounds erupt in the distance.

Her eyes flare wide. She flaps her head left and right as if searching for the source of those noises.

"They're blocks away," I tell her, though I'm not certain of that. "Concentrate on where Sefton might have gone."

She drops her forehead into her palms.

Human screams reverberate from elsewhere in the city, and she flinches. Neither of us can help the poor sods out there. Even I am not strong enough to defeat an army of Echo creatures, and I'm positive Sefton limited my strength on purpose.

Allison lifts her head. "The Kimbell. I told him about it, and later he mentioned he'd gone there."

"What is the Kimbell?"

"It's an art museum. I mentioned to Sefton it was my favorite place in the city." She drinks the last of her water and tosses the empty bottle away. "I told him about a painting I've loved ever since the first time I saw it. Sometimes I go to the Kimbell just to look at that painting again."

"He knows how much that artwork means to you."

"Yes."

I jump up. "Then we should go there."

"The Kimbell is a couple miles away, at least. Maybe you're an invincible caveman, but I can't keep trudging through the city. I'm in good shape, but I never trained for long-distance hiking through post-apocalyptic rubble."

Her mention of being in good shape spurs me to skim my gaze over her body, and I can't resist paying special attention to her breasts. Yes, she is in fine physical condition. Fucking her will be incredible. But she does have a point about hiking through the city anymore today. Even I'm starting to feel knackered. Maybe that explains why I've been…somewhat less nasty to her. I'm too exhausted to snarl and shout at the woman.

I survey the area.

Allison clambers to her feet. "What are you looking for?"

Rather than responding, I amble down the pavement so I can get a better look at the car park across the street. Shattered asphalt and lumps of debris from the buildings nearby obstruct my view. So I jog across the street and climb atop a mound of rubbish to survey the vehicles parked there.

Allison races to catch me up. "Are you thinking maybe we can use one of these cars?"

"Yes."

"Do you know how to hot-wire a car?"

"No, but I'm hoping someone might have left their keys in one of these vehicles or hidden a spare one on the underside."

"Good idea. Maybe we'll get lucky."

I shuffle down the sloping mound of debris and start to search the cars. Most are locked, and I'd never learned how to break into a vehicle. Allison searches too, and she's the first to locate an unlocked car. We don't find a key inside it or hidden anywhere on its exterior. After several more minutes of searching, we find a vehicle that's unlocked and has a key stashed under the sun visor.

Allison doesn't complain when I take the driver's seat. It feels odd to sit on the left side. I'm having trouble adjusting to the change since I literally dropped into this country with no idea where I was. It hardly matters if I accidentally drive on the wrong side of the road. There are no other cars in sight, no movement visible anywhere, no sign of life other than the distant screams and roars.

Luckily, we find a way out of the car park that doesn't require driving over the rubble heap. I doubt this vehicle could handle that. But Allison suggests I should drive onto the rubble because it's a "shortcut" and we need to "scram" as fast as possible.

"This is an older saloon, not an SUV," I tell her. "It isn't built for that."

"A saloon? I guess that's the British word for a sedan, huh?"

"Yes."

"So it doesn't mean there's a wet bar in the backseat."

"No."

She sighs. "Darn. I could use a stiff drink."

When I glance at her sideways, I catch her smirking. Is she teasing me? Considering my behavior, I can't believe she would do that. But her statement about needing a drink had sounded almost playful. I don't want her to get comfortable with me. Her fear of what I might do to her assures her compliance.

"Don't get used to riding in a car," I say, making sure to growl the words while I veer the car around a corner. "Once I get what I want, you will be of no further use to me."

"Gee, you sure know how to sweet-talk a girl."

"Why would I bother with that?" I swerve around a pile of debris, and the headlights flash across the ruined facade of a building, revealing several creatures hunkered there. "You would do well to stop harassing me, unless you want me to finish what we started in the tunnel. I won't be nice to you when I take your body. It will be—"

"Mean and nasty, blah-blah-blah. I've memorized your little speech, so you can shut the hell up about it now."

Allison looks annoyed again, and she's hugging herself too.

Maybe I feel uneasy about upsetting her, but I can't let her see that. I force myself to relax into my seat. "Tell me how to find the Kimbell."

CHAPTER EIGHT

Allison

WE DON'T SPEAK FOR THE REST OF THE JOURNEY TO THE MUSEUM, EX-cept when I give him directions. The streets look so different now, and the darkness doesn't help matters, but I manage to get us there. Dax drives too fast, but I don't bother telling him to slow down. He'll do whatever he wants no matter what I say. Maybe I had, for a brief time, thought he might be turning into a semi-normal person. But then he snapped at me again and said nasty things to me again, and I remembered he's nothing but a brute.

I cannot trust him. Not ever.

The drive to the museum is a bumpy one, and Dax has to zig-zag around small groups of monsters from the Echo, all of whom look far more danger-ous than he does. I don't see any normal humans. They can't all be dead, can they? Some must have survived the "first wave," as Dax called it. I don't want to think about what the second wave will be like. Maybe the people who lived in this city have hunkered down to hide from the beasts. Maybe they aren't all dead.

I survived only because Dax captured me and spirited me away from the worst of the madness.

We make a detour when I spot a sign for the street Sefton gave as his address, but he doesn't live there. It's an empty lot. Where did Sefton live? Solving that mystery can wait.

Our journey takes longer than it would have pre-apocalypse, but that's no surprise. We pass by buildings that have been reduced to rubble with no evidence of what they were before the destruction began. Just glimpsing the damage as we rush through the darkened city makes me feel nauseous. My eyes start to burn too, and my throat thickens. I can't help teetering on the verge of tears. Who wouldn't get choked up under these circumstances?

Dax, that's who. He doesn't seem to care about anyone or anything except getting what he wants.

Miraculously, we reach the cultural district. Some of the buildings have survived with moderate damage rather than total devastation, while the Kimbell Art Museum seems to have remained mostly intact. Right across the street, the parking lots have suffered major wounds. Yet the museum has survived with cosmetic injuries, though a small section of the roof has caved in. How is that possible? Dax claims Sefton Stainthorpe created the apocalypse, and he seems to think Sefton did that because of me. Could he have spared the museum because he knows I love it?

No. This can't have anything to do with me.

Dax parks in the driveway of the museum, right next to the huge modern art sculpture that marks the entrance. We head for the glass doors that access the building and find them intact and unlocked, as if everyone fled in such a hurry that they didn't bother to secure the premises. As much as I love art, protecting the collection wouldn't have been my priority either. Getting the hell away from the lightning and fireballs, not to mention the monsters, matters more.

As we make our way into the building, Dax turns on the battery-powered lantern. It provides a surprising amount of light considering how small it is, and we have no trouble navigating through the building. Artworks lie scattered on the floor or hang askew on the walls, as if the place has been looted. But nobody took the paintings or sculptures. Whoever did this rampaged through the building in search of something else. There's a restaurant in here and a gift shop too, so maybe they looted those for supplies.

I trip over a small object on the floor. As I reach down to pick it up, I recognize the item. It's an ancient Mesoamerican statue from the Olmec culture. The six-inch-tall figurine depicts a broad-shouldered man with a large, rounded head and a mouth that curves down in a partial frown. Something about his eyes has always struck me as sad. The whole sculpture feels that way, more today than ever before. This poor little guy survived the end of his civilization thousands of years ago only to experience a genuine apocalypse today. He deserves better than to lie on the floor like a discarded toy. So I gently set him on an empty display pedestal.

"What are you doing?" Dax demands.

"Showing a little respect."

"For what? It's a stone statue." He stalks toward me. The jerk had gone halfway across the room before he noticed I wasn't right behind him.

"Excuse me for wanting to preserve one little thing when the world is ending or transforming or whatever." The start of tears burns in my eyes, but I do not want to cry in front of him. I suck in a breath and will the tears to go away. As if that ever works. "If you want to threaten me some more, go ahead. I don't care. Showing emotion is not a crime."

"Perhaps not, but it will get you killed."

"By you? Go on and try it." I throw my arms wide. "Rip me to pieces."

He stares at me for several seconds, breathing hard, his teeth bared. Then he whirls away from me. "Get moving. We need to find that bloody painting and hope Sefton is there or that he at least left you another note."

Naturally, he speaks those words in a vicious tone like the beast he is.

With only the light of Dax's lantern to guide us, I lead the way as we navigate around the debris and hop over artworks that have fallen onto the floor. Maybe it's a dumb reaction, but I can't help feeling a little sad when I see those beautiful works of art strewn across the floor, damaged and abandoned. I'd visited this museum more times than I can count, and coming here had always given me a sense of peace. Now, it's a war zone.

I almost walk past the painting I'm looking for, but then Dax raises his lantern, dispelling the shadows—and the picture we've been searching for comes into view. I stop six feet away from it, entranced as always by the stark beauty of the image. It's a not a scene of war, though. The painting evokes the perils of the sea while a storm rages around a jetty and a beacon meant to guide ships to port. Two men struggle to aid a boat as its occupants make way for the harbor. The drama and starkness of the imagery has always fascinated me.

"This is it?" Dax says. "The painting you love is of a storm at sea?"

"Yes."

"And you told Sefton about this painting."

"That's right. But I don't see him anywhere around here. Do you?"

Dax peers into the shadows at the edges of the room where the lantern's light peters out. "We should wait here for a while to see if he shows up."

"How long do you plan on waiting?"

"Overnight." He glances at the collapsed ceiling, then scans his gaze over the room again. "If Sefton hasn't turned up by morning, we will move on."

"To where, exactly? If Sefton is still in town, he could be anywhere. Assuming those monsters haven't killed him."

Dax grunts. "They won't. He created them."

"It's time you explained yourself. Tell me how you know so much about Sefton, how you know he created the Echo, and what the hell all these creatures are that apparently came out of the other world." I round on him, stabbing a finger into his chest. "Cough up some answers. No more sidestepping."

"What gives you the idea that you have leverage to make me do anything?" He leans in to glare into my eyes. "I have the power, not you. When and if I feel like explaining myself, I'll tell you."

He's wrong. I have leverage, because he believes he can't find Sefton without me. So I lift my chin and march past the jackass.

Dax grabs my arm. "Where do you think you're going?"

"To the cafe." I shake off his hand. "There might be edible food there, and what you've got in your backpack won't last long. Might as well gobble up whatever's available here."

He squints at me.

I start walking.

The clomping of footsteps behind me lets me know Dax is following. I'm getting damn sick of his behavior, and if he tries to grab me again, I'll sink my teeth into his nose.

In the cafe, we find both food that still seems edible and paper bags to store it in, so we gather as much of the food as we can. We put the bags in a plastic tub we discover in the kitchen. This part of the building suffered minimal damage, but it's getting awfully warm in here thanks to no central air and the Texas summer heat.

Dax takes us back to the South Gallery, where the painting we came to see resides. He thought Sefton would leave a clue for me here, but we found nothing.

On our way back to the gallery, Dax ripped the cushions off a pair of benches and hauled them in here, carrying both under one arm. Each cushion is as long as I am tall. Yeah, the jerk is very strong. He lays the cushions down on the floor after clearing an area, creating a space where we can sleep in relative comfort. A breeze wafts down to us through the hole in the ceiling and makes this room a lot more tolerable, temperature-wise, than the cafe had been.

Maybe I should appreciate the fact he tried to make our sleeping spot comfortable. I can't feel gratitude, though, not for the man who abducted me. Besides, he positioned his makeshift bed in front of mine, essentially trapping me against the wall. I promised him I wouldn't run away as long as he stopped threatening to dismember me, but he clearly doesn't believe I'll stick to my oath. Somehow, I manage to fall asleep. After a day of trudging back and forth across the city, I'm exhausted. But still, it seems like a miracle that I can get any rest when I hear unearthly screams and roars reverberating through the night outside our little sanctuary.

In the morning, Dax announces we need to get moving again. When I ask where he thinks we're going, he just grunts and orders me to move my "arse." We find our borrowed car again, and of course, he insists on driving. I've decided to think of this vehicle as borrowed rather than stolen since the person who owns it is probably dead. The thought gives me a shiver.

Dax has no idea where he's going, but he drives like he has a plan, his gaze fixated on the road and his jaw tight. He makes turn after turn, his choices clearly random. But I've given up on trying to convince him to let me take the wheel. Every time I suggested it, he snarled one sexist statement or another, all related to the idea women are too silly and stupid to be trusted to drive.

I can't believe I kissed the jackass. Can't believe I had a dirty dream about him last night either. Maybe he is hot, in a scruffy caveman way, but I will never do the things I fantasized about in my dreams.

When he turns onto River Drive, I can't stop myself. I need to speak up. "Do you have any idea where you're going?"

"Away from where we were."

"Fabulous plan."

We're approaching the railroad trestle that spans the Trinity River, but he veers off the road mere feet from the bridge and heads across the grassy expanse of Trinity Park.

"You really have no clue what you're doing," I say. "Randomly swerving around doesn't help anything."

He stares straight ahead as we bounce across the walking paths, then he swerves right to duck under the trestle. I'm about to say something when he slams on the brakes, making the car fishtail briefly, and we jerk to a halt at the edge of the grassy riverbank. Dax flings his door open and leaps out.

"What are you doing now?" I ask.

He slams the door shut.

While I watch, probably with my mouth gaping, he traipses down a rocky path that leads to the water. What on earth is he up to? We can't drive across the river or swim to safety. Well, I suppose we could drive over the railroad bridge, but it would be a very bumpy ride. And where would we go, anyway? He still hasn't answered that question.

I climb out of the car and stumble along the rocky path, jogging to catch up as he stomps down the shore. I assume he wants to get away from the lumpy area and avoid the drop-off where the water dives into a swirling cascade. He finds a calmer part of the river and halts.

Then he kicks off his boots and starts to remove his clothing.

I stop a dozen feet from him, suddenly frozen. He's not going to undress all the way. Is he? No, he must want to get rid of his coat, that's all. But the idea he might strip naked gives me a strange fluttery sensation in my tummy. I watch in mute fascination, glued to this spot, while he removes every stitch of his clothing.

Dax now stands buck naked on the shore.

Swallowing hard, I try to look away. But my eyes have other ideas. I drink in the sight of his nude body, all muscles and sinews, from his thick biceps to his taut ass and those powerful thighs. When we met, I'd noticed hints of tattoos peeking out from under his shirt, but now I can see the sweeping designs that cover one arm and half of his torso. Though I want to ask him about his tattoos, I get distracted when he turns halfway toward me.

And I get a good look at his dick.

The long, thick length of it is impressive even though he's not aroused. I can't imagine how big he is when he gets an erection. Well, yeah, I kind of can imagine. But I wish I couldn't. That fluttery sensation grows stronger, and a sultry tingle sweeps over my skin, awakening a deep, wet throbbing inside my sex. No, I cannot want a jerk like Dax.

But heaven help me, I *do* want him.

Dax wades into the river. Then he turns around and looks straight at me. "Come in, Allison. Join me."

CHAPTER NINE

Dax

ALLISON STARES AT ME WITH WIDE EYES, BUT SHE'S NOT GAWPING AT my face. Her attention is fixated on my body. She can see everything since I've waded in only up to my knees. I need to shag that woman. Right now. I'll take her in the water or on the grass or anyplace she wants as long as I can have her this instant. It's been too bloody long since I felt a woman's body wrapped around me. Even longer since I had a girl who wasn't from the Echo.

I wade in deeper, glancing over my shoulder at Allison.

She's rubbing her arms and biting her lip. She wants me, and she wants to disrobe in my presence. I can tell. Understanding a woman's amorous responses had been the key to my success in the bedroom before the Echo.

Allison edges closer to the water.

I drop to my knees and fall backward into the current. My whole body sinks under the surface, and I whisk my fingers through my hair to cleanse the filth from it. When I emerge from the water, I see Allison has removed her boots. She just tossed them onto the grass, and now she pulls her shirt off over her head and lets it flutter down to join her boots on the ground. Her gaze locks on to mine as she shimmies out of her jeans.

The sight of her almost naked transfixes me. Her pale blue bra reveals the inner slopes of her breasts, and her skimpy knickers barely cover the hairs at the apex of her thighs. My breathing grows labored as I watch and wait for her to strip off the rest of her clothing. But she doesn't do it. Allison wades into the water in her underwear, and once she's in up to her knees, she whirls around and flops into the water backward, unleashing a miniature geyser around her.

The splash rains down on me.

She sinks under the surface, then shoots back up, smiling at the sky.

Christ, she's beautiful.

Allison tips her head back to rinse her hair in the water. The movement pushes her breasts up, and her wet bra reveals the hard peaks of her nipples.

Movement catches my attention out of the corner of my eye. Though I turn my head to look, I can't see anything. But I know there had been motion. I slowly scan the river until I see it—an odd ripple in the water that seems to be traveling toward us, fast. The ripple reminds me of when I'd once seen a shark racing through the water, but its dorsal fin had protruded above the surface. Still, whatever is causing the ripple seems to be moving just as fast and creating a similar profile in the water.

The beast is heading straight for Allison.

"Get out of the water!" I shout.

She freezes with both hands in her hair and stares at me.

"Out of the water!" I roar.

I swim for the submerged object that's still racing toward us, placing myself in the path of the beast.

Allison swims toward the shore.

I dive under the water just as the mystery object collides with me. Teeth nip at my flesh, but I grasp what feels like the head of the beast and yank it hard, feeling cervical bones crack. I've snapped the creature's neck. Its limp body floats to the surface.

"What the hell is that?" Allison calls out to me. She's standing at the edge of the water, clutching her clothes.

The beast I've just killed has a humanoid body, but its skin consists of flesh-colored scales, and I see gills on its torso. It's brown eyes look disturbingly human, though now they are vacant.

I stalk back to the shore, halting beside Allison. "Get dressed."

"What was that thing?"

"A creature from the Echo." I'm breathing hard from my struggle with the beast, and water dribbles down my body. "It wanted you."

"Me? Why?"

"You tell me."

She scowls and starts reassembling her clothes. "How many times do I have to say the same thing? I have no idea what's going on."

I seize her arm. "I'm beginning to wonder if the creatures that confronted us in the shopping mall were there for you, just like this beast."

"What? That's crazy."

"Really." I drag her closer. "Sefton left you a note. He planned to come for you, but he reached the library before you could find your way back to it. Whether you want to admit it or not, you are the key to everything that's happening. You are the catalyst."

"And you're the anchor. That's what you said." She wrenches free of my grasp, though only because I let her. "That means you're in this up to your eyeballs too."

"So you admit you are an integral part of what's going on."

"No. I admit you're an asshole and a murderer, and I should never have agreed to go anywhere with you."

My gaze flicks to the dead creature floating down the river, headed for the drop-off and the swirling current below it. "You continue to refuse to cooperate, even though I killed that beast to protect you."

"I came with you. That's cooperation." She combs her fingers through her wet hair to push it away from her face. "Gee, I would've thought you'd want that thing to get me, since you hate me so much."

Why had I intervened? If the creature had wanted her, as I believe, then I doubt it would have harmed her. "You aren't telling me everything. Don't deny it."

She crouches to tie her shoelaces. "I know nothing about the apocalypse, and I am not a catalyst for anything."

"If that's true, then you are of no further use to me." I don't believe for one second that she's not the catalyst, or that she knows nothing. Maybe the truth is buried inside her memory. Either way, I will get what I need from her.

Allison straightens. Her attention flicks down to my cock. She clears her throat and focuses on my face.

But her cheeks have turned faintly pink, and I don't think it's embarrassment. I'd seen the way she admired my body earlier. We dislike each other, but we both suffer from the same overpowering lust. Perhaps I can use that to my advantage and get more out of her than answers. I need something else, something that has no bearing on the apocalypse. I need it badly.

I sling an arm around her waist and haul her into my body, lifting her feet off the ground just enough that we now gaze into each other's eyes head-on. "If you want my protection, you need to do more than simply come with me while we search for Sefton."

"Listen good this time. I know nothing—"

"Stop talking." I slide my free hand onto her arse and shove my fingers between her legs. When she gasps, a bolt of white-hot need shoots through me. My voice grows even rougher, even deeper. "Here's the new arrangement. I will protect you from whatever beasts hunt you and ensure you have enough food and water, as well as safe shelter. In return, you will give me your body to do with as I please, whenever I please, as often as I please."

"No way."

"Accept my terms, or I'll toss you back into the water and let the next creature rip you apart."

I can't believe I'm suggesting such an arrangement. What would my mother think of me now? I glance at the heavens and pray Mum can't see or hear me. I have never been so desperate to get a leg over that I'll do anything to make that happen. But I am now. Perhaps it has been far too long since

I had sex, but I don't want just any woman. I want Allison—only Allison. I need to have her.

No excuse, you sodding arsehole.

Allison glowers at me. But her pupils have dilated, and her breasts heave against my chest. "I hate you."

"I don't care." While she wriggles, with little conviction, I slip my hand inside the waist of her jeans and thrust it down until my fingers push between her arse cheeks. Her wetness teases the tips of my fingers. "Don't deny you want me. I can feel how much you do. Agree to my terms, and I will do more than protect you. I will give you pleasure that will make your eyes roll back in your head."

She's breathing so hard now that she's almost gasping. "I can't—This is wrong."

Whether she means her lust for me or my demand that she give me her body, I don't care which it is. I need to be inside her soon or I will go mad. So I push my hand further between her arse cheeks until my fingertips slide between the soft, slick flesh of her folds. "Yes or no. Tell me your answer in the next five seconds. Four, three, two—"

"Yes. I'll do it."

I flip her legs out from under her and lay her down on the grass, kneeling over her. "Remember, you wanted this as much as I do."

She unzips her jeans.

An explosion detonates in the sky, the shock wave spiraling outward and ricocheting off the buildings as the force of the concussion generates a violent wind that rushes toward us. The tempest generates an animalistic roar. Some structures that had been almost destroyed in the first wave now crumble. Iridescent green ripples of energy pulsate within the gateway to the Echo.

And winged beasts flood out.

"Back to the car," I shout.

Allison doesn't hesitate this time. We both bolt for the car and get inside, slamming the doors shut just as the hellish invasion hits. Winged beasts overrun the city, spewing fire from their mouths. As they draw closer, I can see the humanoid bodies attached to those gigantic wings.

Allison cranes her neck to peer up at the sky through the windscreen. "What are those? Dragons?"

I start the engine and floor the accelerator. The car rockets away, throwing dirt and grass up around us. "Those aren't dragons, not in the traditional sense. They are creatures from the Echo."

Perhaps I've left out significant information, but I won't tell her more until she gives me Sefton. Do I still believe she knows how to find him? The angry part of me, which dominates my behavior, says yes she knows—and I need to force her to confess. But the part of me that I've sublimated, for good reason, has begun to wonder about Allison. She might be telling the truth.

I can't worry about her intentions right now.

"We need to hide somewhere," I say as the car jounces onto the road. "The second wave has begun, and the last place anyone should be is out in the open. We should go back to the tunnel."

"That's too far away. I know of another tunnel, but to get there we'd have to double back to get across the river."

"Why?" I slam on the brakes. "We can reach the other side from the place where we swam in the river."

"That's a railroad bridge. And besides, it's elevated above the road. You can't drive onto it."

"I'm not talking about the bridge." No more explaining. It's time to take action, whether she likes it or not. "Buckle up your seatbelt and hold on."

Yanking the wheel, I jam the accelerator down to the floor and swerve the car back around to go the other direction. Allison yelps, but I don't give a stuff about that. Flames erupt in the sky as more dragon-like creatures emerge from the Echo, heading in this direction. We have minutes at most to get to a relatively safe place. I grip the steering wheel tighter as the car rockets off the road and across the grass, barreling toward my destination.

The rock outcropping beside the railroad bridge.

We swam near that manmade pile of rocks, which has an opening at its center. That's where the water becomes turbulent. I'd seen it when I was washing off in the river. Now, we're racing across the landscape alongside the railroad bridge.

"Stop!" Allison screams. "You'll crash in the river."

Instead of slowing down, I aim straight for the rocks.

The car hits the boulders, bouncing up and thumping down over and over, jerking sideways so I need to grip the wheel even harder until my knuckles ache from the effort.

When we reach the gap in the rock barrier, Allison shrieks.

And the car flies across the gap, slamming back down on the other side. I yank the wheel to veer onto a path that leads up, away from the river.

"You're insane," she snaps. "We could've died."

"If we had crashed in the river, I would've survived."

"But you don't give a shit if I die."

Do I care about her safety? Only until I get everything I want from her. That's what I keep telling myself.

She bars her arms over her chest and turns her head away to stare out the window. "I'm reconsidering the deal we made earlier. Don't want to have sex with an asshole who's also a lunatic."

"You won't renege. You want me too much."

Allison flashes me a nasty look. "I hate you."

"But we both know you want me to fuck you. That's how I can be certain you'll keep up your end of our arrangement." I turn onto a street, the car jouncing over holes in the asphalt. "But right now, I need you to give me directions to the tunnel you know of."

"Fine."

She provides the information, guiding us through the streets to a building that I recognize as a hospital only because the sign is still visible, though it has suffered some damage. The building itself is completely destroyed. Even if we could find the tunnel, I wouldn't trust the structure to hold, not when I'm looking at its battered remains.

"What now?" Allison asks.

"I don't know." For a moment, I stare at the ruined building while my entire body sags. But I don't have the luxury of feeling sorry for myself, so I turn the car around and head back the way we'd come.

The engine sputters and dies.

As the car rolls to a stop, I turn the key in the ignition several times, but the engine won't start up again. Then I see why. The gauges on the dashboard make it clear.

"Why did you stop?" Allison asks.

"Because we're out of petrol."

"I guess that means gas."

"Yes." I smack my fist on the steering wheel. "We're not going anywhere, except on foot. Unless you know of a place within walking distance where we can fill up the tank."

"Even if I did know of a gas station, I doubt there's anyplace that has power of any kind, even from generators. No electricity, no gas pumps."

She's right, of course. And I'm a bloody moron.

I grab the backpack and swing my door open. "We walk, then. And pray we'll find a safe place to hide."

CHAPTER TEN

Allison

WHILE I WALK ALONGSIDE DAX, AS WE MAKE OUR WAY THROUGH THE remnants of the hospital district, I can't stop thinking about what I agreed to do with him. He demanded I have sex with him and swore he won't protect me anymore unless I do it. I could've said no to his devil's deal. Instead, I agreed.

More proof that I've lost my mind.

That's the only excuse I have for agreeing to give my body to a stranger who treats me like dirt and snarls at me. It's his fault I'm making horrible decisions. Dax makes me so angry, and I fight the constant urge to slug him, fight it only because I'm sure I'd break my hand if I tried to punch his granite jaw or his rock-hard abs.

It doesn't help that I've seen him naked.

The man might be an evil prick, but he has a body any woman would drool over, with hard muscles flexing under every inch of his flesh and a dick of jaw-dropping size. I should not want him to touch me. But every time he pulls me close, whether it's to growl at me or say crude things, I want to rip his clothes off and ride him until we're both slicked with sweat and we come so hard we can't speak afterward.

He doesn't always treat me like dirt. Maybe that's the real reason I agreed to let him fuck me—because I've seen his softer side too. Well, not softer. More like his less prickly and snarly side.

We've just passed a street corner, one I might've recognized if the world hadn't exploded. The street signs are gone, probably buried under a mountain of rubble. Dax has stopped us here, though I don't know why. When I start to ask, he holds up a hand in the universal gesture for "shut up." He tilts his head to the side.

Since he doesn't want me to speak, I mouth, "What?"

"We are not alone," he mouths back.

Then I hear it. Scrabbling sounds. Faint grunting. Whimpering.

Dax claims my hand, leading me toward the noises, which seems like a horrible idea to me. When I kick his shin to get his attention and mouth "no," he ignores me. The brute drags me down the side street, forcing me to climb over a mound of debris in the process, and we don't stop until we've come within view of whoever or whatever is making those noises.

A gang of four creatures has surrounded a young woman at the entrance to an alley. Two more creatures hang back, holding on to a young man who struggles against their grip. The girl keeps trying to get away from the four demons, but they've got her penned. She whimpers and keeps calling out to the young man, but he can't get free to help her.

I look at Dax just as he looks at me. When I open my mouth to suggest we should do something, he rolls his eyes and growls.

Then he whips out his knife and charges across the street.

Since I've gone crazy, I race after him and grab a battered length of pipe from the ground, wielding it like a baseball bat.

"Let her go," Dax commands. "Or you will regret it."

The creatures give up on harassing the girl and rotate their gazes to Dax and me. Every demon in the gang has scaly skin, though two have fangs, one has long talons on its fingers, and the fourth sports spikes on its back. The two holding on to the young man boast spikes on their heads.

"What's this?" one creature says. "Snow White and the Wolfman came out to play. She's juicier meat than this scrawny little thing." The beast nods toward the young woman. "We'll have her for dessert. Snow White looks like an entrée for sure."

Dax widens his stance, brandishing the knife. "Last chance. Run away or die."

"We ain't running. This is our territory."

"Not anymore." Dax glances at me sideways and whispers out of the corner of his mouth, "Get the girl."

Then he charges at the creatures, roaring and slashing his knife in such quick strokes that I can't see what he's doing. I run to the girl, but now it's the young man who needs help. Dax is keeping the other creatures busy, so I summon all the fury and fear I've held in since this morning and unleash it on the two creatures who hold the man. I slam the pipe into the side of one beast's head, and it staggers sideways, releasing the man's arm. Now held by only one creature, he slugs the monster in the gut. That knocks the beast off balance. The man mutters "thank you" as he rushes past me to grab the girl.

They disappear into the night.

I don't blame them for running without trying to help me or Dax. He doesn't need help. And I know he won't let anything happen to me, at least until we find Sefton. When I turn around, I see Dax encircled by four dead creatures. His clothes, hands, and face are spattered with blood.

He goes perfectly still, his gaze riveted to something behind me. "Don't move."

Then he bolts past me.

I spin around just in time to see him gut the other two creatures. A strange thrill shivers through me, and my nipples go hard. I don't enjoy violence. But there is something darkly erotic about watching Dax neutralize those monsters.

Dax brushes past me. "Let's go."

He pauses to let me catch up. Well, that's new.

As we trek down the street, we see figures lurking in the shadows here and there, but we don't stop to investigate. Nothing good ever lurks in darkness. We pass by a broken fire hydrant that's spurting its contents five feet into the air, and Dax stops to rinse off the blood from his fight with those creatures.

He grasps my hand as we continue on our journey.

I suppress my shock as much as I can. He wants to hold my hand? Maybe he worries I'll run away. He can't feel protective of me.

Four creatures jump out of an alley to block our path.

Jeez, won't these demons ever give up? Though the preternatural darkness has gotten darker, a strange yellowish glow emanates from the hole in the sky.

The creatures in front of us look more human than the other beasts I've seen, but still not human enough to ease the anxiety trickling through me. Two of them seem female, and two male. They might pass for human if not for their fangs and red eyes.

"Look what we found," a male creature says. "Bigfoot and his hot girlfriend. Maybe I'll screw your girl to show her what a real monster can do."

Dax's hand tightens around mine. "You will not touch her."

The fanged cretin glances around with fake surprise. "Wow, a tough guy. I'm so totally terrified right now. I mean, there's only eight of us and two of you. But your threat was wicked scary."

He cackles. His friends laugh too.

"Eight?" Dax says. "I see only four of you."

Several more monsters traipse out from behind a trashed SUV.

"Well, ten counting those guys," the cackling creep says. He waves toward the other side of the street. "They're almost done with their dinner. Then we'll have ten of us against two of you."

A female emerges from the group that just appeared.

I recognize her. I mean, she looks very different now. But yeah, I know her. "Sherry? Is that you?"

The green-haired woman with a smattering of scales on her face smiles at me. "Ally, imagine bumping into you out here."

"Are you okay?" I don't see how the answer could be yes.

"Sure, hon, never better." Her gaze shifts to Dax, and she smiles with a strange hunger. "Damn, the apocalypse has been good to you, Ally."

Dax clamps a hand around my upper arm, bending to hiss into my ear, "She is not your friend."

"What? Something's happened to her, but—"

"You don't understand. She is *not* your friend."

"How would you know? I worked with Sherry at the library for more than a year, and you met her thirty seconds ago."

Dax mashes his mouth to my ear. "That creature is not Sherry. It's her Echo."

I don't know what that means because Dax has refused to explain much of anything. Sherry looks different, but I still recognize her. What does "it's her Echo" mean?

A roaring sound, like a massive gale, sweeps by overhead while streams of fire streak across the sky. The chaos above distracts both me and Dax. He releases my hand, turning sideways to observe the heavens.

Arms lash around me, hauling me backward while a rough, lumpy hand seals over my mouth.

Dax is still staring up at the sky to watch humanoid dragons that soar past us. I can't scream with my mouth covered up, and clawing at my captor's arms doesn't help. Neither does kicking. Sherry joins the beast who's dragging me away, but their pals rush at Dax.

He sees me too late. The other beasts have surrounded him, fangs bared, claws at the ready.

My captor slides his hand up just enough to cover my nostrils. I struggle to suck in air as my ears start to ring and black spots pop up in my vision. Can't move. Can't think. The entire world fades away, and everything goes black and silent. When I regain consciousness, I'm lying on my back in a dark place that stinks of blood and rotting flesh. Voices murmur, but I can't see the creatures who are speaking or understand their words. Pushing up on my elbows, I blink rapidly to clear my vision.

This is an alley. I'm lying on a concrete surface near a dumpster, but I doubt the stench comes from there. No, the fetid odor clearly emanates from the decaying corpses piled up against the giant trash receptacle. The bodies are so mangled that I can't identify them as human, though an instinct warns me they are. The creatures who abducted me must have murdered these people. Though I don't want to do it, I force myself to stand up and walk over to the pile of human refuse to get a closer look at the damage done to the bodies. I swear those are tooth marks. Fang marks, I assume. Something ripped these poor souls to shreds.

Shadows obscure the figures gathered at the alley's entrance. But I hear growling and demonic chuckles.

I need to get out of here. Fast. Before I become another corpse tossed away like garbage.

Though I glance around, I don't see a way out. The buildings on either side look solid, less damaged than elsewhere in the city, with only a few small windows high above my head. The concrete block walls would be impossible to scale even if I climbed on top of the dumpster.

Two of the beasts turn away from their buddies and saunter toward me.

I have no means of defending myself. Nothing but my fingernails and my teeth.

As the creatures draw closer, I can tell one of them is Sherry—or the Echo version of her. I didn't get the chance to make Dax explain what that means. The being who resembles Sherry halts an arm's length away, and her male pal stops beside her.

"Mm, aren't you scrumptious?" she purrs. "Your flesh will taste like filet mignon, I bet."

"What are you?"

"Does it matter? Might as well think of me as Sherry."

I fist my hands and grit my teeth. "You are not my friend. You're from the Echo."

"Your big hunk of man candy told you that, didn't he?" She licks her lips, flicking her forked tongue. "Maybe I'll eat him next."

"You'll never catch him."

"Won't we? He might be big and tough, but we're stronger." Anti-Sherry aims a feral smile at her companion. "Time to show her."

Her cohort sniggers. "Yeah. It'll be a shocker."

She sashays over to the heap of corpses and uses the heel of her stiletto shoe to push some of the bodies aside. Then she steps back. "Take a look, hon."

I inch toward the pile and peer down between the bodies she just moved. There, I see the unmarred face of a woman. A human. The woman I'd worked with for more than a year—the real Sherry.

Just yesterday, I would've been horrified at the sight. Today, I feel nothing but a vacant coldness inside me, though only for a moment. Then I fist my hands again, grit my teeth, and seethe at the realization of what these beasts did to Sherry. The world shouldn't be like this. It was far from perfect before, but now it's a demonic fun house that chews up and spits out good people who got trapped in this nightmare. The anger burning inside me grows stronger, hotter, a boiling but hidden rage that I can't release and certainly can't reveal to these beasts.

I want to murder every last member of this gang of monsters. But I'd get myself killed that way, which wouldn't solve a thing. Yes, I want to live. Despite the horrors the Echo has unleashed, despite the fact I have nowhere to go and no one to comfort me, I do not want to die.

But I still need to figure out how to get away from Anti-Sherry and her carnivorous buddies. *Think, Ally, think.* Can't overpower them. Can't climb up the walls of these buildings. Can't fly away either. Distraction seems like my only option. But how can I distract these creatures so I can run away?

Anti-Sherry comes up beside me again, gazing down at the real Sherry with mock wistfulness. "I just couldn't wreck that pretty face. Ruined every other part of her body. Tanner had his fun with her too."

Fun? I grit my teeth and clench my fists, forcing myself to suppress the seething, boiling rage.

In the distance, an engine rumbles. Not a car. Something else. It's probably another member of this monster gang coming to join the party.

"She was pretty, but I'm way stronger," Anti-Sherry says. Then she grins at me, her jagged fangs glistening. "And now I'm hungry again."

The engine roar gets louder and louder, zooming closer every second. The roar has a growling quality to it, but I'm still not sure what kind of vehicle it is.

Voices cry out in surprise, and someone shouts, "Watch where you're going, moron!"

Anti-Sherry and her pals shout and scatter, getting out of the way of the big black motorcycle that just swerved into the alley, heading straight toward…me. The rider brakes hard, tires squealing, the motorcycle angled sideways. It has stopped three feet away from me.

Dax sits astride the big, black machine with his backpack secured to a metal luggage rack at the rear. "Get on."

I jump on behind him and strap my arms around him.

He guns the engine, and we rocket back down the alley, out onto the street, racing away from the monsters.

A tingle rushes over my skin. Dax came for me. He rescued me. I know he only did it because he thinks I can find Sefton for him and because he wants to screw me. But still, he came. No one has ever done that for me. I know I can't trust him. For now, though, I can at least count on him to keep me alive.

Until I learn how to protect myself.

CHAPTER ELEVEN

Dax

THE MOTORCYCLE'S ENGINE SNARLS WHEN I GIVE IT MORE POWER, AND we barrel through the streets in a blur of motion. I have no idea what possessed me, but I didn't think about what I was doing. I dispatched the creature that had attacked me, though my victory came too late. The others had already taken Allison. Finding her became my only goal and the sole focus of my thoughts. Get to her. Save her. Why? I shouldn't care what happens to the woman. I don't care, except for the fact that she has a connection to Sefton and I need to find him. Without Allison, I can't do that.

But I'd experienced a strange sense of relief when I'd tracked her down, and when I saw she wasn't injured.

Where are we going? Somewhere else. That's the extent of my plan. I'll keep driving until this machine runs out of petrol or I spot a place that looks like a promising hideout. We do need to hide, now more than ever. The second wave is underway and will complete itself soon. That means the next phase won't be far behind. How many waves will ravage this world? Only Sefton knows.

Allison has her body glued to mine and her cheek pasted to my shoulder. Her delicate hands are linked over my belly. I swear I can feel the heat of her flesh even through my leather jacket. The wind created by our flight whips her hair against my face as I grip the handlebars more tightly and veer around another corner. We seem to have reached an industrial zone where factories and warehouses once occupied the area. Most of them have been destroyed now. All I need is one mostly intact structure, even a small one, that I can easily defend and where we will be relatively safe.

Nothing is for certain anymore. Everything is relative.

The feel of her body wrapped around mine gives me a feeling of…safety. That's bollocks. I haven't felt safe in years, and I might never again experience a sense of security.

Because of Sefton.

I hit the brakes and plant one foot on the ground to hold the bike up while I survey the area. One building had caught my eye as we approached this area. It looks like the remnants of a warehouse. Half of it has been destroyed, but the remainder seems intact. Since a wall separates the halves, the undamaged section should provide enough shelter. I check the petrol gauge. We're down to a quarter of a tank, and I don't want to waste what's left in case we need this bike to save our lives again.

I drive up to the door of the half-ruined warehouse and stop, setting one foot on the ground. Then I glance over my shoulder at Allison. "Open the door."

"What? Why?"

"I don't want to leave this bike out here where anyone might see it."

"Oh. Yeah, I guess that makes sense."

She slides off the motorcycle and trots to the warehouse door. Getting it open takes a moment, since it seems to be stuck. Maybe I should help Allison, but I can't have her thinking I give a damn about her. My only leverage is her belief that I will let her die if she doesn't cooperate. Whether I might do that or not is irrelevant. The unease I feel while watching her struggle with the door does not change anything.

Allison finally yanks the door open, then steps aside to hold it for me.

I drive the motorcycle through the opening, parking it just past the threshold, and dismount the bike.

She closes the door with a thunk, stumbling from the effort. "Thanks for not helping. It was so much easier doing that by myself."

"You managed."

"Wow, I'm so lucky to have a knight in shining armor on my side."

"I saved you from a horde of ravenous beasts. You could try thanking me. I didn't have to do that."

She stalks up to me, tipping her head back to give me a nasty look. "You only rescued me because you want to fuck me."

"No, I also mean to drag the truth out of you by whatever means necessary."

The insolent woman rolls her eyes and huffs. "Oh yeah, I'm so frigging grateful you saved me. Thanks a whole bunch, caveman. I might've been better off with the cannibal freaks."

I lash an arm around her waist and tug her into my body. "If you want to be devoured, we can skip straight to me fucking you. Right here. On the concrete floor."

Her chest heaves with every breath, crushing her breasts to my torso, and their rigid tips prod my chest. "Do it."

My cock jerks, but I can't move. Might've stopped breathing too. She wants me to ravish her. Right here, right now, on the grease-stained floor of a half-demolished warehouse while fire-breathing monsters set the city ablaze. But Allison doesn't want *me*. She agreed to let me shag her only because I vowed I would not protect her otherwise. I shouldn't care if she really wants this. But thoughts of our deal trigger an itch deep under my skin.

I glance around the space, then shove her away. "I need to surveil the area first."

Her mouth kinks up at one corner. "Surveil? Nobody talks like that."

Grunting, I push past her and tear the door open.

"Don't worry about me," she says. "I'll be fine here all by myself. Might eat all the food while you're gone, but you probably don't need to eat, anyway. You're a monster from another world, after all."

Why does she insist on harassing me? The woman ought to know better after spending two days with me. Yet I haven't forced myself on her. I haven't even taped her mouth shut to silence her. Perhaps she has reason to believe I won't harm her, not the way those creatures back in the alley would have done. Allison knows this, which means I've lost my leverage with her.

My surveillance of the area surrounding the warehouse reveals nothing of consequence. I do find a half-full can of petrol, so I carry that back to the building in which I left Allison. When I kick the door open, she leaps up from where she'd been sitting on the floor.

"Oh, there you are," she says, in a casual tone that I'm sure is an act. "Did you 'surveil' the area thoroughly with your monster senses?"

"I am not a monster." Perhaps I am. I don't know anymore. But I do not like her calling me that.

"What are you, then? *Who* are you?"

To avoid looking at her, I pour the petrol into the motorcycle's tank. "You know who I am."

She shakes her head as she ambles up to me, her hips swaying and her gaze locked on mine. "When I asked who you are, you told me that if I needed a name, I could call you Dax."

"We can discuss that after."

"After what?"

Oh, she knows exactly what I meant. The way her pupils are dilating, darkening her eyes, attests to that fact.

I drop the petrol can and take off my leather jacket, tossing it onto the floor. "Strip."

"You could at least say please."

"Why? You want me the way I am, so I have no need to seduce you with honeyed words." I remove my boots and shed my socks, then start to unbutton my shirt. "Strip, Allison. Do it now, or I'll rip the clothes off your body."

She kicks off her boots and begins unhooking her shirt buttons one by one.

My cock throbs. I want her body, but that cannot explain why I'm breathing harder and my pulse is racing. I've shagged more women than I could count, and none of them made me feel this way. It must be the intensity of the circumstances affecting me, not the appeal of the woman.

Allison drops her shirt on the floor and shimmies out of her jeans, leaving only her bra and knickers. But she just stands there, half-naked, with her hard nipples pushing against the fabric of her bra.

"Take off the rest," I growl.

"You first."

I strip off my shirt, then unzip my trousers and let them fall down to my ankles. The vision of Allison's almost naked body distracts me, though, and I stumble when I try to kick my trousers away. I throw out a hand to stop myself from hitting the floor. My palm smacks onto the wall.

And she smirks. "Kind of excited, huh?"

Finally rid of my trousers, I stalk up to her. "Don't think it has anything to do with you. I haven't gotten a leg over with anyone in a long time, that's all."

"Why haven't you—"

I sling my arms around Allison and crush my mouth to hers, trying to convince myself I do it only because I couldn't think of another way to make her stop talking. But the truth is that I need to taste her again. She opens for me and teases my lips with her tongue, all but begging me to kiss her deeply. I can't stop myself. I plunge my tongue deep and ravage her like the beast she thinks I am. I might not like hearing her call me a monster, but it is what I've become. The Echo made me this way. She will never understand that, because I will never explain it to her.

She responds to the lashes of my tongue with hungry swipes of her own, and we consume each other like the world is exploding around us and this is the last time we will ever experience passion. The Echo hasn't destroyed the entire world, not just yet. But the apocalypse has begun. If this is the last time I will ever feel a woman's body wrapped around me, then I need to make this last as long as possible.

Without giving up her lips, I unhook her bra and tear it off. She moans with such intensity that the ravenous sound steals my breath. I grasp her knickers and rip them off too, flinging them away. The hairs on her mound brush against my flesh, and her soft skin is plastered to my body while the scent of her envelops me and inundates my senses. I grip her arse with both hands, hoisting her off the floor, and stagger toward the nearest wall. I crack one eye open, though I can barely keep track of where I'm going. I know only that I need to fuck this woman now, take her hard, brand her body the way I've done to her mouth.

Her back hits the wall.

I growl like a ruddy animal, but I don't care.

She lifts one leg to latch it around my hip, then raises the other and locks her ankles behind my arse. She pulls her head back, severing our kiss. "Do it, Dax. Right now. Take me any way you want."

Can't speak anymore. Can barely breathe.

I thrust into her hard, but I freeze with our bodies joined. My heart pounds so fiercely that I feel like I might pass out, which is bollocks. But I can't think about that, not with her silky flesh enveloping me and her gaze nailed to mine. I punch into her even harder, every thrust driving me deeper inside her and making her body bounce. She throws her head back and lets out a hoarse cry that reverberates through the building. Her cream dribbles onto my balls, which only spurs me to fuck her harder and faster while my grunts and her sharp cries fill the air along with the wet slapping of our bodies colliding.

Every muscle in her body goes rigid, and I know she's about to come.

But I'm not done with her yet. I lift her off my cock and set her down, taking a step back. Though my breaths have become harsh gasps, I manage to speak two words. "Not yet."

"What?" she breathes, gaping at me.

"I said not yet." I need a few more quick breaths before I can say anything else. "You won't come until I let you. And I won't do that until I've satisfied my needs."

She smacks my chest. "You asshole."

"Call me whatever you like." I grasp her chin. "But your body belongs to me."

Chapter Twelve

Allison

He owns my body? Like hell. I might've agreed to let him have sex with me, but no part of me belongs to him. Maybe I have to let him do whatever he wants to me, so he'll protect me from the monsters outside. That doesn't make me his property. I should tell him to go to hell, then get out of here as quickly as I can. He thinks I need him. I thought that too, but I can find another way to protect myself.

So what if my body is throbbing with the need to come? I'm not a slave to lust, and I'm definitely not his property.

He palms my ass, then massages it with sensual movements of his strong fingers.

I can't stop myself from sagging into him just a little. When he lowers his head to my neck and nips my flesh, I suck in a sharp breath. I try to steel myself to his seduction, but somehow he knows exactly which buttons to push inside me, exactly how to touch me and arouse me until I'm panting for him. He clamps a hand over one breast, then closes his mouth over the tip and the areola, suckling it so hard that a sharp electric shock fires down my nerves and straight into my sex.

Maybe I am a slave to my lust for Dax, because I sag against him even more. Without his body propping me up, I'd collapse into a heap on the floor.

Dax flips me around so I'm facing away from him, his callused hands rough against my skin.

"Hands on the wall," he says, his voice as rough as his palms.

I slap my hands on the cold concrete.

With one knee, he shoves my thighs apart. Then he takes hold of my hips and thrusts his cock between my legs, though he doesn't push inside me. He pumps his hips while keeping his length nestled between my thighs, rasping it up and down my cleft while alternately hissing in breaths and groaning with what sounds like agony. I feel that way too as my body ramps up toward orgasm again, second by second, every movement of his cock spreading my slickness over his skin.

I grit my teeth and claw at the wall with my fingertips while the pressure inside me intensifies. "Dax, please."

He pistons his hips faster and faster, grunting like a rutting animal while his balls smack into my ass.

Suddenly, he pulls away.

I'm on fire, dammit, so close to climax that I swear I can taste it. But he stopped. Again. I glance over my shoulder, and the bastard is just standing there with his erection jutting straight out from his body in a way I've never seen with any other man. The head is bright red, and his flesh glistens from the tip straight down to the base, coated with my cream and the beads of moisture poised on his crown. I can't catch my breath, overwhelmed by the need to turn around and take him into my mouth just so I can taste him.

But damn, I need to come so badly. I can't stop myself from reaching down to slip my fingers between my folds, where my juices have made my flesh so slick and hot.

Dax seizes my wrist, yanking my hand away from my body. "No."

"I can't stand it anymore."

"You will stand it for as long as I want you to."

He drops to his knees, gripping my ass with both hands, and shoves his face between my thighs. In one long, sensuous lick, he drags his tongue up my cleft from my opening to the rigid head of my clitoris. I cry out, the sound half whimper and half demand. But I don't come. He won't let me. And heaven help me, I don't want him to set me off yet.

He scrapes his teeth down my inner thigh and back up to my mound. With a hungry groan, he sinks his teeth into the flesh there while breaths bluster out of his nostrils to tease the hairs.

I clutch his head and let out a long, guttural moan.

Dax lifts his head to look at me. "Beg me to do it."

"What?"

"Beg me to fuck you until you come."

I'm breathing so hard I can barely understand his command, and I don't have the willpower to resist. "Please, Dax, fuck me until we both come."

His nostrils flare as he rises and rakes his gaze over me from head to toe. With one hand, he strokes his length. "Lie on the floor, facedown."

Why argue? I want this, and I'll consider the consequences of that need later. Can't focus on anything except his dick and what he'll do to me next.

I lie down on the floor with my arms folded under my head. The position grants me a peripheral view of his naked body.

He kneels over my legs, skimming his hands up and down my thighs. While I moan and squirm, he grasps my ankles and pushes until my knees bend, lifting my ass into the air.

"Please, Dax, please," I moan.

He pushes my knees apart and roughly rubs his hand along my folds. "You will scream my name when I finally let you come."

"I'll scream your name right now if that'll make you do it."

He seizes my wrist and bends my arm behind my back, gripping my hip with his other hand. His hold is solid but also gentle, as if he's taking care not to hurt me. When he punches into my body hard and deep, I let out a sharp cry that echoes inside the building. He pummels my body with punishing thrusts while I teeter on the edge, about to plummet over it, and the second he shifts his hand off my hip to reach down and pinch my clit, I come so hard and fast that I can't scream or move or even breathe. My ears start to ring, and black spots appear in my vision. The orgasm goes on and on, the muscles inside me clenching his cock in fierce waves, though the rest of my body has gone stiff, frozen in the throes of ecstasy.

Dax bellows, thrusting a few more times while I feel his release erupting deep inside me.

While he pulls out of my body, I lie flat on the floor, unable to do anything except struggle to regain my breath. Did that really happen? Did I let a beast of a man use my body for his pleasure? Yeah, I did. I agreed to give myself to him, then begged him to take me without caring what he might do to me. And I loved it. Dax made me feel things I've never experienced before, an intensity of sensations that overwhelmed me. If he ordered me to give in to him again, I'd succumb. Not sure if I can reasonably blame the apocalypse for this. I made the decision to surrender my body and soul to a man who hates me and terrifies me.

Does he still scare me? My wits haven't recovered enough for me to answer that question.

I push up off the floor, my arms quivering slightly, and sit back on my heels.

Dax lies beside me, his entire body slack, his eyes closed and his lips curling into the faintest of smiles. A smug one, naturally.

I punch his arm. "Wake up."

He cracks one lid open. "I am not asleep."

"Good. Then you can answer my question now."

"No."

He shuts his eye and links his hands over his belly. His dick is still semi-firm, but he doesn't seem inclined to take possession of my body again. Can't decide if I want him to do that. I stifle a pathetic moan. Of course I want it. I shouldn't, and I hate that I do, but Dax knows every secret way to stoke my deepest, darkest desires until I'm on fire for him. My willpower can't withstand it.

But I need answers, and he will give them to me now. No more passive Allison. No more cowering Allison either. Maybe it's hormones influencing me, but I don't care. If I can handle sex with a man like Dax, I can absolutely tap into my inner warrior—if nothing else, to make the man lying beside me at last tell me everything.

"I want answers," I say. "No more sidestepping my questions. I let you get your rocks off with my body, so it's time you confessed."

"You let me fuck you so I would defend you from the rampaging horde. No part of our arrangement included an exchange of information."

"Fine. Have it your way." I get up and start hunting for my clothes. My panties are trashed, thanks to him. So I crumple them in my hand and toss them away, then pull on my jeans. "I'll take my chances with the horde."

Yeah, I'm playing a dangerous game. But I have no choice. I need answers from Dax, and he thinks I know more about Sefton than I've told him. I don't, though maybe I can use his belief to get what I want.

Dax springs to his feet and stomps over to me.

I've just done up my bra, and now I'm shrugging into my shirt. Despite the way he's glowering at me, I keep my demeanor casual while I fasten the buttons.

"You are going nowhere," Dax snarls, "unless I tell you so. You wouldn't last five minutes out there."

He wants to goad me into snapping at him, so I do the opposite. I stay silent and calm while I tug my socks on and tie my boots.

Dax grabs my arm. "Have you gone deaf? You are going nowhere."

I shake my arm free of his grip and march toward the door.

"Stop." His barked command resounds through the warehouse. In a softer tone, he adds, "All right, have it your way."

Did he just offer to answer my questions? Since his statement was a tad vague, I turn around to get clarification. "Are you going to tell me everything I want to know?"

He fists his hands, then loosens them. "Yes."

I walk straight to him. "Maybe I should tie you up to make sure you can't ditch me."

"That won't be necessary." He shuffles a little closer. "Before I answer your questions, tell me one thing. Why don't you have real mates? You told me it was none of my business the last time I asked. I'd like to know the answer now."

Oh, what the hell. "I was in the plane crash with my parents. They died, but I survived—with serious injuries. Took me months to recover, physically. Not sure I ever fully recovered from the mental damage. Survivor's guilt or whatever. I guess I avoided getting too close to anyone after that because I was afraid another disaster might ruin my life. I've dated, but I steered clear of serious relationships. Guys can be such dicks, anyway. God, I can't believe I just told you all of that."

Because I've never told anyone. Why am I confiding in Dax? Maybe I sense a similar pain in him, or maybe I'm suffering from apocalypse shock.

"I'm sorry, Allison. You've been through hell, even before the Echo."

"Um, thanks. I guess." When he starts to ask another question, I wag a finger at him. "Uh-uh-uh. I answered one of your questions. It's your turn to cough up some info."

"All right." He winces, though only for a second, and rubs his forehead. "What do you want to know?"

"Everything. But we can start with an easy question." I inch closer, and despite my determination not to notice that he's still naked, I can't stop myself from glancing down at his dick. "Um, don't you want to get dressed?"

"Suddenly, it bothers you that I'm naked." He cups my chin with his hand, brushing one finger over the sensitive underside. "You didn't mind a few minutes ago."

"Stop trying to distract me. It won't work."

But yeah, it kind of is working. What we just did, on that floor, makes it impossible for me to ignore the luscious warmth that sweeps through me simply from the touch of his hand. If I live to be ninety, I'll still remember every second of how it felt to have him buried inside me. I wish he'd let me face him while we had sex, but I'm not that surprised he preferred to avoid looking me in the eye.

"Get dressed," I say. "Please."

He gathers his clothes and reassembles them. If I'd thought Dax clothed would eradicate my desire for him, I was a damn idiot. Of course it doesn't. He's still...visible. That's all it takes.

I clear my throat and focus on his face instead of his groin. "What's your name? Your full name, I mean, not just the three-letter version. Who are you?"

He scrubs a hand over his mouth and bows his head briefly. Then he looks straight into my eyes. "I am Daxton Stainthorpe. Sefton is my twin brother."

CHAPTER THIRTEEN

Dax

I'VE TOLD HER WHO I AM. WHY DID I DO THAT? SHE DEMANDED I EXplain myself, and I gave in. Perhaps I can blame sex for relaxing me so much that I lost control of my mind and my mouth. But no, that's not the reason. Allison told me about her family, that she's alone in this world much like I'd been alone in the Echo, and I felt...connected to her.

Which is rubbish.

She stares at me without blinking. "You're not identical twins, obviously."

"We *are* identical twins. Or we used to be."

"I don't understand. How can you not be identical anymore?"

She wants to understand. And after what we did moments ago, I feel a strange need to explain. I've treated her like my enemy. She shouldn't have stayed with me, and she should not have let me claim her body, yet she has done both. The least I can do is answer her questions.

"Sefton and I were born identical twins," I say. "But the magics he used to create the Echo and anchor me to it had...consequences. I was changed. I no longer resemble my brother or sound like him."

"You aren't from the Echo."

"No. I was born in England."

"I was born in Wisconsin, but I've lived in several places around the country. Guess that doesn't really compare to being thrown into a different world."

Are we having a civil conversation? Not sure. Either I'm hallucinating or we are chatting to each other like normal people.

"Did you volunteer to be the anchor for Sefton's magic?" she asks. "Or did he force it on you?"

"My brother tricked me." I can't help grinding my teeth when I remember how it happened. But I force myself to relax my jaw and exhale a long sigh. "This will take time to explain."

"Well, I guess I better cancel my manicure and the appointment with my hair stylist."

"Don't get comfortable with me. I'm still the monster who ruthlessly pursued you, took you hostage, and forced you to give me your body."

"I haven't forgotten that." She leans against the wall, hands jammed into her trouser pockets. "But I need to know how all of this happened and what might come next. You mentioned a first wave and a second wave. I assume you meant the two events we've experienced since the sky split open—the fireballs and lightning, then the fire-breathing dragon-people. Will there be a third wave? Seems like you're the one who knows what Sefton has planned."

"Whatever you think of me, if I knew what would happen next, I would tell you."

"Are you still convinced I'm responsible for everything?"

That's a tricky question. Lying seems ill-advised, but honesty might prove even worse. I may need to bind her hands again to keep her from fleeing. I'd rather not do that, but I will take whatever measures are necessary to uncover the truth.

"Sefton is clearly obsessed with you," I tell her. "He sent his beasts to find you—and to bring you to him, I assume. That's why he left a note encouraging you to wait in the library. But he cocked it up and forgot to exclude you from whatever trance he cast over the people in this city. That's why he needs his minions."

"Only one creature tried to get to me—the fish-beast. And the only evidence I have to support that theory is your claim that it was aiming for me and not you."

"It was." Growling at her won't help matters, but I can't stop myself. The woman is so bloody-minded. "That beast wanted you. So did the creatures in the alley, the ones who abducted you. And I've begun to suspect the beasts in the shopping mall wanted you too."

"Based on what evidence? The fact that you want everything to be my fault?"

Perhaps I am biased. But I know she is the key to understanding what's happened and to finding my brother. Only he knows how to stop the worlds from merging.

I slap a hand on the wall beside her shoulder. "If you knew what Sefton did to me, you wouldn't think I'm the monster. You'd know he is. I had a normal life once, with family and friends, but my own brother stole that from me and threw me into a nightmare world he created."

"Why did he do all of this? I don't understand. Why would anyone want to destroy the world and remake it into hell on earth?"

I doubt she expects a response. Her questions are rhetorical. Even if she genuinely wants to know, I can't explain why my brother has done any of this.

Allison spears me with her gaze. "I want some answers. Here are the questions. You said the Echo is a world populated with desecrations of the human form. What does that mean?"

"They are twisted copies of the beings who inhabit this world. I doubt Sefton planned for them to be that way. It must be an unintended side effect of creating the Echo."

"So when you said Sherry wasn't the woman I knew, you meant that literally."

"Yes."

"But Anti-Sherry knew me."

I try not to groan and end up hissing out a sigh instead. Anti-Sherry? I suppose that's an accurate description of what the Echo creatures are. "I don't know why Sefton's magics caused everyone in this world to be duplicated, with distortions. But my brother called the other world the Echo for a reason. I doubt he chose the name at random. It probably refers to the fact he created twisted copies of everyone on earth and populated his parallel world with them."

The ground beneath my feet begins to vibrate, as if a giant machine has been switched on somewhere nearby. The vibrations bring with them the grumbling, grinding racket of a machine too.

Allison stiffens. "What's that?"

"Not sure."

I walk toward the door, trying not to make noise with my footsteps, and carefully crack the door open to peer outside.

Behind me, Allison gasps.

Yes, I would gasp too if I hadn't lost the ability to move or breathe. What I'm seeing can't be. What Sefton has done so far unleashed horrific terror on the world, but this...

The disk-like opening where the Echo tore through the fabric of this world is expanding. The grinding cacophony seems to emanate from the ever-growing rift in the two worlds. As the opening spreads across the sky, glistening darkness roils outward in its wake like the trail of an obsidian comet.

Allison grips my forearm. "If it keeps going like that, it will—"

"Consume the sky, then the earth."

Her fingers press harder into my flesh. "What should we do? Run?"

"I doubt that would help. Perhaps the best thing we can do right now is to stay here and wait—and hope Sefton isn't about to destroy the entire universe."

She huddles closer to me as we both stare up at the sky, helpless to stop the onrushing blackness. Nothing will stop what my brother has set in motion. The darkness sweeps across the heavens while the mechanical grinding and grumbling becomes almost deafening, vibrating my eardrums until I have no choice but to slap my hands over my ears. Allison does the same, grimacing and squinting her eyes until they're almost shut.

An explosion detonates overhead.

The warehouse shudders. And the doorway to the Echo vanishes.

"What just happened?" Allison asks. "The portal or whatever... It's gone."

"I know."

The sky shimmers with shades of obsidian and darkest crimson, while pinpoints of purple stars glitter there. I can't explain why, but I slip my arm around Allison's shoulders and pull her close. I feel something is coming, something unspeakable, something that my brother has dispatched. To do what? I believe everything I told Allison earlier—that Sefton wants her—but my conviction about his goal does not explain this wriggling unease.

"Do you feel that?" Allison whispers. "It's like the air is electrified or something."

The hairs at my nape go stiff, and awareness tingles over my skin. I grab her wrist and drag her toward the motorcycle. "We need to go. Now."

"Why? Where are we going?"

"Anywhere that's not here."

I throw open the door and jump onto the motorcycle, twisting the key in the ignition. The machine roars to life.

Allison just stands there, her brows furrowed, and bites her bottom lip.

"Get on," I snarl.

She hops on behind me. We rocket out of the warehouse, past the ruins of other buildings, and onto the asphalt street.

Whump. Whump.

The purposeful pounding of footfalls shakes the earth and rattles my eardrums. No creature borne of this earth or the Echo could create a sound like that with its feet. The thing approaching us from behind must be like nothing else in the universe.

Whump. Whump.

Allison wraps her arms around my midsection, clutching me as if she thinks she might fly off into the sky. I doubt that's what Sefton has in mind. The motorcycle wobbles faintly with every footfall of the pursuing monster.

"Dax!"

Allison's cry makes me glance back to see what she's gaping at, and I halt the bike so fast that the tires squeal. Then I plant one foot on the ground to keep the machine upright.

The monstrosity pursuing us towers above every building in the city, its monstrous form a combination of living thing and machine, with metal plates fused into its flesh and eyes that burn with an electric red gleam. Those twin beams sweep side to side as they scan the city. The creature's massive, metal-encased feet pulverize the asphalt with every step.

Whump. Whump.

"What is that thing?" Allison whispers.

"It must be a golem. A creature created by magic to do its master's bidding."

The golem stops moving and swerves its gaze in our direction. Though the monstrosity is at least four blocks away, its attention zeroes in on Allison.

I press my lips to her ear. "Still think Sefton didn't send those other creatures for you?"

"Oh please," she hisses. "You can't tell which one of us that golem's looking at. Maybe he's got a crush on you."

"That thing wants *you*."

"Just get us the hell out of here."

The golem's eyes pulse once.

I get us the hell out of there, pushing the motorcycle to the limits of its capabilities as we roar down the battered streets. The golem starts walking again, one gigantic step at a time, but I have a feeling it's not as ponderous as it seems. The thing had been searching for Allison, so it took its time. But now...

Though I shouldn't do it, I can't stop myself. I glance back at the golem.

Its mouth cranks open with a mechanical ratcheting noise. A spark of light flashes deep inside its maw.

Oh no. That spark...

The golem bends its knees and breaks into a run, barreling straight for us. A stream of fire erupts from its mouth, spewing the golem's molten breath over our heads, past where we rush down the street.

And the asphalt melts.

I slam on the brakes, tires squealing, and struggle to keep the bike from flipping onto its side. We come to a stop inches from the seething pool of asphalt. The only way past the barrier is to turn around and go back the way we'd come.

Straight into the arms of the golem.

"Fuck," I growl.

"We need a weapon," Allison says. "Something really big."

"Unless you have a missile in your bra, we have nothing big enough to defeat that thing."

Since we've stopped sideways in the street, we both have a good view of the approaching golem. Does it have a weak spot? If it does, I have no sodding clue how to find, much less exploit, its weakness.

Whump. Whump. The creature keeps barreling toward us.

Allison jumps off the bike and jogs toward the golem.

I leap off the machine, not caring that it tumbles onto its side on the ground, and reach Allison in three long strides. I seize her arm to halt her. "What the bloody hell are you doing?"

"That thing is coming for me. I'm giving it what it wants, to stop it from doing any more damage."

"Have you lost your mind? You can't surrender to Sefton's monstrosity."

She flaps her arms. "I have no choice. If I don't go to Sefton, that thing will kill—" She stares straight into my eyes while hers shimmer with the start of tears. "It will hurt people, I know it."

For a moment, I thought she was about to say she's worried the golem will kill me. No, she wouldn't be upset about that. Not after the way I've treated her.

The golem halts half a block away.

Allison raises her hands and shouts, "I surrender."

She can't—I need to do something. Anything.

The golem slowly raises an arm and points a finger at the building to our left.

"I think it wants us to go in there," Allison says.

That is the last thing I want to do. Sit in an abandoned, partially ruined building and wait for my brother to appear? I assume that's what the golem is directing us to do. But it's insanity. I need to find an escape route so I can—

I glance at Allison, my throat suddenly tight. I need to protect her, though not because I promised I would if she had sex with me. I don't want any harm to come to her.

But we're trapped. So I take her hand and lead her into the building.

CHAPTER FOURTEEN

Allison

I CAN'T TELL WHAT THIS BUILDING USED TO BE, THANKS TO THE DAMAGE from the apocalypse and the fact it seems to be a vacant structure. It doesn't look like a warehouse. The building was constructed with bricks. But it hardly matters what this place used to be. Today, it's a prison for me and Dax.

The golem has taken up a position in the street, right in front of this building. Through the shattered windows, I can see that hulking monster, and I know we won't get away unless we can take that thing down.

Yeah, sure. Piece of cake.

We're standing maybe twenty feet from the windows. No point in moving deeper into the building. We have nowhere to go. Rubble blocks the back of the structure, spilling down onto the concrete floor. I think I see the remnants of a countertop inside that mound of debris, so maybe this had been a store.

My palm feels warm. When I glance down, I realize Dax is still holding my hand. His palm is warming mine. Why does he want to hold hands? I guess it's an unconscious action, not a sign that he likes me. I'd be good with him just accepting that I'm not in league with the devil, aka Sefton Stainthorpe—his brother.

"How long do you think we'll have to wait?" I ask.

Dax grunts. "Until Sefton feels like showing himself."

A good, specific estimate.

The man I'd labeled a monster releases my hand, then shuffles up to the broken windows to peer out at the golem.

Dax might be a cretin a lot of the time, but he's not a monster. That thing outside is. The Echo creatures are too. But I think the man himself, Dr. Sefton Stainthorpe, might be the worst monster of all. I should've known, shouldn't I? Right, because alchemy and quantum physics inevitably lead to an apocalypse.

I come up beside Dax and gaze out at the monstrosity that guards us. The golem hasn't moved since it took up that position. Its eyes glow steady red. Just looking at the thing makes my skin crawl because it's a nightmare come to life.

Movement draws my attention to street level.

In a spot near the golem's left foot, the atmosphere begins to shimmer, the way hot air can do on a sultry summer's day. But it isn't that hot today. The darkness enveloping the world creates a cool, yet humid, atmosphere. A pinpoint of what looks like sunshine pierces the shimmering air, the light telescoping out until it fills the oval area.

A figure steps through the opening.

It's a portal. From where, I have no clue.

The figure walks toward the building, limping slightly, and the portal winks out of existence.

Sefton Stainthorpe enters the building and halts just inside the doorway. "Good morning. Or is it evening? It's hard to tell today, isn't it?"

He wears a suit with no tie and speaks in a casual tone, like we're all meeting here for lunch.

Dax lunges for his brother, snarling like a wild animal. But when he gets inches away from Sefton, he's thrown backward by an invisible force.

Sefton shakes his head. "Did you think I wouldn't anticipate your reaction? Though, honestly, I think you should be grateful for what I've done. You are now powerful and fearsome."

"Grateful?" Dax snarls. "Your botched magic turned me into a freak. I had no choice."

His brother chuckles. "Botched?"

Dax looks like he might try again to throttle his brother. I need to change the subject. "Where have you been living? The address you gave me was bogus."

"Of course it was." He brushes his hands over his pants and shirt as if he's removing filth. "I dislike visiting any city, but my calculations required me to start the transmutation here. Fortunately, I was able to travel back and forth as needed via portals, rather than living in this place. I prefer England."

"That's, um, interesting."

"All will become clear, eventually." Sefton scuffles toward me, but his brother steps between us. "Really, Dax, it's hopeless. I have more power than any living thing on earth. You needn't worry, though. I have no intention of harming either of you today. In fact, you are both essential to my plans."

I step sideways to get around Dax. "What is your plan, Dr. Stainthorpe?"

His gaze jerks to me. "I told you to call me Sefton."

Could that be a touch of annoyance in his voice? When I'd first met him, he seemed like the kind of guy who would never raise his voice, the kind who was always polite and opened doors for women. Now it turns out he's a lunatic. If I could be that wrong about Sefton, maybe I've been wrong about Dax too. But is he better or worse than I believed?

Time to play along.

I take one step toward the madman. "I'm sorry, Sefton, I forgot. But I really would like to hear what your plan is. And maybe you could explain what your note meant. The part about the alchemy of worlds."

"You should know," Sefton says. "This is my gift to you."

"What is?"

"The alchemy of worlds and of souls, the change that will make everything better." He moves half a step toward me, his expression alight with an excitement that infects his voice too. "I am creating a new and better world, where no one will be able to disguise their true nature because it will be on display for all to see."

"No more crackbrained rubbish," Dax snaps. "What does any of it mean?"

"Why do you think I transmuted you into this"—Sefton waves at Dax's body—"thing that you are now. I did it to reveal your true self. The chancer who shagged every woman he met, took pleasure wherever he wanted without regard for how his actions affected others. *You* are the monster, Dax. I transmuted you to make your inner self show on the outside."

Dax freezes, his face going blank. His voice becomes a harsh whisper. "You did this to me on purpose?"

He had assumed it was an unintended consequence of the magics that Sefton had employed to create the Echo. Now he knows his brother made him this way on purpose.

I want to hug him. But that would be a catastrophically bad idea. Besides, I shouldn't feel sorry for the man who held me hostage and accused me of being Sefton's cohort in creating an apocalypse.

But I can't help it. He looks so...stricken.

Sefton seems oblivious to his brother's reaction. He waves a dismissive hand. "Alchemy is the transmutation of one substance into another, or one being into another. In the classical sense, it's also the quest for eternal life."

"You want to live forever?" I say.

He scuffles closer, now mere inches away. "I want *us* to live forever. Allison, we can rule the world together. Just think, no one will ever look down on us or mistreat us because we will be invincible."

"I don't want to be immortal."

Sefton lifts a hand near my cheek, like he wants to touch me but can't quite do it. "I did all of this for you, pet. We can be together at last, with nothing to stop us. The Echo is my gift to you."

"But I—"

He seizes my hand, gripping it tightly. "I love you, Allison."

Love? He barely knows me. But I don't think it's a good idea to point that out or to tell him I don't feel that way.

My gaze flicks to Dax.

He's still staring at his brother, but his stark expression has hardened into something much darker and angrier. His attention stays nailed to Sefton as he speaks through clenched teeth. "Did you know what would happen to me when you threw me into the Echo?"

"Of course."

Dax lunges for his brother but ricochets off whatever shield Sefton has erected around himself. "We are brothers. How could you do that to me?"

"Because I've never liked you." He rakes his gaze over Dax, his lip curling. "I explained all of this when I gave you the gift of being the anchor." Sefton returns his attention to me. "Come with me, pet, and I will tell you everything."

He holds his hand out to me, palm up.

Go with him? No way. Even before he revealed his madness, I wouldn't have done that. From the start, I'd sensed something off about him, and I'm not going anywhere with Sefton Stainthorpe.

But telling him that seems like a bad, bad, bad idea.

Sefton thrusts his hand out to me again. "Come, Allison."

Come? I am not a dog.

But I need a plan. Can't discuss it with Dax, not when his lunatic brother is standing right in front of me. So I'll need to do this on my own.

Sefton told me the Echo is his gift to me and that we will be invincible together. He also said we would rule the world. Given his personal force field, or whatever it is, I assume he meant magic would give us the power to protect ourselves and control everyone else. He created a frigging golem that could smash a city with one step of its gigantic foot. So yeah, Sefton is very powerful.

But he said "we" would be invincible.

That implies I have power too. I'm the catalyst, that's what Dax said. Without me, Sefton couldn't have created the Echo. I can't prove that, but the evidence suggests it's true. If Sefton has insanely powerful magics, then maybe I do too. Can I use the power he gave me to escape from him and his monsters?

Yeah, if I had any clue how to do that. This is magic, right? Maybe I can just...will it to happen.

Since I don't want to let on that I'm trying to do that, I force myself to focus on Sefton and maintain a neutral expression while I wish with all my mental focus that I were somewhere far away, somewhere Sefton can't find me. While I do that, I need to keep Sefton talking.

"Will there be more waves of beings coming out of the Echo?" I ask.

"No, but there will be waves of...other sorts."

"Like what?" *Get me out of here,* I command the magics. *Get me out of here now, do it, right now, far away from this place, somewhere safe.* "I have to admit what you've done so far is impressive."

"We can discuss that later. Now, it is time to go."

Come on, you stupid magics. Whisk me away.

Peripherally, I see Dax squinting at me. Has he figured out what I'm doing? If Sefton realizes… I am so screwed. He seems a touch annoyed, rather than incensed, so I don't think he's figured it out yet. But I'm pretty sure Dax has. How? I can ask him that later, after we escape from his brother.

My heart stutters. *We.* I thought that word. I want Dax to come with me.

No time to consider the repercussions of that impulse. I keep chanting in my head, keep willing the Echo to do my bidding, though I have no idea if this is how magic works. *Do it, you goddamn magics, do my bidding. I command it. Take me and Dax away right now.*

Sefton squints at me, just like his brother is doing.

A strange sensation sifts through me, like electricity and cool water in my veins. I can't breathe. Can't move. Not because I'm paralyzed, but because I sense the magics heeding my command. It's about to happen.

"No!" Sefton shouts. "You can't—"

He lunges for me just as I lunge for Dax and throw my arms around him.

And we vanish.

CHAPTER FIFTEEN

Dax

THE WORLD SPINS AWAY FROM US, AND WE RUSH THROUGH A VOID deeper and darker than the furthest reaches of outer space. Then we drop down onto a solid surface, swaying for a moment. Allison still has her arms around me. I don't understand what just happened, but I'm certain she is responsible for it. The brightness that engulfs us blinds me for several seconds, but then my vision returns.

I blink swiftly as I try to make sense of our surroundings.

We stand in a meadow filled with wildflowers. The sun shines down on us, warm and soothing. The scent of the outdoors suffuses my senses, and I find myself wrapping my arms around Allison, though I don't know why. It feels…good. That's all I know.

Allison glances around. "Where are we?"

"I should ask you that. This is your doing, isn't it?"

"Well, I tried to use magic to whisk us away. Didn't know if it would work." She takes two steps away from me so she can turn in a circle to inspect the area. "Guess it did work. I wished for us to be far away from Sefton and his apocalypse, in a safe place."

Her statement stops me for a moment as I digest its full meaning. "You wished for me to come with you?"

She faces me, hunching her shoulders and biting her lip. "Yeah. I guess I, um, kind of did."

"Why?"

Yes, I sound stunned. Of course I do. After the way I've treated Allison, she should despise me. But she seems to have stopped hating me and decided to… What? She can't like me. No, she must want me around to protect her from any monsters that might come for us.

She sits down in the grass, closes her eyes, and inhales deeply. Her lips curl into a faint smile. When she looks at me again, she pats the grass beside her. "Sit down. We should talk."

Despite her filthy clothes and disheveled hair, she is beautiful. I can't stop a memory from rushing through me, a replay of our time in the warehouse before Sefton came for us. I remember being inside her, taking her body without mercy, relentless in my need to claim this woman for my own. I hadn't realized that's what I was doing until after we had sex. The act hadn't dulled my hunger for her at all. I still crave her like mad, but now I want to do more than fuck her. I need to make her feel something for me because...I feel something for her.

I drop onto the grass an arm's length from her. "I assume 'talking' involves you demanding information from me."

"Not demanding. Requesting. I'd like it if you volunteered information instead of making me drag it out of you."

The worst part of me insists I should remind her of our arrangement, but I can't speak the words. I need her to want me willingly.

Allison pokes my arm. "Don't you want to remind me that my body is your property?"

"No. Forget our deal."

"Really?" She squeezes my thigh gently. "For the record, you don't need a contract to make me sleep with you. I'll do it anyway."

"Why?"

"Because it feels good. Duh."

I resist the urge to apologize and to explain my behavior. She wants answers now, not my pathetic excuses. "What do you want to know?"

"Tell me what happened between you and Sefton. Why he hates you. Why he made you the anchor for his so-called gift."

"He gave *you* a gift. But he cursed me."

She wriggles her arse to turn toward me. "I'd like to know why Sefton did that. Please."

"We might be twins, but we have never been identical—except in our appearance." I take a deep breath and exhale it slowly. The time has come to tell her everything. "It happened a week ago, back home in England. Sefton asked me to meet him at our ancestral home, in front of the gravestones for our parents."

One Week Ago
Fallenmouth Manor, England

I STRIDE ACROSS THE LAWN, PAST THE SPRAWLING HOME WHERE I ONCE lived with my parents and my brother, heading behind the house toward the family cemetery. Acid roils in my gut, because I never wanted to come back here. This is the property of the Earl of Fallenmouth, not of the Stainthorpe family, not anymore. Without Mum and Dad, I don't want to live here. When the household staff started calling me "my lord," it was too much. I had to leave.

But my brother kept living here. I told him he could. Let Sefton have the place. It holds too many memories for me, too many feelings that I've avoided confronting.

I find Sefton standing at the graves, head down.

"What's going on, Sef?" I ask as I halt beside him. "You made it sound urgent. I rushed here from London, so it had better be good."

"You need to know that I'll be making some changes."

"The estate is your business, not mine. Redecorate all you want."

He lifts his head, aiming his gaze directly at me. "That's not what I meant. The changes I intend to implement are more far-reaching than the upholstery in the house or the shrubs in the garden."

I sigh and shove my hands into my trouser pockets. "Why don't you tell me what it is? I have things to do."

"You mean women to do. Honestly, Dax, Father would be ashamed of you."

No, I won't deny that. It's true.

Sefton's lip curls. "I'm ashamed of you. That's why I've chosen you to be the anchor in my plan to change everything."

A car horn blares three times on the other side of the house.

"Claudia is here," I say. "She's dying to be shagged by an earl. So get on with it, Sef."

"That girl won't want you anymore once I'm done."

"Are you threatening to steal my lover?" I laugh and slug his arm. "Good one, Sef. You almost had me."

"Of course you assume I could never seduce a woman. I'm the quiet one who no one understands, the boy who has no mates." He fists his hands and faces the graves again. "I'll show Mum and Dad. I'll show you too. Soon, everyone will know."

"Know what?" I hold up a hand to stop him from speaking. "Never mind. I'm going to spend the weekend shagging Claudia in the earl's bedroom. She loves that idea. Do what you want, Sef."

As I walk away from him, I hear his voice. "I will, Dax. I will."

I return to the house and do exactly what I told Sefton I would do. I spend the afternoon fucking a woman I sort of like but have no intention of dating, much less marrying. That's who I am. A chancer of an earl who doesn't care about anyone else. My brother can brood by our parents' graves all he wants. They're dead, and I prefer the living.

Especially when the living person with me is a sexy little thing who can't get enough of me.

Just as the sun begins to set, I'm lying in bed with Claudia. We've just shagged, and she is gazing at me with soft eyes warmed by desire. Her body feels warm against me, for sure, and I can't resist gliding a hand up her arm in a teasing caress.

She shivers faintly. "I'm hungry, Dax."

"For food? Or do you mean…"

"I'm hungry for your body." She snuggles up to me. "One more time before we go downstairs for dinner."

Someone knocks on the door.

"Go away," I shout.

"It's me," Sefton says. "I urgently need to discuss something with you."

"Can't it wait? I'm in the middle of an urgent matter myself."

"No, it can't wait."

I sigh, then slap Claudia's arse. "Stay here, darling. I'm sure this won't take long."

She watches me while licking her lips as I pull my clothes on and walk out of the bedroom. My brother gestures for me to follow him, not saying a word about what urgent matter he needs to discuss. Sefton has always been a bit odd, and I've always indulged him. That's what brothers do, isn't it? I've never had any other siblings. I know only that I was expected to look out for Sefton, and I never saw it as an onerous duty.

But I have noticed something else, something I'd overlooked when I was determined to get Claudia upstairs. "Where's the staff, Sefton? I know they like to stay out of the way, but Fallenmouth seems quieter than usual today."

"I sent the staff away. They are no longer necessary."

My brother leads me outside, back to the cemetery.

I groan. "The graves again? Really, Sef? I don't understand your sudden fascination with our parents' headstones."

"They died thirteen years ago today."

"Yes, I know. It's getting dark and chilly, and I didn't bring a coat. So tell me what the bloody hell we're doing out here."

He leans toward me, his voice hushed yet filled with a strange intensity. "Thirteen is a magical number. It's imbued with the frequencies of metaphysical power, ascension, and oneness. But most importantly, thirteen is indivisible in the mathematical sense, which makes it the essence of incorruptible perfection."

What is he on about? This can't be my brother, the logical scientist, spouting New Age rubbish.

I lay a hand on his shoulder. "I think you need to take a holiday, Sef. You've clearly been working too hard."

He shrugs away from my hand. "I resigned."

"You quit your position at Oxford? Why?"

"Because I realized the truth. Humanity is irredeemably corrupted, and the only salvation is to rewrite everything." He tips his head back to gaze up at the darkening sky where the first pinpoints of stars have emerged. "The power of thirteen is vast, but three is of paramount importance. I need two more to complete the spell."

"What spell? Since when are you interested in magic? You are a physicist, Sef, not a sorcerer."

"You understand so little. Ever since we reached puberty, all you've cared about was chasing a bit of skirt." He stabs a finger into my chest. "Now at least you will serve a higher purpose."

Nothing he's told me makes any sense. He must be off his rocker.

"Let's go back inside," I say. "We can break out the Scotch and talk this through."

"There is nothing to 'talk through,' Dax. I have a plan that must be enacted tonight, under the full moon on the thirteenth day of the month."

"All right, Sef," I say slowly. "Time to go back inside and have that drink."

"Stop patronizing me," he hisses. "Allison will understand, but I knew you lacked the intelligence and sophistication to envision the true scope of my plan."

"Who is Allison? Have you met a girl, Sef? About bloody time."

"You will never meet her." He picks up a bag that had been lying on the ground, though I hadn't noticed it before. The twilight concealed it. "Allison Dahl is mine, and you won't get the chance to steal her away from me."

"I've never stolen a girl from you."

He stares down at the graves. "You will be the anchor, which means you'll remain in the Echo even after the beginning of the end arrives. But Allison... She is the catalyst, the reason for everything I do. She wants what I want, as fervently as I desire it."

"This girl of yours wants...what, exactly?" She must be as insane as he has become. The Echo? The catalyst? It's bollocks. "I'm confused, Sef. What are you trying to do?"

He pulls something out of his bag, though it's concealed by his thigh. My brother sidles up to me, his eyes wild and his voice a harsh whisper. "I'm going to create an apocalypse."

"I see. Well, good luck with that." I assume this is an elaborate practical joke, though I've never known my brother to do something like that. "I'll see you at dinner."

"You arrogant prat." Spittle flies from his lips with every word. "Of course you can't believe I could envision a plan as elegantly conceived as this. But in a matter of moments, you will believe."

I rub my eyes and sigh. "No, I won't. I'm done. You can stand out here howling at the moon, but I'm going back to bed. Claudia's waiting for me."

Though I start to turn away, Sefton seizes my wrist and clamps an object around it. Something cold and metallic. I freeze, glancing down at my hand, where a shiny metal bracelet encircles my wrist so snugly that it pinches my skin. My pulse speeds up as a strange sensation of electricity tingles through me. Unusual symbols engraved on the bracelet begin to flicker with a golden light.

I turn toward my brother, but I don't recognize him anymore. "What are you doing?"

He pulls out his mobile and turns the screen toward me. "Look at this woman. Allison Dahl is mine. You could never win her because you are a callous and selfish wanker. I will win not only her, but the entire world."

My gaze lands on the photograph his mobile displays. A beautiful girl with dark hair. Allison Dahl. In the image, she stands behind a waist-high counter while holding a stack of books. Head down, she seems unaware someone is taking her picture.

Sefton steps away from me and starts to chant in another language, maybe Latin, I don't know. He pulls more items out of his bag, laying them on the ground, though I can't see exactly what they are. Night has taken full control of the world, obscuring everything.

The bracelet vibrates, shooting spikes of pain up my arm and out into my entire body. I cry out as my knees buckle and I slump to the ground.

"Stop this," I shout to Sefton. "Please."

My bones begin to crack and shift, forcing me to collapse onto my side on the ground, directly over my parents' graves. My body convulses as an agony unlike anything I could have imagined shreds me from the inside out and the bracelet melts into my flesh, sinking under the skin to scorch through my veins.

And I scream.

Sefton bends over me, holding a knife. He slices a long cut down my inner arm, then carves out another on my cheek. "This is your just punishment. You were always the golden boy, the darling of Mum and Dad's eyes, the perfect son they loved more than me. Why should you inherit an earldom simply because you were born six minutes and fifteen seconds before me? The Echo will right the wrongs done to me, and I will rule the world with Allison at my side."

The cuts on my arm and face burn like acid. The tang of blood seeps into my mouth as the scorching agony becomes overpowering, and numbness rushes through me. Darkness consumes my vision. My brain stops processing sound and sight and sensation as I drift in an abyss, weightless and free of pain. But the blessed release lasts only for a moment.

Then I'm thrust out into hell.

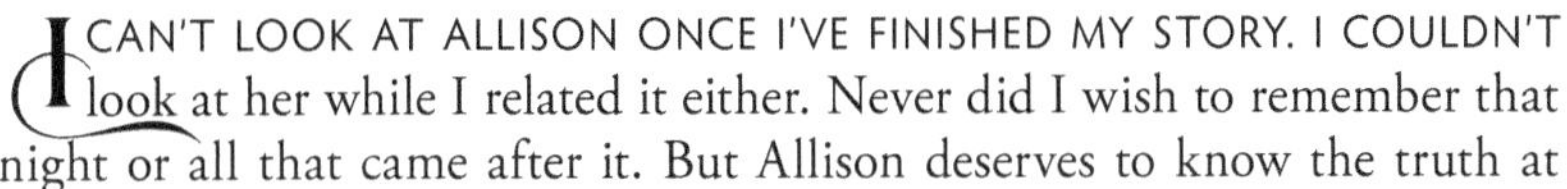

I CAN'T LOOK AT ALLISON ONCE I'VE FINISHED MY STORY. I COULDN'T look at her while I related it either. Never did I wish to remember that night or all that came after it. But Allison deserves to know the truth at last, and so I've told her. My own brother did this to me while I lay atop the graves of our mother and father.

"What was it like in the Echo?" Allison asks, her voice hushed and almost tender. "If you'd rather not talk about it…"

"The Echo is hell. Every depiction of that domain you've ever seen or read about can't come close to the reality." I bend my knees to rest my elbows on them, only so I can hide my face in my raised hands. "I woke up a monster, alone in a brutal world. Gradually, other creatures began to appear, but they were not allies. You've seen what the Echo beings are like. Over the years, I ran into people I recognized, but I quickly realized they were not the men and woman I'd known. They were twisted copies created by my brother."

"Years? Sefton did that to you last week."

I have to look at her now, though I don't want to do it. "Time behaves differently in the Echo. Sefton might have created that world last week, but I lived in it for five years."

She stares at me, not blinking, her lips parted, for a long moment that I don't even try to measure. Though I aim my gaze straight ahead, I can see her peripherally. And I swear I can feel her attention on me, prickling my skin.

At last, she speaks. "I'm so sorry, Dax. I had no idea you'd been in the Echo for so long. Can't imagine how horrific that was."

"Don't feel sorry for me." I swerve my head to glare at her. "Have you forgotten how I treated you until a few hours ago? I abducted you, tied you up, shouted and snarled and accused you of conspiring with Sefton. And let's not overlook the deal I forced you into accepting, the one that requires you to fuck me."

She starts to speak, but I don't let her.

"Remember what I did," I growl. "Sefton was right. I am a monster."

CHAPTER SIXTEEN

Allison

IS DAX A MONSTER? JUST A FEW HOURS AGO, I WOULD'VE SAID YES. I haven't forgotten the way he treated me, but I also haven't overlooked the glimpses of goodness—or at least not-so-awfulness—in him. Yesterday, when I couldn't walk any further, he picked me up and carried me for two miles. He didn't have to do that. He could've dragged me along with him. Then he got me food and water, and he commandeered a car so I wouldn't have to walk anymore.

Yes, he kidnapped me. Yes, he tied me up and snarled at me. And yes, he vowed he wouldn't protect me unless I had sex with him. The fact I wanted to do that doesn't excuse him. But I'm beginning to understand why he behaved the way he did. Five years in a literal hell world? Yeah, that could turn anyone into a monster.

But Dax isn't a monster. He's a damaged man.

Do I want to save him? Not sure that's a good idea, but then, I have no one else. The most important question seems to be whether he wants to be saved.

I try to lay a hand on his arm, but he scoots sideways to get away from me. I decide not to push. "You are not a monster, but you are traumatized. Even before the apocalypse hit, you were trapped in a horrific place."

He bows his head, hands on his knees. "Sefton was right. I deserve to be in hell."

"No, you do not."

"I don't want to talk about this anymore."

"Tough shit. I *do* want to talk about it." I clamber to my knees and grasp his face with both hands to force him to look at me. "Don't let Sefton mess with your head anymore. He's the demon, not you. I get that you were a player, and you didn't act like an earl or whatever. But that doesn't make you evil."

"Believe what you like."

"Thank you. I will."

Since he won't believe me anytime soon, I stand up and look around. We're in a meadow filled with wildflowers, and rolling hills extend toward the horizon. I recognize this place. It's on the outskirts of Fort Worth, probably twenty miles away, far enough that I can see only the skyline. It's always reminded me of the Emerald City in *The Wizard of Oz*, but not today. The city has become a heap of ruins. Luckily, I'd driven past this rural area before the Echo, so I know where we are.

Too damn close to the epicenter of the apocalypse.

A dark smudge on the horizon draws my attention. What is that? A chill frosts over me from head to toe as I realize the truth. That's the apocalypse, and it's spreading outward, coming this way. In the minute or so while I watch it, the darkness and devastation swarms closer and closer until it overtakes the sun. Clear sky remains above us, but the shadows draw ever nearer.

"We have to go," I say. "Now."

Dax wrinkles his brow. But then he sees what I see, and a muscle jumps in his jaw. He leaps up, grabbing my hand. "Where can we go? It's coming this way. I'm sure anywhere we try to hide, Sefton's apocalypse will find us. He wants to destroy the world and remake it to his liking."

"We need to go someplace that he won't destroy. Got any ideas about that?"

Dax studies the approaching darkness while booms echo in the distance, signs that the fireballs and lightning are coming closer. "I can think of only one place that Sefton might have left untouched."

"Where is it?"

"Our ancestral home. Fallenmouth Manor."

"It's amazing you didn't turn out to be a whackjob like your brother when you both grew up in a house with a weird name like that. Does it have gargoyles on the roof?"

"No." He gives me that squinty-eyed look he always gets right before he's about to snarl something nasty at me. "And I *am* a whackjob. Don't start to think I'm the sort who will cuddle with you and soothe your fears. I'm a monster, just as my brother intended."

"Bullshit." I throw my arms wide. "He's the one who destroyed the freaking world. You've helped me."

He slings his arms around my waist, hauling me into him. "Strictly because I wanted your body."

"Oh please. Your threats no longer impress me, and I'm not scared of you either. Quit trying to tick me off."

He cuffs my wrists behind my back with one hand. "You should be afraid, love. Because I am going to tear my brother limb from limb the next time I see him."

"Can't shock me that way, Dax. Not anymore."

Behind him, the roiling darkness creeps ever closer, and lightning bolts slam into the earth with enough force to make the ground beneath us shiver. Fireballs punch into the earth too, sending volcanoes of dirt and debris pluming into the air. Soon, this beautiful landscape will be a wasteland.

"Sefton might be at Fallenmouth Manor," I say. "Why do you think we'll be safe there?"

"We won't be. But he won't kill you, that much I'm certain of. Sefton believes he loves you, which means he will protect you."

"He hates you."

"But he won't kill me, not yet. He still needs his anchor, or else he would have murdered me already." Dax releases my wrists but keeps his arms around me. "Your body belongs to me. Remember that."

"You just opened up to me in a big way, and now you're feeling weird about it. I get that." I wriggle against him, rubbing against the bulge in his pants. "Your body belongs to me too. But the next time we have sex, I'll be the one who decides when and how it happens."

One corner of his mouth twitches upward the tiniest bit, but only for a split second. "Can you transport us to Fallenmouth Manor?"

"Not sure. I've only done the transporting thing once."

"You are a part of the Echo. You control at least some of its power. Harness that again."

"Don't remember exactly how I did it before."

He releases my wrists and holds me close in a much less obnoxious way. It feels almost tender. "What did you want most of all in that moment, when you took us away from Sefton and his golem?"

"I—" Wanted to save myself, yes. But I also fervently wished to save Dax too. That's probably a sign I've gone crazy, but everything about this new world is bonkers. "I just wanted to escape from Sefton and his creatures. It was too much, and I was afraid of what he might do next."

"Tap into that fervent desire to escape. Use it now."

Wrapping my arms around him, I squeeze my eyes shut and take his advice. I wish with everything I have that we could be at Fallenmouth Manor. I don't even know where that is, but I'm tapping into magics now, not plotting a course on a map. That weird sensation of electricity and cool water rushes through me, and I sense the world shifting around us. The bomb blasts of fireballs and supernatural lightning fall silent as a temperate breeze kisses my cheeks.

I open my eyes. "Is that Fallenmouth Manor?"

"Yes." Dax pushes away from me. "I've come home at last."

He doesn't sound happy about that.

The house squats inside an expansive clearing, its boxy shape a sharp contrast to the almost whimsical way the shrubs and flower beds around it have been sculpted. The gray stone structure features windows with wrought iron sectioning the panes and wrought iron benches in the garden that I can just see to the left of the house. I can't see the cemetery from here, but I imagine that's situated out of sight on purpose.

Dax and I are standing in a circular driveway covered in pea gravel that crunches under our shoes. A concrete fountain hunkers in the middle of the circular drive, and water pours out of the mouth of a leaping stag.

Something about this place creeps me out. Maybe it's the apocalypse doing that, but I think it's this estate too. It feels…haunted. I know we will meet Sefton here. It's inevitable. But I dread the moment when he'll arrive and bring who-knows-what kind of creatures with him. His golem? God, I hope not.

Dax takes my hand to lead me into the house. Wooden double doors block our way, but he twists the knob—and it turns. Nobody locks this place up, I guess. Maybe Sefton has the whole estate surrounded, guarded by his Echo minions. Dax pulls the doors shut as we waltz into the entryway, and shadows envelop us. But dim light spills out of a room further down the hall.

A chill sweeps over my skin, raising every hair.

Sefton steps out of the room at the end of the hall. "Come inside and join me by the fire. I know it's summer, but a crackling hearth is soothing."

He sounds calm and almost friendly.

Dax doesn't move. Neither do I.

Sefton waves for us to follow him. "Come, join me in the drawing room. We have much to discuss."

Discuss? The man who brought hell to earth wants to sit down by the fire and have a chat.

I glance at Dax.

He shrugs.

We shuffle down the hall to join Sefton in the drawing room. Our host sits in an armchair while Dax and I settle onto padded wooden chairs.

"Thank you for coming," Sefton says. "I assume you, Allison, are responsible for getting the two of you here. I hadn't anticipated you would share in the power of the Echo."

"Uh-huh." I squirm in my seat. It's not uncomfortable, but I feel uneasy about everything right now. Especially Sefton Stainthorpe. Considering what Dax told me about his brother, I decide playing nice is my best move. "Didn't mean to horn in on your power. You must be annoyed."

"On the contrary. It's perfectly right that you and I should control the Echo together." Sefton leans forward, his gaze pinned to mine. "But I can't have you defying me."

No, I won't comment on that. Instead, I clear my throat and ask, "Where's your golem?"

"Sleeping. I will rouse him when it becomes necessary." Sefton keeps staring at me with unnerving intensity. "But do not ever run away from me again. If you try, you will wish you hadn't. The world outside this sanctuary will grow even worse as time goes on and the alchemy of worlds reaches its conclusion."

"But your sanctuary will be untouched."

"Precisely." Sefton leans back in his chair, resting one ankle on the opposite knee, wincing slightly. He sets both feet on the floor. "Would you care to join me for dinner? Or are you both too knackered? I can take you straight to your quarters if you prefer."

"Sleep sounds great." I glance at Dax. "What about you?"

"Not hungry. Your idea is best."

Sefton rises, wincing again as he puts weight on his leg, clearly favoring his left knee.

Dax and I both stand up. He eyes his brother with a narrowed gaze and tight lips.

"Come," Sefton says. "Let me show you to your quarters, where you will sleep every night for the rest of your lives."

Chapter Seventeen

Dax

MY BROTHER IS INSANE, BEYOND REDEMPTION. BUT THEN, I'M PREJU-diced because he ripped me apart and remade me into a monster, without my permission, without caring what damage his spell would do to me or anyone else caught in the crossfire. Allison was in the crossfire. She might've died, and Sefton did nothing to protect her. He claims to love her, yet he left her alone and defenseless during a catastrophe of biblical proportions.

He created an apocalypse. My brother. Quiet, shy Sefton Stainthorpe has turned the entire world into his own demented experiment.

Sefton mounts the stairs one step at a time, favoring his left leg.

"How did you injure yourself?" I ask.

"During your transformation, you thrashed like a mad beast and kicked me hard in the knee."

I will not apologize for that. He deserved much worse.

We reach the landing, and Sefton pauses to catch his breath. Mounting those stairs seems to have left him winded. That's odd, since he had seemed quite spry earlier, aside from his bad knee. He leads us down the hall toward my old room. I remember this house better than I wish I did, and every room seems filled with the ghosts of the past. I would never have chosen to come back here. This place reminds me that I am not the man I was and never will be again. Isn't a five-year sentence in the Echo enough punishment? Haven't I earned my freedom? But I won't be free, not ever again. Sefton has made certain of that.

At the door to my old room, Sefton halts with his hand resting on the knob of the closed door. "This will be your quarters, Allison. It used to be-long to my parents, the Earl and Countess of Fallenmouth."

Allison flicks her gaze to me, then back to Sefton. "Isn't this Dax's room now? He's the Earl of Fallenmouth."

"There are no earls anymore," Sefton hisses. "No dukes, no viscounts, no fucking queen or king. There is only me. I rule over everyone and everything in both worlds, which means I decide which of you sleeps in this room. Do you understand?"

She nods, seeming to have decided speaking is a bad idea.

The best I can do is to partially restrain my anger. I thrust an arm between Allison and Sefton, thumping my palm on the door. "You will not sleep in the same room with her."

"He didn't say he wanted to," Allison tells me while she gently settles a hand on my outstretched arm. "Relax, huh? We're all wiped out. A good night's rest will make us feel better, and then we can have a nice talk in the morning. Okay?"

Nothing about this is okay, but I understand what Allison is really trying to communicate to me. She wants me to placate my mad-as-a-hatter brother so he won't hack off our arms and legs to stop us from escaping.

I lower my arm.

My brother opens the bedroom door. "Your room, Allison."

"Thank you," she says as she steps across the threshold.

"But it will be our room soon."

I glower at Sefton.

He feigns nonchalance fairly well, but the lines tightening around his eyes attest to his true state of mind. "Good night, Allison. You may lock the door if you wish."

He hands her a key.

The wanker had hoped to sleep with her tonight, hadn't he? Sefton changed his mind only when I let my displeasure show.

Allison shuts the door and locks it.

Sefton waves for me to follow him. "You will stay in your old room. The one you slept in until our parents died and you became lord of the manor strictly based on the accident of fate that pushed you out of Mother's arse before me."

"Don't talk about Mum that way. She loved you."

"But she loved you more. Everyone did. I was invisible, drowned out by the sparkling light of your brilliant personality." He stops at the door to my childhood room and hurls it open. "You always looked down on me."

"That's not true. I was proud of you. We might be twins, but I couldn't have hoped to be as clever and accomplished as you. Two PhDs? I didn't try for one." Maybe I'm desperately attempting to convince him that he wasn't invisible all our lives because I don't want my brother to be the maniac who destroyed the world. But since I can't rewind time and stop him from doing that, I lay a hand on his shoulder and try again. "I never hated you, Sef. I loved you. But I can't understand what you've done."

"Of course not. You don't have the vision to comprehend it."

"Sef—"

"I never loved you, Dax. I always despised you, and I always will."

He stalks off down the hall, his footfalls echoing in his wake.

Sefton and I might not have been best mates, but I thought we got on well enough. Now I find out he has always despised me. The dark energy he ingested to become powerful must have emboldened him to become a monster, but he clearly harbored those desires inside him for years, maybe all his life.

I want to go to Allison's room and lose myself inside her body, erase the pain with sex. But I won't use her that way, not anymore. Seeing my brother again, knowing what he has done, I feel like my entire life has been one long dream and now I've woken from it to discover the real world is a nightmare.

Shuffling into my room, I kick the door shut. I had slept in this room until I turned eighteen and went away to university. My parents died two months after my twentieth birthday, and I became the Earl of Fallenmouth. That's another thing Allison and I have in common—losing our parents at a relatively young age—though I had mates and lovers to help me through it while she had no one.

Allison has me now, but that's hardly a blessing.

I kick off my boots and toss my leather coat onto the chair in the corner. Then I drop onto the bed on my back, still clothed, and shut my eyes. Outside the window, far in the distance, creatures scream and shout, but eventually, I manage to sleep.

The sun is just rising when I wake up. Can't believe I slept at all, but exhaustion had overpowered me. I push up into a sitting position and swing my legs off the bed, yawning and stretching. I need to find Allison and make sure she's all right. I pull on my boots, then head for her room.

The door hangs open, and the room is empty.

I take the steps two at a time as I rush downstairs and stop in the foyer. Voices originate from the dining room. I stomp down the hall and through the doorway.

Sefton sits at the head of the long table while Allison occupies the chair beside him.

When she sees me, she smiles—though only for half a second. I'm sure she worries about my brother's reaction if he should notice that she seems rather pleased to see me. I don't blame her for veering her gaze away.

"Good morning, Dax," my brother says, and he sounds almost sincere. "Join us for breakfast. I made this meal myself."

"Because you fired all the staff." I sit down opposite Allison. "When did you learn to cook, Sef?"

"No one taught me. I figured it out on my own."

Oh yes, that makes me want to eat his food. Allison seems to be pushing it around on her plate but not actually consuming any of her meal. Maybe she's afraid Sefton will poison us. He would only risk that with me. Allison is more than a tool for my crackbrained brother to exploit, but right now, my most pressing problem is how to get her to eat. I doubt the food is poisoned, and we both need nourishment. So I spear a piece of blackened sausage with my fork and eat it. "Not bad, Sef. The faint taste of charcoal gives it a distinctive flavor."

"Glad you approve. But that's not charcoal. It's a honey glaze."

"Sure it is. Honey is so often black."

This is bizarre. I'm having a normal conversation with my brother, the madman responsible for the world's ruination, as if we're just two blokes enjoying a morning meal.

Allison still hasn't tasted the food. I consume a mouthful of mashed potatoes and make a noise that implies I like it. Well, the food isn't the worst I've ever had. It's not the best either, but starving refugees from the apocalypse can't be finicky. Allison bites her upper lip, watching me eat. After I've devoured another bite of sausage and two forkfuls of baked beans, she finally starts to eat.

I relax, just a bit. Can't completely relax under the circumstances, but at least Allison won't be malnourished. It seems impossible to believe I kidnapped her a few days ago and treated her like my enemy. Now I'm determined to make sure she has a good breakfast.

After our meal, and more bizarrely mundane conversation, we all walk out into the foyer.

I haven't forgotten what Sefton said last night—that Allison and I will be in this house for the rest of our lives—and it's time to ask him the obvious question. "What do you mean to do with us?"

"I'll share my plans with you when I return."

"Return? From where?"

Sefton shrugs. "I need to survey the areas that have already been transformed. Alchemy on this level is extraordinarily difficult to achieve, and I can't be sure a few things haven't been cocked up in the process. I need to see for myself."

"I'll go with you."

He lets out a harsh laugh. "Are you off your trolley, Dax? I can't let you leave this compound because I can't trust you not to try to escape. Besides, it wouldn't be clever to leave Allison alone here. The entire five-hundred-acre property is warded, magically, to prevent anyone from entering. But the guards... Well, I can't guarantee they'll mind their manners."

"What sort of guards? I haven't seen them."

"No, you wouldn't. They have their orders." He throws a hand up when I start to speak again. "Enough, Dax. I need to say goodbye to Allison."

Sefton clasps her hands, leaning in until their faces hover a hair's breadth apart. "I regret leaving you so soon after our reunion, but it can't be helped. When I return, we will be married. And we shall at last consummate our union."

Consummate? I don't care if he is my flesh and blood. I will murder him if he touches Allison.

"Married?" she says, her jaw dropping. "We hardly know each other. No offense, but I don't love you."

"But you shall." He presses his lips to hers. "We are going to rule the world together, pet."

He shuffles away from us. A portal appears just behind him, and he walks backward through it. The portal vanishes.

"You are not marrying him," I snarl.

"No, I'm not." She bars her arms over her breasts. "But not because you commanded I won't do it. No more growling orders at me. Got it?"

"I can't stand to see him touch you or speak to you as if you're already his."

"He thinks I am." She approaches me, tilting her head back to meet my gaze. "But he is mistaken. Nobody owns me. Not him, not you, not anyone."

"Yes, I know. But I feel…possessive of your body."

"Get over it. If and when I decide to have sex with you again, it will be my choice."

"Of course it will."

She angles her head to the side and squints at me. "Are you being amenable? That can't be right. I must have misheard that, and you really said something nasty."

"I did not. But if you persist in harassing me about it, I might turn back into a beast."

"Don't do that unless I ask you to."

Though I want to know why she might ask me to behave like a beast, I realize we have other matters to discuss.

"Let's go outside," I say. "We could both use some exercise and fresh air. Then we need to discuss our situation."

And figure out how to undo the apocalypse. No, that's not an impossible task at all.

CHAPTER EIGHTEEN

Allison

I MARCH OUTSIDE, DETERMINED TO...DO SOMETHING. NO IDEA WHAT. I stop in the middle of the yard, or whatever the grassy area around an English mansion is called. I need to do something, anything. Can't just hang out in the ancestral home of Dax and Sefton, sipping tea and nibbling on cucumber sandwiches. Everything seems tranquil and normal here at Fallenmouth Manor, but I know the rest of the world is in ruins or soon will be.

The horror is spreading. I'd watched it rush toward us back in Texas, like a malevolent sandstorm. How many more people have died since then?

Dax hurries to catch up to me. "What are you doing?"

"Gee, I don't know." I throw a scowl his way. "Thought I'd go for a little stroll in the woods to see the wildlife. That's the right thing to do when the entire world, maybe the entire universe, is collapsing around us."

"Sarcasm is not appropriate right now."

"I think it is. But I suppose it would be more appropriate to snarl at you and threaten to kill you or at least tie you up."

The idea of tying Dax up kind of makes me horny. Which is so not helpful right now.

He steps in front of me. "You are behaving irrationally."

"Like you haven't done that too. Does the word kidnapping ring a bell?"

"Why are you in such a foul mood?"

A harsh laugh bursts out of me. "Seriously? Mr. Scowling-Growling Demon from the Echo thinks I'm bitchy."

He grasps my shoulders. "You aren't acting like yourself. What happened?"

What the hell. He'll find out, eventually. "When I woke up this morning, I tested my powers. Tried to whisk myself away like I did yesterday, but it didn't work. I started to feel the tingly electricity thing, then poof. It was gone."

"Perhaps you were too anxious."

"Like I wasn't yesterday when Sefton's golem was hovering behind me?"

His voice and his expression turn gentler. "I'm sorry. Five years in the Echo has made me far less understanding than I used to be. Not that I was a particularly self-aware man before that. But I want to help you, Allison."

For a moment, I can't speak. I gaze into his eyes and wonder how in the world this happened. The beast who had treated me like the enemy has become a man who wants to make me feel better. It's been maybe three days since I met Dax—I've kind of lost count—and I can't process everything I've experienced since then. All I know is that now I trust this man, and I need him.

To help me fix what his brother has done. That's all.

"I appreciate that you want to help," I say. "But if I can't magic us away from here, that means we need to get out the old-fashioned way."

"We used to have several vehicles on the premises. The garage is behind the house."

He clasps my hand, leading me around the backside of the huge mansion where I see the garage he mentioned. It has four big doors in front, but we head for the human-size door on the side. Once we enter the building, he flicks the light switch.

The garage houses super-expensive vehicles. I'm no car expert, but even I can tell the two sedans, one SUV, and one sports car boast price tags so far out of my budget that I couldn't afford to buy a tire for any of these vehicles.

"You're super rich, huh?" I say as I scan the interior of the garage.

"Money hardly matters anymore." Dax approaches the nearest vehicle, a four-door sedan, and opens the driver's door. "I doubt creatures from the Echo accept dollars or pound notes. They want payments in blood."

He finds a key tucked under the visor and tries to start the car. Nothing happens. He pops the hood and gets out to inspect the engine. Screwing his mouth up, he slams the hood shut.

Something I'd almost forgotten springs up in my mind. "I meant to ask you something earlier, but I didn't want to do it in front of Sefton."

"What is it?"

"You said your parents died exactly thirteen years ago on the day Sefton cast his world-destroying spell."

"That's right."

"Well, um…" I hunch my shoulders and avert my gaze, but then force myself to look at him. "My parents died on that day too."

Dax goes completely still, his body rigid, his gaze unblinking. "What?"

"Our parents all died on the same day thirteen years ago. I don't know what that means—"

"I do. Sefton believes the number thirteen is vastly powerful, remember? He somehow discovered the coincidence and used it in his spellcasting."

"Coincidence?" I move closer, tipping my head back to meet his gaze. "Sounds more like fate to me."

"Perhaps it is."

Dax resumes his search, checking the other three vehicles and screwing up his mouth even more with every peek under a hood.

Finally, he returns to me. "Sefton has removed the batteries."

"Of course he has. I knew the garage was too easy. But why can't I teleport or whatever you want to call it?"

"I assume he cast a spell to prevent it."

"Aw, come on. I only got to do that whisking thing twice, and now he's taken it away."

Dax isn't wearing his leather coat today. That fact had escaped my notice for a while, but I don't feel stupid for not realizing it until now. I mean, we're in the middle of an apocalypse, and our host is a lunatic who expects me to marry him and "consummate" our so-called relationship. So yeah, I'm not thinking at the highest level today. Or yesterday. Or the day before.

"Perhaps your 'whisking thing' isn't gone," Dax says. "Not for good, at least."

"Sefton is way more powerful than I am."

"Is he? Sefton keeps talking about sharing the Echo power with you. And you are the catalyst, which must mean all the magics he employed to create the Echo originated from within you."

"That's an awful lot of supposition."

He slides his hands over my shoulders, down my arms, and all the way to my hands. Then he slips his fingers between mine. "Nothing is a certainty anymore. We have to accept that."

"Maybe. But I don't plan to sit around twiddling my thumbs while Sefton is out there doing who knows what."

I like the feel of his fingers threaded with mine a little too much. It feels so good that I want to forget everything and just be here with him. It's crazy. But the whole world has flipped upside down, so maybe I need to stop judging my actions and his based on the way things used to be pre-apocalypse. Yes, he behaved horribly at first. I understand now why he did that. I don't agree with his actions back then, but I get it. He's as scared as the rest of us, though he also needs time to recover from his years in the Echo.

But I cannot, will not, just sit here doing nothing.

Pulling my hands free of his, I march toward the periphery of the woods. The darkness inside that domain gives me a wriggly sensation in my gut, but I won't let fear constrain me anymore.

"Allison, stop!" Dax shouts.

Without looking back, I tell him, "You can come with me or not. Your choice."

"Stop!"

I hear his footfalls pounding behind me, coming closer. But I realize too late why he's running and shouting.

Echo creatures close in around me, emerging from the shadows as if they'd been lying in wait for me.

Oh shit.

I freeze, but the creatures have surrounded me. Everywhere I hear the sounds of gnashing teeth, growling, talons clicking, and even slurping. I don't want to know what these monsters have in mind for me.

Dax crashes through the bushes and stops alongside me, breathing hard. "What the bloody hell did you think you were doing? Running off on your own?"

"Sorry, it was a dumb thing to do. Got any ideas for getting us out of this mess?"

"Afraid not. These creatures were already here on the property, and I doubt Sefton would've left without casting wards around the entire estate, including the forest."

I glance sideways at Dax because moving my head, or even my eyes, strikes me as dangerous right now. "Are you saying these creatures work for him? I wondered if that was the case, but Sefton didn't specify who his guards are."

"The Echo creatures clearly protect the estate. Sefton means to keep us locked in."

Oh, perfect. We're trapped. And what a deceptively beautiful snare it is.

A creature with bronzed skin and hairy flesh moves away from the others as if he's the leader of Sefton's gang of monsters. Yeah, I know for sure the creature is male. He's not wearing any clothes, unless a coat of hair counts.

"You aren't meant to leave," the creature says. "The master forbade it."

I glance at Dax. He has clenched his fists and his jaw too. I've seen that look before. He's about to charge into battle, but he shouldn't do that. We're outnumbered. I close my hand around his fist. "Don't. They aren't going to hurt us. They can't. Sefton wouldn't like it if they did."

Dax grasps my hand. "Turn around slowly."

We rotate in unison, one tiny step at a time, and begin to walk back toward the house. I risk a glance over my shoulder, but the creatures aren't following. They stay in the shadowy confines of the woods, almost as if they can't come any closer to the house. Maybe Sefton created a boundary to keep the creatures where he wants them. He needs us, for now, so I doubt he would give his minions free rein. Too much temptation for vicious beasts.

Dax halts halfway across the lawn, angling sideways to see the woods.

I turn too. The creatures have retreated out of sight. The lawn is off limits to them, apparently, like everything beyond the house and the lawn is off limits to me and Dax.

"What should we do now?" I ask.

"No idea. Wait, I suppose."

"Uh-uh. Told you I won't twiddle my thumbs until His Majesty comes home."

Dax folds his arms over his chest. "What do you suggest we do, then?"

"Oh, I've got an idea. But you won't like it."

"Tell me anyway. Then I'll know whether I need to restrain you again."

I think he's joking. It can be hard to tell with him, but I'm pretty sure he's teasing me.

He arches one brow. "Did you come up with a plan? Or were you having me on?"

"Yes, I have a plan." I square my shoulders and lift my chin. "Teach me how to fight."

"No."

I give him my best stubborn look. "I need to do this."

"You do not need to fight. I will protect you."

"Not good enough. What if you get disabled? Or we get separated?" I poke his chest with my finger. "Teach me how to fight, Dax. I won't give up until you agree to do it. I'll pester and harass and annoy you until—"

"All right." He scrubs a hand over his face and sighs. "What you need to learn is basic self-defense techniques. Once you've mastered that, perhaps we can move on to more advanced maneuvers."

"Great. Let's get started now."

"Not out here. We don't want our watchers to witness everything I teach you."

"Where, then?"

He whirls away and waves for me to follow.

I trot after him only because I need his help to learn how to protect myself. I do not follow because he silently ordered me to do it with his hand-waving. Whether he realizes that or not, I don't care. If he turns all snarly and rude again, he'll get a piece of my mind.

We go inside the house, though calling it a "house" doesn't really describe this enormous structure, and he hurries down the hall. I have to jog to keep up with him. We finally veer into a room at the opposite end of the hall from where the dining room lies. It's a large space with high ceilings and tall windows, though big shrubs block most of the view. The sun shines into the space just enough that it doesn't feel like we're trapped in a box.

I see paintings high up on the walls, each one a depiction of a person—men and women, young and old. Down at eye level, a collection of skinny sword-like implements hangs from hooks on the wall. The floor is wood, but in one section it features a padded mat.

"What is this room?" I ask.

"It's where generations of Stainthorpes learned to fence."

"Fencing is when you play with skinny little pseudo-swords."

He compresses his lips, and I'm sure he wants to growl at me. But he doesn't. "Fencing is a sport. It requires dexterity, control, and skill."

"Don't see how fencing is going to protect me. Besides, it'll take too long for me to learn that."

"I have no intention of teaching you to fence today." He rolls up his sleeves. "I'm going to instruct you in basic self-defense techniques. Just as I told you a few minutes ago."

"Yeah, I remember. I have a brain, you know."

He grunts. "Then act like it."

We're back to Dax the jerk. Maybe he's just scared, which I can understand, but that's no excuse.

I rub my palms together. "I'm ready. Come on, teach me."

CHAPTER NINETEEN

Dax

PERHAPS I SHOULDN'T BOTHER TEACHING ALLISON HOW TO PRO-
tect herself. I can protect her, and the creatures outside are far stronger than any human being in this world. I'm not at all sure any sort of self-defense technique will be enough. But it's all I can offer her.

I saunter up to Allison, halting an arm's length away. "First, you need to learn a few basic principles."

"Go on. I'm ready."

"Avoid the chest. It won't be effective without a weapon. Also avoid the knees. That requires a particular technique, so don't risk it. You're better off sticking to the most vulnerable areas—eyes, nose, throat, and groin."

"Got it."

"When you're in a threatening situation, don't hold back. Make plenty of noise too. Not only will that potentially confuse your attacker, but it will also attract attention that might scare them away." I don't think she fully understands how difficult it will be to ward off an attack, which means I need to make it painfully obvious. "Hit me."

She pulls her head back. "What?"

"I said hit me. Try to knock me down."

"Okay."

Allison bends her knees slightly and raises her fists. Then she just stands there studying me.

"You won't have time to think," I say. "Just do something, or I'll do it for you."

She rushes at me and lunges her knee up to strike me in the groin, but I seize her knee. I push her away, which knocks her off balance, and she tumbles to the floor.

I bend over her. "I wasn't even trying. Imagine what I could do if I really wanted to hurt you. You will never survive an encounter with an Echo creature if you keep holding back. Attack me. Don't think about it. Just do it."

Straightening, I raise my hands, palms up, and wiggle my fingers in a "come and get me" gesture.

Allison scrambles to her feet, planting them wide. Her lips tighten, and her gaze narrows.

Her determination makes me want to kiss her. Hard.

"Remember what I told you," I say. "Or are you so stupid that you can't hold on to a thought for more than five seconds? Maybe you're simply a coward."

She lets out a primal cry as she surges forward to pound her fists on my chest and stomp her foot down on mine.

I catch her wrists and cage her legs by lashing one of mine around both of hers. "Wrong tactic. If I were a murderous beast, you'd be dead."

A frustrated noise erupts out of her as she struggles against my hold.

"Try again," I hiss.

I shove her away with more force, and she tumbles to the mat again. This time she rolls across it and slides off onto the wood floor. Her elbow smacks into the hard surface.

Allison winces and scowls at me. "You asshole."

Stalking over to her, I kneel at her side. "Do you think an assailant will care about your tender feelings? They won't give a toss. Unless you want to be raped and murdered, your body ripped apart, you had better start taking this training seriously."

"How does throwing me across the room help?"

I lean in closer until our noses almost touch. "Now you understand the stakes. I could have killed you without breaking a sweat."

She glares at me for a moment, but gradually, the anger fades from her expression. With a sigh, she struggles to get up off the floor. I offer her my hands, but she scrambles to her feet without my help. When I lead her onto the mat, she faces me with her shoulders back, her chin lifted, and a new resolve evident in her expression.

Now she's ready.

"It's time to teach you," I say. "When an attacker threatens you, grab whatever is to hand—car keys, a brick, anything—then aim for the vulnerable areas."

"Eyes, nose, throat, and groin."

"That's right." I grasp her wrists and hold them between us. "Keep your hands ready and your knees bent."

She bends her knees a bit and keeps her hands raised even after I release her wrists. "Like this?"

"Yes." I back away from her. "First, you're going to try the groin kick. Make sure you've stabilized yourself as much as possible, then lift your leg with the knee bent and swing it upward. Straighten your lower leg just as you make contact with the attacker's groin. This isn't a knee jab. It's your calf doing the damage."

"Think I get it."

"All right. Give it a go, slowly at first." I smirk. "And try not to ram my bollocks. This is training, not an exercise in castration."

"I doubt I can actually whack your balls off with my leg."

"Try the groin kick now."

She rushes toward me, raises her bent knee, and straightens it just as her calf contacts my groin. Luckily, she's restraining herself. I let her try it several more times while I lunge at her and duck side to side while keeping our movements deliberate and painless. Though I'd told her to hold back, now I think that might be the wrong tactic. The only way she'll know for sure she can manage this maneuver is if I let her go all the way.

My balls ache just thinking about it.

"Enough practice," I say. "Time for a live demonstration."

Her eyes widen, and she blinks twice slowly. "You want me to ram your 'bollocks'? A few minutes ago, you told me not to do that."

"I was wrong. We don't have any time to waste. You need to know you can do this, and you need to realize that right now." I wave for her to back away, and I do the same until we're standing at opposite ends of the mat. "I'm going to come at you, but I won't give you any warning."

"You just did warn me."

"I meant I won't warn you when I do it. Understand?"

"Uh-huh. Whatever you say, oh wise master."

I just manage to stifle a growl.

Allison smirks at me, her lips twitching like she's trying not to laugh.

Perfect. She's relaxed and off her guard.

I run at her.

She rushes forward, arms raised in front of her face, and swings her bent knee up, then straightens it to ram her calf into my groin.

Pain slams through me, making me double over and gasp. I look up at her. "That was perfect."

The fact that I'm still gasping and bent over tells me she has mastered that technique.

She grins. "Do I get a gold star?"

I straighten and blow out a breath, cocking one hip to take some of the pressure off my privates, which haven't completely recovered yet. "Next, we'll try the heel palm strike."

Allison bites her lip, eying my groin. "Are you okay? Looked like that really hurt."

"It did, which is a good thing."

"Are you sure you'll be okay? Maybe we should take a breather so you can recover."

"No breaks. With those creatures out there guarding the estate, we both need to be ready for anything."

"Okay. Let's keep going."

I show her the heel palm strike, which involves thrusting a flat palm backward and up into either the attacker's nose or the soft spot under the chin. She masters that technique too. Next, we try the elbow strike—swinging an elbow up crosswise to the attacker to hit the jaw hard. She has no trouble with that move either, even when I have her try performing the elbow strike while I'm behind her. The more we practice, though, the less force she uses, and I have to ask her why.

"Because I'm hitting you, of course," she says. "Don't want to leave you bruised and bloody."

"I can take it. Trust me. I lived in the Echo for five years, and no one in that world pulls their punches." I cup my groin and pretend to grimace. "But I don't think I'll ask you to practice the groin kick again."

Her gaze drops to my cock, and her tone turns husky. "No, I wouldn't want to damage your manly parts."

The way she spoke those words threatens to send all the blood in my body flooding into my "manly parts." I need to change the subject, or I'll be shagging her on the mat.

"Let's try a more advanced technique," I say. Then I crook my finger at her. "Come here. This is a close combat move."

Her lips curve into a sexy smile. "I like the sound of that."

She's flirting with me. I can't imagine why, not after everything I'd done to her before we came to Fallenmouth. Perhaps she thinks I need encouragement to keep up the training since I've been letting her genuinely assault me.

Allison walks up to me, our bodies inches apart.

"Turn around," I tell her.

She obeys my command, which must be a first in our relationship. Or rather, our acquaintance. We don't have the sort of dynamic that the word relationship implies.

I wrap my arms around her midsection, locking my hands and pulling her tight against me. "Now I've got you."

The cheeky woman rubs her arse against me. "Yes, you do."

With every breath I take, I smell our sweat but also the scent of her desire. Christ, she's aroused. How can that be? I'm pushing her hard, testing her limits, forcing her to defend herself against my attacks. Her reaction seems barmy. But I'm getting aroused too. For me, it makes sense. I'm a man, and we blokes don't require much stimulation to get randy. But women aren't meant to like fighting with a man. Are they?

"Break free of my hold," I rumble into her ear. "Do it now."

"Don't know how."

"First, bend forward from the waist." When she follows my instructions, I tell her, "Good. Turn into me and ram your elbow up into my neck, and keep doing that, switching sides every time, until you can get leverage to spin around and execute a groin kick. You can also stomp on the top of my foot."

"Are you sure you want me to do all of that? You said you didn't want me to ram your balls anymore."

"Changed my mind." I tug, crushing my locked hands into her torso hard enough to make her gasp. "Do it now. Don't hold back."

She swings her elbow up, on one side and then the other, striking me in the neck or shoulder every time. When she slams her foot down on mine, my grip loosens a little, just enough to let her spin around and nail me in the groin. I grunt and let go of her, not because I chose to do that. She genuinely outmaneuvered me.

Once I've recovered my ability to breathe and speak, I say, "That's enough for now. You're a quick study, so I doubt it will take many lessons to get you ready to defend yourself. I can't say if these techniques will work on Echo creatures."

"I know. But I feel better just having a few tricks I can use. Being helpless sucks."

"You were never helpless. It takes a strong woman to stand up to a brute like me."

"Inner strength is great." She bumps her hip into me. "But I love being able to beat the crap out of you."

When she says that, while aiming a teasing smile at me, I find myself doing something I haven't done in years. I chuckle. "Yes, you did beat the crap out of me quite well."

Her eyes go wide. "Did you just laugh? Or was I hallucinating?"

I flash her a scowl. "Don't make an issue of it."

Allison raises her hands. "Okay, okay, relax. I'll pretend you never laughed. But for the record, you are not a brute."

"Of course I am."

She studies me for a moment, but then sighs as if she's given up on trying to convert me to her viewpoint. Despite the fact I'm still scowling at her, she walks up to me and splays a hand over my cheek. "Your beard has gotten longer and scratchier. It's kind of like sandpaper, but I might kiss you anyway."

Kiss me? Why on earth would she do that? Yes, I want to fuck her again. But she shouldn't want that, which means she should not want to kiss me either.

I pull away from her. "Let's explore the study for clues to what Sefton has done and what he still plans to do."

Chapter Twenty

Allison

I MUST HAVE EMBARRASSED DAX. WHY ELSE WOULD HE GO ALL CAVE-man again and change the subject so fast I think it caused a minor air disturbance? All I said was that his beard is scratchy and I might kiss him. I'm guessing it was the part about a potential kiss that made him uncomfortable.

He whips his shirt off and uses it to wipe sweat from his brow.

Uh, what? He didn't need to remove his shirt to do that. I wish he were still covered up because the sight of his naked chest makes me flash back to when we got it on in the warehouse. I can't explain why I suggested I might kiss him, but I guess it was the heat of the moment, when we were both sweaty and amped up, that made me say it. I can't deny that sparring with Dax was hot.

Jeez, the world is literally going to hell, and I'm thinking about sex.

"I need a new shirt," Dax announces. "Wait for me in the foyer."

"Sure, because I follow orders when you command me to do something without explaining why."

"I did say why. Should I drop to my knees and beg you to do what I tell you?"

"Yeah, sounds good to me. I beat the crap out of you just now, so maybe you shouldn't try to boss me around."

Rather than snarling at me, he spins around and stalks out of the room.

I follow him into the foyer. Not because he commanded it, but because I need a change of clothes too, which means I have to walk through the foyer to go upstairs. Earlier this morning, I'd found a ton of women's clothes in the closet of the bedroom I'd slept in. A note taped to the closet door had said, "For you, Allison." Sefton bought clothes for me before I set foot in this house.

The creepiest part of all is that Sefton thinks I'm going to marry him.

Dax takes the stairs two at a time, leaving me to scramble after him. The idea of being alone when those creatures are outside makes me uneasy. But Dax goes into his room and shuts the door. Message received. He doesn't want to talk to me or even see me right now. So I retreat into my room and change into clean clothes, despite the fact wearing things a madman chose for me gives me a weird slithery feeling in my gut. Knowing he picked underwear for me is just plain icky. Once I'm dressed in jeans and a T-shirt, I march down to Dax's room and knock on the door.

It swings open.

Dax is wearing nothing but a towel that looks like it's about to fall off his hips.

I shouldn't be ogling him. It's inappropriate when we have important things to do. Things I suddenly can't remember. His hair is wet, and droplets of water trickle down his chest, drawing my focus to the edge of the towel. I can see a few dark hairs poking out above the terry cloth.

"Did you take a shower?" I ask.

"Obviously."

My attention shifts to his face, and I suddenly realize something. "You shaved."

Besides getting rid of his beard, he slicked his wet hair back to tame the wild locks. He looks, um, kind of good clean-shaven. Kind of? *Ugh*. He's hot. Even the scar that slashes across his jaw can't diminish his sex appeal.

Dax frowns. "What is wrong with you?"

"Huh? Nothing." I tear my gaze away from his pecs. "Are you ready to go search the study?"

"Does it look like I'm ready?"

He doesn't wait for my response, instead stomping over to the bed where he's laid out clothes for himself.

I should leave. Wait for him downstairs. But I can't convince my muscles to move. I also can't talk my eyes out of staring at him.

Dax whips the towel off and flings it onto the floor.

Suddenly, I'm breathing harder and my skin feels warm all over—warm and tingly. I can see everything, from his hair down to his toes and all the bits in between. But it's his dick that captivates me. I've seen it before, felt it inside me, so I shouldn't get breathless and tingly from seeing it again. My hand drifts up to my throat, and I can't stop myself from petting my skin while I imagine him touching me.

He stands there for a minute, just gazing down at the clothes he laid out on the bed.

Is he doing that on purpose? To get me horny? If he is... Well, mission accomplished.

Finally, he gets dressed. The charcoal slacks and golden tan dress shirt he chose look damn good on him. He slips on a pair of socks and brown loafers too. I'd chosen casual clothes—jeans, a T-shirt, and tennies—because I assumed we'll be running for our lives again any minute. But he looks like he's heading out to a corporate lunch meeting.

"Did you have a job before Sefton dumped you into the Echo?" I ask.

"I was the CEO of Stainthorpe Limited, our family's marketing firm."

"You made it sound like you were a ladies' man who didn't care about anything but sex."

"Maintaining the company my father started was important to me." He saunters closer, leaving only the barest gap between our bodies. "I admit I was an arse who treated women like toys. But whatever you might think of me, I took my work seriously."

"Never said you didn't. Your brother made it sound that way, though."

"Sefton was jealous when I inherited the title and the business, but I didn't realize how jealous until he…" Dax shuts his eyes briefly and sighs. "Until he destroyed the world."

"It's not your fault he did that."

"Perhaps not. But I should've noticed the signs that something was wrong." He pushes past me. "I'm going to the study. You can follow me or not."

I get that he doesn't like talking about his brother, and I decide to let it go for now. So I hurry down the stairs after him. When we reach the study door, Dax tries to turn the knob, but it won't budge. Sefton keeps his inner sanctum locked.

"You didn't really think he'd leave it open, did you?" I say. "Sefton might be crazy, but he's not stupid."

"But I am. Is that what you're implying?"

"Don't get grumpy with me because your brother locked the study door. You damn well know I never implied you're stupid."

He stares at me, his lips puckered and his body tense.

I stare right back at him, brows raised, arms crossed over my chest.

Dax growls and backs away from the door. Then he runs at it, slamming his large foot into the wood. The door flies open.

He saunters into the study. "Not locked anymore."

"That's just great." I finger the broken lock while I cross the threshold into the room. "Now the lunatic holding us hostage will come home and realize we broke into his study. Good job, Dax."

"I don't give a toss if he knows."

"Start giving 'a toss.' Your brother has an enormous amount of power, and we have no way to stop him."

Dax leans over the big wooden desk that sits in front of a large window and begins to rifle through the papers and notebooks neatly stacked on the desktop. "Let Sefton do what he wants to me. I don't care."

What happened between the moment when I saw him in a towel and the moment we reached the study? I asked what he'd done for a living before the apocalypse, and then he turned into a growling jerk again. He really has some kind of complex about his brother. Jealousy? Guilt? Maybe it's both.

I grab his arm to make him stop and look at me. "Maybe you don't care what happens to you, but I do."

He freezes. His expression goes blank, and he might not be breathing either. "Why would you say that?"

"Because it's true." I grasp his face with both hands. "I don't want you to die, Dax."

"You want me alive to protect you."

"I want you alive, period."

He shuts his eyes, releasing the breath he must've been holding in, and his posture slackens. "You shouldn't care about me."

"Of course I should. I haven't forgotten about the way you treated me at first, but I've seen more sides of you since then." I move closer until my body is brushing against his. "It's too late to tell me not to care about you."

He opens his eyes but doesn't meet my gaze. "We need to search the rest of the study."

Okay, I'll let him get away with pretending he didn't hear what I said. Can't believe I did say it. But I meant every word. Maybe he's right and I shouldn't care about him, but I can't help it. I have seen different sides of him, like earlier when he taught me how to defend myself. That's only the latest in a series of little things he's done that prove he's not a total bastard.

So I help him search the study.

Mostly we find papers on which Sefton wrote down notes that make no sense. I should've gotten a PhD in physics and taken an intensive course in alchemy before walking into this room. Dax is clearly just as confused as I am. If we'd hoped to find the key to stopping the apocalypse inside the study... Well, we were complete idiots.

One of the desk drawers is locked. I don't bother trying to talk Dax out of smashing his way into it because I know that won't do any good. Besides, we've already broken into the room. Sefton will know we invaded his study the second he sees the door.

Dax uses a letter opener to break the lock on the drawer.

We find neatly arranged stacks of cash in there, each block sealed with a strip of thick paper. Empty spaces suggest he spent most of the money, though I can't imagine what he might buy that would help him trigger doomsday.

I shut the drawer.

We give up on the study and search the rest of the house. Dax wants us to split up so we can cover more ground in less time, but I reject that command. Neither of us should be alone, not with those creatures outside and the possibility that Sefton might return at any moment. Safety in numbers, I say, even if the number is only two. None of the many rooms in this mansion provides anything useful. But when we get to the cellar door in the kitchen, it's locked.

"What's down there?" I ask. "I mean, is it usually locked?"

"No, it is not." He takes a large step backward. "And it won't be for long."

I don't even bother trying to stop him. He kicks the door open with a bang that reverberates through the kitchen and hurts my ears. Then we clomp down the stairs into the cellar.

Dax flicks a switch at the top of the stairs, which turns on a light bulb in the space below us.

"Haven't you wondered how this house has electricity when the rest of the world doesn't?" I ask as I follow Dax into the gloom below.

"Sefton used magic to spare the estate from the devastation elsewhere. Why should it surprise you that he ensured his home would have electricity?"

"Fair point."

We've reached the bottom of the stairs when he stops to turn toward me. "Did you just admit I was right? Perhaps I imagined that."

I roll my eyes.

A draft wafts over me, so cold that it raises goosebumps on my arms. I get the strangest feeling that something is in here with us, something dark and strange and intangible. The dank basement is weirding me out, that's all.

The chill teases my skin again.

"Do you feel that?" I ask.

"Yes." Dax walks further into the cellar, fists clenched, scanning the area with his gaze. He halts in the middle of the cramped, shadowy space. "I have felt this before."

"What is it?"

"Dark magics."

"They're just floating around in here?"

He glances at me over his shoulder. "No. I believe Sefton is storing them here."

"You can't know that. Can you?"

"I suspect it, and I can find out for sure."

Dax creeps toward a row of metal shelves that hold various sizes and shapes of boxes, all fashioned from wood or metal and featuring strange symbols etched on their surfaces. He stops inches away from the shelves, scrutinizing them while he just stands there, not even moving his head. Then he stretches out a hand to touch one box.

He jerks and gasps, yanking his hand away.

"What happened?" I ask as I come up beside him.

"It stung me." He rubs his palm. "Felt something like an electrical shock combined with a jellyfish sting."

"Ouch. I guess your brother protected these boxes. That must mean they hold something important, huh?"

"Yes. I suspect they're part of the magics he used to create the Echo and start an apocalypse."

I touch one of the boxes, and my entire body jerks, making me stumble backward half a step. Yeah, that felt a lot like electricity and a wasp sting. I've never been stung by a jellyfish, but wasps have gotten me a time or two.

"Are you all right?" Dax asks.

"I'm fine. I was hoping I'd be able to get into these boxes, but I guess I'm not sharing Sefton's magic anymore."

Which means we're screwed.

Chapter Twenty-One

Dax

I'M NOT CONVINCED THAT THE FACT ALLISON CAN'T ACCESS THOSE BOX-es means she no longer shares the power Sefton has gathered for himself. But she believes that, and I have no evidence to the contrary. For once, I keep my mouth shut. Well, that's what I should do. I've never been good at not speaking my mind, and I manage to stay silent only until we've gone back upstairs and stand in the foyer, neither of us having any idea what to do now.

"You might still have the power of the Echo inside you," I say. "Perhaps the spell Sefton cast to stop you from escaping again is also dampening the magics you share with him. Or maybe it's not sharing at all."

"What do you mean it's not sharing?"

"Sefton told us you share the Echo power. We don't know if that's true. Your magics might stem from a different source."

"I guess that could be the case. Doesn't help me now, though."

"When did you first notice something different inside you?"

"Back in the warehouse." She hugs herself and looks away, biting the inside of her lip. "When we, um…"

"When we what? You need to tell me everything."

"Oh really." She lifts her chin. "Have you told me everything? No, of course not."

I thought we were past all this rubbish, but of course we're not. Did I expect her to trust me implicitly just because I fucked her? Yes, I'm that sort of idiot. And perhaps I've misunderstood her mood right now. She told me she noticed a change "back in the warehouse." She can't mean… No. It has nothing to do with me.

Even when I'd been popular with women, I hadn't known a ruddy thing about intuiting their feelings and needs—other than the sexual kind. I'm even worse at it now. Allison won't tell me what she wants, and that fact irritates me. Which explains why I resort to growling at her.

"What are you claiming I haven't told you?" I demand. "You know about my past and what Sefton did to me."

She huffs. "You seriously think that's everything? Come on. You were trapped in the Echo for five years."

"I'm aware of that."

"Tell me about it."

"About what?"

She throws her arms out and growls, not unlike the way I often do. "Tell me what happened to you in the Echo."

"You don't want to know."

Allison throws her head back and makes another frustrated growling noise. "You are so pigheaded. I want to know. I need to know. Has it never occurred to you that what happened in the Echo might have some bearing on the current situation?"

"Not what I went through. It was torture, not information gathering."

She stares at me for a moment, lips puckered. Then she exhales a long sigh. "Do what you want. I'm going to the kitchen to get a snack. All that self-defense training made me hungry."

Allison whirls around and marches down the hallway toward the kitchen.

I hurry after her.

Yes, I've now been reduced to trailing after a woman like a lost puppy. In the Echo, I was fearsome. I'd needed to be, thanks to the brutality inherent in that world. I became a monster out of necessity. But the longer I'm with Allison, the less I feel like a beast. I haven't reverted to the old me, but I have begun to feel less like the monster who abducted Allison and more like a human being. Something has shifted inside me, but I can't explain or describe the change.

I find Allison in the kitchen. Though she was only a few seconds ahead of me, she already has the refrigerator open and is grabbing items from inside, then tossing them onto the island. Tossing them with more vigor than seems necessary.

Allison wants to know everything. And I suddenly realize I want to tell her.

She has dumped so many items onto the island that I can't believe she really intends to eat all of it. She's angry with me, and hurling packaged foods is her way of expressing that frustration.

I wrap an arm around her waist and hoist her off her feet, setting her down beside the island. Then I slam the refrigerator door.

Allison leans against the island. "What are you doing?"

"Shut up and listen."

"You shut up. That's what you're best at."

Naturally, I want to growl at her. But I resist the impulse and instead cage her to the island with my hands framing her body. "I grew up in this house. After my parents died, I moved to London and rarely came home unless a bird I was shagging wanted to see Fallenmouth. Hiding out in my London flat was easier than dealing with my brother. He wasn't insane back then, at least visibly, but I knew he felt slighted. So I left him alone."

"What does any of that have to do with the Echo?"

"It should be obvious. He turned me into a monster and threw me into the hell world he had created." I lean in closer. "One minute, I was a normal bloke who loved to shag women. The next, I became a genuine monster and found myself living in a world I didn't understand and could barely cope with. But I had no choice. I had to cope with all of it, and I didn't do that very well."

"Can't imagine what that must've been like."

"Yes, you can. We are both living it. Sefton turned the Echo inside out and brought hell down on the earth." I scrub a hand over my eyes and bow my head. "I killed living creatures. They would have killed me, so I justified it as self-defense. After a while, though, I couldn't tell the difference between benign monsters and the sort who only wanted to destroy anything they came across. I'm not proud of what I did to survive."

"Were there any normal people in the Echo?"

"No. Only beasts like me."

She lays a hand on my cheek. "You are not a beast. Even when we first met, I saw glimpses of who you really are. You are not a creature from the Echo. You're a man who lost his way through no fault of his own."

I'm about to point out that it *was* my fault, but something else she just said finally sinks into my brain. "What do you mean you saw glimpses?"

"At first, I hated you. But even then, I noticed little things you did that contradicted the idea you were nothing but a monster." She slides her hand down to my shoulder. "You found food for me. You carried me when I couldn't walk anymore, and later, you found a car for us for the same reason. You saved my life several times, and I've stopped believing you did that strictly because you wanted to have sex with me."

"I forced you to be with me. Vowed I wouldn't protect you unless you gave me your body."

"Yeah, you did that. But it's bullshit that you 'forced' me to get naked with you. Despite all your snarling and nastiness, you never assaulted me." She seals two fingers over my lips when I try to protest. "You never forced me. I wanted to be with you back in the warehouse. I wanted you, period. Maybe that desire terrified me at first, but not anymore."

I peel her fingers away from my lips. "But you shouldn't want me."

"Stop telling me what I should or shouldn't feel. Without you, I never would've survived the first wave, much less everything that came after."

Bloody hell, she's stubborn. I can't convince her to despise me again, though that would be safer for her.

Allison drums her fingers on the island and studies me. "When you were in the Echo, did you have sex with, um, female creatures?"

"Only a few times, when I first arrived in that world."

"Why not after that?"

I can't help it. I snarl again. "Because they are hideous, vile creatures that may look female, but they are not women."

"Mm-hm." She insists on studying me more, as if she thinks she can ferret out my deeper motivations that way, which is bollocks. "Are you saying you were celibate for the better part of five years?"

"Yes."

"Well, that does explain a few things."

I push away from the island, away from her. "What do you claim it explains? I couldn't stomach shagging monsters anymore, but there's no deeper meaning in that decision."

"Sure there is." She slants toward me. "It means you're a good person underneath all the growling and snarling and generally rude behavior. If you were scum, like you want me to believe, then you would've screwed whatever humanlike monsters you met."

Though I try to respond, to deny her claim, she doesn't give me the chance.

Allison jabs a finger into my chest. "You're not fooling me anymore. I'm on to your game. And I finally understand why you were so desperate to get me naked that you threatened to throw me to the wolves if I didn't have sex with you."

"No, you—"

"Zip it, Dax." She raises onto her tiptoes, leveling our gazes. "You were so pent-up when we first met that you couldn't admit you like me. But here I was, a normal human female, and you needed to let off steam. That's why, when we had sex, it was so explosive."

She's right, of course. I hadn't been with a woman for so long that I couldn't control my lust for her. But it's more than that. I want her because, as she said, I've come to like her. I trust Allison and want to protect her in any way I can. She's the opposite of all the women I used to shag as a normal man, and when I'm with her, I feel things I've never experienced before. But it doesn't mean anything, it can't. We aren't two people navigating a romance. We're an integral part of the apocalypse, and nothing we say or do will change that. I am the anchor. She is the catalyst. What if she wants me only because of the magics that connect us?

Enough talking. I need action.

I push past her. "I'm going to search the entire house. Must be a ruddy clue somewhere in here."

"Think I'll go outside and get some fresh air."

Spinning around, I jab a finger toward her. "You will not leave this house on your own."

"Come with me, then."

"There's no time for relaxation. We have no idea when Sefton might return, and we need to find out how he created the Echo."

"We both know those boxes in the cellar are the key. Since we can't get into them, we might as well stretch our legs and get some sunshine."

"I can't play silly buggers with you while the rest of the world is burning."

She clasps my hands. "You need to relax, or we'll never find what we're looking for. Trust me. Nobody on earth is more pent-up than you. It's time to take a break."

"And do what?"

"Go for a walk."

I see no point in arguing, so I let her lead me outside and onto the lawn. We wander aimlessly while Allison admires the flowers that lie in ground beds or climb up the trellises attached to the house. She holds my hand the entire time. I should pull away from her, to get some necessary distance, but I can't make myself do it. The feel of her hand in mine gives me a strange sense of peace. I wish we could stay here at Fallenmouth forever, safe in the bubble my brother created around the estate, and pretend the apocalypse never happened. Above us, the sun shines. But it's a deception. I know that beyond the perimeter of the estate, human beings are fighting for their lives against impossible odds.

Too many have died already. Many more will die soon.

Allison stops and faces me. "You suck at relaxing, don't you?"

"Yes."

"Let me help."

She takes my face in her hands and kisses me. I should push her away, but I can't do it. I should stop her from deepening the kiss, but I can't manage that either. All my body will allow me to do is reciprocate, coiling my tongue around hers and wrapping my arms around her body to pull her close.

Perhaps, in this one moment, I can forget about the world beyond Fallenmouth.

But only for a moment.

Chapter Twenty-Two

Allison

OUR KISS LASTS ONLY FOR A MINUTE, THEN DAX INSISTS WE RETREAT into the house. I go along with that because I can see those creatures patrolling the perimeter of the lawn, just inside the woods. I can't see their faces, only their shadowy shapes. So yeah, I'm good with going back inside. Fallenmouth might look like a beautiful and serene place, but that's an illusion. Magic ensures the estate remains as it was before the apocalypse.

Dax insists we need to search every inch of the house, and I decide to go along with that idea. I think it's bullshit. The boxes in the cellar are clearly the source of Sefton's "alchemy of worlds," but Dax needs to do something. It's a guy thing.

Naturally, we find zip after searching the whole house.

By then, it's after dark, and I'm too exhausted to do anything other than eat a sandwich and go to bed. Dax insists I should lock my bedroom door. I bite my tongue instead of pointing out that Sefton could teleport into this room anytime. At least those creatures out there can't storm the house, unless their master removes the invisible boundary around the yard. The beasts are wickedly strong, and Sefton has powerful magics on his side.

Nobody storms the house. Not that night or the next morning.

After breakfast, Dax announces that I need more training so I can learn how to fight instead of only knowing how to fend off an attack. He starts with fencing, which he describes as "a combat sport."

I roll my eyes. "That foil thingy looks like a skinny metal stick that wouldn't hurt a fly."

"The foil is a dangerous weapon," he says. "Especially if the blade breaks. A Ukrainian fencing champion died that way. Perhaps I should demonstrate how dangerous a foil is."

We both wear protective clothing and full-face masks, plus gloves. I've seen this stuff in movies, but never could I have imagined I'd need to learn swordplay.

Dax removes his mask and makes a come-on gesture. "Strike my cheek with the tip of your foil."

"What? If it can hurt you, I'm not doing that."

"You need to know what a foil can do." He sets his weapon down and makes that come-on gesture with both hands. "Cut me."

I thrust my foil out to nick his cheek, drawing a thin trickle of blood. "Are you okay?"

"You'll need to be more aggressive when we're sparring." He plucks his foil off the floor. "Especially if you want to graduate to a larger, deadlier sword."

"You have bigger swords around here? I've only seen the fencing foils."

"That's because you insisted on searching the solarium while I was ransacking the sitting room. My father kept a pair of eighteenth-century cutlasses on the wall above the fireplace mantel, as well as a medieval broadsword."

"You're going to teach me how to use a real sword? Cool. A cutlass sounds like a pirate sword."

He frowns at me, which is a somewhat softer expression than his usual scowl. "You need to take this seriously. Your life may depend on your ability to fight."

"I know. And I do take it seriously. But if I don't crack a joke now and then, I'll go bonkers. Wouldn't kill you to lighten up on occasion."

"To 'lighten up' in the Echo means death."

"Okay, message received." I square my shoulders and raise my foil. "A death match it is, then."

No, I don't kill Dax. I meant that as a dig at his "every moment is a life-or-death event" attitude. An affectionate dig. Because yeah, I've realized I do like him, especially now that I understand more about what he's been through, in and out of the Echo.

Following a morning of sparring with Dax and an afternoon of more self-defense training, I am once again too exhausted to do anything except gobble up a sandwich and go to bed. Dax tries to talk me into waiting while he makes a big dinner for us, complete with vegetables, though he claims he's never been good at cooking. I'm too wiped out. Maybe living on sandwiches and soda pop isn't the healthiest choice, but for crying out loud, there's an apocalypse going on out there. Screw green beans and spinach. I need cheese and chocolate.

For the next three days, Dax teaches me how to fence and graduates me up to a cutlass. Swords are kind of awesome. The cutlass isn't as heavy as a broadsword, so he tells me it's a good weapon for a woman. There were female pirates, after all. If those ladies could handle a cutlass, so can I. Despite his constant admonishments that I need to stop making jokes, I do take my training seriously. The world outside this estate has no electricity, no running water, just devastation. When we go back out into that new world, which I know we will do eventually, I need to be prepared.

Dax's family armory doesn't include guns or explosives. I never used to want stuff like that, but now I wish we had some.

Every day, we both go down to the cellar multiple times and try to open those boxes. Dax gets more frustrated with every attempt. Maybe I should tell him my theory about why I was able to teleport us away from Sefton and the golem, but I don't know how he'll react. My theory isn't scientific. It's very, very personal. I doubt he'll want to consider the idea, much less accept it.

Because I've become convinced that sex with Dax gave me the power to spirit us away.

It's crazy, I know. And sooner or later, I'll have to share my theory with him. But not today. I'm enjoying this time with Dax, learning to fight and taking walks around the lawn. We kiss now and then, but he hasn't even suggested sex. I'm starting to wonder if he's lost interest, but I think it's more likely that he's as tired as I am. A tough guy would never admit to that.

On the fifth day since our mad host left us here, I realize I need a day off from combat lessons. I've gotten a little sore from all the physical activity. I used to exercise, pre-apocalypse, but I didn't do this kind of intensive training.

"I need a break," I tell Dax. "Please. I'm getting sore."

He stares at me for a few seconds. Then he marches over to a door I hadn't realized was a door, since it blends into the wall and has no knob. He pushes on a section of the wall, and the door pops open. He ducks inside what looks like a closet, emerging with a folded-up table under one arm.

"What's that for?" I ask.

Dax being Dax, he grunts instead of speaking. Then he carries the folded-up table over to the windows and sets it up there. He glances at me and pats the padded tabletop. "Lie on this."

I walk over there, but I can't help eying the table with a touch of suspicion. "Why do you want me to do that?"

"You are sore. I'm going to give you a massage."

Pretty sure I'm gaping at him. My hot but grumpy roommate wants to rub me down? The idea both shocks me and turns me on.

Dax scoops me up and deposits me on the table, on my back. "Roll over and cross your arms above your head."

Only now do I notice the bottle of massage oil he has tucked under his arm.

I roll onto my stomach and link my hands above my head.

He pushes my shirt up to expose nearly all of my back, then he unhooks my bra and lets the halves fall to my sides. With one cheek on the table, I can see him sideways. My nipples harden while I watch him pour oil onto his palm and rub his hands together to spread it around. By the time he lays his hands on me, I'm already wet for him. He slides his palms over my back, massaging tight muscles and getting me more turned on every second. When he pulls my sweatpants and underwear down to my ankles, I start breathing harder. To feel his hands on my ass, rubbing while he works his way down my thighs, gets me so hot for him that I want to squirm and moan. I just manage to suppress that response. But damn, this man knows how to touch a woman.

"Turn onto your back," he says, his voice rougher and rumblier, the way he sounded that day in the warehouse when he vowed to fuck me on the concrete floor.

Just as I start to roll over, a scream echoes outside the house.

I jump off the table and yank my clothes back into place. "What was that?"

Dax grabs a cutlass and sprints out of the room.

Another scream pierces the air, followed by the ravenous howls and bellows of the Echo creatures.

I race after Dax, catching up to him just as he flings the front door open and bolts outside. But as he sprints across the lawn, I lag behind him in my pursuit. His legs are longer, and I can't quite catch up.

A girl tumbles out of the woods, crashing through a hydrangea bush, and collapses on the lawn.

Dax reaches her first, but the girl shrieks when he tries to help her up. I get there a few seconds later and drop to my knees beside the girl.

"Are you hurt?" I ask. "What did those creatures do to you?"

Her blue eyes home in on me. She's breathing hard, and her cheeks are pink, but I can't see any wounds on her. She seems like a teenager. The girl bites her lip, glancing back and forth between me and Dax.

"It's okay," I tell her. "He's a good guy. We want to help you, if we can. Will you let us do that?"

She nods.

"Can you walk?" I ask.

"Y-yeah. I think so."

"Good." I offer her my hands. "Let me help you up."

The girl sounds American, and I want to ask where she's from and how she got here. But questions can wait.

Snarling and the snapping of teeth makes me glance at the woods even while the girl takes my hands and we stand up together. The creatures who guard this estate are watching us. Glaring at us. Ravening for blood they know they won't get, not today. No one can penetrate the estate, Sefton had said. It's magically warded. The Echo creatures are allowed to guard the perimeter and the woods, but they can't cross into the yard. So how did this girl get in? I remember Sefton saying he couldn't guarantee the creatures would "mind their manners." I think he was just trying to scare me. It seems like the so-called guards can't step onto the lawn.

I brush leaves out of the girl's hair. "My name is Allison, and that's Dax. What's your name?"

"Willow."

"Are you sure you aren't hurt?"

She nods. "I'm okay. Those monsters didn't chase me until I got almost to the yard."

The creatures are still observing us from a discreet distance, so I lead Willow and Dax back into the house. We go into the sitting room, and I take a seat on the sofa. Willow drops onto the sofa too, with one cushion separating us.

Dax stands nearby, arms barred over his chest.

Willow keeps glancing at him sideways while wringing her hands.

I look at Dax. "Why don't you get some food and water for Willow? She must be hungry."

He narrows his gaze and flattens his lips, which I've come to realize means he's worried. Grumpiness is a cover.

"Please," I say. "Find something for our guest to eat."

Dax lowers his arms and sighs, then walks out the door.

"Is he a monster?" Willow asks.

"No. Dax is a good man, but he can be grumpy when he's worried. Don't let it get to you." I lay my hand over hers. "First, I want you to know you will be safe here. Dax and I will not hurt you. Do you believe me?"

She chews on her lip and nods.

"How old are you, Willow?"

"Fifteen."

Christ, she's so young. I don't want to grill her, but I do need to know more about the girl. Though I hate thinking that way, I can't help worrying Sefton has used this girl to get to me. Not sure how or why he would do that, but I can't shake the worry.

"Where are your parents?" I ask.

She bows her head, wringing her hands more vigorously. "They died in the first wave. Mom and Dad hid me in a sewer drain, but they had to go out to look for food. Monsters got them."

"I'm so sorry, Willow. I lost my parents too, but it was a long time ago. You were very brave to get past those creatures in the woods."

She shrugs. "Heard there was a place in the countryside that hadn't been destroyed. So I came here. Nobody else could get into the woods, but I did."

"Do you know how you did that?"

Willow shakes her head. "The other people I was with kind of bounced off the air or something. They couldn't get in."

"I'm sorry your friends didn't get in too."

She throws me a sidelong look. "I'm not. They weren't my friends, and they weren't nice like you."

Dax returns with food for our guest, and I don't ask any more questions—for now. Willow scarfs down the food and water Dax got for her, then she starts yawning. Though it's late afternoon, we take Willow upstairs and let her choose which bedroom she wants. She picks the one next to mine. I sit on the bed until she falls asleep, then leave the room and shut the door as quietly as possible.

How did this girl get through Sefton's safeguards?

If someone else has the power to breach the wards around Fallenmouth... Maybe Dax and I aren't the only ones connected to the Echo.

Chapter Twenty-Three

Dax

ALLISON DOESN'T WANT TO GO FAR FROM OUR HOUSEGUEST, SO she stays in her bedroom with the door open in case the girl needs to call out for help. I go into the cellar and try yet again to break into the boxes. No luck, of course. I wonder if the young girl who broke through the wards can help us. I don't want to upset Willow, though. She seems frightened of me, and those creatures outside don't help matters.

Willow trusts Allison. They seem to have forged an instant, if fragile, bond.

Unfortunately, I can imagine what Willow might've gone through since the alchemy of worlds began. I'd rather not envision it, but my mind has other ideas. Maybe she didn't experience the full terror of the Echo, like I did, but the strangers she took up with could have abused her.

After giving up on Sefton's boxes, I go outside to patrol the grounds and make sure none of those creatures managed to pierce the wards the way Willow had done. I see no evidence they have. Just before I left Allison upstairs, she suggested the girl might have a connection to the Echo that allows her to circumvent the magics that bar anyone from getting onto the estate. Is that possible? Given the cataclysmic power my brother has amassed, I can't rule out anything.

I return to the house just as Willow and Allison are coming down the staircase. We all need to eat, and I insist on cooking for the girls. Allison offers to help. We wind up collaborating on a meal while Willow sits on a stool at the island watching us. We bicker over which dishes to make, but it's not a real argument. I think we're teasing each other. It seems odd to do that when the rest of the world is in chaos, but I've decided Allison was right. We both need to relax once in a while and allow ourselves to "lighten up." I'd forgotten how to do that after five years in purgatory.

Our mutual teasing encourages Willow to sit up straighter and almost smile.

When I drop a fish finger on the floor, Allison plucks it up and holds it to my mouth. "Five second rule. You dropped it, you eat it."

"No thank you."

She pulls her hand away, then moves it toward my mouth again while making train whistle noises. "Open up."

I tickle her belly, making her laugh so hard her eyes water. She tosses the fish finger into the sink.

"Are you surrendering?" I ask as I pause in my tickling.

She raises her hands. "Yes, I surrender. That fish stick was my white flag."

"I'm not sure a fish flag is a proper way of surrendering, but I will accept it."

Allison bows deeply. "Thank you, Lord Fallenmouth."

She rises and smiles at me, looking so beautiful that I want to kiss her. But we are not alone.

Willow is grinning at us.

By the time we finish cooking and eating our meal, our guest seems much more relaxed than when we first met her. We all retreat into the sitting room to drink hot cocoa. I would've preferred vodka, but we do have a minor in the house. I feel odd about drinking in front of a teenage girl. Instead, I sit in a large armchair while sipping cocoa.

Allison takes a few sips of her drink, then sets her mug down on the end table. "Willow, do you mind if I ask you a few questions?"

The girl stares down into her cocoa mug. "Okay."

"How did you end up in England? You sound American."

"My parents always wanted to see the UK, so we came over on vacation." She clutches her mug with both hands. "We would've been flying home today."

I assume Allison started with an easy question before she gently prods the girl about other matters.

"You said the people you were with weren't nice," Allison says. "Did they hurt you?"

Willow says nothing, though I can see the movements in her throat every time she swallows hard.

"I should leave so you two can discuss this," I say, half rising from my chair.

"No," Willow says, her head popping up. "You can stay."

"Are you sure?"

"Yeah. You're okay."

I've passed muster with a fifteen-year-old girl. Not sure if that means she trusts me, or if she simply trusts Allison's opinion of me. Maybe my ridiculous behavior in the kitchen convinced the girl I'm not a monster after all. I sit back down.

"They said mean things to me," Willow tells us. "Called me bad names, told me I was dragging them down. When I cried, they would slap me hard. They didn't give me much food, even when they found a big box of granola bars. They decided we should head out this way because other people were saying there's a place in the country where everything is still pretty and nice."

"How did you get here?" Allison asks. "You couldn't have walked the whole way."

"The people I was with found a car that still had gas in it. That got us most of the way here. We walked after that."

Allison nibbles on her lower lip as if she's considering what to say next. "How did you get away from those people?"

"When I saw the woods, I just ran. Not sure why, but I felt like I needed to be here." The girl stares down into her cocoa mug again. "Then those creatures came after me. They didn't hurt me, just made a lot of noise and chased me."

"You're safe now, sweetie." Allison chews her lip again, glancing at me as if she wants my approval. For what, I have no idea. She looks at the girl again. "Willow, do you, um, have any idea how you got here when nobody else has been able to cross into the woods?"

Willow takes a big gulp of cocoa, then sets her mug on the table. "You mean how did I get through the magic barrier or whatever. Don't know. I heard people talking about that, but I have no idea how it works. My parents never believed in supernatural stuff, but now everybody knows it's real. I mean, that's how all of this happened, right? Magic made the world crazy."

Yes, that's exactly what my brother has done. He made the world as crazy as he is.

The girl yawns.

Allison and I escort her upstairs. Though we tell Willow she can lock her bedroom door if she wants, she prefers not to do that. She does close the door, though. I walk Allison to her room, right next door to Willow's.

Allison grasps the doorknob.

"Wait," I say. "I was, ah, wondering if perhaps…"

"Spit it out, Dax." She gives me a teasing smile. "Never heard you hem and haw before. It's cute."

"I was trying to ask if you would, well…" I feel my face tightening into a pinched expression, and for some bloody stupid reason, I scratch the back of my neck. "May I come in?"

"Sure."

We enter the bedroom, where I had slept before Sefton banished me to the Echo and where my parents had once slept. It feels odd to do what I'm about to suggest, and do it in this room, but it also feels right somehow. Not that I've had much experience with doing the right thing.

Not until Allison.

She stops at the foot of the bed. "What did you need to ask me?"

"I want to make love to you."

"That's not a question." She leans into me, spreading her palms over my chest. "But yes, I would love that."

"We should undress, then. Shouldn't we?"

She laughs. "Ya think?"

I can't move, my body seemingly rooted to this spot while Allison strips off her clothes. I hadn't given myself time to appreciate the beauty of her body when we'd shagged in the warehouse. But I can't resist poring over every inch of her as she undresses now, here in my ancestral home, in the bed where I had seduced more women than I care to remember.

Tonight, it's different. *She* is different.

Have I changed? Allison seems to think so, and I trust her judgment.

While I've been admiring the swell of her breasts and the curve of her hips, she got rid of all her clothes. Flipping the covers back, she lies down on the bed. "Your turn."

I strip quickly and crawl up the bed until I'm straddling her body on my hands and knees. Perhaps I should say something, but it feels wrong to interrupt this moment with words, especially since I have no bloody idea what to say. Instead of speaking, I seal my mouth over hers, deepening the kiss until we're devouring each other with our tongues and lips and teeth. She slides her hands up and down my arms, then runs them over my back to grasp my nape.

Peeling my lips away from hers, I open my eyes.

Allison is gazing straight at me with a soft smile tightening her lips.

I press my mouth to hers again, only for a second, while I lower my body until every inch of me touches every inch of her. I drag my mouth across her cheek to her ear, where I pull the lobe into my mouth to suckle and nibble on it. She arches her neck and pushes her fingers into my hair. I shimmy down her body while kissing, nipping, and licking her skin, starting with the delicate curve of her throat and moving down to her chest, inching ever closer to her breasts. Her skin feels so soft, and it smells like sweet, womanly things that I can't describe. I find myself inhaling the scent of her skin, reveling in it, as I keep moving lower until my head rests between those lush mounds. I kiss a path toward her left breast and at last seal my mouth around its rigid peak.

A breathless cry rushes out of her. She grips my head with both hands and spreads her thighs.

She wants me to take her right now, but I won't rush this. Allison deserves better than what I gave her the first time. She deserves to be worshiped. And this time, I need to gaze into her eyes while I push her toward climax.

I tease her nipple with light nips and sweeps of my tongue until she's writhing beneath me and her breathing becomes labored, her chest rising and falling in a faster rhythm. I release her peak and drag my tongue down her belly, pausing to swirl it inside her navel, then slither lower until I reach her hips. The thatch of hairs on her mound tickles my chin and lips, and the scent of her desire suffuses my senses. Fuck, it makes my cock throb.

"Please, Dax," she moans. "Oh God, I need you inside me."

I need that too, but I will not sacrifice her pleasure to satisfy my own needs. Not anymore.

Sliding further down her body, I push my mouth between her folds to latch on to her nub. The flavor of her coats my tongue as I lick and suckle her clit, and she thrusts her hips up as if she needs me to consume her completely. I shove my hands under her arse to angle her body up, giving me deeper access to her slick flesh.

"Dax!" she cries out as her release tightens her entire body, lifting her head off the pillow. More cries of pleasure erupt out of her while she clenches the sheets in her fists.

I lift my head just as she goes limp. "Allison, I have never seen anything as beautiful as you, especially when you come."

"Call me Ally. Please."

"All right—Ally." I love the way those syllables feel on my tongue. She wants me to use her nickname. Part of me relishes that, but another part of me feels unworthy of it. "Have I exhausted you?"

"Oh no, not even close." She smiles and tickles my nose with her fingertips. "Don't stop now. It was just getting good."

"Not stopping. Couldn't if I wanted to. I need to feel your cream all over my cock."

She bends her knees, framing my head with her thighs. "Then make it happen."

I rise to my knees, plant my hands at either side of her shoulders, and plunge into the silky softness of her body, loving the way her flesh molds to mine. We gaze into each other's eyes as if an invisible rope binds us together, while I thrust into her again and again, groaning every time I sink inside and sucking in a breath with every retreat. Her slickness coats my length, and the wet sounds of our bodies merging and separating echoes around us.

Allison grips my wrists and struggles to catch her breath, though she can't seem to do it. I can't control my ragged breathing either. The sensation of her body wrapped around my cock steals my breath and my thoughts. All I know is how good this feels, how beautiful her eyes are, and how much I need to lose myself inside her.

"Oh yes, Dax." Her spine bows up, and she throws her head back.

I punch into her harder and faster, grinding myself into her flesh, rubbing that nub until she stops breathing. Her body curls into itself, and I know she's about to climax. She squeezes her eyes shut, her mouth drops open, and the waves of her orgasm milk me so fiercely that I splutter. But I keep thrusting and marshal all my willpower to hold back my release until she's done. Just as the last spasm of her climax wanes, I let go.

With two more punishing thrusts, I'm done. Spasms fire through my cock so hard and fast that I lose my breath, and I come with such force that I grit my teeth and struggle for breath while my fingers dig into the mattress.

Then I collapse on top of Allison.

She brushes her fingers through my hair and sweetly kisses me.

My cock is still inside her. I should move my arse to pull out, but I have no energy to do that. I'm exhausted in the best way, and besides, I don't want to move when she's gazing at me with tenderness in her eyes.

"Ally, I—"

The door explodes inward.

And my brother storms into the room.

CHAPTER TWENTY-FOUR

Allison

DAX YANKS THE COVERS OVER ME AND LEAPS OFF THE BED. SEFTON hobbles into the room while Dax stalks up to him without bothering to put any clothes on. The brothers stand an arm's length from each other, both wearing furious expressions. Dax has his hands fisted and his shoulders bunched. Sefton seems to be quivering slightly from the intensity of his rage.

"You bastard," he snarls at Dax. "You had no right to touch her. Allison is mine."

I'm what? Nobody owns me.

Yanking on my shirt and pants, I jump off the bed and move to stand beside Dax.

Sefton's eyes narrow to slits. "You have betrayed me, Allison."

"No, I didn't. You said I was going to marry you, but I never agreed to that."

"You didn't need to agree." He clenches his jaw, baring his teeth when he speaks again. "You belong to me."

I want to tell him to go to hell, but considering the vast power he has amassed, I don't think I should annoy him any further. But I will not marry him or sleep with him. Will I have a choice if he employs magic to get what he wants?

"Sefton, please stop this," Dax says, sounding calmer than I would've expected. "You can't force Allison to love you. Please let her go. You don't need the catalyst anymore."

"Oh really." Sefton leans toward his brother and lowers his voice to a harsh whisper. "You are the one I don't need anymore."

Sefton steps back a few paces, raises his hands, and shoves them toward Dax. He can't touch him, not from several yards away. But a visible wave of energy, like heat rising up from the pavement in the summer, rushes toward Dax and slams into him. He's thrown backward just as a portal opens behind him.

He sails through it. The portal telescopes shut.

I stand paralyzed, my mouth open and my eyes wide, unable to speak or comprehend what just happened. Dax is gone.

"Whuh—" I swing my head toward the spot where Dax had stood, then veer my attention back to Sefton. "What did you do to him? Is he dead?"

"Does it matter?" Sefton seizes my arms, hauling me into him. "The answer is no. You will do as I say, or you will suffer the consequences. Do you understand?"

The fury in his voice and on his face convinces me that I need to play along, at least until I can figure out what to do. Can I do anything? Well, maybe I should test my theory that sex with Dax amps up my Echo power. If I can open those damn boxes...

Willow. The thought blasts through my mind, and I wrench free of Sefton to race past him and get to the girl's room.

She isn't there.

"Did you honestly think I wouldn't know about the sniveling child you brought here?"

I whirl around, coming face to face with Sefton. "What did you do to her?"

"She is irrelevant."

"Where is she?"

"Forget about Dax and the child. You will never see either of them again."

I want to pound my fists on his chest, slug him in the gut, run him through with a cutlass. But I can't be sure that would kill him, or even hurt him. He has that damn force field or whatever that protects him. He also has those creatures outside. *Shit.*

As much as I don't want to do it, I know I must placate him. Play along, at least for a while. He'll have to let his shields down if he wants to have sex with me. That might be my only opening, unless I can access those boxes in the cellar.

Without Dax's help? Yes, I can do it. I must do it.

My chest aches when I think about Dax. Sefton wouldn't have killed him, would he? The use of a portal to get rid of him suggests he sent him away. Don't need teleportation to commit murder. I must believe Dax and Willow are alive, somewhere. To believe the opposite... That would destroy me.

"All right," I say. "No more talk of Willow or Dax."

Sefton's entire demeanor softens, though I sense the tension crackling under the surface.

"Did your trip outside the estate go well?" I ask. Might as well engage in inane conversation in the hopes of learning something useful from him.

"The alchemy of worlds is progressing as expected."

"So that's good news. Right?" Not for me or anyone else on earth, except for Sefton and maybe the Echo creatures. I've become a spy, haven't I? Pretending to be something I'm not, pretending to believe in things I don't subscribe to, all to keep a madman from lashing out at innocent people.

"There is no good or bad news," he says. "Only truth and power."

Whatever that means. "I get what the alchemy of worlds is. But I'm confused about the alchemy of souls."

He clasps his hands behind his back. "You will find out soon enough anyway, so I suppose you might as well know now. The alchemy of souls will transmute the Echo version of every human being, merging the Echo soul with the human one to create a hybrid. Since both souls are entangled at the quantum level, the result should be quite interesting. That is how the Echo shall reveal all—as in the true nature of every person on earth."

He's going to jam our souls into the bodies of Echo creatures and force us to become one with those monsters. How that equates to revealing our true nature is a question only the madman can answer. But since I have no response to his statement that won't enrage him, I change the subject. "What will you do now?"

"It's time for our union."

Oh, how I wish he meant we were joining a labor union. No such luck. I'm sure he's talking about our sham wedding and the sex he expects to get afterward. Do I have the power to stop Sefton from transmuting the souls of every human on earth? Even if my sex theory for teleportation is valid, that doesn't guarantee I can save Dax and Willow. If I bring them back here, Sefton might kill them or send them away again. I have no idea how long my power boost might work.

Better save it for opening those boxes.

Hang on, Dax. Hang on, Willow. I will never forget about you.

I shove my hands into my pants pockets. "What now? You must have more important stuff to keep tabs on."

"Yes, I do." He takes a step toward me. "Why did you let my brother shag you?"

There is no way I can answer that question unless I lie. "Dax threatened to give me to the Echo creatures if I didn't have sex with him."

"You seemed to be enjoying it."

"Did it ever occur to you that I faked it so he wouldn't kill me?"

Sefton studies me with squinted eyes while his fingers twitch. "If you despise him, why were you so upset that I sent him away? You demanded to know what I did with him."

Damn, I suck at lying. *Say something to convince him, do it now.*

I resist the urge to bite my lip and force myself to look him in the eye. "Dax is the anchor. I was afraid all your hard work might be destroyed if he dies."

Sefton slants toward me. "Should I believe you? I'd like to, Allison, but your behavior suggests otherwise. You did escape from me a few days ago. And you fucked my brother. These actions must have consequences."

My throat has gone tight and dry. My pulse beats so fast that I'm starting to feel lightheaded, but I can't give in to the fear. I need to stay calm, at least on the outside.

He grabs my arm and drags me out into the hall, then shoves me into the bedroom where Dax and I had made love a matter of minutes ago. The sheets are still rumpled. Dax's clothes lie on the floor beside my underwear.

Sefton hovers on the threshold, one hand on the knob. He's breathing hard, almost wheezing.

"Are you okay?" I ask. "You seem tired."

"Yes, I am tired—of waiting to get what I want."

I suddenly wonder if he's suffering from power drain. All the magics he keeps tapping into might have weakened his body.

He twists the doorknob in his hand. "You will remain here while I prepare for the ceremony."

Sefton slams the door shut.

I stare at the door, immobilized by shock and fear and so many other emotions that I can't sort them out. Ceremony? He intends to force me to marry him so he can…rape me.

A chill shudders through me, making my teeth chatter. Yeah, I'm terrified of what Sefton might do next. But I can't just stand here waiting for it to happen. Dax taught me how to defend myself—and how to fight.

I hurry to the door and try the knob. It twists freely, but the door will not open. I yank as hard as I can. Nothing happens. Sefton must've sealed the door from the outside via supernatural means.

Should I risk using some of my power to break out of this room? I wish I had a magical power meter that would let me know how much I can afford to use.

The door swings open, forcing me to stumble backward out of its way.

Sefton locks his hand around my upper arm. "Soon we will be wedded, and the power of that union will reinforce the merging of the worlds. You will be one with me."

"But I don't love you. How will a forced union give you what you want?"

"It will. I need only your power." He hauls me out the door. "Our sexual union will cement the bond."

"No, it won't. We have no bond, Sefton. I barely know you, and quite frankly, I don't like you anymore. You are insane."

Yeah, I've thrown the "placate him" plan out the window. I know what he intends to do to me, and I will never let him do it, even if I have to die to stop him.

He tries to drag me down the hall, but I dig my heels in, which forces him to stop. With his bad knee, I don't think he can fight me if I resist, at least not enough to make me go where he wants.

Sefton halts and half turns to look at me, still cuffing my arm with his hand. His lips compress into a hard line, his gaze narrows and sharpens on me, and he hisses words through his gritted teeth. "Give yourself to me willingly, or I will take you by force."

Like hell he will.

I relax as if I'm giving in, and his grip loosens a touch. Seizing the opening, I yank my arm free of his grasp and run for the staircase. Sefton reacts a split second too late. I leap onto the railing and slide down it faster than his bad knee will let him get to the stairs. The instant I reach the bottom, I race through the foyer and rip the front door open to sprint outside into the light of the full moon. Just as my bare feet touch down on the grass, figures jump out to block my way.

The Echo creatures have surrounded me.

I halt so quickly that I stumble and almost hit the ground. I'm gasping for breath, my heart thrashing.

"Did you really think I wouldn't have a backup plan?"

The sound of Sefton's voice right behind me raises every hair on my body.

He lashes his arms around my midsection with his hands over my navel, pinning my arms to my sides. His lips scrape against my ear as he hisses, "You are mine."

Everything Dax had taught me, all the hours I spent practicing with him, suddenly comes crashing through my mind, and I know what I need to do. I lock my hands together, slant forward, and twist sideways to slam my elbow into his throat, then twist the other way to hit him again. His grip falters. I don't need to do the rest of the moves Dax had shown me. I shove away from Sefton and dash through a gap between two of the creatures. Before anyone has time to react, I'm pelting across the lawn toward the woods, crashing through bushes, mere feet from the cover of the trees.

A figure leaps out in front of me, catching me in mid stride and hoisting me off my feet. Powerful, scaly arms bind my body to the creature's.

My face is mashed to the beast's throat while my feet dangle above the ground. I can't get any leverage. This wasn't one of the moves Dax taught me, and this creature is way stronger than any human being. Out of the corner of my eye, I can see the person hobbling toward us now.

Sefton stops inches away. His horde of fiends gathers behind him.

For a moment, he just stands there, his hands trembling and his breathing uneven, until he recovers his composure. Then he traces the backs of his fingers over my cheek. "Why did you do that? Fighting me is useless, and now I'll have to punish you."

"I will never stop fighting, you sick son of a bitch."

"You lied to me, pet." He slants in, our chins almost touching. "You will regret this."

He takes a step back, waving his hand in my face.

And darkness consumes me.

CHAPTER TWENTY-FIVE

Dax

AM I DEAD? SINCE I'VE NEVER DIED BEFORE, I CAN'T TELL IF THAT'S what happened to me. I can't move and don't feel or hear anything. As my senses gradually rouse, I detect a solid surface beneath me and feel warmth on my face. The sun? Not sure. My muscles still refuse to function, and my brain seems to be having trouble revving up again. Soon, though, I begin to detect sounds—birds chirping, wind rustling, my heart beating.

Not dead after all.

Something nudges my leg. "Are you in a coma?"

That voice. I've heard it before. Peeling my lids apart, which requires an enormous effort, I squint at Willow. "Does it look like I'm in a coma?"

She hugs herself, hunching her shoulders. "Sorry. Glad you're not dead."

"As am I."

"What happened? Where's Allison?"

"Back at Fallenmouth, I assume. That's the house we were in before…" Before my lunatic brother hurled us to somewhere else.

Willow nods. "I remember the house. Allison will be okay there, right?"

"She knows how to take care of herself."

But I have no idea what Sefton might do to her.

I lever myself into a sitting position, my legs stretched out, and take a look at my body. I am no longer naked. Sefton apparently saw fit to clothe me when he discarded me like a broken toy. I'm wearing my old clothes, the things I'd had on when I was thrown out of the Echo. The warmth of the air and the sun make me start to sweat, thanks to my leather coat.

Why did Sefton clothe me? He sacrificed some of his precious power to make sure I was no longer naked. *He did it because he's crackers, you moron.* And of course, he did not send me here with my knife, the one I keep hidden inside my coat.

I clamber to my feet and brush grass and dirt off my clothes.

"Where are we?" Willow asks.

"Not a bloody clue."

I turn in a circle to take in our surroundings, but I still can't say for sure where my brother sent us. Or why he sent us. He could've simply killed us both. We seem to be on the side of a mountain, based on the sloping terrain, though I can't see what lies below us. Trees block the view. If I knew anything about old-school navigation, I could chart our location based on the sun's position in the sky or some such bollocks. I am not versed in navigation techniques. We're in the mountains. That's all I can deduce.

"Are you growling?" Willow asks, her eyes widening. "Are you a bear-man or something?"

"No." I hadn't realized I growled until she said that, but I don't sound like a sodding bear. Do I? Perhaps I have sometimes behaved like a wild animal, but I do not sound like one, and I am not a bear-man. "Have you seen anyone else here?"

Willow shakes her head.

Sefton undoubtedly dropped us in the middle of nowhere, in a place where we would have little chance of running into other humans and potentially finding help. Since he'd been enraged at the time, I can't help speculating, or perhaps hoping, he cocked it up somehow and left us near some sort of civilization.

"We need to get to higher ground," I say. "Someplace where we can see what's around us. If we're lucky, there will be someone nearby."

"Might be the monsters."

I glance at Willow. The girl is still hugging herself. She was terrorized by strangers and Echo creatures, so I can't blame her for being ill at ease. Allison would know what to say to the girl to make her feel better, but I haven't got a ruddy clue. After five years in the Echo, I've forgotten anything I might have known about how to comfort another person.

Especially a child.

Naturally, I react like the prat I am. I pat the girl's shoulder. "I doubt the monsters live here. Besides, if any of them show up, I will rip their heads off."

Her eyes bulge.

Yes, here is proof positive that I know nothing about children. I've terrified the girl, so I try to backpedal. "Ah, well, I meant that metaphorically. I'm sure the monsters are...lovely people deep down."

Willow still stares at me, her face blank.

Then she starts laughing, spluttering so much that she needs to slap a hand over her mouth. When she finally stops laughing at me, she wipes her eyes with her shirt.

"What is so bloody funny?" I snarl.

The girl might not be laughing anymore, but she is smiling. "Lovely people? You're funny, but you're kind of a dork too."

"I'm a what?"

"A dork. It means you're clueless." She pats my arm the way I had patted hers. "You don't know much about kids, do you?"

"No." I squint at the girl. "A matter of hours ago, you were screaming and cowering on the lawn. You would only speak to Allison. Now you're harassing me."

"I was scared because those people-things were after me. But you and Allison are cool."

No one has ever called me "cool" before. I was an earl, so most people referred to me as Lord Fallenmouth, whether I wanted them to or not. But Allison calls me "hot." I like that term best.

A fierce pang stabs into my chest. *Allison.* I abandoned her, though not by choice, and I can't imagine what my brother is doing to her right now. No, that's a lie. I *can* imagine it, though I wish I couldn't. Allison is strong and clever. She knows how to defend herself. I have to hope that's enough.

"If you're about to hurl," Willow says, "could you go behind a bush or something to do it? I might blow chunks if I see that."

Hurl? Blow chunks? I'm suddenly grateful that I don't have any children if that's how they speak. Could Allison and I raise a baby in this new world? No, she wouldn't want that. She can't want it. Not with me.

Willow squeezes her eyes shut and cinches up her entire face. "Okay, go on and do it. I can't see now."

"Go on and do what?"

"Hurl."

"What are you talking about?"

She cracks one lid to peek at me. "Throwing up."

I growl. Can anyone blame me? This child speaks nonsense, but at least I understood that phrase. "I am not about to throw up or 'blow chunks' or 'hurl.' Satisfied?"

Willow opens both eyes, and her features relax. "Sure, yeah. What kind of school did you go to where kids don't talk that way?"

"I attended a prestigious boarding school."

"Rich kids don't barf, huh?"

"We need to get moving."

Together, we hike up the mountainside. I still can't determine where we are in the world, other than on a forested mountain. That's so bloody helpful. I hear birds high up in the boughs, and I see a squirrel racing up a tree. This place, wherever it might be, clearly has not been affected by Sefton's apocalypse yet. Will it be spared?

That's doubtful. My brother won't stop until he has destroyed everything except Fallenmouth. Perhaps he will destroy that too once he's finished with the rest of the world.

"How did we get here?" Willow asks. "I fell asleep in my room. But when I woke up, I was here."

"My brother opened a magical portal and flung us to this place, which I assume is the location furthest from where he is."

"Don't you get along with your brother?"

"No." I clench my fists without meaning to as the memory of Sefton storming into the bedroom replays in my mind. "He is the madman who instigated the apocalypse."

"Seriously?"

"Yes."

"Wow, that's harsh. Why did he keep Allison?"

I grumble out a sigh. Are all children so intrusive? "Sefton is obsessed with Allison. She and I are two sides of the triangle my brother needed to create the Echo and instigate the apocalypse. She is the catalyst, I am the anchor."

"That's freaky."

"Yes, it is." At least I understand what the word freaky means. "Do you know what the Echo is?"

"Uh-huh. I heard people talking about it. I guess those monsters like to tell everybody where they came from."

I grunt.

Mercifully, she does not speak while we cross into a less wooded area. I pause for a moment to take in the view, though not because I feel like doing a bit of sightseeing. I'm hoping to find clues to where we are and if there might be settlements nearby. I see nothing, so we continue up the mountain. When we crest its summit, I turn in a circle to inspect the area and perhaps find a place where we can camp for the night. It's still daylight here, though the sun is sinking toward the horizon.

Below us, on the other side of the mountain we've just hiked up, I see a beach stretching out along the coast of an ocean while waves crash on the shore. This mountain range is high, but small compared to the sort they have in the Himalayas or the Andes.

Where are we? Someplace far from England, that's for certain.

"Bloody hell," I grumble. "I have no idea where we've wound up, or how to get back to Allison."

I hadn't meant to say that out loud, but the words poured out anyway.

Willow slips her hand into mine. "It's okay. We'll find her again."

A child is comforting me. And for some reason, I find myself clasping her hand.

"Maybe we should go down there," Willow says. "Might find a town or something if we walk far enough."

The terrain leading down to the beach is steep, which forces us to take it slow. I keep hold of Willow's hand strictly to ensure she won't tumble off a cliff. Allison would not be happy if I let her new mate die in a terrible accident. I do *not* like the child. She asks annoying questions and uses bizarre words.

At last, we set foot on the beach. The girl immediately rushes into the waves to get herself soaked by the three-foot swells. She laughs and shrieks, splashing around in the water. Though she waves for me to join her, I do not do that. Maybe I had jumped into the river back in Fort Worth, but that had been different. I don't feel like playing in the swells, not when Allison is trapped at Fallenmouth with my mad brother.

Once Willow has grown tired of splashing and shrieking, we head off down the beach, following the coast with steep mountain slopes on one side and the ocean on the other. I wish I could figure out where we are. I wish I had a weapon too. But most of all, I wish I were with Allison.

We've just rounded a corner into a small cove when movement catches my eye. Someone is walking away from us, apparently not having noticed our presence, and the individual carries an armload of what looks like driftwood. I lay a hand on Willow's arm as we halt to observe the other person. It's a man, I think. But with the deepening sunset and the distance between us, it's hard to tell for certain.

I tighten my grip on Willow's hand while we edge along the cliffs, following the stranger.

He turns toward us. "You can stop trying to hide. I saw you two before you came around the cliffs. Might as well come to my house for dinner. Hope you like fish."

Trusting a stranger seems unwise, but I am quite hungry, and Willow must be too. I have no weapons, but I'm bigger and stronger than this man, just as my brother remade me to be. So I let the bloke guide us around an outcropping, where he has a makeshift tent set up using what looks like a vinyl tarpaulin and several pieces of tree branches.

The man drops his load on the sand. "I'll get the fire started. Either of you know how to gut a fish? If not, you can start the fire while I handle dinner."

"I can gut the fish," I say.

Willow wrinkles her nose. "Ew. That's way too icky."

The only reason I know how to prepare a fish for eating is because my father loved fishing. He would take me and Sefton to his favorite river, then show us how to gut the fish he caught. I'd hated the sport, but I wanted to spend time with my father. Sefton always thought it was a ridiculous way to waste time.

The stranger offers his hand to me. "I'm Grant Larson."

I shake his hand. "Daxton Stainthorpe, but I prefer Dax. And this is Willow, ah…"

"Willow Greenwood," the girl says. Then she shakes Grant's hand too. "I don't use a nickname."

"Can't tell you how nice it is to meet both of you," Grant says. "I was beginning to think nobody else had survived."

I glance around. "This area clearly hasn't been touched by the Echo."

Grant's brows rise. "The Echo? Is that what they call it? At first, I thought it was a meteor, but then the crazy lightning started, and the demons flooded out of the hole in the sky."

"Where are we?"

"You're on the Lost Coast. Fitting name, hey? I used to come here to go hiking before... Well, you know."

"I'm afraid we have no idea where the Lost Coast is." And I will not admit to him that the girl and I were thrown into this region by magic. Not until I decide if I trust him.

"Not from around here, huh?" Grant says. "The Lost Coast is in Humboldt County."

"I'm not familiar with that area."

"California, buddy. You're in Northern California."

Chapter Twenty-Six

Allison

I WAKE UP SLOWLY, LIKE CRAWLING UP A MUDDY SLOPE IN THE PITCH dark. What happened? A fog envelops my mind as if I've been drugged, which slows my progress in rising from sleep. But slowly, I begin to sense things—the rustling of leaves in the wind, the warmth of sunshine on my face, cushy softness beneath me, and the scent of leather. Why would I smell that? With more effort than seems possible, I pry my lids open and try to make sense of my environment.

This is the bedroom I've slept in since coming to Fallenmouth. The window is open, allowing a pleasant breeze to waft through the space. The leaves on the ash tree rustle, though I can only see the top branches. I realize I'm lying on the bed, on top of the covers, but I can't seem to move my arms or legs. Blinking rapidly, I struggle to clear the haze. At last, I understand why I feel immobilized. It's not sleepiness holding me down.

Leather straps tie my hands to the headboard rails and my ankles to the footboard posts. Sefton must've ordered his minions to tie me to the bed. I'm spreadeagled and can't even move enough to scratch my nose.

Where are Dax and Willow? Did Sefton kill them?

I can't worry about that right now. First, I need to get free of these bindings. But if I tap into my Echo power to do that, I have no idea how much energy I'll have left for either zipping myself to wherever Dax and Willow are, or for opening those boxes in the cellar. My teleporting isn't exactly…exact. The first time I'd done it, I dropped us in a random location. The second time, I'd gotten us to Fallenmouth, but I can't be sure that wasn't a fluke. What if I whisk us straight into a war zone where Echo creatures reign?

Suck it up, girl, that's fear talking.

The door swings open, and Sefton approaches the bed. "Good morning, Allison. Today is the most important day of your life. I've given you the night to reconsider your actions yesterday, and I trust you will not attempt to escape again. But whether you've changed your mind is irrelevant. We will be bound in every way after the ceremony this morning."

Never going to happen. I'm with Dax, not this creep.

Sefton leans over to kiss my cheek. "You will be a beautiful bride."

Then he hobbles out of the room, shutting the door.

Screw this. I am not going to lie here and wait for Sefton to "consummate" our so-called union without my consent. If I can free myself and get downstairs to the exercise room, I can grab a cutlass. That's the best weapon available to me, and I've gotten pretty damn good with a blade. That, combined with my self-defense skills, should give me just enough of an advantage. Echo creatures might be wickedly strong and vicious, but they don't seem like the brightest bulbs. And yeah, I've had plenty of time to reconsider my choices. Sefton won't like what I've decided.

No more waiting. It's time to save myself.

I shut my eyes and focus on the leather restraints as I imagine them popping open. I focus so hard that a stabbing pain fires up in my temple, but I don't care. *Open, dammit, set me free.* I grit my teeth, clench my fists, bluster breaths out through my nostrils even as the pain gets sharper and harder. *Open, open, open.*

The instant the restraints break, my arms fall onto the mattress. I sit up and swing my legs off the bed. After hours of lying here tied up, my arms and legs feel a little sore, but I can handle that. The real test is whether I still have the agility to fight.

I slide off the bed until my bare feet touch the floor, then gently settle my weight onto my legs. I'm standing now, and I don't feel wobbly at all. So I take one step. That seems okay, and I take another step, then another, and another, until I've walked past the foot of the bed. Then I kick it up a notch by walking briskly toward the window, pivoting on my heels, and walking briskly to the door. I feel a few minor twinges, but I think those will iron themselves out the more I move.

Time for the final test.

I run to the window, whirl around, and run back to the door.

No twinges, no wobbling, nothing that indicates I can't handle a fight. I want to throw my arms up and shout "woo-hoo," but I don't do it. The noise might alert my captor and his minions. But in my mind, I am fist-pumping and shouting.

Once I find some socks and shoes, not to mention a bra and panties, I'm ready to go. I'd only pulled on my pants and shirt last night. Feels good to be fully dressed again. This is my battle armor.

I turn the doorknob with care to avoid making any noise, and pray the door isn't magically barred anymore. But when I try to open it, the door won't budge. *Dammit.* I risk sending out a small pulse of power. Though I don't hear or see anything, somehow I know I've unsealed the barrier. Yanking the door open, I tiptoe into the hall.

Nobody around. Guess they all assume I can't escape.

Tiptoeing swiftly down the hall, I head to the stairs and pause there to listen and watch. The coast seems clear. I continue down to the foyer, but freeze with my hand on the banister.

Although the sitting room door is shut, I hear voices in there. I want to know what they're talking about, but I have more pressing issues. I skirt around the staircase to scurry down the hall, staying on the opposite side from the sitting room, and make my way to the cellar door. Its lock is still broken from when Dax kicked the door open. Why Sefton doesn't guard it, I have no idea. Maybe he believes no one else has any chance of touching, much less opening, all those boxes. His arrogance is hard to overlook, but I shouldn't assume anything.

I ease the cellar door open and slip inside. The single bulb positioned in the center of the subterranean room can't squelch the shadows that seem to writhe in every corner. A damp odor suffuses the space, and the faint creak of each step sends a shiver down my spine. One step at a time, I slink down the stairs with my pulse beating faster and my breaths growing shallower. I force myself to take deeper breaths and exhale slowly because the last thing I need is to get lightheaded while I'm breaching Sefton's creepy basement lair. As I hop off the last step, the magics inside those boxes slither out to lick at me, though they hadn't done that the other day. Something has changed. I can feel it, but whether the change is good or cataclysmically bad, I need to keep going and find out what Sefton is hiding.

The closer I get to the shelves that hold the boxes, the stronger the magics grow, until they're prickling my skin with electrical currents of energy. Every hair on my body stiffens as a tingling sensation sweeps over my flesh. I raise my hand, inching it ever closer to a metal box on the middle shelf, and focus on utilizing the power within me. I wish magic came with an instruction manual, but I'll have to wing it. As I will the box to let me open it, the tingling becomes stronger and sharper, like a thousand needles pricking my skin, digging in deeper and deeper. I suck in a breath and hold it because I can't breathe anymore, not with a strange pressure bearing down on my chest. When I stretch my arm out to reach for the box, the pressure makes my hand tremble. It's like pushing through quicksand. My entire arm begins to quiver from the effort, and my ears start to ring. Black dots speckle my vision.

The box's lid pops open. The electric tingling vanishes.

Blowing out a breath, I sag against the shelves. The box lies open six inches away, but I need a minute or two to catch my breath and recover from the assault of those magics.

Holy cow, I beat them.

Once the ringing in my ears fades away, I straighten and pick up the box. It's heavy, but not so ponderous that I can't hold it. The sides of the box are half an inch thick, and the exterior is engraved with strange symbols. I'd noticed the symbols before, but now I sense their importance. One looks like a crescent moon. Another appears to show a circle with a dot in the middle. I also note the symbols for male and female, as well as various triangle symbols, some of which have lines drawn through them, and even more symbols with stranger designs.

Within the box lies...nothing. While velvet lines the interior, there's nothing inside it but air. No, it must contain something. I'm not seeing it, that's all. Not seeing or not feeling? I spread my hand over the box and gradually lower it into the vacant space until my palm settles onto the velvet lining.

Symbols on the exterior begin to glow and flash in some kind of sequence, but I have no idea what it means.

"You are very clever, Allison, to find these boxes and open one."

Sefton's voice sends a chill skittering down my spine. I glance over my shoulder and see him standing halfway across the room. "Why don't you guard the boxes the way you guard everything else? A locked door isn't a real fortification. Your creatures protect the estate, but these precious containers of magic are just lying here undefended."

"Are they undefended? I know you and Dax broke into my study and explored the cellar while I was gone. I sensed it every time you two tried to access the boxes." Sefton shuffles closer, coming up alongside me. "Only one who is worthy may open the vessels and access the magics in them."

"That doesn't answer my question. Why don't you protect these boxes?"

"But I did explain. Only the worthy may use the boxes. No further security measures are necessary, and besides, the magics need to roam free."

I had removed my hand from the box when he approached, but now I settle it inside the "vessel," triggering the engraved icons to glow. "What are these symbols? I recognize a few of them, but—"

"They are alchemical symbols." He pulls my hand out of the box and encloses it in his palms. "I needed years to research and uncover the secrets hidden within ancient texts and at last realize that alchemy holds the key to remaking the world. When I met you, I recognized I had found not only the catalyst I needed to begin the transmutation but also a soul mate who would stand beside me while the alchemy of worlds unfolds."

"You never said any of that to me. I'm not your soul mate. I'm just the employee who happened to be manning the check-out counter on the day you showed up at the library."

"I know, and that was fate at work." He moves closer, still clasping my hand. "How many others would have understood what I needed when I asked about alchemy and quantum physics? You knew, and you gathered the information."

"Any librarian could've done that. I found what you asked for by searching a computer system. That's not fate, it's dumb luck."

"Look at the symbols." He releases my hand, then throws an arm around my shoulders to hold me to his side. "*Look* at them. Until today, the symbols had only been activated when I touched them. They obey me—and now you. Notice which symbols activate when you touch the box. Do it."

I do what he says only because I need to know what the symbols mean. Maybe he's going to explain. So I stretch my hand out again and flatten my palm on the box's bottom.

The symbols begin to glow in a repeating sequence.

"Do you see?" Sefton whispers into my ear. "Watch as the sequence restarts. Venus, the symbol for woman and for copper. Jupiter, the king of the gods who represents the chemical element tin. Terra, the earthly embodiment of woman and the symbol for earth itself, the basis upon which all else rests. Ignis, the fire of passion and the burning flame of life that shall turn the world to ash so that it may be reborn anew."

To change the world, we must first dismantle it. One of his notes to me had said that, but I didn't understand what he'd meant until it was too late.

He points to the wooden box adjacent to the one inside which my hand lies. "Open that one and see what its symbols reveal."

Might as well let him tell me everything. I swallow against a constriction in my throat and open the other box. The second my hand touches the velvet interior, the symbols on the exterior begin to activate.

"The sun," he says, "symbol of warmth and life, also associated with the element gold. That is you, Allison. The warm and radiant woman who sparked the alchemical reaction. The moon represents darkness and the metal silver, and it binds me to you."

Sounds like baloney to me. Why would the moon bind me to him?

Three symbols light up in unison.

Sefton plasters his mouth to my ear and whispers, "Tria Prima. The three elements that triggered the original transmutation, the change that created all other matter. That's why I needed the three of us together—to recreate the Tria Prima. In ancient alchemy, three physical elements comprised the triangle, but I needed more than mercury, sulfur, and salt to achieve my goal. Only a trio of humans could accomplish the feat. Well, that and the quintessentia, which is the unknowable essence of everything, the prime catalyst that generated the universe."

Quintessentia? Tria Prima? The scariest part of all this is that I'm beginning to make sense of his lunatic ramblings. Because he's not just rambling anymore. He's telling me how he created the Echo and started the transmutation of two worlds into one.

He pulls me away from the shelves, dragging me backward, and rests his hands on my shoulders. "On that day when Dax and I stood before our parents' graves, I had already planted the seed of the transmutation within you. We are entangled, the three of us, bound at the quantum level."

"You planted the seed when you kissed me."

"Exactly. You didn't need to be present when I triggered the Tria Prima. I already possessed the requisite magics, and all I needed on that day was Dax."

Though I want to push away from him, I know I shouldn't. Not yet. I need more answers. "What did you mean about the three of us being entangled?"

"Quantum entanglement links discrete particles, even across vast distances. What affects one affects the other. That is how we share power. Eventually, I will find a way to sever Dax from the entanglement. But you and I shall forever be entwined."

Bound to him forever? No way.

"Once I achieved the entangled state," Sefton says, "the pieces fell into place. And voila, the apocalypse began. The elegance and beautiful horror of the transmutation is stunning. Don't you agree?"

My God, he really is insane. Nothing can save him now. He's gone too far beyond the edge of sanity, so far that he can no longer see reality as anything but a distant star in another galaxy. If I'd ever thought I might somehow bring him back from the madness, talk sense into him, now I realize that can never happen. He has murdered countless human beings, destroyed entire cities, and created monsters that do his bidding. No one should have that much power, and there's only one way to stop him.

Sefton Stainthorpe must die. And I'm going to kill him.

Chapter Twenty-Seven

Dax

LAST NIGHT, WILLOW AND GRANT SLEPT. I DID NOT. AT LEAST, I DIDN'T sleep soundly, but that was on purpose. My years in the Echo taught me the life-threatening consequences of letting my guard down in the presence of strangers. I met Willow less than two days ago, yet I trust the child. Perhaps because Allison trusts her.

Our host, Grant, is another story. He seems amiable and as normal as anyone can be under the circumstances, but I have an intuition that he's keeping something from us. I can't blame him for that. We just met, and I am not the most...friendly person. Everyone in this world has known the Echo for only a matter of days, while I lived in it for five years. Of course I'm a growling, snarling beast.

But I need to know what Grant is hiding.

I stand watch on the shore while Grant and Willow wade out into the water to catch our breakfast. They use sticks with sharpened tips, punching them into the gentle swells whenever they see a fish. While they focus on their task, I scan the shore and the mountains behind us, the sky too.

But my thoughts keep circling back to one question.

What has Sefton done to Allison? If that bastard has hurt her, I will tear him apart. I don't care that he's my brother. He lost the right to expect me to feel sorry for him when he turned the world inside out.

Willow sprints up to me, grinning, and holds up her spear—with a fish impaled on it. "I caught one. Isn't that awesome?"

"Yes, it's awesome." I probably sound less than enthused, but I can't help that. What if Sefton starves Allison to punish her for shagging me? I need to get back to her, but I have no idea how to accomplish that feat.

"You sure worry a lot," Willow says. "Mostly about Allison, right? You're scared about what your brother might do to her."

"I have no way to get back to Allison. So yes, I am deeply concerned."

She nods gravely. "Yeah, not having cars or planes or even scooters really sucks."

"Yes, it certainly does suck."

Maybe I should tell Grant that Sefton created the apocalypse. But our host is within earshot, and I still can't figure him out.

Grant saunters out of the water wearing only a pair of long swim trunks and carrying a spear loaded with two fish. They're both smaller than the one Willow caught. She is a clever child, and a brave one considering that she ran through a crowd of Echo creatures to reach Fallenmouth. She reminds me of Allison in some ways.

Grant leads us back to his campsite along the rim of the mountain. "Dax, why don't you prepare the fish while I get the fire going again?"

"I can do that."

"What about me?" Willow asks. "Don't I get a job?"

"You can help me," I say. "Learning how to gut and clean a fish is a useful skill. But if you still feel it's 'too icky,' I can handle the task alone."

She wrinkles her nose. "Still sounds yucky. But I'm in."

Willow learns quickly, and I only need to demonstrate the techniques for her once, then she takes care of the other two fish on her own. I keep an eye on Grant the entire time. He reignites the fire and creates a makeshift spit for roasting our catch, and soon we're all enjoying a hearty breakfast. Well, "enjoying" might be an overstatement. We're too hungry to care that our meal is slightly burned.

After breakfast, Willow wades out into the waves to hunt for seashells, though I'm not convinced she will find any. I order her to remain within my sight. She rolls her eyes and calls me "such a dork."

Grant excuses himself to find "a boy bush." I decide that's his polite way of saying he needs to relieve himself.

And I take the opportunity to explore his makeshift shelter.

Last night, it had been essentially dark by the time we found Grant and he offered us shelter. The interior of the shelter had been too gloomy for me to see what he keeps inside it, but I need to know more about our host. That requires reconnaissance.

I quickly search the shelter but find nothing of interest—until a spider lands on my boot and I stomp my foot to shake it off. The sole of my boot hits something hard. Metal, I'd say. The object lies buried under the sand alongside the spot where Grant had slept. He *is* hiding something. And I need to know what it is.

Leaning out of the shelter, I check whether Grant is coming back yet. I see only Willow building a sandcastle.

But our host might return at any moment. I need to hurry.

Pulling back Grant's sleeping bag, I dig in the sand to excavate the mystery item, which turns out to be a metal box. I brush the sand away from its top and open the lid.

A gun lies inside the box, nestled on top of a sheaf of folded papers.

"It's a Beretta .9mm semi-auto, in case you were wondering."

When I glance over my shoulder, Grant is hovering just outside the shelter. He's wearing jeans and a T-shirt now, with hiking boots and a denim jacket. I hadn't seen him change clothes, but I did notice he took a pile of clothing with him when he wandered off into the woods.

I rise from my crouch and exit the tent with the box in my hand.

Grant waits while I approach him, his expression as calm as his voice had been.

"Where did you get a gun?" I demand.

"Took it off a dead body. I didn't kill the guy. But I did take his weapon since I figured he didn't need it anymore." Grant taps the box's rim. "Only one bullet in there. Check and you'll see."

I pop the magazine out and see no rounds inside it. Then I check the chamber. One bullet.

"What did you mean to do with a single round?" I ask. "That won't stop an Echo creature."

"I know. But I thought if things got tough…" He raises a hand to his temple with his thumb and forefinger forming a gun-like shape, then snaps his thumb down. "Pow. I'd rather be dead than get tortured by those creatures."

"That's understandable." I pull the papers out from under the gun and set the box down on the sand. Another object tumbles out too—a photograph. I pick it up and study the picture of a blonde woman hugging a sandy-haired toddler. "What is this?"

Grant snatches the photo from me. "It's personal."

"Is this your family?"

He grinds his teeth, making his jaw muscles work. "Yeah. They were."

Clearly, he doesn't want to discuss the matter. If his family died, I have no desire to dredge up his pain. Unfolding the sheaf, I feel my brows rise as I realize what I'm holding. "Scientific papers? These look like they all relate to quantum physics."

"Bingo."

"Are you a scientist?"

"No, I was a deputy sheriff. When the shit hit the universal fan, I was hiking in the mountains just outside Los Angeles." He bows his head and rubs the back of his neck. "Didn't have my service weapon with me, so I couldn't do much when the creatures came. Tried to save people, but…"

"You couldn't fight them. The Echo creatures are incredibly strong and completely focused on destroying anything and anyone they encounter."

I am one of those creatures, at least in part. Sefton's transformation granted me more strength than any normal human could muster. Though I can fight those creatures, it's no easy task to defeat them. For a man like Grant, it must be terrifying to realize that not even his muscular physique, strength, and police training could save him if a horde attacked. So yes, I understand the need for one bullet.

Willow screams.

I drop the papers and run across the beach toward her, where she's been kneeling to create her sandcastle. In the sky above us, a winged Echo creature dives straight down at her.

The beast extends the claws on its hands and feet, preparing to snatch the girl.

My heart pounds so hard and fast that I almost can't breathe. Just as I reach Willow, the beast swoops in for the grab. I latch on to its hind legs, but that only slows it down. The creature is too strong and too determined. It flies up until my feet lift off the ground, and the thing flails its legs to shake me off. Its tail smacks me in the face, and I tumble to the sand.

Willow is running toward the shelter, toward Grant.

The beast swoops down again to grab Willow.

Grant raises the gun and fires at the creature's head. Blood spurts from its forehead. The beast loses its grip on Willow.

I race over to the girl, scooping her up in my arms just as the creature shrieks and soars away over the ridge of the mountain. I carry Willow to the shelter and set her down on her feet. "Are you injured?"

"No, I'm okay." Tears trickle down her cheeks, and her lips tremble. She flings her arms around me, hugging me tightly. "That creature almost got you. Why didn't you run away?"

"I was more concerned with not letting it get you." I caress her hair the way my mother had always done for me when I was a little boy and something scared me. I glance at Grant. "Why did you sacrifice your only bullet?"

"Couldn't let either of you get taken. I've seen what those creatures do to their prisoners." He tosses the gun into the brush behind the shelter. "I was a cop. Saving lives is what I do."

How can I not trust him after this? Maybe I shouldn't, but I feel that I can. "Let's all sit down and talk about things. We should get to know each other a bit more."

"Sounds good."

We sit on the sand just outside the shelter, near the fire that still smolders.

And I tell a stranger everything. Well, almost everything. I will not divulge my connection to the Echo or Allison's link to it, and I leave out the fact that the creator of doomsday is my twin brother. I might trust Grant now, but I have no idea how he might react to those truths. I do tell him about the golem Sefton sent to retrieve Allison, but I omit the fact that she whisked us both away. Keeping that bit of the story somewhat vague will let

Grant reach his own conclusion—that Sefton abducted us both. He does seem to decide that's what happened, which means he won't develop any suspicions about how Allison and I reached Fallenmouth.

"Allison's alone with that crazy guy?" Willow says once I've finished my story. "We have to go get her."

"I know. But I don't have a ruddy clue how to do that."

Grant picks up the papers I'd dropped on the ground and holds them out to me. "Maybe this will help. I found these in what's left of the Stanford University library. Heard some of the creatures talking about how their leader was fascinated with quantum physics and thought maybe I'd find something useful in these papers. I didn't."

I take the documents. "How far is Stanford from here?"

"About three hundred miles."

"You walked that far?"

Grant chuckles. "No. I found an abandoned boat, and that got me most of the way. I walked the last ten miles and decided to make camp here. Still don't know where I'm going, just that I needed to get away from LA. It's truly apocalyptic down there."

"As is Fort Worth, Texas."

"London too," Willow says. She looks at me and bites her lip. "Can't we get back to Allison the way we got sent here? You know, like, poof."

She makes a hand gesture that seems like an attempt to emulate an explosion and makes a matching noise. That must not be what she meant since we were not thrown here by an explosion. But I don't understand how a detonation sound indicates "poofing."

"Unfortunately," I say, "I can't reproduce the 'poof' that brought us here."

Grant pokes at the coals in the fire with the toe of his boot, triggering tiny sparks that float into the air. "Sounds like you need a portal."

I freeze, my gaze glued to him. "Portal? I thought you didn't learn anything from those papers."

"No, I said I didn't find anything useful in them. But I learned a lot." He stands and kicks sand onto the fire, dousing most of the coals. "Knowing how to open a portal isn't the same thing as being able to do it, though. I've tried. Guess you need some kind of hoodoo inside you already for that to work."

"What makes you think Willow or I have that 'hoodoo'?"

"Look, man, I don't like to comment on other people's looks. I'm one hundred percent committed to accepting everyone the way they are, even those creatures." Grant folds his arms over his chest. "Come on, you can't deny you aren't an average guy. It's obvious from the way you look and the way you growl. You've got some Echo blood in you, right?"

Bloody hell. How did he figure that out? This man is cleverer than I'd assumed, and now he knows my secret.

"I'm not judging," Grant says. "You look human, mostly, but no mundane man I've ever seen has muscles like yours or that animalistic quality. You also seem to know an awful lot about the Echo and the creatures that come from there. Most of us have been dealing with the creatures for less than a week, but you seem awfully knowledgeable about them."

Why should I lie? If he wanted to kill me, he could've fired his only bullet at me, square between the eyes.

"Yes," I admit. "I do have Echo blood in me. I was a mundane man until the architect of the apocalypse turned me into a beast and threw me into the hell world he had created. I lived in the Echo for five years."

"Thanks for sharing."

He doesn't sound sarcastic. I think he is genuinely thanking me for telling him about myself. Grant behaves nothing like any copper I've ever met. A deputy sheriff who behaves like a hippie? I can't fathom that. But nothing makes sense anymore, so I need to stop assuming I understand other people.

Grant claps his hands together. "Okay. Let's make you a portal so you can rescue the girl."

Chapter Twenty-Eight

Dax

I lever my body off the ground and fold my arms over my chest. "You say you know nothing about quantum physics, yet you're implying you can open a portal. Have you been toying with me?"

"No, I don't roll that way. I say what I mean and do what I say."

"Then how do you know—"

"Don't *know* anything. That word suggests certainty, and I've got none of that." Grant raises his hands in a placating gesture. "Relax. I'm not a spy for the creatures or for whoever created the apocalypse. But I have seen things."

"Such as?"

"When I was getting the hell outta Dodge—Los Angeles, I mean—I had to stop and hide in a trashed convenience store. A big bunch of those creatures had swarmed the street." Grant shoves his hands into his trouser pockets, his features pinched. "They were doing things I'd rather not describe in front of a minor."

Yes, I can imagine. The creatures I've met had no qualms about performing lewd acts out in the open.

"I don't care about the creatures' antics," I tell him. "You can skip that bit."

"Well, after a while, they all stopped moving and went real quiet. Every single one of them turned in the same direction like they were waiting for something or someone." Grant shakes his head. "It was the damnedest thing. A hole opened up in the air, at ground level, and I could see another place through that hole. This happened before I read all those physics papers. The creatures just stood there, seeming almost awed, while a man walked out of that opening—a portal, I realized later."

Every muscle in my body tenses because I know that man's identity. But I need to be certain. "What did this man look like?"

"Blond hair. Blue eyes. Fit, but not the way you are. He walked with a slight limp too."

Sefton. Grant had witnessed my brother exiting a portal. But I need to know more. "What did the man do next?"

"He started talking to the creatures, but I couldn't hear what he said. They seemed to be entranced by him, so I kinda figured he's their god." Grant tips his head to the side, eying me with curiosity. "You said one man created the apocalypse and the creatures. Was it the blond guy?"

"Yes."

Grant sighs, and his shoulders slump. "Sorry, I can't tell you more about what happened that day. The creator guy and his pet monsters walked off down the street. And I scrammed in the opposite direction. I should've stayed to find out what they were doing, but I, uh…chickened out."

"I doubt that. You reacted as anyone would have under the same circumstances. There was nothing you could've done to stop them, and if they'd seen you, they would have killed you."

He shrugs and stares down at the sand.

"Tell me what you've learned about portals," I say. "Anything you know could be helpful."

"The math of it all is way too complicated for me, but some of the papers I found seemed to be aimed at a more general audience. I'm no expert, but here's what I think it means." He crouches and picks up a small stick, using it like a pen while he draws figures in the sand to illustrate his points. "To create a portal, you need a wormhole. That's basically a tunnel through space, with a mouth at either end. Even if you could find a wormhole, you probably can't just walk through it, because the structure is very unstable. You need exotic matter to hold it open."

"Would magic qualify as exotic?"

"No idea." He scrapes the stick across the drawing he'd made, erasing it. "But I'm guessing the creator guy didn't search the universe for exotic matter. Magic seems like the best bet for tapping into a wormhole."

How bizarre that we no longer doubt the existence of magic. Last week, I laughed at my brother when he suggested such things exist. Now, I'm calmly discussing how magic and theoretical physics converge to create a portal.

Grant rises and studies me again. "If you're really from the Echo, maybe *you* could be the exotic matter."

If I knew how Sefton had generated enough of that material to hold a wormhole open, perhaps I could use the same method. But he failed to share that information. He would have needed an external source, I imagine, since he is not from the Echo and has not altered his essential makeup the way he changed me.

Perhaps I am exotic matter.

"How do I create a portal?" I ask. "Assuming my body contains that sort of material."

"I think that's where magic comes into it. You need to find and lasso a wormhole."

"Brilliant. Where do I find a unicorn I can ride into the wormhole?" Perhaps I did snarl those words. I hadn't meant to, but this discussion is making my head hurt. "Sorry. I have no bloody clue how to lasso anything, much less a hypothetical tunnel through space."

"You're doing this to find your girl, right?"

Not sure if Allison would agree that she's my girl, but Grant doesn't need to know that. "Yes, I need to get back to Allison."

"Maybe what you should do is focus on her and let everything else go. If you're connected to exotic matter, I guess it's possible you'll find a portal that way."

"Your words don't inspire confidence. Maybe? Possible? You guess?"

He shrugs. "This is all new territory—for everyone."

"I know, you're right. If I'm going to try this, I should move away from you and Willow. In case I cock it up and create a black hole instead of a wormhole."

Grant chuckles. "If you do that, we're all toast no matter where we're standing."

When I glance at Willow, she doesn't seem frightened. After witnessing the start of an apocalypse and being tormented by humans and creatures alike, I suspect the girl has developed a thick skin. She'd been terrified when that winged beast attacked us, but she recovered from that quickly. She's as brave as Allison, and as clever too, but she shouldn't be left alone.

"If I succeed in creating a portal," I say to the girl, "you'll be here alone with Grant. Are you all right with that?"

"Sure. He's cool."

"I'll take care of her," Grant says. "You have my word."

From his tone and his expression, I know he means that.

Willow hops up on her tiptoes to kiss my cheek. "Go help Allison. I'll be fine."

I march across the sand, staying as far away from the wooded cliff as possible, and edge around an outcropping so I'm out of sight of Grant and Willow. This is the best I can do. Whether anything can protect them if I make a terrible mistake, I have no idea. But I must try. This is more than a quest to reunite with the woman I love. She and I have a connection to the Echo and to the magics my brother crafted, a link that might help us stop the alchemy of worlds.

I freeze, barely noticing the wavelets that lap around my feet. Did I just think... Yes, I did. I've known Allison for such a short time, and yet I know what I feel, know it with a conviction that sinks deep into my soul. I am in love with Allison.

Could she ever feel that way about me? After the things I've done, the answer must be no.

Forget about everything else. Focus on Allison.

I shut my eyes and picture her face, her smile, the way she looked at me when we made love the other night. I hear her voice whispering "you are not a beast" and feel her arms wrapped around me. Pressure bears down on me from everywhere and nowhere as a prickling sensation sweeps over my body.

The pressure releases with such suddenness that I stumble sideways and bump into an object. I should open my eyes, but I feel like I can't move even the smallest muscles.

Arms wrap around me. A familiar scent envelops me, and familiar lips press against mine.

I pry my lids open and gaze straight into Allison's eyes.

She grins at me. "You're here."

"Yes, I—" Something incredible happens to me, something I haven't experienced in years. I grin at her like an idiot and laugh too. "It worked. I found you."

She throws her arms around my neck and kisses me.

"Uh, just FYI, you guys aren't alone."

Grant's voice jerks me back to reality. I keep one arm around Allison as I turn toward him. Willow stands beside Grant, and they can't be more than six feet from me. When I'd left them, they were much further away, out of my sight.

It's magic, you bloody moron. Line of sight doesn't matter.

Allison breaks away from me to rush over to Willow and give the girl a firm hug. Then she notices our other guest, and her brows wrinkle. "Who are you?"

"Grant Larson," he says, offering his hand to Allison. "I met Dax and Willow on the beach yesterday."

"Beach?" Allison turns her attention to me. "Where did you end up?"

"The Lost Coast," I tell her. "It's in Northern California."

But now we're in the bedroom where Allison has been sleeping.

Grant seems a bit confused as he walks up to the window and gazes out at the estate. "Where exactly are we now?"

"England," I say. "This is Fallenmouth Manor, my ancestral home."

"Really? Are you royalty or something?"

"I am the Earl of Fallenmouth. Not that titles matter anymore." My attention swerves back to Allison. "Where is Sefton? If he has hurt you in the slightest, even a tiny scratch—"

"He hasn't. Sefton had to go check on some outpost of the Echo, though I have no clue what that means." She grasps my hands. "But he did tell me everything about those boxes."

"What do you mean?"

"Sefton explained to me how he created the Echo and the alchemy of worlds, and I think I know how to stop him—now that you're here."

"Me? I know nothing about that."

She clasps my face in her hands. "We are two elements of the Tria Prima, the original alchemical reaction that started everything."

"What?" If I sound baffled, that's because I am. Clearly, I've missed a lot during my brief time away from her.

"I'll explain everything," she says. "Should your new friend be included in the discussion?"

"Yes. Grant is trustworthy, and he helped me figure out how to get back to you."

"I'm glad he did." She gives me a quick, soft kiss. "But we'd better get to the explaining before Sefton comes back."

We all sit down on the bed, Grant and I on one side while the girls occupy the other side, and Allison fills us in on everything that happened while we were apart. When she tells us that she can now open the boxes in the cellar, I have to interrupt.

"How did you manage that?" I ask.

"Opening the boxes?" She bites her lip and glances at Willow and Grant. "That's something we should discuss in private, just you and me."

"Why?"

She seizes my hand and drags me to the opposite side of the room, in the corner near the window. Then she speaks in a hushed voice. "We have, um, a sort of shared power."

"What sort? I don't understand."

She raises onto her tiptoes to whisper in my ear, "Sex."

"I don't think it's appropriate to shag right now."

Allison snorts, apparently trying not to laugh at me. "I didn't mean I want to do that right now. But when we have sex, it kind of amps up my Echo power."

"Oh. Well, that's, ah...interesting."

She leads me back to the bed and continues discussing what she learned from Sefton.

I have trouble focusing on what she's saying. Sex with me gives her more power? That's barmy. I can't help wondering if she means that when we're in the throes, she feels more connected to me and—No, I will not finish that thought. She can't love me. Should I tell her how I feel? Not yet. That conversation can wait until later.

What a bleeding coward I've become.

After Allison finishes her recap, Grant shares his experiences and what he learned, concluding with when Willow and I stumbled onto his makeshift campsite.

"The Lost Coast was untouched?" she asks.

"Not completely," Grant says. "The land itself is intact, but at least one creature is hanging around there. The gargoyle thing tried to swoop down and grab Willow, but Dax and I thwarted that attempt."

"I wonder how many other enclaves have survived."

"We can find that out later," I say. "Right now, we need to develop a plan for stopping Sefton from destroying whatever is left of this world."

"Oh, I have a plan for that," she says. "It came to me while Sefton was explaining how awesome it is to murder millions of innocent people and start an apocalypse."

The coldest chill I've ever felt sifts through me, from my skin down to the core of my being. Suddenly, I know what she means to do. "No, Ally, you can't."

Grant raises his brows. "She can't what?"

Allison straightens and clears her throat. "I am going to kill Sefton Stainthorpe."

Like hell she will. If anyone kills my brother, it will be me.

Chapter Twenty-Nine

Allison

GRANT KEEPS HIS EYEBROWS RAISED, THOUGH HE SEEMS UNUSUALLY calm considering that I just announced my plan to murder a man. A psycho, but still, a human being. I don't want to do it, but I know the only way to stop the alchemy of worlds is to destroy the creator of the apocalypse. Sefton has gone too far down the rabbit hole for anyone to pull him out again, which leaves me with no other options.

Willow has wrapped her arms around herself, but she doesn't seem horrified by what I just said. Maybe I shouldn't have included her in our discussion, but this is an unprecedented situation—for the whole world—and even a teenager deserves to know what's at stake.

Dax has been staring at me with squinted eyes and compressed lips while a muscle in his jaw pulses. He fists and loosens his hands repeatedly while his gaze drills into mine. "You will do no such thing."

"It's the only way. Weren't you listening when I told you how Sefton created the apocalypse? The Tria Prima has to be demolished. That means I have to kill him."

"Will that make the world the way it used to be?" Willow asks.

"No, I think it's too late for that. But I'm hoping we can at least stop any further damage." I give her shoulder a squeeze. "And one day we will find a way to make things better. Might take a long time, but I know we can do it. All of us together."

I glance at the three people who are watching me. Yes, I believe that one day we won't live in hell on earth anymore. I have to believe it. Stopping the Echo from swallowing up this world is a start. The fact that at least one enclave has survived virtually untouched gives me hope.

And we desperately need that now.

Dax stalks up to me, seizes my arm, and drags me back into the corner we had retreated to earlier to have a private conversation. He backs me into the corner, penning me with his body, though he doesn't touch me. "You will not kill Sefton. I will do that. You'll be safe on the Lost Coast with Grant and Willow."

"No. I'm the catalyst, which means I need to be the one to take down Sefton. Besides, you don't know how to access those boxes."

"I am the anchor. That means I should be the one to do it."

"This is ridiculous." I let my head fall back against the wall and groan. "We're both a part of the equation—Tria Prima, the reaction that sparked the alchemy of worlds. Arguing about who gets to kill Sefton is not helpful."

"What are you saying?"

"Maybe I was wrong. Maybe we both need to be there to stop him and break the cycle."

He lifts one brow. "Maybe? That's rot. You are going to the Lost Coast with Grant and Willow. I will break the cycle."

"Give it up, Dax. I'm not letting you do this alone."

A throat-clearing from the other side of the room spurs both of us to look at Grant.

He scratches his cheek. "You were talking kinda loud right at the end there, so we heard what you said. And I have a different opinion."

"I don't give a stuff about your opinion," Dax snarls through clenched teeth.

Grant raises his hands, palms out. "Hey, man, I'm just trying to help. I'm not as useless as you seem to think."

"No one thinks you're useless," I say. "But taking out Sefton will require a real battle. His creatures will defend him, and he has powerful magics on his side. Dax and I will need to get into the cellar, which means fighting our way past a lot of insanely strong creatures."

"I was an Army Ranger before I became a deputy sheriff." Grant's expression hardens, his posture stiffens, and he suddenly looks every bit the cop slash soldier. His voice sounds rougher too, like he's summoning his inner badass right before our eyes. "I lived through all kinds of shit, way before the apocalypse hit, including deployments in Iraq and Afghanistan. I fought my way out of LA after those creatures overran the entire city and the county too. Stop acting like I need you to protect me. The truth is, you need me."

He could be right. I hadn't realized until just now that we have a real warrior on our side. With Dax and Grant on the team, we just might get this done—and maybe even survive it.

My gaze flits to the teenager in the group, then back to Dax. "What about Willow? We can't send her to the Lost Coast alone."

Willow leaps off the bed and hurries over to us. "Please don't send me away. Maybe I didn't fight in a war, and maybe I don't have magic, but I can take care of myself. That's what I had to do before I found you guys."

I grasp her shoulders. "You can't be a part of the battle. Those creatures are way too strong."

"But I can hide. Just please don't send me away."

The poor kid doesn't want to be abandoned again. I pull her into a hug. "Okay. You can stay, but you have to keep out of sight."

Dax clears his throat deliberately. "Willow might have magic, you know. She did breach Sefton's wards."

"Even if she does have powers," I say, "she needs to hide for her own protection. We don't have time to figure out what kind of magic skills she has."

"I suppose you're right." Dax walks up to Grant. "Are you sure you want to do this with us? It's quite likely we will die."

"I lost my wife and son in the first wave. Got nothing left to lose."

And Willow lost her parents. Dax's parents passed away years ago, and so did mine. We're all orphans in one way or another, but we've found a new family here in the middle of an apocalypse.

We will live or die together.

"Slight problem with the plan, though," Grant says. "We don't have any weapons. I doubt fists and teeth will do the trick with those creatures."

"There are weapons downstairs," I tell him. "Swords and knives, mostly. I did see a couple cricket bats in a closet too."

Dax bars his arms over his chest. "We need to get downstairs before we can even try to retrieve weapons."

"You'll have an opening soon." I glance at the clock on the bedside table. "Sefton said he'd be back by one o'clock, and that's only fifteen minutes away. You guys should hide."

"I will not hide. If my brother means to assault you, he will need to get through me first."

"That's sweet, Dax, but I need you and Grant to get those weapons."

He sharpens his gaze on me and virtually growls his words. "You are not to be alone with Sefton."

"Oh, you mean like I have been while you were gone. I can handle myself. You know that." Because he taught me how to defend myself. I know I can't beat the Echo creatures, but I have the skills to stop Sefton from assaulting me. "We don't have time to argue about this. Promise me you will do what I ask."

I watch him grinding his teeth while his shoulders bunch up and his nostrils flare. Yeah, he hates my plan. But it's all we've got, and the only way to stop the final phase of Sefton's global transmutation is to take life-threatening risks. Dax may not like it, but he understands we have no other options.

He slumps his shoulders. "All right. We'll do this your way."

"Good." I turn to Willow. "Sweetie, please go hide. I need to know you're safe while this goes down."

"Is anybody safe anymore?"

The answer is no, of course. "Please do this for me. Please."

She chews on her lip, eyes glistening as if she might cry. But she sucks in a breath and squares her shoulders. "Okay. I'll hide."

I give her a quick, firm hug. "Thank you."

"Where do you want me to go?"

"The three of you should fit inside that huge closet over there."

Grant and Willow head for the walk-in closet, but Dax does not move. He stares at me, though he no longer seems annoyed. I know he's been scared, not angry, but growling at me is how he shows his concern. Now, he stares at me in a different way, one that makes me stride up to him, boost myself up on my toes, and meet his gaze head-on.

I lay my hands on his chest. "I need you to believe we can do this, because if you don't, everything will fall apart. Our connection, to Tria Prima and to each other, is the only chance we've got. Do you trust me enough to believe we can get this done?"

"Of course I trust you." He pulls me close, and I swear his lower lip trembles the tiniest bit. "I've never trusted anyone more."

"I trust you too, with all my heart and soul."

He presses his lips to mine, holding that sweet kiss for several seconds. Then he takes a step backward. "I will never let you down."

Dax walks into the closet and shuts the door.

The rest is up to me.

I try to psych myself up with a mental pep talk, but I know nothing can prepare me for what's to come.

The door swings open, and Sefton hobbles across the threshold. "It's time."

A lump forms in my throat, but I will not let him see my anxiety.

He waves for me to exit the room. "The ceremony will take place downstairs, then we will consummate our union."

"What, in front of all your minions?"

"Yes. They are the witnesses." He waves his arm again, and an icy coldness colors his voice. "Come now, Allison."

I follow Sefton out of the bedroom, resisting the impulse to glance back, and let him lead me downstairs and into the sitting room where Dax, Willow, and I had shared hot cocoa last night. Half a dozen creatures have formed a semicircle around the room's periphery. My guards. If I try to run, they'll attack. Dax and Grant won't let that happen. All I need to do is hold the line until they get the weapons.

Then comes the hardest part—breaching the cellar and accessing the boxes so I can shut down the alchemy of worlds.

"Don't I get a wedding dress?" I ask, strictly as a delaying tactic. "I should at least have a veil. Don't you think?"

Sefton shoves me toward a large creature who has tiger-like eyes and whiskers too. The beast also holds a book that has a brown cover. I want to punch Sefton for shoving me, but I need to play along for now. So I take my position in front of the book-holding creature while Sefton comes up beside me.

"Is this guy our minister?" I ask.

"He is the officiant. And that book is not a bible, but an alchemical manuscript I nicked from the Getty Research Institute just before the transmutation began." He smirks, lifting his chin. "Being able to summon portals is quite handy for committing thievery."

"Yeah, you're so damn clever. I'm in awe."

He seizes my arm, forcing me to turn so we face each other. "Sarcasm will do you no good."

"Do you even care if I enjoy you screwing me? Or have you always been a sexual predator?"

"You will enjoy it because I will make certain of that with a spell."

I swallow hard, resisting the urge to lash out at the bastard. *Not yet.*

"When we make love," he says, "it will be more than sex. We shall replicate the moment of creation, when the world was born."

Sefton nods to the beastly officiant.

The creature begins to chant in what sounds like Latin. He wraps up his spiel, holding the book to his chest.

And Sefton grasps my upper arms. "Time to consummate."

Magics unfurl around me, their slippery tongues invisible yet palpable, coiling around me and unleashing electric shocks that sink deep inside me. My sex tingles, growing wet little by little. *No, no, oh God no.* This can't be happening. The tingling spreads throughout my body, forcing me to feel a desire that turns my stomach. I must act before the magics take control and I can't save myself.

I raise my arms, bend my knee, and swing my calf up between Sefton's legs.

The breath explodes out of him. His eyes widen, and he tips forward.

Before he can react, I thrust a palm out and up, ramming it into his nose.

The madman cries out, stumbling backward.

I can't wait any longer. Dax and Grant must have found the weapons by now, so I suck in a deep breath and summon the magics. A portal opens behind me.

"No!" Sefton bellows, his face crimson, his eyes wild.

I step backward through the portal and watch the opening telescope shut just as Sefton staggers toward me with his teeth bared. He thrusts out an arm as if to hold the portal open, or maybe grab my neck to wring it, but I hit him with another groin kick that sends him tumbling to the floor while cradling his privates.

The portal closes, and darkness envelops me.

I can feel the magics zinging in the air around me. How much power do I have left? One way to find out. I wish for the overhead bulb to come on, and it flickers to life. Wan light illuminates the cellar, showing me that I'm standing halfway across the space, facing the collection of spooky boxes. I hurry to the shelves and trail my fingers over the tops of the boxes in hopes I'll sense which one I need to accomplish my task. I shut my eyes, focusing on one thought.

Show me how to stop the alchemy of worlds.

The thought repeats in my mind over and over, almost like a prayer. I suppose I am praying—for the power and wherewithal to end the worst of the horrors one man unleashed.

Click. Click.

My lids fly open, and I scan the shelves. Two boxes have sprung open.

Noises erupt upstairs. The pounding of feet. The shouts of male voices. The metallic clang of blades connecting. The inhuman roars of Echo creatures.

I force myself to block out the melee upstairs and focus on my task. Spreading my arms, I lay one hand inside a box to my right and settle the other palm within a box to my left, with two closed boxes directly in front of me. Magic slithers into me, cool and electric, winding its way through my veins to spread into my entire body. From head to toe, hairs lift and goosebumps pebble my skin.

Yes, almost there, almost.

A portal opens right beside me.

Willow stumbles out, whipping her head left and right as if she's confused. The portal closes. "Holy cow! I did it."

I have no time to consider the ramifications of what she has done. I need to focus on the boxes. Symbols light up on each box in a rotating sequence. The power within me rises and expands, tingling down my arms and into my hands.

Peripherally, I see Willow staring wide-eyed at the boxes.

The sounds of the battle upstairs grow louder.

"Stop this now!" Sefton roars from behind me. But his enraged cry crumbles into wheezing.

He must have opened a portal to get here, and the action drained him. That gives me an opening. I summon everything I have to ramp up the energy in the boxes and funnel it into me.

Willow clamps her hand around my forearm. A surge of power rushes into me from her.

Someone tumbles down the cellar stairs. Though I hear Sefton shouting, my awareness of his angry words has retreated into the recesses of my mind. Only the boxes matter. Only the power they have. Only what I can command them to do.

A scuffle erupts behind me.

"Hurry!" Willow says. "That guy looks really mad."

With a suddenness that steals my breath, the flow of magic stops. I have what I need, and I know how to do it. I raise my arms high and release the magics.

My head falls back, my body stiff and immobile, as the power I'd consumed floods out of me and straight up through the house into the sky. I don't need to see the sky to know what happened. I can feel the change in every cell in my body, the seismic shift that first slows the alchemical reaction and then grinds it to a halt.

Silence yawns around me in the pitch darkness.

The overhead light flickers on again, but I'm breathing too hard to speak or move. Willow still has her hand on my arm, though she gapes at me like I've turned into a human-size light bulb. I'm not glowing, though.

"Wow, Allison," she says, her tone as awed as her expression. "You stopped it, didn't you?"

"I think so. With help from you and Dax."

Though I hadn't consciously taken power from them, I had experienced an invigorating sensation of feeling them both inside me, more so with Dax than with Willow. Only now that we've completed our task do I understand what I felt. Dax has been a part of me since before we ever met, thanks to the Tria Prima, and we will remain connected in a deep and irrevocable way. Willow holds the Echo power inside her too, though not as deeply as Dax and I feel it. She is a part of me too. The alchemical reaction that created the Echo and started the apocalypse bound her to me, which makes me wonder if others out there share the same power and the same link to the Tria Prima.

"Allison, you faithless bitch."

The harshness in Sefton's voice spurs me to whirl around and face him. He stands a few yards away with every muscle in his body bunched up, his entire demeanor electrified by a fury that warps his face into a hideous mask. He clenches his fists so hard that his hands tremble.

Sefton takes one step toward me, his teeth clamped shut and his lips peeled back. Sweat trickles down his temples. "You tricked me, Allison. But you've done worse than that. You have stolen my power."

"It's over, Sefton. The alchemical reaction has ground to a halt." I can't explain how I know that or exactly how I did it—or rather, how I, Dax, and Willow did it. "The alchemy of worlds is over, and I disentangled you from Dax and me. No more quantum connection. You've lost."

"Stopping the process won't reverse what has already been done."

"I know, but it's a start." I glance up at the ceiling, where I can still hear the noises of the battle going on upstairs. "We will find a way to reverse everything you've done. Maybe the world won't be exactly what it was before, but it can be a good place again."

He glares at me for a moment, then his demeanor abruptly shifts. His body relaxes, and a bizarre calmness sweeps over him. "I'm afraid I can't let that happen. You and Dax are bound to me forever, and I will use you to restart the alchemical process. Now that I know you and the girl share the power of the Echo, I can amplify the process by draining that energy from every human who possesses those magics. Thank you for pointing that out to me."

How did he know? I thought he just got here a minute ago.

Sefton chuckles, but it's a dark sound. "You didn't notice when I opened a portal to get here? Took a significant amount of energy to do that while you were siphoning off my power. But I succeeded, and I saw the two of you sharing the energy of the vessels."

Oh shit. I must kill him before he tells anyone else what he knows. With a burst of power that makes my head throb, I conjure a weapon. Since I don't want to steal anything Dax and Grant might be using, the weapon I now hold in my hand is a fencing foil.

A foil is a dangerous weapon, Dax had told me.

Sefton laughs. "You mean to fight me with that flimsy blade?"

I rush forward and slash the foil toward his throat.

He scuffles backward and trips over…the corpse of a creature that lies in the corner, shrouded in darkness until Sefton moved and I could see that body at last. The creature's weapon—a carving knife—is still clutched in the dead beast's hand.

Sefton grabs the knife and lunges toward me.

I slice the foil across his throat. Blood trickles from the wound, but it's not a deadly blow. Dax told me a foil can kill if the blade breaks.

Just as Sefton staggers forward, stabbing his knife at me, I duck sideways and jam the tip of my foil into the earthen floor, then stomp my foot down on it. The blade snaps. I roll out of the way as he jabs at me again. Springing to my feet, I slash the jagged tip of my foil at his neck.

He pulls back, and the blade misses him.

Before I can strike out again, he thrusts his knife into my chest.

Willow screams.

I crumple to the floor and fumble with the hilt of the blade that's sunk deep into me—into my heart. Blood stains my shirt, spreading inexorably outward as the life pours out of me. I feel it happening. I know I'm dying.

My lids slide shut, and the world vanishes.

CHAPTER THIRTY

Dax

SEVEN CREATURES LIE DEAD ON THE FLOOR IN THE EXERCISE ROOM, THE foyer, and the hallway. Grant and I have battled our way through the house, with the former deputy wielding a cutlass while I commandeered the broadsword. Five more creatures continue the fight, but we keep making headway toward the cellar.

A scream reverberates through the house.

Not Allison. It sounds like Willow.

"We have to get to the cellar now," I shout to Grant. "Something's wrong."

Grant glances at me, nodding once. His expression of grim determination becomes more intense and deadlier as he swings his cutlass toward the nearest creature. His blade slices the beast's head off. While the head rolls across the floor, Grant rams his cutlass into another creature's belly and yanks it upward, gutting the monster.

I dispatch two more creatures, but Grant gets the last one.

And we run for the cellar.

The door hangs open, the darkness below broken only by the wan glow of a single bulb. Down there, someone sobs.

"I warned her," Sefton hisses. His face has taken on a grey pallor. "She should have obeyed me."

A rage like none I've ever experienced before descends on me, hot and feral and unstoppable, because I know what has happened. I feel it before I see it and pound down the stairs, leaping over a dead creature, roaring as I punch my brother in the chest hard enough to send him flying into the wall.

I fall to my knees beside Allison. The broadsword tumbles from my hand.

Willow crouches across from me while tears stream down her cheeks and sobs rack her body.

Allison is pale and covered in blood. I check for a pulse but can't feel anything. My hand trembles as I lay my palm on her cheek. She can't be dead. We haven't come this far and stopped the alchemy of worlds together for everything to end this way.

Sefton starts laughing.

I turn my head toward him slowly, my fingers curling into my palms while my pulse surges in my ears.

He keeps laughing. He points a quivering finger at Allison. "You lose again."

My focus telescopes down to Sefton alone as a cold rage infiltrates every cell of my body and the certainty of what I must do erases everything else. I see only him, hear only his manic laughter. As I rise and walk toward him, he still won't shut up. By the time I reach him, standing inches away, his eyes are watering and his cheeks are red from the strength of his laughter. He's begun to wheeze, but I spare not one millisecond of thought for his condition.

"Shut up," I say, my tone deceptively calm, "or I will silence you permanently."

My brother stops laughing, but he still wears a look of manic glee. "I took the thing you wanted most. I won."

"You murdered Allison."

Laughter splutters out of him. "Of course I did."

I take hold of his arms and lift him off the floor until his face is directly in front of mine. "You murdered her."

"Keep saying that. I love hearing it."

"Why, Sefton? Why did you do any of this? You had a good life, but you threw it away to become a monster. Our parents didn't raise you to be like that."

He huffs. "They only cared about you, the golden boy."

I stare at him while cold certainty solidifies in my gut. "You know I have to kill you now."

"Do it. Prove you are the monster I turned you into."

I shake him hard. "You are the monster, not me."

He sneers and cackles. Then something past my shoulder catches his attention. His eyes widen, and his sneer disintegrates. He struggles to get free of my grip, almost whimpering in his desperation. "No! You can't do that."

I swivel my head and...drop Sefton.

Willow crouches beside Allison with a palm flat on Allison's chest, over her heart, and her other hand inside a box that lies on the floor beside her. Silvery light emanates from Willow's palms and spreads outward to encompass Allison's body.

Sefton and I both stand paralyzed, our gazes locked on whatever the girl is doing. I sense energy crackling through me, drawing from the magics my brother had instilled in me, growing every second until, with a rush that sucks the air out of my lungs, the energy reels back into...Allison. I feel that's what happens.

And I feel it when her heart thuds back to life.

"No!" Sefton wails. "I'm meant to win, not you."

He rushes for the broadsword, but I snare him around the waist and haul him backward into me. Shackled by my arm, he can't escape. I lay a hand on his forehead. "I'm sorry, Sefton, but you cannot be allowed to live."

I yank my hand, snapping his neck.

Allison's chest rises on a deep breath, and Willow grins at her even while tears pour down the girl's cheeks.

I drop my brother's body and kneel beside Allison, cupping her face in one hand. "Wake up, love, we need you. I need you."

Her lids flutter open, and her shimmering eyes focus on me. Her lips curl into a soft, sweet smile. "Can't get rid of me that easily."

"Don't want to be rid of you." I touch my forehead to hers. "I love you, Ally."

"I love you too."

Once, I'd told myself she shouldn't feel that way about me. But now, I realize I am not the monster my brother convinced me I am. Allison wouldn't fall for a vicious beast, but she loves me. That's all the proof I need that, despite all my mistakes, I am nothing like the Echo creatures.

Allison pushes up onto her elbows. "This isn't a complaint, but how am I not dead?"

I nod toward the girl. "Willow saved you."

"She did what?"

The teenager hunches her shoulders and bites her lip. "Don't know how I did it. I wanted you back, so I got one of those boxes, shoved my hand into it, and wished hard for you to come back to us."

"Willow shares our Echo power," Allison says. "I realized that right before Sefton attacked me. And I also realized that might mean more people out there have the same gift."

I help her sit up and brush hair away from her face. "But I don't understand how that power could resurrect you from death."

Her brows lift a touch. "I actually died, didn't I?"

"Yes. Please don't ever do that again."

"I'll do my best." She slings an arm around my neck and kisses me. "Don't you want to know my theory for how Willow brought me back?"

The girl raises her hand. "I do."

Pulling Allison closer, I hold her while I rise to my feet, then set her down. "Tell us your theory."

"Sefton told me that he wanted to reenact the moment of creation, when the world was born." She turns slightly to see both me and Willow. "Sefton also said alchemy is the quest for eternal life. I think both of those elements gave the three of us the power to bring me back. A new creation, as in a rebirth. Eternal life, which means to cheat death. I doubt I'm immortal, though the Echo power we all share brought me back."

"But Sefton hadn't achieved either of those goals."

"He was trying, and the magics he gathered in that quest became a part of me and you, and by extension, Willow and any others who have the same power. Sefton had also ensured that you and I were entangled on a quantum level along with him. But I severed his connection to us." She hunches her shoulders. "Do you mind being bound to me? I can sever that link too if you want."

"There's no one else I'd rather be entangled with."

I'm not certain her explanation of how she managed to stop the alchemy of worlds accounts for everything, but I don't care. She came back to me. Nothing else matters.

Footfalls pound in the hallway above the cellar.

We all glance up just as Grant appears in the doorway, breathing hard. "What did I miss?"

Allison shrugs. "Oh, just me dying and being resurrected. Plus, Dax offed his brother."

"Sounds like a good result."

"What took you so bloody long?" I ask. "You were right behind me."

"Yeah, sorry," Grant says. "The creature you skewered with your broadsword didn't quite die. He bounced back and attacked me. Damn, those things are tough."

Allison leads me and Willow out of the cellar, and Grant suggests we go outside to see what effect, if any, halting the alchemy of worlds has caused. Willow sidles up to me as we pass by the corpses of Sefton's minions. I find myself wrapping an arm around the girl. I hold Allison's hand too, which leaves me with no hands free to fight, if the need should arise, but I don't care. After five years of torment, I've found peace in the middle of an apocalypse.

We stop halfway across the lawn and tip our heads back to take in the sight above us.

Fireballs and lightning streak across the sky, slamming down to penetrate the earth. The concussions of those impacts vibrate under our feet, growing stronger every second as they draw ever closer to Fallenmouth. Darkness pours out of the Echo, rushing toward the estate in a tidal wave of dark energies that will soon engulf us.

Allison grips my hand more firmly. "The alchemy of worlds hasn't stopped. We failed."

"No, I don't believe that's what is happening."

"What, then? Looks like the apocalypse all over again."

I nod toward the sky. "Look. You can see the alchemical reaction hasn't started up again in the distance. It's only here at Fallenmouth. Sefton had created wards around the estate to protect it from the chaos. Now, with him gone, the last gasp of the alchemy of worlds needs to fill in the gap."

"There's only one way to know for sure. We need to zip ourselves to various places and see if the reaction has ended."

"I agree."

And we do just that, though I grab the alchemical manuscripts Sefton had collected before we leave. We discover the books in the library, laid out on the chaise by the windows. Sefton must have put them there after we searched the house and didn't feel the need to protect them, arrogantly certain of his impending victory. They might come in handy. We check London first, then Fort Worth and several other cities around the globe. After satisfying ourselves that the reaction has ceased, we return to the Lost Coast. The four of us might be the only people living here now, but things will change. We will make certain of it, together.

My brother believed he had cursed me to eternal torment, but he never predicted the one variable neither of us could control—Allison Dahl, the woman who saved my soul and the world.

EPILOGUE

Allison

A BONFIRE CRACKLES IN FRONT OF US WHILE DAX AND I CUDDLE ON the grass nearby, his arm around me and my head on his shoulder. Not that long ago, I hated and feared him. Now, I love to cuddle up with my sexy beast and gaze at the stars or the ocean or a bonfire. Today, we're celebrating the Fourth of July—a little late. With no clocks or calendars to go by, we didn't realize until this morning that Independence Day had come and gone weeks ago. Everyone in our camp agreed that we should do something to commemorate the holiday.

Why? Because everyone who lives in our new enclave on the Lost Coast has escaped from the horrors of the alchemy of worlds. We have broken free of Sefton's vision for the world and created a community out here in the wilds. The cities are still ruled by Echo creatures, and the opening to the Echo still hangs in the sky above us, though we can't see it as long as we're outside the invisible boundaries around the cities and a good chunk of the suburbs, not to mention sections of the rural areas. Whenever a solitary creature manages to reach this enclave, we take that monster down. Everyone pitches in. Even the former nun in our group has taken up arms to help defend the community.

At first, we didn't seek out new members. They would find us, though no one could explain how they discovered our enclave. I think it's the Echo power in them. It just hasn't surfaced yet in a way that anyone can recognize. How many people harbor that power inside them? Nobody knows. These days, when we venture out into the world, we invite the lost souls we meet to join our community. Some do, some don't. We rely on our instincts to decide who to trust.

Grant has become a good friend to both me and Dax—and our adopted daughter, Willow. He still grieves for his wife and son, but I hope one day he will find someone new. Grant is such a good man that he deserves to know love again.

Seven weeks have gone by since the day Dax killed his brother and the alchemical reaction ground to a halt. We returned to Fallenmouth a few days after that and found the estate in ruins, ravaged by the apocalypse. But over the weeks since then, we've checked on other areas around the globe. The alchemy of worlds has clearly ended for good, though the consequences of what Sefton did haven't been erased. One day, we will undo the damage. I believe that with all my heart and soul.

Grant ducks into his tent and emerges holding a plastic bag. He waves it in the air. "Look what I found today. Who wants toasted marshmallows?"

Willow jumps up and down. "Me! Yes!"

That's right. We hunt for more than essential supplies when we head out into the post-apocalyptic world. Allowing ourselves to enjoy the occasional treat makes living out here seem less like escaping from danger and more like coming home.

As much as I love toasted marshmallows, I have something to tell Dax—alone. So I lift my head to whisper into his ear, "Grab the lantern and let's go for a walk."

"Now?"

"Yes. Please."

He retrieves our oil lantern from our tent and takes my hand as we amble away from the group, into the woods. We stop just inside the canopy of trees.

"What is it?" he asks.

Yeah, he knows me well enough to realize I need to say something. "Well, it's, um..."

"Relax, Ally. You can tell me anything."

"When we were in LA today, in that pharmacy, I grabbed something. While you and Grant were hunting for medicine and food."

"What did you take?"

"A home pregnancy test."

He goes perfectly still, his eyes glimmering in the lantern light.

I take a breath and just say it. "I'm pregnant, Dax."

The lantern drops to the ground, and his mouth falls open.

"Are you okay with this development?" I ask. "It's a lot to process, I know. We're living in a post-apocalyptic world, which isn't the ideal place to raise a child."

He wraps his arms around me, tugging me close. "We can do this, Ally, I know we can. All that matters is our family—you, me, Willow, and our baby."

"I'm so glad you feel that way, because I want our baby so much."

"And I do too."

We wander back to the bonfire and share our news with everyone. I cry. Willow cries. Even Dax gets a little choked up. This will be the first baby born in our new community.

That night, we make love in our tent, slowly, sensually, celebrating our impending parenthood the best way we know how. Willow has her own tent, as any teenage girl should. That means Dax and I can spend all night reveling in the love that saved us both and made this baby.

A month later, a newcomer arrives. The raven-haired beauty catches Grant's eye, though he won't admit to that. So he does what any red-blooded man would. He ignores her. I know Grant can't admit he's attracted to Erin yet, not until he has more distance from the loss of his family. That might take years. Of course, the pace of life during the Echo has changed things for everyone. Time seems more precious, every day more meaningful.

Dax and I have become the unofficial leaders of this ragtag group. Everyone expects us to have a plan to undo the apocalypse, but we are not experts on the topic. Not long after we settled here, Grant asked if he could study the alchemical manuscripts Sefton had stolen from the Getty Institute and that Dax had rescued from Fallenmouth before the Echo ravaged it. Grant isn't a scientist or a philosopher, but he has become engrossed in understanding those books.

One day, we will find a way to restore the world. I believe that. I feel the truth of it. Someone in our community is destined to uncover the secrets of the Echo. Will it be Grant? Who knows. But it will happen.

If a beastly man from the Echo can win the heart of a librarian, anything is possible.

The apocalypse isn't over yet.

**Grant Larson returns in *Echo Dominion*,
book two of the Echo Power Trilogy.**

ECHO DOMINION

Echo Power Trilogy, Book Two

CHAPTER ONE

Grant

I PLUNGE MY CUTLASS INTO THE CHEST OF THE ECHO CREATURE, punching the sword's blade straight into the beast's torso and out through its back, skewering the monster's heart. The creature gurgles. Its jaw slackens, and blood dribbles out of its gaping mouth. When I pull the sword free, the beast crumples to the ground.

Maybe I should feel a flush of triumph, but I don't. Killing is never a good thing, even when the monster before me had tried to assault a child. I'm glad the creature is dead and no longer a threat to anyone. That doesn't mean I enjoy meting out lethal punishment.

I glance around the alley, searching for my partners.

Bobby had gotten cornered by an Echo creature at the entrance, but I don't see him now. Erin did what she always does—run off on her own and get into trouble. I can't see her either, so I have no proof she's gotten herself in trouble again, but it's a safe bet she did. That woman must have a suicidal streak.

A triumphant cry of "hooh-yeah!" echoes down the alley.

That would be Bobby. Christ, I'm working with immature daredevils. I sprint out of the alley, then pause to survey the area. Yeah, there's Bobby. He stands over a creature that lies prone on the ground. I rush to him and peer down at the beast. Blood streams out of a wound in the center of the creature's forehead.

"Nice shot," I say. "But we can't be sure it's dead. The only surefire way to take out an Echo creature is to pierce the center of its heart."

"Yeah, I know," Bobby says. "But a shot to the head will at least slow him down for a good long while."

I grasp the straps of my backpack and wiggle them to get the weight more evenly distributed. The medical supplies in my pack could save lives, but it's damn hard to fight these monsters while saddled with a full load. I glance at Bobby. "Have you seen Erin?"

"Yeah. She went down that street over there." He points toward the next intersection, about a hundred yards away. "Told her not to go because you'd be mad. But you know how Erin is."

Oh, yeah. I know.

"Come on," I tell him. "Let's catch up to her."

And then I'll strangle the woman. She is single-handedly eroding my belief that I don't want to kill anybody without serious provocation.

We jog down the street until we reach the intersection, then I stop us both so we can scan the crossroad.

That's when I see her. Three creatures have surrounded Erin, circling her while they taunt her with verbal jabs I can't quite hear and fake-out lunges that keep her on her toes.

Bobby and I raise our weapons—my cutlass and his .9mm handgun—as we pelt down the road toward Erin. The creatures hear us coming. All eyes, including Erin's, rotate toward us. Two creatures break away from their buddy to sprint in this direction, clearly aiming to murder me and Bobby. He fires three shots, two of which hit one creature. Neither shot results in a kill, but the beast hits the pavement facedown.

I try to skewer the other creature, but it dodges my strike and hunches to ram its head into my stomach. The force of the blow sends me reeling backward while I gasp for breath. The creature straightens and pulls out a wickedly serrated blade half the length of my sword but just as deadly, if not more so.

The monster roars and rushes at me.

With one swift movement, I pierce its heart.

And the beast collapses.

Erin lets out a primal shout.

I leap over the dead creature and run toward her. But I know that wasn't a scream of fear. She often hollers that way right before she delivers a serious blow to an Echo creature. I see Erin and the last creature dancing around each other. She hollers again and thrusts her cutlass, but the beast kicks her in the gut. Erin drops, clearly stunned by the blow.

The creature raises its knife and plunges it toward Erin's chest.

Grasping the cutlass in both hands, I ram it straight through the creature's back and out through its chest. I wrestle the blade free while Erin lies there on the ground, her eyes wide, breathing hard as her gaze locks on to me.

"How do you do that?" she asks. "Hitting the exact center of the heart is tough enough, but doing that from behind… Nobody else can manage it."

"Glad you're impressed. Maybe you'll start listening to me now."

She pushes up into a sitting position and puckers her lips. "Never said I was impressed."

I lean over her and offer my hands. "Come on, we need to get moving."

Erin narrows her gaze, flattening her lips, but she accepts my help in getting up. "You must have Echo power in you. No way in hell anybody could punch straight through the center of a creature's heart that way every time without magic involved."

"Shut up and get moving."

I spin around and stomp down the street toward Bobby.

Erin huffs but hurries after me, falling into step beside me. "Everybody says you're such a nice guy. Did you bribe them to spread that propaganda? You're a dick."

"Yeah, I am."

"Can't understand why Willow thinks you're amazing. Must be a teenage crush caused by hormone overload."

"For once, could you please shut up?" I squeeze the words out between my gritted teeth. "We need to get back to Sanctuary before any more creatures come out of the woodwork."

Peripherally, I see her flash me a scowl.

We stop when we reach Bobby. "Okay, kid, do your thing."

He shuts his eyes and fists his hands as if that helps him focus his Echo power. But I've spent enough time with him to realize it's a crutch, not a necessity. The apocalypse that transformed the world gave certain people a special kind of magic that lets them teleport themselves and others to anywhere they want to go. I don't have that power, so I need someone like Bobby with me on every supply run.

Energy tingles over my skin, and the ruins of Phoenix, Arizona, vanish. Sunshine and greenery take its place. The scent of meat cooking on a barbecue grill wafts toward us, and birds chirp in the trees. We've come home to Sanctuary. We don't call it that just because it's a relatively safe place. This has become our home, and all these people are our family.

A teenage girl rushes up to me and throws her arms around my neck, standing on her tiptoes. "Sooo glad you're home."

I stroke Willow's hair. "Hey, kiddo. Yeah, we're glad to be home too."

Willow lets go of me and hugs Bobby, then tries to fling her arms around Erin. But she scuffles backward to avoid the girl's attempt.

Unfazed, Willow shrugs and returns to me, grasping my hand. We walk into the main area of the camp, which lies in the center of a large clearing. Forest surrounds us, and I've always thought that might be why Echo creatures rarely make it into our Sanctuary. Anybody could get lost in these woods.

Bobby jogs over to his buddies, the youngest adult members of our ragtag family.

Erin flashes me a scowl, then hustles into her tent.

Willow and I approach the group that's gathered around the barbecue grill. We had scored a huge grill a couple of months ago in Des Moines, Iowa, of all places. Now we can cook our meals without needing to gather wood. Because yeah, we find lots of bags of charcoal on our trips into the wider world.

Dax and Allison, the leaders of our community, stand at the grill. Dax flips a hamburger and slips an arm around his wife's waist. Allison smiles up at him. Nobody voted on who would lead our group. Didn't need to vote. Dax and Allison earned the right to be head honchos because they stopped the alchemy of worlds, the magically powered reaction that started the apocalypse. They know more about the apocalypse than anyone else.

The savory scent of hamburgers makes my stomach growl. Finding meat has gotten harder, since nobody has electricity anymore. As much as I don't like to kill anything, even I realize we need meat to survive, especially with a pregnant woman in our ranks. Allison needs protein, iron, and all that good stuff. I'd prefer to eat only things that were never breathing, but fighting Echo creatures and hunting for a way to reverse or at least end the apocalypse requires tons of energy.

"Grant is back," Willow announces as we reach Dax and Allison. "Isn't it awesome?"

"Yes, it is awesome," Dax says, though he still sounds uncomfortable every time he uses Willow's teen-speak. It took him a while to adopt her slang, and being British probably didn't make the transition any easier for him.

I still can't get over the fact that Dax, a man with Echo blood in him and giant muscles to boot, cooks burgers and plays go fish with Willow.

"Welcome home, Grant," Allison says. "How did your trip go? Looks like you found a lot of supplies for our little pharmacy."

"Yeah, we did. And I got you something." I shrug out of my backpack and dig inside it until I find Allison's gift. Dropping the backpack on the ground, I hand the plastic bottle to her. "It's not an exciting or fun present, but I figured you could use these."

She takes the bottle and reads its label. Then she grins and kisses my cheek. "Thank you, Grant. Look, Dax, he got me prenatal vitamins."

Dax nods at me. "That was very thoughtful. Thank you."

"No problem."

"Care for a venison burger?"

"Nah. I'm not hungry. The three of us ate back in Phoenix. We scored some MREs at an army surplus store, so we had a nice warm meal and even dessert." Prepackaged meals never used to appeal to me, though I ate MREs in the army. Can't be finicky these days.

"Did you bring home any of those desserts?" Allison asks. "I'd love something sweet."

"Our mandate was to grab as many medical supplies as possible. But somebody could go back and grab the MREs, either us or another team."

Dax gets a thoughtful look while he studies the flames inside the grill. "Perhaps we should send two teams."

"Good idea." I pick up my backpack, hooking one strap over my shoulder. "I'll drop these supplies off at the med tent, then head back to my place to do some more studying."

"Can I help?" Willow asks. "I got straight A's back when there was, like, actual school."

"That reminds me," Allison says. "It's time for your math lessons. Eat your lunch, then go find Sister Muriel."

Yeah, a former nun has become our schoolteacher. Since Willow is the only kid among us, Muriel doesn't have an arduous job. And she's technically still a nun, though we all call her "former" because there's no church here—or anywhere, as far as we've seen. I wonder if Sefton Stainthorpe planned it that way. The architect of the apocalypse was a total nutjob, after all.

I leave Willow with her adoptive parents, Allison and Dax, and head into my tent on the outskirts of Sanctuary. When I decided to make my little home in a secluded spot away from everyone else, nobody minded. Maybe I'm a bit of a loner, but I do try to matriculate with the group sometimes too.

My mission doesn't leave much time for that.

Inside the tent, I pull out my trunk I'd insisted on dragging home a few weeks ago. I needed a safe place to store the precious antique documents I'd saved from the ruins of Fallenmouth, the English manor where Sefton and his twin brother Dax had grown up. I'd seen Fallenmouth not long after the alchemy of worlds destroyed it. The place looks like a haunted house now. Feels like it too.

Pulling the key out of my pocket, I unlock the trunk and flip the lid up. My notebook lies on top. I take that out and open it to the last page of my notes, then carefully bring out the book I've spent two weeks studying. Alchemy isn't the easiest subject to master, but quantum physics is even harder. I need to understand both, though, and figure out how the magical and the scientific intersected to create the Echo.

I remember the day the world ended. Vividly.

The sky had split open, and monsters poured out of the hole to ravage our world and murder any humans they found. Fireballs and freakish lightning pounded the earth, punching holes straight through solid concrete buildings. But that wasn't the worst part. No, I'd seen things I still can't force myself to relive, not even in my own thoughts.

The flap on my tent is flung open, and Erin marches inside. "What's your problem?"

"Excuse me?"

"I said what is your problem. Getting damn tired of you treating me like dirt."

"No, I don't treat you that way. I like dirt. It smells good after the rain."

Her brows pull together, and her lips fall open.

Ignoring her, I carry the book to my desk—aka a folding table—and set the volume on the plastic surface along with my notebook.

"What have I ever done to you?" Erin asks. "You've hated me from day one."

"I have work to do. Could you please leave?"

She huffs and stomps out of the tent.

Erin Harding might drive me batty, but she's also beautiful and sexy, with long raven hair and emerald-green eyes. But I will never admit to anyone that I'm attracted to her. I can't. It has nothing to do with her reckless behavior on our supply missions. No, my reasons are entirely personal and too painful to discuss with a woman I've known for a matter of weeks. Maybe I should do what most guys would and take my pleasure any way I can, but I've never been that kind of man. As much as I'd love to have sex with Erin, I will never do that.

What's my problem? It's simple.

My wife and son died at the hands of Echo creatures, and I cannot watch that happen to anyone I love ever again.

Chapter Two

Erin

GRANT LARSON IS A JACKASS. I'VE KNOWN HIM FOR SIX WEEKS AND three days, according to the calendar on my watch, but I still can't get the man to have a normal conversation with me. It took fifteen days for him to look me in the eye, and even longer before he spoke to me. I shouldn't keep track of the timing of my acquaintance with Grant, especially since my watch battery will die one day soon, but I've become slightly obsessed with him.

With his behavior. Not the man himself.

Sure, he has a hot body and a beautiful face, gorgeous blue eyes and wavy brown hair too, but his looks don't make me like him any better. What did I ever do to him? Nothing. He hated me from the moment I walked into Sanctuary. Not long after I arrived here, I asked Allison about Grant's attitude toward me. She said, "Cut him some slack. He'll warm up to you eventually."

Yeah, I'm still waiting for that warm-up.

I shouldn't have waltzed into his tent to gripe at him. I know that. It was childish and stupid, but the man honestly drives me insane. I can fight almost as well as he can, and I'm ex-military like he is. We should get along fine. He's nice to everyone else in Sanctuary, and they all love him.

Oh, for heaven's sake. I need to stop thinking about the jerk.

Since I'm always kind of wired after a trip into the hell zones formerly known as cities, I decide to blow off steam by practicing my archery skills. We have firearms in the camp, but we reserve those for emergencies. Or for Bobby. He doesn't like swords or knives, but he does well with a .9mm pistol.

I grab my bow and my quiver of arrows, then head for the outskirts of Sanctuary where we've set up a practice range with equipment we took from sporting goods stores. Nobody owned the stuff anymore. We found the owner and several employees dead and buried under a mountain of debris. Part of the roof had caved in, probably because a bolt of Echo lightning punched through it.

The world ended. What took its place... Well, the only person who wants to think about that is Grant Larson.

"Erin! Wait up!"

I spin around and see Willow sprinting toward me. She's carrying her bow and a quiver of arrows.

When she reaches me, she's breathing hard. But she still manages to grin. "Can I practice with you?"

"Sure. Come on, sweetie, let's see who can hit the first bull's eye."

"Only you do that. The rest of us are still trying to get inside the circles on the target."

"You do a lot better than that." I start walking, with Willow keeping step. "You're even better than Allison and Dax."

"Thanks, Erin. You're awesome. Did you really fight in combat?"

"Uh-huh. I was a Marine."

"Wow, that is so amazingly awesome."

Everyone around here knows Willow's favorite word is "awesome." She also likes to tell Dax, the huge and shockingly muscular man with Echo blood, that he looks like he's about to "hurl." It's an inside joke between the two of them, and Dax always fake growls at her when she teases him that way.

Willow and I reach the practice range, which already has two targets set up. They're pinned to stacked straw bales, providing a safe backdrop. I give Willow a few pointers, but honestly, she knows the rules and doesn't need my help. I hit one bull's eye, and Willow shrieks while jumping up and down to celebrate my victory. Her shots all fall within the circles on the target, and several get close to the center. She doesn't hit a bull's eye, but that doesn't matter. We had fun and got in some necessary practice.

Life isn't all warfare and devastation these days. The sun is shining, the sky is blue, and birdsong fills the air. At times like this, I can almost forget that the world was destroyed. If birds can survive, maybe there is a chance that one day we will figure out how to repair the damage.

The ground shudders.

I stumble sideways and bump into Willow.

"What was that?" she asks.

"No idea."

I stand still and tilt my head to the side to listen and watch. The air feels different somehow, and the sky turns a darker shade of blue while silence descends on the world as if someone has flicked a switch. The air feels different, smells different, though I can't explain how or why. A shiver tingles down my spine, and every hair on my body stiffens.

A ratcheting noise originates from somewhere overhead, growling louder every second.

I seize Willow's arm. "Run! Go!"

We bolt toward the main camp area.

Screams erupt as the sky above us roils and darkens. People scurry around like mice trying to find a hole to hide in while they crash into each other because they aren't watching where they're going. The barbecue grill has fallen over, spilling hot coals onto the grass and spewing sparks.

I slam into a big body and yelp.

The man whirls toward me and Willow. Grant's eyes widen for a heartbeat, then he grabs us both by the arm and drags us toward the center of the camp. He flips over a crate full of melons and stands on it.

"Everyone, calm down," he hollers, and somehow, he manages to sound calm. "I know this is scary, but someone might get injured if we panic. Come on over here, please."

Willow wraps her arms around my waist. I hold her to me, though I don't normally like to hug or be hugged. Yeah, I'm not ashamed to admit I'm terrified right now. As the others gather around us, we all bend our heads back to stare at the heavens. A circular section of the sky has begun to rotate, the maelstrom shifting to a darker shade of blue.

A deafening crack of thunder explodes. The maelstrom snaps shut.

Within seconds, the hole in the sky starts to enlarge and spin again.

The entire camp has fallen silent. No one even yelped when that unearthly thunder shattered the air. We've all seen something like this before, though the entrance to the Echo looks nothing like this maelstrom in the sky.

Dax and Allison push through the crowd to reach Grant, who still perches on the wooden crate. He stares up at the sky just like Willow and I do. Dax and Allison stare at the maelstrom too. So does everyone.

I hug Willow tighter. My pulse pounds so hard and fast that I feel a little weak and nauseous. No, we can't lose our camp. Sanctuary means more than a place to sleep and eat. It's our home, our family, our everything. Is it all about to be devoured by the Echo?

Another explosion of thunder shakes us and the ground too. I instinctively shield Willow with my body, as if that will help.

The maelstrom telescopes shut and vanishes. Utter silence blankets the world.

A breeze kicks up, then the birds resume their chirping. I loosen my death grip on Willow, but she still clings to me. The sky looks normal now, and the air feels like air with no supernatural weirdness.

I look at Grant. "What was that?"

"Not sure." He hops off the crate. "But I'm going to find out."

He pushes past Allison and Dax, whispering something to them, and they follow him toward his tent.

I release Willow. "Go hang out with Sister Muriel for a while. I need to do something."

"But—"

"Please, Willow. Go with Muriel."

She twists her mouth into an expression of teenage annoyance, then stomps off toward the nun.

I march into Grant's tent.

He, Dax, and Allison all swerve their attention to me.

"You guys know something," I say. "Don't you?"

Dax glowers at me. "This is a private conversation."

"Unless you're talking about how to manage childbirth in a tent, it's not private. You're discussing the maelstrom in the sky, right?"

"Yes," Allison admits. "We don't want to scare the others. That's why we came in here to talk."

"I get that. But I've been fighting alongside you guys for long enough that you should know I can handle whatever's going on. I was a Marine—in combat situations. Only one other person in this camp has military training and battle experience."

We all know the other person is Grant.

Dax and Grant exchange looks that I can't decipher. Then Dax and Allison exchange a similar look.

Finally, Dax nods at me. "All right. You can stay."

I wonder briefly if the three of them share a psychic bond or something, but I dismiss the idea. They've been through actual hell together, so I imagine that forged a deep connection.

"What just happened out there?" I ask.

The trio trade more meaningful looks that I can't puzzle out.

"We should tell her," Allison says. "Bringing another person into the loop could be helpful, and she can handle knowing the truth."

Dax rubs his jaw. "Perhaps you're right."

Grant shrugs when his friends look at him. "Whatever you think is best. She might be reckless, but she knows how to fight and getting into a fracas with Echo creatures doesn't faze her."

"I'm standing right here," I say, not even trying to squelch the annoyance in my voice. "You could speak *to* me instead of talking *about* me."

"Sorry," Allison says. "We've gotten used to keeping this stuff between the three of us. But it's time to initiate you."

"You guys have a cult?"

Allison smiles, though only a little. "No. But we've kept secrets for a damn good reason."

They exchange yet another group look.

"We're not sure what just happened," Grant tells me. "But it seemed like the Echo was trying to restart the alchemy of worlds."

"The what? I know I'm relatively new here, but I haven't heard anyone else talk about the alchemy of worlds. I'm assuming that's one of the secrets you three keep."

"Yeah." Grant shoves his hands into his pants pockets. "Everyone knows that Sefton Stainthorpe created the Echo and the apocalypse, and that he and Dax were brothers. They know Dax killed Sefton to save Allison, but that's all anyone outside the three of us knew—until right now."

"Okay. I'm ready to listen."

"Let's all sit down." Grant waves toward two folding canvas chairs that are set up in the corner of the tent. "You and Allison take the chairs. Dax and I will sit on the ground."

Whatever they plan to tell me, it must be awful if we need to sit down before I hear about it. I do what Grant said, though. Allison and I settle onto the chairs while the men take the dirt floor.

"Have you heard of alchemy?" Grant asks me.

"Yes. Don't know anything about it except that it's supposed to be a way to make gold out of other metals."

"Alchemy is way more than that." He has his knees bent in front of him, but now he rests his arms on them as he gazes at me. "Alchemy is the transmutation of one thing into something else. It's a medieval science that has mystical aspects too. With the Echo, it became more than that. Sefton Stainthorpe combined quantum physics with alchemy to create another world and then use that world to trigger the apocalypse."

"I don't understand."

"Yeah, it's complicated." He stares down at the ground for a moment as if he's considering how to explain. Then he meets my gaze again. "Think of it this way. Quantum physics provides the scientific framework, but alchemy fills that in with magic. You see, quantum entanglement was a key part of the apocalypse. Entanglement used to be theoretical, until Sefton used it to bind Dax and Allison to him. The science of it says that two particles can be linked across vast distances via entanglement, and whatever happens to one particle also happens to the other."

"What does that have to do with Dax and Allison?" I ask. "They're not particles."

"No. That's why Sefton added magic to the mix. He used alchemical principles to cast a spell that bound him to Dax and Allison through quantum entanglement. Sefton called it the alchemy of worlds."

Okay, I think I understand what he's saying—sort of. But it brings up a question. "Do you think what happened in the sky a few minutes ago means the alchemy of worlds is starting up again?"

Grant's eyes widen for a heartbeat, then he blinks rapidly, as if I've surprised him. "You're smarter than you seem."

Should I thank him for the compliment? No. I'm not sure it was a compliment.

"Yes," Grant says. "I'm concerned the alchemical reaction has either restarted or never completely stopped in the first place."

"What can we do about that?" I ask.

"Someone needs to visit Fallenmouth."

It's my turn to blink rapidly and stare at Grant. "Fallen-what?"

Dax clears his throat. "Fallenmouth was my ancestral home. And it's where Sefton plotted his apocalypse."

CHAPTER THREE

Grant

"WHY DO WE NEED TO GO BACK THERE?" ALLISON ASKS. SHE LOOKS TO Dax, but he shrugs and shoves a hand through his hair. "Grant, you know how dangerous it would be to go back there. Even if the house is still standing, the last time we saw it, the place had been devastated by the last gasp of the alchemy of worlds."

Dax sighs heavily, shaking his head at me. "The only way to get there is via teleportation. Only Allison, Willow, and I can manage that. Besides, Fallenmouth Manor is in ruins now."

"I know that," I say. "But the bones of it are still there, and we might be able to get inside and search for Sefton's notes."

"His notes?"

"Didn't you ever think your brother might've written his plans down in a notebook or on a computer?" I pick up one of the alchemy books. "He made a few notes in these manuscripts. But he must've had records of his calculations and plans. Sefton was a scientist before he went completely insane. Scientists document everything."

"What do you hope to gain from reading the ramblings of my mad-as-a-hatter brother?"

"Don't know. But somebody needs to check it out." I flip through the pages of the alchemy book, which makes the strange drawings inside it seem to move. It's an illusion. I know that, but watching the pictures shift and blend into each other rattles a shiver up my spine. "I need to go back to Fallenmouth. Not asking any of you to go with me."

"Then how, precisely, do you mean to get there? You can't teleport."

"No, but someone with a strong link to the Echo power can do it. You three aren't the only ones who have a touch of the Echo." I set the book down, but I swear I can feel those images licking at my skin. The sensation is a remnant of what happened in the sky a few minutes ago, nothing more. "Not asking Allison or Willow to help me get there."

"You want me to do it."

"No. We all agreed you need to stay with Allison to protect her and the baby."

Their child is barely a fetus right now, but we have no idea if Echo creatures might be able to find Allison. If they can, she needs Dax, our strongest warrior, to stop them. Since they both served as part of the Tria Prima, the reaction that started the alchemy of worlds, they might be connected to the creatures in ways we haven't recognized yet. And their unborn child might become the golden fleece of the apocalypse.

It's all conjecture. But we need to take every precaution.

"No one else in this camp can teleport," Dax tells me. "Your plan cannot succeed."

"I'm not so sure nobody else *can* do it. We only know that nobody else *has* done it."

Dax's brows wrinkle.

"Oh, I get it," Allison says. "Grant thinks that somebody else in our community might have the latent ability to teleport."

"Exactly," I say. "Some of the people in this camp got here when we found them in one of the cities and you or Dax teleported them to Sanctuary. But others just wandered into camp with no idea how they found it. We've assumed that means they have the Echo power inside them, but not strongly enough to do any magic. I think we were wrong. Maybe those people just need a nudge in the right direction."

Erin eyes me up and down, lifting her brows. "What about you? The way I heard it, you wandered aimlessly until you found the beach that's just over the hill from Sanctuary."

"I was escaping from the apocalypse. And that was before we founded Sanctuary."

"What does that matter? You found the place. According to your half-assed theory, that means you might have the Echo power too."

"I don't have it." Okay, I kind of snarled those words. I've always tried to stay calm under any circumstances, a skill I learned the hard way in the army and as a deputy sheriff. But Erin knows every way to tick me off. I take a deep breath and exhale slowly until the anger sifts out of me. "Look, I get what you're saying. But I don't have the Echo power. I've tried to teleport, tried many times, but it never works."

"You tried?" Allison says. "When?"

I avert my gaze and scratch my cheek. "It was, uh, occasionally over the past few months."

"But you never told us. Maybe we could've helped you figure it out."

"Doubt that would've worked. From what you and Dax told me about the instances when each of you teleported, it required a strong emotional connection." I hesitate because it's really not my business to point this out. But I need to convince them that I don't have the power in me. Why I need to convince them... Well, that doesn't matter. Mostly because I'm not sure of the answer. "Willow managed to teleport for the same reason. She desperately wanted to get to you when the creatures attacked Fallenmouth. Dax was desperate too, after Sefton sent him and Willow to the other side of the world. They both love you, and that emotion empowered their magics."

Allison and Dax both nod as if they agree with me.

But Erin huffs and throws her arms up. "Oh, come on. Why do you automatically believe him? He's not an expert on anything about teleportation or Echo magics. Everything he just said might be true—or it might be total bullshit."

I shrug. "You're right. But since the apocalypse hit, nothing is for certain. All we have is guesswork. That's why I need to get to Fallenmouth."

Dax rubs his chin, his gaze narrowed as if he's thinking. "Perhaps I could send you there without traveling myself."

"What makes you think that?" Allison asks.

"It's worth a try. Don't you think?"

"Sure. But how would Grant get back to Sanctuary?"

"We could arrange a specific time when I will bring them home, using our watches as a guide."

Allison bites her lip. "Well, that might work. But Grant shouldn't go to Fallenmouth alone."

Erin straightens and looks directly at me. "I'll go with him."

"Maybe I should ask someone else," I say. "You don't know how to follow orders, which is odd since you served in the military."

"Yeah, I did. And when I got out, I'd had enough of taking orders from jackasses like you."

Allison clears her throat to get our attention. "She would be the best choice. You and Erin have worked together a lot lately, and she has military training. If you need to fight your way out of Fallenmouth, you'll have a better chance with someone like Erin beside you."

I hate that she's right. The suicidal chick is the only one who has the training to fight Echo creatures. Others in our community know how to defend themselves, and a few have become good fighters, but none can claim to have genuine battle skills. None except Erin Harding.

Well, and me. So yeah, that makes us the perfect team to go to Fallenmouth. *Damn.*

"All right," I say. "Erin can come with me. But I'm in charge, which means she needs to follow my orders."

Erin rolls her eyes. "Yes, sir. 'She' will do what you say as long as your orders make sense."

She just had to tack a qualification onto her statement.

"How did you survive in the Marines?" I ask. "You should've gotten booted out for insubordination."

"I followed orders then. Had to. But I'm not in the Marines anymore, and you are not in charge of me."

"For this mission, I am."

Erin glances at Allison, who shrugs. "Fine. I'll do what he says—as long as it makes sense."

She couldn't stop herself from adding that qualification again. Whatever. I have more important things to worry about than what one obnoxious woman might do. I need to gather equipment and supplies. That means weapons and water. We can't assume we'll have access to clean, safe water at Fallenmouth, and we don't want to get dehydrated while fighting those beasts.

Yeah, I assume we'll need to fight. Fallenmouth lies within an exclusion zone, after all. We call it that, and we defined which areas qualify for that title. We had to call them something. "Post-apocalyptic wasteland" is too hard to say five times fast. "Exclusion zone" sounds official and less like hell on earth. The places we identified as exclusion zones are the areas that suffered the worst damage during the alchemy of worlds.

Nobody wants to live in those areas. Nobody except the creatures.

"Let's go," Dax announces as he marches out of the tent. He pauses to glance back at us. "It's time to test my teleportation skills."

By "test" he means "try to send you two morons to Fallenmouth and hope you survive the trip." Well, I signed on for this. If Dax messes it up, I'll probably die without ever knowing what happened.

I grab my backpack and head to the supply tent to get water and ammo, though I prefer my cutlass to firearms. Erin joins me a minute later to stock up her pack too. Dax loiters outside while we get what we need. Then we all tromp out to the edge of the camp, to an open area where no one has set up a tent. Though we stand a good hundred yards from the nearest tent, I can't help worrying we might accidentally hurt somebody if our test goes sideways. At least Allison stayed in the tent she shares with Dax. It's farther away from ground zero.

Dax waves at the air in front of him. "Stand over there."

Erin and I take our positions, facing Dax.

He fists his hands and clenches his jaw, then shuts his eyes.

Nothing happens.

Dax growls and glares at us.

"Try again," I say. "Let all the tension go and relax into the magics."

Erin shoots me a skeptical glance. Okay, it's more like a nasty glance.

I might be full of crap, but all I was really trying to do was to help Dax get in the zone.

This time, he shuts his eyes but keeps his body relaxed. He takes a few slow, deep breaths. And he seems to disappear. But I know he hasn't moved.

Instead, Erin and I moved, which I can tell because we now stand in a different spot than before.

"Over here," Dax shouts.

I swerve my gaze toward the direction of his voice. He stands about fifty feet away. I holler, "It worked."

"No shit," Erin mutters. "Thanks for the completely unnecessary statement."

We jog back to Dax.

"That wasn't so hard, was it?" I say. Then I slap his arm. "Good job."

"Don't congratulate me yet. I transported you a short distance, but Fallenmouth is thousands of miles away across an ocean."

"You can do it, Dax."

Erin snorts. "Now you're the head cheerleader."

I ignore her statement and grab her arm to drag her a short distance away from Dax. "If this works, bring us back in three hours."

"One hour."

"That's not long enough."

"I will not wait longer than two hours." Dax clenches his fists. "If I can't bring you back…"

"We know the risks." I glance at Erin. "Are you sure about this? Last chance to back out."

"I'm sure."

Don't think either of us can be positive about this mission, but we need to try. "We're ready, Dax. Do it."

He shuts his eyes again.

The world vanishes. A powerful force hauls us into a darkness deeper than the furthest reaches of outer space and sucks us down, down, down. Can't breathe. Can't see. My only tether to the world is the sensations that bombard me, things I can't describe but that disturb me at the deepest level of my soul.

Light blinds me.

I squint and struggle to sort out what I see. Not only am a little disoriented from the trip here, but I also have trouble figuring out what the ruins before me are supposed to be. I'd seen Fallenmouth before its demise. Back then, the boxy house had squatted inside a large clearing, surrounded by manicured shrubs and flowering bushes. The house itself had consisted of gray stone with windows that had wrought-iron holding the panes together, and the garden had featured wrought-iron benches. Fallenmouth also boasted a cemetery, which I assume is still here.

But everything looks different now.

Though the sun shines down on us from a blue sky, the house hunkers inside a barren clearing scarred by the scorch marks I've come to recognize as the aftermath of the supernatural lightning bolts and meteorites that had battered so much of the earth until the alchemy of worlds ended. The incident today, back in Sanctuary, might suggest otherwise. That's what we need to find out. The gravel driveway is unrecognizable, though I can see the remnants of the track that used to lead through the woods to Fallenmouth Manor. Chunks of scorched concrete serve as reminders of the fountain that had once stood inside the circular driveway.

As for the house itself... The third floor is gone. Only jagged pieces of walls hint that the building used to have another level. The second floor has suffered major damage, but it retains about half of its ceiling. The ground floor appears to be intact, though who knows what kind of wounds it suffered on the inside. The ground-floor windows have cracked in some spots and shattered in others. Only a handful of the panes have stayed intact.

This place looks even worse than the last time I'd seen it, shortly after the alchemy of worlds finally consumed Fallenmouth.

Erin stares at the house with her mouth partway open. "This used to be a mansion? It looks like something out of a horror movie."

"Yeah. That's what the alchemy of worlds did. You lived through that, so how can you be surprised by what Fallenmouth looks like now?"

"I just am." She scans her gaze over the house again. "Every time I see another devastated city, I feel this way. It should never stop being a horrific sight."

Well, she's right about that. The day we get blasé about it is the day we lose our humanity.

"Come on," I say. "Let's go inside and see what we can find."

Erin follows me to the massive wooden doors that form the entrance to the manor. They hang askew, almost off their hinges, the wood singed by the apocalypse. I pause at the doorway as a strange chill rushes over me. I feel like I'm about to walk on someone's grave. I suppose I am. Sefton Stainthorpe died in this house along with his Echo minions. Though I've never believed in ghosts, I can no longer swear they don't exist. If a madman could create a parallel world and start an apocalypse, then anything is possible.

"Are you going inside or what?" Erin asks. She just came up alongside me, and now she peers into the darkness within the house. "This is one spooky place."

"Glad you told me that. I thought we were walking into a Christmas party."

"Why are you always mean and sarcastic to me? I've seen the way you treat everybody else. They call you Mr. Zen because you're calm and easygoing."

Maybe I am usually that way. I can't explain why Erin makes me behave like a jerk. Allison suggested recently that I dislike Erin because I'm attracted to her but I'm afraid of getting involved with anyone since I lost my wife and son. She might have a point. But that doesn't change anything. I will never let another woman into my heart. The apocalypse took my family from me. That's why I must dedicate my life to reversing the alchemy of worlds. Nothing else matters.

Erin doesn't need to know any of that.

She huffs and jabs her finger into my arm. "Get moving. We'll never find anything if we just stand here staring at the doorway."

"Maybe I'd be nicer to you if you tried being nicer to me."

"Just go inside already."

I stomp across the threshold and stumble over chunks of debris. Pieces of a wall, I think. Since I'd only visited this house once before it was destroyed, I don't remember what rooms are where. There was a library, and a sitting room too. Within half an hour after Dax teleported me and Willow to Fallenmouth with him, we had been thrown into a battle with Sefton's minions, the Echo creatures who guarded the estate. I didn't have much time to explore the place.

Yeah, I had a solid plan for this excursion. Find mysterious things I've never seen before while navigating the ruins of a house that has many rooms I've never seen before.

This might be a lot harder than I expected.

CHAPTER FOUR

WE WANDER THROUGH THE HOUSE, CLIMBING OVER WRECKED FURNI-ture and doors that got knocked off their hinges. Grant really has no clue where he's going or what he's looking for, except that it must be something vital. Yeah, sure, I believe him. He's given me so much reason to trust his instincts. If he has a nice-guy side, he hides it well.

I brought my bow and arrows, and he brought his cutlass. We used to have guns, but it's gotten much harder to find usable ammo when we search the cities and small towns. I have a machete in my arrow quiver too, but I'd feel a heck of a lot better about creeping through an eerie mansion if I had a fully automatic handgun or at least grenades.

The apocalypse doesn't care what I want. And neither does Grant Larson.

While we search Fallenmouth Manor, we stumble onto the decaying bodies of Echo creatures. Though I'd known we might see those corpses, I couldn't prepare for how I would feel when it happened. I get slightly nauseous the first time, but after the seventh body, I just feel cold inside. I've killed creatures like these. But seeing their lifeless forms crumpled under debris... I can't help experiencing a twinge of empathy. Then I think of Hayley, and I lose all empathy for the creatures.

Because monsters just like the ones whose bodies I'm stepping over murdered my baby sister.

In the library, we find books. Duh. I could've told Grant we'd find those, but they aren't the ones he wants. I've asked him repeatedly what sort of books he hopes to recover from this place, but he just grunts and tells me to keep searching. Great. I'm hunting for unidentified junk.

Grant's backpack looks heavy, and he's sweating like a pig roasting on a spit. His face has turned kind of gray too.

I grab his arm to stop him just as he's about to clamber over a pile of rubble near the staircase. "We need to rest and drink some water."

"Can't stop. We only have two hours."

"Then at least let me get a couple of water bottles out of your backpack."

He exhales a heavy sigh. "Fine."

I unzip his pack and bring out two water bottles, then zip it shut again. He snatches a bottle from my hand and marches up the stairs while unscrewing the cap. Swigging his water, he climbs the stairs to the second floor.

So much for taking a break.

After opening my bottle and downing half its contents, I race up the stairs after him. I find Grant standing in the hallway, staring through a doorway that has no door. Or rather, its door no longer hangs from the hinges. It lies on the floor, half propped on the bed. The wrought iron on the windows remains intact, though the glass has shattered, leaving jagged fragments stuck to the iron.

Grant stares into the room with a blank expression, and his gray pallor has deepened. His lips have turned paler too.

I lay a hand on his arm and try for a gentle tone. "Hey, are you all right? Look like you've seen a ghost."

He shakes his head slowly. "Not a ghost. A memory."

"Of what?"

"The day we stopped the alchemy of worlds." He takes a few steps into the room, and I follow him. "This is where I entered the house. Dax teleported me, Willow, and himself into this room—the bedroom of the Earl of Fallenmouth."

"Dax's room?"

He nods. "But Sefton had locked Allison in here while he planned his next move. He was going to force Allison to marry him and use her Echo power to bolster his own."

I can't believe Grant is telling me all of this. He barely speaks to me except to gripe at me. But this room has some kind of hold on him, something more than the events that might've transpired here. If he wants to tell me, I'll listen. But I will not push him to share the details.

"We hid in the closet," he says, "while Allison waited for Sefton to come for her. She went with him. She had to, or else he would've killed us all. Willow stayed in the closet, but Dax and I went downstairs to get weapons."

Though I've heard parts of this story before, from Dax and Allison, I feel like Grant is about to tell me something the three of them have never told anyone else. So I stand beside him and wait for him to continue.

"Sefton planned to rape Allison," he says, his voice flat. "But she got away by using her Echo power to teleport into the cellar. Dax and I were on the ground floor fighting the creatures. Lost count of how many heads I sliced off with my cutlass. Back then, I didn't know you could kill an Echo creature by piercing its heart straight through the center."

All the bodies of creatures we had stepped over during our search of this house had died at the hands of Dax and Grant. I'd noticed the severed heads, though not all the corpses had been decapitated. I understand how, in the heat of battle, a person can avoid thinking about what they've done, what they had to do to survive. Later, the reality of it creeps into your psyche. I don't regret any of my kills, not even the ones that happened before the apocalypse when I'd been a Marine. But I wish I had never needed to take even one life.

"Sefton found Allison in the cellar," he says. "And he killed her."

"What? I never heard about that."

"That's because we've kept the details of what happened here at Fallen-mouth a secret. We want to trust the other members of Sanctuary complete-ly, but we don't really know all of them." He turns his pallid face toward me. "You can't ever tell anyone. Everybody knows Allison and Dax have the Echo power, but they don't know how powerful those two are. If anyone found out Willow had resurrected Allison… Well, we still keep her powers a secret for a damn good reason."

"I won't tell anyone. You have my word." But I can't believe he shared those secrets with me. Does that mean Grant trusts me? I don't know why he would since our relationship has always been strained at best. Since he opened the door to this story, I decide to walk in. "Did something else happen in the cellar?"

"Yeah. Dax killed his brother. He snapped Sefton's neck because he'd murdered Allison."

"Did you see it happen?"

"No. I was still upstairs fighting the creatures. I got to the cellar right after Willow brought Allison back." He turns toward the doorway, still seem-ing almost like a zombie. "The cellar was the key to Sefton's plans, and he wanted to start the next phase—the alchemy of souls. The boxes in the cellar contained powerful magics. Allison used them to stop the alchemy of worlds, but we still don't know if that means the other part stopped too."

"Other part?"

"The alchemy of souls." He looks down at his water bottle, which he still holds in his hand. The bottle quivers faintly. His voice sounds weaker when he speaks again. "Sefton wanted to transmute the souls of every human left on earth and force them into the bodies of Echo creatures."

Oh dear God. What would that do to us? Make us monsters? Or would we become normal humans trapped inside the bodies of the Echo creatures, unable to control the horrific acts they commit?

Grant's knees buckle.

I try to grab his arm to hold him up, but he tumbles to the floor before I get the chance. His eyelids flutter closed. His body goes slack. Kneeling beside him, my heart thudding, I check for a pulse. He's alive, but his pulse feels thready. I'm no doctor, but I'd learned a thing or two from Navy med-ics. I think Grant might just be dehydrated and exhausted.

So I drag the door off the bed and haul Grant onto the mattress, which leaves me gasping and drenched with sweat. I'm in good shape, but Grant is a tall, muscular man. He weighs a lot. Once I've got him on the bed, I wrestle with his limp form so I can remove his jacket. Taking his shoes off is much easier. Now he wears only his T-shirt, jeans, and socks. He seems more comfortable now, but I can't tell if Grant would agree with that statement since he's unconscious.

A search of the room nets me a pillow and a blanket. I carefully lift his head and slide the pillow under it, then I lay the blanket over him.

Now what? I have no idea how long it'll be before he wakes up.

I should stay in this room in case Dax needs us to be close together when he teleports us. But when I check my watch, I see we still have nearly an hour left before Dax will even try to bring us back. Might as well explore the second floor. I won't go too far from Grant, though, in case he rouses.

My exploration doesn't give me any helpful information. Most of the rooms don't have anything other than furniture in them. Unless I want to carry a few chairs home with me, I can't get anything useful out of these rooms.

I return to the earl's bedroom and find Grant still sleeping.

What if he never wakes up? I hardly know the man, but I don't want him to die or languish in a coma forever. So I dribble water onto his lips in the hopes it will seep into his mouth and refresh him. Maybe that's a dumb thing to do, but I can't think of anything else. I've seen too many people die before and after the apocalypse, and I don't want to watch that happen to Grant, however much he annoys me.

Grant told me what really happened on the day the alchemy of worlds ended. He shared secrets with me. Why? He doesn't even like me, and he thinks I'm reckless. Maybe I am. But he's obsessed with alchemy and quantum physics, though he never studied those subjects pre-apocalypse, and he exhausted himself to the point of passing out. He has no right to criticize my actions.

I've just set the water bottle on the nightstand when he groans.

Grant's eyes flutter open, and he squints at the sunlight streaming through the windows. "What happened?"

"You passed out. Have you eaten anything today?"

He ignores my question and tries to push up into a sitting position but falls back onto the mattress. "Shit. I feel like I've got the flu."

I press a hand to his forehead. "No fever. I think you wiped yourself out. So I repeat, when did you last eat?"

He screws up his mouth and wriggles, then shoves the blanket off himself. "Don't remember."

"Come on, Grant. If you had traveled to Fallenmouth alone, like you wanted, you'd be dead by now. I dribbled water into your mouth and put you on the bed."

"Didn't need your help. Still don't." He tries once again to sit up, but once again falls back down. "How long have we been here?"

I check my watch. "An hour and forty-five minutes."

"Dammit. I need to search the rest of the house."

"I already ransacked this floor. The only thing left is the cellar."

He freezes, his eyes widening the slightest bit. "No. We can't go down there."

"Why not?"

Grant scrubs his hands over his face and sighs. "Sefton's body is still down there."

"We've stepped over how many dead creatures today? I can't believe you're squeamish about the remains of one lunatic."

"Don't you care that he was a human being? He might've gone nuts and destroyed the world, but Sefton Stainthorpe was still a man. He deserves to rest in peace."

"Of course I care that he was human." I stand up and cross my arms over my chest. "You might think I'm a heartless, reckless bitch. But I care about every damn living thing that died because of the apocalypse, even the creatures. Sefton and his minions had to die. That doesn't mean I threw a party to celebrate those deaths."

He sighs again and manages to sit up this time, though he shimmies backward to lean against the headboard. "I'm sorry, Erin. I didn't mean—Well, let's just forget about that, okay?"

"Forget about what?"

"That I kind of accused you of being a heartless bitch. I don't really believe that."

But he believes I'm reckless, otherwise he would've apologized for that too. Well, he might have a point—one that also applies to him.

"How long has it been since you ate or slept?" I ask. "You've been obsessed with those books, haven't you? So I'm betting you haven't taken care of yourself."

He makes a pained face and bows his head. "Yeah, I've been obsessed. For a good reason."

"I get that you want to save the world or whatever, but you need to take care of yourself. I repeat, when did you last eat or sleep?"

Grant glances out the broken windows. "I haven't slept well for a week or so, and not at all last night."

"And food?"

He shrugs. "Lunch yesterday, I think."

"You think yesterday? Grant, you need to eat three meals a day like everybody else. Three good meals."

"What does it matter? We'll all die if I can't reverse the apocalypse."

I stare at him, frozen by the stark words he spoke in a casual tone. "What do you mean reverse the apocalypse? Is that possible?"

"Don't know." He throws his head back, shuts his eyes, and groans. "Didn't mean to tell you that."

I study him for a moment while I try to understand. No such luck. "Have you told anyone else that you want to reverse the apocalypse?"

"No."

"But that's what you're obsessed with doing. Have you come up with a plan?"

He shakes his head slowly, his eyes still closed.

"Do you have any food in your backpack?" I ask. "You need to eat something."

"Got some energy bars I took from that army surplus store."

I retrieve his backpack from where he left it on the floor and sit on the bed next to him while I search for food inside the bag. I've just pulled out an energy bar when one fact finally penetrates my brain.

"How could you have not eaten since yesterday?" I ask. "When we got back from Phoenix, you told Dax you weren't hungry because the three of us ate MREs from the army surplus store."

"Did you see me eating?"

"No." I hand him an energy bar. "You lied to Dax, didn't you?"

He nods while he takes a bite of the food I gave him.

"Why would you do that?" I realize the answer a second after I asked the question. "You don't want anyone to know you aren't eating or sleeping. Your obsession has gotten so strong that it's taken over your entire life."

"Life? I don't have one of those anymore. Nobody does."

We need to talk about his issues more, but Fallenmouth is not the right place to do that.

I hand him two more energy bars. "Eat these. Then we need to search the cellar before Dax brings us home."

"No. There's nothing down there that either of us needs to see."

"If you're scared, you can stay in the kitchen. I'll check out what's down there."

He wolfs down half of a second energy bar and glowers at me. "I'm not scared. We'll check out the cellar together."

"Can you walk? We'll need to go down two flights of stairs."

"I'll manage."

Once he's finished his snack and guzzled more water, I try to help him get off the bed. He scowls and shakes my hand off his arm. I grab his backpack. Grant does manage to walk on his own with only a little shakiness that dissipates by the time we reach the top of the staircase. We climb down the steps to reach the foyer, then swerve right toward the kitchen and the cellar beneath.

All the while, one question haunts me. Will his obsession get us both killed?

Chapter Five

Grant

I SWEAR I'M NOT A JACKASS, AND I'M NOT STUPID EITHER. MY RECENT behavior doesn't support my claim, and I can't deny what Erin said. I am obsessed. When I first began to study the alchemical manuscripts, I made it my goal to ensure the transmutation that destroyed much of the earth would never swallow up any more of it. But that goal has mutated over the past few months. Now I need to reverse what Sefton Stainthorpe did.

Is that even possible? I don't know.

The longer I obsess over the answer to that question, the less I care about trivial things like eating and sleeping. Yeah, I'm being sarcastic, sort of. I know I need food and rest, but I just can't muster any enthusiasm for either thing. How can I sleep when the entire earth is in chaos? When people are still suffering and dying out there in the world beyond our Sanctuary?

While I follow Erin into the kitchen, I can't stop the memories that unreel in my mind. Blood. Screams. Death. Destruction. Maybe I should adopt Erin's mindset and just murder everything I see that's not a human being. But I can't do that. It's not in my nature.

The doorway to the cellar stands open—because the door itself got torn off its hinges and now lies on the floor near the shattered marble island.

Erin goes through the cellar doorway but hesitates on the top step to glance back at me. "Are you coming?"

I've stopped moving, haven't I? Didn't realize that until she spoke. My feet don't want to move. Why the cellar disturbs me so much, I can't explain. I've been down there before, once, but I didn't witness what happened when Dax, Allison, and Willow stopped the alchemy of worlds and Sefton died. I have no firsthand experience of those events and know only what I saw when I finally reached the cellar.

A dead creature. A dead man. That's what I saw. Sefton and his minion had suffered similar fates.

"Okay, fine," Erin says. "You wait here. I'll check out what's down there."

"No. I'm coming with you."

I follow her down the stairs. Every hair on my body stiffens and tingles as if an electrical current has enveloped me. But I keep trudging down the steps into the darkness below. Even when Erin switches on a flashlight, I swear I can feel the darkness around me. Yeah, the apocalypse can make a believer out of the most die-hard skeptic of the paranormal.

We both halt when we reach the dirt floor of the cellar.

"Do you feel that?" Erin asks. "Never believed in ghosts, but I can only describe this feeling as like a spirit passing through me."

"Yeah, I feel it too."

She rubs her arms. "Suddenly, I get why you didn't want to come down here."

Well, at least I'm not paranoid. She feels the weirdness too.

Erin sweeps her flashlight over the cellar. A mostly decomposed body, not much more than a skeleton, lies in the corner a few feet from us.

"That's one of the Echo creatures," I tell Erin. "Sefton's body would be over there."

I point toward the middle of the space.

Erin swings her light toward where I pointed, revealing another mostly decomposed body that consists of bones with bits of decayed flesh and scraps of clothing stuck to it.

"And that would be Sefton Stainthorpe," I say. "Dax broke his brother's neck."

Erin winces. "I've seen that done before. Heard the crack when the vertebrae snap."

I don't need to ask when she witnessed that. Even before the apocalypse, we'd both seen things no one can ever unsee.

"What are those boxes?" Erin asks.

My gaze lands on the metal shelves that take up one wall of the cellar. A bunch of boxes occupy those shelves, with some made of metal and others fashioned from wood. Every box sports unusual symbols carved into it. I recognize many of them from my research into the alchemy books, though I haven't figured out how they relate to the apocalypse. My gaze is drawn to a circle with a dot in the middle that represents gold, the sun, and the heart. Next to that one, I see the symbol for air, a triangle with a line drawn across it, which also represents life-giving energy and blood.

"Those were the vessels for the Echo energy that created the apocalypse," I say. "The patterns etched into their surfaces are alchemical symbols. The images used to light up in a specific sequence, but only when someone with the Echo power touched the boxes."

"Used to?"

"Yes. They're dead now, apparently. When the alchemy of worlds ground to a halt, the boxes no longer lit up. Allison said she felt the energy inside them had been drained."

"She felt it? That's awfully indefinite."

"We're dealing with magics here, stuff nobody really understands. Can't give a definitive answer."

And for reasons I can't explain, I don't want to point out the gold and air symbols to her. It feels…forbidden. Or maybe I'm losing my mind and those shapes hold no darker meaning.

Erin approaches the shelves and traces her fingertips over the symbols on one of the boxes. Then she opens the lid and explores the velvet lining inside the box. "Don't feel anything."

"Told you, the magics must be depleted."

She turns toward me. "What now?"

"We go home." I check my watch. Luckily, it has glowing numbers on it so I can read the time even in the gloom down here. "It's been one hour and fifty-eight minutes. Dax should be calling us home any second."

She walks back to me, and we both stand here waiting. And waiting. And waiting. I check my watch again. Dax should've retrieved us five minutes ago. Well, we didn't synchronize our watches, which means he might think it's not quite two hours yet. So we wait some more.

After ten minutes, I know something has gone wrong.

"We're stuck here, aren't we?" Erin asks. "I knew this plan would go sideways."

"Let's give Dax a little more time. He's never done this before. Retrieving people via teleportation, I mean."

"Maybe we should get out of the cellar. If this room used to house powerful magics, it might be blocking other paranormal signals or something."

I want to roll my eyes and tell her that's bullshit, but I can't swear it is. So instead, I head for the stairs. "Come on. Might as well test your theory."

We climb up to the kitchen and stop there to wait for a little longer.

The world shifts, and sunshine blinds me for a moment. I squint and hold up a hand to shield my eyes.

"Finally," Dax growls. "What took so bloody long?"

"Don't ask me," I say. "You're the teleporter general."

Erin drops her backpack on the ground. "We were in the cellar. Apparently, something in that place blocked you from retrieving us. Once we reached the kitchen, voilà. We got zipped home."

Dax's brows scrunch up in the way I've only seen him do when Allison says something that confuses him. I guess the big guy doesn't get Erin's description of what happened. Well, he did live in the Echo for five years, thanks to the way time moves differently there. He still hasn't fully readjusted to life on earth.

For the rest of us, the apocalypse started a week after Sefton banished his twin brother to the Echo, and Dax emerged from the other world on that day.

"Did you find anything useful?" Dax asks.

"No joy."

Now he gives me that scrunched-up eyebrows look. "What does that mean?"

"It means we didn't find anything."

"Except dead bodies," Erin says. "We found plenty of those."

Dax averts his gaze to the ground. "You found Sefton there."

"Yeah," I say. "Not much of him left. The boxes in the cellar seem to be dead just like the last time we were there."

The big guy grunts. "I suppose that's good news."

"It is. If the boxes have stayed dead, the alchemy of worlds won't restart."

Erin gives me a puzzled look. "Then what caused the thing in the sky earlier? We went to Fallenmouth to get answers, but we found squat to explain it."

I shrug. Honestly, what else can I do in response to her question? I have no answers.

"Need to study the books more," I say. "The answers must be in there somewhere."

Erin squints at me. "Thought you needed Sefton's notes to solve the mystery. That's why we went to Fallenmouth."

"I hoped we would find Sefton's notes there. We didn't, so I have to make do with what I've got."

When I start to head for my tent, Dax claps a hand on my shoulder to stop me. I glance at him. "Did you need something else?"

"Yes. Allison has requested that you greet our newest arrival. She swears you are the best at 'meeting and greeting and schmoozing.' I defer to the woman I love on these matters."

"Sure, I can do that. Where is the newcomer?"

"Over there." He gestures toward the area in the middle of the camp, where we all have our tents set up in a circle around the perimeter. "His name is Roger Thompson. Willow is currently entertaining him."

That's Dax's way of telling me I need to rescue the poor guy before Willow scares him away with her teenage enthusiasm. I can see she and Roger are sitting on the logs that serve as benches positioned in a circle around where we often have bonfires.

"Allison is taking a nap," Dax tells me. "You know how I am with newcomers. Willow enjoys reminding me that I 'bite the big one' when it comes to making people feel welcome."

"No problem. I can handle it."

I trot over there and sit down beside Willow—between her and the new guy. He slumps on the log next to ours. I hold out my hand to him. "I'm

Grant Larson. Welcome to Sanctuary, Mr. Thompson. Mind if I call you Roger?"

"No, I don't mind." He shakes my hand. "It's nice to meet you too."

Despite his words, he sounds confused and looks that way too. Maybe it's more like fear mixed with confusion. That's a common reaction when a person stumbles onto Sanctuary without having any idea how they found it.

"Where are we?" Roger asks as he glances around. "I have no idea how far I traveled."

"This is the Lost Coast, which used to be in Humboldt County in Northern California." I wave toward the woods. "The beach is just over the hill there. Did you come from that way?"

"Yes. I hitched a ride on a boat with some people, but they turned out to be not very nice. That's when I struck out on my own and somehow ended up here."

"How long did your journey take?"

Roger shrugs one shoulder. "Not sure. Don't have a watch or a calendar. But I think it was at least a month."

He does look kind of thin and bedraggled, though not as bad off as some people who find Sanctuary. In the wider world, lots of horrific things happen. That's why we guard our enclave. Everyone takes turns patrolling the beach and the woods.

"We're glad you found us," I say. "This is a community of good people who want to make a better life post-apocalypse."

"Thank you for letting me join your community. I can't tell you what a relief it is to find a place like this."

He fingers the gold band on his left hand.

I nod toward his hand. "You're married?"

"Yes." He bows his head and starts twisting the ring around and around. "No idea what happened to my wife. We'd only been married for two months when the apocalypse hit. On the day that happened, she was in Tacoma visiting her sister, who just had a baby. I've been trying to get there, so I can look for her, but... no luck."

Though I want to tell him we have a way he can get there, I shouldn't blurt that out yet. I need to confer with Dax and Allison first. This guy seems nice, but appearances can be deceiving. Instead of sharing our special mode of transportation, I give him our standard newcomer offer.

"We don't have a tent available for you," I say. "But we can find someone who will share theirs. Are you okay with that? Or you could grab a sleeping bag and camp out."

"Sharing a tent is fine. I'd rather not camp out." He looks up at the sky and hunches his shoulders. "I've seen those things that can fly. They tried to get me a couple of times."

"I'll find you a good roommate, don't worry. And we patrol the area day and night just in case any Echo fliers try to penetrate Sanctuary."

"Echo fliers? I guess that's as good a name for them as anything."

I stand up. "Let's find you a roomie. But maybe we should get you some food first. Are you hungry?"

"Starved."

For the rest of the afternoon, I help Roger get settled in and make sure he eats a good meal. Lunch was over long before Erin and I got back from Fallenmouth, but she actually volunteers to scrounge up food for the newest resident in Sanctuary. She surprises me even more when she volunteers to hang out with Roger until his new roommate comes back from his turn patrolling the beach. She smiles and laughs too, telling him jokes to help him relax.

Maybe she's not a heartless bitch, and maybe her recklessness has a reason. But I will never become friends with Erin Harding.

She throws her head back to laugh at something Roger said. He smiles in response, but I'm not really looking at him. My focus gravitates to Erin. The column of her throat. Those pink lips. Her long raven hair fanning out around her face. The long locks draw my gaze down to her chest and the mounds of her breasts hidden beneath her shirt, though not hidden enough. I can imagine what her tits look like naked, can picture it in detail far more vividly than my willpower can stand. This always happens to me when I catch her behaving like a normal person. I start to see her as a woman, not just a tough chick, and that realization makes my dick twitch and my hands curl into fists. Fighting my lust for her only makes the problem worse. But I cannot, will not, ever have sex with her. She's a loose cannon, and I'm hung up on the wife I lost.

Erin will never know how much I want her. Never.

CHAPTER SIX

Erin

I LEARNED SOMETHING NEW TODAY. GRANT ISN'T AS ZEN ABOUT life after the apocalypse as he wants everyone to think. He loses sleep and forgets to eat because he's become obsessed with finding a way to save the world. I can't deny he knows how to make strangers feel welcome when they stumble onto Sanctuary. He didn't ask Roger many questions, but I've noticed he and our leaders, Allison and Dax, always wait awhile before they gently prod someone for details.

At sunset, we all gather wood to start a bonfire. Why? Because it makes us feel less like a colony of outcasts from the apocalypse and more like a family. Everybody needs that, now more than ever, considering what the sky did today. Anxiety levels run higher in our community now. No surprise. We worry the alchemy of worlds might start up again, though Grant seems sure it won't.

I share a log bench with Roger and his new roommate, Patrick. I know Patrick, though I haven't gotten close to anyone since I came here. It's hard to feel comfortable sharing my innermost thoughts and feelings with another person, but I'd had that problem before the Echo ravaged our world. Still, I try to make more of an effort for our newest member, but only in part because I hope Grant will see it and stop treating me like his enemy.

Why do I care what he thinks?

Though we all ate dinner earlier, everyone agrees it would be fun to toast marshmallows while stargazing. I saw Grant eating food at dinnertime, so at least the moron isn't starving himself, at least for the moment. Maybe I should've told Allison or Dax or someone that Grant has a tendency not to eat or sleep lately, but I feel weird about doing that. If I keep an eye on him, it won't happen again. Great. Now I've appointed myself guardian of a man who dislikes me as much as I dislike him.

Somebody has to do it.

Patrick and Roger wander off to chat with other people, leaving me alone on my log bench.

A hand thrusts a stick in front of my face, though I can't see the person that hand belongs to since they're standing behind me. "Try a marshmallow."

The sound of Grant's voice makes me twist around to look at him. "What are you doing?"

"Bringing you a toasted marshmallow. Call it a peace offering."

"Uh, thanks."

I accept the stick—just a twig, really—and face the fire again. I've been sitting at the furthest edge of the bonfire, a short distance from everyone else. Yeah, okay, I still suck at socializing. Not because I have no idea how to talk to people. I just don't feel comfortable here yet. It's been slightly more than a month since I found Sanctuary, if I've counted right with no calendar to guide me, but I haven't settled in here.

Grant sits down beside me on the log. "Have you eaten toasted marshmallows before?"

"Of course I have."

"I only asked because you're staring at the marshmallow like it might come to life and eat you."

"You're the one who has food issues."

The corner of his mouth kicks up. "Yeah. Thanks for taking care of me while I was unconscious."

"No problem. If I let you die, Allison would clobber me."

"Glad you saved her from needing to do that. Might not have been good for the baby." He watches me nibble on the warm, gooey marshmallow. "You gave me water while I was asleep."

"Yeah."

"Thank you for that too."

"Um, you're welcome." I take another bite of the marshmallow. "Mm, this is really good."

"Everything tastes better post-apocalypse."

"MREs still taste like shit."

He smiles. "Yeah, they do."

Grant looks surprisingly good when he smiles. Well, he's always attractive. But I've never seen him looking happy before. That smile lights up his face, and the bonfire casts a glimmer on his eyes and his hair, making him seem less like the jerk who snaps at me and more like a normal person. Everyone here loves him. Maybe I just haven't seen what they do until right now.

My life would be a lot easier if we could be friends.

"Enjoy your marshmallow," Grant says. Then he heaves himself off the log and saunters over to Allison and Willow.

What the… Did he just stop by to give me a marshmallow? That's weird. I assumed he'd want to talk about our trip to Fallenmouth, but instead he walked away. I will never understand that man.

For some reason, talking to Grant made me want to socialize with my fellow Sanctuary inhabitants. I start up conversations with several people until everybody gets tired and wants to go to bed. I hang around by the fire for a little longer, by myself, and watch the glowing coals. The first night shift is still guarding the camp, so they'll keep an eye on the fire too until it dwindles and eventually dies.

After a few minutes, I give up on staring at the coals and head for my tent on the outskirts of the camp. I pass by Grant's tent on my way there. A light burns inside. Grant is still awake. I wonder if he'll have trouble sleeping again tonight, and then I wonder why I should care. Well, I seem to have become his regular partner on trips into the wider world, so maybe I should care if the guy sleeps. His insomnia might jeopardize both our lives—and the life of anyone else who goes with us on our supply missions.

Damn. That means I need to talk to Grant.

Tents don't have doors, just a flap for an opening. But by the time I arrived in Sanctuary, they had already developed an etiquette for how to let someone know you want to enter their tent. We have doorbells. Yep, every tent features a small clump of jingle bells tied onto the canvas to the left of the flap. I have no idea where they found those bells, since I wasn't here then, but it was a clever idea.

I jingle the bells.

"Come in," Grant says.

Pushing the flap aside, I walk into the tent.

Grant lies sprawled on his cot, shirtless, his muscular torso gilded by the light from an oil lantern.

Holy shit, he's hot.

No, no, no. I am not attracted to him. Noticing his body is…a reflex or whatever.

"Did you want something?" he asks. "Or did you just miss me?"

He can't be flirting with me. That would be too weird. So what if I'm kind of staring at his bare chest? It means nothing. I might've taken off my denim shirt, leaving me with only a tank top to cover my upper body. But he can't be speaking in a sexier voice because he's attracted to me.

"I'm checking to make sure you're okay," I tell him. "You did pass out earlier today. And you said you haven't been sleeping, so I thought maybe I could help you relax."

He sits up, swinging his feet off the cot. "Help me how?"

Good question. How had I intended to relax him? By singing a lullaby? "I could read you a story. That always worked for me when I was a kid. My mom would read to me."

"Don't think we have any bedtime storybooks in this camp."

"I could probably remember one." *Stop yammering about bedtime stories, woman.* "Well, I guess this was a bad idea. I'll leave you alone."

Just as I turn to leave, Grant says, "Have a drink with me."

"What?" I turn back to him. That's when I notice a bottle of amber liquid sitting on the ground near his feet. "Is that bourbon?"

"Yeah." He pats the cot. "Sit down and have some."

"Where did you get booze?"

"On a mission a while back, before you showed up. I kept it in case of emergency."

"What's the emergency tonight?"

He picks up the bottle and unscrews the cap. "Can't sleep. Finally decided to try the Jack Daniels method for getting a good night's rest."

I amble over there and sit down beside him. "Getting drunk won't help. You'll wake up with a hangover."

"True. But I wasn't planning to get drunk."

He takes a swig from the bottle and sighs with satisfaction. Then he offers me the bottle.

What the hell. I grab it and take a swig. The bourbon burns down my throat, but then a delicious warmth spreads through me. Yeah, Grant's method is a good way to relax. So I toss back another mouthful. Mm, yeah, warm and cozy.

He takes the bottle and drinks more bourbon. "You're good with people, especially Willow. I didn't expect that."

"Because I'm a crazy person you got saddled with on supply missions."

"No. Because you take unnecessary risks."

I snatch the bottle from him and swig more bourbon. "I take risks because nobody else wants to. Maybe offing a few Echo creatures won't save the world, but it's a start."

"You could get yourself killed that way."

"Why do you care?"

He reclaims the bottle and gulps down a mouthful. "I have to care. Your recklessness could get someone else killed."

"I've saved lives."

"Yeah, I know." He sets the bottle on the floor and turns toward me. "Maybe I don't want you to die in the process."

"Like you care what happens to me."

He leans closer, his body inches away and his gaze boring into mine. "I do care."

Maybe it's the booze affecting me, but I suddenly feel warm in a very different way that has nothing to do with alcohol. I can't stop my gaze from traveling down to his chest and all those muscles. How does he stay in shape post-apocalypse? I haven't seen any workout equipment here. But damn, whatever he does to maintain those muscles, it works.

When I lift my gaze to his again, his pupils have dilated. He licks his lips while staring into my eyes. "Maybe we'd get along better on missions if we blew off some steam together."

Blow off steam? Yeah, the rough tone of his voice made it clear he's suggesting sex. But no, Grant wouldn't do that. He despises me.

My nipples have hardened, and slickness gathers between my thighs. Maybe we should have sex. It won't make me fall instantly in love with him, and we'll probably hate each other again in the morning. I glance at his chest again. To feel all those muscles flexing against me while he thrusts inside me...

"I want to kiss you," he murmurs. "Right now."

The bourbon has made me feel so deliciously warm and relaxed. I bet his lips are soft. When he slants even closer, his mouth brushes mine, and I realize I'd been right about those lips. His breaths whisper over my skin, and his blue eyes transfix me.

I haul him into me, crushing my mouth to his.

Grant wraps his arms around me just as he pushes his tongue between my lips. We both groan. I wriggle to get my arms around his neck while I glide my tongue around his and he devours me like I'm that bottle of bourbon and he wants to get drunk on the taste of me. God, this man knows how to kiss. He lays me down on the cot, his body covering mine, and I feel his erection mashed to my belly.

The bells jingle.

We keep kissing and start groping each other.

And the bells jingle again. "Grant, are you awake?"

He freezes. We both open our eyes while we still have our tongues in each other's mouths. Then Grant leaps off the cot and hurries to the entrance, pulling the flap back just enough to speak to whoever is out there.

"Oh hey, Allison," he says with a nervous little laugh. "What's up? Thought you'd be asleep already."

"I was. Then I got nauseous, but I realized I'd run out of that herbal tea you found for me. Do you have any?"

"Sure. Just a sec." Grant lets the flap fall shut as he races to a box in the corner. After rifling through its contents, he brings out a small cardboard box of tea. Then he rushes back to the flap to hand it to Allison. "Here you go."

"Thanks. Do have a friend in there with you?"

"No. Just me."

"Uh-huh," she says, like she doesn't buy his story for one second. "Well, I'll see you in the morning."

"Good night, Ally."

He closes the flap almost all the way, but leaves enough of a gap that he can peek out. After a moment, he returns to the cot, towering over me. "Better go to your tent and get some sleep."

Grant skims his gaze over me from head to toe, and his tongue darts out to wet his lips. Then he moves aside, waving for me to leave.

I want to tell him I don't appreciate being groped and kissed and then ordered to leave, but there's no point. I can tell he's in stoic mode again, which he seems to reserve only for me. I jump off the cot, straighten my shirt, and walk out.

What just happened? No idea, but it will never happen again.

CHAPTER SEVEN

Grant

I MANAGED TO SLEEP LAST NIGHT, THANKS TO THE BOURBON, BUT I endured long and erotic dreams about Erin. I might enjoy that if I didn't know the woman is reckless and destined to get somebody killed—herself or an innocent person, maybe both. No idea why I kissed her. It must've been the alcohol. Okay, maybe I enjoyed kissing her, and maybe I wanted to fuck her right there on my cot.

Thank goodness Allison showed up.

So sure, I slept last night. But only after waiting half an hour for my erection to go away. Of course, I woke up with another one, but that's a normal thing that happens every morning. It has nothing to do with Erin. I'm attracted to her, and I hate myself for feeling that way. That's why I've decided to blame the booze and forget about it.

Problem solved.

Yeah, I'm highly skilled at self-deception.

When I head out to the main area where we always gather for meals, I don't see Erin. Willow tells me she went down to the beach. The teenager also offers me food and won't leave me alone until I eat something. Since I don't think Erin would've told anyone about my forgetfulness when it comes to meals, I decide Willow just wants to be helpful. I appease her by eating a breakfast burrito. Yeah, somebody found tortillas during a recent supply mission. Beans, rice, and salsa taste better than ever postapocalypse. Even rice cakes taste better, though I don't have any of those for breakfast.

After eating, I tell Willow I'm going to find Erin so we can discuss our next mission. The girl wants to go with me, but I convince her that she should stay with Allison. A pregnant woman needs company. Yes, I actually spoke those words to Willow. Maybe my IQ dropped overnight thanks to the bourbon.

Finally, I leave the camp and head through the woods on my own. We've all worn down a path by walking over the mountain so many times to get to the beach. Salt water isn't ideal for bathing, but we also found a natural spring. And yeah, we've worn down a trail to that too. Right now, I'm headed for the beach to find out what Erin is up to down there. Fishing? I doubt that.

I shouldn't care what she's doing. I'm not her keeper.

Just as I crest the mountain, I notice a lone figure on the beach. That must be Erin. I'm too far away to recognize her, but I don't see anyone else.

While I hike down the hill and onto the beach, I get closer to the person on the beach and see I was right. That is Erin. She had been standing on the sand gazing toward the ocean, but now she crouches to untie her shoes. While I amble toward her, she removes her shoes and socks, then takes off her shirt and pants.

I freeze. She can't be about to… No, Erin wouldn't take off her bra and panties.

But then she does.

Erin drops her underwear on the pile of clothes she made on the sand. Though she hasn't noticed me, I get a clear view of her body from the side.

I can't move anything except my eyes, which insist on following her as she wades into the surf and finally jumps into the deeper water just offshore. I clench my fists, struggling to stave off the lust that threatens to seize control of me. I've never experienced such intense desire before. It's wrong and weird.

Last night, it hadn't felt wrong or weird. Kissing Erin had made me feel something I haven't allowed myself to experience in months, not since I lost the love of my life to the apocalypse. No, I can't want Erin. Adele was the only woman I ever loved and the only one I ever wanted. To lust for someone else must be adultery.

Erin dives under the water, then springs up out of the waves with her eyes closed and a rapturous smile curving her lips. She stands amid the swells, visible from the waist up, and brushes her wet hair back with both hands.

Fuck, I'm getting hard.

I long to go over there and pull her into my arms to kiss her right before I drag her onto the beach and lose myself inside her body. I grind my teeth, breathing so hard my ears start to ring.

What else can I do? I spin around and stomp back toward the mountain path.

"Grant?" Erin hollers. "Is that you?"

I don't stop and do not look back. She calls out again, but I walk faster and disappear into the trees before she can run over here to stop me. I maintain my breakneck pace until I crest the hill and start down the mountain's rear flank. Then I slow just enough to keep from getting overheated. But yeah, seeing Erin naked has ensured I will feel overheated for quite a while. Thankfully, by the time I get back to Sanctuary my lust has faded.

Still, I march past everyone I come across in the camp, even Willow and Allison, without speaking or acknowledging I notice them. I glare down at the ground instead. Back inside my tent, I drop onto the cot and rest my elbows on my knees so I can cover my face with my raised palms.

The doorbell jingles.

"Go away," I snarl. "Wanna be alone right now."

"It's Allison. Are you okay, Grant?"

"Fine, yeah. Just need to…take a nap."

"Um, you just woke up two hours ago."

Shit. Of course I did. And I'm not at all tired. But I need to be alone right now, and I don't want to insult Allison by lying. I have no choice, though. If I tell her the truth, she'll want to play matchmaker or something. I love Ally like a sister, but I do not want to get involved with any woman ever again.

That means I have to lie. "I want to study the alchemical manuscripts for a while. Need peace and quiet for that."

"Oh. Sure thing, Grant. I'll let everybody know you're in monk mode."

I hear her footsteps recede.

Monk mode? I guess she means because monks holed up alone in their monasteries to create books. But they didn't make these manuscripts. I'm celibate, so that kind of makes me seem like a monk.

A memory of Erin's nude body blasts through my mind.

"Shit," I grumble. Then I grab the bottle of bourbon. But no, that won't make me feel better. I set the bottle down. "Shit, shit, shit."

I need to calm down and forget about that woman. The best way I know how to do that is with meditation. I get down on the floor, seated cross-legged, and rest my hands on my knees. Then I close my eyes, take a deep breath, and exhale it slowly. Starting from the top—literally, since I begin with the crown of my head—I let all other thoughts go and focus on feeling my skin without moving a muscle. I picture my scalp, ears, nose, and eyelids while sinking into the experience of feeling each of them.

The rest of the world fades from my perception.

I envision the rest of my body in the same manner as I let my psyche travel across my cheeks and lips, down my throat and over my shoulders. I sense every inch of my skin, and my breaths have become slow and regular, whispering through me on a level much deeper than sound or touch. A soft, warm sensation begins in my chest as I let my awareness glide ever downward. That warmth spreads throughout my body as I feel a soothing weight settle onto me. And my lips curve into a slight smile, relaxing the muscles there.

At last, I've reached a state of total relaxation, floating on a sea of warm, tingly contentment.

Bells jingle, but I barely notice the sound. It drifts out of my consciousness a split second later.

The bells jingle again. "Grant? Are you in there?"

My quiet bubble pops, and all the noise of the world rushes back into my awareness. *Aw, shit.* Why can't that woman leave me alone? "Go away, Erin. I'm busy."

"I think we need to talk. About what happened on the beach."

"Nothing happened."

She lifts the flap on my tent to peer in at me. When she notices me sitting on the floor with my hands on my knees, her brows knit together. "What are you doing?"

"I was meditating." With a groan, I push myself up off the ground. "Until you shattered my Zen moment."

"You actually meditate."

"No, I sit here pretending to meditate as a joke to make myself laugh when I'm all alone in my tent."

She steps inside, and the flap falls back down. "I'm serious, Grant. We need to talk about—"

"Wrong. We don't need to talk about anything." I glance down at the bottle of bourbon. Yeah, I'd really love to guzzle the entire contents right now. Erin drives me to drink. "You were being reckless again, end of story."

"Reckless? I took a bath in the ocean."

"Nobody bathes in saltwater."

"I do." She stalks up to me and plants her hands on her hips. "How can someone who meditates be so uptight?"

"Go away, Erin."

"No. I want to know why you were secretly watching me bathe in the nude."

I huff. "Nothing secret about it. I went down to the beach and stumbled onto you acting like a brainless bimbo. I turned around and left as soon as I saw you."

"Bullshit. You stood there gawking at me."

Maybe I had. Even a man who practices meditation has a weak moment now and then. I saw a naked woman and needed a minute to recover from the shock.

Erin moves a little closer. "Did you like what you saw?"

"Anything I think or feel is irrelevant and none of your business."

She opens her mouth—to chew me out some more, no doubt—but the jingling of my doorbell stops her.

"Who is it?" I call out, sounding grumpier than I would've liked.

"Allison. Everyone can hear you two arguing in there. Might want to dial it back a little."

"Sorry. We'll try to keep it down."

"I'd rather you didn't argue. Should I come in there and help you guys talk through your issues?"

"No, we can handle it ourselves. Thanks, Ally."

I hear Allison walking away.

Erin is still staring at me, but now with her chin lifted and her arms crossed. "How are we going to 'handle it' when you won't discuss the 'issues'?"

"You leave, that's how."

She puckers her lips and jabs a finger into my chest. "I will not leave until we talk about—"

An explosion detonates above our heads, the ka-pow sending palpable shock waves through the air that flutter the tent and rattle my eardrums.

Erin and I race outside and halt so fast that I stumble into her.

Above our heads, a black disk spins in the sky while streamers of blood red snake out from it, whipping around like the tails of demonic serpents. A crackling noise erupts in the wake of the explosion, and static electricity tingles over my skin, raising every hair.

"What is that?" Erin asks, her voice hushed.

"No idea. We need to find Dax and Ally."

I seize Erin's arm and drag her with me as I sprint through the camp to Dax and Allison's tent. I don't need to ring the bell. They're already standing outside with their heads tipped back, staring at the heavens.

A mechanical grinding noise originates from the sky and reverberates all the way down to ground level. The earth begins to shudder. I instinctively throw an arm around Erin just as Dax pulls Allison against him. What can we do? Nothing, except gaze in rapt horror as the entrance to the Echo opens wider and wider, grinding along at a snail's pace, accompanied by that earsplitting mechanical noise.

Everyone in Sanctuary has rushed outside to do the same thing—gape at the heavens.

Suddenly, the expanding radius of the Echo freezes.

A silence deeper than anything I've ever experienced falls over the world. No one moves. No one speaks. I'm pretty sure not a single one of us breathes either. The only sound I can hear is the pounding of my own heart.

The entrance to the Echo slams shut with a thunderous racket that shivers through the ground.

I glance at Erin and realize I've been clutching her to me. She doesn't seem to care. Her wide eyes remain glued to the sky, and her face has turned a shade or two paler.

"What the hell is going on in the Echo?" I ask, though I don't expect anyone to respond.

Dax does. "This is an omen. The Echo is struggling to reassert itself and expand to swallow the world."

"Let's not go all 'oh shit, we're about to die' just yet," I say. "The only thing we know for sure is that the Echo is having conniptions."

"Perhaps. But until yesterday, the entrance to the Echo could only be seen from the cities and some of the small towns."

"A few rural areas have seen it."

"But the entrance vanished from those places shortly after the alchemy of worlds ended."

"True." Dax hugs Allison more tightly, though his attention stays focused on the sky. "We need to figure out why this is happening. If the Echo has become volatile and unstable…"

"I have an idea for how to get answers."

Dax, Allison, and Erin swivel their heads toward me at the same time, though Erin does that while still nestled against me.

"What idea?" Allison asks. "I thought you didn't find anything at Fallenmouth."

"That's true. But I came up with this idea while I was meditating this morning." Right before Erin ripped my Zen serenity to shreds. But I won't mention that to Ally. "My plan is radical and crazy dangerous, but I think it's our only option for getting answers."

"What's your idea?" Erin asks. "You're the expert on the alchemy of worlds, which means it's your call."

I look at her, surprised by the sincerity in her voice and her expression. Maybe I like having her tucked against me with the warmth of her body chasing away the chill that had shivered through me while the Echo expanded overhead. Maybe I shouldn't like it, but I do.

"Here's my plan," I say. "We go inside the Echo."

CHAPTER EIGHT

Erin

"GO INSIDE?" I STARE AT GRANT, BECAUSE HE MUST HAVE GONE IN-sane. The Echo is a hell world populated by, as Dax phrases it, desecrations of the human form. Every creature living in that world was created as a twisted copy of someone in this world. "Dax barely survived the Echo. Now you want to jump in there just for the hell of it?"

"Not for the hell of it." Grant squeezes words out between his gritted teeth. "We need to get into the Echo so we can find answers. I still believe Sefton kept notes on his plan to create another world and an apocalypse, and he must've left those notes in the Echo. Otherwise, we would've found something at Fallenmouth."

"The house had been destroyed. Sefton's notes probably got burned up."

"I don't think so. But Dax knows more about Sefton than I do."

Dax lifts his brows. "Do I? My brother changed, and I didn't realize it until he created an apocalypse. Not sure my opinions will be helpful. The only thing I can tell you for certain is that Sefton was very clever and completely insane."

"True," Grant says. "But a smart guy would want to keep his most important notes in a place where no one would ever think to look for them. Got any ideas?"

"No."

"Then it's my plan or bust."

Are we seriously talking about going into the Echo? Into hell? The creatures that live there are wickedly strong and vicious. We've gotten a taste of their power and brutality during our supply missions, but we only see a handful of creatures at one time. A world full of them...

I push away from Grant, even though I kind of liked feeling his body plastered to mine. "Your idea is reckless. Wouldn't you say?"

"Yeah. But that doesn't mean we have to go about it in kamikaze fashion. We can come up with a game plan."

"Oh, I get it. My recklessness is dangerous, but yours is mature and thoughtful."

"Exactly."

I want to deck him. Or possibly rip his clothes off. *Ugh.* I wish we hadn't made out last night in his tent because that experience has knocked me off balance. Never again will I kiss Grant Larson or let him kiss me, and we will absolutely never have sex. He's too infuriating.

"No one is going into the Echo," Dax pronounces. "We will find another way to get answers."

"We don't have time for that," Grant says. "Two days in a row, the Echo had a conniption. And it was worse today."

"He's right," I say. "We can't wait. Grant and I need to go into the Echo today."

Grant raises his brows at me. "You're volunteering us both? Could've asked me first."

"We both know you want to do this. I'm volunteering. You can't volunteer for your own plan."

"This is a bad idea," Allison says. "Time moves differently in the Echo. You might get trapped in there for years while only a few days have passed in this world."

"That might not happen this time," I say. "Things have changed. The alchemy of worlds has stopped, and the Echo has clearly been altered because of that."

Grant nods. "She's right. But even if we wind up living in the Echo for years, it will be worth it to save the world."

"If you can save it," Allison says.

"We can. We will."

The intensity in his voice almost convinces me that we can save the world.

Dax exhales a long sigh. "All right. But you should take more volunteers with you."

"No," Grant says. "Just me and Erin. I won't risk anyone else's life. We both have military training and saw combat before the apocalypse."

Just the two of us? In the Echo? Yeah, I'm not ashamed to admit the idea terrifies me. But I've lived in a war zone before, and I can handle it again. I must do this.

"If you're determined to do this," Dax tells us, "you'll need to start your journey at the epicenter of the apocalypse. You need to go to Fort Worth, Texas."

Grant's lips curve into a grim smile. "Well, at least we've got somebody who can teleport us there."

"Once you're inside the Echo, no one can bring you back. You'll need to find your own way out."

"We'll manage."

How can he sound so positive of that? Neither of us has ever been to that world before.

"Even if you escape the Echo," Dax tells Grant, "we won't have any way to know when I should bring you back to Sanctuary."

"When we leave the Echo, we'll wait at the library. You can try to bring us back every day at noon. Agreed?"

"Yes." Dax makes a pained face. "I should go with you, but…"

"Ally needs you more than we do," Grant says. "I know that, and nobody expects you to take an insane risk like this. Besides, you're the best defense this community has."

"When would you like to go?"

"As soon as we can gather supplies."

Grant and I spend the next hour scrounging up whatever supplies we can reasonably carry in our backpacks. I never use a backpack, but Grant found one for me after he declared that I must have it. We can't carry everything we might need with us. Once we breach the Echo, we will need to find more supplies on our own.

I've experienced real war, and I know fear is a necessary and reasonable reaction to a situation like this. The key to survival is not letting the fear hold you back. Not that a war in the mundane world can compare to what the apocalypse has done or what might await us inside the Echo.

We run into Willow during our search for supplies, and she already knows what we plan to do. Allison and Dax had felt that everyone should know. Though we do keep some secrets from the others, this is one instance where we all agreed we should inform the community. If Grant and I fail, the Echo might swallow our world.

"Please don't go," Willow says as she hugs me. "I love you guys."

"We love you too, baby," I say while I stroke her hair. "And we're coming back. Don't worry. We've got a solid plan."

Grant lifts his brows. Yeah, maybe I shouldn't have essentially promised we will come back. But I can't let Willow spend who knows how long worrying we might never make it home.

Now that we have our supplies, Grant and I find Dax. The three of us tromp out to the edge of the camp, away from any other people.

It's time to go.

Allison rushes up to us, breathing hard as if she ran all the way here from the other side of the camp. She thrusts a canvas bag at Grant. "You forgot the books."

He accepts the bag, gripping it in one hand. "Thanks, Ally."

"Good luck." Allison hugs Grant and kisses his cheek, then hugs me too. "Be careful."

She walks away.

Once Allison has disappeared from view, Dax faces us. "It's time."

Grant and I take a few steps backward.

Dax clenches his fists and grits his teeth, his eyes narrowed to slits.

Whoosh. The world shifts around us in the space of a single heartbeat.

I glance around and try to get my bearings. We've landed in a city, I can tell that much for sure. "Is this Fort Worth? I've never been here before."

"Yeah, it's Fort Worth." Grant surveys the building directly in front of us. "I'd been here a few times on supply missions, before you showed up at Sanctuary. This is the public library."

The building once had tall columns that supported a portico. I know that because I see the columns, though they've been shattered, and the roof of the portico has collapsed on top of them. The remains have spilled down the steps and onto the street.

"Last time I was here," Grant says, "only the front pillars had been broken. Not sure what happened since then to cause more damage."

"If this is the epicenter of the apocalypse, then what happened earlier might have been much worse here and destroyed the rest of the portico."

"Yeah, you could be right." He removes his backpack to stuff the bag full of books inside it. At least, he tries to do that. The bag won't fit. "You got any room in your pack?"

"Maybe. Let me try." I slip out of my backpack and rummage inside it to make room for the books. "I can probably fit some of the books, but not all of them."

"For now, I'll just tie the bag onto my pack. Might find a better way to carry them as we make our way through the city."

"We're going into the Echo, not exploring Fort Worth."

"But we have to walk to the epicenter. It's thataway." He gestures vaguely behind and to the right of the library building. "Let's get moving."

I have no choice but to follow him since I know nothing about this city, before or after the apocalypse. When I'd caught him meditating in his tent earlier, the peaceful look on his face made me wonder why he never looks that way when we're together. I peeked into the tent before I rang the bells, mostly because I wasn't sure if he was in there. Okay, it might've partly been that, but mostly it was my nosiness. I wanted to snoop, just a little, to peek at those alchemy books. But he had been there, and I saw his blissful expression.

Have I ever felt that way? Don't think so. Maybe I need to meditate.

As we hike through the ruined city, I have nothing to do but ask questions. "Weren't you a deputy sheriff before the apocalypse?"

"Yes."

"And in the army before that?"

"Why are you interrogating me about things everybody knows? I should get to interrogate you too. What did you do for a living back then?"

"I owned a little sporting goods store." I stumble over a piece of rubble but catch myself, so I don't fall. "I thought we could get to know each other while we're trudging through the remnants of doomsday. We're about to go inside the Echo. Before we do that, we need to trust each other."

"We've been traveling into exclusion zones together for more than a month. Now you suddenly need to hug it out so we can forge a wartime bond?"

"Don't get sarcastic about it. I'm serious. You don't trust me, and that's a problem."

He stops walking and turns to look at me. "You don't trust me either. Why else would you take off on your own during every single mission we go on together?"

"You always need to be the big man, the hero, the only one who knows how to kill an Echo creature by driving a sword straight into its heart." I grip the straps of my backpack and gaze straight into his eyes. "Have you ever showed anyone else how to do that?"

He screws up his mouth and shifts his weight from one foot to the other. "No."

"Why not?"

"Because it's hard to do, and if you miss the exact center… Well, let's just say you won't be home for dinner that night."

"What does that mean? Did someone get killed on one of your previous missions because they tried to skewer a creature?"

He turns his head to stare at the huge black disk in the sky that is the entrance to the Echo. "Nobody died doing that. Nobody else almost died either."

I'm about to say something when I suddenly realize what he said. "Nobody *else*? Did you almost die trying to kill a creature that way?"

Grant bows his head and sighs. "Yeah."

"Were you alone when that happened?"

He winces and still won't look at me. "I made a stupid mistake. I let a creature lure me away from my team. Once he had me alone, he went for me. I tried to pierce the center of his heart, but he parried at the last second, and I missed. He kicked me in the chest so hard I couldn't breathe, and the cutlass fell out of my hand. Luckily, Dax came looking for me and killed the creature before it could kill me."

"Did he stab its heart?"

"No. He beheaded the creature."

I tip my head to the side while I study him. "You've always told me that the only surefire way to kill an Echo creature is to pierce its heart."

"That's true. The creatures seem to have a slightly different anatomy than humans, and their hearts are the weakest points. I learned that the hard way. Beheading a creature in the heat of battle is damn hard work." He lifts his head. "Trust me. I've done it before."

"I've heard Dax mention that their spines are much harder than the human version, almost like stone."

"Some of them have spines like that. We got lucky early in the apocalypse and fought creatures that had weaker cervical vertebrae. That's how we managed to behead them." He rubs his neck and winces again. "Another lesson we learned the hard way, before you found Sanctuary."

I want to ask him if someone died because no one understood the anatomy of Echo creatures or if not all creatures have identical bone structure. But I've quizzed him enough for now. "Thank you for answering my questions, Grant."

His eyes go wide, but only for a second. "Uh, you're welcome."

"You can ask me questions too."

"We should get moving again."

No, I won't get any other information from him until he decides to tell me.

Chapter Nine

Grant

I LEAD THE WAY AS WE START OFF DOWN THE WRECKED STREET AGAIN, and I avoid looking at Erin, even peripherally. She wants to understand me, I guess, but she shouldn't care about that. I've given her no reason to want to know me better. But after wending our way through the rubble for three more blocks, I realize I should give her what she wants—information about me—whether I feel comfortable telling her or not. "There are a few things you should know."

"Like what?"

I feel my expression tighten, and I'm pretty sure I wear a grimly determined look. Can't be Zen when I'm about to share the details of the worst moments in my life. But I keep my gaze riveted to the road ahead while I speak. "My wife and son died in the first wave."

"I'm so sorry, Grant. What happened to them?"

"We left our son, Billy, with a babysitter while Adele and I went hiking in the mountains near our home." I halt and glare up at the Echo, but inside I feel cold and hollow. "When the apocalypse hit, we were fifty miles away from our son. We tried to get home, but the fireballs and the lightning made it almost impossible. The forest was on fire. Creatures poured out of a hole in the sky."

Erin waits for me to go on, almost as if she's giving me time to collect myself before I finish the story. The fact that I've decided to tell her doesn't mean I have feelings for Erin, not even the friendly kind. But we need to learn to trust each other, and that requires sharing personal information.

I bow my head and suck in a shaky breath. "A creature took Adele. Two of his buddies grabbed me, and I wasn't strong enough to get away from them." I squeeze my eyes shut, but nothing can ward off the memories. "I watched while those monsters…did things to my wife that I won't describe."

Erin doesn't speak. Well, at least she has a modicum of good sense.

I remember every second of what those monsters did, though I wish I didn't. Life post-apocalypse is bad, but life in the early days of the alchemy of worlds was beyond hell. "Luckily, Adele passed out pretty quick. Never felt the worst of what they'd done to her. Then they just let me go and went who knows where to do who knows what. I collapsed on the ground and sobbed."

"Oh, Grant, I… That's horrible."

"Yeah." She has no idea how horrible it was, and I will not explain it. Some things should never be spoken of again. "I managed to get back to our house, though I couldn't carry Adele's body, so I had to leave her in the woods." My throat goes thick, and I want to stop talking about that day, stop thinking about it. Instead, I pull in a deep breath, blow it out, and continue. "Our house was destroyed—by the crazy-powerful lightning, I think—but I found the remains of my son and his babysitter. After that, I fought my way out of Los Angeles County, eventually found an abandoned boat that still had fuel, and made my way north."

"That's when you ran into Dax and Willow."

I almost smile as I remember bumping into them, but the expression crumbles away as memories of Adele and Billy torment me. I marshal all my Zen training and force myself to focus on the here and now. "Yeah, that's when I met Dax and Willow. They happened to stumble onto my little campsite on the beach. The same beach where we all go to fish and swim now."

"It couldn't have been easy to relive those events, and I'm grateful you shared it with me."

She's grateful? I can't see why. When I look at her, she seems almost…sympathetic. I've never shared my whole story with anyone, not even Dax and Allison. Why did I spill my guts to Erin? "You are the only one who knows the details. Guess that means I trust you."

"Maybe we only thought we didn't trust each other because we're still recovering from our losses."

"Who did you lose?"

"My sister. Our parents died years ago." She bites her lip and gazes at me for a moment, then seems to reach a decision—to tell me her story. "We flew to New York City on vacation. Hayley had just graduated from Penn State, with honors, and I was so proud of her. The trip to New York was a graduation present. But when the apocalypse hit, we got separated. I searched and searched for her, fighting my way past Echo creatures and dodging fireballs and lightning."

"Did you find her?"

She bites her lip again, harder this time so the skin turns white. "Kept searching for two months. When I finally found Hayley's body, she had been…eaten. But her face was the least damaged, and I knew it was her. She was still wearing the little diamond earrings I'd given her for her birthday."

I experience a strong urge to hug her. But I doubt Erin would appreciate that.

"The creatures in New York had blocked every borough," she continues. "I had to find ways to break through their barricades, but I finally discovered a weak spot and escaped the city. Caught rides with people whose cars still had gas, even rode a horse for a while until somebody else needed that mare more than I did. Walked and walked and walked."

"You hiked all the way to California?"

"No. I met a woman who had an airplane. Her husband had been on a business trip to San Francisco, so she offered to let me fly there with her because she'd heard a rumor the apocalypse hadn't touched that part of the state. But we ran out of gas. Made an emergency landing in a clearing maybe ten miles from the beach where you met Dax and Willow. Kept walking until I met someone from Sanctuary."

"I wish you'd never had to go through all of that. I wish none of us had."

"Me too. Things were getting really bad in New York by the time I got out of there. I mean, the deepest level of actual hell kind of bad." Her gaze goes distant for a moment, as if she's concentrating on a memory or devising a plan. "I think New York might be the capital city of the apocalypse."

"Why would you think that?"

"The way they fortified the whole thing." A sigh gusts out of her, and she lets her shoulders sag. "Even if that's true, it doesn't help us. Does it?"

"Not sure. Right now, we need to focus on our mission." I cup her elbow with my hand while we start walking again. "We need to get inside the Echo."

We travel at a brisk pace, and soon the Paddock Viaduct comes into view. The bridge spans the West Fork of the Trinity River. I've come to this city several times with Dax and other members of our community, but never with Erin. She joined our group about a month ago, after we'd given up on scrounging for supplies here. It's too dangerous.

If the Echo creatures have a capital city, it should be Fort Worth, not New York. This was ground zero for the apocalypse, after all.

"Why haven't we seen any creatures?" Erin asks. "I thought all the cities were overrun with them."

"They are." I stop dead, mere feet from the on-ramp to the viaduct. "You're right. We should've seen some creatures."

"Does it matter that we didn't? Maybe they've killed each other off."

"I doubt that. All the creatures I've met stuck together." I turn in a circle to survey the area, but I still can't see or hear anything other than the whispering of a breeze and my own heartbeat thumping in my ears. "I don't like this."

"Neither do I."

"We don't have time to explore the city for answers." I grasp her elbow again, urging her to walk with me. "Let's get into the Echo fast."

As we step onto the bridge, we walk faster and faster until it becomes jogging, then sprinting. The entrance to the Echo hovers directly above our heads. The black disk at its center rotates like a whirlpool, and spinning serpents of black and golden yellow unfurl from its edges. A faint mechanical sound emanates from the opening.

I stop us when we reach the center of the viaduct.

"What now?" Erin asks. "How do we get inside the Echo?"

"Not sure. It's up in the sky, so we need a way to climb or jump in there."

"Climb or jump?" Erin's voice is filled with genuine disbelief, and her jaw has gone slack. "Are you insane? I don't see any way that either of us can jump into the sky high enough to climb inside the Echo."

I scratch my jaw as I gaze up at the spinning black disk above our heads.

Erin plants her hands on her hips. "You didn't have a plan at all, did you? No, you just dragged me here and... What? Hoped for a miracle?"

Maybe I had brought us here with a plan that amounts to squat. That doesn't change the fact that we must get into the Echo. *Think, moron, this was your idea. Find a way.*

Growling originates from directly behind us.

We both turn sideways to see the other end of the viaduct. Echo creatures have swarmed the on-ramp. Every sort of monster imaginable stalks across the bridge toward us. When I glance in the other direction, I notice shadowy figures approaching the off-ramp.

Aw, shit. I got us trapped on a bridge. What a fantastic job I'm doing.

I channel all my Zen energy to remain calm and seemingly unaffected by our situation. Then I wave to the creatures coming toward us. "Hey, nice to see you guys. We were getting lonely out here by ourselves. Any of you know how to jump into the Echo, by any chance?"

Erin gapes at me again like she thinks I've gone insane. Maybe I have. My cutlass is inside the scabbard attached to my backpack, and I know Erin has a sword too. We've got handguns, but those are reserved for only the most desperate situations. We don't have an unlimited supply of ammo.

The creatures jog toward us, growling and snarling and gnashing their teeth. Some sport scaly skin, others have horns and bumpy flesh, and even more display other types of weirdness. The beasts approaching from behind will reach us soon too.

"Got any brilliant ideas?" Erin asks. "You're the genius who got us into this mess."

"Shut up and let me think." Yeah, Erin always knows how to shatter my Zen energy.

"Maybe we should ask one of those nice monsters to give us a ride on his back."

"Sarcasm doesn't help."

Erin saunters toward the creatures and waves her arms in the air. "Hey, y'all! Wanna play?"

What the hell is she doing? And why is she speaking with a southern accent?

The largest and scariest-looking beast stops within ten yards of Erin, towering several feet above our heads. His long hair flies wild around his face and shoulders while yellow liquid oozes from the two horns on his forehead. "Yeah, girlie, I'd love to play with you."

"You can have me any way you want." She whips out her cutlass. "After you give me what I want."

The sultry tone of her voice has a bizarre effect on me. My dick twitches. Oh great, that's just what I need—to get an erection in front of a horde of monsters. Can't believe my dick thinks now is the right time to wake up and beg for sex. Maybe it's her fake southern accent that gets me aroused, or maybe it's something weirder and darker that I don't have time to think about right now.

Since I have no other options, I decide to play along with her game. I come up beside Erin and sling an arm around her waist. "Hey, baby, are you starting the fun without me?"

The crazy chick gives me a sexy smile. "Don't worry. I'm sure this guy would be glad to share me with you." She winks at the creature with the weeping horns. "I bet you'd like to screw us both, huh?"

"Yeah," the beast growls. "Let's do that now."

She wags a finger at him. "Uh-uh-uh. Not until you take us into the Echo. I've always wanted to fuck in a hell world."

Erin is more than a crazy chick. She's stark-raving mad.

And I'm beginning to have doubts about her so-called plan. "Erin, maybe we should—"

The weeping-horns beast flies at us, scooping us both up in his massive arms, then bends his knees and vaults into the sky.

I crane my neck to peer up at the entrance to the Echo. It zooms closer and closer while the beast holding us growls and snarls. The mechanical noise we'd heard from ground level grows louder, but it doesn't deafen us. I can still hear the monsters below making all sorts of bizarre noises.

We crash through the portal—and the creature lands flat on his feet. He does not release us.

"Great plan, Crazy Chick," I mutter under my breath.

Erin flashes me a scowl, then aims a sultry smile at the beast. "Let us go and I'll give you the best striptease you've ever seen."

The creature growls softly. "Then I fuck you."

"Uh-huh."

Amazingly, the beast releases us.

We back away quickly. Erin still has her cutlass in her hand, so I whip mine out too.

The creature chuckles. "Stupid humans. I'm stronger than you puny things."

I rush at the beast and ram my sword straight into his heart. But the tip breaks off. *Oh, shit.* "Run, Erin! Now!"

Erin seizes my hand, and we bolt.

CHAPTER TEN

Erin

WHY DID WE RUN? BECAUSE EVEN I'M NOT RECKLESS ENOUGH TO fight an Echo creature that outweighs us, is six feet taller than us, and apparently has armor plating. Jeez, who knew that might happen? Piercing a creature's heart kills it, but only if we can penetrate its skin. Now we're trapped in the Echo with who knows how many beasts that have armored bodies. Our best offensive tactic has been stolen from us.

"Got any ideas?" I ask while breathing hard because we're racing around a corner and down an alley. This place is clearly a city, but I've never seen another one like it. No time for sightseeing, though. That beast is still on our tails.

"Yeah, I've got an idea," Grant says. "Keep running."

Like I needed him to tell me that.

We race out of the alley and onto another street, this one featuring a wide roadway that could accommodate four lanes, though I don't see any lines demarcating them. I'm in the Echo, so I shouldn't expect the rules here to mirror those on earth. But the creatures in this world are twisted copies of human beings, which makes me wonder if they share more than a passing resemblance.

No time to ponder that idea.

When I glance back, that damn beast is still rushing after us with his massive feet pounding so hard that I feel tremors beneath me. I haven't seen any vehicles in this world, but I glimpse a shape up ahead that might be an SUV or a similar-size car.

Grant veers left as if he intends to turn down another street.

I grab his arm, halting us both. Though I'm gasping for breath, I manage to tell him, "Go straight. Think there's a car."

"Are you hoping a creature left his keys in it?"

"Yeah. But if not, I can hot-wire it."

His brows shoot up, but he doesn't get the chance to speak. That creature barrels toward us, and needing to stop to talk to Grant has given the monster a chance to narrow our lead.

We run.

The shape I'd noticed in the twilight gloom resolves into a familiar object—an SUV-type vehicle, though it looks quite different from the versions back home on earth. Its boxy shape has many sharp angles, almost like the exterior of a stealth fighter jet. When I yank on the handle of the passenger door, it doesn't give. Damn, the car is locked.

"Allow me," Grant says as pulls out a Beretta .9mm handgun he had kept holstered under his jacket. "Stand back."

We both move away a few yards.

Grant fires at the car window. The glass shatters.

I guess Echo creatures haven't reinvented tempered glass.

Grant reaches inside the vehicle to unlock the doors, then pulls it open and waves for me to jump in.

"I need to hot-wire this thing," I say, "so I'll drive."

"No way. You start it, then I drive."

The creature roars as he barrels toward us, only one block away now.

"Fine," I hiss.

Grant smirks as we hurry around to the driver's side. He yanks the door open, and I shrug out of my backpack, handing it to him once I've retrieved my mini toolkit from an outer pocket. I hope to hell this car isn't the kind that requires unscrewing the steering column to hot-wire it. I lean inside and find the ignition tumbler on the right side of the steering column. Still can't tell for sure. So I bring out a mini screwdriver and shove it into the tumbler, then twist it.

The engine rumbles to life.

Hallelujah. We caught a break.

"Want my due!" the creature bellows, while his footsteps pound even louder, their vibrations rattling my bones.

That beast will reach us in a matter of seconds.

I leave the screwdriver in the ignition tumbler and sprint to the passenger door while Grant leaps in on the driver's side. I've barely slammed my door shut when the vehicle launches forward like a rocket with the engine snarling.

Our big, gnarly friend throws an arm out to sideswipe our car, but he misses. His infuriated roar makes my ears hurt.

"Got any idea where we're going?" I ask. "Because I have no fucking clue."

"Neither do I. We'll wing it."

I twist around in my seat to check on our angry buddy. His figure is swiftly receding from view. Guess he can't run sixty miles an hour. Good to know.

"Thanks for getting us into hot water with your recklessness again," Grant says, his gruff tone not unlike that of the beast we just swatted off our tails. "That was really helpful."

"Hey, I just saved your sorry ass. Try being grateful."

"I said thank you."

"Sarcastically. That doesn't count."

Grant veers around a corner so fast that I get thrown against my door. "At least we're in the Echo now. But you ticked off a huge monster. What if he comes looking for us?"

"Keep driving until we get well away from where we left him."

"Glad you had a solid plan when you got us thrown into a hell world."

"Shut up and drive."

My partner in this insanity continues driving very fast and swerving around corner after corner. I search for a seatbelt, but the car doesn't seem to have those. It could stand to get some new shocks, but otherwise, it isn't half bad—for a post-apocalyptic vehicle.

"The Echo has only been around for a few months," I say. "How did the creatures make all these buildings and cars and who knows what else in such a short time?"

My partner grunts. "How do you think? Magic. For all we know, Sefton didn't just create twisted copies of humans, but also warped versions of everything else, including cars and buildings."

"Good point. I didn't think of that."

He glances at me sideways and smirks. "Did you just give me a compliment?"

"I said you made a good point. Don't read too much into that."

Grant relaxes into his seat while he slows the car a bit. "I might not agree with your methods, but you did get us here. Your crazy idea got us in."

"You can say it. I won't gloat or make fun of you."

"I can say what?"

"Do the words 'thank you' ring a bell? And this time, you could try being sincere when you say it."

He doesn't respond, but instead focuses on the road ahead.

Though I have no idea if the time on my watch corresponds in any way to the time here in the Echo, I have no other way to gauge how long we've been driving. Ten minutes go by, then fifteen, and then twenty. Finally, he pulls over at a gas station. The charred sign hangs at a sharp angle, seeming to dangle from a single nail, and the pumps look like they survived a gun battle. A giant hole gapes in the center of the roof, probably thanks to one of the Echo's ultra-powerful lightning strikes or a hit from a fireball.

Grant parks near one of the pumps.

"What are you doing?" I ask. "Kinda doubt the Echo takes Mastercard. If these pumps even work."

"Need to try. Not much left in the tank."

"But gas pumps need electricity to work."

He swings his door open and hops out, then points toward the left side of the building. "There's an emergency generator. I'll check if it's got any juice left."

"Oh. Okay." I hadn't thought of that, but I'm still not convinced it'll work.

"Stay in the car," he says. "I'll be just a minute."

I watch Grant jog over to the generator that sits on the ground near the gas station's wall. He kneels to fiddle with the thing. Soon, the generator grumbles to life. He grins at me over his shoulder and gives me the thumbs-up sign. Then Grant jogs back over here. I roll down my window, which I have to do the old-fashioned way by cranking a handle, and peer at Grant while he unscrews the fuel tank cap and slides the pump nozzle inside. When he squeezes the handle, he once again grins and gives the thumbs-up sign.

He is kind of cute when he smiles.

Okay, all right, he's completely adorable when he does that. I've seen him grin at other people, though not often. He never smiles that way at me. Until now. And I suddenly realize I'm grinning at him too.

I pull my head back into the car and face forward. Not because he caught me smiling. No, what disturbs me is the fluttery sensation in my tummy when Grant grinned.

Once he's filled up the tank, he screws the cap back on and trots into the half-destroyed gas station building. I'm just about to rush in there to make sure a creature hasn't eaten him when Grant trots back out carrying four plastic gas cans. He fills them up and stashes them in the rear cargo area of our vehicle.

Then he jumps into the driver's seat and pulls the door shut. And he smiles at me again. "Well, you might've dropped us into the deep end with no life preservers, but at least we have gas now. Enough to last awhile."

"Why are you suddenly Mr. Optimism? Five minutes ago, you were preaching doom and gloom."

"I never preach."

"But you don't deny the doom and gloom part."

He shrugs one shoulder while he twists the screwdriver to start up the engine. "Think what you want. I believe everyone should have the freedom to believe and behave as they like."

"Oh really." I turn partway toward him while he steers the car back onto the road. "Then why do you harass me about my recklessness? You are a hypocrite."

"No, I worry—Never mind. You're too pigheaded to listen, anyway."

Did he just almost admit he worries about me? Can't be sure. He didn't finish the sentence.

"Got any clue where we're going?" I ask. "You're the one who wanted to get inside the Echo, but we seem to be aimlessly exploring this city or whatever it is."

"I'm looking for a hideout."

"We came here to hide from the Echo creatures? Jeez, we could've done that in our own world."

He huffs, then snarls, "Not hiding. We need a relatively safe place to hunker down while we figure out our next move."

"And you complained that I didn't have a plan."

"Stop bitching and help me look for a hideout."

I open my mouth to issue a scathing retort, but decide against that. We're partners now, whether we like it or not, and we'll both need to make concessions if we have any chance of figuring out why the Echo is having conniptions. I stare out the window and watch for a good hideout. Grant does the same, though he also has to keep an eye on the road. We travel into an area of the city that has fewer buildings and no houses, which I take for an industrial zone. I see warehouses but also buildings that look like abandoned stores. This whole world seems abandoned, at least the parts I've seen so far.

"How about there?" I ask. I'm pointing to one of the smaller buildings that has a parking lot, though the asphalt has been reduced to rubble. "It's away from other buildings, but not conspicuously separate."

"Yeah, that looks pretty good. Let's check it out."

Grant pulls into the wrecked parking lot. Its pitted surface makes my teeth clack together, and I wind up tensing my jaw to keep from breaking my molars. He parks right beside the building's main doors. Grant pulls the screwdriver out of the ignition tumbler and hands it to me.

I stuff it into my backpack.

He climbs out, leaving his pack in the car.

Following his lead, I leave my pack too and trail after him as he pushes through the double doors and wanders into the building. Without electricity, we have no lights to guide us. But Grant pulls a flashlight out of his jacket pocket and flicks it on. The glow spreads out to illuminate a radius of maybe fifteen feet around us, with most of that area ahead of us.

We stand inside a hardware store.

Grant halts near a bin full of penny nails and turns in a circle to take in our surroundings. "Not exactly the Hilton, but we can make it work. Don't you think?"

Am I hallucinating, or did he ask for my opinion? I need a moment to process that fact before I can respond. "Sure, I guess so. Maybe they've got sleeping bags in here. You know, as part of a display."

"Let's go a little deeper and find out exactly what supplies we can find here."

We walk side by side into the bowels of the building, discovering more than just hardware supplies. Though I'd first taken this for that kind of store, I soon realize it's more like a home improvement center than a hardware store. We find a furniture department too, with a full bedroom set on display, bedding and all. Damn, I could live here. Sleeping on an actual mattress? I vaguely remember when I did that every night.

I can't resist. I flop onto the bed on my back and sigh with deep contentment. "Oh yeah, let's make a home right here."

Grant sits on the bed's edge. "We're making this our hideaway, then?"

"Sure. Might as well take comfort where we can find it." I rise to a sitting position, propped up by my straight arms, with my legs outstretched. "Doesn't it seem weird that the Echo was apparently devastated just like the earth, but it seems like it was a normal world before that?"

"Yeah, it's weird."

"What does it all mean?"

"No idea. But we're going to find out."

CHAPTER ELEVEN

Grant

I WISH ERIN HADN'T JUMPED ONTO THE BED AND SIGHED WITH ALL the satisfaction of a woman who just had amazing sex. Now that she's sitting up, I still wish she would climb off the damn bed. Something about seeing her lying on a cushy mattress while smiling with sheer pleasure makes me horny. Yeah, that's exactly what I need right now—to get a hard-on. I cannot and will not have sex with her.

Okay, I *can* do it. I'm fully capable of performing the act. But slaking my lust would be a mistake.

I jump off the bed. "Let's bring our stuff in here and find a way to get more light."

We grab our junk from the car and stash our backpacks in the bedroom display, then hide the gas cans in the front among the aisles of hardware. We find food too, though it's all the prepackaged and not entirely healthy variety. Apocalypse outlaws can't be picky. I'll even eat pork rinds if it comes down to that. But I doubt it will be necessary since I plan for us to take surreptitious trips out into the wider world of the Echo—to find more supplies, but mostly to search for answers. We came here to uncover the reason for the strange things emanating from this land that have bled into the normal world, and I will never forget our goal.

After gathering some stuff we found inside this building, we return to our new "bedroom" to talk about our next moves. But first, Erin has a different topic in mind.

"Doesn't it seem a little too easy?" she asks. "I mean the way we found a car that could be hot-wired, found a gas station that had a generator, and found a store that has almost everything we need to survive."

"What's too easy about hot-wiring the car? You did that."

"You're not a car guy, are you?"

"No. I can change a flat and fill up the wiper fluid, but that's about it."

She moves the puffy pillows to make them into a pile, then she wriggles backward to lean against them. "In our world, not many cars can be hot-wired anymore. Every break we got seemed way too coincidental for my taste. One break, sure. But three? And we found exactly what we needed every time."

"Maybe you have a point, but I prefer to be optimistic."

Erin snorts out a laugh. "Since when? You're Mr. Doom, not Captain Optimism."

"You haven't seen me at my best. I'm usually upbeat and relaxed."

"I've heard a rumor to that effect, but I assumed it was baloney. All you do is growl and snarl and snap at me. Oh, and let's not forget the dirty looks."

She's right, but not the way she thinks, and I will not explain to her that I only act that way when she's around. The annoying woman will think that means something. I refuse to consider what it might suggest. Yeah, denial is my best friend.

"I apologize for treating you that way," I tell her. "We're stuck in the Echo together, so we should find a way to get along without beating each other senseless."

"Sounds like a reasonable idea."

"The sun is setting out there, so I think we should hunker down for the night. Okay?"

"Yeah." She bites the inside of her lip and scrunches her brows. "I wonder how long day and night last in this world. Would it be the same as on earth since the Echo is a twisted version of our world?"

"Not a clue."

"But you've been studying physics and alchemy. You're the expert on the Echo."

I laugh, but it's a bitter sound. "Expert? Nobody can claim that title except for Sefton Stainthorpe, and he's dead."

"Complain about my word choice all you want. The fact is that you know more about Sefton's original plan than anyone else."

Maybe I do, but I haven't been able to make sense of that information yet. Sefton must have left his notes here in the Echo. I just need to figure out where. Does he have a place like Fallenmouth here in this world? I'm too damn tired to think about that right now.

I climb onto the bed and crawl across to the other side, lying down next to where she sits. "I'm going to sleep now."

"Just like that?"

"Yeah."

"Mind if I leave the light on?"

"Do what you want."

Though I don't open my eyes, I can hear her moving around on her side of the bed and feel her movements jostling the mattress as she settles in for sleep. We had found a battery-operated lantern and some batteries earlier. If she wants to keep a light on, that won't bother me at all. I can sleep anywhere. Well, not lately. I've had trouble getting any shuteye, and knowing our home world might be razed at any second if the Echo consumes it doesn't help me relax.

Naturally, I toss and turn, though I avoid bumping into Erin.

After a while, she blows out an annoyed sigh. "How am I supposed to sleep while you're bouncing around?"

"I'm bouncing? You wriggle and jump more than anybody I've ever met."

"Me? I haven't moved in the past twenty-three minutes, but for you, tossing and turning is an aerobic workout that apparently lasts all night."

"Shut up and let me sleep."

"Happy to—if you ever do fall asleep."

I grumble and roll over onto my side, facing away from her. But I still can't sleep. I sneak a look at my watch several times and learn the dismaying fact that I've been trying to rest for an hour and a half, not including the first twenty-three minutes that Erin counted. I gently turn onto my back, so I won't disturb her.

"Still awake too," she says. "This has to stop."

I mumble things that don't turn out to be words.

Erin wriggles closer and reaches for the zipper on my pants.

"What are you doing?" I demand.

"Helping you relax." She bats my hand away when I try to block her from pulling my zipper down. "Close your eyes, be quiet, and you'll feel better very soon."

She can't intend to—No, Erin hates me.

Well, we did almost have sex last night.

No, I must be misinterpreting her motives. She wants to remove my pants to make me more comfortable. Yeah, because her hand brushing my dick makes me feel totally relaxed.

She finishes unzipping me, then slips a hand inside my pants to pull my dick out.

"Erin, what—"

"Shush. Lie back and enjoy the gift I'm about to give you."

Considering the way my heart is pounding, I won't get any sleep for sure. Guess I might as well let her do what she wants. Yeah, it's a common-sense decision. I haven't surrendered because I know she wants to give me head and I haven't experienced any kind of orgasm in a long time.

She closes her fist around the base of my cock. "Can't deny you have a gorgeous dick. And you got hard so fast." She drags her tongue up my length and back down again. "Mm, you taste good too. Can't wait to suck you off and swallow everything you give me."

Fuck, she's actually going to do this.

Erin massages my balls with one hand while she swallows my cock. Her cheeks cave in while she gently sucks, and her other hand pumps me in sync with her mouth movements. I groan and sag into the mattress. While she keeps working me, I can't stop myself from watching everything she does, and I start breathing harder. She closes her eyes and moans as she pumps faster and sucks harder.

A strangled sound emerges from me.

She removes her mouth from my dick and wriggles around to crouch over my thighs facing me. Then she sets her hands on my hips and swallows me again, licking and sucking while she makes little grunting noises and my back arches. I clench the covers under me, and though my body wants me to shut my eyes, I need to keep watching her. Erin's gaze remains nailed to mine, which is the hottest thing I've ever seen.

"Fuck, Erin, ah…" Pressure mounts inside me, and I feel it barreling down my spine. Any second now…

She reaches up to pinch my nipple.

Rapid-fire spasms grip my cock, and I shout wordlessly while I come inside her warm, soft mouth. She keeps working me until I'm done, then sits up and licks her lips. "Mm, yeah, that was good."

"What was good?"

"You, Grant. I could devour you all night long." She returns to her side of the bed, rolls over, and sighs. "Good night. I'm sure you'll sleep better now."

I do feel more…relaxed now. So I close my eyes and try to let what she just did for me slacken my muscles and ease me out of consciousness, down into sleep.

"Time to rise and shine, Grant."

"What?" I mumble.

"Get up. We have world-saving to do, remember?"

"But I just fell asleep."

She laughs. "Just? You've been asleep for eight hours."

My lids fly open. I spring into a sitting position and glance around, whipping my head left and right several times. Though we're in the back of the store, I can see the first rays of sunrise throwing their pink and gold light all the way into our little sanctuary. "I haven't gotten more than one consecutive hour of sleep in weeks. I toss and turn, wake up repeatedly, and—"

"You're welcome." She's being sarcastic, of course. Erin doesn't know how not to harass me.

I rub my eyes. "Excuse me?"

Erin gives me a wry smile from her perch at the foot of the bed, where she kneels. "I said 'you're welcome,' to save you from needing to lavish me with your gratitude. I did give you amazing head last night, after all."

Oh yeah, she did that. But I still can't understand why.

"Men always fall asleep after sex," she says. "At least, that's been my experience. You are a stereotypical guy."

"Gee, thanks." A yawn overtakes me, and I stretch my arms out. "I do feel better. Rested, I mean."

But also feel kind of weird about what happened last night.

I suddenly notice what she's wearing—gray shorts that hug her hips and barely cover her ass, a blue tank top with matching blue socks, and a pair of hiking boots. "You changed clothes? What you're wearing barely qualifies as clothing, but still—"

"Ugh. I made sure you're well rested, and all you can do is complain about my outfit." She slides off the bed to stand near the foot, which lets me see nearly all of her sexy body. "My clothes were dirty, so I found new ones."

The way her hair hangs in loose waves around her face and kisses her shoulders doesn't help me avoid the morning erection issue. I feel myself getting firm already, but I don't think I can pass it off as completely because I just woke up. She looks too damn hot in that outfit.

I jump off the bed. "Think I'll find some new clothes too. But you really need to change into something more appropriate for battling monsters. I'm sure we'll meet plenty of those when we go out to search for Sefton's private hideaway."

"Wear whatever you want, but I am not changing my clothes. It's already hot outside. Since our car doesn't seem to have air conditioning, I need to dress for the weather, so I don't get heat stroke."

"Your legs are fully exposed. Any creature that attacks you will go for your vulnerable areas." I point at her thighs. "Like your legs."

"They won't get the chance."

"You aren't invincible."

She rolls her eyes.

"Grow up, Erin. Acting like a spoiled child doesn't suit you."

I stalk over to the clothing section of the store and hunt around for appropriate stuff to wear. She's right about the weather here, or at least in this part of the Echo. I have no idea how big this world is, and Dax couldn't tell me either. I guess he stuck to one section of the Echo, though he never mentioned anything that resembles this region.

Erin didn't follow me, which makes me suspicious of what she's up to now.

I pull on fresh clothes and new boots, then march back to our bedroom. She isn't there. That woman loves to tick me off, so she's probably hiding somewhere watching me look for her. "Erin! Where the hell are you?"

"Over here. I found awesome stuff."

I jog in the direction her voice seemed to originate from and see her standing behind a glass-topped counter in front of a display of firearms, knives, and other weapons. She's holding a machine gun and test sighting it.

When I reach the counter, she gives me a smug smile. "While you were feeling self-righteous, I found us loads of weapons."

"Yeah, I can see that." I nod to her machine gun. "Does that have a full magazine?"

"Not yet. I need to load the rounds. But I think it's fully automatic."

She dry fires the machine gun, and her lips curl into a satisfied smile.

"Got another one of those?" I ask.

She hooks a thumb over her shoulder. "Take your pick. This store has every kind of weapon you could want."

Well, maybe the Echo isn't quite so awful after all.

CHAPTER TWELVE

Erin

GRANT HAS STOPPED COMPLAINING ABOUT MY CLOTHES EVER SINCE he discovered we hit the jackpot—in terms of weaponry. I've got new knives, a fully automatic machine gun, a fully automatic handgun, grenades, and a bulletproof vest. If any armored creatures attack us now, we'll give them a hell of a fight.

And we might even win.

Despite bitching about my clothes, Grant chose similar items for himself. He wears olive-green cargo pants, big black boots, and a black tank top with an olive-green, short-sleeve shirt over it. He left the shirt half unbuttoned, so I get a nice view of his pectoral muscles. It's not fair that he saw me naked, but I still have no idea what he looks like in the nude, except for his dick. That part of him is impressive.

I still can't believe I gave him a blow job. My only excuse is that his constant tossing and turning, combined with the irritated little breathing noises he kept making, drove me bonkers. I needed some serious rest, but I couldn't get even forty winks until I found a way to make him fall asleep. So naturally, I went down on him. Well, at least it worked. We both slept after that, though I dreamed about Grant doing naughty things to me with our naked bodies entangled. Maybe I, um, kind of loved taking him into my mouth, and maybe I want him to screw me for hours and hours. I doubt he wants that. Yes, he clearly enjoyed the gift I gave him, but he seems to have reverted to his usual uptight demeanor.

He did smile in the sexiest way when he saw my machine gun. I guess Mr. Zen has a hard-on for powerful firearms. He chose a similar complement of weapons as I had, minus the machine gun, so we are both now heavily armed.

We replenish our backpack supplies and load big water-cooler-size bottles into the back of our vehicle. Don't want to get dehydrated while battling Echo creatures. I insist that we also put some cardboard boxes full of nonperishable food items into the car too. I search for any kind of electronics that might help us navigate this world, but it seems like the Echo doesn't have computer technology.

Grant seems not the least surprised by that fact. He gave me peevish looks while I searched for electronic items, but I refrained from pointing out he was behaving in the "childish" way he accused me of doing earlier. Guess that makes me the adult in the room. No, I don't tell him that. Despite what he thinks, I am not immature.

I don't find any paper maps. How do these creatures find their way around this world?

Once we've returned to the car, I ask, "So, wise and grumpy master, where are we going?"

"To find Sefton's hidden lair."

"You had a vision of where it is?"

He flashes me a nasty look. "No. We're going to search for it."

"With no clue where it might be. How do you know it's even in this city?"

"Because the entrance to the Echo leads here." He starts up the engine and rolls the SUV out onto the street. "Sefton traveled back and forth between the Echo and the earth. He would've done that via Fort Worth."

I won't point out that for all we know the entrance moves around and drops people off in a different place every time. He's clearly in no mood to discuss the issue.

But I can't keep my mouth shut about something else. "How are we going to find our way back to our base camp, meaning the store we slept in last night?"

Grant slams on the brakes, which shoves me forward. I throw my hands out to keep from smacking into the dashboard or the windshield.

"Shit," he hisses. "I didn't think about that."

I twist around to reach behind my seat and dig a spiral-bound notebook out of my backpack. I'd snagged it this morning, thinking it might come in handy. Smiling, I hold up my notebook. "I'll make notes to keep track of where we turned. And I'll even draw a crude map."

"That might work. Good thing you thought to grab a notebook."

"Gee, somebody rolled his eyes and frowned at me for doing that."

He wrings the steering wheel with both hands. "I was wrong. You have good instincts, Erin."

"So do you, but your insomnia gets in the way of it sometimes."

"You're right about that." He throws me a sly sideways glance. "But you helped me with that problem."

"For one night." I cross my legs, which draws his attention to my bare legs, though I didn't intend to lure him to look there. "Unless you think I'm going to give you blow jobs every night so you can get some shuteye."

With his gaze still riveted to my legs, he licks his lips. "Maybe it could be reciprocal next time."

Did he just offer to go down on me tonight? I can't believe Grant would say something like that. "Don't you hate me?"

"No, Erin. I don't understand you, and I worry about your gonzo tactics."

"Fair enough. I don't fully understand you either, but I'm sure we'll get better acquainted now. I mean, there's nobody else to talk to—unless you like chatting with slavering monsters who want to screw you."

Grant gives me a sexy smile. "The beast we met wanted to screw *you*, but I can't blame him for that."

I feel tingly all over because of that simple statement. "Actually, he wanted a threesome with you and me."

"Sorry, I only make love to women, and only one at a time." He taps my notebook. "Start taking notes."

I dig a pen out of my pack, set the notebook on my thigh, flip it open, and poise my pen over the paper. "Ready when you are."

"The faded and almost unreadable sign on that store seems to call it the One-Stop Shop. Guess Echo creatures aren't very creative."

I scrawl the name on my paper. "What did you expect? They're vicious monsters."

"But they were created to be like their alter egos in the normal world, albeit with warped bodies and minds. You would think they'd be as intelligent as the humans they resemble."

"Well, I always thought ninety percent of the human race was stupid."

"You're an optimist, then." He starts the car rolling down the street again. "I figured it was more like ninety-nine percent."

We're both cynics, apparently. That means we share not only military experience but also the same opinion about our fellow humans. I don't think we both believe that, not deep down, but our war experiences have left us kind of jaded. Since the apocalypse began, I've witnessed humans of all ages and nationalities coming together to fight for our world. I can't view my fellow humans through the same lens as before the world was destroyed. The aftermath brought us together.

"I don't really think all people are stupid," I say. "Not anymore. Do you?"

"Nah. It's just what everybody likes to say, right? Even before the worlds collided, I preferred to see the good in people."

"That's your Zen attitude. Wish I could achieve that kind of serenity."

His gaze flicks toward me. "I needed years to cultivate it. Give yourself time."

I write down the street name and draw a line on my map when he turns a corner. "Why have you been treating me like a criminal you want to arrest? I never did anything to you."

Grant stares out the windshield while apparently trying to strangle the steering wheel. "I don't feel that way."

"But why—"

"Just keep making notes and watch out for some kind of clue to where Sefton might have hidden his notes."

"No problem. I'll get out my crystal ball."

He doesn't speak anymore as we turn down street after street, but I have to speak up when I realize my makeshift map shows something disturbing. "We're going in circles."

"What? No, that's not possible."

I thrust my map in his face. "Here's the proof."

Grant jerks his head back and squints at the paper, then he brings the car to a halt. He snatches the map from me, frowning at it. "Dammit."

"Aimlessly wandering through a strange city is not helping."

"What do you suggest we do?"

He's asking for my opinion, at last, but I have no idea what to say.

"You don't know either," he says. "We're the dream team that was going to save the world, but now our plan has ground to a halt before we even got started."

"Saying 'we suck' is not useful."

He tosses the map back to me and stares out the windshield while drumming his fingers on the steering wheel. "Let's get out and walk around. Maybe we'll bump into some Echo creatures we can interrogate."

I try not to laugh, but it turns into snorting instead. "Interrogate them? Are you nuts? They don't want to chat, they want to murder us."

"Must be some who aren't homicidal."

"Sure, you hold your breath for that. I'll catch you when you pass out from lack of oxygen."

He flashes me a scowl, then throws his door open and jumps out. "Come on. We're walking."

Grant slams the door, rocking the vehicle.

He left the screwdriver in the ignition, so I remove it and shove the thing into my backpack. Naturally, he left his pack in the car. I grab that one too and climb out. "If your hissy fit is over, you might want this."

I hold up his backpack.

Lips flattened, he plucks the pack out of my hand and stalks off down the street while struggling to get the straps over his shoulders. I pull my backpack on and jog to catch up, but he refuses my help when I try to tug his left strap into position. It takes him another thirty seconds or so to get his pack situated.

That stubborn idiot. Well, no, he's not stupid. But sometimes he does a fine impression of a moron, especially when the pigheaded beast within rears its head.

He keeps glancing at my legs and wincing.

"My clothes really bother you, huh?" I shake my head. "Get over it, Grant. We need to work together, not snipe at each other."

"I'm not bothered."

"Bullshit." I grab his arm to stop him. "Tell me what your problem is—right now."

He grinds his teeth, which I know because I can see his jaw working and the muscles pulsing. "It's none of your concern."

"Everything about you is my business now. Your behavior affects both of our safety."

He squeezes his eyes shut and hisses something I can't make out, but it's probably a curse word. Then he turns toward me. "You're right. What affects me puts both of us at risk, so I need to tell you."

The guy says that like he's just been convicted of murder and condemned to death row. Whatever he needs to tell me must be a doozy.

"It's just that—" He bows his head and shoves both hands into his hair. "I couldn't save my own family. How can I possibly save the world?"

All the annoyance floods out of me as I realize he must've been carrying that guilt around for months, ever since the apocalypse hit. No wonder he's been hell-bent on studying those alchemy books and finding a way to reverse the destruction.

I clasp his face in my hands, touching my forehead to his. "You need to stop blaming yourself for what happened to your wife and son. No one saw the apocalypse coming, and no one had the power to stop it or save themselves, much less the people they loved. It's not your fault."

"But I was a cop and former military. I have the skills—"

"Nobody had the skills to battle Echo creatures, not in the beginning. Since then, we've learned the hard way."

"But I let everyone believe I could find a way to save the world, maybe even put things back the way they were."

I tug to make him lift his face to me, then gaze straight into his eyes. "Only you laid that burden on your shoulders. The rest of us don't expect you to save us. We hope somebody might find a way sometime, but no one told you it's your fault if you can't do it."

He just looks at me, his expression unreadable.

What else can I do to convince him? Nothing. But I need to make him feel better, for reasons I can't understand or explain, so I do the only thing I can. I kiss him. The moment our lips meet, I swear I feel electricity crackling through me, and I press my mouth more firmly to his and just hold that position so I can relish the feel of his warmth and the softness of his lips.

Then he slides his tongue into my mouth.

I moan and coil my tongue around his.

He wraps his arms around me, pulling me tightly against his muscular body. I push my fingers into his hair, then latch my arms around his neck while we ravish each other with our tongues, our lips, and our bodies. The flavor of his mouth excites me though I can't describe what he tastes like, and it hardly matters. To feel every contour of his body molded to mine, it makes me crazy with the need to get us both naked and finally do what I know we've both wanted since the day we met—to have sex.

"There you are. I want what you promised me."

We both freeze. I peel my lids apart to find Grant staring right back at me, though we haven't moved any other parts of our bodies yet. The voice that spoke those words is all too familiar. The creature who had given us a lift into the Echo has found us again.

And he wants to ravage us.

CHAPTER THIRTEEN

Grant

I STARE INTO ERIN'S EYES FROM INCHES AWAY, OUR MOUTHS STILL fused and our arms still around each other. That armor-plated creature has found us again, and neither of us has any idea how to stop him from capturing us. We've traveled too far from our car to safely get back to it. I got us into this mess. My "hissy fit," as Erin called it, pushed me to act like a moron yet again. That means it's my responsibility to get us out of trouble.

Grasping Erin's shoulders, I peel her away from my body.

She glances at the creature. "Got any bright ideas? My brain is stuck in neutral right now."

"Uh…" I notice the machine gun strapped to her backpack. I've got weapons too, but I have no idea if we can get them out and ready to fire before that beast tramples us. Of course, that creature is armor-plated, and we don't have any armor-piercing rounds. "Our good buddy over there must have a weakness. Don't you think?"

"Sure. But how do we find it without getting killed?"

"You're the expert on being insanely reckless. Can't you think of anything?"

Erin lifts her brows. "Now you want me to be reckless?"

"Yeah. Do it quick."

"No more talking," the beast growls, his deep baritone voice echoing off the buildings. "Time to fuck you."

Yeah, that's exactly what I want to do right now. I doubt either of us will survive sex with that thing.

Erin turns sideways to me, facing the creature, and plasters on a sexily teasing smile. "Where have you been, honey? I was hoping you'd catch up. It's a fun game, isn't it? Hide and go seek."

The creature takes two hulking steps, and the ground shudders. "Hide and go seek? I never knew of this game."

"It's lots of fun. Want me to tell you how it works?"

The beast's brows wrinkle, as much as they can with those horns in the way. "How what works?"

"Well, you close your eyes and count to ten. Then you try to find me." Erin trails her fingertips over her breastbone, exposed by her tank top. The beast's gaze tracks every movement of her fingers. "Wanna play, don't you? So start counting."

Our huge buddy squats and closes his eyes. "One—"

He thumps his fist on the ground as he counts.

Erin snatches her machine gun off her backpack while I rummage around in mine to grab the extra magazines for her gun and the rounds for my shotgun. I toss her the magazines, and she catches them.

"Three," the creature says. "Four, five—"

He keeps striking the ground with every count, the noise giving us perfect cover. We spin around and race back the way we'd come. We have our weapons ready if we should need them, but I'm hoping Erin's clever little ruse has granted us enough time to escape before that big dumb beast realizes what we've done.

"Six, seven—"

We stumble as the creature thumps the ground even harder, but we manage to reach the car and climb inside. I reach for the ignition and freeze. "Where's the screwdriver?"

"Oh, shit, I forgot. It's in my backpack."

"Nine," the creature hollers, and we can hear it even inside the car with the windows rolled up.

Erin struggles to get her pack off her shoulders and dig the screwdriver out. She hands it to me.

I crank the thing in the ignition, and the engine sputters but doesn't catch. I try again, with the same result.

"Ten!" the creature bellows as he rises to his full height. "Here I come!"

Erin rolls down her window and roots around inside her backpack. She brings out two grenades.

I crank the screwdriver again. More sputtering. *Fuck.*

She pulls the pin out, thrusts her arm out the window, and hurls the grenade at the creature. It lands halfway between us and our buddy. The explosion rattles my eardrums, but it only makes the creature pause for a few seconds.

The engine catches at last, and I gun it, wrenching the wheel to turn us around and speed off in the opposite direction from the horny beast. Erin rises off her seat to hang halfway out the window and throw the other grenade. In the rearview mirror, I see the grenades strike the beast's calf and erupt. Our buddy roars, but not in agony. He sounds pissed to the extreme.

Erin grabs her machine gun and starts raining rounds on the creature.

I veer around a corner, hoping to hell I can find a place that monster can't get through, but having no clue what such a place might look like.

The rapid-fire rounds from the gun cease. Erin leans into the car to grab another magazine and starts shooting again.

In the rearview mirror, I see the creature still barreling toward us. I lean over to slap Erin's leg.

When she pauses in firing rounds at our buddy, she glances at me with a questioning look.

"That thing must have a vulnerable spot," I tell her. "We need to find it."

"No shit. Thanks for stating the obvious." She raises her gun again, but stops when I slap her thigh again. "What, Grant? I don't have the magical power to know where that thing is vulnerable."

"Try his groin." I'd seen a bulge under his enormous pants. Maybe he's got a dick that's as easy to injure as the ones we human guys have.

Erin drops the gun and digs a couple more grenades out of her pack. Then she pulls the pins and hurls both of them toward the creature's groin.

I watch in the mirror while the grenade strikes the monster's groin and explodes.

The beast screams. He stumbles over an abandoned vehicle, staggers sideways, and clutches his groin.

Our car sideswipes a lamppost.

Erin kicks my arm. "Watch where you're going, genius."

I return my attention to the road ahead. Just as I swerve around another corner, a massive explosion makes the earth beneath us ripple like the waves of an earthquake.

"What did you just throw at him?" I ask. "Did you hide some C-4 in your bra?"

Erin drops back onto her seat, breathing hard. "That wasn't me. The creature collapsed and created a mini earthquake."

I twist my head around to glance backward.

The beast lies prone on the ground, rocking slightly, both hands cupped over his dick.

"Guess we got him," I say, facing forward again. "Score one for the humans."

"That was a smart idea. But I don't think we should assume our ugly friend is out of commission for good."

"I know. But we managed to knock him down once, which means we can do it again." I look at her at the same moment she looks at me. "We make a good team."

"Yeah, we do."

Something ripples through me, a sensation like excitement and relief coupled with desire. My gaze flicks to her legs and the expanse of tanned skin revealed by her minuscule shorts. My dick jerks. How can I be horny when we barely survived an assault from a massive Echo creature just seconds ago? I guess it's the adrenaline rush.

I focus on the road, doing my damnedest to ignore what my body wants, and execute several more turns that seem to take us further away from the creature. I'm trying to make sure I don't drive us in circles again by turning left, right, left, right.

The engine sputters and dies. The car rolls to a stop.

"We're out of gas," I say. "Need to fill up the tank with our handy gas cans."

I get out of the car and retrieve some of the cans. Just as I've finished gassing up, Erin climbs out and stretches her entire body while moaning as if it feels so good.

My attention swerves to her legs. Those long, slim thighs that have strong muscles under the surface. I can tell that much from the way she stretches. My dick jerks again. But then Erin plants her hands on her lower back and stretches again, bending backward. The action lifts her tits, and I can see her nipples stiffening. She's not wearing a bra.

I screw the gas cap back on, suddenly breathing harder.

Erin stretches backward again, this time with her arms extended.

Lust grips me so hard that I can't breathe. I shouldn't want to screw her right now, but I can't resist the impulse. I stalk over to Erin, sling an arm around her waist, and haul her into my body. Despite her taut muscles, she has all the soft curves I love in a woman, and I can't stop myself. I mash my mouth to hers.

She doesn't react for a few seconds. But then she plunges her tongue into my mouth, and we consume each other with a passion so intense that it verges on insanity. With my eyes closed, I fumble with the zipper on her shorts until I finally grasp it and yank the thing down so I can shove my hand inside her panties. She doesn't have any underwear on. My hand slides through the silky curls on her mound. I hesitate there, but only for a moment, then I push my fingers between her folds to revel in the realization of how wet and ready she is.

For me.

This is insane. And a bad idea. But I've careened off the cliff already, and there's no going back now, especially when Erin moans and latches one leg around my hip. I scrape my fingers up and down her slick folds while I peel one eye open just enough to help me find the back door and yank it open. Then I toss her onto the backseat and jump in, straddling her body while poised on my knees. I keep rubbing her cleft even as I bend my head to take her clit in my mouth and suckle it.

She cries out, arching her back.

Though I should make her come first, my desperate need to fuck her overrides my brain. I shove her shorts down to her ankles, unzip my pants, and thrust into her hard. She cries out again, but then grips my biceps and bends her knees. I pound into her so fiercely that the car starts to shake and creak. Braced on my straight arms, I stare into her eyes while she stares right back at me, her mouth open and frantic noises tumbling from her lips. I grunt and gasp while I fuck her like a demon, pumping faster and faster while the wet sucking sound of our bodies colliding fills the interior of the car and her cream coats my cock.

I retain just enough willpower to give her what she needs. I reach down to rub her clit.

She comes so hard and fast that her body curls inward and her scream gets choked off. The spasms of her inner muscles push me over the edge too, and I let out a string of hoarse shouts while my own spasms rack my cock and the sweet bliss of orgasm barrels through me with the power of lightning strikes. After a few more thrusts, I'm done.

I collapse on top of her. We're both struggling to catch our breath.

"Holy shit, Grant," she says while still breathing hard. "That was, um, unexpected."

I suddenly realize I still have my dick inside her. Pulling out, I rise to my knees and gaze down at Erin. "Did I hurt you?"

She laughs softly. "No, I'm fine. That was incredible."

"Can't believe I did that." I glance down at my waning erection. Her cream glistens on it. "Shit. What if I got you pregnant?"

"From one time? I don't think that's likely since I had my period last week." She sits up and shimmies backward so she can get to her knees and pull her shorts up again. "Relax. I won't be demanding you provide child support for our baby. There won't be one."

"Why aren't you mad? I didn't even ask if you wanted to have sex. I just…assaulted you."

Erin waddles across the seat toward me and takes hold of my face. "You didn't do anything wrong. What about me makes you think I'm afraid to say no to a man? I wanted you, and I didn't care how you took me. It was amazing."

She's not upset, but I'm disgusted with myself. Not because of the way I fucked her. No, it's something much worse.

"What's wrong?" Erin asks. "You look like you might throw up."

Maybe I will, since bile is rising in my throat, scorching a path toward my mouth. I can already taste the acrid flavor of it. But I can't move or speak to answer her question. What's wrong? Everything.

She inches closer until our noses brush against each other. "Please tell me why you're upset."

I grasp her wrists and pull them back to peel her hands away from my face. "I betrayed Adele."

"No, Grant, you—"

"When we got married, I didn't promise to honor and cherish Adele until death do us part. I vowed to love her forever." I scuffle backward and fall off the seat, tumbling to the ground. My fly is still open. I yank it closed and struggle to get to my feet. "I'm sorry, Erin. I shouldn't have done this, any of it. Kissing you. Letting you give me head. Fucking you. I've become the kind of bastard I never wanted to be."

She starts to speak, but I slam the door to silence her.

Then I stalk around to the driver's side, get in, and crank the screwdriver in the ignition until the engine snarls to life. Erin climbs over the center console and onto the passenger seat. I gun the engine, rocketing our car down the street.

I wanted Erin since the day we met, but I fought it. I don't deserve to feel good, not even for a minute. Because I betrayed Adele the first time I looked at Erin.

CHAPTER FOURTEEN

Erin

WE DIDN'T DO ANYTHING WRONG, BUT I KNOW I CAN'T CONVINCE Grant of that. He needs to punish himself. I've never been into self-flagellation, not even the mental kind, and I refuse to lie and tell him what we just did meant nothing. When a man tormented by his past finally opens the floodgates of his emotions, he's destined to sink under the water for a while. He'll surface again. By the time he does, maybe I'll have thought of a way to talk him out of the idea that he betrayed his late wife.

I'm not dumb enough to try that right now.

So instead, I gaze out the windows. "The way Dax described the Echo, I expected more fire and brimstone and less…normal stuff."

"What's normal about a destroyed city?"

"I just meant that this place looks an awful lot like Earth. Dax described this world as literal hell."

"He lived here for five years before the alchemy of worlds began. When that happened, he was thrown into the normal world again. Maybe everything here changed post-apocalypse, just like things changed on Earth."

"Maybe." I chew on the inside of my cheek while I contemplate our surroundings. Something still doesn't feel right about this place and our amazingly good luck in finding supplies and a car. "This is supposed to be a copy of the earth, right? Sefton Stainthorpe created the Echo to be a twisted mirror image of the real world, and that's why the Echo creatures look like demonic versions of the people on earth. Right?"

"If you keep repeating everything we've already talked about, I'll go insane."

"Newsflash—you've already done that."

"Yeah." He scowls out the windshield, his fingers wrapped around the wheel so tightly that the knuckles have turned white. "Must be a clue somewhere in this city."

We drive past a dilapidated building that has faded words painted on a scorched sign.

"Stop!" I shout.

Grant slams on the brakes. "What is your problem now?"

"Back up. I saw something on that sign, but we went by too fast for me to read all of it."

He shifts the car into reverse and backs up.

"Stop here," I say. Then I stare up at the sign. The damage has made it harder to read the words, and the muted daylight in this world doesn't help either. But finally, I'm sure of what I see. "It's a shop called Maps of the World."

"Maps?" Grant sounds baffled, and I'm right there with him. "Are you sure you're reading it right?"

"Yep. Look for yourself."

He leans across the center console and peers through my window. His brows furrow. His mouth falls open a touch. Then he swivels his gaze to me. "It does say Maps of the World. It can't mean…"

"Maps of the Echo? Yeah, I think it does mean that."

Grant shuts off the engine and stares blankly at nothing. "This is insane."

"Uh-huh. Still think all our good luck has been nothing but a series of random coincidences?"

"I'll reserve my judgment for after we check out that shop." He climbs out and lays one hand on the top of the driver's door as he bends forward to look at me. "Hurry up, Erin."

He must have seriously sublimated what we did a few minutes ago. I still feel tingly in places that aren't at all helpful to my powers of concentration, but he acts like we didn't just have sex in the backseat so hard that the car shook—and possibly the earth too.

Wow, I loved that. But he thinks it was a horrible sin.

I climb out of the car and follow Grant into the shop. The windows have been shattered, but jagged pieces clinging to the frame make it impossible to enter the building that way. The door is locked.

But Grant doesn't care about that. He kicks it open.

That's hot. Really hot.

"Wake up, Erin."

Grant's snarly command jerks me back to reality. I'd been enjoying a memory of our encounter in the backseat. "I am awake, jackass."

I follow him into the shop, and he turns on a flashlight to sweep its beam over the interior. Metal racks fill the space, but most are empty. I pull a folded map out of its slot, but the paper has been badly scorched. I can read the title, though—Capital City. The Echo has a capital? That implies it also has some type of government. It must be a dictatorship, considering what I've heard about Sefton Stainthorpe. He was not a nice guy or a sane person.

That begs a question. "Who's in charge of the Echo now that Sefton is dead?"

"Nobody, I guess." Grant picks up a hand-size globe. "This world must be a separate planet. We've assumed it's purely a magical construct that doesn't exist on a physical plane the way planets do, but this globe suggests otherwise."

"Maybe it's a parallel universe. Or maybe it's both magical and physical."

He jerks his head up to look at me. "That's a smart observation, Erin."

Why does he seem shocked? I'm not an idiot. I went to college, for heaven's sake.

"You're the first person who suggested that," he says. "Not even Sanctuary's resident expert on the Echo thought of it."

"Dax didn't realize that? Has he ever mentioned the Capital City?"

"No. Unless he found this city and this shop, he wouldn't have any reason to know about it. The Echo is a magical construct, but it must also have a physical presence in some kind of universe."

"This is a fascinating discussion. But aren't we looking for a map of the city we're in right now?"

"Yeah." He rolls the globe in his palm, then sets it down. "Better keep searching."

I wander among the racks but don't see anything useful, just maps that are so damaged they're unreadable. But then I notice something on the sales counter and trot over there to get a closer look. I hold up the booklet. "Found something."

Grant hurries over to me. "What is it?"

"A map booklet." I flip through the pages to let him see. "It's an undamaged map of the Capital City. I think that's where we are. It would make sense that Sefton headquartered his new world in the city where the entrance to the Echo resides."

He picks up the map booklet to thumb through it. "I think you're right about all these convenient discoveries. We just happen to drive by a shop that has a single pristine map for us to find? That's one too many coincidences for my taste."

"You finally came over to my way of thinking. About time."

"Why do you always have to be snarky? I liked it a lot better when you were gasping and moaning."

He said that while casually browsing the map booklet, and his expression stayed neutral, his tone of voice too. I can't figure this guy out. He snarls at me, then screws me, then tells me he betrayed his dead wife, and finally he reminds me of what we did in the car a little while ago. I have no frigging idea how to respond to that.

"I especially liked it when you screamed my name," he says in that same neutral tone as he hands me the map booklet. "You should keep this. I'll drive, and you can navigate."

Yeah, I'm getting whiplash from his mood swings.

But I do what he wanted. Once we get back to the car, I use the map booklet to figure out where we are. It's the Capital City, like I thought. The names of the streets we pass match up with what the map shows. Apparently, this city has no real name, just the generic one. Most of the streets get their names from scientists I've heard of, both modern and historical figures. Other streets are named after alchemical terms like quicksilver and quintessentia. I wouldn't have known what those terms are, but Grant explained they're related to alchemy. Other street names related to alchemy include Alembic, Solifaction, and Touchstone.

He wants to explain to me what those terms are about, but I tell him not to bother unless those things become important to our quest to reverse the apocalypse.

Grant stops the car at an intersection. He compresses his lips while he studies the street signs. We're on Ignis Boulevard, and the cross street is called Decknamen Way. I remember enough of my college science class to know ignis means fire. But that other word? Not a clue.

"Do you have any idea what the word decknamen means?" Grant asks.

"Of course I don't. I'm not obsessed with alchemy."

He eyes me sideways. "A decknamen is basically a pseudonym for an alchemical substance, something that hides its true identify."

"Fascinating. How does that help us?"

He scratches his cheek and winces. "This will sound kind of nuts."

"Like everything else you've said and done was completely sane?"

"Fair point." He sags into his seat, letting out a long sigh. "I have no rational reason for believing this, but I have a hunch we should take Decknamen Way to wherever it ends."

"Okay. Let's do that."

He glances at me. "You don't want to complain about my half-assed plan?"

"Nope. Just get moving."

Grant steers the car around the corner onto the street with a weird and kind of spooky name. "Decknamen" sounds like German or Latin or something, but I won't waste time asking Grant about that. The term's origins hardly matter.

After a few blocks, I stop staring at the buildings along the streets because something else has captured my attention. Directly ahead, at what seems like the end of this street, I see a hulking skyscraper that I swear wasn't there a few minutes ago. "Do you see that? I think that building appeared, like poof."

"You just didn't notice it before."

"Did you?"

He screws up his mouth as he stares straight ahead at the building in question. "No, I didn't see it either—until right now."

"I'm pretty sure that building wasn't there before."

"Okay, I trust your instincts. But a mysterious building that materializes out of nowhere just confirms my suspicion that we're on the right track."

"Or on our way to a horrifically painful death."

"Pessimism isn't helpful."

"I'm not being pessimistic. I'm keeping both eyes peeled and all my senses on high alert for whatever might magically appear next."

Grant braces his elbow on the door frame, tapping his fingers on the steering wheel. "Let's both be hypervigilant."

"Agreed."

The closer we get to the spooky building, the more the hairs on my arms lift and my skin tingles with an eerie kind of anticipation. What awaits us there? Soon, we will learn the answer to that question.

At the end of the street, Grant stops the car and shuts off the engine, but he just sits there staring up at the massive gray structure. Its curving lines and smooth planes remind me of fairy tales, but I doubt a valiant king resides in this castle. The building has suffered no visible damage, but I'd expect that if Sefton created this as his private sanctum. When Grant finally opens his door, I do the same. We grab our backpacks, but first, we gather as much ammo as we can stuff into our bags. I have the machine gun strapped to my pack while Grant slings a shotgun over his shoulder.

We're armed. But are we ready for what might come next? Are we prepared to meet whoever lives in this structure?

Grant holds my hand as we push through the glass doors into a vacant lobby that has no furniture, not even a reception desk. A large clock on the wall ticks off the seconds and minutes without making the slightest sound. I glance at our hands, expecting Grant to let go of mine. But he doesn't. He leads me toward an elevator instead.

The doors glide open for us.

I look at Grant just as he looks at me. He raises his brows. I shrug. We waltz into the elevator, and the doors shut. The car begins to rise while a clock-like device counts off the floors, one for every tick of the minute hand—though the device doesn't make a ticking sound. Like everything we've seen so far, the elevator makes no noise. We know it's rising only because we felt the movement when it first started to lift.

The dial counting floors glides through the numbers. Seven. Eight. Nine. Ten. I suddenly realize I've shuffled closer to Grant, and my body is touching his. I wonder if I should move away, but then he snakes an arm around my waist to tug me closer. Floor eleven. Twelve. I reach for my gun but realize I shouldn't do that yet. Maybe we're about to meet someone nice.

In a hell world? Yeah, right.

My throat has grown tight, and my pulse is racing.

At the thirteenth floor, the elevator stops. The doors glide open.

Grant clasps my hand again to lead me out into a long, blank hall-way. "I'd swear this building has more than thirteen floors, based on how tall it looked from the outside. But then, Sefton was obsessed with the number thirteen. Maybe he built more floors just for show."

"Could be."

The elevator doors slide shut behind us, making me jump.

We stand here looking around, searching for anything that might ex-plain what this building is and why we've apparently been lured here. A door at the far end of the hall eases open just as I glance that way.

"Look," I say. "Guess we're supposed to go there."

"Seems like."

We approach the door and slip inside the room, which has floor-to-ceiling windows on three sides and a stunning view of the post-apocalyptic city. No one waits for us in the large room that I take for an office. But footsteps clap in the hallway, coming our way. We both turn toward the door.

A blond man walks into the room.

Grant's eyes flare wide. "Sefton Stainthorpe?"

CHAPTER FIFTEEN

Grant

I TRY DAMN HARD TO CHANNEL MY ZEN SIDE AND KEEP MY EXPRES-
sion neutral, but I have trouble doing that under these circumstances. The
man whose decaying corpse I saw just a few days ago at Fallenmouth now stands
ten feet away from us. This can't be. Dax told me he snapped his brother's neck,
and I know he wouldn't lie. The body in the cellar must have been Sefton.

The man eying us with curiosity is an Echo of Sefton Stainthorpe. That's
the only explanation that makes even a minuscule amount of sense.

"Hello," I say once I've reasserted my calm demeanor. "May I ask who we
have the pleasure of meeting?"

The blond man has begun to stare at Erin in a way that makes me uneasy. "Allison Dahl?"

She shakes her head.

"Who are you?" he asks, glancing back and forth between me and
Erin. "The signs were meant for Allison, to bring her to Sefton."

This guy looks like Sefton, who was British, but he speaks with an
American accent.

I think it's time for a strategic sharing of information—but only a little
of that. "I'm Grant, and this is Erin. Who might you be?"

"Call me Will."

"You remind me of someone I met once. Are you related to Sefton Stainthorpe?"

"In a way."

"You must know Dax too."

"No, I haven't encountered him." Will tugs at the collar of his dress shirt,
which has the top button unhooked, and he grimaces. "How did you find
the Capital City? No one comes here."

"We did."

Will hasn't met Sefton's brother, though he clearly knows who Dax is.

Our new friend stares at Erin again. "Are you sure you're not Allison? You followed the signs, didn't you?"

Erin clinches my hand more tightly.

"If you mean the literal signs," I say, "as in the ones attached to buildings that drew us here, yeah. We followed the signs. Did you leave those breadcrumbs for us?"

"For Allison, not for you." He sounds befuddled rather than annoyed. His fingers twiddle while he glances around like he's hunting for an escape route. "Sefton will be quite angry when he learns I've let uninvited guests into his city."

"No, he won't. Sefton Stainthorpe is dead."

Will jerks his attention to me, his eyes wide. "That's impossible. The master cannot be killed. He surrounds himself with powerful magics that repel all attempts to assault his person."

This guy talks like a prig with a big stick wedged up his ass, but he mostly seems terrified. Of what? Sefton? Like I just told him, that man is dead.

"Where are all the Echo creatures?" I ask.

"No creatures live in the Capital City—except for the one you two brought here."

"Are you going to kill him?"

Will shakes his head. "I don't have the power."

Erin releases my hand, leveling her gaze on our new friend. "Do you mean Echo power?"

"Yes," Will says. "Only Sefton has that."

Does this guy really not know that other people share the Echo power? That would have to mean he hasn't left the Echo since the alchemy of worlds began on earth. But who is this man? I want answers, and I want them now.

"What are you?" I demand. "You look just like Sefton, but you sound American. You know about Allison but had no idea Sefton was dead. You hide in this building, but as far as I can tell, you're the only living thing in this city other than me, Erin, and that creature."

Will shuffles over to the windows, gazing out at the cityscape illuminated by the glow of a full moon. "I am Sefton's Echo. He called me Will because that's his name too—Sefton William Stainthorpe."

I stop myself a split second before I blurt out something that might get us into trouble and temper my question. "But I thought the Echo versions of humans all had scales or horns or something."

"You fail to understand the scope of what an Echo is."

"Enlighten me. Please."

He touches his fingertips to the glass and begins to draw invisible patterns with them. "Sefton invented the concept of an Echo, which is essentially a copy of a human being. But he took it several steps further. Each

Echo is both an exact copy and a mirror image. What was once hidden inside the person becomes visible on the outside."

"Yeah, we know about that."

"But an Echo is more than a copy. It is the result of turning a human soul inside out. If Sefton had succeeded in creating the alchemy of souls, every person on earth would have been forced to merge with their Echo."

We already knew about the alchemy of souls, but I decide it's not smart to point that out. Will seems timid, but I won't make the mistake of trusting what appears to be true. He's hiding something, for sure.

"There are good creatures in this world," he says. "They each have the appearance of a monster but the heart and soul of a human. Sefton did not anticipate that, and the realization enraged him." Will turns toward us, his expression pinched. "You see, he assumed that if his magics created an Echo of him, that creature would be more powerful than Sefton himself—in bodily strength and brutality. But instead, he got me."

"If you're his doppelgänger, do you know everything he knew?"

"Afraid not. I know only what he told me and what I learned from experience."

I study him for a moment, trying to gauge his honesty, but I'm no mind reader. During the initial phases of the apocalypse, Allison had encountered the Echo version of a woman she'd worked with at the Fort Worth Public Library. Luckily, I haven't come across anyone I knew. Not yet, at least. "A friend of mine bumped into an Echo creature who was a copy of someone she knew. That creature shared the original woman's memories."

"Other Echo creations retain some of the knowledge of their originals. I do not." Will clamps a hand over his nape. "Sefton was disappointed that I have no knowledge of magic, alchemy, or science. He called me a useless byproduct."

As interesting as learning about Will's creation and existence might be, we have more important matters to discuss with him. He's our only lead and our only link to the madman who instigated hell on earth and in the Echo. If he is a copy of Sefton, maybe he knows something useful.

Erin has been unusually quiet until now, but she finally speaks up. "Why does this building seem empty? Devoid of everything including furniture? The way I heard it, Sefton loved the creature comforts."

"Oh, this isn't where he lived," Will says. "I assume that's what you were implying. Only Allison would ever visit his home, if she had come to him as he planned."

But she didn't because he returned to Fallenmouth instead. Based on what Will said, it sounds like Sefton had assumed Allison would find her way into the Echo alone despite the fact he left her a note urging her to wait for him at the library on the day the apocalypse began.

"I've told you all I know," Will says. "Apologies for not being able to answer all your questions. I might be Sefton's Echo, but I do not share all his memories."

Does he share Sefton's insanity? I shouldn't assume this guy is genuinely pleasant and not evil, but my gut isn't giving me any advice. As a deputy sheriff, I'd needed to hone my instincts, so I'm not gullible. I will remain wary of this man even while I trust him with a vital piece of intel.

"I have reason to believe," I tell him, "that Sefton kept notes on everything he did. Magic, alchemy, quantum physics, everything. Do you have any idea where he might've hidden those notes?"

Sure, I have no proof the documentation exists. But my gut tells me it does.

Will grasps his upper arm, almost as if it pains him. "I'm sorry, no. If Sefton kept notes, they would most likely be in his home. The one in this world."

"You really have no clue where that home is?"

"None."

Shit. We'll need to find another way to get what we need.

"We should go," Erin says. "There's nothing for us here."

"You can't leave," Will announces. "The building is warded. Once you enter, you must remain here. You're trapped, just like me."

A coldness rushes through me, and I can do nothing but stare at him. Trapped? Oh, hell no. There must be a way to escape, and we'll find it. Maybe Will is too timid to even try, but Erin and I have skills and training he can't imagine.

"We're getting out of here," I say. "Will, you can come with us if you want. But being trapped is not an option for us."

I seize Erin's hand and turn toward the doorway, which remains open. We march down the hall, and I hear footsteps behind us. A quick glance back shows me Will is following us. Maybe he only wants out of this building. Fine, we'll help him escape. After that, I'm not sure if we should let him tag along on our quest to find Sefton's notes because I'm still not sure we should trust him.

The elevator is gone. A blank wall occupies the space where it had been.

"What now?" Erin asks.

No fucking idea. But I don't say that out loud. "We keep searching for a way out."

"None exists," Will says. "Believe me, I've tried."

Isn't he a ray of sunshine? I need to keep thinking positive and keep trying.

While we all stand here like a trio of clueless morons, Will chews on his bottom lip.

I raise my brows at him. "You got something to say?"

"No. Well, yes, sort of. I was just curious."

"About what?"

"Ah, how did you two and your very large friend get inside the Echo?"

"How do you think? We came in through the front door."

"He means the entrance to the Echo," Erin says. Then she mutters under her breath to me, "He knows nothing."

Maybe she's right. But he's connected to Sefton, literally, and I can't believe he holds nothing useful in his brain, not even a speck of information. Yet he seems utterly ignorant. It's a puzzle, for sure. Why can't anything be simple? I'm damn tired of sorting out mysteries.

"The entrance?" Will says. "But only Sefton can travel through it. The gateway remains locked at all times."

I shake my head. "Maybe it used to be locked down, but it isn't now. Sefton's death might've changed the whole dynamic of the Echo."

Will's eyes widen. "If that's true, then…he might come back."

"Sefton's dead and gone, trust me."

"Not Sefton." Will grasps his upper arm again, this time hunching his shoulders too. "I was referring to the golem."

Erin stares at Will. "The what?"

"Golem," I say. "Dax and Allison told me about that. Sefton had a gigantic creature, part flesh and part machine but completely suffused with magics. It trapped Dax and Ally in Fort Worth and held them hostage until Sefton arrived."

"How gigantic is it?"

"About half the height of this building."

She blinks once slowly. "Oh. Is that all?"

"The golem sleeps," Will says. "But Sefton mentioned he could reactivate his pet anytime he liked."

Oh yeah, things just keep getting better. "Where is the golem now?"

Will shrugs.

I still don't get why he seems relatively sane, but he did mention not all Echo creatures are evil. So maybe whatever glitch made that happen might also have affected Will. Honestly, we have worse problems right now.

Our new friend suddenly freezes, and his eyes widen though his gaze goes distant. "The creature you brought here is on the move again. He will be here any moment." Will swerves his gaze to me. "He is not happy."

Gee, I'm glad he told me that. I might've thought the monster wanted a hug instead of a massacre.

Erin and I still have our backpacks and our weapons. Maybe we can fight our way out of this building. If the creature realizes where we are, I suspect he can shake this building down if he wants. Maybe he won't destroy it, but all he'd need to do is smash the lower floors to destabilize the whole thing. When that beast stomps his feet, the city shakes.

"Stay here," I tell Will. "Erin and I need to have a private moment."

Without waiting for his response, I grab Erin's arm and drag her down the hallway until we've gotten far enough away from Will that he won't hear what we say. Unless he has superpowers. These days, I can't rule out anything.

"Can't stay in this building," I whisper. Guess it's my optimism peeking out, assuming Will can't hear us this way. "We need to blow our way out."

"Not sure even a grenade could do that."

"Worth a shot. If our big, gnarly buddy really is awake again, we need to scram."

"Okay." She pulls out her machine gun and whirls toward the wall, then fires off a volley of rounds that makes my ears ring. She shakes her head. "Damn."

The wall sports pockmarks now, but it's intact.

We are screwed.

CHAPTER SIXTEEN

Erin

GRANT GLANCES BACK AT WILL WHOSE EYES ARE BULGING, AND HE'S hugging himself too. Yeah, Sefton Stainthorpe's Echo has no balls, not in the metaphorical sense. But I guess being created by a madman probably scarred him, and I imagine Sefton bullied the guy too. I mean, he wasn't expecting to create a duplicate of himself, only of everyone else on earth. From what I've heard about Dax's brother, the guy did not like competition. That's why he turned Dax into a part-Echo beast of a man and threw him into the nightmare world he'd manufactured.

"Better try a grenade," I say to Grant.

"Might just wind up deaf but still trapped here."

I smirk. "You're starting to sound like me."

"No, I'm sounding like Dax. You got it from him too."

I roll my eyes. "Please. I have my own style that doesn't come from anyone else."

"Yeah, that's for sure."

Whump.

The thunderous noise seems to emanate from outside the building, though it makes the floor beneath us shudder.

"It's the creature you brought here," Will calls out to us. "I can sense him."

Okay, I didn't expect that. But it makes sense, I guess, considering that Sefton created both Will and the beast.

Grant digs half a dozen grenades out of my backpack and offers me three of them. "Let's try it your way."

About damn time. My way might be louder and more dangerous, but it usually gets the job done.

We jog back to Will.

"Plug your ears," Grant instructs him. "Then shut your eyes and brace for impact."

Will shoves his fingers into his ears and huddles against the wall with his lids tightly sealed.

Good enough, I suppose. Grant could have been more specific and told the guy to assume the tornado warning position with his ass in the air and his head on the floor. But this way will probably do.

"Throw your grenades toward the left wall," Grant tells me. "Then plug your ears. I'll throw mine toward the right. Pitch them as far as you can."

"I played softball in high school. You don't need to coach me on how to throw."

"Good. Then we'll do it on the count of three. That means three, two, one, throw."

I give him an oh-please look, but then palm my grenades and face the end of the hall.

Grant bends his knees slightly, holding two grenades in his left hand and the remaining one in his right, ready to lob his first pitch. "Three, two, one, go!"

The two of us hurl our first grenades at the same time, then quickly throw the rest. They land close to the walls. We both plug our ears and turn our backs to that end of the hallway, huddling near the wall as we squeeze our eyes shut. The explosions reverberate through the air, the concussions rattling my bones as the floor shudders hard enough to make Grant stumble sideways into me. Once the dust has settled, literally, I peel my lids apart and shuffle around to see what damage we've done. Grant does the same.

Chunks of drywall or whatever these walls are made of have crumbled away to reveal metal underneath.

Aw, shit. What is this building made of? Steel walls and magic, apparently.

"The only way we're getting out," I say, "is if one of us develops Echo power."

Will shuffles away from the wall to face us. He wears a confused expression, like he thinks I said something weird. But he knows about the Echo and the power it confers on some people. Or does he? Maybe Sefton never told him that.

The building shakes as the Echo beast's feet stomp outside. *Whump. Whump.*

"At least one of you does have the Echo power," Will says. "I sensed it the moment you entered the building, but I was afraid to let on that I knew."

Yeah, he is one big bundle of nerves and fear.

"It's Grant," I say. "Has to be."

Will shakes his head. "It's you, Erin."

"Me? That's crazy. If I had that kind of power, I wouldn't have needed to stumble through the woods for days before I found sanc—a good place to stay."

I almost blurted out that I stumbled onto Sanctuary. Though Will can't know what that really means, I won't risk him figuring it out. He seems okay, but trusting strangers is always a risk these days. The people in Sanctuary welcomed me into their community, but they didn't loop me in on the bigger picture until recently. That means I need to treat Will in a similar fashion. He is the doppelgänger of a madman, after all.

Grant's eyebrows hiked up a touch when I almost revealed the name of our new hometown. He recovered from his surprise quickly, though.

"Perhaps you fought your Echo power," Will says. "You seem averse to the idea."

Averse? Yeah, I guess I am. Having freaky apocalypse powers doesn't appeal to me. But we need a way out of this building. That creature's footfalls pound louder and closer every minute, and the building shivers more with every concussion. Bits of the walls keep falling off. It's also getting harder for us to stay upright.

Grant seizes my upper arms and pulls me closer. The intensity of his gaze ripples a shiver through me, though not the bad kind. His voice is imbued with that same intensity. "You can do this, Erin. You need to do it. Please try."

Or we will die a horrific death. I already got that memo.

I gaze into his eyes, and for some reason, I flash back to the times we kissed and what we did earlier today in that SUV. My breaths quicken, and a warm tingle sweeps through my entire body, settling between my thighs. My tongue sneaks out to moisten my lips, but I swear I didn't mean to do that. How can I be getting horny when we're about to die?

Grant drags me into his body and slants his head to murmur into my ear. "Listen and don't complain. Just believe what I'm about to say. Desire and pleasure can trigger the Echo power."

He can't seriously be suggesting we get it on right here, right now.

"I have an idea," he says, "but I need to know you trust me. I trust you, Erin."

Boom. The building shudders and…sways. Did that really happen? Or am I so high on hormones that I imagined it?

Will lets out a sharp whimper. "Do something quick."

Grant clasps my face in both hands and kisses me.

For a few seconds, I don't move or react. He's kissing me now? Why? But I can't resist the feel of his lips pressed to mine and his rough hands cupping my cheeks. My lids flutter closed of their own volition. While the building shudders and sways around and beneath us, Grant pushes his tongue between my lips and wildly explores my mouth like he wants to devour every inch of me, and I can't stop myself from thrusting my tongue into his mouth too while I moan and clutch at his shirt. When he drops a hand to my ass, I melt into him. Maybe I'd be embarrassed if I weren't lost in a haze of lust. I feel his dick starting to stiffen. My nipples ache and grow sensitive.

Whoosh.

I swear I hear that sound just as I sense we've shifted through space, landing in a different location. My lids drift open.

Grant slowly peels his lips away from mine, though his eyes remain hooded. "Good job, Erin."

"Huh?" Somewhere in the back of my mind, I know what I've done. But that kiss fried most of my neurons. They need time to recover. I need time. But I manage to say, "Did it work?"

I sound kind of dazed, not like me at all.

Grant steps back and pats my upper arm. "You did it. You transported us out of that building."

My senses recover quickly, but my wits need a little more time.

He chucks me under the chin. "I knew you could do it. With a little help from me."

The smug tone in his voice snaps me back to reality. I plant my hands on my hips. "You knew it? Get over yourself, Grant. Kissing you isn't a life-changing experience, much less a world-shifting one."

I've never seen Grant smug before. It's hot, but I will not tell him so.

That kiss was definitely hot. Sizzling, actually.

"Is it over yet?" Will asks, almost whining.

"Yes, it's over." I tap his fingers, which are glued to his eyes. "You can look now. We got away from the big bad Echo beast."

He lowers his hands, but his gaze darts like he's not one hundred percent convinced we've gotten away scot-free.

I settle a hand on Will's arm. "Relax. We're safe now, relatively speaking."

Grant shakes his head, his lips puckered. "You just can't be optimistic all the way, can you?"

"Me? You've been Mr. Gloomy Pants lately." I turn in a circle to take in our surroundings. "Looks like we're still in the Capital City, but we got shifted to another part of it."

"It is the Capital," Will says. "But since we and that beast are the only living things in this sector, he will find us again rather easily."

Throwing my head back, I groan at the sky. "I take that back. Grant is Captain Grouchy, and you are Mr. Gloomy Pants."

Grant slings an arm around my waist and tugs me into him. "Maybe we are those things, but you are the Great Teleporter."

"Wow, thank you," I reply with more than a hint of sarcasm. "Your compliment is making me blush."

"Don't downplay your accomplishment, Erin." He gives me a quick kiss. "I'm proud of you."

"Um, thank you." This time I mean it. No sarcasm. "We need to figure out how to find Sefton's hideout."

Yeah, I changed the subject because I'm embarrassed. Only Grant has ever made me feel like a schoolgirl having her first crush on a boy. But it's more than that. He makes me feel alive again for the first time since the apocalypse ravaged our world. I think I might also be experiencing something far more shocking—hope.

"Perhaps you can wish yourself to be there," Will says. "Teleporting is an intuitive art, or so Sefton always told me."

"Can't hurt to try," I say. "What do you think, Grant?"

"Sure, try it." His hot smirk returns. "Should I kiss you again?"

"I think I can handle it this time without your lips involved."

"Maybe I can't." He nuzzles my neck. "I might get scared."

"Sure, I believe that. Mr. Zen is terrified."

A steamy thrill shivers through me when he flicks his tongue out to tease my throat. Oh, what the hell. I grasp his face and lift his head, then crush my mouth to his. It's like no time at all has elapsed between when he pressed his mouth to mine a moment ago and when I just did the same. We resume our wild, hot kiss, but this time we grope each other just as wildly as our tongues tangle.

The world spins, but I think that's only in my mind.

Will yelps.

Grant and I can't stop kissing.

"What have you done?" Will says in a panicked tone. "No, no, I don't want to be here."

Something in his voice shatters the lustful haze around me, and I jerk my head back. Grant still has his eyes closed, so I give him a quick shake. "Wake up, Romeo. You need to see this."

His lids flutter open. "What?"

"Look around."

Grant takes a few steps back, then scans the space. "Well, I'll be damned."

We've wound up inside an underground cavern that has rough-hewn walls and no visible means of exit or entry. Bookshelves line one wall, while a table in the middle holds scientific equipment like beakers and petri dishes. All the containers are empty. On the table, one book lies open.

Grant and I walk over there, and he picks up the book to flip through it. "Quantum physics. It's on loan from the Fort Worth Public Library. Way overdue."

"I doubt Sefton Stainthorpe will pay the fines, considering that he's dead."

Will keeps whimpering off and on, and now he hugs himself.

"Hey, what's wrong?" I ask. "Look like you saw a ghost."

"I have. The ghosts of the magics he invoked in this place." Will glances around, his face growing paler by the second. "This is where I was born."

He means that literally, I think. Well, he didn't emerge from a mother's womb, but Sefton created him with the magics he invoked to trigger doomsday. That's a kind of birth. A very creepy kind.

"Sefton is long gone," I say. "And his magics are gone too."

"No, they aren't. I feel their remnants nipping at my skin."

Grant starts wandering through the cavern, picking up books to flip through them, bending over to peer under the chair and table.

I cautiously slip an arm around Will's shoulders. "Take it easy, hey? Maybe what you feel is triggered by your own anxiety."

"That could be the case," he says cautiously. "You're a smart person."

"No, not really. I do a good impression of a smart person, though."

My lukewarm attempt at humor does not make him laugh or even make his lips twitch.

"Eureka!" Grant shouts. He jumps up from where he'd been perusing books on the shelves and hoists one bound volume above his head. He grins. "I found it."

"Found what?" I ask.

"Sefton's notes."

CHAPTER SEVENTEEN

Grant

I CAN'T STOP GRINNING, WHICH IS IDIOTIC. I FOUND SEFTON'S SECRET notes, and I want to jump up and down and whoop. No one knew if the madman kept any records, but I had a hunch and risked everything to get into the Echo to find the book I now hold in my hand. God, I hope it was worth the trouble. If the handwritten notes scrawled in this journal turn out to be the incoherent ramblings of a lunatic, I just might lie down on the floor and sleep for ten years.

Maybe the apocalypse would be over by then. Of course, that would probably mean the world exploded, leaving nothing behind but cosmic dust.

Erin rushes over to me and plants a firm kiss on my mouth. "Congratulations, Grant. You rock."

"I haven't actually found anything yet. Just a book."

"Haven't you read any of it?"

"Just a few sentences to verify that it seems to be what I think it is. I'd need Dax to confirm the handwriting belongs to Sefton."

Erin pats my cheek. "Stop looking for reasons to be bummed out. Open the damn book and read it already."

I used to hate her bossiness, but now I kind of like it. Erin knows what she needs to do and doesn't waste time vacillating. So I do what she would. I flip the book open and start reading. "I, Sefton Stainthorpe, vow to commit to the pages of this journal every bit of information I need to achieve my goal. The world has become too dirty and vile to go on as it is. A change is required. Only a massive and violent upheaval will bring about the necessary alterations."

Erin sidles up to me, leaning against my side, and peers down at the journal. "This is super creepy."

"No shit." The rest of the first page consists of complex equations I don't understand. I flip to the next page. "I know what the world needs, though no one would agree with my assessment. My fellow humans have become unconscionably addicted to technology and creature comforts, too settled in their hedonistic ways, more like animals than highly evolved beings."

The rest of this page is taken up by a rendering of Da Vinci's *The Vitruvian Man*. I've seen that image before—just about everybody has at some point—but for some reason, today the careful reproduction of Da Vinci's study of human anatomy sends a shiver through me. Why would Sefton care about making beautifully rendered drawings and equations when he planned to destroy the world?

Well, maybe I'll find answers on the next page.

But that page contains more ramblings about how evil and unworthy of life human beings are, plus more equations that I can't figure out. My studies of alchemy and quantum physics didn't prepare me for wickedly advanced math. Maybe these equations are nonsense, anyway.

I look at Will and hold up the journal, turning it so he can see the math gobbledygook. "Do you understand these equations?"

He shakes his head. "Sefton never taught me math."

But he is the madman's Echo. Other doppelgängers I've met knew things their originals knew, which suggests they inherited their original's memories.

I grasp Erin's arm and turn us both around, so we face the wall with our backs to Will. Then I whisper, "Something about that guy doesn't add up. He claims to be Sefton's Echo, but then he says he knows nothing about math. He should have at least some of Sefton's memories."

"Because Echo creatures do remember."

"Yeah. We shouldn't trust Will. He might be lying about everything."

"Does he look like Sefton?"

I shrug. "Guess so. But I only saw the man once, and he was already dead. Well, make that twice, counting when you and I visited Fallenmouth. His decaying corpse was hard to identify, though."

"Let's not read anymore of the journal aloud. Okay?"

"Agreed."

She leans in until her lips meet my ear, then whispers even more softly. "We can't just ditch Will, in case he's on the level, but we can't risk keeping him with us or sending him to earth."

"I know."

"Let's rummage through the rest of the books in here, then get back outside to come up with a plan."

"Good idea."

We thumb through the other books, but most of them are just textbooks on alchemy and physics. I've already read similar information in the papers I rescued from the remains of the Stanford University library. We don't need to bring these books with us. I stuff the journal into my backpack, and we're ready to go.

Erin can't seem to teleport. She didn't want me to kiss her again because she claimed it's unnecessary. But she seems to have suddenly become shy about what we need to do to get out of this cavern. No more waiting. We need out now, so I pull her into my arms and kiss her like there's no tomorrow. Which there might not be. I'm not doing this because I need to kiss her. It's an exit strategy.

Okay, maybe I just wanted to feel her up and taste her lips again. The exit strategy thing is an added benefit.

We pop out inside the Capital City, but nowhere I recognize. Since we'd driven through a lot of this town yesterday and this morning, I can't help wondering why I don't see anything familiar here. The skyscraper we had gotten trapped in earlier is nowhere on the horizon. Did our creature buddy destroy the whole building? Grenades couldn't pull that off, so I kind of doubt his big ugly feet could do it.

"Are you done fondling my ass?" Erin asks.

I jerk my hands away from her body. "Yeah, sorry."

"Don't apologize. I liked it, but we have stuff to do. Like, you know, saving the world and other inconsequential things."

Yeah, I've even started to like her snarky attitude.

The pattering of footsteps erupts behind us, retreating swiftly.

We both turn to look—and see Will fleeing. What the hell is he doing?

"Hey!" I holler. "Wait up."

Will does not stop or even slow down. He pelts down the street like an Olympic athlete and disappears around a corner. Erin and I race after him, but our backpacks hinder our speed. We get there too late. Will has vanished.

No, that's not weird or suspicious.

Erin and I halt halfway down the alley, breathing hard from sprinting while wearing fully loaded backpacks. Sweat dribbles down my temples.

"Where did he go?" Erin asks, and I take it for a rhetorical question. "Why did he run? I thought he was terrified and wanted us to protect him."

"Either he panicked, or he's a liar." Since we don't have our car, we can't search for Will. Even our eerily handy map of the city won't tell us where Sefton's Echo might have gone. "We have no choice. Let's find a place to hunker down and study the journal. If Will hasn't turned up by this evening, we should head back to earth."

"Okay." Erin bites her lip while she scans the alley in both directions. "Still not sure about Will, but I feel bad about leaving him behind."

"We didn't abandon him. He ran. That's his choice, and we need to move on."

"Maybe I should whisk us away to someplace outside the Capital City."

I consider the idea while we amble back onto the street. "I'd rather wait a few more hours to see if Will finds us. Then you can whisk us away."

"Fair enough."

The signs that led us to Will and the creepy skyscraper had also shown us where to find supplies and a safe place to sleep. We have no such luck now. Whatever magics had helped us before seem to have evaporated. But we find a building that hasn't been trashed inside as much as the other ones we checked out, so we decide to hunker down here. The vacant store is part of a larger building that extends down the entire block. This seems like it was an auto parts store, but it's hard to tell for sure what any post-apocalyptic structure might've been originally.

We don't have sleeping bags, but we find a partially scorched fabric car cover that we fold over to create a makeshift bed on the floor. Lying on our backs, we take turns reading the journal aloud. Do we learn anything? Yeah. We realize just how irretrievably insane Sefton was. Do we learn anything of practical use? Not really. Not yet, at least. But Erin keeps poring over the journal after I've given up. I'm staring at the ceiling when she speaks.

"Look at these weird symbols," she says, pointing at the book. "What are they?"

"Alchemical symbols. I saw the same designs in one of the medieval manuscripts Sefton stole from a university library, but I didn't understand why he had drawn them in the margin. Still don't."

"What do the symbols mean?"

"One is the sun symbol, which also represents the heart. The other is the symbol for gold, and it illustrates the concept of blood or the essence of life." I study the notes on the page and suddenly realize something. "Look at that. Sefton wrote that the heart and the lifeblood must be joined with the Tria Prima after the alchemical reaction has begun or else control can't be established."

"And that means what?"

"No idea."

She dog-ears that page and flips to the next. After an hour of scouring the journal, we take a break to eat some energy bars. We need real food soon, but that can wait a little while longer. I'm already feeling not up to my usual energy level, despite the name of those bars we ate. Red meat, that's what I need. We both do. But I also need to understand the journal because I feel like the fate of the world depends on it.

"You're so tense," Erin says. "Mr. Zen seems to have forgotten how to relax."

"We're in shit so deep we can't see the sky above us. Excuse me for feeling less than Zen right now."

"Try meditating. I'll do it too."

I glance at her sideways. "Have you ever meditated before?"

"Nope. You can teach me."

Erin the hardcore badass wants to learn about meditation while we're trapped in another world full of evil creatures. Go figure.

"All right," I tell her. "Let's get you up to speed on meditation. It's pretty simple."

"How do we start?"

"Ideally, we would find a comfortable place to settle in. That's not likely around here, so we'll have to make do." I sit up and get into a cross-legged position facing her. "You can sit however you like or stay lying down. I prefer a half-lotus position."

"Might as well try that too." She sits up and mimics my cross-legged pose. "I'm ready."

"We'll start with a basic mindfulness routine. It's all about staying in the moment."

"So, it's nice and vague. Which moment? This one? The next moment?"

"Right now. Are you ready?"

"Mm-hm."

"Good." I straighten my spine and take a deep breath. "Sit up straight, but keep your overall posture relaxed."

"That makes no sense."

"Shut up and do what I say."

Erin sputters like she's desperately trying not to laugh at me. "That doesn't sound very Zen, oh wise master."

I groan. "Just listen to my instructions and follow them. Okay?"

"Sir, yes, sir."

This time, I ignore her sarcasm. Telling her to shut up does no good. Instead, I channel my inner calmness and speak in a soothing voice. "Close your eyes and take slow, deep breaths to relax your entire body. Begin with your head and gradually move down to your toes. Keep breathing deeply while you do this and feel all the negative energy sifting out of you."

I peek through my mostly closed lids to watch her and make sure she does what I said. To my surprise, she obeys my instructions. Her lips curl into the barest of closed-mouth smiles.

"Next phase," I say. "Continue breathing deeply and slowly while you take note of every sensation in your body. Warm, cool, painful, whatever. Just let yourself experience all of it while remaining still and relaxed."

Her lips curl up a little more. Perfect. She's getting into the gentle relaxation of mindfulness. I'm feeling more peaceful too.

"If your mind drifts away from you, just ease it back into yourself," I say. "Your thoughts might wander occasionally, but keep bringing your focus back to your deep breathing and the sensations your body gives you."

My mind wanders, for sure—to her breasts and their enticing roundness. Her skintight tank top lets me see every contour of those tits as well as the flatness of her belly and the muscles in her arms. But I drag my focus back to the routine and close my eyes all the way, inhaling deep breaths and releasing them little by little. "How do you feel?"

"Good. Relaxed." Her voice has an almost dreamy quality. "Feel like I'm floating on a cloud while the sun warms my face."

"I feel that way too." I've never experienced this kind of sensation while I meditate. The warmth spreads down my throat and into my chest, sliding down toward my belly. "Keep breathing, slow and easy."

At this point, I would normally open my eyes. I've achieved relaxation and should move on to another exercise, but I can't make my lids part. That warmth spreads even lower, encompassing my groin, and I suck in a breath when my dick jerks and starts to swell. I've never gotten aroused while meditating, but then, I've never done it with a partner before.

The warmth suffuses my entire body now.

I hear soft whispering inside my mind, but it's not my voice. Whose, then? I sink into the mindful meditation and let go of all questions, but that voice keeps whispering to me in a sultry tone, though I can't understand the words yet.

Touch me, Grant.

Erin's voice shimmers through me like a wave of heat radiating off pavement in the summer. I inhale a deep breath, exhaling gradually while an arousing sensation ripples through me, almost like fingers caressing my skin. Erin's fingers. A blurry vision of her nude body intrudes on my meditation, and I can't resist allowing myself to dive into the fantasy. Everything remains slightly out of focus, but the feel of her skin brushing against mine grows more powerful every second.

My dick is rock-hard.

And I need to fuck her right now.

CHAPTER EIGHTEEN

Erin

"GRANT," I WHISPER, SOUNDING NOTHING LIKE MYSELF. I'VE BECOME A sex addict who needs another fix right now. My Zen master didn't warn me mindfulness meditation would lead to scorching sex and a strangely hot mental connection. My nipples have gone hard, and I can't shut my stupid mouth. "Oh God, please, Grant. Touch me everywhere."

"Fuck," he growls. His voice has become a rough and growly whisper that I swear I can hear in my own head. "Look at me, Erin."

His Zen tone has turned rough and rife with hunger.

I slowly part my lids, but I still feel dreamy and warm in all the best ways. "I want you."

Like I've never wanted anyone in my life, but I manage not to blurt that out. What I've said so far is embarrassing enough. The ardent desire I feel seems rooted in magics, though I can't explain why I believe that. I know it with a strange conviction.

His gaze gravitates to my lips. "I want you too. But this isn't the time."

"Please. Don't make me wait. I'm so turned on, and it feels incredible. But I need you inside me right now or I think I might go crazy."

Based on his expression and the iron hard-on straining his pants, I know he's experiencing the same phenomenon. What is happening to us? I swear I can feel him inside me already, like a sexy ghost inhabiting my body while giving me an erotic massage.

"Oh, yes," I moan. "Take me deep inside you and penetrate me to the core."

What the hell? Why am I begging for sex? And why do I kind of not mind that I'm begging?

Grant strokes his dick through his jeans.

I can't stop myself. I palm my tits and flick my thumbs over my nipples, gasping when a bolt of pleasure fires down my nerves and straight into my clit.

Grant surges forward and pins me to the blanket with his entire body, rotating his hips to grind his erection into my belly. His breaths come as short, harsh gasps, just like mine. I wrap my legs around his hips and drag my tongue up his throat, afflicted with a sudden craving to taste every inch of him. Groaning, he pushes up on his straight arms so he can reach down to unzip his jeans and push a hand inside his boxers, pulling his dick out as if plans to fuck me any second.

I latch on to his earlobe and suckle it.

He growls something unintelligible.

A ratcheting noise erupts outside, the mechanical sound echoing off the buildings.

Whump. Whump.

Grant and I both freeze, our gazes locked. Our horny friend from the Echo made a similar sound when he tromped through the city, but this noise is so much louder and imbued with a mechanical undertone.

"What is that?" I ask as if Grant could possibly know the answer.

Instead of responding, he leaps up and hauls me to my feet with him. He holds my hand as we approach the broken windows of the former store and peer out into the darkening twilight.

"Don't see anything," I say. "But that noise seems to be coming closer."

Grant compresses his lips as he stares out the window with his head cocked to one side and his gaze narrowed. "Something about that sound is familiar. Not like I've heard it, but like somebody told me about it once."

"Who told you?"

The ground trembles as massive footfalls crash down on the asphalt, and the cracking of the roadway reverberates through the city. I feel the vibrations in my body. The city itself begins to shiver visibly, from the subsurface all the way up to the tops of the buildings.

I grab Grant's arm. "We need to get out of here. Fast."

He tears his focus away from what's happening outside and looks at me. "You should teleport us away right now."

"Okay, I'll try." I seize his shirt and pull him into me, then squeeze my eyes shut as I concentrate all my willpower on one task—*get us away from here.* Nothing happens. I peek out between my half-closed lids to make sure. Nope, we haven't moved one inch. "Didn't work."

Grant cradles my face in his hands and kisses me.

I pull my head back to see him. "Still nothing. Sorry."

"Where did you try to go?"

"Anyplace else."

He squints like he's thinking hard. "Try aiming for a specific place."

"Like where?"

"The gateway to the Echo. From there, maybe you can whisk us back to earth."

The whumping footfalls of whatever lurks out there grow louder every minute, and the shaking beneath our feet may soon become a genuine earthquake. I have no choice. I must do what Grant suggested—and do it now.

"Should I kiss you again?" he asks.

"Why not? Can't hurt."

He plasters his mouth to mine and plunges his tongue deep while I concentrate harder than ever, so hard that my head starts to hurt. I don't sense any change. When I open my eyes, I realize we haven't moved at all. Grant still has his tongue in my mouth, so I slap my hands on his chest and push him away.

"Did it work?" he asks.

I spread my arms to indicate our surroundings. "Does it look like it worked?"

"Dumb question, you're right. I got a little, uh, mentally scrambled."

He can't mean because he kissed me. Well, his lips and his body turn me into a human omelet too, so I probably shouldn't judge him for that.

Whump. Whump. Whump.

The bits of jagged glass that still cling to the store window's frame begin to rattle with every step our mysterious visitor takes. I grab Grant's hand and haul him out the door, onto the sidewalk. There, we stop. As one, we tip our heads back to glimpse whatever is coming for us. The crown of a monstrous head pops up above the buildings on the cross street two blocks over, and the little of it I can see does not ease my anxiety in the least.

"What on earth is that?" I ask, my tone hushed and filled with a terrible awe I can't disguise.

Grant shuts his eyes and grimaces. Then he blows out a breath. "That is Sefton's golem."

"His what? You and Will mentioned that before, but I don't understand what the word means."

"A golem is a creature created by magic and bound to obey its master's commands. I never saw the golem, but Allison and Dax told me about it. They described it in detail." He throws an arm around me as more footfalls slam down and their concussions make the ground shudder so much that I might've fallen over if Grant hadn't held on to me. "Sefton said he put the golem to sleep after he captured Dax and Allison. Either this is a different golem, or somebody woke it up."

"Will could've done it. Don't you think?"

"Maybe. He claims not to know about Sefton's plans or his alchemical experiments, but he might've been lying."

The crown of the monstrosity's head rises above the buildings again, giving me enough of a glimpse that I know that thing can't be more than two blocks away now. I close my eyes and slide my arms around Grant, hugging him tightly. Then I try one last time to whisk us away.

Pain slams into my head like a lightning bolt.

I scream, and my legs buckle. Grant catches me. The intensity of the pain makes me feel like my skull has exploded and my brain has melted, but I force myself to suck in the tiniest of breaths to quell the ringing in my ears and prevent myself from passing out. What on earth is this? I got shot during my time as a Marine, but that was nothing compared to the mind-shattering agony I'm experiencing now.

Grant holds me to him and kisses the top of my head. "Easy, Erin. Remember the mindfulness routine. Try to focus on one thing—my voice. Can you do that?"

The golem stomps ever nearer, and the ground pulsates with every footstep.

But I manage to nod weakly.

"Good," Grant says. "Just listen to me. Tune out everything else. I won't let anyone hurt you ever again, so you don't need to worry about that. Just relax and take slow breaths, shallow ones at first, then try taking deeper ones as the pain subsides." He combs his fingers through my hair in a soothing gesture. "Shh, it's okay. Picture a sandy beach, blue skies, palm trees, and a hammock. You walk over to the hammock and lie down on it, letting the hammock rock gently side to side. I'm there with you, massaging your feet."

A tingling sensation begins in my arms and blossoms out through the rest of my body, reaching my head last. The soft, sensual tingling relaxes my muscles. The pain subsides while I focus on the lovely sensation of his fingers in my hair and the image of a tropical beach.

I lift my head. "I'm okay now. Thank you."

He kisses me. "Glad to hear it."

We turn toward the cross street again. With no options left, we stand here to await the arrival of the golem. Oddly, I experience only a twinge of anxiety. Grant got me so Zenned out that I can't worry at all, but I know the feeling will pass. I also know I can get it back anytime I need to, thanks to the man who taught me how to relax.

All of the golem's head emerges as he passes the shorter buildings near the intersection.

I glance up at Grant. "That thing looks like it's part machine and part living thing."

"Looks that way because it is that way."

The asphalt on the cross street buckles and rises like waves on an ocean, the ripples racing across the intersection to follow the track of the cross street. Their motion causes much smaller ripples in the asphalt where we stand. Though they might be smaller, those waves create enough energy to make the brick building across from us crumble.

The golem steps into the intersection and swivels to face us.

Holy shit, that thing really is man and machine combined. The metal plates fused to its skin flex with every muscle in its body. Solid metal shoes cover its feet. The dark gray and black shades of its flesh seem to shimmer as if its entire body is infused with metal. The monstrosity's eyes shimmer an electric crimson, like demonic headlights.

The golem moves only those eyes as it scans the street where we loiter.

"Don't suppose that thing has a weak spot," I say. "Looks like an unstoppable monster."

"From what Allison told me, that's exactly what it is. But the golem obeyed Sefton's commands. Who woke it up today?"

I slip my hand into his and thread our fingers, taking comfort from the simple contact while I consider his question. I'm sure it was rhetorical, but I can't help wondering. "Do you think Will did this? Could he control the golem now that Sefton is gone?"

"Maybe. He seems like a scaredy-cat, but that might be an act."

"What if he used us to find Sefton's secret journal?"

The idea only occurred to me a second ago, and I expect Grant to scoff at the suggestion.

But he doesn't. Instead, he gives me a sly smile. "You're one smart cookie, Erin. You may be right about that. I think we'll find out the answer any minute now."

The golem swerves its demonic gaze to us. The machine-beast tips his head down, then a ratcheting sound starts up as the thing slowly cranks its jaw open.

"Oh no," Grant says. "I remember what Dax said the golem does with its mouth."

"I'm guessing it doesn't sing lullabies."

"Nope." He grips my hands harder. "Time to run."

We take off in the opposite direction from the golem, still holding hands.

The ratcheting noise of the thing's jaw opening ceases.

I know I shouldn't look, but my mind has other ideas. It forces me to glance over my shoulder.

A red glow burns deep inside the golem's mouth.

"Stop gawking," Grant snarls. "You're slowing us down."

I face forward again. Between gasping breaths, I ask, "What is that thing doing now?"

"Getting ready to fire."

No chance to ask what sort of weapon the thing will fire at us. I've barely formulated the thought when the golem roars and flames shoot past us over our heads to strike the asphalt street half a block away.

Grant jerks me to a halt.

The heat of the golem's fire breath rushes over our heads, and I raise my free arm to shield myself from it. Then silence falls over the world, or at least this part of it. I gingerly lower my arm and peek out through half-closed lids.

Oh shit.

The golem has melted the asphalt ahead of us, the sidewalks too. His breath set several buildings on fire. That damn beast has blocked our way out. I glance at Grant, and he nods. We rotate to face the golem, which now stands not quite a block away.

"Should we raise our hands in surrender?" I ask. "Don't think we can overpower that thing."

Grant releases my hand and raises both of his.

I do the same. What choice do we have? For the moment, we must surrender.

The golem, which still has its maw wide open, reaches behind its head to hold its hand palm up. A small figure trots out from behind the monster's head, or maybe from inside it, and hops onto the giant metal-and-flesh hand. The golem lowers itself into a kneeling position, emitting grinding noises, and sets its hand on the ground. The small figure leaps off the monstrosity's palm to land on the roadway.

Will saunters toward us, halting several yards away. "Thank you for finding the journal for me, but I now have no use for you."

He snaps his fingers, and the sound echoes off the buildings.

That red glow fires up again inside the golem's mouth.

We are about to get flambéed.

CHAPTER NINETEEN

Grant

I MIGHT BE THE KIND OF MAN WHO MEDITATES AND DOESN'T LIKE TO argue with anybody unless it's absolutely necessary, but that doesn't mean I'm a coward. Surrendering does not appeal to me. I need to fight, but I won't risk Erin's life to do that. Sure, she can handle herself like the seasoned military vet she is. But the thought of that golem or his master injuring Erin… It makes me feel a kind of anger I haven't experienced since the day Sefton's apocalypse ripped my family away from me.

"Why are you doing this?" I shout to Will. "We helped you."

"You are tools who have outlived their usefulness."

"Did Sefton really leave those breadcrumbs for Allison? Or did you lead us to that building so we could rescue you?"

He lifts one shoulder in a slight shrug. "I was genuinely trapped in that building, and I took advantage of your presence to effect my escape. But the clues you followed were the ones my original self planted for Allison."

Will seems much more confident now, but I have an intuition that he wasn't faking when he behaved like a terrified, abused child. Maybe his success in reactivating the golem has emboldened him. I mean, the guy has a giant cyborg with asphalt-melting fire breath. That probably made him feel invincible, and the power has gone to his head.

How can we teach him a lesson in humility without getting killed in the process? I have an idea, but Erin might not like it. Well, it's nothing she hasn't done before.

I lean toward her to whisper directly into her ear. "Flirt with him."

"What?" she hisses out of the corner of her mouth. "Are you insane?"

"You did the same thing with that creature who carried us into the Echo. Why is it insane to use your special skills to distract Will right now?"

"What if my flirtation makes him angry? He's got a gigantic cyborg on his side. And I doubt the golem will fall for my charms."

"Just try it with Will. The goal is to stop him from telling his golem to squash us under his metal boots."

"They're shoes, not boots."

She just has to argue with me about everything, doesn't she?

"Whatever," I growl. "Just do it."

Erin rolls her eyes and pushes me away.

I decide to assume that means she's about to test her flirty charms on Will.

"Are we still friends, Will?" she asks. "I can't believe you were lying about everything. You like me, don't you?"

Will squints at her. "What are you doing?"

"Just chatting. We helped you, and we want to go on helping you. *I* want to help you. How can I do that?"

"You're still alive only because I need that journal. Hand it over."

Why didn't he steal that before he fled from us? He must've thought he couldn't wrest it away from me or Erin. That implies he views us as stronger and tougher than he is. Erin must realize that too. She's too smart not to figure that out. She has the journal in her backpack, but we took our packs off to meditate. They're still inside the store—a block behind us, beyond the wide expanse of melted asphalt. The road surface back there still bubbles, the heat of it warming our backs.

I hope she remembers that's where we left the journal. If she doesn't remember… No, she will.

"The journal," Will snaps, though his lips tremble the slightest bit. "I want it now."

Erin sashays a little closer to him. "I'm so proud of you, sweetie. Awakening the golem would've terrified anyone, but you did it. You're stronger and better than Sefton ever was."

"No, I—" He makes a frustrated noise. "Bloody hell, you're trying to confuse me."

His accent just switched from American to British. Had he been faking his American persona? If so, he did a bang-up job. I completely bought his performance. Or is he faking this time? Since Sefton was British, I tend to believe that's Will's natural accent too.

As if it matters.

Erin holds her hands palms out, raised slightly in front of her in a conciliatory gesture. "Relax, Will. I want to help if you'll let me. I'm your friend, remember?"

She isn't flirting, but her tactic seems more likely to convince Will than my idea would have.

"I thought we were friends," Will says carefully. "But you ran away from my golem."

"No, we ran away from his fire breath," Erin tells him. "If we'd known you were controlling the golem, we wouldn't have tried to run."

His anger softens into an almost hopeful expression. "You want to be with me?"

"Of course we do." She takes another step toward him. "Please tell me what has you so scared."

"You'll laugh at me. Sefton always did."

"No, we won't." Erin glances back at me. "Come over here, Grant. Show him we're all friends."

I approach her, and though I want to hold her hand, I stop myself from doing that. Will might not like it. And she's right, we need to placate him, not trick him. The guy was locked inside a vacant, creepy skyscraper—for months, at least. Maybe he just needs reassurance.

But I'll keep my cop senses on high alert.

Erin glances at me and tips her head toward Will.

She wants me to play nice with the guy who controls a frigging golem. Well, why not? If it stops us from getting pancaked on the asphalt, I'll give it a try. "Hey, Will, I'm glad you're okay. We were worried about you after you took off. In fact, we hung around hoping you'd turn up."

His brows knit together, and he bites one corner of his lip.

Yeah, he wants to believe us. That's a good sign.

"You must have been alone for a long time," I say. "Time moves differently in the Echo, right?"

Will gnaws on his lip for a moment. "Yes, that's right. I've been trapped here for more years than I can count."

"Trapped in that building?"

He nods.

"Can't imagine how awful that was. But you're free now. And we really do want to be your friends. What do you say?"

Will chews on his lip even harder.

I slowly approach him and nod for Erin to do the same. We halt a few feet from Will. I offer him my hand. "Friends, right?"

He stares at my hand, but then takes it. "Yes, friends."

Erin kisses his cheek and smiles.

But we still have a gigantic cyborg looming ahead of us with its maw gaping wide and its crimson eyes scanning the area. Yeah, that's not disturbing. The way every hair on my body is stiffening has nothing to do with that thing staring at us.

Being sarcastic in my own head isn't helpful.

"I do need that journal," Will says. "Please give it to me."

Erin and I exchange glances. I shrug.

She faces Will. "We left our backpacks in a store about two blocks away, on the other side of the melted asphalt. The journal is in my pack."

Will turns around to face the golem. "Get their backpacks for me, would you?"

The golem closes its mouth with a ratcheting sound, then nods and straightens. The grinding noise as it rises grates on my ears even more than the ratcheting sound had. The metal monster lifts one foot and swings it forward to stomp down on the asphalt just behind us. Its other foot whumps down a second later. The golem hesitates there, as if analyzing its options. Finally, the thing bends its knees and launches itself off the ground. The golem lands on the other side of the melted asphalt.

"How does he know which building it is?" I ask.

"My golem is imbued with tracking spells," Will says. "He knew exactly where you were the moment I awakened him and told him your names."

"But you only know our first names."

"Sefton created the tracking spells. I don't know the details, only that they work."

All this magic stuff can be amazing, but in the hands of a whackjob, it's damn annoying. Will seems a lot more reasonable than Sefton was, but I'm still balanced on that fence when it comes to our new buddy. After all, when he gets mad, he sics a golem on us.

Since he already knows why we came to the Echo, I see no reason I shouldn't ask him a question related to that. "We need to figure out what the information in Sefton's journal means. Would you help us?"

"I've already told you I know nothing about those magics or quantum physics."

"But you woke the golem up. That must've required magic."

"The spell to awaken the sleeping giant required nothing more than chanting a specific phrase. I heard Sefton recite the words when he first created the golem."

"I appreciate your honesty, Will." But if he was there when Sefton created that thing—a fact he didn't mention when we met him—then he might have more secrets.

"You appreciate it?" Will says, seeming genuinely baffled.

"That's right. I always appreciate it when someone tells me the truth. When I was a deputy sheriff, I spent every day listening to people lie to me."

He still seems confused, but I think that means he understands I meant what I said.

"We're both grateful, Will," Erin says, "that you've been upfront with us. Honesty between friends is important."

The mechanical noise of the golem on the move starts up again. Just as we turn our heads to look at the thing, it leaps over the melted asphalt, which seems to be cooling now, and lands just behind its master. The golem faces us.

And it drops our backpacks at our feet.

Saying "thank you" seems like a bad idea. Not sure that cyborg understands words, anyway, unless they're spoken by its puppet master. I kneel to unzip Erin's pack and pull out the journal. Will wants it, but if he has no knowledge of magics, I can't see what good the journal will do him. He got angry when we told him we didn't have it, and he repeatedly demanded we hand it over to him.

I rise and hold the journal in one hand. "Here it is. But since you don't know anything about magic, this thing won't do you any good. It's full of spells and alchemical junk, not to mention quantum physics. Are you an expert on that?"

Will puckers his lips while staring at the journal like it's a juicy rib-eye steak, and he hasn't eaten in days. "Please give me the journal."

"Let's find a place to sit down and go through it together. I've already spent some time studying it."

He thrusts out his hand. "Give it to me."

Okay, now I'm back to thinking he's a nutjob like the original Sefton. I am not giving up this journal without a damn good reason or at least some serious proof that I can trust this guy. I might not fully understand the info in the book, but I know it holds vital clues that might let us reverse the damage done by Sefton's apocalypse or at least stop the convulsions the Echo has experienced lately.

So no, I'm not handing over the journal.

Will's chest heaves as he blusters breaths out through his nostrils and clenches his fists tightly enough that they tremble. He clenches his teeth too, which I can tell because his lips peel back from them when he speaks, his voice raspy and harsh. "I want the fucking journal. *Now.*"

Erin raises her hands. "Take it easy, sweetie. We're friends, remember?"

"Friends do not refuse to give me what I need." Spittle sprayed from his lips when he snarled those words. "If you defy me again, I will exact punishment. Last chance."

I hold the journal to my belly and shake my head. "No dice, Will. We study this book together or not at all."

"You think you can stop me from taking it?" He makes a strange noise deep in his throat, almost like an animal growling. Then he tips his head to the side, seeming curious now. "Have you not figured out why Erin couldn't teleport you away?"

She got a massive headache but couldn't do it. That's all we know, but I won't admit that to him.

Will straightens and rolls his shoulders back, his chin lifted. "I prevented it."

Yeah, I really trust him now. He just admitted to lying to us again, didn't he? The guy keeps telling us he has no magic skills, but then he admits to awakening a golem and now, apparently, stopping Erin from whisking us away.

"I imagine she suffered intense pain when she tried to do it," Will says with a smug little smile. "Sefton might have believed I was useless and impotent, but I watched everything he did. I heard every spell he cast." Will taps his temple. "And I memorized them. I have a photographic memory, but Sefton didn't seem to realize that. He never bothered to learn much of anything about me."

A chill slithers down my spine, raising the hairs at my nape. I'm getting an inkling, but nothing I can articulate just yet.

"I must have that journal," Will says. "I'll give you ten seconds to relinquish it. Count it down for me, golem."

The cyborg emits a weird ticking noise. One, two, three…

Erin pulls a switchblade out of her pocket, flicks it open, and races up to Will. She holds the blade's glistening edge to his throat. "Stop the countdown, or I'll slit your throat."

He smirks.

She nicks his skin. Blood trickles down his throat. "Stop the countdown."

"Stop," he shouts.

The golem goes silent.

"I have a better idea, anyway," Will says. "Golem, seize them."

The great cyborg slowly bends down, stretching out a hand as if to grab us.

We snatch up our backpacks and run.

CHAPTER TWENTY

Erin

WHERE ARE WE GOING? NO IDEA. BUT IF GRANT THINKS WE NEED TO RUN, I'll follow him anywhere. I can't teleport, which leaves us with no means of escaping except to bolt. The golem seems too slow to catch us, but since we're dealing with a magically created monstrosity, I can't rule anything out. Maybe that thing has a stick shift inside it that will push it into overdrive.

So we run, run, run.

A mechanical screeching reverberates through the city, seeming to emanate from above our heads. I risk a glance up—and my heart thuds. "Grant! It's overhead!"

He tips his head back while still sprinting down the street. "Shit!"

Yeah, lots and lots of swearing is appropriate right now because the golem is flying toward us from above. Does it have propellers? A jet engine? Given the haphazard way it flies toward us, I wonder if the thing just jumped into the air and intends to flop down on top of us. We would die, but the journal might remain intact.

"Don't watch the golem," Grant shouts at me. "Focus on the road ahead."

I do what he suggested, but my legs have started to burn and I'm having trouble catching my breath. My ears ring too. I might be hyperventilating. Who can blame me? A monstrous robot-man thing wants to turn us into red smears on the road.

Whump.

The ground shudders so violently that we both stumble and fall, rolling across the pavement because the pavement itself is rolling like waves on a turbulent sea. Cracking noises accompany the buckling of the roadway. Grant hits the curb, and I slam into him. Once the dizziness lessens, my brain manages to process what I'm seeing.

The golem lies flat on its belly on the street. Steam rises up from beneath it as if the monster slid down the roadway after crash landing on it and skidded so hard and fast that the pavement heated up. Maybe the golem got injured, and it can't get up again.

Grant crawls out from under me and struggles to his feet. He sways a little, but only for a few seconds. Then he grasps my arms and hauls me up too. "Can't run anymore. What about you?"

"My legs feel like jelly." I nod toward the golem. "Think it's damaged?"

"Kinda doubt it. We should get moving, as fast as we can. I realize that probably won't be fast at all, but still…"

"Yeah. No choice and all that jazz."

A ratcheting noise starts up, and the golem pushes up with its arms, slowly rising into a crouch.

We run. Well, it's more like a fast walk, and we weave around instead of taking a straight path. I feel a touch woozy, so I imagine he does too. My jelly legs can't carry me as fast as I need to go.

The ratcheting stops, replaced by a grinding noise that makes my ears hurt.

Dammit. We need to move faster.

Giant fingers curl around us like a barricade.

We both stumble to a halt, but we're confused for half a second too long. By the time we try to escape the literal clutches of the metal beast, its fingers have encompassed us and are closing tighter and tighter every second. I can't move my arms or legs, not with a gigantic hand wrapped around my entire body, leaving only my head and neck exposed. Grant suffers from the same problem.

The golem has caught us.

With more mechanical noises, the metal monster rises to his feet and turns around to face his master. Will stands at the intersection where we'd left him, but now he strides down the street toward us.

I can't believe I felt bad for the guy. Once a coward gets a taste of power, he gorges on it. The only way to stop a bully is to take away that power and remind him what it feels like to be the weak one. I can't stand up to him right now. Literally. I can't move my body.

The golem waits patiently for his master, standing so perfectly still that I wonder if the thing can fall asleep while standing up. Does it sleep at all? No idea.

Will halts right in front of the golem, mere feet from his mechanical slave. He tilts his head up to look at us. "You two should have obeyed me."

I want to smack him down so hard.

"Now, you have forced me to be unkind to you." Will waves a hand in a grand gesture. "Golem, take them to the palace."

Sefton had a palace? What, did he wear a crown too? I assumed nothing could surprise me anymore, not after the alchemy of worlds, but Will has done that. King Sefton died. Does his doppelgänger plan to anoint himself Lord of the Echo now? I'm beginning to suspect that what everyone, including Dax, thought they knew about Sefton was only the tip of a blood-red iceberg.

The golem starts walking. He picks up Will along the way, holding him gently in one palm with those enormous fingers half curled.

I still have my knife in my hand. If I could wriggle a bit and get a sliver of leverage, maybe I could... What? Prick the golem's finger? Yeah, I'm sure he'd collapse and writhe in agony if I did that. *Use your brain, woman. Think of something.*

Grant, who remains squished in the golem's hand with his back plastered to mine, twists his head around to see me. "Our cyborg pal doesn't seem to have a brain of his own."

"Duh." We're both speaking in hushed voices to keep Will or the golem from hearing us. "This thing is a magical construct, right? That means no brain."

"Not quite. All the Echo creatures, and Will too, are magical constructs. They have brains, even if they use them for evil purposes."

"How does this conversation help us? I hope you're not about to suggest I should flirt with the golem."

"No. But I think there might be... I don't know. Feel like an idea is hovering just out of my reach, and if I could stretch a little farther, I might catch it."

"Keep trying. We've got nothing else." I make a pained face. "My best idea so far is to get stabby with my knife."

Grant's expression goes blank. He stares at me for a moment while our golem buddy lumbers down the street and rounds a corner. Then Grant grins. "You're a genius."

"As much as I love a compliment, I think you're overdoing it. I haven't done anything genius-level yet."

"Oh yes you have." He grins. "Get stabby, baby."

Grant has never called me "baby" before. He never called me anything but my name. Well, that and "reckless." I shouldn't read too much into what he just said, though, because I doubt he means it as an endearment.

But I do what he suggested. I wriggle, though only enough to get a better grip on my switchblade, not enough to alert the golem—I hope. Once I've got my hand positioned right, I tell Grant, "Ready."

"Thrust as hard and deep as you can." He smirks. "I didn't mean for that to sound so erotic."

"Sure you didn't. I'm on to you, Larson. You're a closet sex addict, aren't you?"

"Only for you."

I need to change the subject. It's too weird for us to be making suggestive comments to each other while we're literally in the grip of a cyborg. So instead, I "get stabby." I thrust my blade as deep and hard as possible, but I don't stop with one strike. I gore the golem's hand repeatedly and even manage to slice a gash through its palm. Is that enough to distract it? Not sure, so I keep going. My blade bumps into one of the metal plates embedded in the thing's flesh. At first, I assume I can't do anything about that, but then I realize something vital. The golem's metal plates are fused to its flesh, yes, but I can slip my knife under this one. I take a deep breath and shove the blade under the plate and tug it upward to separate the metal from the flesh.

The golem roars.

And it stops moving.

Its grip on us loosens a touch, just enough that I can wriggle around and get both my hands on the knife. I manage to pry my arms free of the cyborg's grip, then slash it down toward the top of the metal plate and slice it free too. Two sides of it gape open with blood trickling down from the wound.

The golem roars again, but this time its voice has a note of pain in it.

And its fingers pop open. Not all the way, but enough.

Grant and I climb out of the beast's palm. Far below us lies the roadway. If we jump, we will probably become pancakes for real this time.

Will howls like a wounded animal. "Stop them, golem! Stop them! I command you!"

The golem pays no attention, too distracted by its own pain to worry about its master.

Grant holds our backpacks. He hands me one, and we quickly slip into them. But we can't jump, not from this height. Does he have a plan? Of course he does. Grant is amazing that way.

"Let's climb up the golem's arm and stab him on the inside of his elbow," Grant says. "That might be a weak spot." He pulls out the cutlass I'd seen him stash in his pack and slides it out of its scabbard. "With your switchblade and my cutlass, we can slay this giant. Or at least make him fall to his knees."

And then we can jump onto the ground. Damn, he's brilliant. We need to have sex again soon.

Grant and I scramble up the golem's arm while he raises his wounded hand, which means we're running downhill. I stumble and wind up sliding toward the monster's elbow, bouncing over the edges of metal plates. Grant sees what happened to me and decides to follow suit, though he slides down the beast's arm on purpose. Luckily, the golem raises his arm halfway and stops. He stares at his palm, those crimson eyes glowing less brightly than before.

Grant thrusts his cutlass into the crease of the beast's elbow, pushing it in to the hilt.

I kneel and stab my knife into the golem's flesh, hard and deep, over and over, while blood begins to pour from the wounds. Grant yanks his cutlass free, then punches it into the cyborg's flesh yet again. Even more blood pours from the wounds he inflicts. We keep piercing the elbow again and again, plunging ours blades as deep as possible and getting covered in the golem's blood in the process. It's red like ours.

The golem emits an ear-splitting sound, a cross between a howl and machinery screaming. Then the creature's knees buckle.

Whump.

The metal monster strikes the ground and starts to fall forward.

Grant and I leap off the golem's arm, landing on our feet. But we only have seconds to get out of the path of the monster's body before it crushes us. I glance back and see Will trapped in the golem's other hand, though its fingers have slackened. That gives him a shot at escaping alive, but I can't worry about the crazy son of a bitch right now. He brought this on himself.

"Hurry!" Grant hollers as he seizes my hand and half drags me away.

The golem's body seems to tip forward in slow motion, but I think that's adrenaline heightening my senses and altering my perception of time. I can smell the cyborg's blood, acrid and metallic but with a hint of motor oil. We race down the street, headed to who knows where, knowing only that we need to get far away from what's about to happen. When the golem dropped from the sky, it had nearly shattered an entire block of buildings and pavement. The creature will fall from a much lower altitude this time, but something about the way his blood smells makes me worry that we won't be safe until we get farther away.

Because I smell something I recognize, and it means big trouble.

"Run faster," I tell Grant. "That golem might have explosives inside it."

"What? Why do you think that?"

"Trust me. I worked alongside the bomb squad when I was in the Marines. I swear I smell C-4." We have to shout to hear each other over the groaning, grinding, ratcheting, roaring noises coming from the golem.

"What does it smell like?" Grant asks.

"Motor oil."

"Why would Sefton make his toy explosive?"

"No idea."

The mechanical noises end, plunging the city into a silence deeper than normal. Whatever normal is in the Echo.

Whump.

We stagger sideways as the earth shudders, but I catch Grant before he tumbles into a mailbox. They have mail in the Echo? Who knew.

The golem has fallen. But will it rise again or explode? It might just lie there on the ground, dead in whatever way a magically made construct would be. We stand still for a moment, waiting for something else to happen. I glance back the way we'd come, but I can't see anything, not even a cloud of dust. Maybe the golem disintegrated when it ceased to function.

I look down at my body and suddenly realize I'm covered in Golem blood. Grant is soaked in the stuff too.

A human roar of anguish reverberates off the buildings.

We whirl around.

Someone has rounded a corner, exiting the street where the golem had been and limping down this road toward us. The person wails again, throwing both arms in the air and tripping over who knows what. The individual manages not to fall down and keeps struggling to cross the distance to us. As the figure draws closer, I recognize that face.

Will has caught up to us. And he's royally ticked.

Chapter Twenty-One

Grant

Erin and I remain motionless while we watch our former friend shuffling toward us, favoring his left leg and cradling his left arm. When the golem fell, it must have injured Will. Though I feel like I should experience a twinge of empathy for the guy, considering how Sefton treated him, I can't pull that off. He threatened to kill us, and I believe he would have done it. Then he sicced his golem on us. So yeah, I don't feel bad for that guy anymore.

We should get out of here, but I can't move, and Erin seems to have the same problem. I think we're still in shock. About everything. Nobody has had much of a chance to deal with the losses and the horror of what Sefton unleashed on the world a few months ago. Just when we thought at least things couldn't get worse, the Echo started to freak out.

"Should we run?" Erin asks. "He sounds beyond angry."

"Yeah, but he has no leverage anymore. Without the golem, he's just a spineless nerd who can't even teleport."

"Can't believe I felt sorry for him. Or that I tried to comfort him."

"He put on a good show. His true colors only surfaced when he got out of that skyscraper."

Since I'm known as the guy who never gets upset and accepts everyone the way they are, maybe I should muster a little bit of empathy for Will. But no, I won't do that. He tried to kill me, which I find slightly annoying. He also tried to kill Erin, and I will murder anyone who endangers her.

When I glance at Erin, I feel a strong urge to kiss her. Since we're both blood-soaked, I think I'll wait. But a familiar odor wafts into my nostrils every time I inhale, a smell that reminds me of what Erin said a minute ago.

C-4 smells like motor oil.

"Do you smell that?" I ask. "On your clothes. Doesn't that odor remind you of motor oil? I assumed any explosives would be hidden inside the golem, not on us."

Erin lifts the collar of her shirt and sniffs. Her eyes widen. "Oh, shit. The golem's blood must be infused with C-4 or something similar. I kind of doubt it's actually motor oil."

"Maybe the golem needs a lot of lubrication to function."

"Grasp at all the straws you want. But if there's even a slim chance we're covered in the blood of a creature that might contain explosives, we need to act accordingly."

I ignore the limping nerd slowly coming toward us and ask, "Act according to what?"

"Decontamination protocols. We have to get this gunk off us ASAP."

"You see any bathtubs or showers around here? We can't clean ourselves off with anything but dirt."

"I know." She flattens her lips and narrows her gaze, an expression I've decided means she's thinking. Then she shrugs and shakes her head. "I've got nothing."

A shuffling sound draws our attention back to Will. He stops several yards away to pout at us. Okay, maybe his lips don't actually form a pout, but his expression and his attitude create the effect. He stands there with slumped shoulders, messy hair, torn clothes, and one shoe missing its sole. Dirt and blood spatter his body, though he's not soaked like we are.

When I glance at Erin, I know she's thinking the same thing I am. So I face Will. "Does that golem have explosive blood?"

His expression goes blank. He doesn't blink for several seconds. Then he starts laughing.

Does that mean no, the golem doesn't have C-4 blood? No idea.

When Will finally stops laughing, he wipes tears from his eyes. "Thank you for reminding me."

I don't know what that means, but I'm getting a prickly feeling on my skin that's telling me to run.

He shoves a hand into his pants pocket and pulls out a cigarette lighter. "This was the only gift Sefton ever gave me. He said it would either light my way or reduce me to ashes, and he didn't care which one happened."

"Erin," I whisper out of the corner of my mouth. "Run."

Will flicks the lighter. A small flame ignites.

And we bolt.

My leg muscles burn because I haven't recovered from our escape from the golem, but we have no other choice than to run. I can tell from the grimace on Erin's face that she feels the same agony. We both served in the military and learned how to push through the pain and fear, but nobody has ever received training in how to defeat a golem and his nutjob master, much less how to neutralize the incendiary blood of a magical construct.

An object flies past my shoulder.

I skid to a halt and throw out an arm to stop Erin.

The object is a glass bottle that shattered on impact. The makeshift wick—a piece of fabric stuffed into the bottle's neck—burns with a small yellow flame.

If I'd ever wanted to save Will, that impulse has disintegrated. Fuck him. He just tried to ice us with a Molotov cocktail. I take a step toward the bottle and lift my foot, intending to squelch the flame.

But Erin seizes my arm to stop me. "We're covered in possibly explosive blood, remember?"

I mutter a curse under my breath and retract my foot, then back up a couple of steps. "Thanks for reminding me."

"What are friends for?"

She is more than a friend, though I can't quite make myself consider the full import of that thought. Not yet. Maybe never.

I study the broken bottle while its flame fizzles out. "A Molotov cocktail has gasoline or alcohol in it, right?"

"Yeah."

"The bottle is empty except for the wick. He can't even get that right." But he could still hurt us if we really have incendiary blood on us.

Another bottle soars over our heads, smacking down on the pavement. This one lands too damn close, its flaming wick nearly grazing my shoe.

I grasp Erin's hand, and we sprint down the street.

"You won't get away forever," Will hollers. "I know this city better than you do. I'll track you down wherever you go."

He's right that we don't know the city. But we will never give in to Sefton's wimpier but no less deranged doppelgänger. We swerve around a corner just as Will lobs another bottle at us, though it strikes a building instead of us.

I see a sign up ahead and drag Erin into that building. Its wooden door is mostly intact, so I push it shut. A chair lies on its side nearby, and I grab that to brace the doorknob. In Will's condition, he won't be able to kick the door down—if he even realizes we've entered this building. He was still around the corner when he hurled the last bottle. I keep hold of Erin's hand while I take us deeper into the building, sidling around a swinging door that barely clings to its hinges.

"Did that sign say 'physical therapy'?" Erin asks.

"Yeah. This must've been a clinic at some point. Assuming anything in this world is what it seems."

"Wouldn't bank on it."

I guide us down a hallway until I see a door labeled "water therapy."

"Where are you going?" Erin asks.

"Hopefully, someplace where we can get cleaned up." I push the intact door open. "Oh yeah, this will do."

I lead Erin to the big round tub at the center of the room, which still contains water. Releasing her hand, I kneel to dip my fingers into the water. Cold, of course.

Erin crouches beside me. "Still confused, Grant. What are we doing here?"

"Do you want to rinse the potentially explosive golem blood off before it dries?"

She stares at me for a moment, then her mouth slides into a sexy smile. "You're a genius, Grant."

Genius? No, I'm not that good. "We need to get clean and get out of here before Will realizes where we are."

We strip off our clothes and jump into the pool to scrub ourselves with our hands and wash our hair out by dunking our heads under the water. Once we feel relatively clean, we dump our clothes into the water. I find a broom in the corner and use its handle to create an agitation effect like a washing machine would have. It does the trick. Now that we're cleansed of golem blood, we struggle to pull on our wet stuff. My boots make a squishing sound when I walk. We had to wash our footwear too since they got doused with golem blood too.

Instead of leaving through the front door, we leave by the rear exit and step out into an alley. To our right, it dead-ends. To our left, it's blocked by a slumped figure.

Will has found us.

Shit. Won't this guy ever give up?

"You're not getting the journal," I shout to him. "Might as well forget about it. You can barely walk, and we're in top condition."

Maybe I'm not in as top condition as I was before we jumped into the Echo, but I've got more stamina and strength than Will does. He looks even worse than he had a few minutes ago on the street. His face is pale, and he seems to be breathing harder.

"The journal belongs to me," he whines. "I am the only living version of Sefton Stainthorpe."

"He had a twin brother," I say. "That means the journal belongs to Dax now, and he wants me to read it."

Maybe I didn't actually ask Dax about that, but he won't care. Since the law doesn't exist anymore, no one can argue with my assessment of who owns the book.

"Give it to me," Will snarls while saliva sprays from his lips.

"Don't think so."

"But that—The journal is mine." He starts sobbing, and his knees buckle. He hits the ground hard. "It's mine."

I grab Erin's hand. "Try whisking us away."

"The last time I did that, it hurt like hell."

"Since when are you afraid of pain?"

"That's a low blow."

I tug her closer. "But did my evil plan work?"

She sighs and shakes her head. "Yeah, it worked."

Erin wraps her arms around me and shuts her eyes. I can tell she's trying to teleport because she always scrunches her face up when she does that.

The world shifts around us.

Will's anguished cry echoes in the alley but fades into silence as we land in another place.

Erin opens her eyes and glances around. "Where have I taken us?"

"Not sure, but it looks sweet."

We're standing inside a fancy bedroom with stone walls and a stone fireplace. Flames flicker in the hearth. A huge canopy bed with a crimson blanket sits in the center of the room, pushed against the wall. A spiffy rug fills the center of the space, extending under the bed, while two ornate dressers stand against the wall beside it.

"Where did you want to send us?" I ask. "To Cinderella's castle?"

"No." She hunches her shoulders. "I wished for us to be far away from Will and the golem, somewhere warm and comfortable and safe."

"You got all that into your one-second wish."

She slugs my arm. "Don't tick off the woman who saved your ass—again."

"I would never do that. You're a badder badass than I am."

"Very funny."

"Not joking." I cup her cheek in one hand. "You are amazing, Erin."

"As much as I love it when a man gushes over how badass I am, we should explore our new digs. Make sure we haven't crashed somebody's house."

"Good idea."

I hold her hand while we exit through the big wooden door and step out into a long hallway. Oil lanterns in sconces attached to the walls provide flickering light. A long crimson carpet covers the floor but doesn't reach the walls, leaving the stone floor visible at either side.

What is this place?

Erin and I wander down the corridor and peek inside other rooms, but we don't see anything that explains where we are. The other rooms contain various kinds of furniture but no books or other stuff that might give us a clue about…anything. We keep exploring the corridor until we reach its end.

Large wooden doors bar our way. It must be another room.

The doors swing open, forcing us to scuttle backward. In the space now revealed, I see something that doesn't jibe with the old-timey decor in this place.

Because it looks like an elevator.

Chapter Twenty-Two

Erin

A MYSTERIOUS ELEVATOR IN A MYSTERIOUS PLACE WITH NO SIGN OF life anywhere? Nah, that's not creepy. Who doesn't want to step inside a little box that goes who knows where? Down to hell, for all I know. Maybe I like taking chances and being reckless, but even I'm not stupid enough to jump right into the elevator car. So I glance at Grant. "Should we, um, go inside?"

"What the hell." He walks into the car first. "At least dying in an elevator crash would probably be quick."

"Uh-huh. I see we're back to Mr. Sunshine."

In Command Grant is the sexiest version of him, but I get why he has reverted to Mr. Doom and Gloom. This place gives me a creepy-crawly sensation all over my body.

The doors swing shut, and the car begins to move. A dial on the wall, similar to the one in Sefton's skyscraper, indicates that we're rising. We started on the second floor, apparently, and now we're heading up. The car keeps rising until we reach the fifth level, which seems like the top.

And the doors open for us.

Grant and I step out into another corridor. As the elevator doors shut behind us, we start walking down the crimson carpet, though we have no idea where we're going. Maybe I should suggest that I whisk us away to a different place, but I'm curious about where we've ended up. I know it must've piqued Grant's curiosity too. So we explore this new corridor, checking out every room we pass but not finding much of anything other than more fancy furniture.

Why did the elevator bring us here? We didn't push a button because I saw no buttons. Someone wanted us to come to the fifth floor. At the end of the hall, we find one room left to explore and push the door open.

This room is enormous. Cavernous might be a better description. It looks nothing like a cave, but it could certainly house one. As we cross the threshold, I notice a half-open doorway that looks like a bathroom. The bedroom features a four-poster bed even bigger than the ones in the other rooms we've explored. The suite also has a huge walk-in closet stocked with clothes for both men and women. Jeez, who lives here?

Grant comes up beside me. "Maybe we should steal some new duds. Doesn't seem like anybody's here, and our stuff has seen better days."

Yeah, I'd love new duds. My shorts lost their appeal after I got doused with golem blood. Though we'd washed that out of our clothes and off our skin, I swear I can still smell the motor oil odor. Still, stealing clothes from an unknown host seems like bad manners. I mean, I didn't even knock before I teleported us in here.

"Let's go into the closet," Grant says. "Just to look."

"If the door slams shut behind us and we're locked in, I'm going to beat you to death with my fists."

He chuckles. "I love it when you're vicious."

Grant used to hate that about me. Now he likes it. Maybe it was never my behavior that got to him, but something else entirely. I want to ask him about that. This isn't the time or place, though.

We set our backpacks on the floor.

As we enter the huge closet, he says, "You might still be able to teleport even if we get locked in here."

"Back to Grant the Optimist, hey? I should buy you a mood ring so I can tell at a glance whether you're going to growl at me or seduce me."

"You'll know if I want your body. No mood ring required."

As I skim through the clothes on the hangers, I realize everything here is my size. Grant is still browsing the racks when I head for the cubbyholes that house wooden boxes full of underthings. The bras and panties are also my size. I might dismiss that as a coincidence, but life post-Echo has taught me to be suspicious of everything. Magic rules the world—in the Echo and on earth.

"Everything here would fit me perfectly," Grant says. "Is the girlie stuff sized for you too?"

"Yeah. It's kind of creepy, but I've decided to be grateful I can steal some clean, fresh clothes."

"Seems like somebody expected us."

"Is Skeptical Grant gone for good? Or will he come back in a few minutes and dismiss all of this as a coincidence?"

He rests a hand on the metal bar of the clothes racks and huffs out a breath. "Do you always have to be so combative?"

"Yes. It's the only way I can get you to admit what you really think without studying the issue for a month first."

"Get changed, Erin. We need to search this place to see if anyone else is here."

Discussion over, that's what he means.

I pick a pair of butter-soft brown leather pants that mold to my thighs and have pockets where I could hide smaller weapons. I slip my switchblade into one pocket and stuff some extra rounds for my handgun in the other pocket. I've also chosen a tan T-shirt and a leather jacket that matches my pants as well as boots in the same color. One cubbyhole contains hair doo-hickeys, and I use a scrunchy to hold my hair back. It's harder to fight when my hair keeps falling over my eyes.

Grant and I turn to face each other.

Holy cow, he looks even hotter in the outfit he selected for himself. Black leather pants, a blue T-shirt, and a dark-blue denim jacket. His boots match his pants, which conform to every inch of his thighs and groin. The bulge in his pants draws my attention, and my breasts begin to feel swollen, the nipples taut. I want him, but not here in a freaky, vacant mystery building.

Well, okay, I want him right now despite the fact we're trapped in a freaky, vacant mystery building. Can't help it. I've never seen Grant in leather pants before.

"I see you found the wardrobe."

The female voice spurs us both to whirl toward the doorway.

A pretty blonde woman stands just outside the closet, hands clasped in front of her, and watches us with a pleasantly bland expression. "Does the clothing fit correctly? Magic isn't always the most accurate way to take measurements."

She sounds American, but I have no doubts she is not from the United States, much less the Planet Earth. Her hazel eyes shimmer with a strange golden light.

"Do you know who we are?" I ask.

"Yes." Her lips curve into a subdued smile. "You are Erin Harding, and he is Grant Larson. You entered the Echo through the gateway and brought a guest with you."

"That thing was not our guest."

She tips her head to the side, her expression turning curious. "He is not your friend?"

"No."

"I'm glad to hear that since I quartered him in the dungeon. He was…rather uncooperative."

I manage to stifle a laugh. Uncooperative? I'm surprised he didn't smash this place to rubble.

"You arrived sooner than I anticipated," the woman says. "I was never gifted with foresight, of course. But I hoped you would find your way here."

"Why?" Grant asks. "Who are you, anyway?"

"My name is Aldith. And I hoped to meet you because my ethereal senses told me you and Erin might be the ones I have waited for."

"You told us your name, but that's not what I asked. Who are you?"

She smiles just enough to dimple her cheeks. "I am the guardian of the Echo's heart."

We both stare at her blankly for a moment. I regain my senses first. "The Echo has a heart? What does that mean?"

"The closest approximation is the human heart, for this world has a pulse and arteries that throb with energy. This stronghold is the essence of the Echo, the only neutral ground within the war zone that Sefton Stainthorpe created." Aldith turns sideways and waves for us to follow her. "Come. I will show you what I mean."

Can we trust her? No way, not yet. Do we have any other choice than to follow her? Doubtful. If we attack her, she might fight back with magics. If we kill her, we might realize too late we destroyed a powerful ally. Life was hardly black and white before the apocalypse, but everything has gotten so much murkier since then.

We trail after Aldith as she leads us out of the bedroom and across the corridor to another doorway. She swings it open, marching inside. We stop just past the threshold.

Aldith gives us her neutral smile again. "This is the Heart of the Echo."

"But it's just an empty room," Grant says. "How can it be the heart of the apocalypse?"

She shakes her head. "You should know better by now. Not everything is as you assume it should be. Sefton Stainthorpe might have created this world and appropriated its power, but he never controlled the Heart. He never controlled me either, which infuriated him."

Might she really be the sole neutral element in this world? If she refused to help Sefton, then maybe she could become our ally. But I still have cynical reservations about this woman and this place. Deception is a mainstay of the Echo and the creatures it disgorged into our world.

"You remain skeptical," she says. "I understand your reticence, and I realize I cannot convince you of anything with words alone. Allow me to demonstrate."

She raises her hands, palms up.

"Hold up," Grant says. "How exactly do you plan to show us we can trust you?"

"I cannot. But I wish to show you that I'm not lying about the Echo's Heart." She glances at me, then meets Grant's gaze again. "Will you allow me to demonstrate?"

He looks at me.

I shrug.

Grant faces Aldith and clears his throat. "Okay. Show us."

He sidles up to me and clasps my hand.

My pulse revs up as Aldith closes her eyes, and I feel energies rising around us. I don't know how I can sense it, but I know these magics won't harm us. They feel warm and soft, despite the way they crackle with power. Maybe my connection to the Echo, which lets me teleport, also gives me the ability to sense that I can trust a stranger who wants to prove her sincerity to us. It's not like we have any other options.

If she fries us, I'll crawl out of hell or heaven or wherever my soul goes and punish her for hurting Grant. I don't care what happens to me, only that no harm comes to him. I won't think about why I feel that way, not now.

Glowing, golden magics emerge from Aldith's hands, the sparkling tendrils spreading upward from her palms. The energy swirls around her in a cloud that soon envelops her so we can't even see her face. I feel the magics licking at my skin, but it isn't a bad sensation. In fact, it infuses me with a sense of peace and contentment I've never experienced before. I don't want it to end, but I know it must.

The magics dissipate, revealing Aldith. Her lips spread into a joyous smile as she lowers her hands. "The Heart is here in this room with us."

"You are the Heart," I say. "You control this place."

She shakes her head as her smile softens into something gentler and almost beatific. "No, dear, I am but the servant."

"You said the Heart is here."

"And it is." She walks up to us, glancing back and forth between me and Grant. Then she lays her palm on Grant's chest. "You are the Heart of the Echo."

Grant stiffens, and even his fingers go rigid, though they still clasp mine. "No, you're wrong. I can't be—I don't have the Echo power."

"Of course you do." Aldith lays one hand on his cheek and the other on mine. "You, Grant Larson, are the Heart. But Erin Harding is the Lifeblood."

My mouth falls open. "Excuse me? That's insane. I'm not the Lifeblood of anything or anyone. I'm just the crazy chick who takes risks no one else would. I kill Echo creatures. Unless spilling blood is what you mean, I am not this…whatever it is."

"Your bravery and your willingness to fight for the world you love are what proves you are the Lifeblood." She moves her hands to our shoulders, and her cheeks dimple again. "You don't believe me yet, but you will. Why do you think I sent signs to guide you?"

"Will sent those signs. For Allison."

"No, dear. He wanted you to believe that, but even Will knows that's not the case." Aldith takes two steps back. "The signs were for you and Grant. The Heart has been without its Lifeblood for too long, and the time has come to reunite the elements."

"What purpose do these elements serve?" Grant asks.

"You have noticed the tremors in the Echo."

"Sure, but—"

"And you came here to stop them. To do that, you must first unite with the Lifeblood."

"How?"

Aldith laughs softly—because we both look stunned and confused, I'm sure. "Make love to her, Grant."

Chapter Twenty-Three

Grant

A STRANGER JUST ORDERED ME TO HAVE SEX WITH ERIN. WHAT THE hell? I don't even know for sure that this woman knows anything or if she's giving us the biggest snow job in history. The Heart? The Lifeblood? This is all starting to sound like bullshit. I can't be the heart of anything since my own heart has felt cold and empty ever since the Echo invaded our world. I lost the love of my life and my precious son. I can't "unite" with Erin.

Maybe I fucked her once. But that's irrelevant.

Yeah, right, it's irrelevant. What a stupid jackass I've become.

"I can tell you are resistant to the idea," Aldith says. "You need time to realize the truth."

"Why are we in this room?" I ask. "There's nothing in here."

"As I said, the Heart of the Echo resides in this room. Right now, it is nothing but a collection of energy. It needs you and Erin to become complete and alive."

"If it has a heart, arteries, and blood, then it is alive. What are we supposed to do for it?"

Can't believe this is what my life has become. A quest for alchemical secrets and magics I don't understand. I was a logical, hardworking deputy sheriff, and now I've become enmeshed in forces I can't comprehend.

No way could I be the Heart. It's crazy.

"Your first task," Aldith says, "is to stop the convulsions in the Echo that have bled into the mortal world. Only then might the end of the apocalypse be within sight."

"The end?" I freeze with my gaze glued to Aldith. A strange shiver races over my skin, though it's not fear. "Are you saying Erin and I could destroy the Echo and end the apocalypse?"

Aldith aims her bland smile at me. "You shall not be the ones to end what Sefton began. But you are important organs within the body. Only your connection might stop the convulsions and begin the healing process."

"This all sounds too convenient. We get naked, and the Echo stops convulsing? Come on."

Aldith shrugs. "You found your way to this place. That means you are the necessary elements. Time passes differently in the Echo, so your friends on Earth might be enduring more spasms while you linger here."

Now she's issuing vague threats. I think. Or maybe I'm just way too cynical these days.

"You mean time moves faster here," I say. "But we already knew that."

"No, not faster. Not necessarily. It might slow down, speed up, hover, or even rewind. The Echo itself decides which way it will allow time to move." Aldith bows her head. "I regret that I have been unable to affect the conditions here or on Earth. Sefton retained that power by removing the Heart and the Lifeblood. And Will appropriated the power when Sefton died. But he could not take control of the Heart or the Lifeblood. Only you and Erin possess that power."

"If nobody's in control here, how can the Echo keep going? A heart and blood seem like critical things for any living…entity." I try not to cringe when I say that, but all this talk of mystical hearts and blood makes my skin crawl.

"Yes, it is critical. The black hearts of the worst Echo creatures have sustained this realm thus far." Aldith raises her head. "They cannot be allowed to continue their reign of terror. Feed the Heart, and the balance of power will shift."

"But Erin and I can't stop the apocalypse."

"Not alone. But that is a tale for another day." Aldith spreads her arms wide. "This room has contained the Heart until its proper owner could claim it. The Echo has been waiting for you, Grant."

"But—No, I can't—"

Finish a sentence? No, I can't do that anymore. This is sheer insanity. I'm not a good enough person to deserve this honor, if it is an honor. Maybe it's a trick to turn us into evil puppets for Will. We have only this woman's word to go on.

Aldith clasps her hands. "You may, of course, teleport out of here at any time. Nothing will stop you from leaving."

Erin shuts her eyes for a moment, then looks at me. "I can teleport. Didn't try it all the way, but I can feel it will work if we want to get the hell out of Dodge."

"Do you want to leave?" I ask.

"No. I'm starting to believe Aldith."

As much as I hate to admit it, I won't lie to Erin. Despite my reservations, or maybe my fears, I need to speak the truth. "Yeah, I'm starting to believe her too."

Erin shifts her gaze to the floor. "So do you want to, um…"

"Get it on? Might as well give it a shot."

She scowls at me. "Well, if it's that much of a trial for you to screw me, we can just hop on back home."

"I didn't mean it like that."

Aldith clears her throat. "This is my cue to leave. If you require anything, simply call my name."

The woman disappears. Literally. Poof, she's gone.

How can I still be surprised by the freaky things magic can do? Of course a woman can vanish into thin air, and of course Erin can teleport us straight into a safe zone. Naturally, we need to have sex to save the world. Makes perfect sense.

Erin and I awkwardly cross the hall and go into the bedroom, then awkwardly stop to glance at each other sideways. I kick the door shut while she starts to sit down on the bed, but jumps up again. Why should this feel weird? We fucked earlier today. Now we both act like virgins who don't know how sex works.

I grasp Erin's shoulders and turn her toward me. "Are you sure you want to do this?"

"Yeah. I'm sure. Sort of." She winces. "Well, being ordered to screw each other is…weird. I want to be with you, but I can't help feeling like Aldith will be watching us."

"I get that. This feels weird to me too." I slide my hands down to her upper arms. "But we're attracted to each other, and we had amazing sex just this morning. That means we have chemistry. We just need to relax and forget about the circumstances."

"Are we going to meditate again? That was surprisingly hot."

"Yeah, it was." I raise a hand to brush my fingers over her cheek. "I wanted you right there in that dilapidated building. I wanted you in the physical therapy clinic too, when we stripped and washed our clothes. You are beautiful, Erin, and the sexiest woman I've ever seen. I love your body."

"I love your body too." She lays a palm on my chest and glides it down to my waistband. "Maybe we don't need to meditate this time. Maybe all we need is to focus on each other and forget about the rest of the universe."

"That's called mindfulness, Erin. It's meditation too."

"No half Lotus position this time. We should meditate on each other's bodies."

I have no idea what that means, but my dick loves the idea. It jerks and starts to stiffen. The sultry tone of her voice has always done this to me, even before we had sex or kissed. I've wanted her since the day she walked into Sanctuary. Making love to her won't be an onerous duty as long as I avoid thinking about everything except for Erin's body.

"Let's undress each other," I say. "Slowly. Sensually. Like we have all the time in the world. Maybe we do. Let's see if we can freeze the clock while we make love."

"Oh God, I want that. With you."

Erin backs away just far enough that I can see her entire body, then takes hold of the hem of her shirt and slowly lifts it. She exposes her flat belly inch by inch while I track her every movement and she shimmies her hips just enough to make my dick jerk again. My breathing grows heavier, and I clench my hands into fists to avoid grabbing her so I can tear her clothes off and sink my cock into her body. I want her like crazy, but I can't focus on why, not right now. It would ruin this moment.

She pulls her shirt up over her head and tosses it onto the floor. Her lips tighten into a sexy smirk while she lays her palms on her upper chest and glides them down her body so slowly that I'm breathing even harder, my chest rising and falling while I struggle not to hyperventilate. She palms her breasts through her powder-blue bra, then slides her hands down her belly to grasp the button on her brown leather pants. Damn, she looks incredible in leather. But I'm so excited to see her naked that I need to remind myself to keep taking slow, even breaths.

Erin unhooks that button and eases her zipper down, revealing her powder-blue panties.

"Fuck," I growl. "You're driving me insane."

"Good. Insane is better than snippy." She kicks her boots off and shimmies out of her pants, leaving only her skimpy blue panties and bra. I see glimpses of the hairs on her mound through the semi-transparent fabric.

And now I'm rock-hard.

She pushes her panties down over her hips and wiggles until they fall to her ankles. While she steps out of her underwear, she unhooks her bra and tosses it away.

I barely have time to salivate over her tits before she turns around, leaving me to admire her taut ass. But when she bends over to remove her socks, I hiss, "Hurry the fuck up, would you?"

She spreads her legs just enough that she can gaze at me through the gap between her thighs. Her head hangs upside down, though that elastic thing in her hair keeps it from falling around her face. "Getting a little overexcited, huh?"

I wish she weren't speaking in that sultry tone again. It's eroding my willpower even faster. Like I had much willpower left, anyway.

Erin removes one sock, then the other, doing it slowly on purpose while she flashes me upside down smiles between her legs.

I rip my clothes off so fast that I probably tore a few seams, but I don't give a shit. Stripping at lightning speed due to extreme sexual frustration isn't the brightest idea. I forget that I still have my boots on and try to yank my leather pants off while the boots are still on my feet. That results in me crashing into the bed, kind of bouncing off it, and tumbling to my knees on the floor.

Erin laughs. Loudly.

And I growl. Seriously, I do.

But I take a few slow, deep breaths and channel my Zen side, closing my eyes while I listen to my heartbeats decelerating.

Something tugs on the button of my pants.

I open my lids halfway.

Erin is kneeling beside me, undoing my pants while seeming intently focused on the task. I can't resist staring at her tits and the way their stiff peaks point slightly upward.

She casts me a sideways glance. "Like what you see?"

"Hell yes."

"You've been seriously pent-up, haven't you?"

I suck in a sharp breath when she drags my zipper down, which makes her fingers graze my cock.

"Think you can get yourself undressed now?" she asks. "I mean without the Three Stooges solo routine."

"Yeah, I can do it. Please get on the bed, Erin. It's taking all my meditative skills not to flip you onto your back and fuck you right here on the floor."

She kisses me sweetly, then climbs onto the bed and pulls the covers back. With a quick jerk of her hand, she ditches the scrunchy thing that had held her hair up. Now the lush, dark waves cascade over her shoulders and kiss her breasts.

This time, I manage to remove my clothes without acting like a buffoon. Finally naked, I crawl up the bed on all fours until my body hovers over her. Christ, she's beautiful. I feather my lips over hers, flicking my tongue out to taste them. Her breaths tease my mouth, and I swear I can almost taste her lips. But it's another part of her I need to devour now.

I lay my body on top of hers and shimmy backward with deliberate slowness, licking and nibbling on her flesh while I move. When I pull one nipple into my mouth and gently lave it, she arches her neck. But when I flick my thumb over the other peak while I suckle this one, she moans, and her back bows up. How many times can a woman come before she's too exhausted to take it anymore? I plan to find out.

Right now.

Chapter Twenty-Four

Erin

GRANT KEEPS TORMENTING MY NIPPLE WITH HIS MOUTH AND HIS hand, and all I can do is moan repeatedly and thrust my fingers into his thick, silky hair. Every time he gently nips that peak, I gasp and moan again, sounding so desperate that it's pathetic. I don't care. I love what he's doing to me, and I never want it to stop.

He removes his mouth from my nipple, but then touches his lips to the rigid tip and groans. The vibrations from that sound penetrate my skin and send a bolt of sheer pleasure straight down my nerves and into my core. He licks the peak and blows a gentle current of air across it while pinching my other nipple. I'm struggling to catch my breath, and the way my sex has started to tingle and throb doesn't help.

Grant swallows my nipple and the areola, then flicks his thumb across my other peak in swift, light motions that drive me insane in the best way. The most incredible sensation sweeps down my nerves from my breast straight into my clit, and my entire body goes rigid. I cry out as the orgasm rushes through me, softer than a regular climax but no less satisfying. I've never come this way before, but I love it.

The man with my tit in his mouth releases my flesh and grins. "Ready for round two?"

I'm still breathing hard from what he just did, but yeah, I need more. So I nod.

He slides down my body, licking a trail in his wake until he reaches my hips. His breaths tease the hairs on my mound, and my gaze has become riveted to his every movement. When I glance at his face, our eyes meet, and he winks. "Don't look at my face. I want you to watch me fucking you with my mouth."

I want that too, but I can't speak to tell him so.

Grant spreads my folds with two fingers and holds them like that. First, he blows a breath over my slick flesh, making me moan, then he flicks his tongue out to tease my clit. I jerk and gasp. He slides his fingers up and down, licking at my nub, and my gaze tracks the movements of his tongue while he coils it around my clit again and again. Holy shit, watching him do that ramps up my arousal until I feel like I might turn into a raving lunatic if I don't come soon.

"You taste so damn good," he murmurs. "I could feast on you all day and all night."

He drags his tongue up and down my cleft while his nose rubs against my nub. I fist my hands in the sheets and spread my legs for him, silently begging him to take me right now, then I bend my knees too and thrust my hips up. He buries his face between my thighs to seal his mouth over my opening, then plunges his tongue inside over and over while I thrash and cry out and clutch the sheets so hard that I hear a ripping sound. Screw the sheets. I need him inside me so badly that I hear myself begging him to do it.

Grant shifts his mouth to my clit. His face glistens with my slickness. He licks his lips and smiles at me with so much heat and hunger that it makes my nub throb, then he pushes two fingers inside me and starts pumping while he latches on to my clit and suckles it fiercely.

The orgasm slams through me like a wrecking ball, shattering my self-control. I scream his name and thrash beneath him, my eyes squeezed shut as I ride out the spasms. The intensity of the climax wrenches my whole body, and my screams turn into hoarse cries.

When the orgasm finally fades, I lie here limp and gasping.

Grant kisses my belly. "Catch your breath. When you're ready, I'll make love to you."

He lies down beside me and combs his fingers through my hair while I come down from the most amazing climax I've ever experienced. How does Grant Larson know what to do, what to say, to make me wild with desire for him? I've never gotten this excited with any other man. But every time he touches me, I melt for him.

Once my breathing normalizes and my ears stop ringing, I turn my face into his palm to kiss it. "Thank you for that."

"We're not done yet."

"Good. I'd be disappointed if that's all we do. I need to feel you buried inside me again, for longer this time so I can watch your face while you take me."

"I want that too." He rolls onto his back and pats my hip. "Get up."

"What?"

"Get up, Erin." He grasps his rigid erection and strokes himself slowly. "I want you to ride my cock."

Just the thought of that makes me grow wetter.

He slaps my thigh. "Get up and fuck me already."

I rise to my knees and crawl over to straddle his hips. Then I need to take a moment to appreciate the masculine beauty of Grant's body. He has defined pecs and abs that make me want to bend down and lick every line of those muscles, and his thighs look powerful too. I already knew he had strong biceps, but what really catches my attention now is that dick. Wow. It's thick and smooth, and the rosy head just begs to be licked and sucked. But I'll do that later. For now, I need to take him into my body and feel that gorgeous cock nestled inside me.

I let myself revel in the look on his face while I grasp his length and slowly pump it. His eyes have gone hooded, his lips are parted, and his chest heaves.

"Hurry, baby," he almost growls. "Don't wanna go off before you've even mounted me."

But I wait a few more seconds, just to watch him squirm and grimace. Then I waddle forward and hold the base of his dick to get it positioned just right. A breath gusts out of him. I bend my knees until the head of his erection nudges my opening. My clit throbs, but I hold my position for several seconds until Grant fists his hands in the sheets and makes a sound I can only describe as a desperate snarl.

Okay, enough torturing him.

I lower myself onto his cock until I've got him seated fully inside me. Oh God, this feels even better than I'd hoped it would. I rock my hips gently, letting us both enjoy the sensation of our bodies merging and my wetness dribbling down his dick. He gasps and grunts, his gaze riveted to the intersection of our bodies.

"Faster, Erin, please."

I speed up the pace, but only a little, and rise up until his crown just nudges my entrance, then I slam back down. The way his cock glides in and out has me teetering on the verge of another orgasm already.

"Erin," he hisses. "Can't wait—ah—much longer."

"Me either." I throw my head back and ride him harder, fondling my tits. "Oh God, Grant, yes."

He surges up, seizes me around the waist, and flips us both over with me beneath him. Staring into my eyes, he plants his hands on the mattress at either side of my head and begins thrusting into me so hard and fast that I come within seconds. While my body convulses around him, he punches into me twice more and freezes, shouting as he goes off. I swear I can feel his release erupting inside me, and it makes me come harder.

Though we've both found our release, he settles his body onto mine, and we just lie here without moving. His dick has softened, but I still feel him inside me. I love that sensation. But I love the way he's gazing at me even more, because his expression resembles affection. Just yesterday, I would've laughed at myself for thinking such a thing, considering the way Grant has behaved toward me. Coming to the Echo changed everything between us in ways I still don't understand—especially since we found the Heart of the Echo. This place feels magical. It's more than the supernatural energies that suffuse the building. I sense a different kind of magic between me and Grant, a sizzling and sweet kind that makes my throat go thick and my chest ache in the best way.

He brushes hair away from my face with two fingers. "Hey, are you all right? I know that was intense, but…"

"I'm fine." Grant seems less than convinced, so I touch my lips to his. "Really, I'm good. Feel fantastic, actually."

"Me too. Which seems wrong somehow, since we're trapped in the Heart of the Echo."

"Whatever that means." I fold my arms around him, and he rests his head on my shoulder. His breaths tickle my throat. "Not sure sex gave us more power."

"Maybe we should try it again."

"You don't need to do that. If sex with me didn't rock the worlds the first time, I doubt it will do the trick the second time either. I must not be the Lifeblood after all."

"Bullshit. You are that and more."

I run my hands up and down his back, not minding at all that his full weight still bears down on me. It feels right, lying here with him. "Thanks for the vote of confidence, but for all we know, Aldith didn't mean me specifically. She might've meant that any woman who found a way into the Heart of the Echo could become the Lifeblood."

"Shut up and listen." He lifts his head to aim his beautiful blue eyes at me and sweeps his thumb over my lips. "I didn't make love to you because a weird girl told me I should. I wanted to be with you, Erin."

"Yeah, but—"

"No buts. You are as critical to the salvation of both worlds as I am, or as Dax and Allison are. Maybe I never believed in magic before the apocalypse, but I've witnessed what it can do—the good and the bad." He shifts his weight so he can clasp my face in his hands with his elbows braced on the mattress. "You are good, Erin. Amazing, actually. Sorry it took me so long to realize that and admit to it. If anyone is the key to reversing or at least stopping the apocalypse, of course it's you."

"What do you mean of course it's me? That makes no sense."

"No, it makes perfect sense." He dips his head closer until our noses touch. His eyes bore straight into mine, imbued with an intensity that takes my breath away. "You're a warrior, a hero, a role model to Willow, and the smartest, bravest person I've ever met."

"But you hated me until earlier today."

"No. I never hated you." He presses his lips to mine and licks at the seam of my mouth until I moan softly. "Later, I'll explain to you why I treated you the way I did. But right now, we need to make love again, this time for real. That means I'll do it slowly so I can show you how I really feel before I try to explain it in words."

"Grant, I—"

He kisses me again, pushing his tongue between my lips, though he doesn't go any deeper. Not yet. He glides one hand down my side, all the way to my hip, then he kneads the hollow there while he explores my mouth with sensual movements of his tongue. I feel myself growing wetter, my body softening as I realize what he wants to do now. This won't be hot sex. Well, okay, it will be hot for sure. But he told me what he wants in the most literal terms.

Grant Larson is about to make love to me.

Chapter Twenty-Five

Grant

SOMETHING HAS CHANGED BETWEEN ME AND ERIN. SCRATCH THAT. EVerything has changed. I don't fully understand why or how, and I have no clue in what ways making love inside the Heart of the Echo will affect us both. But I don't care. Right now, I need to show her what I've been afraid to admit—to her and to myself—because this feels like the right time to let go of the past, at least for a while.

I've never gotten hard again while still inside a woman. Never thought it was possible. But the more I kiss Erin, the stiffer I get. The blood doesn't rush to my dick all at once, though. I feel myself gradually hardening while I let myself revel in our kiss and the way she strokes my back while our tongues tease each other. The first time we kissed, I hadn't wanted to stop. Here and now, in this weird and mysterious place, I know we won't stop until we've both shared our true feelings by kissing and touching and getting lost in each other's bodies.

Erin knows how to kiss. That's one thing I've learned about her. I move my hand up to caress her breast while I dive deeper into her mouth and groan at how good this feels. Damn, I could lie here for days just enjoying the taste of her mouth and the sensation of our tongues melding and separating, over and over, while our bodies start to writhe of their own volition. My dick shifts inside her, and she crooks her nails into my back. I think she tried to gasp, but my mouth prevented her from making a sound. With our mouths still fused, I begin a measured pace of thrusting into her while her body molds to my cock and the scent of her cream teases my senses. I never thought I'd want anyone after Adele, but I won't think about that right now. In this moment, I'm giving myself permission to relish the feel of a woman's body wrapped around me.

I pull my mouth away so I can gaze into Erin's eyes. She looks at me too, and something sizzles between us, something I won't even try to describe. Magic? Maybe. But we don't need spells or Echo power to create a connection between us. It was always there, even when I refused to see it.

"Grant," she murmurs while she grips my biceps. "Oh, Grant, this is—"

"Hush." I graze my lips over hers while I thrust with more power. "Just let it happen, baby."

I can feel her body tensing up, the way it does right before she comes. Her breaths become soft gasps as she struggles to lift her hips into my movements, and her nails dig into my skin. Every time I plunge inside her, I blow out a breath, and when I pull out, I groan. She arches her neck and squeezes her eyes shut, but then seems to force herself to look at me as if she can't stand not to do that. The pressure inside me grows with every thrust, and I raise onto my straight arms to push even deeper inside her.

When she comes, it unfolds in slow motion. Her mouth falls open, and her body freezes. While we gaze at each other, the first spasm of her climax grips my cock. The pressure to come barrels down my spine faster and faster, but I need to make sure she jumps off that cliff first. So I reach down to separate her folds with my fingers, then settle onto her again while rubbing against her clit with every thrust. She cries out, her muscles clenching me in a pulsating rhythm, and I can't hold back one second longer. I shout while machine-gun spasms fire through my cock, punching into her body until I've spilled everything I have inside her.

Then I go limp on top of her.

Erin's chest rises and falls while we both try to recover our ability to breathe without gasping. Even when I make love to her sweetly, we wind up breathless and spent. Guess we just can't help it. Sex with Adele was never quite this…intense.

"Wow," Erin says after a moment. "That was less athletic than the first or second time, but no less mind-blowing."

Yeah, it was that and more. Now it's time I told her why. I slide off her body onto my side and hook an arm around her waist. "I've wanted you since the day we met, but I was afraid of what it would mean if we had sex."

She rolls onto her side to face me. "What did it mean? Aside from Aldith's claim that we can become one with the Heart of the Echo."

"I'm not talking about that." I cup my hand over her hip and move my thumb in lazy circles. "The alchemy of worlds robbed me of my family, and I convinced myself I'd be a cheater and a traitor if I let anyone else into my heart besides my wife. Adele was the love of my life, and our son meant everything to us."

Erin tips her head down so I'm looking at her scalp. "Yeah, I get that. Don't worry. I won't demand you announce to the world that I'm your girlfriend."

Does she think I'm ashamed of what we've done together? I must've given her that impression since I fucked her in the car, then just walked away like nothing had happened. Erin is a strong, capable woman. But even the strongest of us can feel vulnerable when our emotions get tangled up. I can't believe I treated her that way, or that I kept snapping at her and calling her reckless. Her bravery saved us here in the Echo. When she leaned out the car window to fire machine gun volleys at our horny monster friend, it was the sexiest thing I'd ever seen.

So I tell her the truth. "You are amazing, Erin. I've never met anyone as brave, intelligent, resourceful, and unstoppable as you are. We survived traveling into the Echo because of you, not because of anything I did. We wouldn't even be here now if you hadn't taken a crazy risk that turned out to be the smartest thing you've ever done."

The top of her head gradually rises until I'm gazing into her eyes again. They shimmer with the slightest hint of tears. Erin crying? Just last week, I would've said that could never happen. But now, she looks at me with her eyes full of an emotion I wouldn't have tried to describe before tonight. I understand at last because I finally realize what I need to do.

"Never thought I'd say this," I tell her. "But I'm ready to move on. With you."

Her eyes widen. "What? You don't even like me."

"Were you not listening a minute ago? I waxed poetic about how wonderful you are."

"Sure, but it sounds like you mean—Well, it can't be that. What exactly do you mean? Move on? From the Heart of the Echo. That's what you must mean."

"I meant what I said the way I said it, no reinterpretation required." I cradle her cheek in my hand. "Adele might've been the love of my life, but I can't spend the rest of whatever life we have left pining for her. She wouldn't want that. Adele will always be in my heart, but I have room for more than one woman in here." I clasp her hand to my heart. "Got a spot waiting for you, if you want it."

Tears trickle from her eyes, but she doesn't even try to wipe them away. "I want that. If you're sure."

"I'm sure, Erin." I kiss her softly. "It's time we both moved on. The apocalypse taught me that life is too damn precious to waste it on obsessing over the past. Let's live for today, tomorrow, and whatever comes after that."

"Sounds like a plan."

What I need to say next seems moronic in my head, but maybe she won't think it's as stupid as I do. "Aldith mentioned that you and I can stop the convulsions of the Echo. We can control the Heart, that's what she said. Do you think that, uh, we did that when we had sex?"

Erin bites her upper lip while her body quivers.

"You're trying not to laugh at me, aren't you?" I say. "I know it sounds dumb—"

She seals my lips with two fingers. "Not laughing at you. The idea that getting it on will save the world sounds insane. That's why I was trying not to laugh."

"Oh. Good." I scratch the back of my head while avoiding her gaze. "I'm, uh, glad to hear you weren't laughing at the idea of having sex with me."

She smiles and taps my lips with her fingertips. "You are adorable when you're flustered."

"Don't think I've ever been flustered before. Isn't that something only girls do?"

Erin pokes me in the belly. "Don't insult the 'girl' who saved your ass more times than anyone can count."

"I didn't mean it that way." My lips curve into a smile that I'm sure conveys my real meaning. But I palm her tit just to make sure she gets it. "Should we try again just to make sure we've connected with the Heart or whatever the hell we're supposed to be doing?"

"Are you implying sex with me was just a tool for saving the world?"

"No, I—" I'm about to apologize when her expression changes. Her smirk spurs me to slap her ass. "Will you ever stop harassing me?"

"Afraid not."

"Good. I've gotten used to it, and I'd probably die of shock if you stopped."

She slaps my ass. "Are you always this cheeky?"

"You've been hanging out with Dax too much. 'Cheeky' is a British thing."

Erin's expression turns serious, and she exhales a weary sigh. "Do you honestly think we can stop the Echo's convulsions? We had sex, but I don't feel any different. I mean, I don't feel like I've developed the supernatural power to control the Heart of the Echo." She scrunches up her face. "What would that feel like, anyway?"

"Not a clue." I sit up and stretch, feeling better than I have since before the apocalypse. "Let's go across the hall and see if we can get into that other room. The Heart room or the Lifeblood room or... I have no idea what to call it."

"The creepy-ass room?"

I raise my brows. "Doesn't that term apply to this whole building? This whole world?"

"Yeah, I guess it does." She sits up too and stretches, the action lifting her tits. "Guess we should get dressed."

My brain thinks now is a good time to stare at her breasts, or maybe that's my dick's decision. Either way, I can't form any words. I love her body. I love fucking her. I'm starting to think another round of hot workout sex might be just the thing right now.

Yeah, that's definitely my dick talking.

Erin smacks my cheek, though not hard. "Wake up, Grant."

I clear my throat and rub my jaw, though I can't stop staring at her chest. "Sorry, I got distracted. Your body hypnotizes me."

She busts out laughing. "There's a line I've never heard before."

My attention shifts down to her hips and the hairs on her mound. Did I just groan like a man who found a juicy morsel after starving for six months? Erin turns me into a ravenous beast. I won't say that out loud, though. I swear I've never behaved this way before.

Erin pats my chest, her cheeks dimpling. "You really are adorable."

"Uh, thanks. That was a compliment, right?"

She laughs again, though not as raucously as before. Then she clambers off the bed to stand at the foot. "Are you coming?"

No, but we could both be doing that if I just... I squeeze my eyes shut. "Shit."

"What's wrong now?"

"I can't stop thinking about sex." I open my eyes and wince. "Maybe it'll help if you get dressed."

She salutes me. "Sir, yes, sir."

Erin marches into the huge closet where I can't see her anymore. She could've put on the clothes she'd been wearing before we jumped into bed together, but I guess she's a typical woman in one respect. She needs to try on lots of outfits.

I get up and get dressed too, but I stay away from the closet and wear the same thing I'd had on before we got naked.

The woman I can't stop fucking ambles out of the closet. Okay, I have stopped fucking her, but I want to do it again. And again. And again. It doesn't help that she's wearing skintight jeans that hug her hips and a top that stretches barely past her belly button. It has extra-short sleeves too. She holds a denim jacket draped over one arm and taps the toe of one hiking boot on the floor while she angles her head to the side to study me.

"Didn't want clean clothes?" she asks.

"I only wore this outfit for a little while before we, uh..." My gaze darts to the bed and the rumpled sheets that must still smell of sex and Erin. "Well, you know."

Suddenly, I can't speak the words "had sex." Can't say "fucked" either. Even "made love" sounds like a weird thing to say. I know this is just anxiety because I haven't been with anyone since my wife, not until today. The feeling will pass.

I grasp Erin's hand, leading her across the hall to the creepy-ass room.

Chapter Twenty-Six

Erin

I'VE ONLY EVER THOUGHT OF NERDY GUYS AS BEING ADORABLE, BUT I've called Grant that twice. He is not a nerd. I mean, geeks can be hot too, but the words geek and nerd don't describe the man I just got down and dirty with a few minutes ago. Grant can be surprisingly sweet and almost shy at times, which I'd previously seen only when he was with people other than me. But here in this bizarre place, I finally experienced the sides of him everyone else knows well.

But nobody else gets to experience how incredible he is in bed.

What we shared was more than mind-blowing sex. It meant something, though I don't have the time or the brainpower to figure out exactly what it meant. He told me he's ready to move on and that he has room for another woman in his heart. I've never been in love, not really. I had boyfriends I cared about, but those relationships never turned into a commitment. I lived in my apartment, and they lived in theirs. With Grant, I feel…ready for more. Before the apocalypse, I would've thought I should take a lot more time to decide how I feel about Grant. I still don't know exactly what this is between us, but I do know I want to be with him, even if we wind up not working out as a couple. I need to give us a shot.

Like Allison says, the pace of life post-apocalypse has accelerated. I won't second guess what I feel. But I'll still ride Grant's ass if he does something I disagree with—or if we're naked. Yeah, different kind of riding in that case.

We walk into the creepy-ass room and find Aldith already there, standing in the center of the space with her hands clasped and her head bowed. She raises her head when we enter. Her lips curl up the tiniest bit, which seems like the closest she gets to smiling. Well, if I'd been stuck inside a weird place like this, I might have trouble summoning a real smile too. That thought leads to a question, and I decide to ask it.

"Just curious," I say. "Can you leave this building?"

"No. I am bound to the Heart of the Echo until someone else takes control of it." She turns toward us as we stop near her. "Did the ritual engender a feeling of oneness?"

"Um, what?"

Grant squeezes my hand. "She wants to know if sex made us feel any different, like we have Echo power."

"Oh." My cheeks start to feel warm. I never get embarrassed, but I've done that today thanks to the most intimate and powerful sexual experience of my life. Grant gave me that. But did it amp up my Echo power? Not sure. "How can we know if we have the ability to control the Heart of the Echo now?"

Aldith's almost smile curls up a bit more. "There is but one way to know. You must attempt to take dominion over the Heart."

"Good plan," Grant says," but we have no idea how to do that."

"Employ your intuition. It brought you to the Echo, did it not? And it guided you toward your destination."

"You mean this place," I say.

Aldith approaches us, placing one hand on my arm and the other on Grant's. "It is time to channel the strength of your newfound connection and seize control of the Heart. Time is running out."

"What do you mean?" Grant asks. "How is time running out? And for who?"

"For everyone in both worlds. Creating another world and merging it with the earth required magics of such scope and power that it could not be sustained for long. The cracks are beginning to show."

"You mean the convulsions. We saw those in our world."

"Similar incidents have occurred here as well. The fabric of the Echo is falling apart."

I think back on our journey through this world, and I have to point out something. "Where is it falling apart in the Echo? The Capital City seems fine. Empty, but intact except for what seems like damage incurred during the first waves of the apocalypse."

"Let me show you." Aldith turns sideways to us and waves a hand toward the wall. A window appears. "Take a look. The Heart has a panoramic view of the entire Echo."

Hand in hand, Grant and I approach the window to peer out at the totality of the world that invaded our home and wreaked uncountable costs in lives and destruction. The structure in which we stand seems to hover in the sky, far above everything else in this world. Our bird's-eye view reveals exactly what Aldith meant when she said the fabric of the Echo is falling apart. I see the Capital City in the distance, untouched and vacant. Smoke streams up from many locations elsewhere in this magically constructed world, but that's not the most disturbing aspect.

The sky pulsates with shades of purple and black that seem to split and slither around like blood cells in a body. Lightning slams down intermittently, scorching the ground and making buildings explode.

"Without the Brain," Aldith says, "the Echo is without guidance. Sefton Stainthorpe was the Brain, the cognitive entity keeping this world in some semblance of order. Well, perhaps 'order' is an inaccurate description. He kept it from completely disintegrating."

I can't tear my gaze away from the shocking view below us, not even when I speak to Aldith. "So killing Sefton killed the Echo too, or at least injured it badly. Must've taken a lot of energy to hold a magically made world together."

"Yes. That's why Sefton grew weak enough that Dax and Allison could stop the alchemy of worlds."

"Or maybe they were more powerful to start with."

"It is difficult to differentiate the two causal factors."

She talks like a scientist, but we are not discussing physics or mathematics. Those disciplines might have inspired Sefton Stainthorpe, but they didn't lay waste to the earth. Magic did that.

I turn toward Grant. "We need to try. See if we can take control of the Heart."

He rotates toward me. "Yeah, we do need to take control. Right now."

I glance at Aldith. "Do you help us? Or should we try this with just me and Grant?"

"The power is yours alone. I am a caretaker, not an integral element of the Echo."

"Okay." I clasp Grant's hands. "Let's do this."

He threads his fingers through mine and draws me a little closer. "You've used the Echo power before. That means you should get this party started."

"Party? We'll throw one of those once we stop the worlds from convulsing."

"I'll track down some warm champagne for us to celebrate with."

He said "warm champagne" because we don't have ice post-apocalypse. I really miss having a nice cold drink on a hot day. But I need to focus. My task is to somehow start the process of taking control of the Heart so we can stop the Echo's convulsions. I have no clue how to do that. Magic is all about mental power, right? That's the way I've understood it when Allison explained it to me and when Grant explained the alchemy of worlds. Magic isn't something you accomplish with a wrench or a computer. Not that computers work anymore.

Snap out of it, woman, and do your job.

Yeah, babbling in my head won't save anybody. I need to ease my anxiety. So I close my eyes and focus on the feel of Grant's hands in mine, the warmth of his skin, the roughness of his palms. I can hear the whispering of his breaths, and he gently strokes my palm with his thumb. The tension inside me unwinds little by little to relax my shoulders first, followed by the rest of my muscles, until I feel as soft as butter in the sun. My awareness of the world around me recedes, though I still sense Grant with me, and the anchor of his presence keeps me from drifting away into a trance.

Relaxation, check.

I don't realize I've moved closer to Grant until I feel his cheek grazing mine. If Aldith is telling the truth, Grant and I need to channel the energy of our lovemaking to tap into the Heart. Instead of logically trying to figure out how to do that, I let my body sag into him and relive the moment when he'd given me the sweetest, most beautiful climax I'd ever experienced. Right before I came, he'd whispered, "Hush, just let it happen, baby." Those tender yet sensual words had pushed me over the edge and suffused me with a feeling of completeness, like I'd always been meant to share a supernatural connection with this man.

Maybe this was our destiny.

Grant slips his arms around my waist to tug me closer, but he doesn't try to kiss me. He just holds me while I rest my head on his chest and listen to the steady thump-thump of his heartbeats. My heart thumps in time with his, as if we've synchronized our souls. Don't care if that sounds crazy. I know something binds us to each other, something more than our bodies touching, more than the words we might speak. I wrap my arms around him and revel in the deep intimacy of this moment, this connection.

Power sizzles through me.

I feel it, though I can't describe the sensation. Every fine hair on my body shivers and stiffens as a luscious tingle spreads through me from head to toe and dives deep inside my sex. I could almost climax just from that sensation. Grant's dick thickens against me, and I know that means he's experiencing the same effect. Without opening my eyes, I slide my hands up his chest and loop my arms around his neck, rising onto my toes to press my mouth to his.

The second our lips meet, that power zings through me again.

Grant plunges his tongue between my lips and devours me like I'm the last morsel of food in the universe. While our tongues tangle, he grasps my ass to lift me onto my toes and thrusts his hips into me, rubbing the iron length of his cock into my mound.

A crack of thunder explodes overhead, rattling the building.

I stumble backward, out of Grant's arms. "What was that?"

"Though I am far from an expert," Aldith says, "I believe you two just took dominion over the Heart of the Echo."

"How can we tell for sure if that's what happened?"

"Try to halt the convulsions, I suppose."

Grant and I look at each other. He shrugs. I shrug. Some amazing superheroes we are.

I grasp his hand and turn toward the windows, where we can see the convulsions racking the sky. Then we glance at each other again, and I know he understands what I want to do. I know what should be done, but I also realize I can't accomplish the task intellectually. I need to feel it. We both aim our focus out the windows and just do it. Energy crackles on my skin, diving beneath the surface, racing through my body and straight into Grant's at the exact moment when a similar energy rushes out of him and into me.

Another, louder crack of thunder resonates through the Echo. It vibrates in my bones and makes the building shudder so powerfully that we both stumble backward.

Then silence falls over the world.

And the sky no longer roils. It has turned a deep shade of azure that I've only seen once before—when the alchemy of worlds began on earth. This must be the natural sky of the Echo. The sun burns less brightly than in the mundane world, but it still illuminates the entire land. I don't know if the Echo is a globe or just a flat surface, and I suppose it doesn't really matter right now.

"Did we do it?" I ask, not caring who answers my question. "Seems like we did."

"Yes, you have done it," Aldith says. "The Echo is once more stable, though the apocalypse has not subsided."

"At least the worlds won't be destroyed. Right?"

"Correct. You have stabilized the earth as well."

We actually did it. But I still have a few questions for our eerie friend. "We've taken dominion of the Echo's Heart. But what does that mean? Is it a one-time thing or a permanent change?"

"I believe you will remain in control unless and until you die."

"Can we use our shared power to make things better in both worlds?"

"That I cannot answer." She tips her head to the side, and her gaze goes distant. "There is another, more pressing matter you should attend to. I sense Will is out there, desperately seeking a way to find you and secure Sefton's journal for himself."

Great. I'd really hoped I would never need to see that dweeb again. He set his pet golem loose on us, after all.

Aldith's eyes flare wide. "Oh my. He is rather angry with you two, and I fear he can feel that you have dominion over the Heart of the Echo. He is not well pleased."

Sometimes she talks like a medieval person. Or at least the way medieval people talk in the movies.

"Okay, so Will is ticked off at us," I say. "Does he still have magic?"

"Yes, though not as much power as you and Grant have."

"Can he cause major trouble with his magics?"

Aldith puckers her lips as if she's considering the question. "I can't say for certain."

"Well, that leaves us with one option." I turn to Grant. "I know you agree."

"Yeah, I do." He smiles. "Time for some reckless Erin tactics."

CHAPTER TWENTY-SEVEN

Grant

SOMETHING ABOUT TAKING CO-DOMINION OVER THE ECHO HAS changed my perception of Erin and myself. Why else would I suggest we employ her gonzo tactics to find and stop Will? Either that, or sex with her has melted all my brain cells. The weirdest part is that I don't mind at all. Lunacy sounds pretty damn good today. The apocalypse has made everyone a little nutty, but no one more than Sefton Stainthorpe's doppelgänger.

Before we head out into the unfamiliar world of the Echo, I need a few more answers from Aldith. "Is Will as dangerously nuts as Sefton was?"

"Perhaps. I've had no direct contact with him, so I can't give you a definitive response."

"Okay. Then can you tell us whether the golem is up and running again?"

She shrugs.

"What *do* you know?" I ask. "You tell us all kinds of vague stuff and… What? We're supposed to decipher it on our own?"

"I regret that I cannot be more helpful. I once did have more knowledge to impart, but Sefton managed to delete most of it from my memory."

The way she phrased that statement makes me wonder. "Are you a computer?"

She laughs softly. "No, I am a living being. Though I am different from you."

"In what ways?" I'm getting sick of her vague statements, and I want answers before Erin and I go out there to track down Will. "Come on, Aldith, tell us the truth. Stop making us drag it out of you."

She bows her head and wrings her hands. "The vision you see of me is not what I really am. I didn't wish to upset you, so I used what little magics I do have to create a more palatable image."

"Palatable? You're being vague again."

Aldith raises her head to look straight at me, though she bites her lower lip. "I will show you. Please don't panic. I mean you no harm and only wish to help."

Why would we panic? I have a sinking feeling I know the answer.

She takes a deep breath and exhales it.

The image of a cute, petite woman evaporates, replaced by what I assume is the real her—an Echo creature with scaly, flesh-covered skin and small spikes on her head. She has eerie green eyes that almost glow and inner eyelids that flick out every so often. I've seen much weirder and more disturbing Echo creatures than Aldith. The others I've come across were created by Sefton to resemble their human counterparts, which means I need to ask more questions.

"If you're an Echo creature," I say, "why aren't you trying to murder us? Those monsters are evil."

She shakes her head slowly. "Do not paint all of us with the same brush, Grant. Those of us who are not bent on wreaking bloody havoc will do you no harm. In fact, we will help you whenever possible, for even we wish to escape this world."

Not sure inviting Echo creatures to come home with us is a good idea. But I'll worry about that after we stop Will from doing whatever evil things he's plotting. Being a cop didn't prepare me for this. Neither did the army. All the combat experience on earth couldn't prepare anybody for living in a post-apocalyptic world full of magic and monsters.

But now I have magic powers. *Holy shit.*

"Do you have a counterpart on earth?" I ask Aldith. "A twin who's not a scaly being."

She considers me for a moment. "I would assume so, though I've never ventured into that world."

"Let's grab our backpacks," I tell Erin. "Then try to get out of here."

We retrieve our packs from the bedroom and return to the creepy-ass room where Aldith waits for us.

I clasp Erin's hand. "You should teleport us out of here, and see if you can take us directly to Will. I might have powers now, but I don't know how to whisk us away."

"Like I do? Well, maybe I've gotten better at doing that. But I'm no expert."

"You're more of an expert than I am. I know you can do this. Go for it, Erin."

A smile flickers across her lips. Then she shuts her eyes, and I do the same. Don't think I want to see whatever ether or wormhole we go through to reach our destination. I've had enough surprises over the past few months. A man needs some downtime once in a while, but I doubt I'll get any of that. I wince as I feel the change happening, though it's more of a mental sensation than a physical one.

"We're here," Erin says. "You can open your eyes now, Grant."

I peel my lids apart, which seems to take more effort than it should because I swear my eyelids have become glued together. But when I open them, I get to see the best sight in any world—Erin's face. "Hey, beautiful, you did it."

Her lips twitch, but she doesn't quite smile. "You were worried I'd screw it up, weren't you?"

"No. I have total faith in you, just not in magic."

She stares at me. "Total faith? In me?"

"Yeah, of course." I pull her close. "Sorry I acted like such a dick around you. That's over now. For good."

"I'm glad you feel that way. Because I need my partner to trust me all the way. That's how I feel about you."

"Ditto. Now let's find Will."

We're standing in the middle of a street that seems deserted, but I don't think this is the Capital City anymore. That means we will see Echo creatures and probably have to fend them off. At least I have a solid partner by my side for whatever comes next. I do trust Erin, all the way, because she has proved to me I can. Not by trying to do that. Just by being herself. Yeah, I finally appreciate her way of doing things, even if in the future I might sometimes disagree with her actions. She's been right too many times lately for me to doubt her ever again.

A noise, faint but distinct, catches my attention. I tip my head to the side and listen. Is that growling? Yeah, definitely. Whatever creature is making that sound, it doesn't seem like the friendly type. Erin and I have no weapons. We left them on the street where Will and his golem found us. Escaping from a cyborg didn't give us time to snatch up our weapons, though at least we still have our packs.

"Do you hear that?" Erin whispers.

"Yep, I hear it." I'm speaking softly too, though for all I know, these creatures have super-hearing. "We have no way to defend ourselves."

"We can punch and kick them."

I rotate my eyes toward her. "Hand to hand won't work with Echo creatures. They're too damn strong, and at least one of them has an armored torso. We need real weapons."

"Do you think I can magically create guns for us? Come on."

No, I don't expect her to conjure weapons out of thin air. I have a different idea. "Try teleporting our backpacks to us. You remember where we left them."

"Don't know if I can teleport objects."

"Give it a try. You can do it, Erin, I know you can."

She nods and shuts her eyes. Her shoulders bunch up, and her face does that too. But then a breath gusts out of her as her shoulders flag. She glances at me. "Didn't work. Sorry, I tried."

"That's okay. I have an idea."

I cradle her face in my hands and kiss her.

She relaxes against me and exhales a breathy moan.

Though I'd love to keep kissing her, we have important things to do. So I pull away and glance down at our feet, where our two backpacks slump on the pavement, and I grin. "You did it, baby."

She grins too. "Yeah, I did."

The growling noise I'd heard a few minutes ago has grown louder, clearly closer than before. I yank my cutlass out of its scabbard and shrug into my backpack straps. Erin grabs her machine gun, then gets her pack in position. Whatever is coming for us, it doesn't sound like a friendly Echo creature. Aldith never behaved like a monster, which wrecks my belief that all creatures are vicious killers. How many nice Echo beasts are out there? Don't know, and I can't risk finding out right now.

I lead Erin down the street. "Since you brought us here, I'm assuming Will must be someplace nearby."

"Hopefully. I'm new to this teleporting thing, so I can't swear I got my targeting right. We could be miles away from him."

"No, we're close. I can feel it. Besides, I trust your magics even if you don't."

"You have magics too, Grant. After all, you are the Heart of the Echo."

I don't like hearing her call me that. I'm not crazy about the title, but every time I think about what it means, I get a creepy-crawly sensation all over my body. I never wanted to become a vital link in a chain I can't see or understand. Sefton Stainthorpe served as a part of that chain too, and he was a whackjob.

As we reach an intersection, I notice shapes moving around in the semi-darkness on a side street. Though we stopped the convulsions of the Echo, the apocalypse has not been reversed. The sky above seems darker than it did when we were high above it inside the stronghold where we found Aldith. Just like on earth, here in the Echo, all the buildings have suffered devastating damage. I can't help wondering why, since this world only came into existence maybe a week before the alchemy of worlds began. Then again, Dax and Allison have talked about how he spent five years in the Echo before Sefton ignited the process of merging the worlds. Time moves differently here, just like Aldith said. For Dax, it moved more quickly. What effect will the time distortions have on me and Erin?

I can't worry about that right now.

The sun seems to be setting, which explains why the figures of creatures seem like writhing shadows rather than silhouettes. The buildings on the side street cast darkness on the ground too, adding to the ghost-like ambiance. We both stay aware of our surroundings as we keep walking, hyper-alert to every sound and shadow. The sinuous outlines of creatures become more defined as they inch ever closer to this street. In a matter of seconds, we will have left the intersection behind us—but not the creatures that stalk us. I wish they'd just come out and attack. Waiting and wondering is the worst part.

We've traveled halfway to the next block when it happens.

A horde of creatures rushes out into the next intersection, blocking our way.

Erin and I stop to survey the area. The creatures behind us, who had been mere shadows, now reveal themselves and line up in the intersection behind us. I see every kind of Echo creature—horned, spiked, scaly, fishlike, and other things I can't describe.

"Maybe we can command them," Erin says. "We are the Heart and Life-blood of the Echo."

"Great idea. How do we do that?"

She grasps my hand. "Magic, of course."

To control the Echo, we had to get naked. I'm not doing that out here in front of ravenous beasts. I doubt I could get an erection, anyway. The potential for imminent and horrific death is not conducive to getting turned on.

We don't get the chance to argue about her suggestion. The creatures rush at us as one, like a wall of spiky, scaly, gnarly monsters ready to pummel us. I lash out with my cutlass at the first beast that reaches me, aiming my blade straight for its heart, but the creature hops backward. Then I see it. A figure standing in the doorway of a wrecked building. The person standing there steps out onto the sidewalk, giving me a clear view of him.

It's Will.

I slash my blade toward the creature again, but then I stop. "Need some space, Erin, just for a minute. Can you handle that?"

Erin smirks and fires off a volley of rounds from her machine gun, scattering the creatures.

That won't hold them back for long. I have seconds to do this. So I shout, "Will! Get your ass over here. I've got what you want." I shrug out of my backpack and pull out the journal, but I also grab the cigarette lighter I'd found in the store where Erin and I spent our first night in the Echo. I flick the lighter, igniting a flame, and hold it near the journal high enough in the air that Will can see. "Call off your dogs, or I'll torch this thing."

He steps off the curb onto the street but halts there. "No, you won't. You need it if you're going to reverse the apocalypse."

Clearly, he doesn't realize Erin and I have dominion over the Heart of the Echo. He thinks we're still just two earthlings he can order his minions to trounce.

I move the lighter closer to the journal and flip it open to show the pages. "Call them off, Will."

"No."

The creatures make a move in unison, but Erin blasts them with another volley.

I don't want to reveal too much to Will, but I need to make him understand I will burn the damn journal. Erin's life means more to me than any book, no matter how magical and vital it might seem. I'd also realized after browsing the journal that it contains nothing more illuminating than the ramblings of a nutjob. So yeah, I'll give it up—but only to get what I want.

To make my point clear, I light the first page on fire.

"No!" Will screams as he races across the street to reach us. He glances at the creatures. "Back off now! I command you!"

The monsters retreat to either end of the block. Will halts several yards away from us.

I douse the burning page by laying it facedown on the ground and stomping my foot on it. Then I raise the damaged journal again. "I'll light it up good next time if you don't cooperate."

Will grinds words out between his clenched teeth. "What do you want?"

"Give us your golem."

CHAPTER TWENTY-EIGHT

Erin

MY RECKLESS, INSANE BEHAVIOR MUST BE RUBBING OFF ON GRANT. WHY else would he suggest that Will should give us his golem? What would we do with that thing, anyway? Maybe we could order it to crush the creatures that surround us with its big metal feet. Not sure what else a golem is good for if you aren't a megalomaniac bent on destroying two worlds.

"Are you off your rocker?" Will asks. "Why would I give you my golem?"

"To get the journal," Grant says. "Before I torch it—for real this time."

Grant had been saying that the journal must hold the key to undoing the apocalypse. But now that we control the Heart of the Echo, maybe he thinks the journal isn't necessary anymore because we have all the power we need. Unfortunately, I can't read his mind to find out the answer.

"What's your decision?" Grant asks. "The journal or the golem?"

"I could have my creatures or my golem destroy you," Will says. "You'd be dead before you realized what happened."

"Go on, do it. But I can torch this book faster than you can shout orders to your troops."

Yeah, Grant has definitely absorbed some of my crazy behavior. I should prepare to whisk us both away, just in case.

Will studies Grant for a moment, his expression unreadable. Then he glances at me and lifts one brow.

I have no idea what that means.

"All right," Will says. "You may have the golem. If you can summon him."

Will seems quite smug now, as if he's positive we have no chance of summoning the metal beast. Yeah, he must not know we took control of the Heart, otherwise he would never give us the golem. Sefton's doppelgänger doesn't seem to have the vast magics that the original madman wielded.

Grant moves closer to me and whispers, "Got any ideas about how to summon the golem?"

"No. This was your idea. Don't you know how to do it?"

"Guess we'll have to wing it. Should we make out to improve our chances?"

Since he's smirking, I know he doesn't really think we should do that. Making a joke during a dire situation might've seemed inappropriate to me before the Echo, but life after the apocalypse has rewritten all the rules of etiquette.

And I love it when Grant teases me.

We face each other and hold hands, our gazes connected by an invisible tether that I can feel as a pulsing thread of magic. Just yesterday, I would've denied magic existed. Today, I'm relying on it to save our lives. How bizarre. But I push all other thoughts out of my mind and focus on the task at hand—how to summon the golem. Grant's blue eyes transfix me, almost as if he's hypnotizing me, and I gaze into those irises as I take a deep breath, letting it out slowly. Everything else fades from my perception. I see only him, feel only his hands grasping mine, while we concentrate on a single thought.

Come to us, golem.

I swear I hear Grant's voice in my head while we concentrate on our task. *Come to us, come to us.* A metallic grinding noise emanates from somewhere farther away, faint at first but growing louder with every passing second. Monstrous footfalls draw ever closer. *Whump. Whump. Whump.*

Grant releases my hands.

When I open my eyes, he's smirking again. Cocky Grant turns me on even more than Zen Grant. So yeah, I feel like having sex right now, which is beyond inappropriate.

Whump. Whump. The golem strides ever closer.

Now I glimpse the crown of its head as the cyborg trudges up the side street, heading for us.

Will sputters. "No, you can't—It's impossible. Only I can summon the golem."

Grant chuckles. "We just did, asswipe. Not as all-powerful as you hoped you were, huh?"

I shake my head. "Even Sefton wasn't omnipotent. And you, Will, are nothing next to the mad genius."

"Remember when he whimpered and whined because he heard our horny friend coming for us?" Grant asks me. "This guy is a loser."

Why are we both insulting Will? I think Grant is trying to knock the dweeb off balance, and I'm all in for that. The more upset he gets, the more mistakes he'll make. Will believes he has more power than we do.

Think again, doppelgänger.

Our golem lumbers into view, turning the corner to head for us. It steps over the line of creatures that bars the intersection and halts maybe twenty feet from where we stand, then faces us and just waits. For instructions, I assume. Guess whoever summons the golem gets to command the cyborg.

Will throws an arm out to indicate us. "Kill them, golem. Kill them now. I am your master."

Not anymore. The golem ignores Will as if he doesn't exist.

I sidle closer to Grant. "Um, what now? We summoned that thing, but I'm fuzzy on the rest of your plan."

"No plan," he murmurs out of the corner of his mouth. "Winging it, remember?"

"I'm open to suggestions."

Will stomps toward us, but the golem takes one small step to block his path. He lets out a loud, frustrated cry. "Give me the fucking journal!"

"Sure thing." Grant tosses the book to Will, but the guy fumbles his catch and nearly falls over in his zeal to snag the journal. He gives us a smug look. "You are incredibly stupid, aren't you? This book allows me to control the Echo—all of it."

I stifle a laugh. He really has no clue.

Will flips through the book, his expression turning almost manic.

Since Grant doesn't have a plan, I decide to enact my own idea. I wave my arms in the air to get everyone's attention—well, everyone except Will—and wait until I've achieved my goal. All the creatures watching me snarl and gnash their teeth.

I take a deep breath and go for it. "Listen up, everybody. If you want to live, better run for it right now. The golem will crush anyone who sticks around. Last chance. Go now."

The creatures scoff at me.

Oh, they'll regret that. I crane my neck to look up at the golem. "Would you mind sweeping away these annoying cretins for me? Please?"

The golem swings his foot out and sweeps it leftward.

All the creatures scatter, fleeing in various directions to avoid getting bowled over by the cyborg's foot.

"Golem, stop!" Will almost shrieks. "I command you!"

The golem ignores him and shuffles around to swing his foot at the line of creatures behind us, but they've already started to flee. The only living things on this street are me, Grant, Will, and the golem.

Wow. My idea worked.

Grant grins. "Nice work, Erin."

"Thanks. But we lost the journal."

"Don't worry about that. It's useless, anyway. The ramblings of a madman."

"Useless?" I lodge my hands on my hips. "Why didn't you tell me that before now?"

"Didn't know how you'd react. I mean, that was our only lead for how to stop the Echo convulsions." He rubs the back of his neck and winces. "I'm sorry. Should've told you as soon as I realized the journal wouldn't help us. I was, uh…"

"Embarrassed?"

"Yeah."

"It's not your fault the journal doesn't help us. But maybe we don't need it now, anyway."

No, I won't say out loud that maybe our newfound shared power is better than Sefton's ramblings. Not in front of Will.

"Better run," Grant tells Will. "Or we'll ask the golem to please crush you under his foot. You've got the journal, so go."

Will scowls briefly, but then takes off down the street.

"Should we have just let him go?" I ask. "That guy might be whiny and annoying, but he has Echo power."

"Not as much as we do. I'd rather not kill anybody unless it's absolutely necessary." He lifts his brows. "You asked the golem to chase the creatures away. What happened to killing every last one of them?"

"I guess your Zen attitude has rubbed off on me."

"And your gonzo tactics have influenced me. That's why we make such a good team."

The golem turns around to face us, his head tipped down as if he's watching and waiting for us to command him again.

Maybe this creature captured us earlier, but I don't think he meant to hurt us. I can see the scars where we slashed him in our attempt to escape. The golem has been a slave, first to Sefton, and then to Will. We asked him to come to us, which skirts the line of enslavement. Not all Echo creatures are evil, as Aldith proved to us, and that makes me wonder.

I suddenly have an idea that's so bizarre I'm sure Grant will balk at it.

"What are you thinking?" Grant asks. "I can practically see the gears turning in your mind."

"I have a radical idea that might get us killed."

"Your favorite kind of plan. Tell me about it."

"Let's release the golem from his magical enslavement."

Grant stares at me, his face blank.

Yeah, I figured this plan might be too radical for him.

But then he smiles and kisses me. "You're a genius."

I can't help laughing. "Genius? No, I'm just the kind of girl who loves insanely bad ideas."

"You're an optimist in disguise, huh? Your wacky ideas usually work, after all."

"Are you saying we should do it? Free the golem?"

He glances up at the metal beast. "Yeah, I think we should. Maybe if we give him autonomy, he'll realize we only hurt him earlier because we needed to escape from Will. We should apologize for that, to get the ball rolling."

"Okay. Let's do that. Can the golem speak?"

"Not sure." Grant sucks in a big breath and hollers, "Golem, can you speak to us?"

The creature shakes its head slowly, emitting a metallic noise.

Grant looks at me and shrugs. "Guess we play twenty questions with the big guy. Yes or no responses only."

"Okay. Let's start with that apology." I clasp Grant's hand as we both tip our heads back to meet the golem's glowing red gaze. "We're sorry we hurt you. If we'd had any other option, we would've taken it. Do you accept our apology?"

The golem nods.

"We really appreciate that." I pause to think of what to ask him first. "Are you enslaved by magic to do your master's bidding?"

He nods.

"And we are your masters now, right?"

Another nod.

"We would like to free you, but we aren't sure it will work. Do you want us to try?"

The metal beast nods yet again.

"Okay." I turn to Grant. "What else should we ask him? He served Sefton and Will, so maybe one or both of those guys blabbed useful info to the golem. What do you think?"

"Worth a shot." Grant clears his throat. "Golem, do you know how Sefton Stainthorpe created the Echo?"

Our new friend shakes his head.

"Did Will mention anything about how to stop the apocalypse?"

The golem shakes his head again.

"Let's try to free him," I say, "then maybe ask him a few more questions. It would be a show of good faith from us to give him the option of answering rather than forcing him to do it. I assume we are forcing him, though we don't mean to do that."

"Good point. Let's free him."

We face each other, our foreheads touching, and hold hands again, lacing our fingers. I gaze directly into Grant's eyes while he gazes right back at me. Power crackles between us, an almost palpable force, as I feel the magics gathering inside me. Grant must experience the same thing. An erotic warmth ripples through me, suffusing my body, but I no longer care about whether it's bizarre or wrong to get turned on every time Grant and I use our shared power. It feels right.

Our hunger for each other empowers us.

I can't describe how I sense it, but I know we just freed the golem. He is autonomous now. The risk we've taken might get us killed or earn us a solid ally. Time to find out which way the big metal guy will swing.

We return our attention to the golem, and I say, "You're free now. No one can enslave you again."

I know that's true, though I can't explain why. Magic doesn't come with a user's manual.

"Do you have a name?" I ask.

The big guy shakes his head.

"Would you like to have one?"

He hesitates, then nods.

"You can make one up yourself, or we could help you. Would you like us to do that?"

The golem nods.

Grant gives me a brows-raised look, probably because he thinks it's weird that I'm going to give our new friend a name. I could let Grant do that, but I've already got an idea. "Would you like to be called Jarek? It means strong, which definitely applies to you. But it can also mean spring, as in renewal and rebirth. That suits you too since you're now an independent being. What do you think?"

The golem nods.

"You like the name Jarek?"

He gives me a thumbs-up sign, his metal joints creaking as he forms the gesture.

Well, that's weird. "Okay, I hereby christen you Jarek."

The golem opens his mouth a little, and I swear his lips curl up the tiniest bit as if he's trying to smile. I hadn't realized he had lips until just now. They're thin and gray, not at all like a human mouth. I briefly wonder where Sefton got the flesh to create the living machine, but then I realize I don't want to know.

Jarek kneels amid a cacophony of metallic noises, then touches a fingertip to the ground. He draws a pattern on the asphalt by gouging it out.

The golem has written, "Thank you."

I approach him and settle a hand on his gigantic arm. "You're welcome."

When I glance back at Grant, he's gaping at me.

"Something wrong?" I ask.

"You...made friends with a golem."

"Uh-huh. I took a page from your book and went for a peaceful resolution."

"I don't make nice with Echo creatures, in general. Not wanting to murder every last one of them isn't the same as a peace treaty." His gaping mouth shifts into an appreciative smile. "You are an amazing woman, Erin. I never would've realized that if we hadn't come to the Echo."

He's impressed, I think. What I've done with the golem didn't emerge from a plan or even serious consideration. I had a hunch and followed it. Now we have another ally besides Aldith.

I move to stand beside Jarek's hand, laying both of mine atop his index finger. "Maybe we can work together, hey? Grant and I want to make both worlds better."

He uses the index finger of his other hand to gouge out his response in the asphalt. "Me too."

"Did you like Sefton?"

Jarek shakes his head.

"Didn't think so. He sounded like a total bastard."

My new friend does that sort-of smiling thing again and nods.

I pat his hand with both of mine. "Now you've got friends. If we stick together, maybe we can change the worlds."

Jarek's lips curl up a teeny bit more.

Yeah, my plan worked. But we still have a serious problem. Will is out there somewhere, angry and humiliated, and I have an intuition that he wants revenge.

Chapter Twenty-Nine

Grant

WHAT'S LEFT FOR US TO DO NOW? ENDING THE ECHO'S CONVULSIONS in this world should have stopped them on earth too, though we can't know that for sure unless we go home. But I have no doubts Will is running around searching for a way to get his revenge on us. We shouldn't just go home and forget about this world, especially since we learned the Echo houses decent creatures alongside the murderous ones.

I can't help thinking of Aldith and Jarek. Okay, the golem is right beside us, so of course I think of him. But we left Aldith in the stronghold, alone. What if Will finds a way to get inside the Heart of the Echo and hurt her? Jarek has the size and strength to squash a skyscraper, so I doubt we need to worry about his well-being—unless Will invokes even stronger magics to stop the cyborg.

When I look at Erin, she smiles. "I know what you're thinking."

"Do you? I'm not entirely sure of what I'm thinking. I'm positive I have no idea what your thoughts are."

"Baloney."

"What do you mean 'baloney'?"

She laughs softly. "Haven't you noticed? We share a telepathic bond that started before we took dominion over the Heart of the Echo. I felt it when we meditated together. Didn't you?"

My thoughts rewind to our time in that auto parts store when we got in a meditative groove. I did feel like I could hear her thoughts and sense her desire like a palpable force inside me. Before we breached the Echo, I would've dismissed the idea as ridiculous. Now, I can no longer brush it off. "You're right. We do share a telepathic bond."

"Does that bother you?"

"No. I like it."

"Me too." She glances up at Jarek, then looks at me again. "Now that we've taken control of the Heart of the Echo, I think we should go home. Don't you? We need to check on our world and make sure the convulsions have stopped there too. Even if we can't reverse the apocalypse, maybe we can use our new powers to make things a little better for everybody."

"I agree."

"But I worry—"

"About Jarek and Aldith, and any other nice Echo beings."

Erin raises her brows. "Yeah, that's exactly what I was thinking. Guess we have telepathy even when we aren't having sex or meditating."

"Let's ask our big buddy what he thinks." I turn to face the golem, and Erin does the same. "Hey, Jarek, we need to go home to check on our friends. Would you be okay if we go?"

He nods, then scrawls a big message on the asphalt—*Help your friends.*

"You are a friend too," I say. "And we'll be back to find Will. Can you keep an eye out for him while we're away?"

Jarek nods.

"Maybe you could come home with us." I just thought of that option.

The golem nods, then shakes his head.

"Are you saying you want to come with us, but you can't?"

Jarek nods again.

I clasp Erin's hand. "It's time to go home, but I feel bad for leaving Jarek and Aldith here."

"We'll come back for them." Erin faces the golem. "Can you help us get out of the Echo?"

Instead of responding, he bends down to offer his hand to us, palm up, like he wants to give us a ride.

Erin and I climb into his palm.

Jarek jogs down the street, but we get a surprisingly gentle ride despite his swift gait. As we leave the city, heading out into barren countryside blackened by the apocalypse, I can't help feeling like we've scored a major victory. Our trip into the Echo netted us awesome new powers, new friends in Jarek and Aldith, and more information that might one day help us undo the damage Sefton inflicted on the earth. Maybe we can save the good Echo creatures too.

A dark smudge in the sky enlarges with every massive stride the golem takes. That's the doorway to the Echo. Or from this side, the entrance to earth.

When Jarek halts, we find ourselves face to face with the roiling black disk of the doorway. Our golem buddy raises his hand to his chin level to look at us.

Erin scrambles to her feet and leans over to kiss his cheek. "Thank you, Jarek. We won't forget about you."

The golem stretches his arm out until the doorway lies only feet away, then he pushes his arm through the opening to set us down on the ground. His giant limb retracts, and we can't see him anymore.

Erin and I stand on the Paddock Viaduct, the bridge that crosses the Trinity River and marks the area where the alchemy of worlds had begun. Before we can whisk ourselves away, an external force yanks us out of Fort Worth and teleports us to Sanctuary. It must be noon on the Lost Coast. As we adjust to the bright sunlight, having come from the epicenter of the apocalypse where the sunshine is always muted, I realize Dax and Allison stand a few yards away.

"Welcome home," Ally says as she races over to hug me and then Erin. "Dax was getting pessimistic, but I knew you'd come back eventually."

"How long were we gone?" I ask.

"Ten days."

"Wasn't that long for us. But we met a nice Echo lady who told us time in that world can slow down, hover, or speed up."

Dax stalks up to us. "Slow down? I only experienced the acceleration, though it didn't seem fast to me. Be grateful you weren't trapped in the Echo for five years."

"We are grateful."

He slaps my arm. "Glad you didn't get eaten by Echo creatures."

"Yeah, me too."

Erin gives me an odd look, and thanks to our new bond, I know what she wants to ask me. But not out here in front of everyone. We've touched down in the central commons of our camp, and other people loiter nearby.

"Have the convulsions ended here?" I ask. "They did in the Echo."

"Yes, the conniptions are over," Allison says. "We haven't experienced any of those in several days."

"Good. We have a lot more to tell you guys, but Erin and I need to have a private talk first. If that's okay."

"Of course." Ally eyes me and Erin as a knowing smile curves her mouth. "You two aren't arguing anymore. In fact, I'd say you've gotten to know each other really well."

I claim Erin's hand. "Yeah, we're a couple now."

Ally grins. "That's wonderful. I knew you were meant for each other."

Willow rushes up to us and hauls me into a bear hug, then does the same to Erin. "I missed you guys soooo much."

Erin tousles the girl's hair. "Yeah, we missed you too, sweetie. Have you grown since the last time I saw you?"

"No," Willow says with a laugh. "I'm fifteen. That means I'm too old to grow anymore."

Though Willow wants to know "absolutely everything" about our time in the Echo "including the gross parts," we excuse ourselves to go into my tent. After offloading our backpacks, we sit down on the cot.

"Why didn't you mention that Aldith also said time can rewind?" Erin asks.

"Not sure if we should tell anyone about that."

"But why?"

"Don't you get it?" I fold my hand around Erin's and gaze into her luminous eyes. "Rewinding time to stop the Echo from ever happening would mean you and I never met. We never came to Sanctuary and made all these friends, and Allison and Dax wouldn't be having a baby. Do we have the right to erase the good things we've found since the apocalypse hit?"

"Maybe our new powers will give us the skills to erase only the bad parts."

"We aren't good enough with our powers yet to know what we can or can't do. Until we figure that out, I suggest we keep some stuff to ourselves."

"I guess you're right. We don't know the rules of being the Heart and the Lifeblood of the Echo."

Now that we've agreed to keep a few secrets, we head back out to the commons, where Dax is grilling fish for lunch. I can't even remember what time of day it was when we left the Echo, but I'm famished. Those fish smell like heaven. Willow gives us a detailed description of how Dax took her net fishing this morning and they caught enough to feed the entire camp for lunch today.

But after our meal, we inform Dax and Ally that we need to go back to Fort Worth and make sure the convulsions have really ended there. Dax whisked us away before we had a chance to look around, not that we're complaining. Coming home feels damn good. Dax wants to go with us, but we assure him he should stay here with Allison. Only Erin and I will risk returning to the epicenter.

We emerge near the viaduct.

"Don't see anything weirder than usual," Erin says. "How long should we hang out here?"

"Let's tap into our shared powers to determine if things are stable here."

We hold hands, close our eyes, and focus on our task. I can feel the convulsions have stopped, though I can't explain how I know that. But I trust my intuition, more than I ever had before the apocalypse.

Erin and I look at each other, and she says, "It's all good."

"Yeah, it is."

The doorway to the Echo hovers high above our heads, seeming to be in stasis.

"Should we hang around for a while anyway?" Erin asks. "Just to be sure."

I shrug. "Might as well."

Erin turns to head away from the viaduct toward other parts of the city. I lag a little behind her, mostly so I can watch her sexy ass. Maybe we should waste a little time by having sex while we loiter in this city. Yeah, that's a solid plan based on sound reasoning. It has nothing to do with how much I want to fuck her again.

Erin glances back at me. "Hurry it up, Larson. Are you turning into an arthritic old man?"

"As soon as we find a comfortable spot, I'm going to prove to you how not arthritic I am."

She grins at me over her shoulder. "Can't wait."

I grin too.

But then pressure bears down on me as if someone dropped a big iron blanket over my body. I freeze, suddenly unable to take another step. I manage to open my mouth just enough to squeeze words out between my clamped teeth. "Erin, help."

She whirls around, gapes at me for a second, then rushes over to grasp my shoulders. But she can't do that. Her palms meet an impenetrable and invisible barrier. As hard as I try to break free, I can't do it. Sweat streams down my face from the effort. Erin pounds her fists on the unseen wall, shouting wordless cries of frustration.

The world disappears.

I spin through a dizzying void and pop out into muted sunlight. My brain needs a moment to sort through what I see around me. Devastated buildings. An eerily azure sky. Creatures gathered on the street before me, snarling and gnashing their teeth, ready to chow down on their meal.

Me. I'm their meal.

The creature Erin had tricked into transporting us into the Echo hunkers at the front of the congregation—and Will stands beside him.

At least the force field around me has evaporated. I could run, but I have no clue where I'd go. Without Erin, can I teleport? Or use any magics? I wish somebody had given us an instruction manual.

Will limps up to me, smiling smugly despite the gray pallor of his face and sweat dribbling down his temples. He's breathing hard too, almost wheezing. That's exactly how Sefton had looked after using a shitload of Echo power. Maybe I can exploit his weakness. No clue how, but I need to think of something. Since I don't have my backpack or any weapons, I have little chance of beating these Echo creatures in a fight.

"You ran away," Will says, and even his voice sounds weaker, though no less nasty. He hobbles closer to me, and spittle sprays my face when he snarls, "Give me the real journal."

"I did. You've got the genuine ramblings of the original Sefton Stainthorpe. Not my fault he was a raving lunatic."

"That's rot."

"Sorry the truth doesn't make you happy."

He flaps a hand toward the horny monster. "Seize this arsehole and transport him back to the palace. Now. I need to torture the truth out of him."

The horny beast pulls me into a bear hug, though not the cuddly kind, and his massive arms restrict my ability to inhale. I can pull in only shallow breaths. He lopes down the street. When I glance back, I see Will climbing into a vehicle. Soon, he's driving after us. I try to teleport, but nothing happens.

My only hope is the newfound bond between me and Erin. But will she hear my telepathic cry for help? I have no choice but to try.

Erin, help, I'm trapped in the Echo.

Chapter Thirty

Erin

GRANT IS GONE. HE VANISHED IN A HEARTBEAT AS IF HE'D TELEPORTED, though I've never known that type of travel to involve an incapacitating bubble that envelops the traveler. Something or someone ripped him away. To where? And why did they do it? We stopped the convulsions and gained new powers and new insights into the Echo. We should be celebrating. Why Grant? I don't understand anything that just happened, and I've become frozen in this spot, inches from where he had stood seconds ago. Is he dead?

No, he can't be. I will never believe that.

Tears burn in my eyes, but I swipe them away and take slow, deep breaths. Grant showed me how to meditate, and I need to do that right now. But my hands are shaking, and I feel like I might throw up. No, no, no, I need to keep it together. So I shut my eyes and imagine Grant's voice leading me through mindfulness meditation, the way he had back in that building in the Echo. His soothing tone. The sensation of our minds touching. The intimacy of the connection. I can almost feel him, almost, not quite, so close…

I throw my head back and shout curses at the heavens.

This isn't helpful. What should I do? Go home to Sanctuary and tell everyone I lost Grant? He must be in the Echo. I need to get in there, but my teleportation won't work.

Suddenly, I have an idea. A crazy one. Grant would call it a "gonzo" plan, and he'd be right. I sprint onto the bridge, halting at the center, and bend my head back to glare at the entrance to the Echo. Since I've had no luck contacting Grant, I'll try getting in touch with someone else.

I take a big breath and scream, "Jarek!"

Nothing.

"Jarek!" I scream even louder. "I need you, Jarek. Come and get me."

Growling and snarling noises originate from behind me. I've roused the Echo creatures, and I have no weapons I can use to defend myself.

Don't care. "Jarek! Help me. Please."

The doorway to the Echo telescopes open, and a large metal-and-flesh hand reaches down to pluck me off the ground. Jarek cradles me in his palm as he pulls me into the other world. The doorway shuts, and he sets me down on the asphalt surface of a street.

No time for pleasantries. "Have you seen Grant?"

Jarek shakes his head.

"What about Will?"

He nods.

"Do you know where I can find him?"

Jarek shakes his head.

Damn, I wish he could talk. Yes or no responses are so limited.

Erin, help me, I'm trapped in the palace.

Grant's words slam through me, making me stumble sideways as if they exert a physical force. But I heard those words in my head, in his voice. Maybe our telepathic link only works in this world, since I couldn't contact him until Jarek brought me here.

I tip my head back to gaze into the golem's red eyes. "Do you know where the palace is?"

He nods.

"Thank you for bringing me here," I say. "But I need another favor. I'll understand if you don't want to do it."

Jarek bends his knees and touches my nose with the barest pressure from his enormous index finger, which I think means he wants to assist me.

"You will help?" I ask.

The cyborg nods his assent.

Relief makes my entire body sag, and my knees almost buckle, but I catch myself. "Please take me to the palace. Grant is there."

Jarek offers me his hand, and I climb on for the ride. As he jogs down the street, I have nothing to do but think. Maybe my telepathic bond with Grant only works when we're in the same world. Does my teleportation have a similar limit? Or could I bring something from earth into the Echo using my powers? Might as well try.

I close my eyes and focus on my connection with Grant. The warmth of it rushes through me, and I know we are connected now. So I summon all our shared power and picture the object I need, picture it appearing on my lap. At first, nothing happens. Then a weight settles on my thighs. I open my eyes and grin.

My backpack sits on my lap, with my sword still in its scabbard.

Unzipping the pack, I dig around until I find the rest of the grenades Grant and I had scrounged up in that big store. I have three left. That's not my entire arsenal, though. I also have two more magazines for my machine gun and my switchblade, as well as a handgun.

Oh yeah, this will do.

Up ahead, I see a structure squatting atop a mountain that has steep sides. The closer we get to the building, the more detail I can see. It looks like a castle straight out of a fairy tale. Sefton must have thought Allison would live there with him and they would rule the Echo together. Now Will has holed up in that castle. What is he doing to Grant?

At the base of the mountain, Jarek halts. He raises his hand high above his head, reaching up to the peak. I step off his hand onto a rocky but mostly flat area not far from the castle and pull on my backpack. I wave down at Jarek. "Thank you."

He nods, then assumes an upright posture I take for the golem standing guard.

I race toward the castle, leaping over boulders and holes. By the time I reach the gates, I'm almost out of breath. I allow myself ten seconds to recover, then I knock on the massive wooden door.

Nothing.

Screw this. I fist my hands and clench my jaw, willing myself to zip straight to Grant. The gates vanish, and I find myself inside what looks like a prison cell.

Grant sits on the floor, knees bent, hands on the floor, gaze downcast.

"You needed a hand?" I say.

His head jerks up, and he grins. "Erin. I knew you'd find me."

My pulse accelerates, and every hair on my body lifts. I did it. I found Grant. "Are you okay?"

"Yeah. I've only been here for a few minutes. Will locked me up and left."

"It's only been a little while for me too."

Grant heaves his body off the floor and pulls me into his arms to kiss me. "I love you, Erin."

A thrill chases over my skin, and I can't help grinning. "I love you too, Grant."

The door bursts inward.

We turn toward the figure limping across the threshold. Will props himself up with a gnarled wooden stick, and he seems even paler than the last time I saw him.

"You don't look so good, Will," I say. "Maybe you should dial back the magics and give yourself time to recover."

"No, I will not," he snarls. "Give me the real journal."

"We did. Not our fault you refuse to believe the truth."

Our horny friend the Echo monster hovers just behind Will.

"I want the journal!" Will shouts, but his voice has become hoarse. "Tell me the truth!"

Grant pulls my sword out of its sheath and clamps my hand around the grip while he keeps his palm around mine. "Time to end this."

Somehow, I know exactly what he wants us to do. While both gripping the sword, we lunge forward as one to pierce the exact center of Will's heart.

"Want to know the truth?" I ask. "Grant is the heart. I am the Life-blood. You are nothing."

I know he understands what I mean. I see it in his eyes.

Grant and I combine our strength again, pushing harder than ever to punch the sword straight through until the hilt meets Will's chest with most of the metal protruding from his back. We marshal that physical power again to thrust the blade into the Echo creature's heart too. Will is shorter than the creature, but somehow, we knew the exact angle that would let us kill him with the same blade.

The linked bodies of Will and the beast crumple to the floor.

Grant extricates the sword and wipes the blood off using Will's clothes.

It's over. We prevailed.

But I don't feel like celebrating. I experience a powerful sense of relief, as if the weight of two worlds had settled onto my shoulders but now has been removed.

Grant gazes down at the dead man. "Guess we own this castle now."

"Don't think I want to live here."

"No, but maybe we'll find more answers hidden somewhere in this building."

"Maybe." I grab his shirt and pull him closer. "But not today. We've earned a vacation from death and mayhem."

"Let's get out of here."

"Jarek is waiting to take us home."

CHAPTER THIRTY-ONE

Grant

EIGHT DAYS HAVE GONE BY SINCE ERIN AND I ENDED WILL'S MANIC reign in the Echo. Everything seems to have calmed down, though I doubt we've been given a permanent reprieve. However much time we have to relax, I plan on making the most of it. That means Erin and I go down to the beach for a saltwater bath in the nude. Naturally, that was her idea. We also told Dax to discourage anybody else from visiting the beach until we come back. Nobody says no to Dax—except for Allison. So we climb up to the crest of the mountain and make our way to the shore.

Oh yeah, I plan on making love to Erin on the warm, golden sand.

We amble down the gentle slope that leads to the beach hand in hand, reveling in the sunshine and the sound of waves lapping on the shore. Life might not be what it was before the Echo, but we've carved out a nice little haven here on the California Coast. All I want to think about now is what I want to do to Erin once I get her naked. We've just passed the spot where I had erected a makeshift camp when I first landed here, not long after the apocalypse hit. It seems like such a long time ago.

Erin stops and points toward the shore. "What's that?"

I halt too and follow the track of her finger. A lump lies on the sand. No, not just a lump. A human being. I drag Erin along with me as I sprint toward the figure lying sprawled at the edge of the beach, where waves splash over the person who lies facedown there. We crouch at either side of the person and gently turn the body onto its back.

We gaze down at a woman's face.

She's breathing, though she seems rather pale and scratches mark her arms. I pat her cheek, but she doesn't respond. Checking her pulse, I feel a strong rhythm. So I slide my arms under her body and lift her into a sitting position, then scoop up a handful of water to splash it on her face.

The woman's lids flutter several times, then finally open. She gazes at us blearily. "Who are you?"

"My name is Grant, and that's Erin." I nod toward her. "What's your name?"

Her faces goes blank. "I don't know."

An amnesiac? We've never had one of those show up on our doorstep before.

I pat her hand. "Don't worry, we'll take care of you. If you feel like you can't walk, I can go get a stretcher from our camp. We made one out of tree branches, in case we ever needed it."

The woman bites her lip. "I'd rather walk."

"All right. If you get weak along the way, just let us know."

Erin offers the stranger a bottle of water, and the woman takes a few sips. Then we help her get up. Her dress is dirty and frayed at the hem, but otherwise undamaged. We take it slow as we make our way back to the camp. Everyone is happy to see a newcomer, though they all wonder what caused her memory loss and how she wound up on our beach. Those questions will wait for another day, though. Right now, we need to take care of her.

Naturally, Dax wonders if the woman's amnesia is a trick. I don't blame him for being skeptical, but Erin and I both feel we can trust the stranger. No concrete reason why. We just know it's true. Erin and I share control over the Heart of the Echo, but the parallel world remains a dangerous place. Now that we have allies in the Echo, we all experience something we haven't known since before the alchemy of worlds.

We have hope. And these days, that's the most precious gift of all.

**The apocalypse isn't over yet. Get ready for
the epic conclusion to the trilogy in *Echo Unbound.***

ECHO UNBOUND

Echo Power Trilogy, Book Three

Chapter One

Gabriel

K EEP CLIMBING! WE'RE ALMOST THERE." I LATCH ON TO A HANDHOLD in the cliff and pull myself up another a few feet, then repeat the process again and again as I inch upward. Sweat pours down my face and soaks my shirt. Damn, this is taking too long. The monsters below us will catch up soon. "Faster! No time to waste, people, keep moving."

I risk a glance downward. My friends are still climbing, but some have begun to fall back. I know they can't help it. None of us trained for climbing up a sheer cliff in the dark. Doing this in the daytime would test the best climber's skills. We are not the best of the best. We're only the best this world has got right now. At least the cliff offers a ton of natural handholds. But our job is still a damn hard one.

A scream echoes below me, receding swiftly.

No, no, no. I glance down, and my heart thuds.

Below me, a figure tumbles toward the ground.

I catch a glimpse of Rafiq's terrified face, and though my first impulse is to look away, I refuse to do that. My team, my friends, followed me onto this cliff without reservations. Losing even one person hurts like a knife driven into my heart, but I can't stop to grieve. Not right now. My friends have stopped climbing, frozen in place as they stare at the ground far below us. That's the last thing they should do right now.

"No gawking," I shout. "We have to keep climbing."

Everyone starts moving again, one handhold at a time, slowly making our way toward the summit. Fog shrouds it, but we know what lies on top of the cliff.

The castle created by Sefton Stainthorpe, the architect of the apocalypse.

I reach up, feeling for anything I can grip, and my palm lands on a flat surface. Peering up through the fog, I can just make out the ground. I've done it. I've reached the summit.

"Come on, guys!" I holler. "I'm at the top. You can make it too."

I find a foothold and push my body up, over the edge, landing face-first on flat ground. For a moment, I just lie here, catching my breath. My pulse pounds in my ears, but gradually, it slows down and becomes almost normal. I roll onto my back, wiping sweat off my face with my shirt. Just as I sit up, my friends begin to pour onto the summit.

Kai crawls toward me on hands and knees. Though he looks exhausted, he manages to grin. "We're here. We made it, sir."

I can't respond, not yet, not until I know the rest of my crew has reached the summit. I rattle off their names in my head as each one climbs over the edge, onto flat ground. Once they've all arrived, I relax a little. Can't relax all the way. We lost a member of our family tonight.

And the battle hasn't even begun yet.

Despite several hundred feet separating us from the street below, I can hear our enemies clamoring at ground level, desperate to reach the summit. They've only just arrived at the cliff's base, though.

"What now?" Kai asks.

"Let's go inside. That's what we came here for—to seize control of the castle. Sefton's palace belongs to us."

I get up and offer Kai my hand, helping him rise too. The rest of our friends lie on the ground or slump on their knees. I'd like to give them time to recover from that climb, but I can't do it. The monsters below will not give us a chance to catch our breath.

"Time to get moving again," I shout. "Into the castle. Now."

Nobody complains. They all get up and follow me and Kai as we approach the castle. The structure hunkers on the summit like an abandoned castle from a fairy tale, with sloping lines and rounded turrets. The whole thing feels off, though, like a painting with another picture hidden under the surface paint.

The wooden gates hang open.

Yeah, that's just creepy enough to give me pause. I've fought more battles with Echo creatures than I can count, and I've walked into some of the freakiest quadrants in this world. Yet the fact the castle doors are open, as if they were waiting for us, makes me uneasy.

But we have no choice. We can't turn back now.

I slowly walk through the open doors and into a large, empty entryway. A staircase winds its way up to the second floor. Doors on either side of the entryway stand closed. Light that seems to come from nowhere illuminates the interior of Sefton's palace. It's a castle, really, but apparently the mad architect of doomsday labeled it a palace.

The man who created it is dead. Even his Echo is dead. Sefton cannot ever return to reclaim this place.

Do I have an Echo? If I do, I haven't met him. All humans on Earth supposedly have twisted copies of themselves running around in the Echo or in the normal world, beings who have scaly skin, horns, or a thousand other aberrations.

And yes, that includes my friends.

"We need to search the castle," I announce. "Look for anything that might help us understand what this building was created to do."

Yeah, I don't buy that Sefton just wanted a throne to rest his maniacal ass on, or that he wanted to flaunt his power by creating a "palace" in the sky that everyone would see.

Kai sticks close to me as we explore the ground floor.

Outside, the cries of our enemies have died away. That seems like a bad sign.

"Stay here," I tell Kai. "I need to take a look outside."

"I should come with you, sir. No one works alone, that's what you tell us.'"

Suddenly, I wish I had never said that. I meant that none of them should ever do anything alone. I can handle myself.

I grasp Kai's shoulders and stare straight into his eyes. "Just stay here."

His shoulders flag, and his expression falls. But he does what I told him. He stays in the castle while I hurry outside to check on what's happening. Silence is never a good thing in an Echo battle. It means the enemy is plotting something.

As I cross the open space in front of the castle, I hear faint growling noises. I pull out my longest, sharpest serrated knife and grip it tightly. The noises draw closer and closer. I slow my pace as I approach the cliff's edge and halt a few yards away, tilting my head to the side to listen.

Grunting. Growling. Scrabbling.

That doesn't sound like an army climbing up the cliff.

I inch toward the edge, leaning forward, peering into the darkness below.

An Echo creature vaults over the edge to land inches away from me. The beast charges me, and I thrust my knife at its chest, aiming for the heart. The blade sinks into the creature's flesh to the hilt. Blood oozes from the wound—until I yank the blade free. Then blood pours out, and the beast collapses to the ground. I've heard rumors that some creatures can be killed by piercing the exact center of the heart, but I hadn't tried it until tonight. Did I hit the exact center? Can't be sure.

I punch the knife into the beast's heart again, just to be safe. Since the strike doesn't trigger a new rush of blood, I assume the creature is dead.

Where are this guy's friends? I scuffle up to the very edge of the cliff and peer down into the darkness. I don't see any shapes climbing toward the summit. The moon provides just enough light for me to tell that absolutely no creatures are scaling the cliff.

A chill shivers up my spine, lifting every hair.

Screams erupt inside the castle.

I whirl around and race back inside.

But I'm too late. The screams have ended, and the deepest silence I've ever heard suffuses the entire castle. Bodies lie strewn across the floor of the entryway. The bodies of my friends. I grip my knife so hard that my fingers ache. Where are the monsters who did this? I scurry from body to body, verifying that they're actually dead and not just injured.

I don't find anyone still alive. My people are all accounted for, along with quite a few of our enemies. I find Kai last and pick him up to hold him for a moment. My throat goes thick. The kid had followed me around like a lost puppy, and he became my best ally and battle partner.

Shuffling noises originate from another part of the castle.

My people are dead. Those noises must be the enemy.

I grab my knife and the machine gun Kai had liked to carry, then I stalk toward the noises. It sounds like someone is rifling through stuff, searching for who knows what. I clench my jaw and shove my knife into its scabbard. The machine gun works better—and faster, for sure. Whatever creatures are left in the castle, they will die tonight.

When I stalk into the room from where the noises originated, I find myself inside Sefton's throne room. A single creature hustles around, hunting for something to steal but finding nothing. The room is empty, except for the throne.

The monster faces away from me.

"Hey, turn around," I holler.

Slowly, the beast shuffles around to look at me. "Mm, I am hungry. Maybe I should eat you, human."

"You and your friends murdered my family."

"But you fight alongside my kind."

"No. I fight with my family." I raise the machine gun. "You murdered them. I believe in the eye-for-an-eye approach to justice."

"You want to swap eyes with me?"

These creatures can be incredibly stupid, but they also have a vicious type of cunning. Vicious and gruesome.

"I prefer to eat human eyes," the monster says. "But hearts taste the best."

Fury rises inside me, searing and sharp, and I can't hold back any longer. I roar as I bolt for the beast, pulling the trigger to spray round after round at the thing that murdered my surrogate family. I don't stop firing until the beast hits the floor with a thud that vibrates the entire castle. When the bullets run out, I get my knife and stab it straight into the creature's heart.

He lies dead, his eyes open and vacant.

It's over. The Echo has won. The only decent beings living in this world have died while following my orders. The family I cultivated here no longer exists. I am alone.

The weight of the loss envelops me, and the bitter taste of it seeps into my soul. I trudge over to the marble throne Sefton had erected and drop onto it. Every muscle in my body slackens. The gun falls from my hand, clattering on the floor. I let my head fall back against the throne and shut my eyes.

"You grieve for your friends, but you cannot give up yet."

The female voice that spoke those words makes me crack one eye open. A pretty Echo creature with scaly flesh and small spikes on her head stands several yards away, watching me with a bland expression. When she blinks, her inner lids flick across her eyes, and her green eyes have an iridescent quality that makes them almost seem to glow.

I leap off the throne and rip my knife out of its scabbard, wielding it at the pretty beast. "Your buddies killed my family."

"They were not my friends. I serve no master."

"Who are you?"

She moves closer. "I am Aldith, guardian of the Echo's Heart and Lifeblood. I also protect the Brain."

"What brain?"

"The Echo is a living thing composed of magics. It cannot think or act like a human or an Echo creature. It has no sentience of its own, thus it requires another being to keep the Brain working properly." She steps even closer, seemingly unfazed by the big knife in my hand. "I have waited for you. I had no knowledge of who you might be, but I sensed you would come."

"If you live in this castle, you are not my ally."

She scans the throne room, though she seems only faintly interested in it. "I don't live here. The castle belongs to the one who claimed it. That would be you."

"You think I want to live here?" I shake my head. "You're insane. And I'm out of here."

I stomp toward the doorway.

"Don't you wish to know why I came here?" Aldith asks. "Or would you prefer never to know your true destiny?"

"Don't believe in that shit."

"You, Gabriel Merchant, cannot escape your destiny. Belief is not required, but cooperation is mandatory."

I glance back at her. "Sorry, I'm fresh out of cooperation."

She sighs. "I regret the need to force your compliance. But you leave me no choice. The fate of two worlds depends on you, and I know of only one way to convince you of that. I'm sending you to Sanctuary."

"To where? You're nuts, lady."

I walk out of the throne room—and straight into the entryway, where my friends lie dead, their blood staining the floor. My feet won't move. My eyes force me to look at their faces. They stare at me with the starkness of death.

My friends. My family. Every one of them was murdered by the monsters who inhabit this world. What made me believe I could protect them and bring them to a place where no one could find us? I'd been so arrogant.

Outside, the footfalls of a gigantic beast detonate like synchronized bomb blasts. Then the racket stops.

Aldith appears in front of me. "Your ride is here."

"My ride to where?"

"Sanctuary." She turns to the side, gesturing for me to exit the building. "Jarek doesn't like to be kept waiting."

Why not do what she says? I've got nothing now, except the responsibility for getting my friends killed. Whether Aldith intends to send me to a nice place or the hell I deserve, it doesn't matter anymore. I walk outside and stop a few feet from the cliff's edge.

A gigantic creature made of flesh and metal stands there, his eyes at my chest level. He offers me his enormous hand.

I guess I'm supposed to sit on his palm. "Are you my taxi to Sanctuary?"

The behemoth nods.

He looks familiar, but I know I've never met this creature before. I think I heard stories about him.

"Are you the golem?" I ask. "The creature Sefton created out of magics?"

He nods.

With a heavy sigh, I climb onto the golem's hand. Aldith had called him Jarek.

The golem walks through the city, and no one dares to get in his way or question him about where he's going or what he's doing. Maybe he can't talk, but I wouldn't be surprised if he can write. Eventually, we leave the Capital City behind, heading out into the ravaged wasteland beyond it. The Echo destroyed both worlds, but I have no idea what Earth looks like now.

Jarek takes me to the gateway that joins the two worlds, a spinning black disk high in the sky. For Jarek, reaching that height proves no obstacle at all. He raises his hand just as the gateway spirals open, then stretches his hand through it to set me down on the cracked pavement of a city street.

I turn around just in time to see the golem's hand retreating into the Echo. The gateway shuts.

Where am I? It looks like a city. But which one? The destruction wrought by the Echo might have made it impossible to tell, or at least very difficult to figure out. I don't get why Aldith wanted to drop me here. Sanctuary? I don't think so. But I have nowhere else to go. Might as well explore my new environment.

And pray I haven't been tricked into walking into hell.

Chapter Two

Sarah

I LIE ON THE BEACH, STRETCHED OUT ON MY TUMMY ON A SOFT TOWEL, and let the warmth of the sun penetrate my skin and warm me from the inside out. The apocalypse might have destroyed the world, but I've found a lovely new home here on the Lost Coast, in what used to be called Northern California. I don't remember the day the Echo struck, or what happened after that. But oddly, I do remember where California is.

Yeah, amnesia can be totally confusing.

My new friends here at Sanctuary took me in, despite having no idea who I am or how I got here. I woke up on this very beach two months ago, dressed in ragged clothes and with no memory of who I am or how I came to be here. Months and still nothing. My life before I found Sanctuary remains a gaping black hole.

A few days after I turned up here, Allison, one of my new friends, asked me what I'd like to be called. The name Sarah popped out of my mouth. Is that my real name? I still don't know. How old am I? Everybody took a poll and decided I must be twenty-eight. Works for me.

I roll over onto my back and slip on my sunglasses. I'm glad my friends have the ability to teleport to basically anywhere they want, because they bring home a lot more than food. They grab fun things too. Like Allison says, "Everybody needs to feel normal, even if it's only for a little while." My towel and my shades came from a partially destroyed department store in Yuma, Arizona. Or what used to be Yuma. Echo creatures took control of the city not long after the gang came home.

Ahhh, the sun feels so good on my skin. I asked if I could sunbathe in the nude, and Allison said sure. Dax, her grumpy British husband, threatened to "knock the bloody daylights" out of anyone who might spy on me. But that was unnecessary. The Sanctuary gang obeys the rules of etiquette in our camp. No Echo creatures have come here in months, which is the only reason I'm allowed to sunbathe alone.

Maybe I used to love nude sunbathing before the apocalypse. I definitely love it today. With the trees providing privacy, I feel totally relaxed for the first time since I woke up here.

An angry yell echoes from high above me and further down the beach. It draws closer every second, almost as if the person doing the yelling has been launched through the air.

Whump.

Sand sprays up and rains down on my body.

I jerk into a sitting position, my eyes flying open, and gape at the man lying near my feet. The shock of what just happened ensures that I don't do the smart thing. No, I just sit here staring at the man.

He pushes up onto his straight arms, seeming dazed. He blinks rapidly several times, then his attention lands on me. On my breasts.

I still can't move. While he stares at my body, I can't stop myself from admiring him too. The man has a muscular physique, and his clothes have gotten torn. Only a few scraps cling to his torso, and his pants have been ripped in various places. His hair is a mess.

Suddenly, I realize I'm still naked.

I scurry backward and snatch my towel up to cover my front side. "Who are you? What are you doing here?"

The man rises to his knees and brushes sand off himself. "Where am I?"

"California."

He surveys the beach, seeming satisfied. "Well, that's better than where I just came from."

"You haven't answered my questions."

"Maybe I don't feel like answering."

I glance to my right, where I'd left my clothes in a neat little pile.

"Want your clothes?" the man asks. "Or would you rather fuck right here on the beach?"

"Excuse me? I do not have sex with strangers." Well, maybe I used to be like that, but I don't remember. I hope not.

He licks his lips as he gazes at my bare thighs. "I haven't been with a woman in such a long time."

I leap up and grab my clothes, then bolt for the path that leads up and over the mountain, to where Sanctuary lies. I only make it halfway there before the stranger throws his arms around me from behind and hoists me off my feet.

"Don't run," he growls into my ear. "Tell me one thing, and I'll consider letting you go."

"Gee, thanks."

He rubs his stubbly cheek against my face. "Guess you don't want me to let go yet."

"Just ask your damn question."

"Is this Sanctuary?"

His question stops me for a moment. Sure, people find us here and often join our camp. But they don't know what name we gave it until we tell them. This man already knows. That realization sweeps a shiver up my spine.

My captor gives me a quick, hard squeeze. "Answer my question."

"I can't. Need to talk to my friends first."

"Wrong answer." He rips the towel away, leaving me naked and holding on to my lump of clothes. "Guess it's fucking on the beach, then."

"Threatening me with sexual assault won't convince me to give you information."

For a moment, he doesn't move or speak. I hear only the whispering of his breaths and the pounding of my own heart. Then he releases me. "Go on. Run to your friends, Lady Godiva."

I race for the camp, running faster than I ever have before, and crest the mountain in a few minutes. I stop there. Needing to rest is only part of the reason. I glance around but don't see that vile man. So I take the time to quickly yank my clothes on before I sprint down the mountainside. By the time I reach the camp, everyone is busy preparing for lunch. They've started a small fire to roast over a spit what looks like a chicken. As I draw closer, slowing to a jog, I can tell they have another spit set up on the other side of the fire, and that one seems to have a pig roasting on it.

I approach Grant Larson and Erin Harding, the people who found me on the beach two months ago. They've become my friends, just like Dax and Allison Stainthorpe and their adopted daughter, Willow. Dax's brother was the lunatic who created the apocalypse, but nobody brings up that subject without a really good reason.

Erin smiles and waves for me to go to her. "Did you have a good time sunbathing?"

"Uh, yeah. Until some guy fell out of the sky and grabbed me."

"What? Are you okay?"

I shrug. "Sure, fine. He let me go, and I ran back here."

"You're awfully calm, considering what happened."

Why don't I feel panicky? It's weird.

Erin throws an arm around my shoulders. "If that creep comes within two hundred yards of the camp, we'll know about it—and we'll eighty-six that guy. So just relax and eat some lunch."

The guards positioned discreetly around the camp will never let that jerk past the perimeter. They're armed and well-trained by Grant and Erin, who both have military experience.

"Don't worry," Grant says. "No one in this camp will ever let anyone hurt you."

I wish they wouldn't treat me differently than everyone else in Sanctuary. Amnesia doesn't make me special. All the residents of Sanctuary have a story of loss, the gut-wrenching kind. I have no idea if I've lost anyone, or if somebody out there is looking for me.

"Please, just treat me like everyone else," I say. "And I really wish you guys would let me do something. I can help with the cooking or sewing, or anything."

"Do you remember how to sew?" Erin asks.

"Well, no. But I can't keep sitting around doing nothing." I suddenly remember that maniac on the beach. "Erin, would you teach me how to defend myself? I'd love to know how to shoot arrows like you do."

"Allison can show you self-defense techniques. Dax taught her. But if you really want to learn about archery, I'd be happy to teach you."

"Thank you." I try to restrain myself, but I fail. "When can we start? Today?"

Erin smiles and shakes her head. "You might not remember your past, but you sure know what you want. Yes, we can get started later this afternoon. I need to help Grant with something after lunch, then I'll come find you."

Well, that's a start. I need to feel useful, and after my encounter earlier, I need to develop some fighting skills.

"Maybe you shouldn't go out by yourself anymore," Grant says. "Just to be safe."

No more nude sunbathing. He's right, of course. But I wish he were wrong.

"I should check around," Grant says, "to see if anybody has seen that creature."

"He wasn't an Echo creature," I say. "He was a man."

"Oh. Well, we should send a few people to search the beach and the woods along our favorite trails to make sure that guy has left the vicinity."

"Lunch," Dax hollers. "Come and get it."

Hearing a British man speak those words always strikes me as kind of funny. Shouldn't he announce that lunch will be served in the dining room? But we don't have a dining room, or any type of rooms. Just tents. Grant, Erin, and I head for the fire and the nicely roasted meat waiting for us there. As I eat a hunk of white meat chicken, I can't help wondering for the thousandth time if I used to like meat or if I might've been a vegetarian, maybe even a vegan.

Will I ever find out the truth about myself?

I say goodbye to Grant and Erin, who are going off to do whatever they need to do that I'm not allowed to know about. Despite the fact they've welcomed me into Sanctuary and treat me like family, I often wonder if their secret discussions revolve around me and who or what they think I am.

Someone screams.

We all freeze. I glance at Grant and Erin, who have barely walked halfway to Dax and Allison's tent.

"Out of my way, you moron!" a man shouts.

I recognize that growly, nasty voice. But no, it can't be him. We have lookouts who watch for anyone or anything that might waltz into our camp.

"Hey! Don't push my wife. Who do you think you are, anyway?"

That sounds like Stan Woodruff. He and his wife, Miriam, are the oldest residents of Sanctuary, though they're only in their sixties.

Dax and Allison rush out of their tent and race toward the ruckus, but Dax waves for her to stay away. She is pregnant, so I get why she needs to stay back. Grant and Erin hurry after Dax.

Will I just stand here? That's what I usually do. But I refuse to keep letting everyone treat me like the fairy-tale princess who can't stand to lie on a pea. So I race after my friends, heading straight for the ruckus on the other side of the camp. Halfway there, we stop.

A figure stumbles out from between two tents.

My heart thuds, and a wave of ice floods through me. Oh yes, I know that man. He saw me naked, and I tried to get away from him. I only succeeded because he let me.

The man still wears torn and tattered clothes, but grass stains have joined the dirt stains. "Is this Sanctuary?"

Dax approaches the man. "Who are you? And why have you frightened our friends?"

"Not my fault if they're pansies who screech every time they see a stranger."

"Perhaps you should try a less violent approach to entering a new place."

The man squints at Dax. "Is this Sanctuary or not? Aldith sent me here, and I want to know why."

Dax goes perfectly still, his expression blank. He glances at Allison, who hovers just outside their tent. She shrugs. Grant and Erin shrug too.

"Tell us what you know about Sanctuary and Aldith," Dax demands. "And how you got past our sentries."

The stranger clenches his fists, then loosens them. "What the hell. Aldith is an Echo creature, who must live in the Echo since that's where I met her. She told me I needed to come here. Then she got a golem to dump me on Earth, but nowhere near this place, as far as I can tell."

"Where did Aldith send you?"

"Some city. I didn't get the chance to do any sightseeing. Creatures attacked me."

Dax folds his arms over his chest. "Hmm. If you were in 'some city,' how did you reach this place? There are no metropolitan areas anywhere near the Lost Coast."

"Something threw me here, and I landed on the beach with that naked girl." He glances at me. "Figured she must know where she's going, so I followed her."

I jog over to Dax and the stranger, focusing on the man who threatened to assault me on the beach. "If you followed me, why did it take an hour for you to get here?"

"Reconnaissance, Lady Godiva. I never walk into a strange place without scouting the area first."

"My name is not Lady Godiva."

The maniac smirks. "What is it, then?"

"Like I would ever tell you."

Dax inserts himself between me and the stranger. "Start by telling us your name, and we'll go from there."

The man keeps his focus on me as he speaks to Dax. "Gabriel Merchant. Who are you, mountain man?"

"You may call me Dax. Now, you will follow me. We need to have a discussion."

Dax grasps Gabriel's arm and drags him away to the tent where we store our food. I experience a bizarre impulse to follow them, but I ignore it. The last thing I want to do is spend more time in Gabriel's presence. That man is evil.

I return to my tent and try to read a book, but I can't concentrate on it even though I love detective stories from the nineteen forties. My mind keeps forcing me to wonder what Dax and Gabriel are talking about and whether it has anything to do with me. That's narcissistic, though. Not everything strange in this place revolves around the amnesia girl. But Gabriel did seem extremely interested in me.

After chewing on my bottom lip for a moment, I shut the book and sneak out of my tent. I slip out the back way, so nobody will see me, and tiptoe past half a dozen other tents to reach the one where Dax took Gabriel. I can hear them talking.

"Who the bloody hell are you?" Dax snarls. "I want to know the truth. All of it. Right now."

"And I should cooperate, why?"

"Because I will snap your neck if you don't."

Gabriel chuckles. "I've fought with much worse things than you."

A rustling sound originates from the other side of the tent. "Mind if I come in?"

That's Grant.

"Yes, of course," Dax tells him.

"Maybe I should talk to the new guy," Grant says. "Use my Zen powers on him. After a little forced meditation, he might be more open to talking."

Gabriel chuckles again. "Forced meditation? You guys are nuts."

I really want to see what's going on in there, instead of just hearing it. So I skulk along the backside of the tent until I find a seam where the tent has been held together with snaps. I carefully push two fingers into the seam and spread them. That gives me a partial view of the interior.

Gabriel sits on a folding canvas chair with his wrists bound behind it with duct tape. He keeps smiling with smug satisfaction while Dax glares and Grant just gazes at the man placidly.

"We're not bad people," Grant says. "If you tell us about you, maybe we can help each other."

"I don't trust anyone."

"That's too bad. Trust is a beautiful thing—when it's earned."

Gabriel grunts. "Why should I give a shit about earning your trust? You haven't earned mine."

"Hey, man, we're just trying to keep our family safe. I'm sure you can understand that. Besides, you did assault our friend."

"No, I didn't. I detained her briefly."

Grant clucks his tongue. "Lying won't help us trust you."

"Screw your trust."

Gabriel swivels his head toward the rear of the tent—toward me—and his lips kink into a sly smile.

A shiver races up my spine.

No, I don't like this at all. A stranger with ulterior motives has invaded our Sanctuary, and nothing good can come of that.

CHAPTER THREE

Gabriel

I SIT HERE INSIDE A TENT, WITH MY WRISTS SECURED WITH DUCT TAPE, AND try to figure out if I should trust these people. They haven't made me feel welcome, that's for sure. I haven't given them reason to, so there's that. After months of scrabbling to survive post-apocalypse, I'd finally found a group of allies I could trust. Friends. A new kind of family. But I got them all killed.

Why did Aldith send me here? She claimed it's my destiny or some bullshit like that. I've never bought into the idea of fate. The Echo didn't change my mind about that.

The big guy who has a beard, tattoos, and a British accent walks up beside me and leans in. "You should start answering our questions, mate. Give us a reason to trust you, or we will toss you back to wherever you came from."

"Dial it back a little, Dax, would you?" the other man says. "We're trying to be nice."

The man who just spoke is American, which doesn't surprise me. The British Hulk seems out of place here, though. How many Brits lived in Northern California before the Echo hit? Not many, I'd bet. Of course, this is my first visit to California.

I glance toward the rear of the tent. The blonde sunbather is still peeking through a slit in the tent to watch us. So, she's a nudist and a voyeur.

"What should we do with him, Grant?" the British Hulk says. He told me I could call him Dax, but I prefer my nickname for him.

"Try to make peace," Grant says.

What do I have to lose? Everyone I cared about is gone. I sigh and slump in my chair. "Look, I don't want to hurt anybody. But I don't know you guys, and I've learned the hard way that trusting the wrong people ends in bloodshed."

"Yeah, we've learned that lesson too," Grant says. "Let's untie him, huh, Dax?"

The British Hulk nods.

Grant removes the duct tape, then offers me his hand to shake. "I'm Grant Larson. And that big scary dude is Dax."

"No last name? How chic. He's like a rock singer or an athlete."

"We don't know you well enough to share Dax's last name," Grant says. "It's up to him whether he feels like telling you."

What's that guy hiding? I gave my full name. But the hulk won't reciprocate.

Movement catches my attention, and I move only my eyes to glance at the sexy voyeur. I can see one of her eyes, but their blue color is so pale that it almost seems like silver. I've never seen eyes like that.

"Here's the deal," I say to Dax and Grant. "I'll tell Lady Godiva everything you want to know."

"Lady Godiva?" Grant says. "Oh, you mean Sarah. Why her?"

"We met on the beach. Anything else you want to know about me, you'll have to get from her after I tell the nudist."

Dax and Grant retreat into the far corner of the tent to have a hushed discussion. Then they return to me.

"We have to ask Sarah first," Grant says. "If she agrees—"

"I agree," a feminine voice announces. The pretty voyeur ducks through the rear tent flap. "You guys can go."

"We'll be right outside," Dax tells her.

"Uh-uh-uh," I say. "You'll be out of earshot. That's the deal. Take it or leave it."

Dax pulls a switchblade out of his pocket and tosses it to Sarah.

She catches it. "Thanks."

He nods. Then both men walk out.

The pretty voyeur sits on the cot on the other side of the tent, about ten feet away from me. "Here I am. Now tell me everything Dax and Grant want to know."

"First, I want to know something." I lean forward in my chair, resting my elbows on my knees. "Why do you sunbathe in the nude? Echo creatures might find you and decide you look like a good snack. Or worse, a fun sex toy."

"None of your business. I'm supposed to gather all the intel about you."

"Intel? That's cute. I bet you were a librarian before the Echo."

She bows her head.

"Hey, it's nothing to be ashamed of. Librarians are hot."

"I'm not embarrassed." She lifts her head. "You still haven't given me any information about you."

Well, I did say I'd tell her everything. "The day the apocalypse hit, I got sucked into the Echo."

Sarah stares at me. "Seriously?"

"Yeah, seriously. It's not the kind of thing anybody would joke about." I can't get comfortable all of a sudden, and sitting back in my chair doesn't help. So I get up and start pacing. "I experienced the apocalypse from the Earth side of things for about two hours, and I spent most of that time running away so I wouldn't get ripped apart by the creatures. Then I got thrown into the Echo. Pretty much everything I know about the apocalypse came from my time in that world."

"Did the Echo get destroyed like Earth did on the day the apocalypse started? We've wondered about that."

"Yeah. That happened in both worlds."

She wants to ask more questions, I can tell, and I promised I would spill all the beans—but only to her. Now I'm wondering if that's the wisest choice. I can't claim I made that deal for any good reasons. No, I just wanted to be alone with Sarah. I've seen her naked. She's beautiful and sexy, and I haven't been with a woman in so long that I can't even remember when the last time was. That's the only reason I feel such a strong urge to spend more time with her.

If I stop talking, she'll go get the British Hulk, and he will probably pummel me.

Worse things than him have tried to crush me. They always lose the battle.

Sarah holds the switchblade in one hand, loosely, like she's uncomfortable with the weapon. Every so often, she glances down at it. "Would you tell me who you were before the Echo? Before the worlds collided?"

"Does it matter? Nobody is who they used to be anymore."

"We want to trust you, Gabriel. But evasive answers don't help."

Of course I'm being evasive. I just met these people. For all I know, they're Echo creatures who found a way to disguise their true nature, and any minute they'll hoist me onto a spit and roast me for dinner. Or maybe they're a doomsday cult who believe the Echo is their ticket to the afterlife, and they plan to sacrifice me to get inside the other world.

Yeah, I've spent too much time in the Echo.

Nothing in that hell world is as beautiful as the woman sitting ten feet away from me.

"Would you tell me about your time in the Echo?" Sarah asks.

"You don't want to know what it was like, trust me."

My pulse beats faster, and I start to feel slightly nauseous. Why? Anything I might tell her about the Echo is nothing I haven't experienced firsthand. It never made me uneasy before. But with Sarah's eerily pale eyes fixed on me, I develop a phantom itch that refuses to go away.

"I won't tell anyone else," she says. "Not unless you give me permission to do that."

"But you told your buddies that you'd get the information they want." I shake my head. "Guess you're a liar. Way to build trust, Lady Godiva."

"Please stop calling me that. My name is Sarah."

"What's your last name?"

She bows her head again. "I don't know."

For a moment, I stare at the top of her head. Then I finally manage to ask the obvious question. "Do you mean you have amnesia?"

"Yes."

"Oh. Well, that's, uh…" I have no idea what to say to an amnesiac to make her feel better. Why I care about making her feel better, I have no clue. "Maybe your memory will come back soon. Is it total amnesia?"

She nods. "I have no idea who I am, or how I wound up lying on the beach, facedown, wearing tattered clothes. It's terrifying not to know anything about yourself."

This woman who just met me has shared a secret with me. I don't understand why. But it's pretty clear from her body language that she's telling the truth. She has no idea who she is or how she got here. At least I know my own name. She doesn't know where her family lives, whether they're still alive, or what she might've done to earn a living before the apocalypse. Something about her story makes me feel like I need to share more about myself with her.

"I had friends in the Echo," I tell her. "They were not human. I guess they were Echoes of people who died during the apocalypse. Anyway, they turned out to be good people who wanted to fight with me and find a way out of the new world Sefton Stainthorpe had created."

"You know about Sefton? Did you meet him?"

"Only from a distance. I saw him having a sort of conference with his minions. Then he vanished, and the creatures took off on a rampage."

"I've never seen what the creatures can do. At least, I don't remember seeing it."

"Be glad for that. They're monsters in the truest sense of the word." I sit back in my chair and sigh, letting my shoulders wilt. "Despite the horrors of the Echo, I found allies. We became friends, and eventually, a family."

"Maybe you can find them again and bring them into this world."

"No, I can't." I shut my eyes as the memory barrels through my mind. Screams. Blood. Agony. "They're all dead, and it's my fault."

Soft, warm hands clasp mine.

I open my eyes—and discover Sarah has moved up to my chair, kneeling in front of me. "What are you doing?"

"You seemed like you needed a little comforting. Whatever happened to your friends must have been horrific."

Why does she care about comforting me? I'd behaved like a complete asshole when we first met. Now, she's holding my hand while giving me the sweetest look of compassion and understanding. I should push her away, but

I can't make myself do it. No one has ever looked at me the way she does right now. But it's pity, nothing more.

"I can tell you don't like talking about it," Sarah says. "But would you tell me what happened to your friends? How did they die?"

Weariness drops over me like a lead blanket, and I no longer have the energy to resist whatever she wants. "I'd cobbled together a kind of army, a small one. Then I got the great idea that we should storm the castle and seize control of it. Didn't work out that way. All my friends died."

Did my voice hitch the slightest bit? No, it couldn't have.

"What castle?" Sarah asks, sounding totally confused.

"The one Sefton Stainthorpe built for himself. He's not there anymore, and neither is his Echo, the dweeb who calls himself Will."

"I haven't heard about the castle or someone called Will. But then, I think our leaders have kept a few secrets—to protect us, I'm sure."

"Leaders?" I study her face, trying to gauge how much she might actually know. Is the pretty voyeur as clueless as she seems? I have trouble believing it's all an act. "I'm guessing this camp is run by your friends Dax and Grant."

"Allison and Erin too. But this isn't a dictatorship."

"Then you guys have one up on the Echo creatures. Most of them did whatever their master told them to do." I try to make myself pull my hands away from hers, but I still can't do it. "Not all the creatures are evil. My friends were loyal and brave, but I talked them into breaching the castle and…they all died. Because of me. I didn't realize the bad creatures had found a secret entrance that let them walk right into the castle. My friends and I had to climb up a sheer cliff. We were exhausted by the time we reached the top. I should've known…"

"What? That there was a hidden entrance?" She clasps my hands more firmly while gazing straight into my eyes. "It's not your fault your friends died. I'm sorry that happened. But you shouldn't blame yourself."

"Don't you understand? I taught them to fight. I convinced them they could beat the other creatures, and that together we had a chance at seizing the castle." I yank my hands away from hers and cover my eyes with my palms, then drop them. "There was nothing in the castle. Just empty rooms, and one stone chair. Sefton's throne, apparently. I got my friends killed for nothing."

Why have I told her so much? Maybe because it doesn't matter. Everyone I ever cared about died today. Being alone is nothing new to me, but getting close to other people… I'd never done that before. Never. Then I found a home with creatures created by magic, who live in another world.

But I'm back on earth, and I have no fucking idea how to deal with other human beings.

"Were you in the Capital City?" Sarah asks. "Or did you land somewhere else in the Echo?"

"I didn't reach the Capital City until a few weeks ago. I traveled through the entire Echo world and picked up friends along the way."

"You've seen the whole Echo? Is it a flat plane, or an actual world? Like Earth, I mean. Grant and Erin thought it might be a planet in an alternate universe."

I study her for a moment, trying to decide if she really doesn't know the answer to that question. "Yeah, it's a planet."

Sarah leaps to her feet. "I need to tell Dax and Grant about this. Please stay here, I'll be right back."

The shape of the Echo never seemed that exciting to me, but Sarah clearly thinks it's big news. I guess her friends haven't explored much of the other world Sefton Stainthorpe had created.

Bells jingle. The tent flap flutters.

I look in that direction and see a pale face gazing at me through the partly open flap. The girl can't be more than fifteen or sixteen, I'd guess.

She glances over her shoulder furtively, then tiptoes into the tent. "You must be the guy who invaded our camp. Where did you come from? Are you going to stay? I've never seen anyone who looks like you, but that's probably because your clothes are falling off and your hair is dirty."

"Are you related to Sarah? She's too inquisitive for her own good too. Kids like you should stay away from beasts like me."

Her eyes widen. "Are you an Echo creature? Don't look like the ones I've met."

She tiptoes closer to me.

"Beat it, kid." I bare my teeth and clack them together, growling softly. "Or I'll gnaw on your flesh."

The girl stares at me blankly for a moment, then starts laughing. "You're so weird."

"What's your name, kid?" Not that I care. I'm bored, which is the only reason I'm talking to an annoying child.

"I'm Willow. Who are you?"

"Gabriel."

Sarah waltzes into the tent with Dax, Grant, and a raven-haired woman following her. When Dax notices Willow, her grabs the girl's arm to haul her away from me. "Go to Allison's tent and stay there."

"But—"

"Do it," Dax snarls. "Now."

Once the girl has left, Sarah approaches me. "Please tell my friends what you told me, Gabriel."

"Which part?"

"About what the Echo is."

She must have already told her friends that, but she wants me to explain it all over again. I guess the news really is a big deal to them.

"The Echo is a planet," I say. "Like Earth, only smaller. I think it's smaller, anyway. Since I'm not an expert on things like that, I can't say for sure. But it's definitely a globe. It has a horizon that curves down around the rest of the planet."

"Fascinating," Grant says. "How much of the Echo was devastated by the alchemy of worlds?"

"The what?"

"Oh, sorry. I forgot you don't know about that." Grant sits down cross-legged on the dirt floor in front of me. Then he glances up at Dax. "Should we tell him about it?"

The British Hulk shrugs. "Since you already mentioned it, there's no point in denying you said it. Might as well explain. This bloke did confirm the Echo is a planet."

"Okay." Grant sets his hands on his knees. "The alchemy of worlds is what Sefton Stainthorpe called the method he used to merge the two worlds. He combined alchemy, quantum physics, and dark magics to create the Echo, then he let the alchemical reaction transform the worlds. He intended for the Echo and the Earth to merge into one hell dimension."

CHAPTER FOUR

Sarah

THAT DIDN'T HAPPEN," GABRIEL SAYS. "I DON'T KNOW WHERE YOU GUYS get your information, but it must be from a brain-dead con artist. Both worlds got destroyed, mostly. Well, the Echo did. I don't know how Earth fared after that. But I know the worlds didn't magically merge into one planet."

"You are correct. The worlds did not merge," Dax concurs. "But only because we stopped the alchemical reaction before it could complete the transmutation."

Gabriel seems vaguely confused, though he tries to hide that. Whatever happened to him after he was thrown into the Echo, it clearly changed him in ways that he doesn't want to consider. I didn't know him before the apocalypse. Yet I feel I can trust him, and I feel that he has suffered more than he lets on, more than he wants to admit even to himself.

He shifts uncomfortably in his chair. "That does explain a few things I'd wondered about for a long time after I got thrown into the Echo. Like why I never saw any other humans in that world. And why the creatures were able to come and go as they pleased. I couldn't. That alchemical reaction thing must have been intended to kill all humans. But it was stopped before it finished."

"Indeed."

"So, did you people know Sefton Stainthorpe?"

Dax narrows his gaze on me. "Did you? Can't see why you would bother trying to breach the castle if you had never met Sefton. How would you even know the castle existed?"

"Because it's on top of a big cliff. Everyone in the Capital City can see it. Told you already, I never met Sefton." Gabriel seems incapable of stopping himself from getting annoyed with my friends. He grits his teeth, then loosens his jaw, and his words come out rough and almost snarly. "Are you people stupid? I thought you knew all about the Echo. You sure act like you do. But apparently, I know more than all of you combined."

"Do you?" Dax leans in, squinting at Gabriel, clearly trying to intimidate him. "You had no idea what the alchemy of worlds was. That means we know more."

"All right, boys," Erin says. "Time to dial back the testosterone so you can think like grown-ups again."

I love Erin. She never lets anybody push her around, and she always knows exactly what to do when an argument gets too heated. I don't have that talent. She also knows how to take down any type of Echo creature, another skill I lack.

Erin walks up to Gabriel and plants her hands on her hips. "It would be in your best interest to tell us everything you know."

"Why? If you're in league with the Echo creatures, or some other bad guys, you'll use that knowledge against me. I've been on this ride for long enough to know how things work."

"You're awfully cynical. Is that because you lost your Echo pals? Or because you're hiding something?"

He grunts. "Take your pick."

"What happened to your actual family?" Erin asks. "Parents, aunts, uncles, brothers, sisters…"

"None of your business. Kill me, or let me go."

"If Aldith really did send you here, maybe you should do what she wanted. Work with us, instead of against us."

Gabriel shakes his head slightly. "Aldith wasn't that specific."

I step up beside Erin. "Why don't we try this my way? Bullying him doesn't work."

"What is your way, sweetie?" Erin asks. "No offense, but you don't have the skills to handle a jerk like him."

"You guys aren't having any luck. But Gabriel will talk to me. Alone." I glance at his tattered shirt and pants. "But let's get him some new clothes first. As a show of good faith."

Grant shrugs. "She's right. We need to trust Sarah's instincts on this. And we'll get him new duds."

Our guest huffs. "Let me guess. You'll give me girlie clothes."

I lean in until my face is inches from his. "Say thank you, Gabriel."

His lips kink into the faintest smirk. "Thank you, Lady Godiva."

"No, thank my friends. They're donating the clothes for you."

Gabriel glances at the others. "They haven't given me anything yet, so I don't need to be grateful to them."

He is the stubbornest man I've ever met. Of course, I only remember the past two months.

The others leave to find clothes for Gabriel and to do whatever else they need to do. I'm alone again with the man who grabbed me on the beach, but I don't feel anxious about that. I think underneath all the bluster and snarling, he's just as scared as anyone else.

"How long have you lived here?" Gabriel asks.

"Two months. I washed up on the beach with amnesia."

"It's awfully convenient," he says, "that you have no memory of anything before two months ago. You can't tell me anything useful."

"You're here to share information with us, not the other way around." I sit down on the cot. "But no, it isn't convenient. Maybe I have parents or a husband somewhere. They might be looking for me, but I couldn't find them even if I wanted to."

"Okay, maybe it's not so convenient."

"Thank you."

"For what?"

I give him a tight smile. "For acknowledging the truth."

He shrugs. "Whatever."

Getting through to Gabriel seems like an insurmountable task, but I feel that I need to do it. Can't explain why. On the beach, he'd behaved like a cretin. He'd threatened to fuck me on the beach, or at least I'd interpreted it as a threat. But then he let me go. And he'd mentioned he hadn't been with a woman in a long time. Living among Echo creatures for months couldn't have been easy.

I shouldn't cut him any slack. But I feel like I can trust him. Maybe amnesia has made me insane.

"Why did you let me go?" I ask.

He scrunches up his eyebrows. "What?"

"On the beach. Why did you let me go? If you really wanted to assault me, you should have held on to me. You were in control then."

"Maybe." He eyes me up and down, though it doesn't seem like sexual interest. "Why aren't you afraid of me?"

"Don't know. I guess you just aren't that scary." I tap my fingers on my knees while I consider how to get him to tell me what I want to know—which is everything about him. "Do you trust me?"

"Yeah."

"Good. Then please answer my questions." I look straight into his eyes. "Do you have a family? Friends? Anybody who might've missed you over the past eight months?"

He freezes. His eyes flick left, right, up, down as if he's contemplating an escape route. But I know he won't try to run. My intuition tells me so.

Gabriel seems more tense now, maybe because my question brought up bad memories. But he said before that he was sucked into the Echo before the really bad stuff started happening on Earth. He can't suffer from memories of the horrible things Echo creatures did to his loved ones.

"How long has this camp existed?" Gabriel asks.

"Answer my question first."

The stubborn man flattens his lips and glares at me, but I ignore his behavior. Frightened men get angry much more easily than women do. Finally, he blows out a breath. "I didn't have any family or friends before the apocalypse. That means nobody is looking for me."

"I'm sorry. Being alone is scary." I bite my lip for a moment before I can talk myself into sharing the information he wants to hear. "Sanctuary has existed for eight months. People tend to stumble onto it without knowing how they found us. Getting dumped here isn't the usual way of entering Sanctuary."

"So, I got special treatment. How nice."

The man seems incapable of speaking without being sarcastic.

He abruptly turns more serious, his gaze boring into me. "What was it like on this side of the apocalypse? I mean, when the Echo first hit? I know how things looked from the other side, but not here."

"I don't know what it was like. Amnesia, remember?"

"Oh. Right." He fidgets in his chair, his face pinching up a little. "It's been so long since I was in this world that I just...wanted to know what I missed, I guess."

"The cities are destroyed, mostly. That's what I heard."

Grant marches into the tent and tosses a pile of clothes to Gabriel. "Get changed. Then meet us outside."

He leaves the tent.

And Gabriel smirks at me. "Sticking around to watch me get naked?"

"Oh, no, I—" Jumping up, I glance around because I suddenly can't remember what I was going to do. Then I remember and clear my throat. "I'll wait outside."

I rush out of the tent and stop just past the doorway. Why did I get flustered just because he smirked at me? It's ridiculous.

After a minute or two, Gabriel saunters out wearing jeans, a T-shirt, and tennis shoes. "Where to now, Lady Godiva?"

"Will you please stop calling me that?"

"No." He shoves his hands into his jeans pockets. "Where are we meeting the Three Stooges?"

"The what?"

He raises his brows. "Well, I guess you wouldn't remember those movies since you have amnesia. The Three Stooges were a bunch of morons."

"My friends are not morons."

Grant, Erin, and Dax approach us. But Grant takes the lead in the conversation. "Okay, it's time to have an upfront discussion. We're trusting you, Gabriel, so don't abuse that faith."

"Wouldn't dream of it."

He says that in a sarcastic tone, but something in his eyes makes me think that's baloney. He told me he had no one before the apocalypse. That must've been a lonely existence, and his life after the Echo had to be much worse.

"Gabriel means 'thank you'," I say, "and he'll do his best to become a contributing member of Sanctuary."

"You're his translator now?" Grant says. "Here I thought he spoke English. Must've been hallucinating that."

"Ugh. Just talk to him. All right?"

"Yeah, sorry." Grant nods to Gabriel. "Okay, here's the deal. We've been trying to understand Sefton Stainthorpe's notes and how he created the alchemy of worlds. If we could get a clear understanding of that, maybe we could find a way to counteract what happened."

"Counteract it?" Gabriel says. "Is that even possible? Not sure what that means, anyway."

"It would be like an inoculation for the whole world. We would be immune to the shit going on inside the Echo, and possibly to the assaults of the creatures living here."

"Do you have reason to believe you can actually do that? Or are you tilting at windmills?"

"Kind of both. We're only telling you this because Aldith sent you to us—and Sarah trusts you."

My opinion sealed the deal? I don't understand why. A girl with amnesia doesn't seem like the most trustworthy person. I can't give them any information about my past or who I was before I washed up on the beach. Yet they trust me. Of course, Aldith's opinion must count more than anything I could say.

A light flashes to my right, visible in my peripheral vision, and I turn my head to glance in that direction. Another flash slices across the sky, though I see no clouds. I point toward the area where the flashes had originated. "Is that a thunderstorm?"

Everyone glances toward that area just as several more flashes erupt. Brows wrinkle. Eyes widen.

"What is it?" I ask. "Have you seen something like that before?"

Dax goes stoic, which is never a good sign. "Not exactly like that. But I have seen strange lightning as part of the alchemy of worlds. In that case, it was extraordinarily powerful and could shatter streets and buildings, causing earthquakes."

Still no clouds have formed, but the lightning mutates into silver tongues of electrical energy that sizzle and snap, not quite hitting the ground. We all stand here immobilized by the sight before us, and I can tell my friends recognize what's going on. Allison and Willow race out of the tent she shares with Dax and huddle beside him. He slips an arm around each of them.

Dax glances down at his wife's swollen belly. "You should find a place to hide. Perhaps I should teleport you to…somewhere else."

"Like where? For all we know, this is happening everywhere. I want to stay with you, Dax. The three of us are in this together, forever. Remember?"

"Yeah, that's right," Willow says.

Dax hugs them both more firmly.

If Dax and Allison are worried… Oh, we're in big trouble.

A bolt of silver lightning slams down at the far end of the camp, just shy of the nearest tents. The concussion rattles my eardrums and makes the ground shudder.

"We need to find cover," Grant hollers. "Everybody, head for the woods! The lightning should strike the trees instead of us."

But it's supernatural lightning. Who knows how or where it might strike? Still, the woods feel like our best option.

Slender ribbons of electricity snake across the sky above us, spanning from horizon to horizon. The crackling and snapping grows louder, to the point where we can't hear each other even when we shout. Dax, Grant, and Erin wave their arms to indicate that everyone should flee into the dense woods and seek whatever shelter they can find.

Everyone flees.

The lightning has become so blinding and deafening that I can't see anyone. I can't move either. Something about the cloudless storm raging in the sky transfixes me, and try as I might, I can't convince my muscles to work.

A bolt slams down a few yards away from me.

The concussion makes me stumble sideways and scream. I trip over something—a rock, I think—and struggle to get back on my feet. Slithering tongues of silver continue to snake across the heavens, and I swear they're searching for me.

A figure races toward me, but my vision has become blurred and the brilliance of the lightning has created black spots that further hinder my ability to see. I stumble forward.

The blurry figure draws closer, shouting something I can't understand, not with my ears ringing.

As if in slow motion, a bolt slams down like a ladder of electricity, one rung at a time, seeming to adjust its trajectory as I stagger toward the woods. A crack and a sizzle resound so close that my heart stutters.

Then the bolt strikes.

A figure pushes me out of the way, and the lightning pounds into that person instead of me. My savior falls backward, knocking us both to the ground and pinning me beneath their weight.

The lightning abruptly stops.

A silence deeper than anything I've experienced before descends on Sanctuary. Smoke emerges from inside several tents, and flames ignite on others. But I don't see any people. Except for the man lying on top of me. I push him off and roll him over so I can see his face.

Gabriel's eyes are open, but he's not breathing.
The lightning has killed him.

27

CHAPTER FIVE

Gabriel

A RINGING NOISE DEAFENS ME. MY ENTIRE BODY FEELS LIKE I'VE jumped into a swimming pool while holding a raw electric wire in my teeth. Though my eyes are open, and I can see what's going on around me, I can't move or breathe or speak. Did I leap in front of a lightning bolt? That's insane. I would never do anything like that. But I do sort of recall seeing a bolt heading straight for Sarah, almost in slow motion, and I remember thinking that she would die if that thing hit her.

So, I jumped in front of her.

The bolt must have struck a few feet away. Right? That scorched smell must be the grass that got incinerated.

"He's not breathing!" Sarah shrieks, while she kneels beside me. Her eyes are wide, and her lips are trembling. "Help! Someone, please!"

Footfalls pound. Voices say things I can't quite make out.

"What happened?" That's the voice of Dax, the British Hulk. "Lightning hit him?"

"Yes," Sarah says. "He jumped in front of me and took the bolt for me. We have to save Gabriel."

Another figure approaches, though I see the person as only a shadow. "I had some basic medical training in the army. Let me take a look."

Is that Grant? I had no idea he was ex-military, but that doesn't matter right now. I feel oddly disconnected from everything around me. The only thing that comes through clearly is Sarah's voice.

"Please try," she says. "He might've been an ass at first, but he saved me."

If I could chuckle, I would. She described me perfectly. I am an ass.

Someone starts pushing on my chest, probably doing CPR, and I feel my heart trying to pump. Little by little, my body comes back to life, first with my heartbeat, then with my breathing. I blink slowly and groan.

"Take it easy," Grant says. "We nearly lost you, so you'll need a few minutes to recover."

I try to speak, but it comes out as incoherent mumbling. So this is what almost dying feels like. I have to admit, I expected something more dramatic, like a white tunnel with an angel reaching out to me. Not that I believe in that kind of thing. But if heaven does exist, I won't be going there.

Pain ricochets through my body, but it isn't as intense as I'd expected, considering I got fried by lightning. I push up onto my elbows, groaning again, then try to sit up. Grant helps me.

I scrub my hands over my face, then shove them into my hair. "I don't recommend tangling with Echo lightning."

"Yeah, it's a lot more powerful than the regular kind," Grant says. "Can't believe you survived that. Most people would be crispy critters after a strike half as strong as the one you took."

"Guess I got lucky."

Sarah is kneeling beside me, her eyes wide, staring at me like I've started to glow. Have I? No, I'm pretty sure that hasn't happened. But she keeps gaping at me. It makes my skin crawl.

"What's wrong with you?" I snap.

"You died, then you came back." She reaches out to grasp my hand. "And you saved my life."

"No, I just—It wasn't like that."

"Don't be embarrassed. You jumped in front of a bolt of Echo lightning to protect me."

"I didn't think about what I was doing. Don't take it personally."

She shakes her head slowly. "I don't understand you, Gabriel. I'm thanking you for saving my life, and you act like I've insulted you."

Maybe I've kind of forgotten how to accept a compliment, or how to admit I might not be a total bastard. I've spent too long fighting for my life and the lives of my friends, only to lose everything. Sarah would be better off if she slugged me and told her friends to toss me into the ocean.

Sarah wraps her arms around my neck and kisses my cheek. "Thank you, Gabriel. If you hadn't been here, I would've died."

If she says that one more time… I'll probably growl at her and act like a jerk again.

"We're all grateful," Grant says, "that you were there to help Sarah. That took guts."

I push Sarah's arms away and scramble to my feet. "I didn't do it on purpose. That was instinct, plain and simple."

Though I want to get away from these people, I have nowhere to go. So I stand here glancing around, fisting my hands and loosening them again, over and over.

Men and women pour out of the woods, where they'd been hiding. Several approach Grant and his friends, wanting to know what happened and why. Dax gets me another T-shirt, since the one I'd been wearing got scorched. There's a hole in the fabric smack in the middle of my chest, but my skin suffered no damage. Supernatural lightning has different rules.

But in the Echo, lightning like that would kill whoever got in its way.

After things calm down, I follow Grant, Dax, and Erin into the tent where they'd kept me until they decided I'm not a psycho. Sarah walks right beside me. I pull my hand away when she tries to hold it. I get that she feels grateful, and she's probably latched on to me because I helped her. But I wish she wouldn't do that.

Inside the tent, we all sit down to discuss the event that has everyone panicked and confused. Sarah sits on the chair I'd been tied to earlier, while Erin and Grant take the cot. Dax and I sit on the floor.

The British Hulk squints at me. "How did you survive that strike? Echo lightning can destroy a city, and it incinerates the human body."

"I know. Don't ask me how it happened, because I have no idea."

Dax keeps staring at me with his squinty, flinty gaze, like he thinks that will make me confess that I'm secretly an Echo beast who wants to eat everyone in this camp. "No one survives the lightning."

"Clearly, that's not true. How do you know that nobody else has survived it? You can't be everywhere at once, all the time."

"Perhaps not. But over the past eight months, I and my mates have visited many cities and rural towns to scavenge supplies and help anyone who might need our assistance." Dax rests one arm on his bent knee, leaning toward me. "No one has ever seen a human being survive Echo lightning."

"At least I could be the first. Maybe I'll get an entry in the Guinness Book of World Records."

"I doubt that exists anymore."

"Well, I know I'm the record-holder. That's something."

Grant shakes his head at me. "Is everything a joke to you? We're talking about the end of the world, and you're cracking wise."

"The alternative doesn't appeal to me."

Because going full-on doom and gloom would mean surrendering to the Echo. No, I'll never do that. I fought my way through that hell world once, and I can do it again if necessary.

Sarah stands up. "I should go. Everyone here has a role to play in the apocalypse, but not me."

"Of course you play a role," Grant says. "Something or someone sent you to us. That means you belong in this discussion. Besides, that lightning was meant for you."

"But all of you can fight. I can't."

"There are other ways to contribute, Sarah."

She sits back down, hands clasped on her lap.

And she keeps her gaze trained on me.

For some reason, her unwavering focus on me makes me feel the need to share information. "Aldith mentioned that the Echo has a heart and lifeblood, and a brain too."

"We know about the Heart and the Lifeblood," Grant says. "But this is the first we've heard of a brain."

"I only know what Aldith told me. She said the Echo has been without a brain ever since Sefton and his doppelgänger died." I stare at the dirt floor to avoid Sarah's gaze, because her undivided attention still makes me uneasy. "The Echo is a living thing composed of magics, that's what Aldith told me. It's not sentient, and without its master, it needs another being to keep the Brain working."

"Interesting," Grant says. "Aldith never mentioned that to us. But I guess she's been waiting for whoever will become the Brain."

Sarah's eyes go wide. I try not to see that, but my eyes insist on looking at her. She opens her mouth but seems unable to speak for a moment. Then she points a finger at me. "It's you, Gabriel. You are the Brain."

"What? Come on, that's crazy. I got good grades in school, but I'm no brainiac."

"I doubt a high IQ is required," Grant says. "The Heart and the Lifeblood were chosen based on their strength and dedication to protecting others. The Brain was probably selected for similar reasons."

Though I intend to refute his claim, something he just said stops me. I study Grant for a moment, while I decide whether I should alert them to the fact I've figured out one of their secrets. Maybe I'm wrong, anyway. But I have a gut feeling that I'm right.

I nail my gaze to Grant's. "Two of you guys are the Heart and the Lifeblood, aren't you? I'd bet it's you and Erin. Just a hunch, but I think I'm right."

Grant stares at me.

I take that as confirmation I was right. "You don't need to confirm it for me. And I won't spill the beans to anybody else. Who would want to talk to me, anyway? I'm the jerk who scared everyone when I stormed into your little camp."

Dax and Grant exchange a look that I think means they're deciding how much they should tell me. Then Grant looks at Erin, and she nods.

"We should ask Allison first," Dax tells his friends. "She should be involved in the decision of whether to bring someone new into the inner circle."

This is starting to sound like a cult. But I don't think they meant it that way.

Dax strides out of the tent. Minutes tick by while the rest of us wait in silence. Sarah keeps glancing at me, smiling. Every time she does that, I avert my gaze.

The British Hulk returns—with a pregnant woman. He holds her hand, guiding her toward the cot. Erin takes a seat on the floor to let the woman, who I assume is Allison, settle onto the cot. Dax squats on the floor beside her.

"We should tell Gabriel everything," Allison says. "The Echo needs him."

"But it tried to kill me," I say. "Even if it meant to hit Sarah, it still fried me. I just happened to jump in front of the bolt that was meant for her."

"Exactly. You instinctively protected Sarah, even though you just met her and know nothing about her. She doesn't know herself either."

"Yeah, I know that."

Allison glances at her husband, who nods. "What we're about to tell you is top secret. We've kept most of this from the rest of our community because it's explosive. People might panic."

"Do I seem like the panicking type? I can handle whatever it is. Didn't Dax tell you about me?"

"Yes, he did. That's why we agreed you should know the truth." Allison nods to her husband. "You should go first, honey."

The British Hulk faces me. "Sefton Stainthorpe was my twin brother. He used me and Allison as tools in his mad scheme to create the Echo and start an apocalypse. He transformed my body into what you see now and threw me into the Echo."

"He used me too," Allison says. "But not as violently as he used Dax. Sefton made me the Catalyst for his plans. Dax was the Anchor."

"Allison tapped into magics she hadn't known she possessed to stop the alchemy of worlds. As revenge, Sefton murdered Allison." Dax glances at each of his friends in turn, as if seeking their approval. When they nod, he continues. "What I'm about to tell you cannot leave this tent. We want to trust the members of our community completely, but this revelation might hurt a child if everyone knew. You've met Willow, the youngest member of Sanctuary. She's fifteen years old."

"How we met her is a long story we'll tell you later," Allison says. "But it turned out that Willow has the Echo power inside her, just like I do, and so does Dax. Grant and Erin also hold that power inside them. We believe you have it too. But I'm getting away from the main point. Willow used her Echo power to resurrect me from death."

"I've never heard of Echo power," I say. "And I traveled through the entire world that is the Echo."

"Apparently, not many people in either world know about that power. We've found a few people in Sanctuary who have a watered-down version of it that gives them limited teleportation skills."

"This is all fascinating. But I don't see how it relates to me."

"You gathered a small army of Echo creatures who shared your desire to protect the innocents trapped in that world," Allison says. "Then, after you found Sanctuary, you shielded Sarah from the Echo lightning. You are a protector, Gabriel. Dax and I believe you might be the Brain, the key component of the Echo that has been missing ever since Sefton and Will, his doppelgänger, died."

"What does being a protector have to do with being the Brain of the Echo? I'm not a genius like Sefton Stainthorpe. He was a scientist, right? I've learned that much from exploring the Echo world."

Dax lifts one brow at me. "You assume 'the Brain' refers to intelligence. But even a human brain contains more than knowledge. It's the seat of knowledge, yes, but also the seat of everything that turns a living thing into a human being—the heart, soul, and lifeblood."

"But Grant and Erin are the Heart and the Lifeblood."

"Yes, but they haven't been able to affect much change in the Echo. We've believed for a while now that the Echo lacks the balancing power that will bring it under control, and that's why Grant and Erin can't erase the remnants of the alchemy of worlds."

I stand up and start pacing, which is difficult in a small tent with people sitting on the floor around me. But I try it anyway. Movement might help with the tension that's been building inside me ever since Allison walked into the tent and started explaining crazy things to me. "I am not the Brain of anything. I'm just a guy who got thrown into the Echo and had to learn to survive. And I got my friends killed. That's not heroic, and certainly nothing that would qualify me to become the balancing whatever in the Echo."

My pacing speeds up, and I almost trip over Grant, mumbling a half-assed apology.

"Stop, Gabriel," Sarah says.

And I stop. Why? Because her voice always does something to me. It's like a shot of Valium injected directly into my veins. Well, no, it's more like a double shot of Valium and Viagra. Yes, I'm attracted to Sarah, but it's weird and nothing I'm ever going to admit to or surrender to, no matter what. Sarah and I gaze at each other without speaking, without showing our reactions to each other. But I have the strangest feeling she's experiencing the same things I am.

Thunder explodes overhead, making the ground beneath us shudder so violently that I stumble into Sarah. Without realizing what I'm doing, I pull her into my arms.

"We need to get into the woods," Grant says. "Everybody was safe there when the Echo lightning started."

Dax grabs Allison. "We need to find Willow. Gabriel, make sure Sarah gets to safety. Let's all meet at the hot spring. She knows where that is."

The tent begins to sway as another round of thunder detonates. As we hurry out of the tent, Dax and Allison veer to the left, while Grant and Erin announce they're going to make sure everyone makes it into the woods. I've been tasked with protecting Sarah, and I focus on that. I keep hold of her hand as we sprint toward the trees, which tower so high above our heads that I don't see how lightning could reach us down here. Other people rush into the woods too, and we make sure they know everyone should meet at the hot spring.

Whatever is about to happen, it can't be good.

CHAPTER SIX

Sarah

WHAT ON EARTH IS HAPPENING TODAY? THE ECHO HAD BEEN STABLE for months, with only the occasional hiccup. Now, it seems intent on destroying me. I might think I'm being paranoid if I hadn't witnessed the lightning coming after me, strike after strike. Why me? I'm just an amnesiac who has no special skills or magical powers.

Unless I do have skills and powers. Maybe I just can't remember having them.

Gabriel's hand in mine relieves the worst of my fear, though I can't figure out why. I met him today. We've barely spoken to each other. Yet he nearly died for me, and I trust him to be there if I need him again. I trust him not to lie too. Even when he attacked me on the beach, I felt no fear of him.

The thunder fades away, and lightning sizzles across the sky. I can just see it through the treetops, but I know it will grow closer and more powerful. Am I inadvertently leading the Echo lightning to the others? I don't want my friends to die because of me. If the Echo wants me dead, maybe I should just let it have me.

I stumble to a halt beside a wide tree.

Gabriel tugs my hand, but I still don't move. "Come on, Sarah. We need to keep moving."

I shake my head. "Everyone's in danger because of me. I should go back and face the lightning. Let it take me."

"Don't be stupid. Your friends are waiting for you."

"Go on. I'm staying here."

I'd seen everyone from Sanctuary rush past us, heading toward the hot spring. Allison and Dax, Grant and Erin, Willow too. They're out of the path of the lightning, provided that I don't follow them. The strongest thing I can do is to let the Echo take me.

So I yank my hand free of Gabriel's and run back toward Sanctuary.

I can hear footfalls behind me, and I know it's Gabriel. I run as fast as I can, praying he won't catch up and stop me. I need to do this. Maybe it's my destiny. If this has even a snowball's chance of saving my friends, I'll do it.

"Sarah, stop!" Gabriel shouts. "What do you think you're doing?"

I ignore him and keep running. My legs have started to hurt, and I feel like I can't catch my breath. Doesn't matter. I need to get out of the woods so the lightning can take me. *Please let this end the madness, please let it save everyone, please, please, please.* I've just broken out of the woods, and I can see the camp up ahead, not more than thirty feet away.

Arms lash around me, halting me so swiftly that I stumble, and the man trying to restrain me loses his footing. We both crash to the ground, with Gabriel on top of me. He quickly rises and flips me over, kneeling there as he glares at me and struggles to breathe.

"You fucking idiot," he snarls. "What kind of stunt are you trying to pull?"

"I need to get away from the others."

"Why?"

"Because I don't belong here. They do. You do. I have no useful purpose except to stop the lightning from destroying everything and everyone in its path." Tears burn in my eyes and stream down my cheeks. "Let me go. I need to sacrifice myself to the Echo."

"Are you totally brainless? Or just suicidal?" He grabs my arms and pulls me up into a sitting position, holding me inches away from him. Face to face, we stare at each other. "Killing yourself won't solve anything."

"But the lightning wants me. I need to give it what it wants."

"That's bullshit." He's so angry that his eyes have narrowed and he's gritting his teeth. "What makes you think you're so damn important that the Echo wants to murder you? You're just some girl from who knows where, probably a socialite who never worked a day in her life. I bet you spent your days getting manicures and agonizing over which pair of shoes go best with your hair."

Is he trying to tick me off? To dissuade me from what I've resolved to do? If so, it's working. I want to deck him. But I can't move any part of my body. All my muscles have turned to jelly, thanks to my panicked flight through the woods, and I can't tear my focus away from Gabriel's eyes.

"Don't you think your friends need you?" he asks. "Or do you only care about your own fears? What about that girl, Willow? I guess you'll just leave her to grieve for you, like everyone else. How thoughtful of you."

"Stop trying to piss me off, Gabriel."

"Why? You pissed me off, running away like that. I'm supposed to protect you, remember?"

Something in his eyes convinces me that he's genuinely worried about me. We're essentially strangers, yet he won't leave me alone to sacrifice myself for a stupid belief that only my death can stop the Echo lightning.

"Okay, I won't run out there," I say. "I won't let the Echo kill me."

All the anger in his expression melts away. He's breathing hard, but he no longer seems upset. No, I sense something else from him, something I've never experienced before. He wants me. I can't explain how I know it, but I guess my amnesia is letting me know what it means. He wants to have sex with me. I crave that too. Even while the lightning slams down on the camp, I grow wet and tingly between my thighs, and I instinctively understand what that means.

Lust. Hard, hot lust.

Gabriel pulls me into his body and crushes his mouth to mine. His rough lips scrape across mine, and my stiff nipples rub against his chest. Then he thrusts his tongue into my mouth and devours me so completely that my heart pounds and my ears ring because I've stopped breathing. God, this feels incredible, and I want more, need more, can't take another breath again until he consumes my body in every way imaginable. He slides a hand down to my ass, grasping it firmly, and pushes one finger between my cheeks.

I moan and fling my arms around his neck, pushing my tongue between his lips. My sex throbs while slickness dribbles down my inner thighs. I can smell a musky scent that I instinctively know is the proof of how much I hunger for him.

He drops to the ground with me beneath him. Above us, Echo lightning ravages the sky, crashing down to penetrate the earth too. The ground vibrates beneath our bodies as he yanks my jeans and panties down to my ankles and unzips his pants, then plunges inside me so suddenly that I cry out and arch my back. He slaps his hands down on the ground at either side of my head. I bend my knees to cradle his body with them, and though I have no memory of sex, I realize that what's about to happen will change everything in ways I can't comprehend.

Gabriel begins thrusting, hard and fast, the pace brutal, while I grip his biceps and hoist my hips up into his thrusts. I need him to fuck me like the world is ending, and maybe it is. The Echo started the apocalypse, but our blistering lust for each other might eradicate both worlds.

And I don't care.

He growls and snarls and fucks me even harder, making my body bounce while lightning pulsates above us. He fills me so completely that it almost hurts. I don't care about that either. The ground shudders as monstrous bolts penetrate the earth one after another, zigzagging across the sky.

The thickest, most explosive bolt yet punches into the earth—and I come.

My body curls in on itself while mind-blowing spasms seize my inner muscles, and I scream again and again. Gabriel punches into me twice more, roaring to the heavens as I feel him releasing everything inside me. The sensation makes me come harder.

The entire world falls into a deep, tranquil silence.

Gabriel still has his cock inside me. He gazes down at me with a look of wonder and shock on his face. Then he pulls out of my body, sitting up, and glances down at himself.

His eyes go wide. He jerks his head up to gape at me.

"What's wrong?" I ask, pushing up on my straight arms.

"You, ah…" He rubs his jaw and won't look at me. "This is… I'm sorry."

"For what?" I look down at my hips, which seem to have transfixed him with horror. And I see why. I have blood smeared on my inner thighs. When I glance at his dick, I see blood there too. "Um, I don't understand."

"Did it hurt the first time I, ah, thrust into you?"

"A little. But only for a second."

"Fuck." He tucks his dick back into his pants and zips them up. Then he gets to his feet. "You were a virgin."

"I'm…what? No, that can't be. Everyone thinks I must be twenty-eight years old."

"Maybe you were a—" He winces and averts his gaze again.

"What did you almost say? Maybe I'm what?"

He shoves his hands into his hair. "Maybe you were a nun."

"I don't feel like a nun." Sitting up, I struggle to pull up my jeans and panties. "What we just did, it felt familiar. Like I've done that before."

"That can't be. You were obviously a virgin."

He sounds irritated again. Is it my fault I was a virgin and didn't know that? *Hello, amnesia girl here.* Besides, I do feel like I must've had sex before. But that makes no sense. I recognized what an orgasm should feel like, and I sensed that before I reached my climax. I just knew what was coming and how good it would feel.

Nothing about me makes any sense.

Gabriel grasps my hands to pull me up off the ground. "The lightning stopped."

"I know. It completely stopped right when we came."

"That's insane. Sex has nothing to do with it."

"How do you know? You're not an expert on Echo lightning."

Gabriel snares my hand, half dragging me out into the clearing where the camp lies. A few tents have fallen down. Nothing else seems to have been damaged. Would the lightning have kept going if Gabriel and I hadn't screwed each other? I wonder if the lightning somehow fed us erotic energy. I've been attracted to Gabriel since the moment we met, even when he was acting like a jackass. But I didn't experience intense lust until we ran through the woods together amid an Echo lightning storm.

What does that mean? I don't know, and I'm not sure I want to find out.

Gradually, the residents of Sanctuary wander back into the camp. Though everyone wants to talk about what's going on and what it might mean, I can't focus on the conversation. My mind keeps rewinding to those moments at the edge of the forest when Gabriel had taken me like a maniac and I'd loved it.

Can anyone tell we did that? Does it show on our faces? I can't look at him without my entire body growing warm, and every time Gabriel glances at me, he immediately swerves his gaze away. I wonder if the lightning somehow made us insanely hot for each other. It was paranormal lightning, after all. As much as I'd love to blame the Echo for what I did, what we did, I know I can't do that. I wanted him, and I did something incredibly stupid because of that lust.

Never again.

I sneak away to my tent so I can try to erase that incident from my memory. I got amnesia once without wanting it to happen. Why can't I pull off self-induced memory loss that only wipes away those moments with Gabriel in the woods?

Someone rings the bell on my tent flap. "May I come in, sweetie?"

That's Erin. Every tent has a small clump of jingle bells attached to the outer flap that acts as a doorbell. We all understand the value of privacy.

"Sure, come on in," I say.

Erin walks in and sits on the canvas chair across from the cot, where I sit. "Are you okay? You haven't seemed quite like yourself ever since the lightning came again."

I know she didn't mean that in a dirty way, but hearing the words "came again" makes me flash back to Gabriel in the woods, inside me, thrusting wildly.

"Sarah? What's wrong?"

"Nothing, I'm fine." I shake off the memory and try for a smile. I don't think I pulled it off. "The lightning keeps coming for me, doesn't it?"

Erin says nothing for several seconds, then she moves onto the cot beside me. "Yeah, we think it is after you or Gabriel—or both. You guys were together both times the lightning struck, right?"

I nod.

She lays a hand on my thigh. "Don't worry. We'll figure this out, all of us, together."

Maybe I should tell her what Gabriel and I did, but I just can't make myself speak the words. It's humiliating. But also hot and incredible. How could I still have been a virgin? How could I have let Gabriel seduce me? If I used to be a nun, then I'm going to hell for sure.

"Is there something else?" Erin asks. "Seems like you want to tell me more."

"No, it's nothing."

"Okay." She doesn't sound or look like she believes me. "Do you feel up to hashing out ideas about the lightning and other stuff? Or would you rather take a break? The rest of us can talk about things without you, and you can join us when you're ready."

"No, I don't need to rest. I'd rather be a part of the discussion."

"Okay. Then let's head for Dax and Allison's tent. That's where the confab is happening."

As we head through the camp, I notice people gathering around the spot where we often have bonfires. It looks like they might be getting ready to do that this evening. The sun will set soon, and I wouldn't be surprised if nobody wants to sleep tonight. Memories of the lightning will keep us awake.

Erin and I reach Dax and Allison's tent just as Gabriel walks up to it. I manage not to blush or act like a flustered teenager. Gabriel barely glances at me. He holds the flap open as Erin and I walk into the tent.

I can't figure him out at all.

Someone brought in several more chairs to accommodate our group. Allison sits on a cot, and she encourages me to sit beside her. The others take the chairs.

"That lightning was after something or someone," Dax announces. "On both occasions, it sought out either Sarah or Gabriel. Perhaps the lightning wants a different person, but it can't find them. Either option seems plausible."

I wish I remembered what my life had been like pre-apocalypse. What was the world like before the Echo? I want to know, but I suppose I might never remember.

My gaze flicks to Gabriel.

He glances at me sideways and winces faintly.

I stare down at my hands, where I'm wringing them on my lap. "What are we going to do? If the lightning came back once, it might come back again. I don't want anyone to get hurt because of me."

Allison clasps my hand. "No one has been hurt, except for Gabriel. And he survived. This is not your fault, Sarah."

"I should leave. Go somewhere far away."

"And if the lightning follows you there? Then what?"

"Don't know."

A prickly sensation spreads over my skin, raising goosebumps. It swiftly transforms into a warmth that penetrates my skin and sinks deep inside me, settling between my thighs.

When I lift my head, Gabriel is watching me.

I'm getting turned on in front of all my friends. What is wrong with me?

"No one is asking the obvious question," Gabriel says. "What if the lightning is caused by the Brain? What if it's searching for the right person to take over that role?"

He keeps watching me while he speaks.

"I used to be a computer programmer," Gabriel says. "The Brain might be like a living computer, capable of being programmed. The lightning could be its way of dealing with the missing circuits—the missing neurons and brain cells that Sefton Stainthorpe gave it."

"What do you suggest we do?" Grant asks.

"Tell me everything you know about Sefton's plans for the Echo and Earth."

CHAPTER SEVEN

Gabriel

I CAN'T STOP THINKING ABOUT SARAH, LYING HALF-NAKED BENEATH ME while I fucked her in the woods. I don't know what came over me in that moment, but I couldn't fight the lust. It seized control of me and wouldn't let go until I came deep inside her body. She was a virgin. I took her innocence on the ground, in the dirt, with lightning exploding everywhere. Every time the lightning punched into the ground, I thrust into Sarah harder and faster.

Does that mean the lightning made us want each other? I can't say that's insane and impossible. The rules of the universe changed on the day the Echo breached the Earth and the two worlds merged. But Sefton didn't complete the transformation. Now the Echo is suffering from the loss of the only being in either world who could control the Brain.

And the people seated inside this tent think I'm the new Brain. Finding Sefton's castle hardly qualifies me to become the human controller of the Echo's mind.

Can my computer skills help? Well, we don't have electricity, so I can't do any actual programming. But maybe I can employ the mental skills I learned as a computer geek. I'm no longer the man I'd been before the apocalypse. The time I spent inside the Echo changed me in ways I still don't fully understand.

That's one more reason why I shouldn't have screwed Sarah, and why I will never do that again.

I rest my elbows on my knees and rub a hand over my cheek. "The lightning didn't kill me. Maybe that means the Echo wants me to…do something. To figure that out, I need you to tell me everything about Sefton's plans."

"He wanted Allison to rule both worlds with him," Dax tells me. "She was the catalyst for the alchemical reaction, but he never intended for her to die. He killed Allison out of sheer rage when she ruined his plans. Willow brought her back to life."

"Right," Erin says. "Your brother didn't want Allison dead. He only wanted everyone else on Earth to die."

Dax shakes his head. "That's not quite right. He meant to force every human on earth to merge with their Echoes, which would imprison every human inside the bodies of the twisted copies of themselves. My brother called that the alchemy of souls. But he wasn't able to complete that part of his plan."

"Because you killed him," I say. "What else did Sefton want to do?"

"Turn himself into a godlike figure who would have total dominion over both worlds."

"What about his castle?"

Dax shrugs. "He never mentioned that. I had no idea he created such a place until Grant and Erin learned the truth during their mission into the Echo."

I gaze down at the dirt floor for a moment while I try to digest everything they've told me. How do I fit into this? Am I supposed to be the new Brain of the Echo? Or is my fate to protect Sarah? Now I'm seriously considering the idea that fate plays a role in my future. The world really has turned upside down and inside out.

My eyes force me to glance at Sarah out of the corner of my eye. I try not to wince, but every time I see her, I flash back to earlier in the woods. She had felt so fucking good, and I came harder inside her body than I'd ever come before. The woman annoys me. I don't want to want her. Maybe I shouldn't be surprised that we wound up losing control and screwing each other like crazy, since she loves to sunbathe in the nude. She's got a naughty streak, for sure.

But I have no excuse for what I did. I never even asked if she wanted it.

"Maybe I should give you Sefton's journal," Grant says. "You might see something in it that the rest of us missed. He was a scientist, after all. So are you, Gabriel, in a way."

"Computers are my thing, not quantum physics."

"Give it a try," Sarah says. "I can help you."

I raise my brows. "You're a physicist?"

"No. But I'd like to help. Maybe I was a scientist of some sort. I don't know."

Because she has amnesia. I still think it's bizarre that she just appeared on the beach one day, according to her friends. She looked like she'd been assaulted, though not sexually. I know that for sure because I took her virginity earlier today. And I hate myself for that. But we've got bigger problems than my guilt.

"I will take a look at the journal," I say. "And any other information you guys have. But I need to start where Sarah's story begins."

Her brows knit together. "I don't have a story. I'm amnesia girl."

"But you came from somewhere," I growl. Why? No frigging idea. Guilt, I guess. "We should start on the beach, just you and me."

Dax squints at me. "Why only you and Sarah? The rest of us know more about how the Echo has affected this world than you do."

"Yeah, but I have years of experience with the other side of the apocalypse."

Sarah stares at me, her eyes wide. "What do you mean years?"

"Are you deaf? Or just stupid? When I say years, I mean years."

"I think I understand," Dax says. "The same thing happened to me when Sefton initiated the alchemy of worlds."

"What are you talking about?"

"Time can behave differently inside the Echo. My brother threw me into that world, and I was trapped there for five years. How long was it for you, Gabriel?"

For a moment, I can't respond. My brain is struggling to reconcile what the British Hulk just said with what I'd always taken for an absolute truth of the universe. Time moves forward. Sure, I'd watched documentaries about how time travel might be technically possible. But I treated it as theory, not fact. The Echo changed everything, turning myths into truths and theories into reality.

"Three years," I say. "I lived in the Echo for three years."

Sarah rushes over to me and kneels beside my chair. Her soft, warm hand encloses mine. "I'm so sorry, Gabriel. That must have been awful. But it does explain how you managed to explore the entire Echo world."

"I had nothing else to do. No way out. No way home, if that even existed anymore. Might as well explore, that's what I decided."

She gives my hand a gentle squeeze. "I will go with you to the beach. I trust your instincts, and if you believe retracing my steps will help, I'm in."

"That's a good place to start," Grant says. "But I'm wondering if Gabriel's knowledge of the Echo could provide clues none of us ever found. You've seen all of the other world. That has to be useful."

"I want to go to the beach first," I say. "Just me and Sarah."

"You shouldn't go with him alone," Dax declares, and he almost growls like I did. "He is a stranger."

"Dax and I could go with you two," Grant says. "For safety. Yours and ours."

"Sarah and I need to go alone." Why? I have no clue. But I sense that we need to do this without her friends watching.

"Like hell," Dax snarls.

"I could always kidnap Sarah while you're all sleeping."

The British Hulk looks like he's about to rip my head off.

But Sarah steps in. "Relax, he's joking."

"Let them do this," Allison says. "We're all adults here and capable of making our own decisions."

The gang exchanges glances, as if they're seeking each other's permission. Then Grant says, "Okay. You and Sarah, alone. But you should take some kind of weapons. Erin and I can advise you on what to take."

I smirk at Dax, just to annoy him, though I speak to Grant. "That's a good idea."

This time, I will not have sex with Sarah. It's an informational mission only. I don't care if lightning erupts and makes us both so horny that we can't stand it. I will not repeat my mistake.

What if Sarah is pregnant?

I can't worry about that right now. We have bigger problems.

"Let's go," I say, as I push up out of my chair. "I don't want to waste any time. Who knows when the lightning might come back."

Sarah's cheeks dimple, and her eyes sparkle. "I knew you weren't as much of a jerk as you acted like you were when we first met."

"I'm no hero. But everybody does what they have to do to survive in this new world."

The rest of the gang follows us as we march through the camp. We stop along the way at the tent where they keep the weapons and grab a few things. Then we head for the woods. At the edge of the forest, the others halt and just watch us disappear into the gloom. Our trek over the mountain takes longer than I remember, but then, I've only hiked this trail twice before. The second time, we hadn't gone all the way to the beach. Sarah and I hadn't even made it to the hot spring.

Now, we hike up the mountain until we reach the summit. There, we pause to take a break and drink some water. We both have backpacks filled with supplies, which was something Grant and Erin had suggested. Since they've both trekked into the Echo, they know what we might need if we should "get sucked into hell through the sewer drain," as Erin phrased it. Now, we have weapons, food, and water stashed in our packs.

After our brief rest, we head down the other side of the mountain to the beach.

"What now?" Sarah asks.

"Let's put our stuff down and walk over to the shoreline. Do you know if it was high tide or low tide when you washed ashore?"

"Sorry, no idea. I was unconscious at the time."

"Yeah, I know." I drop my pack on the sand and survey the area. "But when you woke up, what did you see? Anything you can remember might be helpful."

She bites her lip, then gnaws on it as if she's thinking hard. "Erin and Grant found me, and they mentioned something about the tide. I know for sure they said I was lying facedown on the beach with the water washing up around me. And now that I think about it…I'm pretty sure they said it was low tide."

"When is low tide?"

"Around noon, I think. Grant keeps track of it."

I bite back a curse. "We're too late for it today. Better hold off until morning. I want to see where you washed ashore, but at low tide."

Because I'm suddenly an expert on that stuff. But nobody else seems to have a clue, so I might as well pretend I know what the fuck I'm doing. It's been two months since Sarah turned up here on the Northern California coast. Don't know what I think I'll learn by visiting that spot at low tide. Maybe it doesn't matter either way. Or maybe I'm delaying because the thought of what I might find out makes me uneasy.

No, it can't be that.

"Okay," Sarah says. "We'll wait. In the meantime, what should we do? Walk back to Sanctuary?"

"No, let's just settle in for the night here."

She glances around, hunching her shoulders. "Shouldn't we stay in the woods? I mean, if the lightning comes back…"

"You'd feel safer in the woods."

She hugs herself. "Yeah, I would. I know I'm being a wimp—"

"No, you're not. Let's go find a good spot for the night."

We hike back up the slope, but we turn down a path worn down by wildlife and choose a spot there to spend the night. We don't have any sleeping bags, but I made sure we brought blankets just in case. I try to give both blankets to Sarah, so she can lie on one and cover herself with the other. But she won't agree to that. I need to have a blanket too, she says. Sarah might think she's a wimp, but she knows how to be tough when she wants to get her way.

Though she declares that she can't really sleep and will only doze, after a while I look over at her and see she has fallen asleep. Good. At least one of us will get some rest.

I lie on my back and gaze up at the sky, what little of it I can see through the trees. Before the apocalypse, I'd rarely gone out into the suburbs, much less the wilderness. My idea of experiencing nature involved driving through a national park. Now, I'm sleeping under the stars. Would it be weird to thank the Echo for taking away my ability to stare at my cell phone for hours? I might never have studied the stars otherwise.

And I would never have met Sarah.

But I can't get too attached to her. I just lost the only family I'd ever known, and I don't want to watch Sarah or her friends suffer the same fate. I need to keep my distance.

Sarah moans softly, stirring a little. Her eyes remain closed, though her lips have curved up just enough to make her look so pretty that I want to cradle her in my arms. Christ, I met her today. I shouldn't have feelings like that. I don't want to feel that way.

Eventually, I doze off and wake up at dawn.

Can't believe I slept at all. But now, we both need to get up and try to find answers. I yawn and stretch, then grasp Sarah's shoulder to give her a little shake. "Wake up. No time for snoozing."

She opens her bleary eyes and frowns at me. "You're even grumpy when you wake up in the morning."

"Just get up." I scramble to stand, though I keep slipping on the grass, where morning dew has made things slick. "Come on. You're still just lying there."

"I need a few minutes to wake up."

Grumbling, I hunt around in my pack until I find the snack bars I'd stashed in there. Apparently, Sarah's friends like to scavenge food from destroyed cities. Grant told me they also hunt, so they can have meat sometimes. All I've got for me and Sarah is snack bars and jerky. Not my favorite foods. But nobody can be picky these days. Hell, I'd even eat pea soup if I found some, and I hate that garbage.

Sarah finally gets up. "What's the plan?"

I toss her a couple of snack bars. "We go down to the beach. Weren't you listening yesterday? I told you already."

She rolls her eyes at me.

Whatever that's supposed to mean, I don't care. I grab my pack and wave for her to follow me. "Hurry up, Lady Godiva."

"How many times do I have to say it before you listen? I don't like being called Lady Godiva."

"Then don't sunbathe in the nude where even Echo creatures could see you."

She scowls at me as she stalks past me down the hill.

I chuckle and follow her. She's hot when she gets mad.

We reach the shore, but it's too early to see low tide yet. So I decide to search the vicinity for anything out of the ordinary, though I have no idea what that might look like. What's ordinary these days? I suppose I'm searching for evidence of how Sarah got here, but that happened months ago. What are the odds I'll find anything?

Sarah refused to come with me on my perimeter search, but I keep an eye on her peripherally. She chose to stay on the beach where I can see her. Maybe she did that because I ordered her to do it, and I might've also snarled at her. But at least she complied. During my three years inside the Echo, I learned that you can't be sweet and nice, not if you want to survive. The Echo beings I'd befriended didn't follow my orders at first. I had to give them reason to do it, which meant getting tough with them. Becoming the general of our ragtag army saved lives—until the day it didn't anymore.

I need to convince Sarah to follow my orders, even if that means I have to get nasty with her. Noncompliance could get her killed. But I got my friends killed despite my orders. She might be safer back at Sanctuary.

After completing my perimeter search, I trek back down the hillside to the beach, heading for Sarah.

She's lying on the sand, fully clothed. The fact that she's dressed doesn't make her any less beautiful and sexy. She has one knee bent and her arms clasped above her head. The sun beams down on her face. Her lips curl into a sweet little smile. I get a strange pang in my chest as I watch her. That doesn't mean I like the girl.

I will never care about her or anyone ever again.

CHAPTER EIGHT

Sarah

THE SUN FEELS SO GOOD THAT I COULD FALL ASLEEP, JUST LYING HERE ON the beach, and I could almost forget about the apocalypse. I think I understand why Gabriel keeps acting like a jerk, but losing his friends is no excuse for his behavior. I haven't done anything to warrant this kind of treatment. I convinced my friends to let me interrogate him, rather than Dax. That man knows how to scare people without even touching them, sometimes without even speaking.

I doubt Dax's red-hot glare would impress Gabriel.

Though I do not like him, I have to admit Gabriel is attractive and sexy, and sometimes he even does selfless things like taking a bolt of Echo lightning for me. But that incident confused me. Now, he wants to help me understand how and why I washed ashore here. Yeah, I'm totally confused now.

A shadow falls over me.

I crack one eye open. "Find anything, General Jackass?"

"No. Get up. This isn't a vacation."

"Really? I thought you were the hotel concierge coming to tell me my massage appointment is at ten o'clock."

"Just get up. The tide is receding. Might be low enough now that I can figure out where you washed ashore."

"Grant and Erin told you that already."

"I want to see it for myself."

What evidence does he think he'll find two months later? Sheesh, he's stubborn. But I might as well indulge his obsession with the tide. Just as I start to sit up, he offers me his hands. To help me? I stare at his hands for a moment, while that idea sinks in, then I let him help me up.

"Thank you," I say. "But I could've gotten up on my own."

"And you think I'm rude. You could've stopped at 'thank you.' But no, you had to tack on some girl-power BS."

"You just have to be obnoxious, don't you? At least I was speaking in a pleasant tone, instead of growling like you do."

He stalks away from me, heading for the shoreline.

I follow him only because I want to do that, not because he silently ordered me to do it by walking away. Just to make sure he understands that, I walk beside him. That means I need to move fast to keep up with his longer strides, and I start to get short of breath.

"Slow down," I say. "What's the rush, anyway?"

He stops abruptly. "Show me the general vicinity where you think you washed ashore."

"I was unconscious at that point. Duh. I woke up when Grant and Erin found me."

"Yes, but you weren't blind. You must've noticed your surroundings, at least a little bit." He grasps my shoulders, gazing intently into my eyes. "This is important. Please think hard about what happened when you woke up. Close your eyes, try to relax, and let the memories flow naturally."

He's actually trying to help. I appreciate that, so I need to try to do what he suggested. I shut my eyes and listen to the gentle ebb and flow of the surf while the scent of the sea and the pine trees waft over me. The warmth and firmness of Gabriel's hands on my arms lulls me too, though I won't try to examine why, not right now. I've got the Zen mood going, and I need to release my worries, floating on a warm wave of relaxation.

At first, nothing happens. But I let my mind drift, as random thoughts tease the edges of my consciousness.

"Just let go," Gabriel murmurs, his tone smooth and almost sensual. "And when you're ready, tell me what you see."

Sounds tickle my memory, faintly at first, growing louder little by little but remaining an indistinguishable mess.

"That's it," Gabriel murmurs. "Relax into the memories as they flow into you."

His voice has grown so deep and sensual that a tingle starts up between my thighs, and my nipples tighten. But I shouldn't focus on that. I sink back into the Zen moment I've woven around myself—and Gabriel. Somehow, I know what I'm feeling has infiltrated him too. The mishmash of vague noises I've been hearing gradually coalesces into recognizable sounds. Pounding feet. Sirens. The roars of angry beasts. The screams of human beings.

"The Echo," I say. "I was in a city somewhere when the alchemy of worlds began, and the Echo invaded Earth."

"Good. Keep going, but remember to stay disconnected from the memories. You're safe, Sarah."

I feel that way with him, right here, right now. I know nothing will hurt me as long as Gabriel is with me. So I sink into the memories once again, anchored by the steady hands of Gabriel as I float on an ocean of tranquility. Even the screams of terrified people can't raise my pulse, and at last, I begin to experience events of the past as more than blurry images. I don't feel connected to what I see and hear, though, and I don't think that's solely due to my semi-trance state. Angry voices roar while lightning bolts punch into the earth and fireballs rip through buildings.

"Don't let her get away!"

"Wait, she's over there!"

"Stop running, you stupid—"

My lids spring open. My gaze connects with Gabriel's. I can't catch my breath, and my heart is pounding so hard and fast that I feel like I might pass out. Cold sweat dribbles down my temples while my teeth begin to chatter.

Gabriel pulls me into his arms, rubbing my back and murmuring soothing sounds that aren't quite words. My pulse begins to slow down. I let my body sag against him and close my eyes again, with my cheek to his chest, listening to the rhythmic thump-thumping of his heartbeat.

Once I feel able to hold myself upright, I wriggle free of his embrace. "Thank you for…doing that. I started to drown in the memories, though I don't understand any of it."

"What did you remember?"

"Fragments, that's all. Fireballs, lightning, people screaming. That must have been the start of the apocalypse, right?"

He nods. "What else?"

"Angry male voices. They shouted not to let 'her' get away and that 'she' was over there. One guy shouted for 'you' to stop running. I think they were talking about me."

"But you couldn't see who those men were, or in what city that happened."

"No. I'm sorry, I tried."

He lays a hand on my cheek. "You did great."

"Yeah, sure. Vague shouts are super helpful."

"It's a start. And it suggests your memories aren't gone, they're just hidden deep inside your psyche." He makes a pained face. "But I'm hardly an expert on psychology."

"You've helped me more than anyone else has since the day I washed up on this beach."

He scratches his neck and clears his throat, as if he's embarrassed by what I said. "Let's head back to the camp and report what you remembered. Maybe your friends will have some other ideas about how to resurrect your memories."

"They're your friends too, you know."

"Yeah, sure. We're good buddies."

Despite his sarcastic tone, I think he honestly wants to become a part of our family. After three years in the Echo, he's probably forgotten what it feels like to live among a camp like Sanctuary. I'm sure his Echo friends were loyal and good people, but they didn't have the skills that Grant, Erin, Dax, and others in our group can bring to the table. And Gabriel needs a new family. Here, in Sanctuary. Now, how can I convince him that he belongs with us?

A tiny thrill shivers through me. I want Gabriel to join our group. I want him to stick around, even after we discover the truth about me.

I try to hold Gabriel's hand as we start walking toward the mountain slope, but he shakes my hand off.

"They *are* your friends," I tell him. "You're not alone anymore. You have a home here in Sanctuary."

He grunts and refuses to look at me.

A bolt of lightning slams down on the beach just yards ahead of us. The blast throws us backward, and we both go tumbling across the sand into the surf. My ears ring, drowning out all other sounds. I scramble to my knees, hindered by my backpack, and crawl over to Gabriel, who lies flat on his back with his eyes open, seeming dazed. I shake him. He blinks slowly, twice, then grimaces.

A flash overhead makes me tip my head back to stare at the heavens, just as another flash coruscates across the blue sky. I would call it cloud-to-ground lightning, except there are no clouds.

"Get up!" I shout to Gabriel, who still seems a little dazed. "We need to find shelter."

I grab his hand, tugging hard as I rise to a half-crouch. With my help, he gets to his feet.

A bolt slams into the ground, striking so close to us that the sand erupts and showers onto our bodies.

Gabriel seizes my hand, and we take off toward the trees.

Yet another bolt slams down in front of us. But this time, it doesn't retreat into the sky. No, it just hovers there, shimmering and sizzling, the energy rippling inside it. The bolt blocks our path to the trail that leads up the mountain.

We veer to the left, toward the other side of the little cove.

Another bolt punches into the sand and hovers there, like the other one is still doing.

Running for the narrow swathe of beach that skirts the rock outcroppings doesn't work either. The lightning has boxed us in, and we have no escape route.

Gabriel grips my hand so tightly that it almost hurts, but I don't care. Echo lightning has trapped us here, which makes me wonder what will happen next. Will creatures appear to abduct us? In the two months that I've lived in Sanctuary, we've only seen the occasional creature. If a horde of them lived nearby, surely they would've made their presence known.

The sky splits open. The rift spirals outward, forming a black disk high above us that enlarges with every passing second. A ratcheting noise accompanies the ever-expanding disk. Is that... No, it can't be. There has never been an entrance to the Echo in this area. Those are only in cities or some of the small towns. Not here, in the wilderness. Not in Sanctuary.

Something flies out of the opening.

I swallow hard, but my throat has constricted.

A winged Echo creature swoops down to seize us, whisking us up toward the whirling black disk. Before I realize what's happened, we've been pulled through the entrance and into the Echo.

The flying beast drops us and soars away.

We land sprawled on the ground, with me on top of Gabriel.

He smirks. "Well, I'm liking this position."

"Sarcastic come-ons are not appropriate right now." I scramble to my feet. "We're in the Echo, aren't we? How did that happen?"

He sits up and glances around. "Home sweet home."

Yeah, he was being sarcastic again.

I plant my hands on my hips. "But how—"

"What makes you think I have a clue? No idea why a flying monster dragged us into the Echo and dumped us in the middle of nowhere."

I hadn't realized the Echo consisted of more than cities, but we currently stand in a scorched wasteland that seems to have once been countryside, maybe even farmland. I think I see the remnants of corn stalks. Echo creatures farmed? Wow, I have a lot to learn about this world. But my main concern right now is how to figure out why a creature dumped us here.

"Do you think that Aldith woman brought us here?" I ask. "Maybe she wants to talk to us."

"I doubt that. She was in the castle, though she might also have the ability to go into the stronghold. I got the impression she can't roam free, though."

"You mean she's a prisoner?"

He shrugs. "Could be. She didn't give me much info before she tossed me out of the Echo."

"She told you the Brain can't work properly on its own, right? She might be expecting you to take over that role now."

"Then why banish me to Earth? And why bring you here? None of this makes any sense."

Well, I can't argue with that. Lightning has tried to fry me several times. I have nothing to offer in terms of healing the Echo's Brain. Maybe Aldith didn't do this after all. At least we have our backpacks. That gives us some water and snacks, weapons too.

"What should we do now?" I ask. "You've traveled this whole world, so I'll defer to your knowledge of the Echo."

"Do you think I memorized the geography of this entire planet? I don't have a photographic memory."

He's getting grumpy again. Perfect.

A metallic grinding noise erupts behind us, but when we turn around to look, we can't see anything. The ground trembles with every *whump* of what sounds like gigantic feet. Then a white flash behind us makes me spin around and shout, "Gabriel! The lightning is back."

In the distance, bolts pound into the ground one after another after another, sweeping closer every moment.

"Run," Gabriel says, almost whispering the word.

We take off, having no clue where we're going or how to escape from the dual forces coming after us. More metallic grinding. More thunderous lightning. And we keep running, running, running. The ground shudders so violently that we stumble and hit the ground.

A lightning bolt strikes too close.

Gabriel hoists me onto my feet, but just as we turn to run, another bolt erupts from the sky.

A massive metal hand reaches out from behind us, raising its open palm, and the lightning bounces off it. The being that hand belongs to remains shrouded in darkness as the thing deflects bolt after bolt, using both palms as shields. Then the being scoops up both me and Gabriel. Cradled in the monstrosity's palm, we both stare up at the creature.

"Jarek," Gabriel says. "Thanks, buddy. We needed a hand."

The gigantic being seems to be made of metal and flesh, like a cyborg in a sci-fi movie. Gabriel knows this creature, and he doesn't seem angry or afraid of the thing. He called it Jarek.

"Did Aldith send you to bring us into the Echo?" Gabriel asks. When the cyborg shakes its head, Gabriel says, "No, of course you didn't. You would've scooped us up straight off Earth, and whoever brought us here needed an Echo creature to abduct us."

With one hand, Jarek continues deflecting the lightning bolts, but I swear he winces a little every time.

I whisper to Gabriel, "Your friend is getting tired."

"Yeah, he is." Gabriel shouts to Jarek, "Big buddy, can you take us to the castle?"

Jarek shakes his head.

"What about the stronghold?"

The cyborg nods.

"Good. Take us there, please."

Jarek cups his other palm over us, forming a protective shell. Then he lopes away, presumably ferrying us to the stronghold, whatever that is. I can't see Gabriel, but I feel his hand holding mine.

"What is this creature?" I ask. "Everyone says Echo beasts are the size of normal humans, but this guy is like Godzilla."

"He's nicer than that monster. Jarek is good, and he helped me scale the sheer cliff that has Sefton's castle at the top of it."

"But what is Jarek?"

"He's a golem. That's a creature created by magic to serve its master's bidding. But Erin and Grant managed to free him, and he does what he wants now."

I'm glad to hear that, because it means Jarek chooses to help us. The ride in the golem's palm isn't the smoothest, but it seems like Jarek is trying to make it as easy on us as he can. After a while, he slows to a walking pace and pulls one palm away to let us see the landscape. It's vacant land, scorched beyond recognition. I swear I can smell the smoke, though the bulk of the apocalypse has been over for months now. It could've been longer here in the Echo. If time behaves differently in this world, I wonder how long our friends will have to wait for us to return. Will they assume we're dead?

No. They will never give up on us.

Chapter Nine

Gabriel

Jarek's long strides create a slight rocking sensation as we travel toward the stronghold, wherever that might be hidden. The rocking motion seems to be making Sarah kind of dizzy, given the way she keeps biting her lip and gripping her knees. So I sling an arm around her shoulders. "Don't worry. The stronghold is a bastion of good magics, not bad ones. That's what I've heard, anyway. I tried to find it, but I think the stronghold is cloaked to prevent just anybody from getting inside."

"Grant and Erin have been inside the stronghold. They met Aldith there."

"Well, I hope she's still there. I want to know what the hell she expects us to do."

Yeah, that woman did not explain herself very well. Maybe she kept things vague on purpose. I get the feeling she's more than just an Echo creature, but some kind of higher being within this domain. She might even straddle both worlds. I don't know, and that's why I need to interrogate her.

Right, because that worked out so well last time.

As we pass through a blackened and lifeless zone, I notice a familiar shape off to my left, far away but close enough that I can recognize it. That's the castle, poised high up on a narrow and hard to reach cliff. All my friends died there. Only I survived, and I still don't know why.

"Do me a favor," Sarah says. "When we reach the stronghold and see Aldith, don't get grumpy with her."

"Why not? She hasn't been the most helpful person."

"Did you ever think that maybe she's scared too? And she might not be able to tell you more than she already has? You seem to assume she's all-knowing."

I sigh. "Yeah, okay, you've got a point. I'll try to restrain myself." I smirk at her. "But I can't swear I won't get sarcastic."

She smiles a touch and shakes her head. "I figured that would be too much to ask of you."

I know I'm a sarcastic jackass. I never used to be, but the apocalypse changed everything. It changed me, for sure. I don't feel qualified to determine whether I've changed for the better or the worse. Only other people can judge that.

How would Sarah judge me?

I don't care. Her opinion doesn't matter. I asked myself that question because…I'm bored, stuck inside a golem's hand. What else have I got to think about?

Sarah kisses my cheek.

I jerk and whip my head around to stare at her. "What are you doing?"

"Thanking you."

"For what? I didn't do anything, good or bad."

"Of course you did." She rests her head on my shoulder. "You're being much less grumpy. And you helped me recover a sliver of my memories back on the beach."

"You did that. I just stood there."

"Stop trying to downplay how helpful you've been."

I don't bother responding to that. I have no response. If Sarah has developed a hero complex about me, she'll be disappointed, eventually.

But right here, right now, she snuggles up to me.

I resist the urge to grimace and try not to fidget. Nobody has wanted to snuggle with me since way before the alchemy of worlds began. I guess I've forgotten how to accept affection. Three years in the Echo hardened me, and I don't know if I can ever again become the kind of man any woman would want to get involved with for more than sex.

Jarek halts, then raises his hand high above his head, lifting us toward… nothing.

What is he doing? Are we supposed to jump into the clouds?

Suddenly, our surroundings shift. We no longer sit on Jarek's palm. Instead, we stand inside a building, in a long hallway that has flickering oil lamps positioned at intervals along the walls. This place feels like a castle, but I've been inside Sefton Stainthorpe's fortress, and it was nothing like this. His castle seemed vacant and sterile, not at all welcoming. The stronghold we now stand in has warm, flickering light and wooden doors. What lies inside those rooms? Not bare stone, I'm sure. Call it a hunch.

A doorway to our left swings open, and Aldith steps onto the threshold. "Welcome to the stronghold. Please step inside this room, where we can discuss matters in a more comfortable environment."

Sarah slips her hand into mine as we follow Aldith into a spacious bedroom. I consider shaking her hand off, but I can't make myself do that this time. Something about the stronghold makes me uneasy. I guess I need a little comforting too. This room is beautifully decorated, not that I'm an expert on that sort of thing. But even I can appreciate the warm tones and the splashes of brighter colors that make the space feel welcoming.

"It's nice to see you again, Aldith," I say. "But why did you send me away only to bring me back here again?"

She cants her head, seeming curious. "I did not bring you here. I sent you to Sanctuary, that is all."

"But Jarek gave us a ride to get here."

"Jarek is an autonomous being, no longer a slave to anyone since Erin and Grant freed him."

I feel myself about to get grumpy and remember what Sarah told me. I shouldn't get angry at Aldith. She might be as much a pawn in this game as we are. So I take a breath and exhale it slowly to calm myself. "Do you know anything about the lightning on the Earth side of things? It seemed to be going after Sarah. Then it penned us on the beach so a flying creature could grab us and drag us back into the Echo."

"I was aware of the lightning," Aldith says, "but only on this side. The Echo has been enduring strange weather similar to what happened during the alchemy of worlds."

"That wasn't going on when I left here."

"No. It began shortly after your departure." She cants her head again, this time aiming her curiosity at Sarah. "The lightning wished to hurt you?"

Sarah hunches her shoulders. "It kept trying to hit me, that's all I know. Gabriel jumped in front of a bolt to save me. But you just asked if the lightning 'wished' to hurt me. That implies you think it's sentient."

"I regret if I implied that. What I should have asked is whether the lightning might've been directed toward you."

"Of course it was," I say, almost snarling, but not quite. I need to do more work on not getting grumpy. I manage to calm down and unfist my hands. "Sorry. I didn't mean to snap at you. But this is all damn confusing and unnerving."

"Yes, I imagine it is." Aldith clasps her hands in front of her body. "Perhaps we can solve the mystery together."

"Any help you can provide would be appreciated."

When I glance at Sarah, she's smiling at me. It's a small but sweet smile. I'd rather she didn't look at me that way.

"About the lightning," I say, focusing on the pretty Echo creature so I don't have to see Sarah's expression. "Do you have any information about that? Any guesses? I'd like to know why those bolts were after Sarah."

"If I knew, I would tell you. But I cannot see what the Echo is doing on Earth, only what happens here."

"Have you ever known the lightning in the Echo to chase a person? Or corral someone?"

"No. And the fact that an Echo creature abducted you is rather disturbing."

Yeah, no shit. The whole situation is disturbing. Especially since I just realized something. "Jarek was working with the Echo creature that brought us here."

Aldith's eyes widen for the briefest moment. Then she rolls her shoulders back and clears her throat. "I don't believe he would have aided anyone in harming you. There must be an explanation."

"Let's ask him."

Aldith marches past us, through the open doorway and across the hall to another door. She glances back. "Are you coming? This was your idea, after all."

I lead Sarah across the hall as Aldith opens the door. We all tromp into another bedroom. This one features big picture windows that overlook…the clouds. We're in the sky? Well, Jarek had lifted us very high, but I'd assumed he pushed us through some kind of portal to the stronghold.

But no, we're actually floating in the clouds.

Aldith waves a hand. One of the picture windows vanishes. She leans out and tips her head down. "Jarek! We need to speak to you, please."

What on earth is that woman doing? Even Jarek can't reach this place. It's high above his head. I think. We just kind of poofed into the stronghold, so I can't say for sure. Can't believe I thought the word poof. At least I didn't say it out loud.

A large metal-and-flesh hand clamps onto the windowsill, and Jarek's head rises into view.

Did he jump up here? Guess it doesn't really matter how he got here as long as he can answer our questions. Since it's yes or no answers only with the golem, this could take a while.

Aldith pats Jarek's head. "Thank you for coming. We need your assistance, if you're able and willing to help."

The golem nods.

"Go on, Gabriel," Aldith says. "You and Sarah may ask Jarek whatever questions you like."

"Okay." I approach the window and gaze at Jarek's enormous face. "A flying creature brought us into the Echo. Were you working with that beast?"

Jarek shakes his head.

I'm surprisingly glad to hear that. I've only met Jarek a few times, but the golem always seemed like a good, uh, guy. Not sure what else to call a creature like him. So I'll stick with "guy." It sounds weird, though.

"Do you know who sent that creature?" I ask.

Jarek shrugs.

What does that mean? I need to rephrase my question. "Are you saying you aren't sure whether you know who did it?"

The golem nods.

Great. Ambivalence is really helpful. "Do you have any idea why the lightning keeps coming for Sarah?"

Jarek shakes his head.

"Well, thank you for answering my questions." I look at Sarah. "Did you want to ask him anything?"

"I can't think of anything." She bites her lip, her brows furrowed, then leans out the window. "Jarek, why did you bring us to the stronghold?"

"That's not a yes or no question," I point out. "He can't speak. You need to keep it simple so he can respond."

Jarek lifts one finger and points it toward Aldith.

Interesting. I nudge Sarah out of the way and lean out the window. "Are you saying Aldith knows why you brought us here?"

He nods. His arms have begun to tremble slightly, which seems like a sign he can't hold on to the window for much longer.

"Okay," I say. "You can go now, Jarek. Thanks for the help."

The golem lets go of the sill and drops down through the clouds, out of sight.

"Well, that was a waste of time," I mumble.

"No, it wasn't," Sarah says. "At least now we know Jarek didn't conspire with an Echo creature to abduct us."

"And he will help if you need him," Aldith says. "Jarek always wants to help those who deserve to be helped."

Sarah deserves it. Still not sure I do.

"Why does Jarek think you know why he brought us to the stronghold?" I ask. "You claimed you didn't summon us here."

"I did not. But Jarek must believe I will come to understand why he brought you here. I need to think about that. Despite what you may think, I don't have special powers of perception."

A yawn overtakes me, and I rub my hands over my face.

"How much did you sleep last night?" Sarah asks.

I lift one shoulder. "A couple hours, maybe. I've gone with less sleep for much longer."

"You need to rest. We both need to be in top form if we're going to figure out what's happening." Sarah looks at Aldith. "Would you mind if we rest here in the stronghold for a while? It would give you time to think about what Jarek said too."

"Take any room you like. All the doors are unlocked." She walks toward the doorway, then pauses to glance back. "The bedrooms in the stronghold sometimes have an unusual effect on couples, particularly those who make love while in residence here."

Is she suggesting we should have sex? No, I can't get up for that. Even after I get some rest, I doubt I would ever feel comfortable doing that in this strange place.

Right, because fucking in the dirt while crazy Echo lightning bombed the woods wasn't strange at all.

I let Sarah lead me down the hall so we can peek into every bedroom. She chooses one she likes, then asks if I like it too. I shrug. What the room looks like hardly matters. I want to sleep, not admire the sheets or whatever it is she thinks I should care about. A bed is a bed. I haven't slept in comfort for so long that I barely remember what a nice, soft mattress feels like, anyway.

We lie down on top of the covers, and I fall asleep almost instantly. It happens so fast that I think I didn't sleep at all, until Sarah points at a clock situated on a dresser.

"It's been seven hours," she says. "I noticed the time when we lay down. You passed out the second you closed your eyes."

"Did you get any sleep?"

"Yes. But I wasn't as exhausted as you were. I did have a dream, though. It was about what I saw in my vision, the one where men were yelling for me to stop running."

Maybe I shouldn't care, but I have to ask. "What did you see this time?"

"They seemed to want to protect me rather than trying to hurt me."

I suddenly realize we've been spooning. I can honestly say I've never done that before. Pretty sure I fell asleep lying on my back. But at some point, I rolled over to cradle her body with mine, and I have one arm draped over her hip. The warmth and suppleness of her body feels…right.

Which is bullshit.

I sit up and swing my legs off the bed. "Better find Aldith. Maybe she finally realized what Jarek meant."

"There's no need to be embarrassed."

"Why would I be? I got some rest, that's all."

She crawls up behind me and wraps her arms around my torso. "We shared an intimate experience. You get touchy about that kind of thing."

Did we have sex while I was asleep? No, I would've woken up if that happened.

She nuzzles my neck. "We took a nap together, Gabriel. When was the last time you went to sleep with a woman holding you?"

For reasons I can't understand, I tell her the truth. "Never. The women I dated weren't into, uh, cuddling."

"Really? I thought all women loved that. But then, I have amnesia, so maybe I just don't remember disliking cuddling." She kisses my throat. "I loved sleeping with you."

"Uh, yeah, it was…fine."

Her hands, her lips, and her voice are doing things to me that won't be helpful right now. So I peel her arms away and stand up, trying not to let her see the growing bulge in my pants. I'm a guy. I can't help that feeling a woman's body wrapped around me, and hearing a woman's sensual voice, makes my dick wake up.

A woman? No, it's only Sarah who does this to me.

I slither off the bed. "Let's find Aldith."

Sarah tries to hold my hand, but I manage to dodge that attempt. I've let her get too close to me, and that's a recipe for disaster.

Distance, that's what I need.

Chapter Ten

Sarah

GABRIEL DOESN'T WANT ME TO TOUCH HIM ANYMORE. HE HAS pulled away from me before, but not as abruptly as he's doing now. Our sleepover must have disturbed him. We've had sex, for heaven's sake. How can he feel weird about taking a nap with me? Maybe I just don't understand men. Since I have amnesia, I can't be sure I understand anything that other people do.

Aldith appears in front of us.

We'd been walking down the hall, and now we're forced to halt. I try once again to grasp his hand, but he folds his arms over his chest to thwart me. Why is he so determined to avoid even the tiniest amount of intimacy? It must be related to what he went through before he dropped out of the sky and landed on the beach at my feet. Losing his friends must have scarred him more than I'd realized. I wish I had my own experiences to guide me, but I'm flying blind when it comes to helping Gabriel recover from his losses.

Maybe all I need to do is be here for him, whether he likes it or not.

"Did you sleep well?" Aldith asks.

"Yeah, sure," Gabriel says. He seems to be trying to get away from me, shuffling sideways when I rest my cheek on his upper arm. "Aldith, did you figure out why Jarek thinks you know what's going on?"

"I believe so. But I don't have a direct interface with the Heart or Lifeblood of the Echo, and the Brain is still in limbo."

"You said the Brain requires a human being to function."

Aldith's features crimp the slightest bit.

"The Heart and the Lifeblood are humans," I tell Gabriel. "Grant and Erin took over those roles to stabilize the Echo and Earth when the worlds were having conniptions. They don't have any particular duties related to becoming the Heart and the Lifeblood, and they've only come back to the stronghold a few times to check on things."

Gabriel stares at me for a moment, his mood impossible to gauge. "You must be the Brain. That's why the lightning keeps coming for you."

"No, it must be you. I mean, you saved me from the lightning. That has to mean something."

Aldith clears her throat. "You are both ignoring an obvious aspect of the Brain."

"Like what?" Gabriel says, and he's starting to sound grumpy again.

"Every human brain has two hemispheres, which control opposite sides of the body."

"So what?"

Aldith lifts her brows. "The answer is obvious. The Brain of the Echo would seem to require two humans to function properly."

Gabriel narrows his gaze on Aldith. "But you said Sefton Stainthorpe was the Brain. That means one man, not two humans, controlled the Echo."

"And you forget one vital fact." She walks straight up to Gabriel and aims her glowing eyes at him. "Sefton Stainthorpe had an Echo, the being known as Will, his alter ego who was created when Sefton activated the Catalyst and the Anchor to begin the alchemy of worlds. Sefton did not foresee that his plan would result in an Echo of himself being created, but that is what occurred. He also did not appreciate sharing the Brain with Will."

"Allison and Dax are the Catalyst and the Anchor."

"I trust you to keep the information confidential," I tell Gabriel, "because it affects the lives of three people."

Gabriel swerves his attention to me. "I know how to keep a secret, Sarah."

I wrap my arms around myself, rubbing my hands up and down, suddenly feeling a chill. "Allison was the Catalyst, the human who initiated the chain reaction without knowing she'd done that. Sefton used her without her permission. Dax was the Anchor, the human who kept the alchemical reaction from spinning out of control. He was also used by Sefton without his permission. We don't know what might happen if this information got into the wrong hands. For all we know, the Catalyst and the Anchor might reignite the alchemy of worlds or start the alchemy of souls."

"You said the secret affects the lives of three people."

"The third life is Dax and Allison's unborn child. We've been afraid that if Echo creatures found out the Catalyst and the Anchor had conceived a baby, those beasts might try to steal the child. Their baby might become the golden fleece of the apocalypse."

"Because their kid might have the Echo power."

"Or it might have magics that no one can even imagine yet."

Gabriel shoves his hands into his pants pockets and sighs. "Okay, I get why that needs to be kept a secret. But I am not one hemisphere of the Echo's Brain."

"Do not fight your destiny," Aldith says. "When you breached the castle, I knew you must be the one who would join with the other half of the Brain and take control of the Echo."

"But who is the other half?"

"Sarah, of course."

Gabriel glances at me, but he quickly swerves his attention away. "Why would the Echo want two strangers to be the Brain? Neither of us even knows what that means, what we're supposed to do. You must be wrong. Sarah, sure, I can see that. But not me."

Does he honestly believe that I know what the heck is going on here? I don't want to be the Brain either. But Erin and Grant accepted the roles the Echo assigned to them, and they've managed to sort out what they needed to do. They'd known each other for a month or so before they entered the Echo, so they could try to fix the conniptions. Gabriel and I met yesterday. We don't get along, and he clearly wants nothing to do with becoming one hemisphere of the Echo's Brain.

I don't want to do that either. But we have no choice. What the Echo wants, it gets—or else the worlds will be destroyed. How can I convince Gabriel of that?

"Where is this Brain thing, anyway?" Gabriel asks. "Or are we supposed to find it on our own?"

"The Brain is housed inside the castle, but I'm not privy to its exact location. It does not have a physical form, as it is composed entirely of magics."

"Uh-huh. So what the fuck are we supposed to do? Can't become the Brain if we have no way to find it."

I smack his arm. "Don't be rude."

He doesn't look at me even when he hisses, "I wasn't being rude. I asked a valid question."

"You said the F-word."

Gabriel rolls his eyes. "Now you're suddenly a goody two shoes. Didn't act that way back in the woods yesterday."

"Let's not talk about that in front of *her*."

Aldith gazes at us with a neutral expression. Did she hear what we whispered to each other? If so, she doesn't seem to realize what Gabriel was talking about, and I see no reason why she would. Unless she has psychic powers. God, I hope that's not the case.

"You need to digest what I've told you," Aldith says. "Please, take as long as you like. I have frozen time within the stronghold."

I stare at her. "You froze time? I had no idea you could do that. What about time in the Echo and on Earth?"

"Regrettably, I have no control over that."

"So, time will keep moving at the normal pace for our friends."

"Perhaps, or perhaps not. The Echo does what it wants to do."

Wonderful. I love all these vague explanations.

Aldith vanishes.

Gabriel and I both seem unable to look at each other, instead exchanging furtive sidelong glances. But we don't speak or move.

Finally, I can't take the silence anymore. "Should we, um, talk about this?"

"About what? That chick strongly implied we should have sex because the rooms here have a strange effect on couples. We aren't a couple, though."

"She's trying to help. And Aldith does know more about this stuff than we do."

He grunts. "So, what, she's a sex therapist too? Getting laid won't help anything."

"Won't it? Something changed when we had sex in the woods. I know you felt it too."

He grunts again.

We go back to awkwardly standing here in the hall while we awkwardly glance at each other. Though we had sex once, it happened so fast that I have trouble remembering exactly what we did. No, that's a lie. I remember every second of it. But even while I can't stop thinking about that, I also feel like that experience was a blur too. It makes no sense, but I don't care. And I have a weird feeling that Aldith knows what might happen if Gabriel and I get naked again. Will sex make us stronger somehow? More in tune with the Echo?

"Aldith said we should take our time," Gabriel says. "So let's do that."

"Do what?"

"Take our time."

I tip my head back and glare at the ceiling. "You're being just as vague as Aldith."

"Sorry." He scratches the back of his head. "Let's find a place to sit down and then talk about…stuff."

"Fine."

I let Gabriel lead the way, and we wind up peeking inside every room on this floor. We didn't realize the stronghold had more than one floor until we reached the end of the hall and a wooden door magically appeared. It slid open to reveal the elevator car. Gabriel walked right inside, so I did the same. If the elevator wants to kill us, I don't have the mental capacity to think about that. I don't feel physically tired. My brain needs a rest, though.

Crazy revelations will do that to a girl.

On the lower floor, we explore the rooms we find there. Gabriel finally chooses one, and we drop our backpacks on the floor beside the bed. Luckily, this room has four chairs and a comfy sofa, so we don't need to lie on the bed together. I'd be fine with that, though I doubt Gabriel would. He flipped out after accidentally spooning with me.

He sits in a chair.

I drop onto the sofa at the end nearest to him. "What should we talk about?"

"Whether we want to become the Brain."

"Aldith made it sound like that's not optional. I assume the Echo will start to have problems again if we don't do that."

"She told us to think about it. Why bother considering the issue if we have no choice?"

I tuck my feet under me cross-legged and tap my fingers on my knees. "It was my understanding that Aldith meant we need to come to terms with our destiny."

"Our what?" He makes a rude noise and shakes his head. "You're jumping to conclusions."

"No, I'm extrapolating from what Aldith told us."

"We have no choice. Fine." He gets up and starts unzipping his pants. "Let's fuck right now and get it over with."

"Are you insane? I can't get turned on when you're acting like a jackass."

"Of course you can." He stalks up to the sofa, pulls my legs out from under me, and flips me onto my back. Then he kneels on all fours above me. "I bet you're already wet. Back in the woods, I didn't need to do any prep work to get you ready. I've never been with a woman who gets as wet as you do and does it so fast. You're easy, Sarah."

"What? No, I am not." But I get dismayingly turned on when I'm around him, even when we're having a discussion with Grant, Erin, and the others. Nobody could've noticed that. Right?

He lunges his head down to take my nipple into his mouth, through my shirt and bra. The strong sucking motion makes my clit pulsate. I bite back a gasp, because I do not want him to know he's right.

Gabriel ducks his head to shove his nose between my thighs and pull in a big breath through his nostrils. "Damn, I can smell how hot you are for me. Your clothes can't mask it because you want me so badly."

The rough tone of his voice makes my sex throb. I'm trying so hard not to start panting, though my racing heart doesn't help me resist him. How can I want a jerk like him? I wish I could forget that one time we screwed, but I dreamed about it last night in the woods. I woke up with my panties drenched, but I won't admit that to him. He'd just love knowing I'm desperately hot for him.

But I think he kind of figured that out already. *Damn.*

I should order him to stop. Better yet, I should kick him in the head. But I can't convince myself to do either of those things.

He rises to his knees, finishes unzipping his pants, and pulls out his cock. While he stares at my chest, he begins stroking his length with one hand. "Do you want it right here, on the sofa? Or on the bed? Your choice, but it'll be a filthy fuck either way, and I guarantee you'll beg me to do it again once we're done."

No sex, period. That's what I should say. It's not what my mouth decides to tell him, though. "On the bed. Please, hurry."

The desperation in my voice makes me hate myself for being as easy as he claims I am. But I don't care anymore. The way he made me feel when he had sex in the woods… I want more of that. Not for a few minutes. No, this time I want him inside me for hours and hours. We have all the time we want, thanks to Aldith freezing the clock for us. And I need to experience filthy sex just once more before I die.

And yeah, I assume we will both die soon. Neither of us knows how to become the Brain, after all.

Gabriel picks me up and drops me onto the bed without even bothering to remove the covers.

Watching him undress mesmerizes me, and I couldn't move if I tried. I follow his every movement as he unbuttons his shirt and shrugs out of it, revealing all those rippling muscles that I'd seen when he fell from the sky yesterday. But now not even tatters of clothing conceal his physique. I long to lick a path along every one of those muscles.

But then he pushes his pants and underwear down to his ankles and kicks them off along with his socks. He'd already kicked his boots off before he got started stripping. My attention stalls on his cock, that thick, smooth, beautiful dick that I can't wait to feel inside me again.

"Strip," he commands.

And I do it. As quickly as I can, I ditch all my clothes and lie down on the bed again. "Gabriel, I—"

"Don't move."

I watch while he finds his backpack and pulls out a length of rope. "What's that for?"

"Always keep some rope with me just in case." He climbs onto the foot of the bed and crawls up my body on his hands and knees until his face hovers above mine. "And I need it right now."

"Why?"

"You know why, because you want it too. Don't you?"

I can't tell him to go to hell because the power of my arousal has stolen my breath. I feel the slickness of my cream all over my inner thighs, and I can smell it too. Whatever he wants to do, I want him to do it to me.

"Yes, Gabriel, I want it. I want you."

CHAPTER ELEVEN

Gabriel

WHAT AM I DOING? I'VE NEVER GONE ALPHA-MALE ASSHOLE ON A woman before. I never wanted to behave that way. But three years in the Echo changed me in ways I haven't fully explored yet and that I don't fully understand. Now that I have Sarah all to myself, in a place where no one will find us or interrupt us, I've developed a powerful urge to dominate her.

And she seems okay with that.

Fuck, I need to do this.

Sarah's tits rise and fall with her every breath, and her chest has become dappled with rosy pink. Her stiff nipples jut up, begging me to devour them.

But not yet.

I carefully bind her wrists to her ankles with the rope, leaving just a bit of leeway to make sure she doesn't get chafed. "Don't speak unless I tell you to, and don't come unless I give you permission."

"But how—"

"I said don't speak."

She bites her lip, her eyes glossy with desire. Sarah has never looked more beautiful than she does right now.

I push her legs apart, keeping her knees bent, exposing every inch of her glistening pink flesh while I drink in the evidence of how much she wants me. Then I lie down with my head between her thighs and suck in a deep draft of her scent, groaning at the musky, addictive aroma. Now that I have her at my mercy, I need to tease her until she can't stand it anymore. So I drag my tongue up and down the edge of her cleft, flicking my tongue out occasionally to tease her inner folds.

Sarah moans and rocks her hips.

The sound, so erotic and hungry, pushes me to do more, to make her so aroused that she won't be able to think, much less speak. I hoist her hips and seal my mouth around her opening, thrusting my tongue deep again and again until she whimpers and thrashes, her breaths growing shorter and more erratic. When I feel like she's on the edge, I stop.

"Do you like what I'm doing?" I ask. "You can speak this one time, because I'm allowing you to do it."

"Yes," she breathes, "I love this. Don't stop."

I flick my tongue around the rim of her opening, and she writhes, as much as she can when I have her bound. While I keep teasing her entrance, I stretch an arm up to close my hand around her breast and rub my thumbnail over the rigid tip.

Her mouth falls open as she seems to struggle against the need to cry out.

As much as I thought I needed her to stay silent unless I gave her permission to speak, now I realize I want to hear whatever she needs to scream or whisper to me. I need it so much that just thinking about it makes my cock throb. I'm so hard that I don't know if I can last much longer.

"You can speak," I growl. "But I'm still in control."

"Oh, yes, I want you to tell me what to do. It's the hottest thing ever."

She loves having me in control of her. Would I want to give up control to Sarah? I can't think about that right now, because I need to drive her toward a climax that will shatter her. But not yet. I rise to my knees and hoist her hips, then rub the tip of my erection around the rim of her entrance in slow, steady circles. The motion drives me crazy too, but it's the look on Sarah's face that might break me. I'm struggling to catch my breath while she loosely bites her bottom lip and her eyes flutter half-closed. Her mouth curls into the sweetest, naughtiest little smile I've ever seen.

Just as I feel myself on the verge of coming, I pull away and shove my hand into the curly hairs on her mound, teasing them with my fingers. Her slickness dampens those hairs and my fingertips.

Sarah watches me, her breasts heaving.

I hold my fingers to my mouth and lick away the drops of her cream one by one.

"Oh, God, Gabriel," she moans. "Make me come, please."

"Not yet." I trail my fingertips up her belly and back down again, then take hold of the rope and tug it, making her gasp. "You want me to fuck you right now."

"Yes, please."

"I won't do that, not yet."

Rising to my knees, I stroke myself while I gaze down at her nude body. I love watching her writhe as if she can't wait for me to fuck her, but I don't want to do that yet. All right, I *want* to do it. But we have literally all the time in the world, and I won't rush.

"Do that again," she says, her tone sultry and her eyes darkened by lust. "Take me to the edge and leave me hanging. I love what you're doing to me."

I've discovered something about myself since I met Sarah—several things, actually—and I will tell her about it later. Right now, I need to drive her wild again and again until we both can't stand it anymore.

"How flexible are you?" I ask. "Don't want to push you too far and hurt you."

She smiles playfully, then pulls her bound legs and hands up over her head, hooking her ankles in the headboard rails. "Does that answer your question?"

"Hell yeah." I run my hands up and down her legs. "You must do yoga to be that flexible."

"I practice with Grant and Erin. Grant's teaching me how to be Zen too."

My gaze has become glued to her body, where her new position has exposed all that glistening, slick, pink flesh that I need to devour—eventually. I slant forward to grasp the headboard rails, and I start rubbing my dick up and down her cleft. Every time the head of my cock grazes her flesh, I suck in a sharp breath, and she gasps too. I struggle to keep control of my breathing while I rock my hips to rasp her sensitized flesh, and my pulse accelerates, pounding in my chest and thundering in my ears.

I sit back on my heels and wipe sweat from my brow.

Sarah moans and manages to wriggle her ass even while bound to the headboard. She's very flexible. Unbelievably flexible. The fact that she does yoga and meditates turns me on even more.

On my knees, I waddle even closer until my dick hangs right over her face. "Suck me, baby."

She doesn't hesitate. Sarah lunges her head up to catch my cock in her mouth, and she lets out sharp little grunts while she sucks me. I groan and hiss in a breath, clutching the headboard while I let her do whatever she wants. Her tongue coils around me like a sexy snake, and she takes as much of me into her mouth as she possibly can, then she withdraws. With a sly smile, she rakes her tongue over my crown.

"Fuck, Sarah," I growl.

I know I'll come any second, and I don't want that to happen yet. So I back away to kneel near her exposed cleft, then cup both her breasts in my palms. I flick my thumbs over her nipples in a slow rhythm, and her breaths shorten, becoming erratic while I torment her stiff peaks. Just when she's gotten used to the rhythm, I stop. Then I bend over to gently lick her nipples. That makes her jerk and gasp. I blow air over those wet peaks.

"Gabriel, please," she pleads. "Don't ever stop."

I chuckle. "You're a dirty girl, aren't you? Guess that shouldn't surprise me since you sunbathe in the nude."

She must be in agony—the best kind, brought on by intense pleasure with no release—but she wants even more. I feel the same agony, but I'm not ready for this to end yet either.

And she begged me not to stop.

I plant my hands at either side of her body and ease my cock inside her, relishing the silky smoothness of her sheath as it molds to me, hot and wet, the scent of her desire inundating my senses. Once I'm buried as deep inside her as I can go, I hold that position. Yeah, I need to come so badly that I'm clenching my teeth and I can hardly breathe, but I need this to last a little longer. So I pull out completely and just hover here, my dick inches from her opening, and gaze into her eyes. She gazes right back at me, her cheeks pink and her lips a deeper shade of rose.

Can't stop myself. I lunge down to claim her lips, pushing my tongue between them, ravaging her mouth and relishing the taste of her. She thrusts her tongue between my lips. Our teeth clash, our breaths gust over each other's faces, and her heart must be pounding as ferociously as mine, but neither of us can stop. We keep kissing like the world will explode any second, and maybe it will.

The world did explode once, when the Echo punched through into Earth.

If this might be the last day of my life, I need to make it incredible. I thrust my cock into her while we keep kissing, and I punch into her over and over, so hard and so fast that the bed bounces and thumps and our cries fill the room. Almost there… Any second…

With a snarled shout, I pull out of her body and give up her mouth. My ears are ringing. I take some slow breaths and encourage Sarah to do the same. Once we've both calmed down just enough that we won't pass out, it's time to finish. I slide my cock into her sheath inch by inch, letting myself experience every sensation, and I keep my gaze locked on hers. My God, she's beautiful and sensual, the perfect woman, the only one in the universe who could make me feel human again. The heat of her body surrounds me. Nothing else has ever felt this good, but I know what I'm about to do will become the most incredible feeling I will ever know.

I pump into her, slowly at first, then faster and faster until I'm pounding into her and the wet sucking sound of our bodies colliding reverberates in the room.

"Come for me, Sarah," I say, my voice a hoarse growl. "Come right now."

I adjust the angle of my thrusts until my balls rub against her flesh. Her body tightens around me, a sure sign that she's about to go off. The pressure to come builds inside me like an industrial boiler ramping up to an explosion, and I can't do more than gasp and keep pumping faster and harder.

Sarah freezes. She doesn't even blink. Doesn't breathe either, I think. Then her entire body curls in on itself while the spasms of her climax grip my cock, and she screams. The pressure inside me has become too intense to fight, and

I let go. My release erupts out of me while I pound into her twice more, shouting as the last spasms of my cock subside. I'm breathing hard, sweat sheaths my body, and I don't have the wherewithal to pull out of her. All I can do is stare at Sarah.

Did we just do that? Or did I hallucinate the whole thing? When I gaze down at her, I know it was real.

Her lips curl into a smile of intense satisfaction. "That was amazing, Gabriel."

"Yeah, it was." I finally realize she's still bound. "Shit, let me untie you."

I release her bindings and drop onto the bed beside her.

Sarah snuggles up to me, her head on my chest and her arm draped across my torso. She traces little circles on my skin with her fingertips. "I've never felt this good before."

"Me either. Damn, that was…" I can't figure out how to end that sentence. No words feel right.

"What we did in the woods was incredible," she says. "But this was even better."

"Yeah, it was." I slip an arm around her. "Can I tell you something?"

"Of course. You can tell me anything, and I won't repeat it to anyone else."

"I know that." While I caress her hair, I feel more relaxed than I have in years, maybe ever. "The way I've been with you, it's nothing like the way I was before the Echo. And you are the only woman I've been with since then."

She lifts her head to look at me, though she keeps her chin on my chest. "Really? I haven't been with anyone either. Just you. Not sure if I liked this kind of sex before the apocalypse since I have amnesia."

"I can tell you unequivocally that I've never been like this with any other woman." I hesitate because I might be kind of worried about what she'll think of me if I confess. But she needs to know the truth. "I've been celibate since the apocalypse. But even before that, I was never great with the ladies. I had girlfriends, but nothing serious. When I fucked a woman, it was pretty basic, boring sex."

"You could never be boring."

Can't help chuckling. "Thanks, but you didn't know me then. My years in the Echo changed me. Pre-apocalypse, I was a computer programmer—a geek."

"I know that already."

"But I don't feel like the geek I was back then, not anymore. I've changed since the Echo."

"Everyone has. Besides, geeks can be hot."

"How would you know? You don't remember what geeks are like."

She folds her arms on my chest and gazes into my eyes. "I don't care what you were like before. I would've liked you then too, and you can't convince me otherwise."

"Okay, fine, have your way. I was a hot geek."

"That's more like it." She kisses my chest. "Should we get dressed and…do something? You know, something useful."

I close my hand over her ass cheek. "I happen to think sex with you is very useful."

"But we need to understand how the Brain—"

"Yeah, yeah, I know." I sigh with no small measure of sarcasm. "You just can't let me enjoy the afterglow, can you?"

"Sorry." She rests her head on my chest again. "Let's enjoy the afterglow for a while. Time is frozen right now, anyway, so we can do whatever we want."

I wrap my arms around her. "Let's just lie here, then."

Though I know we can't lounge in bed forever, we can take a few minutes to revel in the afterglow. Her body feels warm and soft, and the scent of sex wafts around us. I love the way her breasts are mounded against me, her hair tickles my cheek, and her fingers tease my skin. I've never experienced relaxation like this, and I doubt I ever will again—unless I have Sarah with me. I barely know her, yet I feel like I belong with her.

Nobody can deny anymore that fate exists. The Echo taught us all that the unbelievable can be true.

Are Sarah and I destined to become the two halves of the Brain? I don't even know what that means. We need to find out before we commit to something that monumental. Grant and Erin have become the Heart and Lifeblood, but I don't understand what that means either. When I mention that to Sarah, she props her chin on her folded hands to look at me.

"It means they help keep the Echo in balance," she says. "This world was having seizures, of a sort, before Erin and Grant came to the stronghold."

"Yeah, but what did they actually do?"

"If you're expecting a nuts-and-bolts explanation, no one can give you that. We're talking about magics here."

"Right. But I need to understand what the Brain is before I can sign on for becoming one hemisphere of it."

She sits up and shakes her head. "Honestly, you lived in the Echo for three years. How can you still be skeptical about magics? They exist. We can't explain how or why they work, but we do what feels right to fix any problems."

"You mean problems in the Echo."

"Or on Earth. The two worlds are intertwined, Gabriel."

This conversation is not clearing up the issue for me, not at all. "Living in the Echo didn't give me any insight into how this world works. And it definitely didn't give me knowledge of how magic works."

"You're still trying to squeeze the supernatural into a box designed for the mundane."

"I have no idea what that means."

"Until you can accept that magic exists and you will never understand it, I don't see how we can save the worlds."

CHAPTER TWELVE

Sarah

OW CAN I CONVINCE A STUBBORN MAN TO ACCEPT THAT HE WILL never understand the supernatural? I get that before the apocalypse Gabriel led a life built on logic. But he lived in the Echo for three years. He must have seen all sorts of things he couldn't explain or understand. Yet he refuses to accept that we are the two halves of the Echo's Brain, the only people who might have a chance to change the fate of both worlds.

I don't know how that will work. But I'm willing to accept the unknown. That's the difference between me and Gabriel. We forged a bond when we had sex, both times. But he still won't accept that it meant more than really hot orgasms.

Gabriel slides off the bed and starts hunting for his clothes.

I watch him, only in part so I can admire his body.

Once he's pulled on his pants, he pauses to glower at me. "Why are you staring? Get dressed."

Wonderful. We're back to grumpy Gabriel.

Sex with me must've knocked him off kilter. It threw me for a loop too. Our quickie in the woods had stunned me, but our little bondage experience in this bed had shown me things about myself I never knew. Like that I enjoy being tied up. And I love it when he gets bossy in bed.

Bossy the rest of time? No, I'm not crazy about that.

Time to make him talk. "Did you have a family before the apocalypse? Friends? Anything like that?"

He just pulled on his shirt, and now he flashes me a scowl. "What difference does that make?"

"I'd like to know. Please."

Gabriel grabs his socks and boots and drops onto the bed. "I was alone. Happy now?"

"No, of course that doesn't make me happy. What happened to your parents?"

He shrugs while pulling on his socks. "Never met them. I was an orphan, tossed around to various foster homes."

"Oh, Gabriel—"

"Don't do that. Don't pity me."

I waddle across the bed and wrap my arms around him. "I would never pity you. But I feel for you, Gabriel, for the boy who never had a family. It's no wonder you have trouble connecting with other people."

"What makes you think that?"

"You said yourself that you never got serious about anyone you dated. Did you have friends?"

"Only the people I knew at work. We weren't particularly close."

I lay my cheek on his shoulder. "You aren't alone anymore. You have everyone at Sanctuary—and you have me."

"Because you think I'm the other half of the Brain."

"No." I climb onto his lap while keeping my arms around him. "I'm with you because I like you, Gabriel. You're more than just a guy I had sex with twice."

He grunts.

I think that means he's embarrassed. "It's true. No amount of grumpy behavior will make me change my mind about you."

"What if I growl at you?"

"Nope. That won't work either." I wriggle my bottom on his lap, which makes him wince faintly. "I let you tie me up and order me not to come. How can you think I don't like and trust you?"

He falls back onto the bed and shuts his eyes, leaving me still crouched on his lap. "You're impossible."

"Thank you. I take that as a compliment."

Gabriel peeks at me through one half-closed lid. "You're weird."

I grin. "And I take that as a compliment too. I never realized how spunky and naughty I could be until I met you. But I love it."

He opens both eyes and smirks. "You are a very naughty girl, and I'd love to explore that some more. But I think you'd better get dressed. We need to…figure things out."

"You mean the Brain thing."

"Can we stop calling it that? Makes me feel like I'm Frankenstein's monster."

I pat his chest. "And I'm the monster's bride."

"Uh-huh." He sits up, throws his arms around me, and stands up. Then he sets me on my feet. "You really need to get dressed. Don't know how much longer I can look at your naked body without fucking you again."

Yeah, that would be a shame. I know I shouldn't want to do that again, since we have problems to deal with, but I wish we could have sex one more time. What we've done makes me wonder if I loved sex this much before the apocalypse, or if living under the constant threat of death and destruction has changed me. Does it really matter what I was like before? I want to stay the person I am now. If I regain my memories, maybe I won't like what I learn about myself.

Gabriel likes me this way, that's for sure.

Once I'm dressed, we head back out into the hall. Gabriel suggests we should look for a way out of this place, in case Aldith doesn't come back. I can't imagine she would just abandon us here, but we haven't seen or heard from her since she told us to spend time together. If Gabriel wants to search for an exit, I'll go along with it.

We've just reached the end of the hall, but the elevator door is gone.

Oh, great. We're trapped. I should feel scared by that fact, shouldn't I? But I don't. That's kind of weird. I feel safe, not cornered, and I don't really mind if we stay here for days or weeks, even months. I don't understand my reaction. I almost feel like...

"Someone is using magic on us," Gabriel says. "Can't you sense it? Suddenly, I want to take you into the nearest bedroom and make you scream again."

"Yeah, I do feel it. Not sure what's going on."

Gabriel opens his mouth, but the words we hear are not his.

"The Brain wants you to cement your bond in a deeper way. You won't be permitted to leave until you've done that."

We both spin around to face Aldith. She stands there with her hands clasped in front of her, seeming quite relaxed.

"You can't be suggesting we should have sex again," Gabriel says. "Come on, orgasms aren't the engine running the apocalypse."

"How do you know?" Aldith asks. "Sexual intercourse has powered several important changes in the Echo."

"Like what?"

She bows her head, and I swear she's blushing a little. "You must ask your friends. It's not my place to reveal such information."

"But you know about it. Are you a voyeur? Did you watch me and Sarah getting it on?"

"I do not watch. But it was fairly obvious afterward what transpired in the stronghold."

Gabriel starts to speak, but I can tell he's about to get grumpy again.

So I speak first. "Aldith, what do you mean that we won't be able to leave until we cement our bond? We, um, already did that."

I couldn't help the dopey little laugh that came out of me when I said that. Yeah, I feel very awkward about discussing sex with a woman I barely know who also happens to be an Echo creature.

Aldith shrugs. "I relay the information, nothing more. That's all I can tell you."

She vanishes.

My body wants me to do exactly what Aldith suggested and have bone-melting, earth-shattering sex with Gabriel again. And again. And again. For as long as it takes to finish cementing our bond. But the idea that the Echo's Brain wants us to do that… Yeah, it's beyond disturbing.

"What should we do?" I ask.

Gabriel scratches the back of his neck. "Keep looking for a way out. Screw the damn Brain. I choose when I do things, not some supernatural computer system."

"You think the Brain is a computer?"

"No idea. But it can't be an actual brain, with two hemispheres and blood vessels and neurons and whatever else. It must be more like a computer."

He grabs my hand, leading me back down the hall.

Not sure if a computer brain is less creepy than a real brain. Either way, we're supposed to merge with it or something. Aldith hasn't really explained that part. From what Erin and Grant have said, Aldith simply doesn't have access to all the information that's needed to do the things she informs us we need to do.

Why can't the universe just send me a postcard with all the details printed on it?

Gabriel approaches a door, not the one that leads into the room where we got naked, and throws it open. I see a bed and a couple of chairs. No window.

He shuts the door and moves on to the next one.

We had already searched this floor. But who knows, maybe the Echo decided to change the rooms and one of them includes an exit.

Nope, we don't find anything like that.

Gabriel insists on searching all the rooms three times. Why? Because he's a stubborn, grumpy man who refuses to accept the inevitable. We are trapped in here, until we do whatever the Brain wants us to do. I get that he doesn't like being ordered to do the bidding of a supernatural computer, but I don't see that we have a choice. Gabriel finally gives up and sits down on the floor with his back to the wall.

I pace back and forth in front of him.

What if "cementing" our bond doesn't mean only having sex? There might be another component. Not sure what that would be. Sealing a bond sounds intimate, like something that would involve emotions and trust. I trust Gabriel, but maybe I haven't completely surrendered to the bond between us. Could it be that the Echo's Brain requires us to come to terms with our feelings for each other and accept them?

I met him yesterday. But I already feel closer to him than to anyone in Sanctuary. If I didn't have amnesia, maybe I would find that idea disturbing and slightly insane. But having a giant blank spot in my mind gives me a different perspective. I think. It makes sense, at least to me, that not knowing how I used to feel about anything could make me more open to the idea of bonding with a virtual stranger.

But I know some things about Gabriel. He told me he has no family because he was an orphan, and that he didn't have any real friends.

To bond means to share ourselves with each other. How can I share parts of me with him when I don't even know who I am? Instead of talking to myself about this in my head, I should discuss it with Gabriel.

He'll probably tell me I'm a moron.

But I do it anyway. I sit down beside him and say, "We need to talk about this bond thing."

"It's bullshit. There's nothing else to say."

"Stop that. We need to have a real conversation."

He sighs and leans his head against the wall. "Fine. But it was your idea, so you start the conversation."

"Okay." I resist the impulse to squirm and avoid looking at him. Instead, I turn partway toward him. "We sealed our sexual bond, but there's more to it than that. You saved me from the lightning before you even knew anything about me. You confided in me too. That means something."

"Like what?"

"That maybe we share a bond deeper than lust. You felt protective of me quickly, which makes no logical sense."

He glances at me sideways. "What are you suggesting?"

"That we need to accept our feelings for each other, even though they don't make sense. I think that's what the Brain wants. A real, emotional bond."

"I threatened to assault you on the beach."

"You didn't mean it. I know that. You were scared and doing what I've learned you always do when you're upset. You got grumpy and lashed out."

He grunts.

"And I've also learned that you grunt when you're embarrassed."

Gabriel shakes his head, though it's still leaning against the wall. "You are even more stubborn than I realized."

"And you are even sweeter than I realized."

"Sweet?" His lip curls. "You're insane."

"It's the truth. You are sweet, though you try to hide that fact."

He grunts again.

Well, Allison did tell me that most men don't like to be called "sweet." I'll move on to another topic. "We need to do this bond-sealing thing so we can take control of the Brain. Hopefully, that will give us the power to end the apocalypse. The worst of the devastation might be over, but the Echo keeps throwing things at us. We need to do something before both worlds go nuts."

"You assume they will."

"The Echo already did go nuts, for a while. Erin and Grant stopped it. But now the Brain apparently needs our help. I wonder if it was the Brain that sent the lightning and the Echo creature that kidnapped us."

He swivels his head to look at me. "You never mentioned that possibility before."

"Just occurred to me."

Gabriel studies me for a moment. "That would make sense, I guess."

That's probably the best admission I'll get. He's telling me I'm right without actually saying it.

Of course, I don't know if I am right. Not yet.

He clears his throat. "So, uh, how do we seal our emotional bond?"

"I don't know."

"Of course not." He stands up and offers me his hands. "Come on. We can't do it sitting down."

"How do you know that?"

"Because I just decided it's true." He flaps his hand at me. "Get up, Sarah."

I accept his hand in getting up. "Now what?"

He stares at me. "How should I know? This was your idea."

Of course he expects me to come up with a plan. Well, I think I've got one. I doubt he'll like it, but that's what he gets for making me take charge.

I grasp his hand, then guide him into the bedroom where we'd had sex earlier. "Lie down."

"You said this wouldn't be about sex."

"That's right. But do what I say." I point at the bed. "Lie down, Gabriel. Right now."

I'm really starting to like being bossy, especially when I get to boss him around.

Gabriel lies down on the bed.

And I lie down beside him, rolling onto my side so I'm tucked against him. I lay my head on his chest and slip my hand into his, threading our fingers. "Do you like me?"

"Sure. You're okay."

"Gee, thanks. I got a warm glow all over when you said that."

"I'm a guy. We don't get mushy about this stuff."

"That's the best you can do? Telling me I'm okay?"

He fidgets and screws up his mouth. "I never had a family or friends. You know that."

"Are you saying you don't know how to give affection because you never received it?"

"Uh, yeah, I guess."

I snuggle up to him even more. "I like you, Gabriel, a lot. And I've given up on worrying about the fact that we met yesterday. You make me feel safe and strong and fulfilled. Being with you has changed my life. I'm not just the amnesia girl who needed strangers to give her a name. I'm part of some-thing more, something vital and scary and undeniable."

"What is that something?"

"Us. The two halves of the Brain. But it's more than that too. If you can stop fighting it, I think we could become one with each other and the Brain."

He smirks. "Are you suggesting we should merge bodies, like in some goofy movie?"

"No, I'm suggesting we could merge spiritually and emotionally. Dax and Allison have a supernatural bond. So do Erin and Grant. It's not un-precedented."

"Yeah, you keep telling me about your friends. But I don't know if I can submit to something like that."

He is an alpha-male type. I shouldn't expect him to accept my idea im-mediately. Submission is probably the last thing he wants to do, especially if it means submitting to me. But I let him take control of my body, willingly. He just needs a little more time to get used to the idea.

"Please, Gabriel," I say. "Do this for me."

Chapter Thirteen

Gabriel

SARAH WANTS ME TO BECOME SUBMISSIVE, AT LEAST WHEN IT CONcerns what the Echo's Brain wants. After living in this world for years, I've forgotten how to be anything except hard and tough and the master of my own destiny. I don't even like that the Echo threw me into this world, since I had no choice in that. As a normal guy who was a computer programmer, I didn't have much autonomy. My bosses told me what to do.

But the Echo gave me a kind of freedom I'd never imagined I could have. That might sound weird, since the apocalypse destroyed two worlds, but it's true. Could Sarah ever understand that?

She taps my lips with her fingertip. "I can see that you're mulling over what I've said. You can tell me anything. I won't get mad or make fun of you."

I know that. But I can't help feeling uncomfortable with what she wants me to do. Sarah makes me feel things that I don't understand. Mostly good things. The strength of those feelings disturbs me. But I agreed to try this bonding thing, so I need to tell her all of that. *Damn.* I'd rather sit down in a fire ant mound. But I will do it, for her.

So I blow out a breath and tell her. "I have these, ah, feelings for you. Not sure what it means. When we had sex, I felt it more strongly, but I've been experiencing these feelings more and more often since the moment we met."

"I have the same kind of feelings."

"But you don't fight them, do you? That's the difference between us."

She pushes up on one elbow to gaze down at me. "Our differences can become our strength. Allison—"

"Can we please stop talking about your friends? I get that they all have supernatural bonds, but I'm not ready for that yet."

"The Echo needs us to be ready. Right now."

"Why? Everything seems relatively stable. I'd say there's no rush."

She lifts her brows. "So, you want to stay trapped inside the stronghold forever?"

If we never leave this place, I can fuck her over and over without anything interfering. But I know that's not plausible. I'd make her sore, for sure.

"Time is frozen inside the stronghold," she says. "But the rest of the Echo and the Earth might not be faring so well. We should check that out."

"Great idea. Let's order Aldith to let us out of here."

Sarah drops her head and moans. "Honestly, Gabriel, that's not helpful. We can't leave until the Echo lets us, and it wants us to seal our emotional bond. You're the one holding things up with your stubbornness."

"I admitted I like you and have strong feelings for you. What more do you want?"

The most beautiful woman I've ever seen sits up, growls, and smacks my chest—hard. "Do I need to tie you up to make you comply?"

She wants to dominate me? Not sure how I feel about that. I trust her, so maybe it wouldn't be a horrible thing. But she was probably joking. I should make sure, though.

"Are you seriously suggesting that you want to dominate me?" I ask. "Because, no offense, but you aren't strong enough to do that. I would kick your ass in three seconds flat."

"Kick my ass?" She wags a finger at me. "That's not the way to cement a bond, Gabriel. But yes, I think you need to experience being submissive, so you can give yourself over to our deep, supernatural connection."

A strange tingle of excitement raises the hairs on my arms and at my nape. Maybe her suggestion does arouse me, but I know I can't do what she wants. Not yet. And I need to explain to her why that is.

"I'm sorry, Sarah," I tell her. "I just can't do that, not yet. It isn't because I don't want to. But you have no idea what my life was like inside the Echo for all those years. Showing weakness will get you killed. I got used to always acting like an asshole because anything less would be a cue for the Echo creatures—the bad ones—to attack."

She leans over and kisses me, though it's only the barest brush of her lips on mine. "I understand that. And maybe you don't need to fully give in to the Echo's Brain. It might be enough right now for you to accept that we have a powerful connection. Do you think you can do that?"

"I can try." Though I'd love to say I would do anything for her, I won't lie. When it comes to protecting her at any cost, I'll do that without hesitation. But the touchy-feely stuff is a lot harder for me to embrace.

"Trying is a good start."

"How do I do that?"

She lies down beside me again and drapes half her body over me. "Accepting intimacy is phase one."

"How many phases are there?"

"As many as you need."

I touch my finger to the tip of her nose. "Who came up with these phases?"

She smiles brightly. "Me."

"Uh-huh. I figured as much." I lay my arms on the mattress and take a deep breath, exhaling it slowly to relax my body. "I'm ready. Tell me what to do."

"Touch me, Gabriel."

"I thought this wasn't about sex."

She rolls her eyes. "Do you think 'touching' automatically means the sexual kind? I'm talking about intimacy."

"You'll need to help me out here. We seem to have different ideas about what 'touching' and 'intimacy' mean."

"Right. You're a rough-and-tough guy, and I'm giving you girlie explanations."

She genuinely wants to help me understand and experience intimacy. Nobody has ever cared so much about my emotional well-being. I could fall for this girl, I know it. Maybe I've already started that process. After all, I'm letting her boss me around. That must be a sign of…something.

The fact that I can't even think the words probably isn't a good sign.

"You're tensing up again," Sarah says. "Let me help you with that."

"How?"

She smiles with her lips sealed as she shimmies on top of me, getting herself situated on my lap. I'm still lying down, but she sits on my thighs with her hands resting on my lower belly. When I open my mouth, she wags a finger at me and shakes her head. I guess this must be the submission part of our bizarre ritual. She unbuttons my shirt, and her tongue pokes out between her lips as she focuses on the task. It's the cutest, sexiest thing I've ever seen. Then she spreads her palms on my chest and begins skating them around my torso in slow circles, pressing a little harder with every revolution until she's massaging my muscles. I can't help relaxing into her ministrations. I also can't stop myself from watching her fingers as they work my muscles. My dick starts to thicken, but she doesn't seem to care.

Sarah moves her hands up to my shoulders, pushing my shirt out of the way, and digs her fingers into my flesh to loosen up my tight muscles.

Damn, this feels good.

My eyes drift half-closed, but I don't want them to close all the way. I need to see everything she does and the look on her face while she does it.

The sexy angel unhooks the button on my pants and drags the zipper down.

"Uh, that's not going to relax me," I say. "It'll have the opposite effect. You're getting me turned on."

She rubs the hollows of my hips with her thumbs.

A deep groan resonates in my chest, and I swear all the blood in my body is flooding into my dick.

"You want to fuck me, don't you?" she says. "Tell me why you want that."

"Because you're getting me hot. I thought this little massage thing was supposed to relax me and help me accept intimacy. You told me it wasn't about sex."

"That's right, it's not. I haven't touched your dick or your balls."

A laugh snorts out of me. "Your criteria for not-erotic massage is that you haven't touched my dick or my balls? You are one weird chick."

"Ha-ha." She slides her hands up my belly. "Tell me why you want to fuck me, Gabriel."

"I already told you, and it's obvious, anyway."

Have I started to growl again? I didn't mean to do that. But the more she touches me, the more I need to flip us over so I can tie her to the bed rails and take her again, while she's at my mercy and can't hurt me.

"Come on, Gabriel. Be honest with me. You want to take control again because…"

She wants me to say it, but I won't. I can't. No matter how many times I've tried to convince myself the past doesn't matter, it still does and it always will. Sarah refuses to see that. I push her off me and slide down to the foot of the bed. My feet touch the floor, but I can't move any farther.

She crawls toward me on her knees, halting right beside me, though she doesn't touch me. When she speaks, her voice is hushed and filled with empathy. "Please let me in, Gabriel. I want to help you."

"It's too late."

Memories flash through my mind, vivid and sharp and inescapable. Screams. The crunching of bones. Anguished pleas for mercy. Children running. Monsters pouring out of the newly formed entrance to the Echo, tearing people apart, feasting on their flesh and blood.

I suddenly can't breathe. My chest feels like ten cement blocks have fallen onto it, and I'm starting to hyperventilate. I can't let Sarah see this. I need to get out of here before—

Her arms come around me. She murmurs things that aren't words, just soothing sounds.

And the panic subsides. I shut my eyes, take in slow, deep breaths, and wait it out. That simple act of putting her arms around me has erased the memories. Well, not erased. I will never forget what I saw that day. But her arms around me and the soothing sounds she makes have pulled me out of the past and back into the present.

"What was that?" she whispers. "A flashback?"

"Yeah. How did you know?"

"Because I've seen it before, with people who found Sanctuary. Do you have nightmares too?"

"Not as often as I used to."

She brushes the backs of her fingers over my cheek. "I can't imagine what you went through, and I wish I could erase all of that for you. If you want to tell me about it, I can handle whatever it is."

I believe she can. Sarah might've seemed like an amnesiac with no backbone, but I know now that she's a fighter. Should I tell her everything? If I do, maybe she will finally realize I'm not the kind of man she needs.

"On the day the alchemy of worlds began," I say, "I was walking to work. It was a beautiful summer's day in Oklahoma City, sunny and warm. I'd just passed a park where kids were playing catch, when that eerie music started up and everyone froze. The music was beautiful and terrifying, mesmerizing too, and a force beyond our control compelled us to walk to a specific spot in the city."

"Quite a few people in Sanctuary experienced the music too. Not everyone heard it on that day, though."

"I heard it, and that music always echoes in my dreams."

Sarah hugs me a little tighter, but she doesn't speak.

"When the creatures poured out of the Echo," I say, "I tried to save whoever I could. Those monsters went after the kids first. I tried to help, but I couldn't save even one of them. Then I got sucked into the Echo, and I couldn't save anyone anymore."

"You tried. That's what counts."

"No, it's not," I snarl. "Trying isn't enough. The parents of those kids don't care that I tried. It's bullshit. But the parents are probably dead too."

I set my elbows on my thighs and drop my head into my hands. My eyes sting. I'm not about to cry, no way. I never do that, not even when I watched those children being torn apart and couldn't do a thing to stop it. But when I suck in a sharp breath, it's ragged, which implies that I'm getting choked up. That's bullshit.

Sarah combs her fingers through my hair, her touch gentle and more soothing than seems possible. How she always knows what to do and say, I have no idea. She just knows.

"I apologize for interrupting, but I thought you both would want to know immediately."

The sound of Aldith's voice makes me snap upright. The pretty Echo creature stands there with her hands clasped in front of her, the way she always does, and her slightly pinched expression suggests she thinks she's interrupted an intimate moment.

Well, I guess she has. I just shared the worst experiences of my life with Sarah and almost started to cry. At least Aldith couldn't see that. I hope.

Sarah claims my hand, lacing our fingers. "What is it, Aldith?"

"The Brain has released you and Gabriel. Your connection has been solidified."

"But we didn't do anything," I say. "How did we solidify our connection?"

Aldith shrugs. "That is not for me to say. The Brain has received the information it requires, but you still need to join with the Brain to stop the Echo from falling apart."

"Who cares if it falls apart?"

"The Earth will be destroyed too if that happens. Both worlds will die."

"I thought the whole point of this was to take control of the Brain so we can destroy the Echo."

Sarah leans in to whisper in my ear, "She is an Echo creature. You're suggesting we want her to die."

Oh, shit. I hadn't considered how Aldith might take what I said. Thinking before I speak has never been one of my virtues. Not sure I have any virtues at all.

"I'm sorry, Aldith," I say. "Neither of us wants good people like you to die. Maybe we can take you and any other good Echo beings to Earth with us."

Aldith smiles just a little. "I was not offended, Gabriel. I was created for the sole purpose of protecting the stronghold, and I never expected to leave this place."

"Have you ever left it? Even for a few minutes?"

She lowers her head. "No. I have never seen the world of the Echo or the Earth."

I study her for a moment, trying to decide whether I trust her. After thirty seconds at most, I realize the truth. I do trust Aldith, and I've learned to listen to my intuition about Echo creatures.

Rising, I tug on Sarah's hand to encourage her to stand up too. "Aldith, when we leave the Echo for good, you are coming with us."

Her lips tick up a little more at the corners, and her eyes brighten. "You would do that for me?"

"Yeah, sure. You help people, you don't hurt them. Our friends Grant and Erin vouched for you, and we've gotten to know enough about you that Sarah and I feel the same way."

Maybe I should've asked Sarah if she agrees with me about that, but I somehow know she does.

"That's right," Sarah says. "We would never leave you here alone when the end comes."

I glance at Sarah. "What do we do now? If we already made the Brain happy, I assume our next move is to find a way to destroy the Echo."

"Not necessarily. We need more information."

"How do we get that?"

She nudges me with her elbow. "We have Sefton's journal, remember?"

"Oh, yeah. I forgot." My gaze lands on our backpacks on the floor by the doorway. "Should we study it here? Or go back to Sanctuary?"

"How could we get back there? Neither of us has Echo power."

"Jarek helped me get back to Earth."

"He cannot do that again," Aldith says. "The issues with the Brain have caused problems with the doorways to the Echo as well. Jarek may escort you to and from the stronghold, but he can no longer open the doorway for you."

Chapter Fourteen

Sarah

"WELL, DAMN," GABRIEL SAYS. "I REALLY WANTED TO GET OUT OF HERE. No offense, Aldith, but the Echo isn't the most relaxing place for a vacation. It doesn't even have a good beach or a hot club."

Gabriel is reverting to sarcasm. I've come to realize that's his coping mechanism when things get bad or weird. Reliving his memories of the day the alchemy of worlds began must have made him antsy about staying here. The Echo has previously had "conniptions," as Grant and Erin call them. What if that happens again? We would be trapped here and vulnerable to every kind of horror the Echo can produce.

"Can anyone get into or out of the Echo right now?" Gabriel asks Aldith. "Or are we all stuck here?"

"Only the Brain has the power to reopen the doorways."

Someone had us brought here, and I have a feeling they knew we wouldn't be able to leave. Was it the Echo flier? He abducted us, but then flew away.

"You are wrong, by the way," Aldith says. "You both possess the Echo power. The Brain would not need you otherwise."

We have Echo power, and the Brain needs us. Wow, that's crazy to even think about.

Gabriel rests his hands on his hips and stares down at the carpeting. "A smarter man would know exactly what to do. But I'm no genius, mad or otherwise. You've got the wrong guy."

Aldith tips her head to the side. "You do not believe me, but you will soon."

"We need to find the creature that brought us here," I say. "If we have Echo power, maybe we can do that. Bring him to us."

"You're suggesting we should summon a dangerous creature into the stronghold."

"That's right. But we would contain it. Maybe in one of the rooms that has no windows."

He watches me for a moment, as if he's trying to gauge how serious I am about this plan. I think he knows me well enough by now to realize I'm completely serious about it. Finally, he exhales a big breath. "Fine, let's try that."

Aldith leads us across the hall to a small room that has no windows. Gabriel and I discuss how to make the room safer for us, and that results in removing all the furniture except the bed, which is too big to move. I doubt it would fit through the door.

"Would you like me to assist you?" Aldith asks. "I helped Grant and Erin achieve the necessary state of oneness to access their shared Echo power."

"Sure, help us," I say. "We'd be grateful for your advice."

"Join your hands, one atop the other."

We do that, and Aldith hovers her hand over ours. The air seems to thicken, while invisible energy crackles in the air around us. I can't see it, but I feel that energy on my skin. Glittering light begins to emanate from our hands, and even when Aldith pulls her palm away, the energy continues to build and spread out. My hair stands up, like static electricity has affected it.

Gabriel's eyes have a faint green glow.

Do my eyes look that way too? I don't have time to think about that, because the energy has begun to pulse inside my body. It's not unpleasant. The sensation reminds me of a heartbeat, though it's not my heart causing it. Soon, the rhythm of the magics aligns with the thumping of my heart, and I begin to feel another heartbeat joining mine, merging until I no longer feel it as a separate beat, but simply another layer melding with me.

Gabriel and I are tuned in to each other. I know that, but I could never explain how or why it happened.

An Echo creature appears beside us. Its wings were retracted behind its back when it arrived, but now the beast flutters his wings in a slightly threatening gesture.

"Why have you brought me here?" he asks. Yeah, it's obvious this is a male creature. He's not wearing any clothes, which means I can see his equipment.

"You kidnapped us from Earth," Gabriel says. "I want to know why."

The creature chuckles. "Because the Brain wanted you, of course."

My intuition has kicked into high gear, and I'm getting an idea about what might be going on. "Did you voluntarily do what the Brain said? Or did you have no choice?"

The Echo flier scowls at me. "I choose my own path."

"Okay, then why did you kidnap us? You said it was because the Brain wanted us, but that doesn't explain why you did it. What did you get out of the deal?"

"There was no deal. The Brain commanded, and I—" He scowls again. "No more talking to you."

He spreads his wings wide, forcing us to back away. Then he tries to kick the door open, but he can't do it. After multiple kicks and punches, he's still trapped in this room with us.

The Echo flier throws his head back and roars.

"Not the master of your own destiny, after all," I say. "So answer our question. Why did you kidnap us?"

Our winged friend stands there fuming for a minute or two, then folds his wings and slumps his shoulders. "I had no choice. The Brain command-ed, and I had to obey. I know nothing else. Not why it wanted you, or what it planned to do with you."

Gabriel and I exchange glances, and I know we agree about what to do next.

We send the Echo flier back to where he'd come from, though we have no conscious knowledge of where that might be. We just know we sent him there.

The Echo creature didn't instigate our abduction. That leaves me with another question.

I face Aldith. "How can the Brain command an Echo creature? It's not a sentient being, is it?"

"No, but we are talking about supernatural forces."

Right. I shouldn't expect magic to make logical sense. I don't recall what the world was like before the apocalypse, but I'm pretty sure magic didn't rule the Earth. I miss those days, even though I can't remember them.

Boom.

The entire stronghold shudders, and I stumble into Gabriel. He slings his arms around me.

Boom. Another explosion detonates, shaking the stronghold.

We all race into the other bedroom to peer out the picture windows. Our gazes veer downward, to the ground far below us. Buildings look like toys, but the bolts of lightning slamming into the earth seem all too real. Is the Brain trying to capture us again? I don't see how lightning beneath us will do any-thing except destroy the ground. We're too far away for it to harm us.

But the Brain doesn't want to hurt us. It must not, right? Why else would it try so hard to capture us and stop pounding the worlds once we came to the stronghold? What is it after now? We're here, where it wanted us.

Did the Brain actually stop pounding Earth once we left?

"I don't understand," I say. "Why is the Brain causing mayhem down there? We did what it wanted. We came to the stronghold and sealed our bond."

Gabriel hugs me to his side. "The Brain doesn't have its hemispheres, right? It's basically an empty vessel struggling to fulfill its purpose."

"I guess so. But how can we stop it from destroying both worlds before we have the chance to figure out what we're supposed to do?"

"The Brain can't think on its own. That's the way I see it." He hugs me a little tighter as more lightning bolts strike the ground, sending plumes of dust and debris high into the atmosphere. "It needs to be told what to do. That means we need to give it instructions."

"How? I don't think we're ready to join with the Brain, or whatever we're supposed to do."

"I agree. But we can sort of give it a gift to make it happy for a while."

Though I open my mouth to complain about what he said, I stop short of actually speaking. Maybe he's right. We used our Echo power to summon that flying beast. Why can't we magically send the Brain a gift? A power boost to keep it going while we sort out the details. We need to know a lot more before we take the plunge and take command of the Brain.

Another boom detonates out there, but it sounds much closer.

We peer out the windows again—and my heart thuds.

Two fireballs are streaking down from the highest levels of the atmosphere to rain their fire and destruction down on the land below. One fireball has already struck, setting a large building ablaze and destroying most of the structure. The two fireballs streaking toward the ground seem much bigger.

No time to talk about it. I know Gabriel will agree with my idea, and I feel the energy of our Echo power already surging between us. I grab his hand while focusing on the lightning and fireballs below us, and the magics we share grow warmer and stronger, tingling through me more powerfully than before. Gabriel grips my hand even more tightly. The magics expand and strengthen, invisible yet palpable, a living energy that heeds our bidding.

The two remaining fireballs are snuffed out.

Smoke billows up from the destroyed structures on the ground, but at least we stopped most of the fireballs. The lightning seems to have disappeared too.

I look at Gabriel, and he looks at me. His grim smile probably mirrors mine. Yes, we're glad we circumvented the devastation. But that was only a stopgap measure. Unless we can take control of the Echo's Brain, things could get much, much worse in both worlds.

"We should check on our friends in Sanctuary," I say. "And see what's going on elsewhere on Earth too."

"How? We can't get out of the Echo."

"I think we can. We just stopped fireballs and lightning, after all."

Gabriel gazes out the windows, his grim smile now just a grim expression with no hint of anything resembling satisfaction, despite the fact we saved potentially innocent beings from suffering a terrible death. But I think I understand now why he doesn't seem happy that we might have the power to escape the Echo. I know we'll probably need to come back to fix the Brain, but then we can go home, I assume. Gabriel spent years in this world. He doesn't know how to fit in with normal people on Earth anymore. And he feels like he failed, because he couldn't save his Echo friends.

I grip his hand with both of mine. "You deserve to go home, Gabriel. You don't belong in the Echo anymore."

He tries to pull his hand away, but I hold on. "You're being stupidly stubborn. I am not a hero, or even a good man. I did whatever it took to survive here, and I can barely remember what my life was like before the apocalypse."

"And I don't remember it at all. Don't see me moping and acting grumpy."

"You're different."

I raise my brows. "Because I'm a girl?"

"No. Because you're an angel."

Laughter splutters out of me, though I tried to squelch it. "Angel? I had hot-and-sweaty dirty sex with you—twice."

"I corrupted you."

"Get over yourself, Gabriel. You don't intimidate me, which means I do what I want because I want it. Only I control my desires."

He stares out the window, and his voice becomes flat. "But we're both planning to hand over our free will to something we don't understand and have never seen."

"We'll take control of the Brain, not the other way around."

"You don't know what will happen. Neither do I. Even Aldith doesn't know."

I glance around the room. "Where is Aldith, anyway? She was here a few minutes ago."

"That chick loves to mysteriously disappear."

"Yeah, she has the mystery thing down pat." I lean closer to the windows and lay my palms on the cool glass. "There must be a way to get out of the Echo. Let's ask Jarek to take us to the nearest gateway. Then we can test our powers and see if we can open that door."

"Okay."

For several seconds, I can't move or speak. Did he just agree to my plan? With no growling? No grunting? Yeah, he did just do that.

I open the biggest window and lean over even more. "Jarek! We need you, Jarek!"

Nothing happens. We just stand here waiting and listening.

"Maybe he didn't hear you," Gabriel says. "Let me try."

He thrusts half his body out the window and hollers, "Jarek! Get your ass up here, buddy."

He does shout much louder than I do. Men have bigger lungs, right? So that explains it.

I notice a dark shape rising through the clouds, barreling closer and closer and closer.

Gabriel pulls away from the window, then slings an arm around my waist to drag me away too. "Better not get too close. He might not see you until it's too late."

A large metal-and-flesh hand clamps onto the windowsill, then another identical hand clamps onto the other end of the sill. A grinding noise ensues, as Jarek hauls himself up to the level of the window.

I grin and wave at him. "It's nice to see you again, Jarek. Thank you for coming so quickly."

He nods, and his lips curve into the barest approximation of a smile.

"Can you give us a lift?" I ask. "We need to get to the gateway of the Echo."

He shakes his head.

"Are you saying you won't take us there?" I ask. "Or that you know the gateway is closed and won't open again?"

Jarek doesn't respond.

"He can only answer yes or no questions," Gabriel says. "You made it too complicated."

"Oh, right. I forgot."

"Let me try." Gabriel moves closer to the window. "We know the gateway is sealed. But will you take us there anyway?"

Jarek nods.

"Thanks, buddy. We appreciate it."

The golem stretches out one hand toward us, holding it palm up. His other arm, the one still clamped onto the windowsill, has begun to tremble faintly. Must be really hard to maintain a position like that. Gabriel climbs onto Jarek's open hand first, then helps me up.

Aldith reappears to wave goodbye as Jarek releases his hold on the window.

We sail downward, rushing through the clouds, with the ground zooming ever closer. Just when I think we're about to get creamed, Jarek's massive feet whump down with surprising gentleness. Then he starts striding across the barren landscape, heading back toward the Capital City. Since I have nothing else to do, I take stock of the damage caused by the lightning and fireballs. Scorched earth surrounds the crater where the first fireball struck. The other two never made it to the ground. The lightning had slashed into the ground with electric force, creating glass-encased tunnels.

Gradually, I begin to see signs of civilization ahead of us. Well, I'm using the word civilization loosely. The apocalypse decimated the Echo too, and according to Grant and Erin, not many living things have remained in the Capital City. I got only a glimpse of that metropolis when the Echo flier grabbed me and Gabriel, whisking us away.

Jarek lumbers past the edge of the city, which has a sharp line of demarcation, unlike any city in the normal world. No suburbs, no smattering of shops that peters out the further you go from the skyscrapers. Yeah, I can remember what cities on Earth look like. It's my memories of my own life and the apocalypse that vanished. Jarek speeds up his pace as we head down a four-lane street, and I get my first glimpse of the gateway to the Echo. The sight makes my skin crawl and my mouth go dry.

The black disk in the sky swirls round and round, releasing slithering fingers of darkness that dissipate into smoke-like wisps. The gateway generates no sound, but the gravity of it vibrates in my bones.

Now it's time to find out if the Echo will let us leave—or if it will hold us hostage.

CHAPTER FIFTEEN

Gabriel

AS I GAZE UP AT THE GATEWAY, MY MEMORIES REWIND TO THAT DAY when the sky split apart and the world as we knew it ended. The apocalypse began in the cities with eerie, terrifyingly beautiful music taking over the world, serving as the precursor to the devastation that followed. The spinning tendrils of magics that lashed out from the gateway's center heralded the coming of creatures disgorged from the Echo to wreak havoc.

Today, I see only the placidly swirling disk of darkness.

Despite my mind wanting to pull me into the past to relive my personal journey into the apocalypse, I can't let myself sink into that oblivion. We have too much to do, and no idea how to do it.

Sarah gapes at the gateway like she's never seen it before. We had both gone through the gateway earlier, but it happened so fast that I doubt she got a good look at it. Now we both have no choice but to watch as we draw ever nearer to the disk-shaped abyss that swallows a large quadrant of the sky. Even the damage to the city around us can't tear our focus away from the gateway.

Jarek halts below the black disk, which I can now see lies at his head level. The gateway consumes such a large part of the sky that it's hardly surprising the golem can reach it. When he raises his hand to his chin level, Sarah and I find ourselves staring straight into the roiling blackness of the gateway. Jarek extends his hand toward the opening.

And hits an invisible barrier.

The jolt surprises Jarek, who instinctively jerks his hand away. The sudden movement sends me and Sarah tumbling off the golem's palm, sailing down toward the street far below us. She screams and flails as if to grab on to me. I seize her forearm but lose my grip.

And the ground rushes toward us.

Jarek scoops us up just before we would've hit the ground. We both lie sprawled on the golem's palm, somewhat dazed by our narrow escape from becoming human pancakes. My gaze lands on the gateway, but it's not simply spinning anymore. No, it now roils and rumbles, pulsating with a rhythm that I can feel but not hear.

We just ticked off the Echo.

But we aren't done yet.

I sit up, then cautiously rise to my knees. Once I determine I'm not going to fall off Jarek's palm, I grab Sarah's hands to help her stand too. "We need to tap into our Echo power so we can force the gateway to open."

She nods, though she's biting her lip.

I don't blame her for feeling off kilter. The Echo slammed the door in our faces, and now we plan to kick it in. I clasp Sarah's hands as we face each other, our gazes bound, and summon the magics. The power sizzles between us, hot and liquid, slipping into every cell in our bodies. I concentrate on thoughts of the Echo, of kicking that door open so we can jump through it.

A blast of energy fires into the gateway and bounces right back at us. I fly off Jarek's palm to the left, but Sarah flies off to the right. I tumble toward the pavement below us, face up, and can do nothing but watch as Jarek bends his knees and thrusts out both hands to catch us. We wind up crumpled on separate palms, but Jarek tips one hand over to dump me onto his hand beside Sarah.

Breathing hard, I just lie here recovering from my second brush with pancake-hood. "That worked out well."

"I hope that's a joke." Sarah sounds breathless too. "We failed miserably."

"Because the Echo wouldn't let us out. I'm guessing that means nobody else can get in either."

"That would make sense." She rolls onto her side to look at me. "If the Brain wants our cooperation, why won't it let us leave? We need help from our friends."

"Seems like we aren't allowed to get help. We have to do this on our own."

"What now?"

I sit up and stare at the gateway, with its whirling blackness and slithering tongues of energy. What does the Brain want? Not like we can ask it, since the thing isn't a living being. It's a collection of magics, I assume. Even Aldith seemed uncertain of what the Brain is or how Sefton Stainthorpe used it. I doubt the Echo can keep the Brain functioning for much longer. The desperation evidenced by the lightning and fireballs, and our abduction, proves the point.

The Echo needs us. Maybe we can leverage that.

I scramble to my feet. "Jarek, would you mind taking us to the castle?"

He shakes his head, which I assume means he doesn't mind and will take us there. I sit down beside Sarah, who has already pushed up into a cross-legged sitting position, and hold on while Jarek lopes down the street away from the gateway. He turns down another street, and another, and another, moving faster with each turn until I finally spot the sheer cliff that houses the castle at its summit.

Jarek halts at the base and raises his hand to the level of the summit.

Sarah and I step off the golem's palm, onto solid ground.

"Thanks, buddy," I say. "We'll call if we need you. And let us know if you need anything too."

He nods, then turns to walk away.

Sarah and I stand on the cliff's pinnacle, with the castle looming behind us.

"Now that we're here," she says, "what's the plan?"

"Uh, there is no plan. We wing it."

"Perfect. Guess it was too much to hope for a sliver of a strategy, much less a fully formed one."

I grasp her hand. "Let's go inside and see what we can see."

She lets me lead her across the rock-strewn ground, heading for the castle gates. "How long have you known Jarek?"

"A few days."

"In Echo time, which is different from mortal time."

"According to Aldith, it can be different. I'm no expert on that stuff. I didn't even know time behaved differently here until Aldith told me."

Sarah glances at me, seeming puzzled. "I still don't understand the time stuff. I hope stopping the apocalypse won't involve me needing to understand quantum physics. I don't remember geometry, though I probably took that in high school—or so Allison says."

"Everybody has to endure geometry class."

"Think I'm glad I don't remember it."

I chuckle. "Wish I'd lost that memory. I got a C in geometry. And don't even get me started on trig."

At the castle gates, we pause. Well, I make us pause because I'm a little worried that the castle might reject us too, and we'll end up tumbling off the cliff with no Jarek to catch us.

Sarah gives me a brows-raised look, then sighs and knocks on the gate.

The barrier swings open slowly, creaking all the way.

No, that's not disconcerting. I love walking through creepy creaking gates that lead to a creepy, empty castle. As we cross the threshold, a chill sweeps over my skin, like a ghost has passed through my body. Maybe it has. Sefton Stainthorpe might have died in the mortal world, but he left his Echo here, a man called Will, which must mean he left something of himself, or at least his magics, inside this building.

Something is keeping the Brain going. It has to be those leftover magics.

Hand in hand, we shuffle across the vacant courtyard. The place feels unnervingly quiet and empty. What happened to the bodies of the creatures who died here? My friends hadn't perished in the courtyard, but we had taken out several of our enemies in this place. We continue toward the doors to the castle and find them hanging slightly ajar. I gently nudge one out of the way so we can sidle through the opening into the entryway.

No bodies here either.

I suddenly realize I'm gripping Sarah's hand more tightly, though she doesn't seem to mind. She grips my hand firmly too. We move at a faster pace as we go down the hall to the throne room. The doors should be closed, but instead, they stand wide open. Inside, I see nothing but the throne sitting on its raised dais.

All the bodies are gone. The remains of all my friends have vanished, as if they never existed.

"This makes no sense," I say, speaking in a hushed tone because this feels like a mausoleum. "Who got rid of the bodies? I was the only one left in here after the battle."

"Are you positive of that? Could someone have sneaked in without you noticing?"

"I suppose that's possible. But it doesn't explain what happened to the bodies."

Sarah releases my hand, approaching the dais. "Maybe someone dumped the bodies over the cliff."

I hope that's not what happened. To think of my friends being discarded like trash... It's my fault they died, and it will be my fault if it turns out someone destroyed their remains.

Sarah stretches out an arm toward me, holding her palm up. "Come here, Gabriel. You need to see that it's only a chair, and the demons in this room are all in your head."

But they're not. Real demons murdered the only family I'd ever known.

"Take slow, deep breaths," she says, still offering me her hand. "And come over here. You're almost hyperventilating."

Am I? My chest is heaving, and my ears have started to ring. So yeah, I guess I am almost hyperventilating. Gazing into Sarah's eyes, even from a distance, does more to calm me than any breathing exercise. So I walk over to her and slip my hand into hers. The sensation of her soft, warm fingers threaded with mine relaxes me even more. This connection between us used to scare me, though I would never have admitted it. The time we spent in the stronghold changed things between us so profoundly that I can't even describe how it feels. Magic didn't do it. Sarah was the driving force behind everything inside me that has transformed.

But I still don't know if I can do what she believes we need to do—become one with the Echo's brain. Yeah, the idea of merging with a magically created brain that used to belong to a mad man is kind of…disconcerting. But it's the idea of merging with Sarah that terrifies me. I haven't told her that. Don't know if I can tell her. It sounds weak and pathetic, especially after all the years I'd lived and fought in the Echo. How can having a deep connection with one woman make me feel this off balance?

Right now, here with her, holding hands…maybe I don't feel quite so off balance anymore.

"Tell me about your friends," she says. "The ones you fought with here in the castle. What were they like?"

"Our little army didn't have any training. I didn't either. But when I got thrown into the Echo, I had to learn a lot and learn it fast. Every good Echo being I met became an ally first, and a friend later. It takes time to forge a bond with a stranger." I realize what I just said, and it spurs me to look at Sarah. "But not with you. I felt a connection the instant I first saw you, though I fought it hard."

"I felt the same way." She turns toward me and slips her arms loosely around my waist. "But I'd like to know more about your friends, please. They clearly meant a lot to you."

"Just like your friends mean a lot to you." I can't resist the impulse to slide my arms around her too, linking them at the small of her back. "I never had anyone to start with, no friends or family, just coworkers and women I slept with. In the Echo, that changed, slowly. I couldn't protect myself alone, so I had to ally with anyone I could find who wasn't hell-bent on killing any living things they saw. I met Kai first. He was just a kid, eighteen years old and scared to death. But as we got to know each other and fought together, we forged a bond. Then we picked up more allies along the way, when I decided to explore the entire world of the Echo to understand what was happening."

"Do you understand it now?"

"Not as well as I'd like. But I figured out that the castle on the cliff must be important somehow, and my team agreed that we should check it out. We came back to the Capital City to search for clues. It is Sefton's city, after all. We couldn't find much, so I suggested we should try to breach the castle."

"What did you hope to find there?"

I shrug. "Didn't really know. But after the convulsions in the Echo recently, it seemed like we needed to take drastic action."

"Yeah, the convulsions were what made Grant and Erin decide to go into the Echo. Everyone was afraid it might be the start of something much worse. I wasn't living in Sanctuary then, and I don't remember any of that. It's what my friends told me."

I remember too much, and she has no memory. I still think that's strange. Is it a coincidence? Or does the dichotomy mean something? I should talk to Sarah about that, but first, I need to tell her more about the

Echo beings who became my family. "Kai and the others, they were the bravest people I'd ever met. Even when they were scared, they kept going, kept fighting, kept trying. I was proud of them, especially at the end when they refused to give up despite knowing they were about to die."

Sarah wraps her arms around me more firmly, with her cheek on my chest. "I'm so sorry you lost them."

"I didn't lose them. The Echo took them from me. I spent my whole life as a loner, except for the three years in this world. But even with my friends here, I didn't share everything with them. I held things back. Maybe I deserved to be alone again."

"You're not alone, Gabriel."

With her, I don't feel alone anymore. But I can't make myself tell her that. So I ask a question instead. "Have you seen your friends fight? I mean, in a battle."

"No. They don't let me go on supply missions with them because it's too dangerous. But I've seen them sparring for practice. Dax always beats Grant. But when Grant spars with Erin, you never can tell who will win."

"I thought Grant was a Zen hippie, and Erin was a badass."

"You're half right," Sarah says with a laugh. "But Grant is a badass too, and he's taught Erin how to be Zen. That's what couples do. They make each other better."

Do I make Sarah better? No, I seriously doubt that. But she makes me better, for sure. I don't growl nearly as much as I used to, before I met her.

She lifts her head, aiming a sweet smile at me. "Dax and Allison taught each other lessons too. He was a prisoner in the Echo, banished here by his brother. Allison showed him how to be human again, and he taught her self-defense tactics."

"Hmm, I'm starting to see a pattern here. One half of each couple didn't like to fight, but the badass other halves showed them how it's done."

"You're oversimplifying things. Their relationships are way more complex than that, just like ours is."

We have a relationship, that's what she just implied. I suppose we do in the wider sense of the term. But I suspect she means a romantic relationship. We did have sex, twice, but that doesn't automatically mean we have some kind of emotional connection. Maybe I did sort of share stuff about my past and my feelings, but that's not proof of a relationship either.

So what would be proof? I have no fucking idea.

But something changed between us inside the stronghold, and I'm not sure it's a good thing—for her.

CHAPTER SIXTEEN

Sarah

I SWEAR I CAN HEAR THE GEARS TURNING IN GABRIEL'S MIND WHILE HE struggles to accept that we have a relationship—a real, emotional relationship. It doesn't make sense for us to have this kind of connection so soon after we met, but the Echo has taught everyone that every day is precious and we shouldn't take any moments for granted. I might not remember more than the past two months, but I've listened to everything my friends said and took it to heart.

They're amazing people, and I'd be lucky to find half of what they have.

Why do I care so much about Gabriel? Because he saved my life, yes, but that's only a small part of it. I care because he showed me his pain, he opened up to me in a way I doubt he's ever done in his life before now, and he's determined to stop the Echo from destroying itself and Earth along with it. That's what will happen if we can't command the Brain. The worlds are connected, inextricably. If one dies, so will the other.

Along with all life in both worlds.

"Let's explore the castle," I say. "I know it's full of bad memories for you, but we need to make sure there's nothing in here that could help us. Are you okay with that?"

He blusters out a big breath. "Yeah, I'm okay with it. As long you're with me."

Gabriel winces, like he thinks he said something stupid.

I bracket his face with my hands. "Don't be embarrassed. I feel the same way. As long as I'm with you, everything will be okay."

He peels my hands away from his face and clasps them. "I wasn't embarrassed. But I'm not used to saying things like that—or feeling them." He kisses my hand, then releases both of them. "We should probably spread out to explore the castle, though we shouldn't go out of sight of each other. You take the far side of this room. I'll look around on the dais and behind the throne."

"Sounds good."

We lost our backpacks somewhere along the way, probably one of the times Jarek almost dropped us. Not sure it matters. If we can't figure out how to take control of the Brain and find a way out of the Echo, we're screwed anyway.

I start at the doorway to the throne room and work my way across it in a diagonal pattern. That seems like the most efficient way to explore. As I sweep this side of the room, I search the walls and the floors for any sign of a hidden doorway or panel that might open up to reveal…something. Not knowing what we're looking for makes the search more difficult, but I know we can do this. I wish Aldith could have given us more info about the Brain, but I'm sure she has limitations, just like we all do.

My friends would know how to search. They might even have some equipment that could help. But they aren't here, and we can't go to them.

Gabriel and I can do this. I know we can.

Once I've finished my examination of this half of the room, I wander over to where Gabriel is scrutinizing the throne. He'd been executing a similar search pattern while exploring his half of the room, but he clearly didn't find anything. Now, he's on his hands and knees, feeling around for who knows what.

I squat beside him. "What are you doing?"

"Searching, obviously."

"For what? I haven't found anything. Do you think there might be a hidden compartment or something in the throne?"

"Not sure." He sits back on his heels. "This is pointless. I'm pretty sure the throne and everything in this room is composed of one unbroken piece of stone."

"Everything? I don't see how the floor and ceiling could be like that."

He huffs. "The Echo is a world composed of magic, remember? Sefton could easily have created any damn thing he wanted. The guy had enormous power."

"Good point. We should search the rest of the castle."

We head into the corridor that leads deeper into the castle. Gabriel is right, I think. This entire structure does seem to have been crafted from one continuous piece of stone, which seems impossible. Magics have a way of turning the impossible into reality, though. That makes our task even more difficult.

Every room we find is empty, like it was never designed to house people, not even its creator. The only chamber that seems different is the dungeon, but that room was empty too. Grant had been trapped in the dungeon briefly, until Erin rescued him. But why did Sefton need a prison cell? Why did he build this monstrosity if he never intended to live inside it?

When I voice that question to Gabriel, he stops dead in the middle of the cold stone hallway and stares straight ahead at nothing.

"Are you okay?" I ask. "Gabriel?"

He slowly swivels his head toward me. "That's exactly what he intended—never to live here. It's not a castle in the traditional sense. It's a place to house the Brain."

"I suppose it could be. But we haven't found any evidence of that either."

"We have no idea what the Brain looks like. That means we might be standing right in front of it and not know."

That suggestion sends a shiver up my spine. What if the Brain has a physical form that can reach out to grab us? Nothing is impossible in the Echo.

"So, how do we find it?" I ask. "If we can't see what we're looking for."

He aims a smug smile at me, but it doesn't seem like arrogance. He just looks like he's pleased that he thought of something I didn't. "We made the Brain happy when we sealed our bond. We need to stay here and look through Sefton's journal to figure out how to command the Brain. We also need to do some more bond-forging while we're inside the castle, to make our buddy the Brain happy."

"And you think we should have sex to make that happen."

"Yeah, of course. The Echo seems to like it when we fuck, and I love making you scream."

I can't help smiling. Yes, I would love to get naked with him again. But my smile fades quickly when I realize we have another problem. "We lost both of our backpacks, and the journal was in one of them."

"No problem. We'll bring our packs to us with our wicked new powers."

"Your sudden love for our powers is making me uneasy."

He rolls his eyes. "I thought you wanted me to embrace the magics. I finally figured out how to do that, and you're giving me a disapproving look instead of kissing me."

"I'll kiss you when you explain why you've suddenly changed your attitude toward our Echo power."

Gabriel bows his head and sighs. "Maybe I did get a little too excited about that. But we should try to bring out backpacks to us. Don't you think?"

"Yes, of course we should. Let's try it now."

We sit down on the floor cross-legged, facing each other, and hold hands. When we tried to open the gateway to the Echo, it failed because the Brain doesn't want us to leave yet. We shouldn't run into that problem now, since we're only trying to retrieve our packs. If we get zapped, I will be very annoyed with the Brain. I mean, we're trying to stabilize it. The thing should be grateful.

Now I'm expecting a mystical, formless Brain to thank me. Jeez, I need to get out of the Echo.

Gabriel and I gaze into each other's eyes and focus on bringing our packs to us. The magic rises within us as a gentle, tingling energy that emerges in our chests and spreads outward into our arms, then our legs, and finally up into our heads. I can't explain how I know that he feels the same thing I do. Don't need to explain it. The supernatural energies rise through our skin to waft in the air, swirling and shimmering, zinging whenever they touch us.

Our backpacks appear behind Gabriel.

"This isn't working," he says.

"Yes, it is." I point past his shoulder. "Look."

He twists around to see, and his smug smile returns. "I was right. We did it."

"Get out the journal. We should study it."

"Will do." He pulls both our packs out from behind his body, setting them between us. "Could use a snack and some water too."

"Yes, definitely."

He digs the journal out and offers it to me.

I shake my head. "You should read it."

"Why? You're the smart one."

"Honestly, we're both smart."

"Tell you what." He flips the cover open. "I'll read the first twenty pages, then you can read the next twenty, and so on. Sound good?"

"Yes. Very equitable."

He leans over to lay a hand on my thigh, then slide it up toward my hip. "I love it when you say big words. Makes me want to fuck you again right now."

"Later, Gabriel. We have work to do."

"If you insist."

While he begins reading the journal, I get out some snacks and water bottles, enough for both of us. I offer him food, but he waves it away. I watch him as I eat a snack bar, chewing slowly because I'm fascinated by the look of intense concentration on his face. My friends back in Sanctuary had told me a bit about what the journal contains, but I want to know the details. It might prove vital to figuring out how the Echo's Brain works.

Did Sefton imbue the Brain with his own thought patterns? That would be beyond creepy, but it might also provide insight, if it's true.

Finally, Gabriel raises his head and rolls his head side to side as if ironing out kinks. "This book is boring and full of whackjob nonsense."

"Let me have a go at it."

He hands me the open journal. "Be prepared to go cross-eyed."

"I can handle it." I toss him a snack bar. "Recharge your brain."

While he rips open the foil package, I flip to the next page of the journal to start where he left off. After reading three pages of dense text about quantum physics, and not understanding one sentence of it, I give my eyes a brief rest by shutting them. The light inside the room filters through my lids, creating phantoms of writhing darkness and light. I take slow, deep breaths in the hopes I can achieve a Zen state the way Grant can. He's had years of experience. I've had a few meditation sessions with Grant and Erin. So no, I doubt I can achieve true Zen-ness here in a spooky, empty castle while a hot guy sits across from me, watching and munching on a granola bar.

I can hear him chewing. And breathing.

Let the rest of the world recede from your consciousness, Grant always tells me, *and relax into the silence and mindfulness.* I reel my thoughts backward to the last time I had a mindfulness session with Grant, when I was trying to regain my memories. It didn't work. But I learned how to block out all the noise and focus on my body. I start at my head, feeling my scalp and my hair without touching them or moving even one muscle. Mindfulness is about perception, not physical touch. So I feel my way down my face as I experience my eyelids, my facial muscles, my lips, and my chin.

"What are you doing?" Gabriel asks. "You aren't reading the journal."

"Shush. I'm trying mindfulness meditation to get a clearer perception of the journal."

"But—"

"I said shush, Gabriel. That means be quiet."

He goes back to chewing, and I retreat into my mindfulness again. I work my way down my body, perceiving muscles and skin and hair without touching anything, just sinking into the feeling. When I reach my lap, I experience the sensation of the journal lying on my thigh and my hands resting on the smooth pages. I swear I can smell the paper too, and even the ink Sefton Stainthorpe used to write his nonsensical text.

A strange sensation trickles through me, lifting every fine hair on my body and shortening my breaths. I found something. I can't see it, but I feel it. The journal contains important information hidden beneath the surface of the text itself.

I open my eyes.

Gabriel is staring at me. He narrows his gaze. "You look like you just discovered some vital clue, but all you've been doing was falling asleep while sitting up."

"No, that's not all I was doing. Besides, I wasn't asleep. Mindfulness meditation can release tension and allow you to discover things you might have overlooked."

"Like what?"

I spread my hands over the journal pages. "Not sure yet. But I sensed that the journal is more than a written record of Sefton's plan to create an apocalypse."

He huffs. "That means you found nothing. You wasted time on navel gazing instead of studying the journal."

"Don't turn back into a jerk. I know you're anxious. I am too. But this journal is important, and we need to use more than our physical senses to understand it. Magic was at the heart of everything Sefton did, so we can't treat the journal like it's nothing more than a record of his plans."

Gabriel rubs his forehead. "Yeah, you're right. You'd think I'd be used to all this magic shit by now, but I'm not."

"It's okay. You just relax while I study the journal some more."

He lies down on the floor, hands clasped over his belly, and shuts his eyes. Does he want to take a nap? Well, I wouldn't blame him. We've had a rough couple of days.

I close my eyes and return to the mindfulness routine, starting with the journal on my lap. I feel the texture of the ink on the pages, as well as the leather cover and the stitching that holds the spine together. The scent of the leather wafts into my nostrils, and I suck in a deep breath to experience the scent.

A wriggling sensation begins in my fingers and spreads up through my palms, moving toward my wrists. It stops there, but the wriggling doesn't die away. It teases my skin as if it wants me to do something. What? I have no idea. But the book needs me to explore it, to feel every page and understand its meaning viscerally rather than physically. I flip to the next page.

The wriggling mutates into tingling.

My breaths have become heavier, almost as if a weight has settled onto my chest. I inhale slowly and exhale the same way until the weight lessens enough that I can continue my sightless exploration of the journal. Though I've never had vision issues, I can tell this isn't the kind of blind exploration that some-one with reduced sight would experience. What I feel is magics. They want me to dig deeper into the journal and discover something vital.

Why can't the Echo just say what it wants? Trying to interpret magical signals gets pretty damn annoying.

As I turn the next page, I feel another presence intruding into my men-tal space. No, not intruding. I recognize and welcome the invasion, be-cause it's coming from Gabriel. Does he realize what he's doing? Probably not. He hasn't been entirely comfortable with our shared power. But the silky warmth and sensuality of his presence spreads through me, awaken-ing my body and instigating a slick heat between my thighs.

My eyes fly open.

So do Gabriel's. He springs into a sitting position, his chest heaving and the bulge in his pants much larger than it had been a few minutes ago. We gaze into each other's eyes as the weight of lust bears down on us both, and I know what the Echo wants from us right now.

"We need to fuck, Gabriel. Right now."

Chapter Seventeen

Gabriel

LITTLE MISS AMNESIA JUST DECLARED THAT WE NEED TO FUCK AGAIN, right now, here in the creepy castle. Yeah, I've got a raging hard-on. But we're supposed to be studying the journal, not getting hot and bothered. Maybe I had felt something strange a moment ago, while I lay on the floor trying to relax. Maybe it had felt like Sarah crawled inside my pants and started sucking my cock. But that was a daydream or…something. It hadn't been real.

But it felt real. Not literally, but yeah.

I hate magics. The boring, supernatural-free world was so much easier to navigate.

Sarah sets the journal on the floor and starts unbuttoning her shirt.

"Whoa there, cowgirl," I say, as I rise to my knees. "Slow down. What happened to studying the journal?"

"I did that. And it told me that we need to have sex before we can understand."

"Yeah, that sounds completely rational."

"Don't get sarcastic." She glances down at my dick. "The magics affected you too. Since when does a man turn down an offer of sex?"

"Since you declared that the journal wants us to screw each other's brains out."

"Trust me, Gabriel. We need to do this." She unhooks the last button on her shirt and shrugs out of it. "And we both want it too."

I groan and rub my hand over my mouth, because she just released the first clasp on her front-hook bra. "Of course I want you, but this is too bizarre. A book tells us what to do now? And there isn't even a bed in here. Just hard stone floors."

She tosses her bra away, then crawls over to me. The way her breasts dangle beneath her makes my dick throb. "We can go back to the stronghold, if you'd feel more comfortable there. But I'd love for you to take me on the cold, hard floor."

"Why?" Can't believe I'm resisting so much. I'm insanely hot for her, all the time, and now I keep saying no.

Sarah laughs softly. "Why? Stop asking questions and just strip, Gabriel."

We can't go back to the stronghold, not unless we call for Jarek to take us there. I can't hold out for much longer with Sarah tempting me like a siren luring me to my death on a foggy coast, where I will blindly smash into the jagged rocks. I wouldn't mind if she ripped me to shreds and left nothing but a pile of bones behind afterward. Death would be worth it, if I get to be inside her again.

She unzips my pants and curls her soft hand around my hard-on, pulling it out so she can stroke my length. A deep groan resonates in my chest, and my eyes fall half-closed. I can still see her, though, and I watch while she rests her hands on my thighs and lowers her head to take me into her mouth. I can't move, or even tell her to stop. Not that I want her to stop. But this is crazy, and—

The little siren is devouring me, sucking and licking while making ravenous grunting noises. I throw my head back and growl, then I shove my hand into her hair and let the woman have her way with me. She massages my balls with one hand while pumping me with the other, all while she keeps licking and sucking. Fuck, I know I'll come any second. I feel like I'm on a runaway train that just reached a ninety-degree incline, and now it's inching up the tracks so slowly that I can't breathe anymore. Once the train reaches the peak, I'll go barreling down it toward bliss.

She pulls her mouth away. "Mm, you taste so damn good."

I'm breathing too hard to speak.

"Get naked, Gabriel," she says. "Then lie down on the floor."

"Why?" I actually managed to speak one syllable. That feels like a major accomplishment, considering how turned on I am.

"Stop asking questions. It's my turn to dominate you."

The little siren rises and strips off the rest of her clothes. My gaze stalls on the thatch of hairs between her thighs, the ones I know are as soft as silk. I want to eat her up, but she just commanded me to get naked so she can dominate me. Still not sure I can submit to that. But if anyone can seduce me into relinquishing control, it's Lady Godiva.

While I undress, she breaks into my backpack and brings out the rope. She holds it up, smiling with the sexiest look of triumph. "I'm ready whenever you are."

I shed the last item of clothing—my socks—and saunter up to her. "Sure you wouldn't rather I ordered you around? You loved that last time."

She wags a finger at me. "It's my turn. So lie down on the floor. Now."

I can't refuse her command, because I want her like crazy. But my heart rate has accelerated, and I know it's not entirely because I'm turned on. The thought of letting her tie me up has increased my anxiety. But I do what she wants and lie down on the floor, on my back.

Sarah kneels beside me. "Are you okay? You looked kind of anxious a minute ago."

"Yeah, I was. I still am."

"Why does what I want to do to you make you uneasy? It's nothing you haven't done to me."

"I know. But..." I cover my face with my hands and growl, because I hate talking about this shit.

"Please tell me. I don't want you to let me do this if it will make you uncomfortable."

I should tell her the truth. I want to tell her. But something keeps me from saying the words. When I look into her eyes and see the concern there, I know the time has come to share my last secret. "When I was thrown into the Echo, a gang of creatures caught me. They tied me up and tortured me for three days, until I finally managed to get away. It wasn't sexual, just plain old torture."

"Oh God, Gabriel." She lies down beside me and lays half her body over mine. "I'm so sorry. Forget about the ropes. Let's just make love."

I hold her for a moment while I consider what to do now. She let me take control of her body, tying her up and not letting her come until she was desperate for it. She said she loved that, and I loved it too. But it was a one-sided game. What those creatures did to me has no bearing on the time I've spent making love to Sarah. Now that I've told her my last secret, I feel that weight lifting. It's time to give her what she wants, because I want to do it, not because I feel compelled to satisfy her.

"Have your fun," I say. "Don't hold back. Whatever you want, I want it too."

"What about your past trauma?"

"I'll be fine. In fact, I think letting you be in control will be good for both of us."

"Really?"

"Yeah." I palm her ass. "Can't resist a hot woman ordering me around."

Sarah gets to her knees and grabs the rope. "If what I'm doing bothers you at all, speak up. Okay? Don't go all macho and hold it in."

I smirk. "Yes, ma'am. No macho holding-in. Any other orders?"

"Not yet. But I haven't gotten started yet." She snaps the rope taut, and her lips curl into a sexy smile. "Your ass is mine, Gabriel."

Sarah the dominatrix makes my cock throb again. She is the most incredible woman in the universe. Even amnesia can't keep her down.

The woman who wants to dominate me swings one leg over me to straddle my thighs. Then she tells me to sit up, so she can tie the rope behind my back and bind my wrists there, leaving just enough leeway that I won't strain myself if I can't keep from writhing while she's having her way with me. Can't wait to see what the naughty nudist has planned for me.

She slaps a hand on my chest and pushes me back down on the floor.

Next, she grabs another length of rope to tie my ankles, leaving some leeway there too, and she uses the same length of rope to bind my knees. I should probably feel anxious about this, and my pulse does speed up, but I experience only a twinge of anxiety. With my dick so hard I think I could use it as a baseball bat, I can't think about anything except what Sarah wants to do to me.

She crawls forward on her hands and knees, still straddling me. Though I notice her movements, I reserve all my attention for her body. Those tits sway when she bends over me to adjust the rope behind my back, and I want to lunge my head up to seize one nipple and suck until she cries out. The scent of her cream intoxicates me, especially because I can see it dribbling down her inner thighs.

I need to taste her, but she's in charge.

Her face now hovers above mine. She catches her bottom lip between her teeth and bites down hard, then releases it ever-so-slowly. "I love it when you get me so turned on that I beg for you to make me come. Now it's your turn. Feel free to plead with me to push you over the edge, unless that would make you feel unmanly."

"Don't give a shit about that, not when I'm with you."

"Are you sure you're ready for this?"

"Yes, baby, do it. I trust you all the way."

I could probably manage to flip us over, if I really wanted to, but I realize I need to let her do this as much as she does. Though her nipple dangles millimeters from my lips, I don't even try to latch onto it. She's earned the right to boss me around, after our bondage interlude in the stronghold.

Sarah bends her elbows to lower her head and turns it side to side to tease my lips and my cheeks with her silky hair. I pull in a sharp breath. She skims her lips over mine, barely grazing my skin while her hair tickles me again. "I'm just getting started."

"Good. Not ready for it to be over yet."

The little vixen crawls backward, licking and nibbling my flesh as she moves, catching one of my nipples between her teeth only to let it go gradually, then repeating the process with the other one. I gasp and instinctively arch my back. She licks my nipple, then blows a hot breath over it, and finally nips it hard. I hiss in a breath. She keeps inching backward. Her tits graze my chest when she ducks her head to flick her tongue into my navel, then licks a trail down to my groin.

She sits up and drags her nails down my chest from my shoulders all the way to my hips.

"Fuck, you're a wicked girl," I growl. "Not the goody two shoes I thought you were when we met."

"Never trust first impressions. I thought you were an arrogant, rude jackass."

I smirk. "But I am a jackass."

She shakes her head slowly, then leans in to whisper in my ear, "You're hung like a bull, not a donkey."

"Let me taste you, please."

She sits back on my thighs, and now her wet cleft is pressed into my cock. "Maybe I should let you make me come. You won't be coming anytime soon, though."

"This is your show."

With a wicked smile, she rocks back and forth, spreading her cream all over my erection. Then she rises to her knees and waddles up my body until her groin lies inches above my mouth. "Close enough?"

"A little lower, baby."

I groan when she lowers herself until my nose rubs against her mound and the silky hairs there, and her glistening slickness teases my lips. I lick it off and groan.

"Hurry up," she says, her voice husky. "I need to come now."

"Your wish is my command."

I thrust my tongue out to coil it around her clit, over and over, breathing harder just from hearing her moans and gasps. She rocks her hips into me, and I seize the chance to dive my tongue inside her opening, licking furiously to devour every bit of her cream that I can.

"Oh, God!" she shouts as she begins to rock her hips wildly, and she slaps her palms on the floor at either side of my head. "Hurry, Gabriel. Make me scream."

I capture her clit and suck it hard and fast, letting my chin rub against her folds to get her even more excited. Her breaths have become sharp gasps. A sound like nails on a chalkboard tells me she's scraping her fingernails on the stone floor, so close to orgasm that it won't take much to push her over the edge. I release her clit and frisk my tongue back and forth along her folds until she jerks and cries out, then I go for it. I pull her nub into my mouth and rasp my teeth over it while I suckle her clit.

Her body goes rigid, her nails scrape the floor even harder, and she comes. Her scream reverberates inside the cavernous room. I keep tormenting her clit until she's done and struggling to catch her breath.

After a moment, she crawls back down to my groin and sits back on my thighs. "Wow, you've got skills."

"Thanks, but I need you to fuck me now."

She grasps my dick and strokes it gently, which drives me even crazier than if she'd pumped me fiercely. I make a noise that's something between a groan and a shout. But Sarah isn't done with me. She crouches over my cock and holds it with one hand while she rocks her hips. The movement skates her cleft over me again and again, the pace erratic, not giving me a chance to get into the rhythm, and that's exactly what she wants. Keeping me guessing drives me insane.

Damn, she's amazing.

"Mm, I love how hard you are," she says. "But I want you even harder."

She lowers herself just enough to take the head of my cock into her opening, but she doesn't take me all the way. No, she pulls out, then pushes me inside her again, only a little farther than before. I try to bend my knees, but it's hard to do that when I'm bound at the ankles and knees. Can't really lift my hips either. And when she finally slams down onto my cock, burying me inside her, she just sits there, not moving a muscle.

Her hands glide up my belly, and she pinches my nipples.

The only sound I can make is a strangled shout.

She rises to her knees, leaving me unsatisfied. No, that's not quite right. I love what she's doing. Sex has never been this intense or exciting before. The thrill of never knowing what she might do or when she might let me come… It's incredible.

Her delicate fingers massage the hollows of my hips, like she'd done the last time we had sex—when I wouldn't let her tease me this way. No holding back now.

Sarah shimmies down my body to massage my inner thighs. While she does that, she leans forward to take my dick in her mouth and pump it. Her motions begin at a leisurely pace, but they speed up gradually in sync with her massage. I start gasping again, thrashing though I don't really want to break free. I feel myself teetering on the cusp of a precipice, caught in the second before free-fall, unable to tumble over the edge.

And then she stops.

I suddenly realize I have my eyes closed and open them. Sarah is on her knees again, towering over me. She fondles her tits, pinching the nipples, and moans as she slides her hands down her belly to her mound. Then she slips one finger between her folds and begins to pet herself, seemingly in no hurry. When she slips another finger in there, she rocks her hips in a slow and erotic rhythm, her gaze locked on mine while she licks her lips and adds a third finger, petting herself more vigorously.

The vixen is going to make me watch her pleasure herself.

"Order me to come," she says, her voice even huskier.

"Do it, Sarah. Fuck yourself until you come."

She freezes, moving only one finger to rub herself, and comes with a harsh scream. Then she slams down onto my cock and bucks her hips wildly.

And I explode inside her.

CHAPTER EIGHTEEN

Sarah

HIS RELEASE ERUPTS INSIDE ME MORE POWERFULLY THAN EVER BEFORE, and I cry out again from the bliss of feeling him inside me. Then it's over, and I collapse on top of him. I need a few minutes before I can recover my wits enough to remember I should untie him. I do that quickly, and he folds his arms around me. I love being tucked against his body, feeling his warmth and strength.

Will I get pregnant? I don't care if I do, because I know I want to spend the rest of my life with Gabriel.

He combs his fingers through my hair. "If we hadn't sealed our bond one hundred percent before this, we've definitely done it now."

"You gave yourself to me without hesitation."

"I gave myself to you, body and soul, and I don't regret it at all."

"When I surrendered my body to you, I didn't regret either. It felt right."

For a while, we just lie here in each other's arms and revel in the afterglow. Maybe I shouldn't feel this way when I haven't known him for long, but I refuse to second guess my emotions. I trust him, I want him, and I care what happens to him. We're still trapped in the Echo, but I know we can decipher Sefton's journal and uncover the last secrets of the apocalypse. Then, we will end the madness.

Gabriel hooks a finger under my chin, urging me to look at him. "I'm sorry for the way I acted early on, especially on the beach. I would never have hurt you. The things I said, that was fear talking. I'd just gotten dumped into the middle of an Echo creature gang war, then got ripped away from there to crash down on a beach. That's not an excuse, just what happened."

"I know that. You don't need to apologize for it again. Even on the beach, I knew deep down that you wouldn't hurt me. Having amnesia has forced me to trust my instincts."

He kisses my forehead, then sits up and stretches. He slaps my bottom. "Get up, Lady Godiva. We have more journal pages to explore."

At first, I thought his nickname for me was annoying. But when he says it now, with humor in his voice and a twinkle in his eyes, I love it. But I don't have a nickname for him.

"Do you like being called Gabe?" I ask.

"Not particularly. I prefer Gabriel."

Okay, no nickname for him.

I get up and stretch like he had, but I also yawn. Lying with Gabriel makes me feel relaxed and warm and content. But we still have work to do, so we both get dressed and resume our study of the journal. This time, we sit side by side on the floor as we flip the pages, discussing each one before we move on to the next. Eventually, we come to the drawing Grant had told me about—a rendering of *The Vitruvian Man*, as envisioned by Leonardo da Vinci.

"Grant told me about this drawing," I say. "Da Vinci was inspired by the writings of Vitruvius, a Roman scholar who talked about the perfect proportions for architecture and the human body."

Sefton's version of the Da Vinci drawing looks remarkably like the original, almost as if he traced it. Maybe he did. Sefton Stainthorpe had given himself teleportation powers before he set the alchemy of worlds in motion, and he admitted to Dax and Allison that he had teleported into the Getty museum to steal rare alchemical manuscripts. He might've stolen *The Vitruvian Man* too. But that drawing is so famous that someone would've missed it, surely.

Maybe he hid in the museum after hours to copy it.

Ugh, like it really matters how he managed to reproduce the drawing with such amazing accuracy.

I touch my fingertip to the journal page, following every line of the drawing. Something about it seems vital, like we need to uncover its secrets before we'll have any chance of taking over the Brain. But what then? I have no idea. Can we stop the apocalypse? Sever the Echo from Earth?

Tapping my finger on the drawing, I ask, "Once we control the Brain, what do we do then? There must be a purpose for taking command of the Brain, but we don't know what that is. Do we?"

"I don't know what it is, that's for sure."

"You know, I remember Grant and Erin talked about something called the Tria Prima. The way I understood it, that was the magics that kickstarted the alchemy of worlds. Sefton called it an alchemical reaction."

"He was obsessed with alchemy, right?"

"Yes. There were boxes in the cellar of Fallenmouth that Sefton had imbued with powerful magics to help drive the apocalypse. Allison used her Echo power to circumvent that."

Gabriel squints at the journal, almost like he's trying to divine answers from the page. "Do you know much about the Tria Prima?"

"No. But I think there's more information about it in the journal."

"Let's skip ahead to that." He hesitates, glancing at me. "Mind if I, uh, dog-ear this page?"

"Sure, go ahead. It's not my journal."

Gabriel folds over the page's upper corner, then flips through the journal in search of information about the Tria Prima. We both skim the pages, but it's pretty clear that most of the journal consists of the ramblings of a deranged mind. Very little of it makes sense. But then we finally stumble on to something meaningful.

"Tria Prima," Gabriel says, tapping a page. "Sefton wrote about it right here."

"What does he say?"

"I'll paraphrase, because he tends to ramble like a lunatic for some weird reason." Gabriel smirks at me. "Can't imagine why he would do that."

"Everybody knows he was insane. Just give me the gist of it."

"Okay." Gabriel skims the text. "Here we go. Sefton's obsession with alchemy seems to have led him to an even deeper obsession—with his brother and with Allison. He decided that the three of them were the Tria Prima. That's a reference to the three basal elements of alchemy that triggered the first transmutation and created everything in the universe. Sefton believed that by recreating the Tria Prima with himself, Dax, and Allison, he could generate enough power to tap into the quintessentia, the prime catalyst that created the universe."

"He needed that to start the alchemy of worlds?"

"I think so." Gabriel flips to the next page, his gaze narrows as he struggles to comprehend the text. "There's more rambling, then he talks about the Triangle, which is composed of the Tria Prima. He says the Triangle has the greatest power of all, and he worried that someone might try to appropriate that power from him."

"None of my friends mentioned that. But they don't tell me everything about the journal."

Gabriel lifts his gaze to mine. "Why not? Don't they trust you?"

"Of course they do. But they also treat me like I'm a lost child they've taken in. I understand why, but sometimes, I wish they'd let me in on their deepest secrets."

"Does everyone else in Sanctuary know that stuff?"

"I don't think so. There are some secrets they won't share with anyone outside the inner circle—Dax, Allison, Grant, and Erin."

Gabriel holds the open book out to me. "But they gave you the journal. That means they do trust you. Maybe they just worried all this crazy stuff in the journal would scare you."

"That's probably true. I'm not a badass like Erin, or a fighter like Allison. Nobody taught me self-defense. Erin was going to teach me how to use a bow and arrow, but we didn't get around to that."

"Your friends think you're weak."

I start to object, but then shut my mouth. Do they treat me that way? Maybe a little. I don't blame them. They did find me on the beach, washed ashore like garbage, with no memory of anything before that moment. Of course they want to shield me from the worst truths. I've been coddled, kind of, but not anymore. Coming to the Echo has changed me.

Meeting Gabriel has changed me.

But am I strong enough to handle whatever comes next? I've never fought in a battle or stopped a mad man. But my friends wouldn't have given me the journal if they didn't believe Gabriel and I could handle the secrets hidden within it.

"You mentioned someplace called Fallenmouth," Gabriel says. "The cellar held boxes full of magics."

"That's right. Fallenmouth was the estate where Dax and Sefton grew up, and it became Sefton's home base once he enacted his insane plan."

Gabriel sets the journal on his lap. "The boxes were at Fallenmouth. They contained the magics that Sefton needed to start the alchemical reaction, and apparently, to sustain it after the apocalypse got rolling."

"Yes. Does the journal talk about that?"

"Not in so many words. I read between the lines."

I glance down at the book. "The boxes are dead. That's what Erin and Grant said. They can't power anything anymore."

"Well, I guess that doesn't really matter. We're trying to figure out what the Brain does and why we need to power it up."

"Right. Let's get back to studying the journal."

We browse page after page but don't find anything of interest—until we reach a section of text near the end of the diary. Sefton mentions the Heart and the Lifeblood, two vital elements of the Echo. He believed the world he created from magics would not survive without a "pulsing heart" and "flowing blood," like any living thing must have.

"He cast an intense spell," Gabriel says, "to create those two elements and give them the power to keep the Echo alive. He had discovered a flaw in the alchemical reaction, which meant the new world he created would disintegrate in 'catastrophic fashion' unless he gave it the 'organs' it needed to survive."

"The spell he cast created the Heart and the Lifeblood."

"Exactly."

I chew on the inside of my lip as I stare at the journal and try to comprehend the scope of Sefton's master plan. He screwed it up, though, didn't he? The alchemy of worlds accidentally gave some humans magical abilities, what we call Echo power. That power let Allison stop the alchemy of worlds and destroy those boxes.

"Why didn't my friends know about this?" I ask, though I'm not expecting Gabriel to answer. I'm thinking out loud. "They had the journal for two months and studied it extensively."

"They clearly missed a few things."

"Did they? I wonder. I mean, we are talking about magic and transmutation." I lay my hand on the open journal. "What if the book is imbued with magics too? Maybe it can hide what it doesn't want anyone to see yet."

Gabriel scrunches up his face, like he wants to tell me that's crazy. But then he relaxes and sighs. "Who knows? Maybe you're right. That would explain why we found clues that nobody else noticed. And you did say you felt something strange when you closed your eyes while holding the book."

"Exactly. I think the journal protects its secrets until the right person comes along."

"You are the right person, Sarah."

I lay my hand over his on the book. "We are the right people. You and me together."

"What are we supposed to do? I don't even know where the Brain is, much less how to tap into it. We've searched this entire castle, including the dungeon, and there's nothing."

"But the journal hid pages until we held it in our hands. The Brain might've hidden itself too."

Gabriel slaps the journal shut and jumps up. A muscle in his jaw ticks while he grits his teeth hard. "I'm damn sick of all this cloak-and-dagger bullshit. We're here. We did what we were supposed to do, and still the damn Brain won't show itself."

I scramble to get up and rest my hands on his chest. "Calm down, Gabriel. We're making progress. And we will find the Brain, I know it."

He scrubs a hand over his mouth, and his shoulders sag. "Sorry. I'm getting frustrated. Who knows how many years have gone by while we've been browsing a book."

"Let's go back to the throne room. That seems like the kind of room where Sefton would have hidden his treasure—the Brain."

Gabriel marches toward the doorway, walking so fast that I need to run to catch up to him. When I grasp his hand, he doesn't take hold of mine. Not at first. But I keep my hand wrapped around his while we hustle down the corridor, until he finally gives up and laces his fingers with mine. We hurry into the throne room and halt a few feet from the throne itself.

"Now what?" I ask.

He shrugs.

The floor begins to vibrate, emitting a low rumble.

I grip his hand even more tightly and try not to fall down as the vibrations ramp up more and more. The rumbling becomes a deafening roar, and we both slap our hands over our ears to dull the racket. It makes my ears hurt, so I'm sure Gabriel is experiencing the same thing.

The entire dais sinks beneath the floor.

As the dais and throne vanish from sight, something else rises in its place—a gigantic wall of stone that has its own stone floor attached to it. The new dais consists of one large piece and has symbols carved into its wall. But that's not what has me gaping at the newly revealed dais. The center of the rear wall houses a metal contraption. It has an outer ring with multiple spokes inside it, as well as metal cuffs that seem to have been made to hold a human being in one of two positions—arms spread and slightly raised with legs spread, or arms raised straight out to the sides with legs together.

I've seen this before. Today. A little while ago.

This is the Vitruvian Man.

Gabriel takes a step toward the dais, but I seize his arm to stop him. He rotates his head to look at me, brows raised.

"Don't go any closer," I say. "Please. I have a bad feeling about this."

"But this must be the Brain."

"Maybe. Even if it is, we need to know more before we approach that contraption. Who knows what it might do to us?"

He stares at the machine like he longs to walk up to it and let the thing take him. Maybe it wouldn't hurt him. But who knows? The Brain sent an Echo beast to kidnap us, and it created super destructive lightning, not to mention fireballs. We need to know more before we even think about approaching the machine. The Heart and the Lifeblood were not mechanical, after all. They were Erin and Grant, two humans who took control of those elements of the Echo. Why would the Brain be technological?

A mechanical pulsating noise emanates from the machine.

No, I don't like this at all.

Chapter Nineteen

Gabriel

EVERY TIME THE MACHINE PULSATES, I FREEZE AND STARE AT IT. SARAH keeps tugging on my hand to drag me away from the thing, but I only manage to shuffle a few feet before it pulsates again and I fall into another semi-trance. That can't be good. Sarah was the one who seemed possessed when she touched the journal's pages. But now I've become entranced by the machine. What the hell is going on? We're supposed to take control of the Brain, not the other way around.

Sarah tugs on my arm again. "Come on, Gabriel. We need to get out of this room."

I can't move or speak.

She kicks my shin.

The burst of pain snaps me out of the trance, but I feel the machine's energy licking at my skin, enticing me to walk right up to it and let the device take me. Sarah doesn't seem to feel it. If we're both halves of the Brain, why does it only want me? Or is Sarah just stronger and better able to resist the seductive energies? If the magics push through her resistance…

I won't let the machine take her.

Sarah leads me down the corridor to the entryway, but she hesitates there.

"What's wrong?" I ask. "Are you feeling the pull of the machine too?"

"No. But I hear something. Don't you?"

I tip my head to the side and listen, letting my jaw fall open a little, just enough to enhance my hearing slightly. It's enough. I detect the sounds she must have heard, but I can't tell for sure what they are. It sounds like a combination of noises—grinding, dragging, groaning, huffing, and even shouting. Echo creatures? If so, I doubt they've come to wish us a happy trip back to Earth.

"Wait here," I tell Sarah. "Let me take a look out there first."

She hugs herself and nods.

I approach the big doors and ease one side open a few inches, just enough that I can peer outside. But it's dark now, and I have trouble spotting any creatures that might wait out there. I see writhing shadows, but that's hardly proof of an impending ambush. Damn, I wish I had a pair of night-vision goggles. But I don't, so I need to trust my instincts, and they warn me that something bad is going to happen.

Shutting the door, I try to think of a way to bar the entrance, but I have nothing that would accomplish that feat. The castle is full of empty rooms. Nothing in our backpacks would help either. I have a gun and extra ammo, but not enough to fend off Echo creatures. They're too strong and too vicious. Only a strike to the center of the heart will take them down for certain.

"Grant and Erin teleported themselves out of the dungeon," Sarah says. "Maybe we could use our powers to zip out of here."

"Do something we've never done while being stalked by vicious creatures in a creepy castle that wants to pull me into its web. Yeah, good plan."

"Got a better idea? We did bring our backpacks to us."

That's true. But for some reason, I don't want to try teleporting. No, I'd much rather walk into the throne room again and touch the machine.

Oh, shit. Its magics are still slithering around inside me.

Sarah grasps my face in her hands. "Snap out of it, Gabriel. Your eyes went glassy, and your jaw went slack. You're under the machine's spell again, aren't you? Fight it, Gabriel, fight it hard."

The vehemence in her voice does the trick. It severs the magics from me, at least for now. But we need to get the hell out of here fast.

"Better teleport quick," I say. "Don't think I can keep fighting the machine for much longer."

She throws her arms around me, her cheek against my neck, and holds me tight. We concentrate on transporting ourselves to another place, away from the castle, away from the influence of the machine. It seems to take forever, both of us concentrating on the task so hard that my head starts to hurt, and my jaw aches too. I'm clenching my teeth and fisting my hands, even though I have my arms lashed around her. I must be crushing her, but she doesn't complain. I feel like I need to glue myself to her to stop the machine from sneaking inside me again.

The castle interior vanishes, replaced by the comforting environment of the stronghold and the bedroom where Sarah and I had made love earlier today. The sheets are still rumpled, and the scent of sex fills the room.

My entire body goes slack, with Sarah's arms holding me up. At last, I'm free of the machine's influence.

But will that freedom last?

Our backpacks lie on the floor. Sarah rushes over to them and digs out the journal, flipping the pages in a rush.

Right before we teleported away, the journal had been on the floor in the machine room, where I vaguely remember dropping it when the mechanism powered up. Sarah must have willed it into her pack.

"We've already been through the journal," I say, sounding wearier than I should. I haven't done anything strenuous, like running from monsters or fucking Sarah. I shuffle to the bed and drop my ass onto it, then rub my forehead. "What are you looking for now?"

"More information about the Brain."

"There isn't anything more. It's useless to keep searching."

She stops in the middle of rifling through the journal, while kneeling on the floor, her wide eyes trained on me. "The machine must still be influencing you. Why else would you give up? That's not like you at all."

"You met me yesterday. Maybe I'm a coward at heart, and exactly the kind of jackass who would give up."

"No, Gabriel, that's not true. You're brave and strong and selfless. Giving up isn't your style, and that means the machine still has a hold on you."

"Let's have sex and see if that helps."

She walks over to the bed and sits down beside me, still holding the journal in her hand. "We need to take control of the Brain, so it can't seize control of you. Right now, I think it's still doing what Sefton wanted."

"Which is what?"

"To connect with its creator. Sefton is dead, though, and even his Echo is gone. The Brain must sense that you are part of it now, but it can't comprehend a woman joining with it. Sefton would've wanted to keep the power for himself."

"So, you think the Brain assumes I must be Sefton and that it wants me to command it again."

"Yes."

I rest my elbows on my thighs and let my face fall into my raised palms. "I don't want to become one with a machine that's pining for Sefton Stainthorpe. He was a whackjob."

"But you aren't. Still, it's too dangerous for either of us to meld with that machine until we understand what needs to be done to keep the worlds from imploding."

I raise my head. "When did that become an option? Nobody warned me the worlds might implode."

"No one understands what having no Brain is doing to the Echo or to Earth. We might have enjoyed two months of peace and quiet, but the fact that the Brain brought us into this world to save itself doesn't bode well."

She has a point—a damn good one. The Brain can't function on its own, so it's desperately trying to find a replacement for Sefton. And that's me. Perfect. I feel like I've fallen into a science fiction movie about evil machines taking over the world. But this machine only wants me.

"What should we do?" I ask. "Can the stronghold protect me?"

"No, it cannot."

The response did not come from Sarah. Aldith stands in the doorway, wringing her hands.

"I thought this was a safe place," I say. "Now you tell us it can't protect me from the Brain?"

She bows her head. "I regret that I can't foresee every eventuality, and I can't stop what is about to occur. But if I can help in any way at all, I will."

"It's not your fault, Aldith. Do you have any idea what might be coming?"

She starts to speak but freezes. Her gaze veers to the picture windows. "It is already here."

A black shape speeds past the window.

Oh no, it can't be.

The Echo flier speeds by again, this time squawking like an angry crow.

"I have fortified the windows with wards," Aldith says. "But the Brain is far more powerful than I am. If it has invested the creatures with magics on the level of Sefton Stainthorpe's powers…"

We're screwed. Yeah, I didn't need a diagram to show me that scenario.

Two bird-like creatures soar up from the ground, each hauling an earthbound beast on its back. The fliers aim straight for the windows, then swerve away at the last second. Their passengers slam into the windows, clinging to the outer sill.

And they bash their fists into the glass.

The magics protecting the windows begin to pulsate, just like the machine in the castle had done. But here, the pulsations are clearly aimed at breaking through the shield Aldith had erected. The creatures clinging to the windows pound their fists while still hanging on to the sill with one hand. The wards pulsate even more strongly, creating a sensation of pressure inside the room that makes my ears hurt.

The Echo fliers drop off more creatures, ones even bigger than the beasts currently pounding on the wards, and they join in the party. *Bam, bam, bam.* Big fists batter the windows. A variety of creatures have joined forces with the fliers—big brutes with gnarly skin, scaly beasts with snake-like tongues, fanged monsters, and more.

And all of them want me.

"They've surrounded the stronghold," Aldith says, and for the first time, she sounds panicked. "And the wards are faltering. We can't fight Sefton's magics."

How can a dead man cause this much chaos? The answer must lie within the machine he left behind, but we can't risk returning to the castle to find out. The machine's pull is way too strong for me to keep fighting it.

I grasp Sarah's shoulders. "Get out of here. You can't let those creatures take you."

"They don't want me. They want you."

"But they might use you as leverage. Please, go back to Sanctuary."

"You know I can't." She glances at the pulsating wards and the beasts battering them. "The gateway is closed."

Shit. I'd forgotten about that. My mind has grown fuzzy, and I feel dizzy. My pulse beats so hard and fast that I can't think straight anymore.

"Please, go hide somewhere," I tell Sarah. "Maybe if I merge with the machine, I can reopen the gateway. Then you could at least escape."

"I am not leaving you behind."

Bam, bam, bam. The entire building shudders with every concussion.

"Go, Sarah. Teleport yourself to someplace far away."

She just stands there, chin lifted. I would love her defiance if she weren't endangering herself with it.

I grip her upper arms and drag her closer. "Listen to me, you stupid girl. Do you want to be ripped to shreds by an Echo creature? They love to rape sweet little things like you."

My growling tone doesn't seem to have affected her at all. *Dammit.*

"You can't scare me away," she says. "We're in this together."

"Sarah—"

The obstinate woman throws her arms around me and whisks us away. We wind up in an area I recognize. It's a part of the Echo that lies furthest away from the Capital City and Sefton's castle. I imagine she wished for us to be somewhere far away, and her magics interpreted that literally. We've wound up on the opposite side of the world.

I notice Aldith stands nearby, arms lashed around herself, glancing around with a wary expression.

"You okay, Aldith?" I ask.

She nods.

We find ourselves in what looks like a small town, though I doubt anyone still lives here. Most of the buildings have been reduced to rubble, and the ones that still stand have suffered enough damage that nobody would want to take refuge in them. Burned-out vehicles and burned-out landscapes complete the picture. This is the definition of a post-apocalyptic wasteland.

But at least we're far away from the castle.

For a moment, I just hold Sarah and shut my eyes to enjoy the feel of her body tucked against me. She rests her cheek on my chest. I set my chin on top of her head. I pull in a deep breath and let it out slowly as the tension melts away.

Then the pull of the machine tugs at me again. *Shit.* Even from literally half a world away, that thing can still find me and infect me with its seductive magics. With every fiber of my being, I want to push Sarah away and transport myself straight to the throne room, which now holds the laboratory of a dead lunatic.

Sarah lifts her head, studying me with those beautiful eyes.

Worry taints them. Worry for me. But she should be more concerned with herself because I can't protect her anymore. I can't trust myself. Would I hurt her if that was the only way to get to the castle? Is merging with the machine now my only goal? I don't want to become a monster, but I know I can't fight it for much longer.

So I push away from Sarah. "You need to move on to another location, another city or town, even a cave will do. I don't care where you go, as long as I can't find you there."

"Running away isn't the answer."

"It's all I can do. You and Aldith need to hide."

Even now, I sense the machine reaching out to me. Its magics snake out in slithering tendrils, hunting, sniffing, seeking me out with all the power Sefton left behind. Resisting the call takes every ounce of willpower I have, but I feel it crumbling away bit by bit, more every second. Soon, I will succumb.

But I can't let that happen here. I have only one choice.

I pull Sarah close and kiss her. Then I stumble backward and stop fighting the pull. The magics snatch me away to the castle. As I disappear, I see the look on Sarah's face as she realizes what I've done. Shock gives way to confusion, and finally, grief.

She screams, "No!"

But I'm already gone.

I stand inside the throne room, near the doorway, though the stone chair has been replaced by the machine and its rock housing. The pressure eased the second I materialized inside this room. And I know what I must do. I walk halfway across the room, but pause when I hear odd noises in the corridor.

Even before I glance back, I know what I will see.

A small army of Echo creatures files into the room, taking up positions around the perimeter, avoiding the dais and the machine.

I face the mechanism.

The creatures begin to grunt in unison, as if they're acting out a ritual.

All the hairs at my nape and on my arms shiver and stiffen as awareness teases my senses. *Oh, no, no, no.* I spin around.

Sarah rushes up to me and pounds her fists on my chest. "I can teleport too, you moron. How dare you kiss me and then run away to get yourself killed or melded with a machine or who knows what."

Her eyes shimmer with gathering tears.

Why the fuck did she follow me? Why couldn't she do what I said this one time? I can feel wards lowering over the castle and the entire summit of the mountain. Magics even stronger than the ones that empowered the creatures to break the wards of the stronghold have encased us.

"Dammit, Sarah," I snarl. "You weren't supposed to be here."

"I can't let you do this. There must be another way."

The machine emits a low, growling sound that seems part mechanical and part magics. We both turn toward the dais. The spokes of the Vitruvian Man wheel begin to glow, and the deep, unearthly sound emanating from it grows louder and louder until it finally stops with a thump. The metal clamps that are clearly meant to hold a human body in position pop open.

A soft hum resonates through the room and faintly vibrates into my feet. The call of the machine tugs at me so strongly that I'm breathing hard from the effort of trying to stave it off.

"No, Gabriel, please."

Tears trickle down Sarah's cheeks. I brush them away with my thumbs and cup her face in my hands. "This is how it has to be. I'm sorry."

Chapter Twenty

Sarah

I'VE BECOME FROZEN IN PLACE AS I WATCH GABRIEL STRIDE UP THE STEPS onto the dais and approach the machine. The hum that fills the room throbs once, and the clamps begin to glow faintly. The creatures keep chanting, though I don't think they're speaking words. Or at least, not words in English. Is that Latin? I don't know, and I don't care. Gabriel is about to surrender himself to a machine created by a lunatic.

"No, stop!" I scream, as I fly up the steps to seize his arm. "This isn't right. Please, trust me, don't do this."

"I have no choice. Maybe if I do this, you won't be trapped in the Echo anymore. Maybe I can send you home."

"Maybe? That's your great plan?"

"Don't make this any harder than it already is."

Tears dribble down my cheeks. I don't want to cry. I need to be strong, but I can't control my emotions. The thought of losing Gabriel makes me hurt in ways I've never experienced before. Is this grief? I have no idea. If it is, I'd rather die than live without him, with nothing but the grief to remind me of him.

He turns around, facing away from the machine, and takes a step backward, now inches away from the thing that wants to absorb him or whatever the hell it intends to do to him.

I rush toward him.

A wall of magics blocks my way. I careen off it, falling down the steps and rolling across the floor.

The creatures begin to grunt in unison.

I peel my aching body off the floor, rising to all fours, and glance back at the dais.

Gabriel stands there motionless, expressionless, like he's been drugged. But it's not any kind of drug affecting him. It's the fucking machine.

His clothes vanish.

I clamber to my feet. "Gabriel!"

The machine's clamps reach out to grab him. He doesn't react at all, not even when the clamps snap shut and he's pulled into the machine in a spread-eagle position with his arms slightly raised.

I run up the dais but bump into the wards again. This time, I manage not to fall. My heart thrashes in my chest, and my ears have started to ring. "Gabriel, talk to me, please. Are you okay?"

He blinks slowly, like he's just coming out of a trance. "Sarah?"

"Yes, it's me. I'm here. Are you okay?" I don't see how he could be, when a machine has taken control of his body.

"I'm okay. It doesn't hurt."

But he still sounds weird, like he's half asleep or drugged.

"Please go," he says. "Not safe here. For you."

"No, I will not leave."

The machine emits a series of bizarre thunking and cranking noises that make my skin crawl. What is that thing trying to do?

Meanwhile, the creatures increase the pace of their grunting, growing almost manic.

"It doesn't want you here," Gabriel says, his voice almost a whisper. "If you stay, it will hurt you."

"The machine?"

He nods.

A chill shimmies up my spine. The machine doesn't want me here and will hurt me if I stay. That suggests it's desperate, and in turn suggests I have more power than it does. But I couldn't even save Gabriel from the damn machine.

It blares a long, discordant sound that makes my eardrums vibrate painfully.

Then an invisible force drags me out of the throne room, down the corridor, and through the doors into the courtyard. I struggle against the magics, but they sweep me through the castle gates anyway.

And hurl me off the cliff.

I scream as I hurtle through the air, spinning and spinning.

A giant hand catches me.

While my head keeps spinning, since it hasn't gotten the memo yet that I'm not plummeting to my death anymore, I gaze up at the metal-and-flesh face of the golem. I'm lying on my back in his palm. Jarek looks at me and tips his head to the side, seeming for the life of me like he's worried.

"I'm okay," I tell him, once I can sit up without feeling like I might vomit. "Thank you for saving me."

He nods. Then he glances up at the cliff top.

"We can't help Gabriel right now," I say. "I need to escape the Echo so I can get help from my friends on Earth. Do you know of any way I can force the gateway to open?"

He squints his eyes as if he's considering the problem. Jarek starts walking, away from the castle, carrying me gently in his palm. What about Aldith? Should we find her? Maybe she's safer where she is.

I assume Jarek is taking me to the gateway, and I use this time to think about what to do next. Now that the Brain has taken Gabriel, does it still want to keep the gateway sealed? Since it clearly doesn't want me around, I wonder if it will allow me to leave the Echo now.

Jarek approaches the gateway and halts. He shrugs his shoulders, as if he's letting me know he doesn't know how to get me back to Earth. But it turns out I was right. The gateway spirals open for me. Jarek thrusts his arm through the opening and gently sets me down on the street of a city.

The gateway closes. I am alone in the dark, and nowhere near Sanctuary. I stand on an empty street that shows definite signs of the apocalypse—smashed pavement, wrecked buildings, bent street signs, and piles of rubble. But it's the growling noises emanating from somewhere in the darkness that cranks up my anxiety. Echo creatures make sounds like that.

I teleported myself to Gabriel in the Echo. Maybe I can whisk myself to Sanctuary now. So I close my eyes and wish I were there, wish it with every iota of mental strength I have left in me.

A breeze tickles my arms.

I open my eyes and smile, though it's a faint expression. I'm at the edge of the woods. The light of a bonfire glows in the area between the circle of tents that form our camp. I hear laughter too. My throat goes thick as I run toward Sanctuary, and tears pour down my cheeks until I can barely see where I'm going. Instinct guides me now, and I race up to the bonfire, knowing my friends will be there.

"Sarah!" someone shouts.

I wipe the tears away, sniffling, and see familiar faces heading my way. Erin, Grant, Dax, and Allison hurry over to me. Willow catches up a moment later.

Allison slings an arm around my shoulders. "What happened, sweetie? Where's Gabriel?"

"He's gone." I try not to cry, but a tiny sob bursts out of me. "The machine took him."

"Machine?"

"We can talk about that later," Erin says. "You were gone for three weeks. What happened?"

Three weeks? No, it wasn't that long. But time can move differently in the Echo. Gabriel had been trapped there for three years, though only eight months passed here.

Gabriel. Just thinking his name makes me start crying again.

"Let's get inside," Erin says. "Our tent is closest."

"Yeah," Grant agrees. "We'll take you there."

I let them lead me to Grant and Erin's tent, with Dax, Allison, and Willow following us. But I know they'll want details about what happened, and I don't think I can talk about it yet. I'm exhausted and dehydrated, hungry too. My friends insist I lie down on the cot in Erin and Grant's tent, just until I feel up to walking back to my own place.

Three hours later, I wake up. I hadn't realized I fell asleep, and I feel awful for wasting time while Gabriel is trapped in the Echo, in that machine.

I go to my tent to put on fresh clothes, then look for my friends. I find them all in Dax and Allison's tent. I can tell they've been talking about me, since they abruptly fall silent when I jingle the doorbell, and they stare at me when I walk into the tent.

"How are you feeling?" Allison asks. "We've been so worried about you."

"But not Gabriel. You all think he's evil."

"No, we don't. You know him better than we do." Allison pats the cot she's seated on. "Sit down, Sarah. We'd like to hear what happened. And I'd like to know if you're okay. You look the way I felt when Sefton cast Dax out of Fallenmouth and I had no idea if he was alive or dead."

"I'm okay, physically." I settle onto the cot beside her, but I can't look at my friends. Instead, I gaze down at my hands, which I'm wringing. "I lost Gabriel. Sefton's machine took him."

"Sefton's machine? What are you talking about?"

"When Gabriel and I looked at Sefton's journal, we found that the contents had changed. It showed us different information than what you guys know about."

"I guess that's not surprising," Grant says. "The Echo is a world of magic, and Sefton was its creator. For the journal itself to change based on who looks at it makes a kind of sense."

"None of this makes sense." I clasp my hands tightly to stop myself from wringing them anymore. "The only thing I understand is that Gabriel and I got sucked into the Echo and we couldn't leave. Then we found the machine and…" I wipe at my eyes, but the tears trickle from them anyway. "And now he's gone, trapped in that castle, in that mechanism. The Brain took him and won't let me join him."

I can feel them studying me, but I still can't make myself look at my friends.

"How long were you in the Echo?" Dax asks. "For us, it's been three weeks since we saw either you or Gabriel. We searched the beach and the forest, then went to Fort Worth to search for you more. But we never found even a small clue to your whereabouts."

"It was only two days for us. But it felt like much longer, like we'd known each other forever."

Allison settles her hand over both of mine. "You love him, don't you?"

"Yes. I know it's crazy, but I'm sure of what I feel. I never got to tell him."

"Tell us about this machine."

I take a moment to sort out my memories of my time in the Echo with Gabriel, then I share all of it with my friends. Well, I leave out the stuff about us having sex. But after I'm done, and everyone is digesting what I've told them, I realize I should share everything with them, including the personal parts. My friends don't need the details about our sexual encounters, just the facts about how those experiences changed us both and seemed to change the Echo too.

"There's something else," I say. "It's kind of embarrassing, but I feel like you guys need to know. You have more experience with the Echo than I do, so maybe the information will be useful. It's about me and Gabriel, our relationship."

Jeez, that sounded stupid. I practically stammered when I said the words.

Allison glances at Dax, and her husband nods. She turns to me. "It's about sex, isn't it? You and Gabriel made love, and the Echo responded to that. We've all experienced the phenomenon, though in different ways. Only recently did the four of us talk openly with each other about that stuff. We were uncomfortable discussing the topic."

"I am too. But I realized just now that it might be important, especially for getting Gabriel back."

"When Dax and I had sex for the first time, it amped up my Echo power. And the next time we made love, we both felt something indescribable had changed between us."

"That's what happened with me and Gabriel too. But then the machine got hold of him, and my powers weren't enough to save him."

"Tell us about this machine," Dax says. "My brother never mentioned that to me or to Allison."

"We never heard of it either," Erin says. "Grant and I were in the Echo for a while. Guess that contraption was waiting for Gabriel."

"For both of us, I think. Aldith said the Echo has a Brain, and that it's been adrift without Sefton. He was controlling it. Aldith believed the Brain wanted me and Gabriel to merge with it and take control of it. But if that's true, why did the Brain take Gabriel and kick me out of the Echo?"

Dax rises from his chair and paces the width of the tent. "Perhaps a remnant of Sefton—a ghost, if you will—lingers inside the Brain. It must be cast out before you two will be allowed to assume control."

"But why take Gabriel? I don't understand."

Grant exchanges a glance with Dax, then tells me, "We're all treading on unfamiliar ground here. You said the Brain has two hemispheres, and that it needs both you and Gabriel."

"That's what Aldith said. But maybe she was wrong."

"It's unlikely. She's tapped into the Echo like nobody else in either world. But it's possible the Brain shielded her from seeing that a remnant of Sefton was still in there."

"Yes, that could be," Allison says. "Sefton employed quantum entanglement to link me, Dax, and himself. I severed his links to us when I stopped the alchemy of worlds, but maybe he was also entangled with the Echo. So when he died, something of him survived."

This discussion is reviving more of my memories of the journal. I left it in my pack, and that's still in the Echo. But the more we all talk about these issues, the more I remember. "The machine is modeled after Da Vinci's Vitruvian Man. But Sefton recreated it exactly, with the two sets of arms and legs. If he meant for only one person to enter the machine, why have spaces for more limbs? Aldith must be right that it's designed to accommodate two people."

"But the Echo has become corrupted by the remnants of Sefton," Allison says. "It's interfering with the machine's intended purposed."

Dax halts his pacing and looks sideways at his wife. "Sefton planned to kill me and marry you. He probably wanted you to become the other half of the Brain."

"Yes, that would make sense."

I raise my hand, which is a silly thing to do. "The journal isn't the same as it was before Gabriel and I went into the Echo. I told you the text had changed. But I also felt something strange when I closed my eyes while reading it. I could feel the text, like it was a part of me."

"A part of both you and Gabriel, I'm sure," Grant says. "The way the Heart and the Lifeblood joined me and Erin."

"Can I use that connection to get back to Gabriel and free him from the machine?"

Grant shrugs.

A growling noise erupts outside, growing louder every moment and originating high above us in the sky. We rush outside to see what's happening, but everything looks the same. Something inside that growling sound triggers a memory. The machine made a noise like that.

"What is it, Sarah?" Erin asks.

"It's the machine. It made that noise right before it took Gabriel."

"But it's not here. The noise must be something else. The machine is still inside the Echo."

"Is it? How do we know? It might be interdimensional. I mean, if the Echo can cause lightning in this world, why can't the machine affect Earth too? The worlds are connected, right?"

"Yes, they are." Erin winces as the growling grows even louder, and we need to shout to hear each other. "Got any ideas about how to stop it?"

"Sorry, no."

The racket abruptly stops.

My ears ring, and I keep staring up at the sky, waiting for an Echo flier to swoop down and take me. But I think the machine only let me go with Gabriel because it knew he needed to have sex with me to get primed for melding with the machine. What does that thing want now?

I don't know. But I have no doubts we'll find out soon.

CHAPTER TWENTY-ONE

Gabriel

THE METAL CLAMPS THAT HOLD ME IN POSITION FEEL STRANGELY WARM and silky. Energy buzzes through my entire body, though not enough to hurt. It makes every fine hair on my body stiffen, like an electrical current runs through them. Maybe it is mundane electricity, but I kind of doubt that. Echo power zings through the metal, through me, building up to something I'd rather not think about at all.

What does the Brain want from me? I can't merge with the ghost of a dead maniac. Or can I? Not sure which option is the most disturbing.

I can't even move my head. One big clamp holds it in place.

The gang of Echo beasts hasn't moved since they marched into the room and encircled the perimeter. They've stopped growling, just standing there, silent and motionless. Echo creatures never hang out. They rampage. I think they're in a trance of some sort, waiting for instructions. But from who? Sefton is gone. His doppelgänger is gone too.

I shut my eyes and try to think of a way out of this.

"Afraid there's no time to rest. Wake up, Gabriel."

That voice sounded British.

I open my eyes and blink several times to clear my vision. A blonde man stands several yards away at the edge of the dais. He wears a suit that looks bespoke, though I'm hardly a fashion expert, and his features remind me of someone I sort of know. He reminds me of Dax, though less muscular and without the growling tone in his voice.

"Who are you?" I ask. "Did you bring me here? What did you do with Sarah?"

"That is a long string of queries." He ambles closer, now an arm's length from me and the machine. "Give me time, and I will answer all your questions."

"Start with where Sarah is."

"Gone. She is no longer necessary."

Not necessary? I struggle against my bindings, but the clamps make it hard to wiggle my big toes, much less break free. "What happened to Sarah? You tossed her off a cliff, didn't you?"

"Yes. But unfortunately, she survived. That bloody golem saved her."

Way to go, Jarek. I'll give that golem a big wet kiss the next time I see him. At least I know Sarah is alive.

"I permitted her to leave the Echo," the stranger says. "She will never be allowed to return, and you will never leave. Might as well forget about her."

Never. But telling him that would be monumentally stupid. "Who are you?"

The man smiles, but it's not a friendly expression. "I am Sefton Stainthorpe."

"He's dead."

"Indeed he is. But I am the remnant of his master plan, the entangled Echo of his quantum self."

Yeah, that statement made perfect sense. I should've gotten a degree in quantum physics instead of computer programming.

"How are you a remnant of a dead man?" I ask. "Sefton died months ago."

The pseudo-Sefton sighs with irritation and shakes his head. "You might be the best candidate to fuel the Brain, but you are shockingly ignorant."

"Yeah, I really care what you think of me."

He tips his head to the side, studying me. "I control you. So perhaps you should try being more submissive."

"Wrong. You don't control me, you need me. The Brain doesn't work without me, does it? That's why you needed to use magics to get me here."

A furrow forms just above Sefton's nose, like he doesn't understand what I just said. I'm sure he does. It's more likely that he refuses to accept it.

"You don't have the thought capacity to understand," he says. "Soon, you will be entangled with the machine, and you won't care about petty concerns any longer."

"Why don't you just tell me your evil plan and get it over with?" I'm getting sick of listening to his insults and arrogance. From what I've heard, the real Sefton behaved the same way. So I guess this version of him inherited all the characteristics of his whackjob original.

Entangled Sefton only matters to me because he seems to have control over my body. Once I find a way to break free, I'll scatter his quantum ass into the galactic void. I have no idea if such a thing exists, but I don't care. Screw the scientific terminology. I refuse to become the human puppet of a mad man's ghost.

But I am his puppet right now. Not for long, though.

Sarah and I used our shared Echo power to do a lot of things, like reading the hidden messages in the journal and teleporting our backpacks to us. She managed to teleport both of us and Aldith too. If I can tap into that shared power, maybe I can break free of the machine.

Or at least control it.

Sefton glances at my body and winces. "I wish the machine would allow you to be covered. I dislike seeing unclothed humans."

"You'd be cool with unclothed Echo creatures, then, eh?"

He scowls. "No."

I wonder if the real Sefton had a hang-up about nudity, but that's not important right now. "Go on, tell me your evil plan. I know you're dying to share."

"There is no 'evil' plan. I intend to fulfill Sefton's wishes. He orchestrated the entire plan to create the Echo and initiate the apocalypse, but Dax and Allison circumvented the final chapter. Now that I have the energy provided by your flesh and mind, I may restart the terminal phase."

"You mean the alchemy of souls."

"How does a brute like you know about that? It's beyond the scope of your puny mind to understand it."

Yeah, I can see why Dax snapped his brother's neck. Even the quantum shadow of Sefton is damn annoying and arrogant as hell. Of course, Dax didn't kill his brother for that reason. He did it because Sefton murdered Allison. Thank goodness that girl Willow was able to bring her back. If anything like that happened to Sarah...

I'd rip the throats out of every Echo creature in this room, then I'd find a way to destroy quantum Sefton—and make it hurt like hell.

The only reason I'm listening to him is so I can figure out what he intends to do and how I can stop him.

"Don't you want to tell me all about your grand plan?" I ask. "You know, so I can be awed by your genius."

"Be as sarcastic as you like. It won't save you."

"I'm serious about wanting to hear your plan. If I'm a part of it, I'd like to know what to expect." I try to push against my bindings, but I can't move even one millimeter. "See? I can't escape. Might as well share your ideas. Not like I can tell anybody about it."

"Surprisingly, you've made a good point. Perhaps I will share my plans with you. Saying it out loud is a fine way to hash out a plan."

I didn't really expect him to agree with me, so yeah, I'm feeling proud of myself for tricking him that way. But since I'm still glued to a machine, maybe I shouldn't congratulate myself yet.

Sefton freezes, like a computer that just got unplugged. He doesn't breathe, doesn't move, doesn't blink. Then he abruptly comes back to life. "I am afraid I can't explain right now. I need to deal with another issue first."

He vanishes.

The creatures positioned around the perimeter of the room remain perfectly still, though not as immobile as Sefton had been a moment ago. They make tiny movements, like blinking or minutely twitching a finger, while Sefton seemed as immobile as a statue. That suggests to me that he isn't a living being, but some sort of magical construct designed to act out the desires of the Brain and its machine. Is the Brain separate from the machine? I wish Sarah were here to talk about this with me. I think better when she's beside me.

Yeah, we're a good team. More than a team, actually. We fit together like we were designed for each other. Or maybe destined. I never used to believe in that shit, but now I know it's true.

I wonder if I could summon Sarah here.

No, I won't do that, even if I knew how. She's safer in the normal world than here in the Echo. I'd rather die strapped to this fucking machine than endanger her. But I've still got magics, right? I need to figure out a way to use that to stop the machine.

The creatures begin to moan and grunt, but they still don't move.

A figure appears in front of me.

My heart stutters. "Sarah? How—"

"Don't worry about how. I'm not sure if I have much time, since I can feel the Echo fighting me. It wants me gone."

"Are you really here? Or am I hallucinating?"

She lays a hand on my cheek. "I'm real, Gabriel."

The feel of her palm on my skin makes me almost lightheaded, as relief floods through me. She's here. She's real. I want to touch her, but I can't, so I'll settle for sucking in a big breath to inhale the scent of her. She smells like grass and earth, but I don't care. *She's here.*

"Have you been rolling around on the ground?" I ask. Then I realize what a stupid thing that was to say.

She smiles sweetly. "I tripped and fell down on the grass. Before you panic, I'm fine."

"But I see dirt and grass stains on your clothes. There's something you aren't telling me."

"I was getting there. But I need to do this first."

She rises onto her tiptoes, takes my face in her hands, and kisses me. I relax even more, because the feel of her soft lips and her breaths tickling my skin proves to me that she is real. When she pulls away, she rubs her nose against mine. "I love you, Gabriel."

"I love you too." Maybe I shouldn't, not yet, but life in the Echo taught me the importance of seizing the moment. I should've told Sarah how I feel before the machine took me. I knew it even then. "You shouldn't be here, Sarah. Sefton might come back any second."

"Sefton?"

"Well, not literally him. It's more like a quantum ghost of Sefton Stainthorpe, left behind after the man himself was killed. The being I've met is the entangled Echo of Sefton, and he's somehow infused with the machine."

"That would make sense. I went back to Sanctuary and talked to the others about what's going on. We also wondered if there might be some remnant of Sefton left behind."

"I can confirm that. I've seen him and talked to him."

Sarah still has her hands on my cheeks, as if she can't bear to let go. "I want to try to free you from the machine."

"No, don't do it. Not yet."

"What? Who knows how that machine is affecting you. We need to get you out of there."

"No. Just leave, Sarah. It's too dangerous to try to free me."

She bites her lip and hugs herself. "Gabriel, things aren't going well on the Earth side of things. Something's happening, and I don't think it's good. I have grass and dirt on me because I fell down during an earthquake. Tents were knocked down, and small trees fell too. Then there was the noise in the sky. It reminds me of the sound the machine made when it first activated."

My skin goes cold, and the deep freeze penetrates beneath the surface to chill me to the core. "You heard the machine on Earth?"

"Yes."

"Shit. You need to go home and find out what's going on."

"No. I need to be here with you."

I open my mouth, but I don't get a chance to speak. Someone else does.

"You can't stop what's coming next," Sefton announces as he reappears beside Sarah. "The new alchemy of worlds will begin soon, now that I have you to serve as the power cell. The alchemy of souls won't be far behind."

"You're nothing but a ghost in the machine."

Sefton chuckles. "Don't tax your small mind trying to understand the grandness of my scheme. You don't need to think at all. You are nothing more than a power cell."

"Bullshit. You need me, or you wouldn't be spending so much time trying to convince you're a genius."

"Gabriel? Who are you talking to?"

I rotate my eyes toward Sarah. "You can't see him, can you? It's the quantum ghost of Sefton. He wants to restart the—"

A jolt of electrical energy rips through me, rending a shout from my throat. Spasms rack my muscles, and I feel as if they'll tear me apart. I grit my teeth against the pain, blustering breaths out through my nostrils, until the agony finally subsides.

Sarah tries to touch me, but the last fingers of electricity leap from my skin to zap her. She yelps and stumbles backward. "What was that?"

"The machine doesn't want me to tell you about Sefton's plan."

Sefton laughs. "Of course I don't. Am I a moron? No, that's what you are."

"I can see why your brother snapped your neck," I snarl. "And I'm going to find a way to destroy your quantum ghost too."

"You have neither the power nor the wherewithal."

I want to wring his neck so badly, but even if I could break free of the machine, I can't grab onto a ghost.

"Go," I tell Sarah. "Please. I need to know you're far away from here with people you can trust."

She takes half a step toward me, then stops. Her gaze shimmers with growing tears, but she blinks them away. "This isn't over yet."

The woman I love disappears.

And I'm stuck here with a cadre of monsters and the remnants of a dead man.

Sefton strolls back and forth across the dais in front of me, hands clasped behind his back, a smug smile curling his lips. "You are as stubborn as Dax, but not nearly as strong. I molded him into the perfect monster. He was meant to remain in the Echo, but being a bloody stupid wanker, he just had to leap through the gateway along with the other beasts."

"I bet he's awfully sorry about messing up your plans."

He halts and swivels his head toward me, glaring with all the fire of a mad man. "Do not patronize me. I'm giving you the most incredible gift in the universe."

"Being your Energizer bunny doesn't appeal to me."

"What you want is irrelevant. Together, you and I will restart the alchemy of worlds. It's only the first phase, but I doubt your sweet girl will survive it."

Sarah is much stronger than he thinks. I misunderstood her true nature at first too. But amnesia doesn't make her weak. She's amazing and strong and loyal to the people she loves. The real Sefton Stainthorpe had lacked all those qualities, and his ghost is no different.

If Sarah could teleport into this room, crossing through the gateway despite the Echo not wanting her here, maybe I can summon enough power to shut down this machine.

"No more dillydallying," Sefton says. "It's time to initiate the alchemy of worlds again. And that begins with the quantum entanglement of you and the machine, an unbreakable bond even your friends can't sever."

He vanishes.

And the machine ramps up, grinding and groaning, vibrating the entire room. The creatures begin to chant in grunting, wordless exclamations. Magics inundate the room, invisible yet palpable, nipping at my skin and stinging me like unseen bees. I wince and grit my teeth, but I refuse to give this machine the satisfaction of making me vocalize the pain.

Screw you, Sefton. Not even a remnant of you will fulfill your evil plan.

Because this machine is going down.

CHAPTER TWENTY-TWO

Sarah

LEAVING GABRIEL THERE IN THAT CREEPY CASTLE WITH ALL THOSE CREA-tures and the entangled Echo of Sefton Stainthorpe had been the hardest thing I've ever done. I love him, and he loves me. But that's not enough to save him. We need more than our connection to defeat the machine. We need allies, but not just any allies. Only four other people on Earth understand what it takes to stop the alchemy of worlds and the ghost of its architect.

Sefton let me leave on my own this time, instead of casting me out. He must've hoped I would crash to the ground and die. He no longer seems to view me as any kind of threat, which seems like a bad sign. He believes he holds all the cards, but I will show him how wrong he is. But first, my friends need to know what I've done.

I landed at the edge of the woods and now march across the field to the encampment that is Sanctuary. They haven't lit a bonfire or started up the barbecue grill. It will take time to undo the damage caused by the Echo storm that ravaged our camp. Now that I know for sure the machine is behind the chaos, I also know exactly what needs to be done. I'd had an epiphany while standing in front of that machine, the thing that's holding Gabriel hostage. I felt what he couldn't say, because Sefton was nearby. Gabriel believes I need to stay out of the line of fire, but I know he's wrong. We are stronger together.

Most of the tents have been erected again, so I head straight for Dax and Allison's quarters. When I march inside without even bothering to ring the doorbell, I discover Grant and Erin are there too.

"How did it go?" Grant asks. "Did you see Gabriel?"

"Yes. He's alive and basically okay. But things are about to get much worse for both worlds."

"Tell us everything."

I explain what I learned during my brief visit to the castle. But that's only the beginning. I need to share my plan for stopping the regeneration of the apocalypse, but Dax has a few questions first.

"If you couldn't see Sefton," he says, "how do you know Gabriel wasn't hallucinating? He is trapped inside an Echo machine."

"Can't give you a concrete reason. I trust Gabriel, and I know he actually saw Sefton's quantum ghost."

Dax nods. "Good enough for me."

I hesitate, but only for a few seconds, before I suck it up and tell them the rest. "Any moment, the machine will ramp up and restart the alchemy of worlds. We don't have much time to prepare, but I know what we need to do."

Allison, who had been relaxing on a cot, suddenly springs forward, her gaze pinned to me. "You have a plan?"

"Yes. It will probably sound one hundred percent insane, but please hear me out before knocking it down or duct-taping me to a chair."

"We only duct tape men to chairs," Grant says. "The ones who act like jerks."

Allison rolls her eyes at Grant, then looks at me. "Go on, sweetie. Tell us your plan."

"Here's the short version." I square my shoulders and lift my chin. "We invoke the Tria Prima to take control of the machine and the Echo."

A furrow forms over Allison's nose. "The Tria Prima doesn't exist anymore. It consisted of me, Dax, and Sefton. But I severed our quantum entanglement on the day Sefton died."

"You three were the original Tria Prima. I'm talking about forming a new, stronger version that doesn't involve a wacko who loves dark magics."

"That's interesting," Dax says. "But even a new Tria Prima would only involve three people."

Standing my ground before these four people, my friends, takes all the gumption I've got. For months, I've let everyone else do the hard jobs. I was treated like a delicate princess. But that ends now.

"The new Tria Prima," I say, "includes three couples. The triangle will be formed by those groups, not individuals."

"Couples?" Erin says. "You can't mean…"

"Us. You and Grant, Dax and Allison, and me and Gabriel. We are the real Tria Prima."

Dax gives me a skeptical look. "But the triangle that initiated the apocalypse was three individuals. What makes you think three couples can initiate a new Tria Prima? Especially when Gabriel is being held hostage by a machine."

"You let me worry about Gabriel." If I told them how I intend to ensure our side of the triangle holds up, they would never let me do it. But I'm a grown woman, not a child, and I make my own decisions. "What I need from you guys is your total commitment to this plan. If you don't believe in the Tria Prima, it will never work."

Erin approaches me and lays a hand on my shoulder. "Tell us more about it. Knowing how you came to this conclusion will help us understand."

"Okay." I realize I've been clenching my hands, and I force myself to relax them. "I came to the conclusion that we need a new Tria Prima because I had a revelation while I was studying the journal. Remember I said I could feel the text on the pages? Well, I believe the journal was giving me subconscious clues. Once I understood that, I could more easily see what the Echo needs me to do."

"But the Echo kicked you to the curb, sweetie. Why would it give you clues that might help you destroy it?"

That's another part of my plan that I'd intended to share after I convince them to participate in the most important part. "Let me finish telling you about the Tria Prima first, okay?"

"Sure. I'll zip it." Erin smiles with her lips closed and makes a zipper motion across them. Then she winks and returns to Grant, where they both sit on chairs.

Dax rarely sits down during these kinds of discussions. He prefers to stand behind the others with his arms folded over his massive chest. And that's what he's doing right now.

"To form the new Tria Prima," I say, "we all need to be on board. I know this is a big ask, but let me lay out the scene for you. Dax and Allison were, and as far as any of us know still are, the Anchor and the Catalyst. Erin and Grant are the Lifeblood and the Heart of the Echo, while Gabriel and I are two halves of the Brain. Don't you see? The Echo laid out this plan before we ever set foot in the other world."

Dax seems about to speak—and disagree, no doubt—but I raise a hand to stop him. He smirks a touch but doesn't say anything.

"I believe, though I have no concrete evidence to support the theory, that the Echo is not entirely Sefton Stainthorpe's construct." I wait a couple of seconds, strictly to let that statement sink into their minds. "He created it, yes. But Dax and Allison were integral to the spells that crafted the Echo world itself and the magics that control it."

"Which means what?" Dax asks.

"That you and Allison are a part of the Echo, just as much if not more than Sefton was. Now Grant and Erin have become an integral element too. We have our new Tria Prima, which I believe will be far stronger than the original."

Grant smiles and nods. "I knew you were a genius in disguise, Sarah. Glad you finally let your wings unfurl."

"You don't think I'm insane?"

"No. I think you're amazing."

I can't help blushing a little. Only Gabriel has ever given me a compliment like that.

Dax clears his throat. "I'll reserve my judgment for after Sarah explains the rest of her plan."

And this is the part that will probably convince them I am insane after all. Here we go...

I resist the impulse to bite my lip and glance at each of my friends in turn. "We are going to sever the Echo from the Earth, leaving it as a completely separate world that, I believe, exists only in a parallel universe of magics."

Dax lifts one brow. "That would strand all the Echo creatures who have invaded this world. They will have free rein to wreak havoc on Earth."

"Like they don't already?" Erin says. She shakes her head. "But I'm sure Sarah has more to tell us."

"Yes. That's not my whole plan," I say. "We will also send all the bad creatures back into the Echo just before we sever it from Earth. Good creatures will be allowed to stay here."

Grant raises both his brows. "Are you talking about only Aldith and Jarek? Or other creatures too?"

"All the good ones."

"How are you going to separate the good ones from the demons?"

"With the power of the Echo's Brain, once Gabriel and I take command of it."

"Allison will not enter the Echo," Dax states, his tone fierce. "We will not risk our child's life on a mad scheme like this one."

"I never intended for Allison to go into the Echo. None of you will. I need you here on Earth."

They all stare at me like I've suggested I want them to strip naked and dance in circles around a bonfire.

"Can you guys trust me or not?" I ask. "Because everything depends on you four. No matter what Gabriel and I do, it means nothing without our allies."

"Will you bring Aldith and Jarek in on this?" Grant asks.

"Yes. But I wanted to make sure you guys are in before I tell them." I can't deny I'm a little depressed by their reticence about my plan. But I'd known the moment I conceived it that this would take some serious convincing. "Here's what I need from you guys. Dax and Allison will go to the epicenter of the apocalypse on Earth. That means Fort Worth, Texas. Grant and Erin will go to the point on the planet that is equidistant from Fort Worth."

"Allison cannot go to Texas," Dax snarls. "She's eight months pregnant, and Fort Worth is still a dangerous place."

"I know. But I have a plan for that too."

He sharpens his gaze on me. "It had better be good."

"We will pool our Echo powers to cast a protection spell on Allison. No creatures will be able to touch her."

"Suddenly, you're an expert on magics. That's bollocks."

"No, it isn't." I take a breath and exhale out my frustration. I understand Dax's concerns, and I would never want to put Allison in danger. But I can't figure out how to explain this in a way that will convince Dax. If he says no, my entire scheme falls apart. "You don't know what happened in the castle, while Gabriel and I were there together. Before the quantum ghost of Sefton appeared. We shared more than sex. We forged a bond so deep that I can't even describe it. We met a few days ago, yet I feel closer to him than to anyone else in the world. I know our connection will provide the power we need to complete the mission."

"We're meant to rely on what a book told you to do."

"No, Dax, that's not what I'm saying. Gabriel and I activated the journal, unknowingly, and that's why it provided information to us that no one else had seen."

Erin is watching me with a tight expression. "Don't mean to rain on your parade, Sarah, but we have solid reasons for being skeptical. You have amnesia. That means you don't remember the alchemy of worlds and all the horrific things that happened in the days after the apocalypse began. We do. This world is full of Echo creatures who poured out of the gateway and swarmed the Earth. We fought them. We lost loved ones because of them. Every single person in Sanctuary has experienced the horrors of the apocalypse—except for you."

She's not being nasty or insulting me. I expected this reaction, but I can't deny that I feel completely deflated by having the truth thrust in my face like a pin popping a balloon. But I can't let that stop me. The stakes are too high. So it's time to reveal my biggest revelation.

"While I was inside that castle earlier, with Gabriel pinned to that machine, I experienced what you might call an epiphany." I feel my fingers wanting to curl into my palms, but I order them not to do that. "I believe my amnesia is not a fluke. It's part of a plan so vast and incredible that I don't know how to describe it. The best word would be fate. I remember men trying to protect me when the alchemy of worlds started, and I believe they somehow realized I would become an important link in the chain of saving the world."

My friends exchange surprised looks. But are they surprised by how bonkers I am? Or by how much they believe what I said?

"My amnesia gives me a different perspective," I say. "You might say I have a clean slate on which to draw my conclusions. I'm not riddled with pain and guilt over loved ones I've lost. My opinions and actions aren't colored by experiences during the alchemy of worlds and everything that came later. Maybe I'm the one who thought of this plan because I have no memories of the first days of the apocalypse. And I'm not hindered by constant worry about what happened to my family and friends, if I have any of those."

They all stare at me again. But I think I see a glimmer of understanding in their eyes, and maybe, just maybe, the beginnings of acceptance.

A horrendous racket erupts in the sky, and the ground shudders violently.

I stumble sideways. Dax tries to reach Allison, but trips and tumbles to the ground. Allison slides off her cot to huddle beside her husband. Erin and Grant cling to each other, until they see me struggling to stay on my feet. Then they both rush over to me, and we huddle together while the most bizarre mechanical noises I've ever heard rattle and screech and scrape in the air. The noises are so loud that I wince and squeeze my eyes shut.

Whump. Whump. Whump.

The concussions vibrate through my entire body. As the mechanical noises fade away, screams pierce the air.

Whump. Whump.

The roars of Echo creatures resound everywhere, and the first slashes of Echo lightning stab into the ground. But unlike before, the lightning sizzles and buzzes like electricity racing through a high-tension line.

"Stay here with Allison," Dax tells me. "The rest of us will see what's going on."

"The machine is angry, that's what," I say. "It wants to destroy both worlds."

"Remain here. We will inspect the situation."

Dax, Erin, and Grant rush outside.

I should be out there with them, since I know about the machine and they don't. But I won't leave Allison alone.

Explosions detonate outside, too close and too powerful. They make the ground shudder like an earthquake.

Crack. The sound reverberates in the clearing that surrounds the camp. I've heard that sound before.

A falling tree splits the tent open and smacks down.

Chapter Twenty-Three

Gabriel

THE MACHINE HUMS AND WHIRS AND EMITS A HARSH RATCHETING noise, while the creatures begin to chant again, though I still can't recognize any words in the sounds they make. Energy crackles through my bindings, pinching and biting at my skin. I grit my teeth against the pain and try to focus on a way to escape, or at least halt, the machine's actions.

What is it doing? How many people will it mow down in its determination to complete its task?

The ghost of Sefton appears in front of me. He smiles just like the Cheshire cat, so smug and hungry for blood. "It has begun. Stop trying to find a weakness in the machine. There is none. Once the process has completed, I will no longer require you."

"Bullshit. You don't have the power to keep the alchemical reaction going. Or have you forgotten what happened after Allison shut it down? Fallenmouth was devoured, but the rest of the world went into a kind of stasis."

How do I know that? Through my connection with Sarah, I think.

Sefton lifts his chin. "This time is different."

"Delude yourself all you want. But if you kill me, in six months you'll regret it."

Will he? No idea. I'm snowing him to buy time.

But I don't believe what he said. *It has begun.* I don't think so. The machine has been making all kinds of noises, but I don't feel anything different, certainly not the kind of magics that restarting the alchemy of worlds would require. He'll need me and Sarah for that. But that bastard will never get his hands on her. She's tougher, smarter, and stronger than he thinks.

He clearly has turned the machine up to a higher setting, one that probably uses more energy. Maybe I can leverage that. If it's struggling, why can't I make its job even harder?

I close my eyes and focus all my thoughts on the clamps that hold me in place, funneling every bit of supernatural energy inside me on the task of loosening the bindings. Nothing happens. I keep trying. Slow, deep breaths. Relax my muscles. I need to stop consciously trying to affect the machine and let instinct take over. The energies grow inside me, spreading outward from my chest, into my arms and legs. The magics rush up into my head, buzzing in my brain.

The strength of the magics makes my heart pound and sweat break out on my brow. I struggle to take normal breaths, but I will not give up no matter how hard the energies hit me.

A loud thunk echoes inside the throne room, and the machine winds down. I'm still trapped inside it, but at least the thing has lost power. For how long? At least I can relax, for now, while I consider what my next move is. I let my lids fall shut and sag against my bindings.

"Gabriel? Are you hurt?"

My lids fly open, and I gape at the woman standing a few yards away on the dais.

Aldith has her hands clasped in front of her, as always, but she's wringing them so hard that I wonder if she's abrading her own skin.

"What's up, Aldith?" I ask. "You should be hiding."

"I couldn't stay where you and Sarah left me. Jarek came for me, and I learned that the machine is on the verge of reaching its full capacity." She meets my gaze briefly, then winces. "You are its full capacity."

"No, I'm half of it. As long as Sarah doesn't come back here, the machine will never get what it wants."

"Buy you cannot take control of it without her."

I just manage to stifle a growl. "Yeah, go on and shout that a little louder, would you? Not sure Sefton's quantum ghost heard you."

She tips her head to the side. "I am trying to help you, Gabriel."

"Yeah, I know. I'm sorry, Aldith. It's not your fault I can't stop this machine from destroying both worlds."

"The only way Sefton wins is if you give up. His mortal self wrought untold devastation on two worlds, and now a remnant of his magics may do the same thing. You must keep fighting, please."

She sounds worried. No, more than worried. I think Aldith is terrified of what might happen if the Brain succeeds in recreating the alchemy of worlds. Maybe it already has. I hear explosions outside. Since this room has no windows, I can't see the lightning bolts and fireballs, but I have no doubts they're out there.

"You must find Sarah," Aldith says. "This time, the apocalypse has no boundaries, because no one has control of it."

"I get it, we're in deep shit. Don't need to keep harping on the issue."

She glances around as if she's looking for something—maybe the ghost of Sefton Stainthorpe. "I must go. But please, Gabriel, never stop fighting. Both worlds need you."

Aldith vanishes.

I've never seen another Echo creature do that. Of course, I hadn't seen a human do that until I met Sarah. I suppose Aldith is different from other Echo beings, and that's why she protects the stronghold.

Now what? I shut down the machine, but it still has a hold on me. I stand here, held in place by metal clamps and plates, and listen while the apocalyptic sounds outside draw closer and closer to the castle. The floor begins to vibrate with every concussion. The machine vibrates too, only a little at first, then growing stronger as the lightning and fireballs continue to assault the ground.

What are the odds that Sefton cast a protection spell around this building to spare it from the apocalypse? If he didn't, I won't need to worry about how to get out of this machine. I'll die when the monstrous thing crashes down on me.

The creatures become restless, milling around like they don't know what to do. They begin to grunt, louder than before, and jostle each other as they move around, apparently without any idea what they're doing.

Great. Disturbed creatures are exactly what I need right now.

The room around me shifts and fades away, replaced by a dark void with a single ray of light emanating from above. But when I glance up, I can't see the source, only the diffuse glow.

Five figures appear in a circle that includes me.

"How did you guys get here?" I ask. "And how did I get here?"

Sarah clasps my hand. "We needed a safe place to talk about our plans, and we needed you to be here with us. Since we couldn't risk Sefton hearing what we say, the five of us managed to create a bubble of magic that exists outside the realm of reality."

"Uh, sure, whatever you say." I must be hallucinating. Magic bubbles? Come on.

"I know it sounds crazy." Sarah leans against me, lifting her head to meet my gaze. "But you know what I can do. I teleported myself straight into the castle from Earth. And with four friends to help, it shouldn't be a surprise that we could create this bubble. We're more powerful together."

"You're right, I know. So just tell me what this is all about."

"It's happened. Sefton's quantum remnant has restarted the alchemy of worlds. We need to stop it, once and for all, so neither world will be subject to a mad man's whims ever again."

"Okay, good plan. But how do we implement it?"

Dax steps forward. "We are going to tap into the power of the Tria Prima."

"I thought the Tria Prima was you, Allison, and Sefton."

"Yes, it was. Sarah pointed out that we have a new version of the Tria Prima that may prove even stronger than the original." He hooks an arm around Allison, tugging her close. "The six of us represent the new Tria Prima, the power that can stop the alchemy of worlds. This was all Sarah's idea, and we believe she's right."

"Six of us?"

"That's right," Sarah says. "Three couples whose undying love and strength might be the key to ending the apocalypse forever—Dax and Allison, Grant and Erin, and you and me."

A chill rushes over my skin, but I'm not afraid. This is a shiver of excitement. When Sarah spoke those words, telling me about the New Tria Prima, I felt something indescribable, something so deep and immutable that I know everything she said is true. Three couples. Of course the way to end the apocalypse is for the six of us to flip Sefton's idea on its head. Not one group of three, but three distinct groups that together possess more power than even the original Sefton Stainthorpe.

This might just work.

"How do we do this?" I ask. "You said you have a plan."

Sarah ducks under my arm to slide hers around my waist, and I instinctively wrap my arm around her. "It begins with the two of us seizing control of the machine to shut down the alchemy of worlds."

"How, exactly?"

"Through the power of the Tria Prima. Dax and Allison will go to Fort Worth, which is the epicenter of the apocalypse. Then Erin and Grant will travel to a spot on the other side of the world that's equidistant from Fort Worth. At the same time, you and I will be inside the castle in the Echo, since that seems to be the epicenter of everything in that world."

She really has thought about this. The journal ignited something inside her, and she is no longer just a girl with amnesia. Sarah has become a powerful woman.

I could kiss her right now.

"How do we shut down the apocalypse?" I ask. "I've tried to stop the machine, but the most I could do was shut it down for a while. I can feel it ramping up again even now."

"You haven't been able to shut it down completely because you didn't have me. We're one corner of the Tria Prima triangle, remember? You and I need to stop the machine together."

"Have you found a way to get me out of the machine? Can't see any other way that we can both shut it down."

"I think it's best if I show you what I mean."

Dax chuckles. "Why be shy about it now? We had a group discussion on the subject back in the tent, before everything went to hell—again."

I squint at Sarah. "What is he talking about?"

"The alchemy of worlds has started up again."

"Yeah, I know that. But Dax just said you guys had a group discussion about something that you don't want to tell me."

"I was going to tell you. Just not in front of the others."

Dax is smirking. Allison seems amused. Grant wears a calm expression, while Erin seems to be trying not to smile.

"Somebody tell me what the hell is going on," I say. "We don't have time to dance around whatever it is."

"You're right," Sarah says. "We've realized that sex is a vital component of stopping the apocalypse."

I stare at her. Is my mouth hanging open? I think it might be. For a moment, I can't think, much less come up with words. Sarah just announced that to save the world, we need to fuck. Yeah, I'm pretty sure that's what she meant. Not that I mind. But come on, we can't talk about sex in front of the others.

"We felt weird about it too, at first," Grant says. "But then we realized Sarah is right—and she's a genius."

"I knew that already," I say. "But how does getting naked save the worlds?"

Sarah rests her chin on my chest. "The first time Dax and Allison made love, it increased her Echo power. Erin and Grant experienced the same thing. You and I felt the same thing. Didn't we?"

"Well, yeah. But I don't know if I can, uh, get in the right frame of mind to do that right now. Besides, I'm still trapped in the machine."

"Don't worry about that."

"How do you plan to get around it? Having sex kind of requires physical contact."

She pats my chest. "Let me worry about that. You trust me, don't you?"

"Of course I do."

"Then trust me on this."

How can I say no to her? She's amazing, and I will do whatever she says we need to do. The fact that I love screwing her has nothing to do with my decision.

But I suddenly remember something. "Allison is very pregnant. We can't risk sending her to the epicenter of the apocalypse."

"We've taken care of that," Sarah says. "Using our combined Echo powers, we cast a protection spell around Allison."

"Can't we all get one of those?"

"We didn't want to deplete our magics when we still need to implement the plan. Allison needed the most protection. The rest of us can take care of ourselves."

She's right. We shouldn't waste energy. Because I have a feeling that we'll need every iota we have to defeat Sefton's quantum ghost and end the chaos.

"Okay," I tell Sarah. "Let's get this train rolling."

"There's one more thing we all need to discuss." She glances at each of our friends, then lifts her gaze to mine. "I believe we can restore the Earth to the way it was before the apocalypse, but there's a caveat."

"What is it?"

"I can't guarantee we will remember who we are now. The spell might erase our memories of everything before the Echo, and then we wouldn't know we ever loved each other." She glances at our friends again. "Or that we became a family."

We all just stand here, frozen and silent, as we digest what Sarah said. Forget her? Never. But we're talking about magics, and nothing is ever certain with that stuff. My life before the apocalypse had been dull and lonely. Then I got thrown into the hell of the Echo and became someone I never imagined I could become. The computer programmer turned into a fighter.

I'd love to say adios to the alchemy of worlds and see the Earth returned to its natural state. But I never want to give up the best thing that ever happened to me—finding Sarah. She taught me more than I could ever explain and changed me in all the best ways.

To lose her love... I'd rather die than forget about her.

Dax pulls Allison into his arms. "That's a hefty price to pay for saving the world. But we don't have a choice, do we? And you said you don't know for certain that we will lose our memories of knowing each other."

"That's right," Sarah says. "I believe with all my heart that we won't forget each other. But I won't swear it's a certainty. You need to know the risks."

Dax and Allison gaze into each other's eyes, and he brushes his fingers over his wife's cheek. "We must risk it."

She nods, as tears brim in her eyes.

Erin throws her arms around Grant's neck and whispers into his ear. He nods, and they both seem to be choked up. Grant sounds that way when he says, "We're on board, whatever might happen. Bringing back the world everyone used to know is worth the risk. And I believe, like Sarah does, that we won't forget each other."

I pull Sarah close and kiss her. "Whatever comes next, remember one thing. I will love you until the day I die and beyond, until the universe explodes and there's nothing left. I'll love you forever, and nothing can erase that."

She flings her arms around my neck and rises onto her tiptoes to whisper, "Destiny brought us together, and that's how I know we will survive—and remember."

But we all understand what we're risking and how it might all go sideways.

"It's time to go our separate ways," Sarah says. "Go to your assigned locations, while I find a way to reach Gabriel."

"You're going in well-prepared," Dax tells her. "And we all know you can do this."

The others disappear, leaving me and Sarah alone in this bubble of magic.

She gives me a small smile. "See you soon."

Then she's gone.

And I'm back inside the machine.

Chapter Twenty-Four

Sarah

WE RETURN FROM OUR TRIP INTO THE BUBBLE AND DISCOVER THAT the world has gone insane in the meantime. Not only do fireballs and lightning slam into the earth, but Echo creatures attack every human they see. Everyone in Sanctuary has learned how to fight, and they wield all sorts of weapons to fight off the beasts. Flying creatures keep swooping down in their attempts to snag a meal.

Yes, everyone here can fight—except for me. My friends thought I needed to be protected. But now, I need to breach Sefton's castle, without having any idea what I'll do if I can't simply teleport into the throne room. I don't have training in how to defend myself, but it can't be that hard to stab a monster with a sword.

"I need a weapon," I say. "In case I have to fight my way into the castle. The machine doesn't want me there."

"Okay," Grant says. We're shouting to be heard above the din. "But I think you'd be better off locating a weapon inside the Echo. I can tell you where to find a sporting goods store that has firearms and lots of other stuff."

"That's a good idea," Erin says. "But we should give her a crash course on how to operate a gun."

Dax has his big body wrapped around Allison, shielding her from the melee. "We will head to Fort Worth and find a place to hide that's near the gateway. Let's agree to enact the plan in thirty minutes."

We all agree, and Dax whisks his wife away. I know that they, along with Grant and Erin, have been keeping their watches synchronized just in case something like this happened and we needed to find each other. I also know they had agreed that, if the worst happened, they would teleport to search for each other once every hour.

But I don't have a watch.

Grant and Erin shepherd me into the woods, where the creatures haven't yet decided to hunt. They will soon, I'm sure. The melee is a bit quieter here, the noises dulled by the trees.

"I need a watch," I say. "Otherwise, we won't be synchronized."

"Take mine," Erin says. "I'll be with Grant, so we can share his watch. But time can move differently in the Echo, so we might end up not synchronized after all."

"No choice. This is the best we can do."

For the next ten minutes, my friends give me that crash course Erin had mentioned. It sounds like operating an automatic machine gun isn't that difficult. Of course, hearing about it isn't the same as actually handling such a weapon.

Erin and Grant both hug me, then teleport to their assigned location.

And I transport myself directly into the Echo. The machine didn't try to stop me. Maybe quantum Sefton is distracted by orchestrating mayhem. I can't assume that will keep him occupied for much longer, so I teleport to the shop Erin and Grant had mentioned. I find the items they recommended—a machine gun, extra magazines for it, and a machete. That's a long, wicked-looking knife. Maybe I was a badass in my life before amnesia, because I don't feel weird at all about fighting my way into the castle.

Erin had also recommended a few more items. Grenades are pretty straightforward to use. Pull the pin and throw the grenade. I dump the grenades and the extra magazines of ammo into a canvas bag and sling that over my shoulder.

Then I zip myself to the castle.

But I wind up at the base of the mountain on which the castle rests. It would take forever for me to climb up the steep cliff. I try again to teleport, but the wards around the mountain prevent it.

I hear so much chaos throughout the Capital City that I can't sort out which noises indicate what type of danger. The sky has become crimson. The stench of rotting flesh and blood fills the air.

Oh God, is it this bad in Fort Worth?

I refuse to look back. There's no point. I need to focus on finding a way up the cliff. Only by stopping the apocalypse can I save any innocent Echo beings that still live here.

The ground shudders.

Probably fireballs punching into the earth.

I try to climb the cliff, but I can't even get a hand-hold. The wards prevent it.

A large hand scoops me up, lifting me to the height of the cliff top.

I glance over my shoulder and realize I'm cradled in Jarek's enormous palm. He can give me a lift to the top of the mountain, but I still have the wards to deal with before I can get anywhere near the castle.

But I can feel Gabriel in there, reaching out to me.

Jarek fists his other hand, pulls it back, and slams his fist into the wards. They crackle and shimmer but remain in place.

"Do that again," I say. "And I'll focus on tapping into my connection with Gabriel."

The second I attempt to reach him, I sense the warmth and love and passion he feels for me coming down through our connection, feeding into my passion for him. I suck in a breath, stunned by the ferocity of our shared emotions and desires.

Jarek rams his fist into the wards.

They shatter with a sound like breaking glass and a rush of released magics. But I have no time to waste. I leap off Jarek's palm, shout "thank you" to him, and race toward the castle gates.

A figure appears there just as I reach the gates. Aldith wears an expression I've never seen from her before—resolute determination. "If you have a weapon to spare, I would like to fight with you."

"I'd be grateful for the help. Would you prefer a gun or a machete?"

"Whichever is easiest to use. I have no training in weaponry."

"Neither do I, but my friends gave me a crash course." I dig inside my bag and bring out the machine gun. "Try this. You pull the trigger and it shoots a volley of bullets. I have extra ammunition too."

I get out the extra clips and show her how to switch them out, something I learned less than half an hour ago from my friends. Was I in the military before the apocalypse? Doesn't matter. Today, I have become a warrior—and so has Aldith.

When I check my watch, I see that we have seventeen minutes to break into the castle and enact the plan my friends and I devised. My heart rate spikes, and I feel a strange mix of excitement and fear. What we're about to do… It's beyond epic. If we survive, this will be the most incredible feat in the history of the world.

The castle gates are closed. When Aldith and I try to open them, we can't do it. The wooden barrier is too thick and strong.

A large metal-and-flesh hand reaches around us to tap the gates. They fly open.

"Thank you, Jarek," I shout to the golem.

Aldith and I storm the castle.

But we find only an empty courtyard and an empty entryway. The Echo creatures who guard Gabriel haven't sent any of their brethren to protect the rest of the building. They must assume that no one can breach the castle. We slow down as we approach the doorway to the throne room, which has become the machine room, and we hear a strange humming that does not sound mechanical.

I recognize the sound. It's the creatures who are guarding Gabriel.

Aldith and I stop in the corridor, sidling up to the wall beside the doorway. My watch tells me we have ten minutes left.

I whisper to Aldith, "Get your gun ready. We're going in there, and those creatures won't be happy about it. If you need to run, do it."

"No, I will not leave you."

"Please, Aldith. If the creatures try to swarm you, just run. Teleport away if you can. Getting yourself killed won't help anybody."

"All right."

She doesn't sound happy about what I told her, but I know she will do as I asked.

Now, it's time to storm the throne room.

But we don't burst in, surrounded by a hail of bullets. No, I have a different plan, and it depends on the creatures behaving the way they have since the moment the machine revealed itself.

Aldith stays huddled just out of sight, at the threshold.

I walk into the room, working hard to stop myself from seeming anxious, and casually pass by the creatures who are arrayed around the periphery of the room, including at either side of the doorway. Though my pulse kicks up a couple of extra notches, I remain outwardly calm. The creatures don't seem to notice me, not yet. They're chanting wordlessly while rocking side to side.

Gabriel watches me.

He probably wants to tell me to go away, but he knows as well as I do that any sound might set off the creatures. I hold my machete in one hand, while I have the canvas bag over my opposite shoulder. The grenades are in there. I hope I don't need them, but I won't hesitate if they threaten me or Gabriel.

A shiver sweeps over my skin from head to toe, raising every hair on my body.

I glance around, but the creatures still seem entranced and unaware of my presence. But my intuition warned me to watch out. That's what the shiver meant. Something is about to happen, and I need to be hyper-aware of my surroundings.

Halfway across the room, I stop. Another shiver, much colder than the first, tingles over my skin. I look around but can't see anything. That doesn't mean nothing is going to happen. If my intuition needs to warn me about something, I'll pay attention.

But I won't stop. I can't.

So I start walking again.

Gabriel mouths, "No."

He doesn't really expect me to stop. He knows me too well to believe I'll do that.

A shimmering curtain of magics drops down at the foot of the steps, enveloping the entire dais and the machine. Wards? If quantum Sefton wants a fight, he's about to get one.

I approach the invisible barrier and speak in a calm tone. "Come out, Sefton, and let me see you. Or are you afraid of me?"

"Afraid? Hardly." The ghost of Sefton has appeared on the dais, between me and Gabriel. "You are a foolish child, coming here alone."

He doesn't realize Aldith is in the corridor. Guess he's not all-knowing.

"Why didn't you let me see you last time?" I ask. "If you aren't afraid, you had no reason to hide from me."

"I simply had no desire or need to speak to you."

The sounds of the apocalypse in full swing continue outside, though the ruckus became a background noise the moment Aldith and I entered the castle. I suppose the real Sefton didn't want to hear the agony and suffering of living beings and made sure to dull the noise in his cliff-top hideaway.

"I want to talk to Gabriel," I tell Sefton. "Take down your wards and let me approach the machine so I can speak to him. Please."

Might as well try politeness first.

He glances down at the machete in my hand, then raises his brows. "Why on earth would I do that? You mean to murder me. Not that you will succeed. I have no physical form."

"I know that. This weapon is for your minions, in case they get a little too frisky."

A quick glance at my watch warns me I have only six minutes to complete my task. Screw this. If the ghost of Sefton Stainthorpe won't get out of my way, I'll move him myself.

I shift slightly to the side, where I can see Gabriel, and tap into the connection between us, which makes his eyes flare wide for a split second. Then he reverts to the neutral expression he's worn ever since I entered the room. The power we share sizzles inside me, enlivening my skin and diving deep beneath it to awaken the most sensual parts of me. My nipples tighten. I grow slick between my thighs. The nature of our shared magics has always been erotic, and I no longer worry about why.

I revel in it.

We gaze into each other's eyes, and I feel the Echo energies gathering inside us both.

"Stop that," Sefton snarls. "Stop it now, or I'll have my disciples do it for you."

I ignore him and focus on Gabriel as the energies infiltrate my body, rushing through every part of me and down to my bones too.

"Kill her!" Sefton shouts.

The creatures rouse from their stupor and run toward me.

Automatic gunfire erupts from the doorway, but I don't have time to worry about Aldith or the creatures. The power inside me and Gabriel has reached critical mass, and it's time to unleash it. A ball of sizzling white energy appears between us.

I hurl it at the wards.

They don't shatter, because I don't want them to do that. Instead, the wards let me slip through them, then they seal behind me. Sefton has been ejected from the dais and now lies sprawled on the floor.

"No, Sarah," Gabriel says as I approach the machine. "Please, don't—"

"We've all agreed. This is the only way. You can't back out now, or both worlds will be destroyed."

He shuts his eyes briefly. "I know this is the only way, but I worry about what the magics will do to you."

I clasp his face in my hands. "Stop thinking. It's time to let our instincts take over."

Gabriel's brows knit together, but he seems to be looking at something behind me. I turn to look. Aldith is knocking down Echo creatures like they were bowling balls, though all the bullets in the universe probably can't kill those monsters. But she's buying us time, and that's all I needed her to do.

"Run, Aldith," I shout. "Find a place to hide."

Sefton leaps to his feet and races toward Aldith with his teeth bared, screaming like an enraged animal.

I drop the machete and my bag, then strip off my clothes.

Gabriel's dick is hardening. That's exactly what needs to happen right now. His breathing grows heavier, and he licks his lips as he watches me walk up to the Vitruvian Man device. He shakes his head. "We can't. I'm stuck in this machine and—"

"Let me handle this."

I kneel before him and take his cock in my mouth, pumping the base with one hand while I lick and tease the head. He sucks in a breath. I keep working him with my mouth and hand until I can feel he's on the verge of orgasm. Then I stand up.

"Sarah…" His voice trails off, but the rough tone makes my clit throb.

I climb onto the machine, setting my feet on top of his, then shift my soles onto the inner set of clamps while I place my arms in the second set of clamps that lie just below where his arms are locked in position. The machine wakes up, buzzing and thunking and whirring. The clamps snap into place around my arms, and the action lifts my feet onto my toes. Now I'm attached to the machine in the same way he is. But the fact that I'm shorter than he is means that his cock rubs against me but I can't get him nestled between my folds. The vibrations of the machine increase my arousal, and I've become so wet that the slickness dribbles down my inner thighs.

"Unhook us from the machine," I say, my voice huskier and laden with desire. "We can do it together."

The desire that keeps mounting inside me has stolen my breath. I want him more than I ever have before, and I can tell from the darkening of his eyes and the way his cock jerks against me that Gabriel is experiencing the same intense need.

The machine ramps up, its power vibrating through the floor and into our bodies, as if it's giving us whatever we need to accomplish our task. Only one thing remains.

A surge of power rushes out of the machine and into us. The man-size wheel pops free and falls to the floor face-down. I'm crushed under Gabriel, but I'm not injured. The clamps loosen enough that I can wriggle upward to get his cock into position and slide it inside me.

"Fuck me, Gabriel," I say. "Fuck me now."

Chapter Twenty-Five

Gabriel

I HAVE NO CONTROL OVER MY BODY, AND I DON'T CARE. THE POWER WE share has taken command. The feel of Sarah's body wrapped around my cock steals any thoughts I might've had, and I relinquish myself to her. Even the machine seems to want her, the way it molded itself to her body the instant she stepped into it, then tipped the wheel over to give us the perfect position. So what if we're trapped under the machine? It's feeding us the energy we need. I have just enough leeway to thrust into her, over and over, helpless to stop. Not that I want to stop. Making love to Sarah to save the world is one order I'm happy to comply with, again and again.

The wards around the machine have turned opaque, almost like the Echo wants to give us privacy for this.

She moans when I rock my hips with more vigor and the energies that surround us begin to cling to our skin and sink beneath it. I've never felt anything like it. My ears have started to ring, and black spots appear in my vision, but still, I need to keep fucking her.

The machine is vibrating and shaking, and I can see quantum Sefton standing at the edge of the dais, holding his head in his hands while shrieking in agony.

Don't care. I need to make Sarah come, and nothing else matters. She has her face mashed to my chest, and my flesh muffles her screams, though she hasn't hit that peak yet. I thrust deeper and harder, straining the clamps with the force of my movements, desperate to break free. The pressure inside me intensifies, and my dick feels like it might explode if I can't give her what she needs.

I shift the angle of my thrusts minutely, but it's enough. Now I'm rubbing against her clit with every movement, no longer trying to get as deep inside her as possible, only caring that she needs to climax right now. Faster, faster, I scrape her nub.

Sarah squeezes her eyes shut and screams.

I thrust deep and hold that position, while her body clenches me, her cries become hoarse, and her eyes roll back in her head.

The clamps pop open.

We tumble to the floor, still entangled, and the wheel swings back up into the machine. I lock my hands around Sarah's wrists to hold them above her head.

"Don't stop," she pleads. "Please, don't stop."

No way in hell I'll give up now. Lying sprawled on top of her, I keep pumping into her wildly, grunting and shouting, gazing into her eyes the entire time. Fire scorches down my spine and straight into my cock, like nothing I've ever experienced before. My back bows up, and I explode inside her.

Sarah screams and comes again. Her body milks me while I keep coming, buried so deep inside her that it seems impossible. By the time it's over, we're both boneless and stunned, incapable of moving or speaking. Taking a breath seems like a Herculean task. My head rests over Sarah's heart, every beat thumping in time with mine. After a few minutes—or maybe a few hours, who knows—I slide off her and pull Sarah into my arms.

"Do you hear that?" she asks.

"Hear what?"

"The silence."

I freeze, listening for any sound. But I hear only my own heartbeat and the soft sound of her breaths. The wards have disintegrated, I can tell that much. The machine has shut down. I should hear noises from outside, shouldn't I? And the creatures who guarded the machine ought to be making noises too.

"Did we do it?" I ask. "Did we stop the alchemy of worlds?"

"Seems like it."

I sit up and look around, surprised to find all the Echo creatures lying dead on the floor.

Aldith stands near the doorway, biting her lip.

"Did you do that?" I ask. "You're holding a machine gun, so I figured…"

Aldith nods. "I didn't mean to shoot them all, but they kept coming at me."

"You did what you had to do. They were lunatics." I glance at Sarah, who lies huddled on the floor, as if she's cold. "Better get dressed. Our work isn't done yet."

While she finds her clothes and pulls them on, I stand up and search for my stuff. My clothes kind of just disappeared, so I don't know if I can find it again. Every time I glance at Aldith, she swerves her gaze away from me, then covertly peeks. Maybe she's never seen a naked man before. She did live in the stronghold, all alone.

Sarah squints and flattens her lips.

My clothes appear in her arms. "Better cover up that sexy body. Don't think Aldith knows how to deal with nudity."

I pull on my clothes, then lead the ladies out of the throne room. We bump into a few creatures, but they seem dazed and uninterested in causing trouble. Outside, we find Jarek waiting to give us and Aldith a ride to the gateway. Our job isn't done yet. The most daunting task still lies ahead of us.

Reversing the damage to both worlds.

When we reach the gateway, we discover it's wide open—wider than usual, in fact. The opening stretches across the horizon, though it still hangs high above the ground. Jarek could easily walk through it, but instead of doing that, he hesitates and looks at us.

"Go on through," Sarah says. "You're coming with us. Once all the good Echo beings have escaped, all the bad ones will be locked inside that world. You need to leave now."

A distant rumbling draws all our attention to the city behind us. The castle is crumbling and sliding off the steep sides of the mountain.

Good riddance, I say.

Jarek steps through the gateway.

Echo creatures who had loitered nearby—in hopes of catching someone to eat, no doubt—now turn and run away from the golem. We'll catch them later. Right now, we need to find our friends. Jarek crouches to set us down on the wrecked street.

We're in Fort Worth. The apocalypse began here, and it's only fitting that it should end here too. The nightmare Sefton Stainthorpe crafted will vanish, replaced by the beautiful, imperfect world we'd known before the alchemy of worlds. Sefton tried to transmute the Earth into his vision of perfection, and it cost the lives of countless humans and Echo beings, not to mention his own life. Was it worth it? Only Sefton knows if he was satisfied with the result.

Two figures emerge from the shadows in an alley, striding toward us. As they draw closer, I realize it's Dax and Allison.

"How did it go?" Allison asks. "On our end, it seemed to work."

"Yeah, it worked," I say. "The machine and the castle are gone. The Echo will be just a normal planet now, in a parallel universe, and the beings left inside it will need to teach themselves how to live without magics."

"What about the Heart and the Lifeblood?"

Erin and Grant appear in front of us.

Sarah grins at them. "You're back."

"We heard you guys talking about us," Erin says. "Or rather, we sensed you talking about us. Were you guys discussing the Heart and Lifeblood? Felt like you were."

"Yeah, were," I say. "The Echo doesn't need those elements anymore. The Brain, the Lifeblood, and the Heart were simply magical constructs to keep the Echo from crumbling into chaos that would destroy both worlds."

Dax gives me a skeptical look. "How do you know so much about that rubbish?"

"I was connected to the machine. Everything it knew, I knew." I glance up at Jarek, then look at our friends. "We need to bring all the good Echo refugees here, and toss all the bad ones back into the other world. Once we've unbound the Echo and Earth, we'll reverse the damage done to both worlds."

Growling and grunting noises originate from across the street, and I spot figures moving around in the alley.

Jarek lights up his fiery red eyes and bends his knees, like he's about to pounce on those creatures.

They turn around and run away.

But they won't be able to run once we get started on the next part of our plan.

I smirk at our friends. "So, did everybody have a good time during phase one?"

Dax and Erin smirk right back at me, but Allison bites her lip and bows her head, while Grant scratches the back of his neck and glances sideways at Erin. His lips kink up at one corner.

I take that to mean yes, they had a very good time.

"Please tell me," Dax says, "that phase two does not involve sex. I will not participate in an orgy."

"No sex. Though we will need to hold hands." When Dax compresses his lips and squints at me, I raise a palm. "Calm down, Bigfoot. You'll be holding hands with Allison and Erin."

He relaxes and stops giving me the deadly squint.

I've seen way worse nasty looks. His does not impress me.

"Jarek, stay here," I say. "You too, Aldith. We're about to send all the murderous creatures back into the Echo, and we don't want you guys to get sucked in accidentally."

Sarah and I lead the gang back to the gateway, which has expanded, so it reaches all the way to the ground. We link hands one by one until we've formed a circle, then summon all the Echo power we have inside us, the combined strength of six individuals and three couples—the ultimate Tria Prima. Energies begin to swirl in the air around us, and wind erupts, whirling with tornadic strength. We grip each other's hands harder as the magics grow inside us, and a glittering curtain of golden Echo power forms around our group.

Screams. Far away. Coming closer.

Through the curtain of magics, I spot Echo creatures flying through the air toward the gateway. It sucks them in while they keep thrashing in a desperate attempt to escape. Only the evil creatures will be consigned to the Echo forever, and I have no sympathy for them. They chose to become monsters.

They won't die, anyway. They'll have their own world, and it's up to them how they use it.

Shape after shape gets whisked into the Echo, until finally, the last one flies through the gateway. And it telescopes shut, vanishing from sight.

We keep holding hands, because the most arduous and dangerous part of our plan comes next.

"Time to sever the worlds," I say. "And reverse the damage to them."

Sarah grips my hand harder. "We'll remember each other when this is over. I know we will."

Dax glances at Allison. "Everyone will remember the apocalypse, and each other, but we'll be free of the Echo forever."

I swear I can feel the anxiety inside our circle, like a palpable force that might knock our final blast of magics out of whack and wreck what we're trying to do. "Come on, guys, no wistful gazes or repressed anxiety. I spent enough time in that machine to know the Echo feeds on negative emotions. We all have to believe we can do this, or it will go sideways."

"You're right," Grant says. "No worries. I know we can do this."

"That's better."

Dax touches his forehead to Allison's. "I want our child to grow up in a beautiful world. We can do this—for our baby."

She touches her lips to his. "Me too. Let's make it happen."

I glance at Sarah. "No turning back now."

"We don't want to go back. Everyone on Earth needs to move forward, and what we're about to do will make sure that can happen."

While Aldith and Jarek observe from a distance, we begin the new alchemy of worlds, gathering magics from both worlds and transmuting them from bad to good, weaving a spell of such magnitude that I doubt anyone else in any universe has ever attempted something like this. The power once housed in the Echo, in the castle built by Sefton, reels out of that world and into us, whirling around our group like a hurricane wind. We cling to each other's hands to keep from falling down.

Whatever happens now, it's beyond our control.

A monstrous cracking sound originates overhead, from the place where the gateway to the Echo once hovered. The sky splits apart, but not in the same way as it had on that day when one man's fury and madness destroyed the Earth and unleashed hell on two worlds. The cracking gets louder and louder, and though I want to cover my ears, I keep hold of Sarah and Allison's hands, squeezing my eyes shut as the magics inside the Echo are sucked out of that world and dissipate into the air, gone forever.

Silence descends. The most profound silence I've ever experienced.

Then I begin to hear other sounds, things I haven't heard since before the apocalypse. Birds chirping. Leaves rustling. I open my eyes, and the sun blinds me for a moment. Then I realize we're standing on a grassy hill that overlooks a river and the City of Fort Worth.

"Look!" Allison shouts, grinning as she points toward something in the distance. "The library is back."

"You're excited about that?" I say. "What about the green grass and the wildflowers and the lack of a gaping hole in the sky?"

"That's awesome too," Allison says, still grinning as Dax folds an arm around her. "You don't understand. I used to work at the public library. Seeing it again, the way it used to look, is amazing."

Sarah stares at me, her eyes wide. "We did it. The worlds are unbound, Earth has been restored, and we remember everything."

"But do you remember your life before Sanctuary?"

Her face goes blank. Her gaze is aimed directly at me, but she just stands there as if she's turned to stone.

"Sarah?" I grasp her shoulders. "Are you okay?"

"Gabriel…"

She collapses in my arms.

Chapter Twenty-Six

Sarah

I ROUSE GRADUALLY, AT FIRST HEARING ONLY THE SOUND OF MY HEART-beats and my breaths, then noticing the breeze that tickles my face and the feel of strong arms wrapped around me. I smell the unique and inde-scribable scent of Gabriel, then realize the breeze I thought I'd felt is actu-ally his breaths on my skin. My lids flutter open.

Gabriel hugs me to him even tighter and cradles my cheek in his hand as he gazes into my eyes. "You're awake. How do you feel? What hap-pened?"

"Not sure. I got woozy, and then I must have passed out."

"I know that. But how do you feel?"

"Fine." I sweep my gaze over our surroundings, and I can't help smil-ing. "We did it, didn't we? The worlds are unbound and devoid of magics, and we haven't forgotten each other."

"You already said that, before you passed out."

"Oh. Sorry." I glance around, but stop as I feel something strange inside me. For a moment, I can't understand what I'm sensing. Then it hits me—so hard that I gasp and stumble into Gabriel, clutching his shirt. "Oh, my God. I remember everything."

"Do you have brain damage from all those magics? You keep repeating the same phrase."

"No, no, I'm not." I lift my face to his and grin. "I don't have amnesia anymore. My name is Sarah Delaney, and I was born in Olympia, Wash-ington. My brother and parents were alive before the apocalypse, but I have no idea what happened to them after that. The rest of my memories are still pretty fuzzy."

"You'll get all your memories back, eventually."

I don't see how he could know that, but I realize Gabriel wants to make me feel better. He shouldn't bother. I feel amazing right now, just knowing we saved the world and that I do have a past.

Unfortunately, everyone who died during the apocalypse will stay dead. We couldn't bring them back. Something in the magics that Sefton Stainthorpe used to create the alchemy of worlds prevented that. But we have each other, we have a beautiful world to live in, and we have all the time we need to rebuild the Earth. All the infrastructure has been resurrected, but it might take decades to get everything working again.

"How will we get back to Sanctuary?" I ask. "We need to check on our friends, but we can't teleport anymore."

"Oh, don't worry about that," Erin says. "I can hot-wire any car you want. We'll return it to the original owner later on."

As we wander down the hill to the bridge that spans the river—the Paddock Viaduct, Allison tells us—we don't talk at all. I think we're in shock, still coming to terms with what we've done. We saved the freaking world. Grant will never have his wife and son back, and Erin will never see her sister again. But we've all forged new bonds that mean everything to us, as friends and as lovers.

Do I wish we could've brought back everyone who died? Of course I do. But we can't change the past. It's time to make a new future.

A few blocks past the viaduct, we find an abandoned vehicle that we can all just barely fit inside, but we can find something bigger as we travel. Erin hot-wires the car, and we get on the road.

We don't see anyone.

Maybe they're hiding, unsure of what has happened and whether they should trust it. It will take time for people to accept that the horrors have ended and they've been given a second chance. Still, it feels odd not to see anyone walking around. The city seems normal again, but vacant of human life.

Jarek follows us, loping along at an easy pace that lets him keep up with our car only because he's so enormous.

Allison, who sits up front with Erin, turns on the radio. Nothing but static. She flips through stations but finds none in operation. That's also no surprise.

While we traverse the city, I focus on what I do see rather than what I don't see. Though I had never visited Fort Worth before the apocalypse, I imagine it didn't look as pristine as it does today. Cities never are like that, at least not the ones I've visited. We pull over at the public library so Allison can take a peek inside. We all climb out to join her, mounting the steps to the portico and pushing through the unlocked doors.

While everyone else admires the restored library, which no longer bears the wounds of the apocalypse, I stand near the windows and stare out at nothing in particular.

Gabriel comes up behind me and loops his arms around my waist. "What's going on inside that amazing brain of yours?"

"This will sound weird."

"I'm on board for weird. I did make love to you inside an apocalypse machine, after all."

"Yeah, I know. But, um…" I glance back at our friends, who are laughing and smiling. "Maybe I should wait. Let everyone enjoy the remade world for a while first."

"You can tell me, Sarah. I can keep a secret, and I can handle whatever it is."

Of course he can. I know that. Gabriel is the most incredible person I've ever met.

So I decide to tell him. "I think we still have our Echo powers. Pretty sure nobody else does. Just the six of us."

"Not Aldith either?"

I shake my head.

"What about the creatures here and the ones we consigned to the Echo?"

I shake my head again. "Just us."

Our friends wander over to us, and they can clearly tell Gabriel and I have been engaged in a serious discussion. I can see it in their expressions.

"What's going on?" Allison asks.

I turn toward Gabriel, and he rubs his thumb over my chin. He wants me to share my revelation, and that makes me realize I should.

"We still have Echo powers," I say. "I just realized that a few minutes ago. No one else has them, just the six of us. Are you guys okay with that?"

Our four friends exchange glances and shrugs. Then Allison says, "It actually makes sense that we would keep our powers. Each of us played a vital role in the apocalypse and its reversal. We must be quantum entangled—with each other, at least."

"With the universe," I say. "That's what my intuition tells me."

"And we believe you. But this is one revelation that should never be shared with anyone outside our group."

"Does that mean we have to drive all the way back to Sanctuary?"

Erin grins. "Oh, yeah. But we'll do it in style."

When we leave the library, we find out what Erin meant. She had spotted a big RV in the parking lot across the street, and now she hot-wires it so we can travel in comfort. Jarek will follow on foot.

Our journey takes the better part of two days. The whole time, we debate whether anyone will be waiting for us in Sanctuary and whether that camp still exists. We have to leave our RV and travel the last bit on foot. But when we reach Sanctuary, it still looks like it had before the Brain destroyed it, and our friends are thrilled to see us. Willow races up to give all of us big hugs.

After our homecoming, we begin to take small groups of our Sanctuary friends on little excursions out into the wider world so they can see that the destruction brought on by the alchemy of worlds has indeed been reversed.

I wish we didn't have to tell everyone that their loved ones who died will never come back. I wish we'd been able to save them. But our friends understand.

A week after we reversed the apocalypse, I ask Gabriel to come with me on a private excursion. I've been having dreams about the day the alchemy of worlds began, and I have a hunch I can find more answers about my past by following the clues in my dreams. To make the journey faster, we teleport to Olympia, Washington, being as careful as we can to make sure no one sees us using magic.

We find the house where I'd lived, but nobody is home. Though I'd shared this home with a roommate, my intuition tells me she didn't survive the first wave of the apocalypse.

As we're walking out of the house, three men amble up the driveway.

Gabriel pulls out the revolver he had holstered under his jacket and aims it at the men. "Stop right there. Who are you and what do you want?"

One man holds up his hands. "Take it easy. We've been coming here every week for the past six months, hoping to find Sarah."

"Why?"

"To make sure she's okay. She took off so fast that we never had the chance to explain."

I sidle up to Gabriel but look at the stranger. "I saw you in my dreams. How do we know each other?"

"From the hospital." The man lowers his hands but does not try to approach us. "I was a doctor, and these guys were nurses. We took care of you during your coma."

"My what?"

"Six weeks before the apocalypse, you were in a car accident with your parents and your brother. Only you survived, but you were comatose. Until the day the world went crazy. Then you woke up and ran."

"I remember running. Creatures were chasing me." I inch toward the man but halt a couple of yards away. "You do seem familiar."

Gabriel grasps my arm. "Are you sure you recognize these men?"

"Yes." I freeze as I realize what the doctor said. "My parents and brother are dead?"

The man nods. "I'm sorry. We tried to find any other relatives you might have, but there wasn't anyone. We managed to catch you and protect you from the creatures, but you fell into another coma. Then two months later, you vanished."

I hug myself, suddenly feeling cold. Tears sting my eyes. My family is gone. A force I might never understand must have sent me to Sanctuary, so

Gabriel and I could save the worlds. I will grieve for my family, but I have a new home now and friends who mean everything to me.

Gabriel places a protective arm around me. "Thanks for letting us know about Sarah and her family. But I need to take her home right now."

"Of course. Good luck. It's a new world out there."

We return to Sanctuary, and life goes on. What else can we do? This new world presents many challenges, and we need to focus on the future. Over the next few weeks, we start to improve our camp—erecting permanent structures and bringing in generators to give us some electricity. It will be a long time until the power grid gets up and running again.

We travel around in our RV to meet other survivors and find out what's going on elsewhere, making friends along the way. It helps us feel less isolated and more like the world is gradually returning to normal.

Then the big day arrives. Allison goes into labor. Forty-six hours later, she gives birth to a beautiful baby boy. And three days after that, the camp hosts a double wedding—Erin and Grant, and me and Gabriel, with Willow as our flower girl. Life might not be exactly what it was before the apocalypse, but this new beginning gives everyone hope for the future.

To survivors of the alchemy of worlds, hope means everything.

ANNA DURAND IS A BESTSELLING, MULTI-AWARD-WINNING AUTHOR OF contemporary and paranormal romance. Her books have earned bestseller status on every major retailer and wonderful reviews from readers around the world. But that's the boring spiel. Here are some really cool things you want to know about Anna!

Born on Lackland Air Force Base in Texas, Anna grew up moving here, there, and everywhere thanks to her dad's job as an instructor pilot. She's lived in Texas (twice), Mississippi, California (twice), Michigan (twice), and Alaska—and now Ohio.

As for her writing, Anna has always made up stories in her head, but she didn't write them down until her teen years. Those first awful books went into the trash can a few years later, though she learned a lot from those stories. Eventually, she would pen her first romance novel, the paranormal romance *Willpower*, and she's never looked back since.

Want even more details about Anna? Get access to her extended bio when you subscribe to her newsletter and download the free bonus ebook, *Hot Scots Confidential*. You'll also get hot deleted scenes, character interviews, fun facts, and more!

VISIT ANNADURAND.COM TO SIGN UP.